Bedford Cultural Editions

APHRA BEHN

Oroonoko;
or, The Royal Slave

Bedford Cultural Editions

APHRA BEHN
Oroonoko;
or, The Royal Slave

EDITED BY
Catherine Gallagher
University of California — Berkeley

WITH
Simon Stern
Yale Law School

BEDFORD/ST. MARTIN'S   BOSTON ● NEW YORK

For Bedford/St. Martin's
Developmental Editor: Katherine A. Retan
Editorial Assistants: Nicole Simonsen and Jennifer Rush
Production Supervisor: Cheryl Mamaril
Project Management: Publisher's Studio, a division of Stratford Publishing Services, Inc.
Marketing Manager: Karen Melton
Cover Design: Donna Lee Dennison
Cover Art: Detail of *Mr. Savigny in the Character of Oroonoko,* the frontispiece to
   Oroonoko, A Tragedy (1775).
Composition: Stratford Publishing Services, Inc.
Printing and Binding: Haddon Craftsmen, an R. R. Donnelley & Sons Company

President: Charles H. Christensen
Editorial Director: Joan E. Feinberg
Director of Editing, Design, and Production: Marcia Cohen
Manager, Publishing Services: Emily Berleth

Library of Congress Catalog Card Number: 98-87521

Manufactured in the United States of America.

9   8   7   6
f

For information, write: Bedford/St. Martin's, 75 Arlington Street, Boston, MA 02116
(617-426-7440)

ISBN-10: 0-312-10813-3 (paperback)
          0-312-21065-5 (hardcover)
ISBN-13: 978-0-312-10813-7 (paperback)
          978-0-312-21065-6 (hardcover)

Published and distributed outside North America by:
MACMILLAN PRESS, LTD.
Houndmills, Basingstoke, Hampshire RG21 2XS and London
Companies and representatives throughout the world.
ISBN: 0-333-73074-7
A catalogue record for this book is available from the British Library.

Acknowledgments
Acknowledgments and copyrights can be found at the back of the book on page 473,
which constitutes an extension of the copyright page.

About the Series

The need to "historicize" literary texts — and even more to analyze the historical and cultural issues all texts embody — is now embraced by almost all teachers, scholars, critics, and theoreticians. But the question of how to teach such issues in the undergraduate classroom is still a difficult one. Teachers do not always have the historical information they need for a given text, and contextual documents and sources are not always readily available in the library — even if the teacher has the expertise (and students have the energy) to ferret them out. The Bedford Cultural Editions represent an effort to make available for the classroom the kinds of facts and documents that will enable teachers to use the latest historical approaches to textual analysis and cultural criticism. The best scholarly and theoretical work has for many years gone well beyond the "new critical" practices of formalist analysis and close reading, and we offer here a practical classroom model of the ways that many different kinds of issues can be engaged when texts are not thought of as islands unto themselves.

The impetus for the recent cultural and historical emphasis has come from many directions: the so-called new historicism of the late 1980s, the dominant historical versions of both feminism and Marxism, the cultural studies movement, and a sharply changed focus in older movements such as reader response, structuralism, deconstruction, and psychoanalytic theory. Emphases differ, of course, among schools and individuals, but what these movements and approaches have in common is a commitment to explore — and to have students in the classroom study interactively — texts in their full historical and cultural dimensions. The aim is to discover how older texts (and those from other traditions) differ from our own assumptions and expectations, and thus the focus in teaching falls on cultural and historical difference rather than on similarity or continuity.

The most striking feature of the Bedford Cultural Editions — and the one most likely to promote creative classroom discussion — is the inclusion of a generous selection of historical documents that contextualize the main text in a variety of ways. Each volume contains works (or passages from works) that are contemporary with the main accounts, histories, sections from conduct books, travel books, poems, novels, and other historical sources. These materials have several uses. Often they provide information beyond what the main text offers. They provide, too, different perspectives on a particular theme, issue, or event central to the text, suggesting the range of opinions contemporary readers would have brought to their reading and allowing students to experience for themselves the details of cultural disagreement and debate. The documents are organized in thematic units — each with an introduction by the volume editor that historicizes a particular issue and suggests the ways in which individual selections work to contextualize the main text.

Each volume also contains a general introduction that provides students with information concerning the political, social, and intellectual contexts for the work as well as information concerning the material aspects of the text's creation, production, and distribution. There are also relevant illustrations, a chronology of important events, and, when helpful, an account of the reception history of the text. Finally, both the main work and its accompanying documents are carefully annotated in order to enable students to grasp the significance of historical references, literary allusions, and unfamiliar terms. Everywhere we have tried to keep the special needs of the modern student — especially the culturally conscious student of the turn of the millennium — in mind.

For each title, the volume editor has chosen the best teaching text of the main work and explained his or her choice. Old spellings and capitalizations have been preserved (except that the long "s" has been regularized to the modern "s") — the overwhelming preference of the two hundred teacher-scholars we surveyed in preparing the series.

Original habits of punctuation have also been kept, except for occasional places where the unusual usage would obscure the syntax for modern readers. Whenever possible, the supplementary texts and documents are reprinted from the first edition or the one most relevant to the issue at hand. We have thus meant to preserve — rather than counter — for modern students the sense of "strangeness" in older texts, expecting that the oddness will help students to see where older texts are *not* like modern ones, and expecting too that today's historically informed teachers will find their own creative ways to make something of such historical and cultural differences.

In developing this series, our goal has been to foreground the kinds of issues that typically engage teachers and students of literature and history now. We have not tried to move readers toward a particular ideological, political, or social position or to be exhaustive in our choice of contextual materials. Rather, our aim has been to be provocative — to enable teachers and students of literature to raise the most pressing political, economic, social, religious, intellectual, and artistic issues on a larger field than any single text can offer.

J. Paul Hunter, University of Chicago
William E. Cain, Wellesley College
Series Editors

About This Volume

A critic once called Aphra Behn's *Oroonoko; or, The Royal Slave* "The Earliest American Novel."[1] That description might seem misleading in a couple of ways, for *Oroonoko*'s America is South America and the tale isn't a fully fledged novel. However, the appellation "earliest American novel" tells us something very important about Behn's little book: it is the first literary narrative in English about an American colony. Moreover, its America, in all of its Southernness, is in many ways more representative of the typical early colonial European experience than the seventeenth-century texts from New England that we more often read. Most European settlers headed for latitudes close to the Caribbean, to New Spain, and to the vast tracts of the Portuguese empire, rather than to the frosty shores of Massachusetts. Even in the middle of the eighteenth century, the Western Hemisphere's biggest city was Ouro Prêto in Brazil, which was twice as large as New York. But the most significant feature of *Oroonoko*'s America is the way it gathers European, indigenous American, and African peoples in an explosive mixture. This meeting of the people of three continents had never before been depicted in English literature.

This volume is designed to explore *Oroonoko*'s global historical context. It places the work in literary history as the first English narrative

[1] William Spengemann, "The Earliest American Novel: Aphra Behn's *Oroonoko*," *Nineteenth-Century Fiction* 38.4 (March 1984): 384–414.

with an African hero as well as the most popular tale of the first professional English woman writer. It then goes on to look at each of the three continents the story unites and the relations among them in the seventeenth and early eighteenth centuries. Documents from each of the three corners of the Atlantic triangle are gathered here, and what emerges is a remarkably fluid set of intercontinental relations and perceptions. *Oroonoko* and the dozens of other pieces of writing included in this volume allow us to see the world we now inhabit in the making.

The volume, moreover, breaks down the fixity of the categories "British" and "American" literature. It brings seventeenth-century English literature out of the insular environment in which it is too often treated, and, we hope, it will broaden the horizons of North American students by acquainting them with other parts of Anglophone America, especially England's South American and Caribbean colonies. In short, this volume presents *Oroonoko* as a crossover book, in which an early modern English woman writer engages an enslaved African prince in a startlingly New World.

ACKNOWLEDGMENTS

The volume has benefited greatly from the advice of several generous scholars who read the introduction and organizational plan at an early stage: Margaret Ferguson, Suvir Kaul, Joanna Lipking, and Janet Todd. I'm especially indebted to Janet Todd not only for her valuable suggestions about this volume but also for her help in obtaining permission for us to use her own excellent edition of the text of *Oroonoko*. Thanks are due as well to many colleagues at the University of California — Berkeley, for their perceptive readings of various sections of the manuscript and their guidance on historiographical and bibliographic matters: Janet Adelman, Stephen Greenblatt, Saidiya Hartman, Carla Hesse, Thomas Laqueur, David Lieberman, Thomas Metcalf, and Michael Rogin. I am also grateful to the Bancroft Library at the University of California — Berkeley.

The Bedford/St. Martin's editorial team has been remarkably astute, sympathetic, and efficient from the outset. I have especially appreciated Kathy Retan's cheerful encouragement, admirable editorial judgment, and dexterous coordination, and I wish also to thank Emily Berleth for smoothly steering the book through production. Two young people who prepared materials for the volume, translator Laura Schattschneider and mapmaker Max Landes, deserve special thanks for their patience, diligence, and willingness to meet unreasonable deadlines. I'm grateful as well to research assistant David Brewer, who has expertly attended to numerous last-minute details.

I can only adequately acknowledge Simon Stern's contribution to the volume by naming him coeditor. He originally signed on as a research assistant, but was soon pressed into service as author of most of the headnotes to our documents as well as the volume's annotations and bibliography. Intrepid tracker of sources, editions, illustrations, and the often elusive truth about the many arcane matters the volume touches, Simon Stern is the best coeditor I could imagine.

My daughter Rebecca Jay helped make several crucial decisions about illustrations and maps, and my husband, Martin Jay, was the first, and most perceptive, reader of all of the book's introductions. I thank them and the rest of my family for supporting and encouraging me while I've devoted myself to this enterprise.

Catherine Gallagher
University of California — Berkeley

Contents

Illustrations

Part One

Oroonoko; or, The Royal Slave
The Complete Text

Mrs Behn.

An engraving of Aphra Behn from the frontispiece edition of her *Histories and Novels,* published in 1696, in London. Published eight years after her death, it is the earliest surviving image of the author. Reproduced by permission of The Huntington Library, San Marino, California.

Introduction:
Cultural and
Historical Background

THE WORLD HISTORICAL CONTEXT OF *OROONOKO*

Oroonoko; or, The Royal Slave is the first literary work in English to grasp the global interactions of the modern world. Narrating her hero's journey from West Africa to the Caribbean and his fatal encounter with British colonists, Aphra Behn traces the outlines of a new, interlocking, transcontinental order. The three corners of this Atlantic triangle are called "worlds" in *Oroonoko*: "our world," England, the polite but highly artificial and commercial home of Aphra Behn and her readers, where martial heroes are mainly stage phenomena; Africa, where royal heroes make perpetual war, winning vast numbers of slaves in battle; and Suriname, the roomy but "obscure" American "New World," where friendly natives welcome European colonists and everything is naturally plentiful, except for the one commodity that seems discouraged by such abundance — willing labor.

Although Behn develops the distinctness of these places — the seeming separateness and completeness of each that the word *world* designates — the tale also stresses their mutual interpenetration. Europeans move into Africa and are found even at the court of Oroonoko's grandfather; Africans and Europeans are shipped to America, where they remake its landscape; and American goods are on display in London, where the conquest of Indians becomes a theatrical spectacle.

3

Each place has a different form of wealth: England's wealth is commercial and technological, Africa's riches are mainly in people, and America's in land and natural resources. The imagined surpluses of each continent are thought to supply the wants of another in an interlocking triangle. In sum, *Oroonoko* depicts and, indeed, participates in the differentiation of these "worlds" as components of an unprecedented integral structure.

That structure, which has come to be called "the triangular trade," was an economic, political, and cultural novelty to Behn's readers in the late seventeenth century; English participation in the trade was only about thirty years old when *Oroonoko* was published in 1688. To be sure, large parts of the Americas had long been colonized, and Europeans had dealt in African slaves for centuries, but what distinguished the triangular trade was the forced transportation of a laboring population from one continent (Africa) to another (America) to produce a commodity consumed on a third (Europe). The Spanish in Cuba and the Portuguese in Brazil were the first to use this system; the British came later to the practice but joined in readily and vigorously, demonstrating no hesitation. Their exploitation of African slave labor in the Caribbean massively increased the number of people dislocated, the wealth obtained, the degree of coordination achieved, and the extent of English psychological and economic investment in the institution of colonial slavery.[1]

These developments rapidly followed the discovery in the mid-1640s that sugar cane could be just as successfully grown and processed in the West Indies as in Brazil. Before this realization, English Caribbean colonists were a somewhat hapless lot of largely unsuccessful tobacco and cotton farmers, assisted by "servants" in various, and not very well discriminated, states of unfreedom: indentured laborers and political prisoners from Ireland, Scotland, and England, some of whom were virtual slaves because they were serving life sentences; and black slaves, human property, purchased or kidnapped in Africa. When the colonists converted to sugar cane, their operations quickly outgrew their labor supply: to replenish it quickly, they bought more and more slaves in Africa. Before the sugar revolution, African slaves were a small proportion of the West Indian labor force. By the early

---

[1] Information on the history of slavery in the British Caribbean comes from the following sources: Aykroyd; Bean; Beckles and Shepherd; Beer; Blackburn, *Making*; Bridenbaugh and Bridenbaugh; Curtin, *Atlantic*; Davis; Dunn; Thomas; Sheridan; Watson; E. Williams; Williamson; and Wyndham. Information on the triangular trade comes from many of these same sources, as well as from Inikori, and Inikori and Engerman.

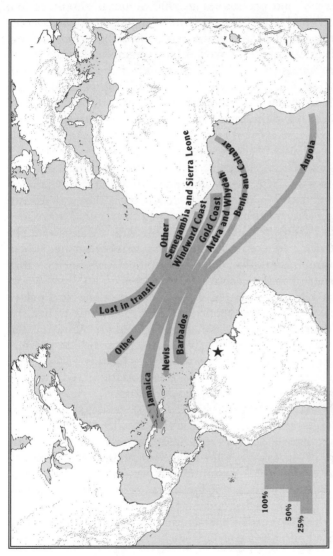

This map shows the proportions of slaves shipped from the various parts of West Africa by the British Royal African Company between 1673 and 1689, as well as their destinations. The majority were from the Gulf of Guinea, many from the Gold Coast, the location of Oroonoko's "Coramantien," and almost all were destined for the West Indian sugar islands. By 1673, England had lost its colony in Suriname, which was the setting for *Oroonoko*. Suriname is southeast of Barbados, on the northern coast of South America; on this map, its location has been marked with a star. Copyright © 1969 The University of Wisconsin Press. Reproduced with permission.

5

1660s (the time of the events depicted in *Oroonoko*), the African population of the largest sugar-producing island, Barbados, was roughly equal to the entire white population (22,000 whites to 20,000 blacks), and by 1690 (around the time of *Oroonoko*'s publication), blacks outnumbered whites by a ratio of approximately three to one: almost 50,000 people of African origin or their descendants and some 18,000 people categorized as "white."[2] The rapidity of the English Caribbean's conversion to slavery is all the more striking when compared with the continuing marginality of that institution in the continental North American British colonies; in Virginia as late as 1689, there were 10,401 white indentured servants, but only 629 African slaves, whereas already in 1680 Barbados had 38,782 slaves and only 2,317 indentured servants from Europe.[3] Slavery became the dominant institution of the English Caribbean in less than a generation; a generation later, the vast majority of the region's people were slaves of African origin or descent. A few decades transformed the region into a ruthlessly efficient machine for supplying Europe with cheap sugar. The English founded a colony at Suriname on the coast of Guiana (where *Oroonoko* is set), and then lost the colony to the Dutch in the heat of this swift conversion to slave labor.

One can quote the statistics, examine the bills of lading for the slave ships, compute the tons of sugar sent to Europe, and try to imagine the misery, inhumanity, and greed implied by those numbers. But the experiences of the people who brought about this transformation and suffered through it remain frustratingly opaque. How did the Africans endure their enslavement and transportation? How did the English, both at home and in the colonies, conceive of what they were doing? When and how did they racialize slavery, that is, attach it exclusively to Africans and their progeny? When, for that matter, did race, as opposed to nationality or religion, come to be seen as the salient feature of Africans and their descendants in the Caribbean? Many historians of the triangular trade treat the colonists as economic automata, creatures comprehensible only as profit maximizers. But if we view them instead as human beings from a specific culture, we can ask which aspects of that culture shaped British-American colonial slavery.

[2] Estimates of the number of slaves in Barbados vary. These conservative figures are from Dunn 320. For a much higher estimate, see Thomas 187. For all references to sources, see the Works Cited list beginning on p. 464.

[3] See Bean and Thomas 386. Totals for Barbados are derived from tables in Dunn 96, 107.

Oroonoko is one of the very few seventeenth-century books that can help us answer these questions. As a heroic tragedy, Aphra Behn's tale exaggerates precisely those emotional experiences that were often suppressed or flattened in the historical descriptions, debates, and documentary records of the period. Instead of rationalizing and normalizing the English trans-Atlantic enterprise, *Oroonoko* churns up its fears and hopes, its sensations of outrage and ambition, confusion and power. The tragedy's formal literary qualities thus create its historical value, for they force to the surface the conflict and turmoil that other records buried. Moreover, since Oroonoko's story was revived in different versions throughout the century that followed its original publication (see pp. 103–40), eventually becoming part of the propaganda of the anti-slave trade movement, its reception both registered changes in English attitudes toward slavery and helped to create them.

If *Oroonoko* is much less directly informative about the other cultures affected by the triangular trade, if its main value is in demonstrating British understandings of African and Caribbean peoples, a skeptical reading of the work can nevertheless indicate the clashes between British patterns of perception and those of the people they encountered. Through the contradictions and elisions of this text, we can catch glimpses of what the enslavers couldn't see. For example, Behn wishes to represent the slave trade as a potentially honorable enterprise carried on with African trading partners, just as she wishes to depict the Indians[4] as naturally generous and welcoming, but the violent coerciveness of the Europeans repeatedly comes to the fore, shattering the pretenses to amicable commerce. The tale, in short, reveals more than the teller can consciously acknowledge.

To explore both what *Oroonoko* reveals and what it conceals about its historical situation, the five chapters in Part Two of this volume include three groups of seventeenth- and eighteenth-century texts, each of which looks at the triangular trade from one of its three corners: England, Africa, and the Caribbean. This organization is designed to stress the local contexts in which seventeenth- and eighteenth-century people conceived of the slave trade and of racial difference. It is designed to challenge the conviction, prevalent since the publication in 1968 of Winthrop D. Jordan's *White over Black,* that the British began their careers as slave traders and slave masters with a stable and securely held ideological justification for slavery built on their belief in

---

[4] We are following Behn's use of "Indians" to designate all indigenous American peoples.

the genetic inferiority of African people.[5] Looking at the issues as perceived from each corner of the triangle demonstrates that there was no single monolithic "British" racial ideology in this period; it shows instead the interplay between beliefs and what we might call "the facts on the ground" in the three locations. By giving separate attention to the three angles over an extended period of time, we can see how ideas about racial difference, for example, adjusted to varying situations and were reshaped by changing desires and political and economic pressures.

The texts pertaining to each location have separate introductions, but there are some general patterns and strange contradictions that we should notice at the outset. First, at the beginning of the seventeenth century the English had no such category as slave in their legal, social, or political traditions. In this they differed from the Spanish — one of their competitors in the West Indies — who had slavery in their own European country and a legal system to justify and regulate it. Some historians have suggested that the English lack of experience with the institution made them unusually harsh slave owners who were very likely to racialize the condition. But the English did not commence with the belief that Africans, and Africans alone, were somehow "naturally" enslavable. There were white slaves in seventeenth-century Barbados (see *Petitions Protesting Slavery,* pp. 408–14), and indentured servants were often bought and sold as if they were exchangeable chattel whose bondage had a limited term (see Ligon, pp. 355–65). Indeed, the narrator of *Oroonoko* calls such servants "slaves for four years" (p. 347). Reports suggest that Indians were also held in slavery; even Behn, who accentuates their freedom at the outset, later refers to Indian servants as slaves.

The English in the Caribbean gradually racialized slavery as they sorted out its differences from other forms of servitude. Over the course of the second half of the seventeenth century, the practice of sending English, Scots, and Irish political prisoners to the West Indies as involuntary laborers was discontinued, and a body of police laws grew up in the Caribbean colonies, specifically and severely limiting the rights and freedoms of Africans and their descendants.[6] Only the

---

[5] Jordan joined an ongoing debate about whether racism grew out of slavery, or slavery out of racism, which continues in the historical literature. For a summary of the debate, see Allen 1–24.

[6] Information on Caribbean slave laws comes from Watson and Dunn.

most minimal justifications prefaced these laws; there was no organized or official body of thought about why Africans could be held
and traded as property but other people could not. Indeed, the question of just what kind of property a slave was went unsettled. The police laws, moreover, were local laws, *lex loci,* which English common
law recognized as valid only in the slave colonies. What, then, was the
status of an African slave when his master brought him to England?
Legal opinions differed widely on this issue (see Ligon and Godwyn,
pp. 355–65, and *Legal Decisions Concerning Slavery in England,*
p. 414–23).

Second, the fact that the colonists were making up racialized slavery as they went along in the seventeenth century and that it was a
local institution at the heart of an intercontinental enterprise led to
marked discrepancies in the way Africans were perceived in the different "worlds" of the trade. For a modern reader of the documents
assembled here, perhaps the most striking incongruity is the double
vision required of slave traders themselves. The men who supplied the
West Indian plantations, especially those who worked directly for the
Royal African Company (a trading monopoly established by Charles
II in 1672), needed to be on very good terms with their African trading
partners in order to have any access to the trade at all.[7] They were
competing against several other European national monopolies, as well
as numerous interlopers, and their success often depended on their
personal relations with African rulers. They were closely involved in
the politics of the "kingdoms" on the Ivory, Gold, and Slave Coasts,
jockeying for monopolies and making alliances with some nations and
leaders against others (see *Correspondence of Slave Traders in the
Royal African Company,* pp. 230–34, and Phillips, pp. 234–44). For
all of these reasons, the trade in Africa forced Englishmen to observe
status and national differences between Africans, pay court to rulers,
display marks of respect for the great men of the region, their wives,
families, and attendants, and maintain a reputation for trustworthi-
ness. Englishmen who by word or deed indiscriminately lumped all
Africans together as barbarians, showed signs of racial contempt, or
behaved treacherously could cause considerable damage to English
interests in the region (see *The Royal African,* pp. 278–302). Hence,
even in the works of British slave traders, there is a palpable tension

---

[7] Information on European traders in Africa comes from Davies; Hewett; Law, *Slave;*
Lovejoy; and Makepeace.

between regarding Africans as just so many potential slaves and responding appropriately to their ethnic and status differences.

But these same Englishmen, once arrived in the West Indies, were equally obliged to regard Africans as indistinguishable slaves. Once an African had been acquired by a trader, whether "legitimately" or not, and sold to a planter in the West Indies, he was simply a slave with no rights whatsoever. Even the Royal African Company might have difficulty retrieving a person of quality tricked into slavery (see *The Royal African,* pp. 278–302). He would have to be manumitted, that is, legally emancipated, in the colony to become a freeman once again, and the racial nature of British West Indian law made that process extremely difficult. In short, the slave trade required its English agents to recognize African status and national differences when trading in Guinea and then to ignore those differences and adopt strictly racial distinctions when in the Caribbean.

Oroonoko registers this disorienting contrast in the stark paradox of its subtitle: *The Royal Slave.* The hero's tragic insistence that his change of place and outward circumstances cannot touch his inner essence — that he remains royal — is certainly credited by the narrator and all of the discerning colonists. Nevertheless, his English friends seem unable to restore him to his kingdom, and legally, despite the respect often shown him, his kingship has been eclipsed by his color. Ironically, his nobility, which had made him the companion and partner of the English in Africa, is the very thing that makes him vulnerable to betrayal and enslavement. The tale requires the reader to feel the impact of the discrepancy between the code of rank that operated in Africa and the code of race that ruled in the West Indies. But the tale reveals considerable distress about the discrepancy, and Behn seems unable to subject her hero or heroine to the actual indignities of plantation labor. Although Oroonoko and Imoinda are not free, they are always distinguished by the narrator and her circle, implying that, no matter what geographic dislocations occur, persons "of quality" will always recognize and attempt to protect one another.

Finally, comparing texts about Africa and the Caribbean reveals not only that early slave traders needed to distinguish between Africans and therefore often spoke out against anti-African prejudice, sounding very much like the narrator of *Oroonoko,* but also that humanitarian reformers sometimes hastened the process of racialization. To be sure, slavery is to be blamed for that process, but it was unwittingly furthered by those who, considering themselves the slaves' advocates, attempted to erase the cultural and religious differences between slaves and masters. As the debate over the 1659 parliamentary petition of two political prisoners indicates (see Part Two, Chapter 5), it was possible to sell not only Christians but also Englishmen into lifelong involuntary servitude in the mid-seventeenth century, but not even the parties to the sale of these Englishmen seemed willing to defend the practice. Instead, the debaters on both sides tended to acknowledge that Christians and especially Englishmen (because members of a peculiarly "free" polity) should not be enslaved. Such a widespread belief that Christians should not be held in bondage made West Indian planters reluctant to baptize their slaves or to suppress their African cultural and religious practices (see Godwyn, p. 365, and Tryon, p. 365). If, in the words of the Barbados Assembly's 1661 Act "for the better ordering and governing of Negroes," Africans required special laws because they were "an heathenish, brutish and an uncertaine, dangerous kinde of people . . . without the knowledge of God in the world" (qtd. in Dunn 239), the efforts to convert them could only work against the rationale of the slave laws, which were based on the assumption of the slaves' religious and cultural inferiority. Christian reformers like Morgan Godwyn, concerned to improve the lot of the slaves and encourage fairer treatment from masters, quite reasonably urged that the bond of a common religion would help the masters to see their slaves as fellow humans, but seventeenth-century masters replied that fellowship was inconsistent with the master-slave relation. Nevertheless, the Christianizers made some headway: some slaves were baptized, and many African ways were forgotten or even outlawed. To be sure, West Indian slaves in general were never as fully acculturated to English laws and customs as continental North American slaves, but nevertheless they became less religiously and culturally distinct in the eighteenth century.

British-American slavery eventually racialized its participants so completely that even its reformers and enemies were trapped inside that dynamic. Lessening the religious and other cultural distinctions between masters and slaves may have encouraged more humane treatment, but it also made the remaining distinctions — the external markers of racial difference, especially skin color — assume even greater prominence. It became increasingly untenable to hold the 1677 opinion that slaves could be owned and traded because they "were infidels, and the *subjects of an infidel prince*" (see p. 417) when they were children born to Christian parents in a British colony. As "Christian" became a less important distinguishing category for masters, they took refuge in the classification "English." But as the slaves became less culturally African, the British West Indies became a discrete entity, and a few black writers even began asserting their literacy, mastery of English culture, and permanent residence in England (see Equiano, pp. 310–25, pp. 391–92, and pp. 458–63, and Sancho, pp. 451–58); "Englishness," too, became an unreliable category for marking the crucial difference between those born into bondage and those born free. What had earlier been a plethora of distinctions was boiled down to one: racial difference. As the slaves ceased to be "Africans," they became merely "negroes," while the masters, and even their Scots and Irish servants, started calling themselves "whites." The conditions were established for modern racial perceptions.

In *Oroonoko*, the words *black* and *white* are certainly used, but the hero normally speaks, in less exclusively racial terms, of his countrymen and the Christians. The narrator presents Oroonoko as learned in European lore but adamantly opposed to European religion, and his opposition is essential to his heroic integrity. As we will see in the next section of this introduction, Oroonoko descends from a well-established line of truth-telling infidels and noble savages (see Mandeville, pp. 166–68, Jonson, pp. 175–79, and Tryon, pp. 368–75) whose criticism is authorized by their very cultural and religious differences from their European interlocutors. Maintaining that distance not only renders Oroonoko consistent as a character but also permits the sharpening of an independent, antagonistic perspective on Christian values as the tale progresses. During his incarceration, the hero begins by scorning Christianity's ignoble and selfish emphasis on punishment in an afterlife, as opposed to his country's code of honor that forbids *"offending and diseasing all Mankind"* (p. 65). After his rebellion is betrayed, he exclaims that the cowards who deserted him "wanted but to be whipt into the knowledge of the *Christian Gods* to be the vilest of all creeping things; to learn to Worship such Deities as had not Power to make 'em Just, Brave, or Honest" (p. 90).

Oroonoko's valiant anti-Christian defiance had a history in European letters, and it also had both a past and a future in the British West Indies generally and Suriname particularly. Seven slave revolts took place in the British islands between 1640 and 1713 (Dunn 256), but Suriname, on the mainland, was the site of the most successful rebellions. As early as the 1660s, a group of self-emancipated former slaves, led by Coromantines like Oroonoko, were raiding plantations there (Price 23–24). And, as the passages from John Gabriel Stedman's *Five Years Expedition against the Revolted Negroes of Surinam* (see pp. 377–90) attest, Africans continued to rebel successfully against their European masters, migrating into the rain forests of Suriname, and establishing independent and populous communities there. Despite numerous efforts to destroy them, those communities won their autonomy, and, according to anthropologists, became preserves of West African civilization transplanted to South America. It is fitting that Aphra Behn's tale of heroic insubordination should have been set in that Caribbean country where thousands of Africans were able to refuse both slavery and Europeanization.

LITERARY TRADITION AND INNOVATION IN *OROONOKO*

Aphra Behn was not trying to provide us with a record of Caribbean slavery or a prediction about its future; she aimed, rather, to blend three popular forms of Restoration literature: the New World travel story, the courtly romance, and the heroic tragedy. There were some precedents for this combination. For example, in 1664, the leading playwright of the age, John Dryden, had coauthored a play called *The Indian Queen* — a play to which Behn specifically refers in the opening pages of *Oroonoko* — and had written a sequel called *The Indian Emperor* the following year (see pp. 180–90). Behn was certainly familiar with both plays. In the latter, Aztec and Spanish heroes act out their amours, jealousies, and a complex code of honor in the course of the Spanish conquest of Mexico. This clash of worlds — the conflict between hitherto completely separate cultures — and the downfall of a great empire seemed intrinsically tragic material to the English. Moreover, both Aztec royalty and Spanish conquistadores are thoroughly heroic in Dryden's play because they are equally susceptible to the promptings of love and honor. The heroes on both sides belong to a universal, natural aristocracy, which allows them to admire each other's honesty, bravery, and chivalry, while a cross-cultural romance between Hernán Cortés and an Indian princess creates the conflict between love and honor that necessitates tragedy. Dryden's play presents the Aztecs as a doomed but noble race. Two decades before Behn wrote *Oroonoko,* then, Dryden had brought together courtly romance and heroic tragedy in a New World setting, imagining the European conquest of the Americas as a catastrophically inevitable event redeemed by heroic self-sacrifice.

By alluding to one of Dryden's American plays in the opening pages of *Oroonoko* (see pp. 37–100), Behn indicates some of the generic assumptions within which her tale will unfold. We will encounter exotic worlds, but the noble heroes will behave according to universally understood codes of love and honor. Europeans are destined to triumph in their encounters with other peoples, but the certainty of the outcome only increases the tragic, heroic potential of the conquered. Finally, a conflict between love and honor will require a tragic resolution. Each of these elements finds its place in *Oroonoko,* but the mixture is far from conventional. Behn, in fact, undertook a much more difficult task than Dryden's. First, her New World setting is the contemporary British Caribbean, not the Mexico of the previous century; hence, her villains are English. She cannot, like Dryden, blame the cruelty she reports on Spanish priests and the decrees of a distant tyrant, but must instead own them as part of current English colonialism. Dryden's tragedy resembles a myth of origins; it describes the remote events leading to European supremacy in the Americas. But Behn brings her readers news of a little-known place, "a Colony in *America,* called *Surinam,* in the *West Indies*" (p. 38), where the natives are friendly trading partners still living in Edenic bliss: "With these People, . . . we live in perfect Tranquillity, and good Understanding, as it behooves us to do" (p. 40). Half of the news in the opening pages is of the peaceful coexistence of Europeans and Caribs, but the other half is of slavery: "before I give you the Story of this *Gallant Slave,* 'tis fit I tell you the manner of bringing them to these new *Colonies;* for those they make use of there, are not *Natives* of the place" (p. 38). Behn assumes her readers must be told of the mere existence of African slaves in the Caribbean. This New World, where the treatment of unspoiled natives sharply contrasts with that of "*Negro's, Black*-Slaves altogether" (p. 41), is unprecedented in English literature.

In the beginning of *Oroonoko,* in other words, the New World is simultaneously a marvelous prelapsarian paradise and the thoroughly commercialized crossroads of international trade, described in alternately lyrical and utilitarian terms:

> [The Indians] will shoot down Oranges, and other Fruit [with bow and arrow], and only touch the Stalk with the Darts Points, that they may not hurt the Fruit. So that they being, on all Occasions, very useful to us, we find it absolutely necessary to caress 'em as Friends, and not to treat 'em as Slaves; nor dare we do other, their Number so far surpassing ours in that *Continent.* (p. 41)

The place seems appropriate to a romantic idyll or perhaps a middle-class comic drama — like Behn's own *The Widdow Ranter* (posthumously staged in 1689) or George Colman's later *Inkle and Yarico* (1787) — but it does not at first appear a promising setting for heroic tragedy. The English are straightforwardly presented as opportunists in their dealings with both Indians and Africans, and their activities are reported by the narrator as neutral facts, devoid of moral significance. The potential for heroic tragedy must be imported, literally, in the person of Oroonoko.

Behn not only portrays a different New World from any before seen in English literature but also tries to envision a different Old World. By following the trade route back across the Atlantic to Africa, instead of Europe, she becomes the first English author who attempted to render the life lived by sub-Saharan African characters on their own continent. Some travelers' accounts of coastal African kingdoms were in circulation at the time, and we can point to the decorative appearance of a few earlier royal Africans in English literature, either as metaphorical figures or as visitors paying homage to the English monarch, but as a narrative exercise, the African episodes of *Oroonoko* are unique. Since it was entirely novel to tell the story of a royal African in sub-Saharan Africa, it should not surprise us that Behn draws on the conventions of the Oriental romance, a popular genre at the time, to give her African episodes a recognizable shape. Indeed, Behn included a conversation that she took verbatim from Gabriel de Bremond's Oriental tale *Hattigé* (1676). Star-crossed young lovers trying to outwit a lustful but impotent and aged tyrant, a harem intrigue, and a farcical subplot in which the hero's friend seduces an older woman were all standard ingredients of the Oriental romance. Although these narrative conventions may seem creaky and inappropriate to modern readers, they probably helped the average seventeenth-century English reader to accept a pair of black Africans as bona fide lovers deserving of their sympathy.

We modern readers of *Oroonoko* feel the strain of the triangular trade's contradictory emotional demands most keenly in the passages that explicitly confront seventeenth-century English attitudes toward Africans, attitudes we now call racial prejudice. *Oroonoko*'s narrator assumes that she must overcome her readers' biases, especially their refusal to believe that Africans could be truly heroic, and yet many of her efforts themselves now strike us as racist. To increase Oroonoko's credibility, she repeatedly stresses his difference from African commoners, giving him a European education and facial features. Twentieth-century readers have reason to complain that Oroonoko, despite his scornful rejection of Christianity, seems in many respects like a European in blackface. We should realize, though, that the modern idea of race as a set of genetically inheritable traits shared by populations, and its concomitant potential for modern racism — the belief that some populations are genetically inferior to others — had not yet been invented in the seventeenth century. The slave trade was establishing the conditions for such beliefs, but the English prejudices against Africans that Behn encountered and shared were a much more ad hoc set of ideas about the barbarous manners and generally uncivilized state of heathen people, whose moral darkness was believed to manifest itself in their complexions.

Sometimes these ideas were supplemented by the opinion that Africans were descended from Cain or from Ham, the accursed son of Noah, and were therefore marked out by God for special punishment. This belief, which takes dark skin to be a marker of an inheritable moral or intellectual baseness, is the immediate precursor of later "scientific" racism. Behn's contemporary, John Milton, seems to endorse such a biblical justification for enslaving Africans in *Paradise Lost* (1667), when he has Michael say,

> Yet sometimes Nations will decline so low
> From virtue, which is reason, that no wrong
> But Justice, and some fatal curse annext
> Deprives them of their outward liberty,
> Their inward lost: Witness th'irreverant Son
> Of him who built the Ark, who for the shame
> Done to his Father, heard this heavy curse,
> *Servant of Servants,* on his vicious Race. (XII, ll. 97–104)

The story of Ham was increasingly read as biblical authorization for British slaveholding and slave trading (Jordan 17–19; Hill 398–99), but the narrator of *Oroonoko* shows no awareness of such thinking.

In *Oroonoko,* slavery is portrayed as a practical, economic matter; it neither needs nor gets transcendental authorization. The English cannot enslave Indians (they would if they could), so they are forced to buy slaves where there is a market in such commodities; the market happens to be in Africa. Some Africans are "by Nature Slaves" (p. 90), that is, cowards, and some, like Oroonoko, Imoinda, Aboan, Jamoan, and Tuscan, are not. For Behn, the distinction is mainly one of rank: black people of "Quality" are brave; commoners are not. We should

recall that *race* in the seventeenth century meant any genealogically
related group: families, dynasties, clans, nations, aristocracies, and
peasantries could all be spoken of as separate races. Behn, like virtually all of her contemporaries, believed that some of these races were
naturally superior to others and deserved greater power. But the natural hierarchy represented in *Oroonoko* is not one of color. Far from
considering blackness a sign of divine displeasure, Behn waxes lyrical
over the fact that Oroonoko is so much blacker than his countrymen.
The narrator, in short, presses no generalizations that apply to all
Africans. She sometimes accedes to certain prevailing European opinions about most Africans — that they were barbarous and ignorant —
perhaps in order to make herself reliable and her claims about the hero
believable. But she also resists and deflects the gathering current of
racial prejudice lest it wipe out the possibility of a noble class of natural African rulers. The narrator wants her readers to be surprised by
the appearance of a tragic black African; to amaze them, however, she
must overcome their stubborn disbelief.

The English literary tradition provided very few precedents for an
African tragic hero. One might, of course, point to Othello, and certainly the two heroes have some things in common: they are both great
warriors and unfortunate lovers; they struggle to maintain their
honor; their enemies are motivated by racial hatred; and they slay their
wives. In adapting *Oroonoko* to the stage in 1695, Thomas Southerne
emphasized the parallels, but the original tale has surprisingly few
Shakespearean echoes. Oroonoko is the noble African conceived
within the new Atlantic context, whereas Othello is the African filtered through the Mediterranean Renaissance world. Unlike Othello,
Oroonoko serves no Christian ruler, but is instead the prince of his
own West African nation. Although he is warlike and passionate, Behn
characterizes her hero as circumspect, skeptical, and astoundingly self-
possessed; he loves an African woman, not a European (Southerne
changed this, too), and his devotion is unwavering. In other words,
Oroonoko is more thoroughly heroic than his predecessor: his initial
social standing is higher, and he falls through no fault of his own.
Shakespeare's hero is certainly one of Behn's models, but Oroonoko
strives to be the nobler Moor.

If the Noble Moor is one of Oroonoko's progenitors, the candid
infidel or noble savage is another. The passages from Mandeville,
Montaigne, and Tryon included in this volume (see Part Two, Chapters 2 and 4) all contain instances of this figure: a pagan or barbarian
whose vantage point inverts normal European perceptions, providing

a satiric foil for reflections on Christian civilization. Passing their judgments through the perceptions of a despised outsider, these works at once estrange "normal" reality, making it seem alien, and create the shock for European readers of being negatively judged by those usually considered their inferiors. Sir John Mandeville's late medieval version of the figure of the Pagan is an Egyptian Sultan, a Muslim and therefore an infidel, who speaks for a powerful, competing civilization. In the Renaissance, Michel de Montaigne relocated the figure to "America" and made "Nature" the source of his superior wisdom. He also attempted a complete overthrow of the reader's moral assumptions by comparing European ways unfavorably to the most outrageously "savage" reported Amerindian practice — cannibalism. In *Oroonoko,* the narrator's claim that it is kinder to practice polygamy, as the Africans do, than to discard former mistresses after the Christian custom, echoes Montaigne's satiric voice. Thomas Tryon, writing a dialogue between a slave and his master in the 1670s, brought together aspects of Mandeville's and Montaigne's characters: Tryon's heathen is African, like the Sultan, but an Ethiopian rather than an Egyptian; he lives in America, like the cannibals. He resembles the Amerindians, too, in his adherence to nature; like Mandeville's Sultan, though, he disdains only the hypocrisy of European practices, not the substance of Christian beliefs.

Tryon's Ethiopian and Behn's Royal Slave, although belonging to the same literary tradition, make a striking contrast. The Ethiopian believes in the superiority of his own country's manners and makes a thorough catalogue of the inhumanity and brutality of his Christian captors; nevertheless he praises Christian doctrine and serves his master obediently, whereas Oroonoko refuses to separate Christian manners and beliefs, nor can he be reconciled to his bondage. Like the tame discursive tool that he is, Tryon's Ethiopian meekly retires after saying his piece. But Oroonoko is more than just another noble savage rhetorically turning tables on surprised Europeans. He is that figure, that trope, that literary device suddenly sprung into violently animated defiance. The narrator may quote Oroonoko's satiric speeches with pride, but she is also terrified that, when he is done jesting, he will "Cut all our Throats" (p. 92).

Indeed, Oroonoko's right to such a revenge is never seriously questioned because he partakes of an essence loftier than mere heroism, one that approaches divinity: kingship. The noble Moor and the noble savage both went into his making, but it was royalty — a quality beyond both of those literary models — that seems to have captured

Behn's imagination. The story of a king encountered as a slave in an English colony was irresistible because it allowed her to explore at close range the mind and behavior of a disempowered prince: from Behn's point of view, the supreme tragic figure of modern history. The Western literary tradition is so thick with instances of deposed, captured, disgraced, and otherwise dishonored kings, that it would be impossible to trace out Oroonoko's long lineage here. Moreover, the association of these unfortunate sovereigns with tragedy has been proverbial since Aristotle.

OROONOKO AND KINGSHIP

In 1688, Behn was not thinking just of the history of tragedy; she was also thinking about the history of England in her own lifetime as a tragedy. *Oroonoko* was written in the last year of the period we call the Restoration, which began with the return of the Stuarts, in the person of Charles II, to the throne of England in 1660. Charles II was the son of Charles I, who had been beheaded in 1649 during the English Revolution, or Civil War, in which the crown and Parliament struggled for control of the state. The restoration of the monarchy followed an eleven-year interregnum, during which the Puritan military leader Oliver Cromwell ruled until his death in 1658; Puritan rule was then precariously maintained for almost two more years. The restoration of the monarchy did not, however, end the conflict between the crown and Parliament. Tory Royalists pressed to restore many of the king's old prerogatives, and some even renewed claims for his divine right to absolute power.[8] On the other side, the Whigs who controlled Parliament strove to limit the power of the restored royal family, and the issue reached a climax during the Exclusion Crisis of 1679–81, when Parliament tried to pass a bill forbidding any Catholic from succeeding to the throne. Since such a law would have excluded the heir apparent, Charles's brother James, the king prevented it, but James's succession remained a sore point. He was peacefully crowned James II after his brother's death in 1685, but his policies seemed to favor Catholics. Defiance in Parliament and dislike in the population at large increased until, on the birth of a son to his Catholic wife and the consequent

---

[8] In this period, for example, Sir Robert Filmer's *Patriarcha* was published. Written in the 1640s, it argued that the king has a divine right of *ownership* over his subjects. Soon after the Glorious Revolution, the first of John Locke's *Two Treatises on Government* (1690) explicitly refuted that view.

prospect of a new line of Catholic monarchs, the powerful peers of the realm invited James's Protestant daughter, Mary (the offspring of an earlier marriage), and her husband, William of Orange, to take the throne. James II fled in 1688, and the accession of William and Mary, known as the Glorious or Bloodless Revolution, settled the balance of power in English politics.

Since Aphra Behn was a well-known royalist and outspoken supporter of James II, writing the story of an unfortunate king in the very year of the forced abdication of her sovereign, her contemporaries would probably have associated her royal hero with her royal Stuart patrons. And the narrator encourages such an association. For example, she has Oroonoko express his abhorrence of the execution of Charles I to prove his own qualification as a prince. Moreover, when the lieutenant governor tries to arrest her hero, she presents the dispute between Oroonoko's defenders and attackers as a replay of the drama surrounding the trial and execution of Charles I. The overseer of Lord Willoughby's plantation at Parham, where Oroonoko recovers after his disastrous insurrection, tells the lieutenant governor and the colony's council that their "Command did not extend to his Lord's *Plantation;* and that *Parham* was as much exempt from the Law as *White-hall;* and that they ought no more to touch the Servants of the Lord [Willoughby] — (who there represented the King's Person) than they cou'd those about the King himself" (p. 94). In this passage, Oroonoko is a literal stand-in for his lord, Willoughby, who in turn stands in for "the King himself" — Charles II by the early 1660s — and is thus above the law and reach of common men. Oroonoko here is also a metaphoric representative of Charles I, who tried, after his defeat by parliamentary forces, to defend himself against the charge that he was guilty of treason for levying war against Parliament. Like the subjects of the Stuarts, moreover, Oroonoko's own people betray him and are consequently bitterly reproached. Behn considered the treatment of James II to be a replay of the trial and execution of Charles I, and contemporary readers would certainly have recognized the fate of James II, deposed and exiled, in this tale of a king who endures a crushing reversal of fortune. The excessive violence at the end of Behn's story, therefore, leaves behind not just images of one "mangled King" (p. 100) but of many. And yet the mangling, imagined as both a stoic ordeal and a martyrdom, results in the apotheosis of the king, who is memorialized, and therefore perpetuates his kingly essence, in the very tragedy we have just read. *Oroonoko* must be read as a paean to kingship in general and a lament for its recent indignities and defeats.

OROONOKO IN THE CONTEXT
OF APHRA BEHN'S CAREER

Aphra Behn identified with mistreated monarchs. As a playwright, she styled herself "a King of Wit" and cast her audience in the role of "A Parliament, by Play-Bill, summoned here"[9]; but her theatrical parliament, like Charles II's real one in 1682, refused to supply the poet-king's tribute, that is, to support the playwright financially. She also identified with people who were turned into commodities, who were bought and sold, especially with prostitutes and middle-class women forced into unhappy marriages for money. She sometimes compared such women to slaves, and recent critics have noticed[10] that the early episodes of Imoinda's story in *Oroonoko* resemble those of other forced brides in Behn's works. Married women at the time belonged to their husbands as a form of nonalienable property, and Behn's portrait of a heroine who is actually sold into chattel slavery seems to be on a continuum with her vivid depictions of the many ways in which European women were also bartered. In her play *The Luckey Chance* (ca. 1686), for example, a husband gives his creditor the sexual use of his wife for one night in order to cover a gambling debt. Some form of commodification is the fate of most women in Behn's stories and plays, and she even ironically likened her situation as an author, striving to please a novelty-seeking public, to that of a prostitute in the prologue to her first play, *The Forced Marriage* (1670). Oroonoko, as a king who becomes a commodity, seems a conflation of the author's two favorite metaphors for her own profession. The tale, in other words, can also be read as a reflection on the career of this writer who has gone down in history as the first professional woman author in English.

Scholars are still pondering the mystery and significance of Aphra Behn's career. Since most of her works are seldom read today, and since we continue to believe in a strong prejudice against women writers in the seventeenth century, we have trouble making sense of her

---

[9] "Epilogue" to *The Second Part of the Rover.*
[10] See, for example, Ballaster 82–84 and Margaret Ferguson 159–81.

early acclaim. It strains our historical imagination and our sense of cultural continuity to realize that, after John Dryden, Behn was the most prolific and probably the most popular playwright of her time, the author of at least eighteen plays, as well as several volumes of poetry and numerous works of fiction that were in vogue for decades after her death. She was second only to Dryden also in the number of plays (four) produced at court. Moreover, most of the male writers to whom we might compare her had advantages of education and family that she lacked. Behn's origins are obscure; she was certainly not what she claimed to be in *Oroonoko,* that is, the legitimate daughter of the governor or intended governor of Suriname. We simply do not know how she received her education or her introduction to literary and theatrical circles.[11]

Behn's works, however, show that she capitalized on her femaleness and even sought, playfully, to intensify the odor of scandal that hung about her as a woman earning her living in public. Her writings were risqué, roguish, and outspokenly partisan; she purposely courted controversy and made herself into a sensational commodity. In the first decade of her literary career, 1672–82, her authorial persona is usually seductive, coaxing, and comical. But a somewhat more serious strain emerges in the works of the mid-1680s. These were very bad economic times for both the London theaters and the court, Behn's two best sources of income, and we might reasonably conclude that the writer's self-sale was beginning to seem more pathetic than comical. A slackening demand for plays forced Behn to write tales, scandalous chronicles, translations from works in languages she only half understood, and numerous poems. Her sense of being an exploited hack seems to have increased as the decade wore on, as did her identification with the equally unappreciated and mistreated heir to the English throne. Two of her last compositions were a celebratory ode on the coronation of James II and a "Congratulatory Poem" on the birth of his son (see pp. 154–56). Another of her last compositions was *Oroonoko.* Dying in 1688, Behn did not long survive these testimonials to the sovereignty of kingship.

Oroonoko can also be read as a testimonial to an ideal of sovereign authorship, authorship that is self-sustaining. It is the most self-

---

[11] Biographies of Aphra Behn speculate about her early life and education, coming to very different conclusions. See Todd, *Secret Life,* for the most recent and authoritative account. See also Duffy and Goreau. For a concise overview of Behn's career, see Todd's introduction to *The Works of Aphra Behn* 1: ix–xxxv.

referential of Behn's narratives. In many of her tales, the narrator is anonymous or is a person who gets her information secondhand from servants or other marginal characters. In contrast, the narrator of *Oroonoko* loudly announces herself as Aphra Behn, a writer already known to the public as a playwright, whose established reputation should guarantee her veracity. She even discusses her next play, stressing that, like *Oroonoko,* it is based to some extent on her life experience (p. 92). Clearly, Behn highlights narratorial-authorial continuity as a guarantee of the tale's authenticity. As a character in the tale, Behn also parallels herself with Oroonoko. Like him, she arrives a stranger in Suriname but is immediately recognized as superior to the local inhabitants; like him, she appears a shining marvel when she travels to the Indian village; and like his words, hers are always supposed to be truthful. The sustained authorial presence in this book is thus closely connected to the hero's black luster; as the story moves forward, narrator and hero brighten each other's celebrity. Although, in the beginning, Oroonoko had the misfortune "to fall in an obscure world, that afforded only a female pen to celebrate his fame" (p. 69), by the end the narrator presumes to hope "the Reputation of my Pen is considerable enough to make his Glorious Name to survive to all ages" (p. 100).

This is a degree of self-congratulation unprecedented in Behn's writings, but the sentiment is, after all, elegiac: what is left of Oroonoko is only his "Glorious Name." Indeed, Oroonoko could not be a hero of the very highest order — a tragic hero — unless he had sacrificed his life. The last sentence also hints at a certain reciprocity: if Behn's reputation preserves Oroonoko after his execution, then Oroonoko, as the author's greatest hero, will also keep Behn's name alive "to all ages." This implicit bid for her own immortality evokes the author's consciousness of her impending death; the posthumous adventures of herself and her kingly hero, she seems to realize, will be closely intertwined.

OROONOKOS

Behn's *Oroonoko* did, in fact, keep her name in the literary histories for hundreds of years after her death. Even the Victorians, who thought her other works obscene, praised it: "When Mrs. Behn's shortcomings are remembered against her 'Oroonoko' should be put to her credit; it is instinct with real feeling and womanly sympathy"

(A. M. Williams 590). *Womanly* is the key word here; readers in each century have been able to reconcile this one story of Behn's with their ideas of what a *woman* writer should accomplish. Late seventeenth- and early eighteenth-century readers saw *Oroonoko* primarily as a heroic love story, complete with a royal protagonist who performs deeds of superhuman strength and stoically suffers unbelievable torments for the sake of his honor. For these readers, Oroonoko's slavery was significant primarily because it allowed him to illustrate the belief that nobility is inborn and manifests itself even under the most adverse circumstances. Later eighteenth- and nineteenth-century commentators, like the Victorian quoted above, read *Oroonoko* more as a sentimental than as a heroic tale. They thought its ruling emotion was sympathy for the downtrodden in general and slaves in particular. When Harriet Beecher Stowe's antislavery novel *Uncle Tom's Cabin* came out in 1852, Behn's tale was frequently identified as one of its emancipationist forerunners.[12] Twentieth-century readers have continued to categorize *Oroonoko* as social or political commentary, often stressing that the author's marginal position, imposed by her gender, provided her with the vantage point of a critical outsider. Thus some twentieth-century commentators remade this Restoration Tory into their own favorite, feminist-inspired version of the prototypical woman writer: the subversive. *Oroonoko*'s most recent critics have produced more multifaceted formal and historical analyses that regard the author's gender as one element in a complex textual mixture. Over the centuries, Behn's narrative has yielded, and continues to yield, many different *Oroonoko*s, most of them the products of "womanly" writers.

There were, moreover, later Oroonokos with different fates, for the hero had a life of his own beyond Behn's text and its interpretations. In the French translation of 1745, for example, the ending is completely revised to allow the hero and heroine to return to Africa and live happily ever after. The more typical revisions, though, were the theatrical versions. First adapted to the stage in 1696 by Thomas Southerne (see pp. 107–31), *Oroonoko* was a huge hit; contemporaries thought it as good as, if not better than, *Othello*. As the passages from the play reprinted in this volume attest, Southerne's hero is more decorous and conventional than Behn's. He cannot bring himself, for example, to deliver the coup de grâce to his European Imoinda, who stabs herself with the dagger he holds, and he certainly does not cut off her face or lie down beside her rotting body. Moreover, the play begins with

[12] See, for example, "England's First Lady Novelist" 854.

Oroonoko's arrival in Suriname, and no mention is made of his previous involvement with the slave trade. In later theatrical revisions, the slave trade becomes a more prominent thematic issue. In 1760, John Hawkesworth excised Southerne's comic subplot as unworthy of such a weighty drama and an anonymous writer added the dialogue on slavery reprinted in this volume (see pp. 132–40). Later versions are even more outspokenly antislavery, and we might surmise that one reason Behn's slave-trading king could be read as an antislavery hero by the 1850s was that most Victorians filtered her text through the stage versions they had seen.

This volume adds even more Oroonokos to the number already in circulation, inviting you to reflect on the many versions of this character that inhabited the seventeenth- and eighteenth-century British imagination. In the century after *Oroonoko*'s publication, English literature became increasingly thick with "Guinea's Captive Kings"[13]; it is hoped that the collection of surrounding texts in Part Two of this volume will encourage you to think beyond the literary works into the general discourse about slaves and their destinies. Stedman's rebellious Baron is an Oroonoko whose insurrection succeeded; the Young Prince of Annamaboe is another whose father forced the English to send him home. Equiano is a third who purchased his freedom and agitated for the abolition of slavery. The more these alternative stories resonate with and against Aphra Behn's tragedy, the deeper its significance for us becomes.

[13] For a history of this figure in English literature, see Sypher.

Chronology of
Behn's Life and Times

1640
Probable year of Aphra Behn's birth. Her parents might have been Bartholomew and Elizabeth Johnson of Kent. Nothing is known of her early life and education.

Marks the beginning of the devotion of English holdings in the Caribbean to sugar production.

1642
Outbreak of the Civil War, sometimes called the "Puritan Revolution," in England.

Theaters closed.

1643–45
Short-lived English settlement in Suriname.

1649
Charles I tried and executed. Oliver Cromwell becomes head of state of the newly established Commonwealth.

1651–52
Guinea Company founded to trade on the West Coast of Africa for ivory, gold, and slaves.

Francis, Lord Willoughby, establishes a colony in Suriname.

Thomas Hobbes publishes Leviathan, an argument for absolute monarchy on secular, rather than religious, grounds.

1653
Oliver Cromwell named Lord Protector.

1658
Oliver Cromwell dies, and his son Richard is unable to maintain the Protectorate.

1660
Charles II, who has been in exile in France, returns to England, and the Stuart monarchy is restored.

Two theater companies chartered, the King's Players and the Duke's Company.

Company of Royal Adventurers into Africa is chartered, replacing the Guinea Company. They begin major trading activity for ivory, gold, and slaves under a new charter three years later.

Samuel Pepys, an administrator in the Navy Office, begins keeping his diary, which he continued for nine years. Published in the nineteenth century, it is the fullest account of life in Restoration London.

1662
Charles II charters the Royal Society of London for the Improving of Natural Knowledge, thus granting official approval to the fledgling natural sciences.

Samuel Butler publishes first part of *Hudibras*.

1663–64
Behn probably a visitor to Suriname.

1665
The last major outbreak of the Plague in England ravages the nation.

1665–67
Second Dutch War effectually destroys the Company of Royal Adventurers and also results in the ceding of Suriname to the Dutch.

John Dryden's *Indian Emperor* produced.

1666
Great Fire of London destroys two-thirds of the city.

John Bunyan's *Grace Abounding to the Chief of Sinners* published.

1667

Behn serves as a spy in Antwerp.

Publication of John Milton's *Paradise Lost*.

1670

Behn's first play, *The Forced Marriage,* performed by the Duke's Company.

1671

Behn's *The Amorous Prince* produced.

1672

Behn edits a collection of poetry, *Covent Garden Drollery.*

Royal African Company established, replacing the previous Company of Royal Adventurers.

William Wycherly's *The Country Wife* produced.

1673

Behn's *The Dutch Lover* produced.

Passage of the Test Act, requiring all holders of civil and military offices to conform to Anglican church rites. It excluded both nonconforming Protestants (Puritans) and Roman Catholics from public life.

Between this year and 1689, the Royal African Company ships 26,245 enslaved Africans to Barbados.

1676

Behn's only tragedy, *Abdelazer,* and *The Town-Fopp* produced.

George Etherege's *The Man of Mode* produced.

1677

Behn's *The Debauchee* and her most successful play, *The Rover,* produced.

John Dryden's *All for Love* produced.

1678

Behn's *Sir Patient Fancy* produced.

John Bunyan's *The Pilgrim's Progress from This World to That Which Is to Come* published.

1678–81

Popish Plot divides England and forces the creation of the first political parties, the Whigs and the Tories.

1679

Behn's *The Young King* and *The Feign'd Curtizans* produced.

1680

Behn's *The Revenge* produced.

1681

Behn's *The Second Part of the Rover* and *The False Count* produced.

Dryden's *Absalom and Achitophel* published.

1681–82

Behn's *The Roundheads* produced.

Whigs in Parliament try to exclude Charles II's brother James from the line of succession to the throne because of his Catholicism, precipitating the Exclusion Crisis.

1682

Behn's *The City-Heiress* produced.

Dryden's *Mac Flecknoe* published.

1684

Behn's *Poems upon Several Occasions* published, as is the first part of her *Love Letters Between a Nobleman And His Sister*. This scandalous tale, which was destined to be continued in two much longer volumes, retailed amorous intrigues in the circle of the banished James Scott, Duke of Monmouth and bastard son of Charles II, whom many Protestants wished would succeed his father.

1685

Charles II dies; James II is crowned his successor. The Duke of Monmouth returns from abroad and tries to lead a rebellion against his uncle. He is defeated and executed.

Behn publishes poems mourning Charles's death and celebrating the succession of James in *Miscellany, Being a collection of poems By several Hands*.

The Second Part of Behn's *Love Letters* appears, attacking Monmouth.

Behn publishes her translation of François, duc de La Rochefoucauld's *Réflexions ou sentences et maximes morales* (1675) as *Seneca Unmasqued*.

Import taxes are doubled, significantly increasing the cost of such products as sugar, and the West Indian interests increasingly complain about taxation and monopoly.

1686

Behn's *The Luckey Chance* produced.

Behn's very loose translation of Balthazar de Bonnecourse's *La montre* published under the same title.

1687

The Third Part of the *Love Letters* is published.

Behn's *Emperor of the Moon* produced.

1688

Behn publishes *Oroonoko, The Fair Jilt, Agnes de Castro,* and numerous poems in *Lycidus . . . Together with a Miscellany of New Poems by Several Hands.* The latter volume also includes her translation of Abbé Paul Tallemant's *Le second voyage de l'Isle d'Amour* (1664).

Behn translates Bernard le Bovier de Fontenelle's *Entretiens sur la pluralité des mondes* (1686) as *A Discovery of New Worlds* and his *L'histoire des oracles* (1687) as *The History of Oracles.*

1689

Behn dies on April 16 and is buried in Westminster Abbey.

Behn's *The Lucky Mistake* and *The History of the Nun* posthumously published and her *The Widdow Ranter* posthumously produced.

The Glorious Revolution leads to the abdication of James II and the coronation of William and Mary of Orange.

Official support for the Royal African Company weakens.

1690

Behn's *The Widdow Ranter* posthumously published.

John Locke's *Essay Concerning Human Understanding* and *Two Treatises on Government* published.

1694

Mary Astell's *A Serious Proposal to the Ladies* published.

1695

Price of slaves in the West Indies begins to increase, stabilizing at approximately £8 sterling in 1705.

William Congreve's *Love for Love* produced.

1696

The Histories and Novels of the late Ingenious Mrs Behn, which includes works previously unpublished, is brought out.

Behn's *The Younger Brother* posthumously produced and published.

1698

Ten Percent Act formally terminates Royal African Company's monopoly; private slave trade becomes legal.

A Note on the Text

This volume reprints Janet Todd's 1995 edition of *Oroonoko; or, The Royal Slave,* published in London by William Pickering in *The Works of Aphra Behn,* volume 3, pp. 50–119. We thank Pickering & Chatto Publishers for permission to use this edition. Todd based her work on the text of *OROONOKO: Or, The Royal Slave* in *Three Histories . . . By Mrs. A. BEHN,* published in London in 1688, "printed for W. Canning, at his Shop in the Temple-Cloysters." Earlier in the same year, Canning had issued *Oroonoko* in a single volume; in *Three Histories* it is bound with *The Fair Jilt* and *Agnes de Castro.* Students should be aware that the Pickering edition retains the original seventeenth-century spelling, punctuation, and other textual peculiarities. We have added footnotes when seventeenth-century usage departs significantly from that of our day and have put in quotation marks spellings of place names that differ from the modern.

In Part Two, texts are normally either from first editions or from the standard scholarly editions; they have not been modified, although the long "s" has been modernized where it appears. When first editions have not been used, the text is specified in the headnote to the selection.

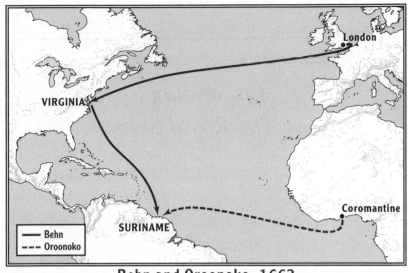

Behn and Oroonoko, 1663

The narrator of *Oroonoko* claims to have traveled one side of the Atlantic triangle, from England to the Caribbean. It is speculated that the historic Aphra Behn might have stopped off in Virginia, since she wrote a play about that colony demonstrating considerable familiarity with it. Oroonoko is said to have been shipped directly from the Gold Coast of Africa to Suriname. The solid line on the above map represents Behn's probable route, and the dotted line represents Oroonoko's journey.

Oroonoko;
or, The Royal Slave

To the Right Honourable the Lord Maitland,[1]

My Lord,

Since the World is grown so Nice[2] and Critical upon Dedications, and will Needs be Judging the Book by the Wit of the Patron; we ought, with a great deal of Circumspection, to chuse a Person against whom there can be no Exception; and whose Wit and Worth truly Merits all that one is capable of saying upon that Occasion.

The most part of Dedications are charg'd with Flattery; and if the World knows a Man has some Vices, they will not allow one to speak of his Virtues. This, my Lord, is for want[3] of thinking Rightly; if Men wou'd consider with Reason, they wou'd have another sort of Opinion, and Esteem of Dedications; and wou'd believe almost every Great Man has enough to make him Worthy of all that can be said of him there. My Lord, a Picture-drawer, when he intends to make a good Picture, essays the Face many Ways, and in many Lights, before he

---

[1] *Lord Maitland:* Richard Maitland (1653–1695) was, like Behn, a strong supporter of the Stuarts, and he became a member of James II's court in exile after the Glorious Revolution of 1688. Despite his own Catholic inclinations, which Behn commends on the next page of her preface, Maitland would later object to James's extreme Catholic policies, and in the early 1690s he was banished from James's court.

[2] *Nice:* Cautious, fastidious.

[3] *want:* Lack.

begins; that he may chuse, from the several turns of it, which is most Agreeable, and gives it the best Grace; and if there be a Scar, an ungrateful[4] Mole, or any little Defect, they leave it out; and yet make the Picture extreamly like: But he who has the good Fortune to draw a Face that is exactly Charming in all its Parts and Features, what Colours or Agreements[5] can be added to make it Finer? All that he can give it but its due; and Glories in a Piece whose Original alone gives it its Perfection. An ill Hand may diminish, but a good Hand cannot augment its Beauty. A Poet is a Painter in his way; he draws to the Life, but in another kind, we draw the Nobler part, the Soul and Mind; the Pictures of the Pen shall out-last those of the Pencil, and even Worlds themselves. 'Tis a Short Chronicle of those Lives that possibly wou'd be forgotten by other Historians, or lye neglected there, however deserving an immortal Fame; for Men of eminent Parts[6] are as Exemplary as even Monarchs themselves; and Virtue is a noble Lesson to be learn'd, and 'tis by Comparison we can Judge and Chuse. 'Tis by such illustrious Presidents[7] as your Lordship the World can be Better'd and Refin'd; when a great part of the lazy Nobility shall, with Shame, behold the admirable Accomplishments of a Man so Great, and so Young.

Your Lordship has Read innumerable Volumes of Men, and Books, not Vainly for the gust[8] of Novelty, but Knowledge, excellent Knowledge: Like the industrious Bee, from every Flower you return Laden with the precious Dew, which you are sure to turn to the Publick Good. You hoard no one Perfection, but lay it all out in the Glorious Service of your Religion and Country; to both which you are a useful and necessary Honour: They both want such Supporters; and 'tis only Men of so elevated Parts, and fine Knowledge; such noble Principles of Loyalty and Religion this Nation Sighs for. Where is it amongst all our Nobility we shall find so great a Champion for the Catholick Church? With what Divine Knowledge have you writ in Defence of the Faith! How unanswerably have you clear'd all these Intricacies in Religion, which even the Gownmen[9] have left Dark and Difficult! With what unbeaten Arguments you convince, the Faithless, and instruct the

---

[4] *ungrateful:* Displeasing.
[5] *Agreements:* Attractions.
[6] *Parts:* Talents.
[7] *Presidents:* Precedents, examples.
[8] *gust:* Taste.
[9] *Gownmen:* Clerics.

Ignorant! Where shall we find a Man so Young, Like St. Augustine,[10] *in the midst of all his Youth and Gaiety, Teaching the World divine Precepts, true Notions of Faith, and Excellent Morality, and, at the same time, be also a perfect Pattern of all that accomplish a Great Man? You have, my Lord, all that refin'd Wit that Charms, and the Affability that Obliges; a Generosity that gives a Lustre to your Nobility; that Hospitality, and Greatness of Mind, that ingages the World; and that admirable Conduct, that so well Instructs it. Our Nation ought to regret and bemoan their Misfortunes, for not being able to claim the Honour of the Birth of a Man who is so fit to serve his Majesty, and his Kingdoms, in all Great and Publick Affairs: And to the Glory of your Nation[11] be it spoken, it produces more considerable Men, for all fine Sence, Wit, Wisdom, Breeding, and Generosity (for the generality of the Nobility) than all other Nations can Boast; and the Fruitfulness of your Virtues sufficiently make amends for the Barrenness of your Soil: Which however cannot be incommode[12] to your Lordship; since your Quality, and the Veneration that the Commonalty naturally pay their Lords, creates a flowing Plenty there — that makes you Happy. And to compleat your Happiness, my Lord, Heaven has blest you with a Lady, to whom it has given all the Graces, Beauties, and Virtues of her Sex; all the Youth, Sweetness of Nature; of a most illustrious Family;[13] and who is a most rare Example to all Wives of Quality, for her eminent Piety, Easiness, and Condescention,[14] and as absolutely merits Respect from all the World, as she does that Passion and Resignation she receives from your Lordship; and which is, on her part, with so much Tenderness return'd. Methinks your tranquil Lives are an Image of the New Made and Beautiful Pair in Paradise: And 'tis the Prayers and Wishes of all, who have the Honour to know you, that it may Eternally so continue, with Additions of all the Blessings this World can give you.*

---

[10] *St Augustine:* St. Augustine of Hippo (354–430), a church father who converted to Christianity at the age of thirty-two and established a monastic Christian community in North Africa. Lord Maitland, whom Behn praises for his youthful dedication, was thirty-five at the time of *Oroonoko's* publication.

[11] *your Nation:* Lord Maitland was from Scotland.

[12] *incommode:* Inconvenient (French).

[13] *a Lady . . . of a most illustrious Family:* Maitland's wife, Anne Campbell, was the daughter of the Earl of Argyll, who had participated in a plot against Charles II; Maitland himself was wrongly suspected of having aided the conspirators, and was removed from his position as lord justice general in 1684.

[14] *Condescention:* Graciousness to inferiors (not in a derogatory sense).

My Lord, the Obligations I have to some of the Great Men of your Nation, particularly to your Lordship, gives me an Ambition of making my Acknowledgments, by all the Opportunities I can; and such humble Fruits, as my Industry produces, I lay at your Lordships feet. This is a true Story, of a Man Gallant enough to merit your Protection; and, had he always been so Fortunate, he had not made so Inglorious an end: The Royal Slave I had the Honour to know in my Travels to the other World; and though I had none above me in that Country, yet I wanted power to preserve this Great Man. If there be any thing that seems Romantick, I beseech your Lordship to consider, these Countries do, in all things, so far differ from ours, that they produce unconceivable Wonders; at least, they appear so to us, because New and Strange. What I have mention'd I have taken care shou'd be Truth, let the Critical Reader judge as he pleases. 'Twill be no Commendation to the book, to assure your Lordship I writ it in a few Hours, though it may serve to Excuse some of its Faults of Connexion; for I never rested my Pen a Moment for Thought: 'Tis purely the Merit of my Slave that must render it worthy of the Honour it begs; and the Author of that of Subscribing herself,

My Lord,

Your Lordship's most obliged

and obedient Servant,

A. BEHN.

The HISTORY of the Royal Slave.

I do not pretend, in giving you the History of this *Royal Slave*, to entertain my Reader with the Adventures of a feign'd *Hero*, whose Life and Fortunes Fancy may manage at the Poets Pleasure; not in relating the Truth, design to adorn it with any Accidents, but such as arriv'd in earnest to him: And it shall come simply into the World, recommended by its own proper Merits, and natural Intrigues; there being enough of Reality to support it, and to render it diverting, without the Addition of Invention.

I was my self an Eye-Witness to a great part, of what you will find here set down; and what I cou'd not be Witness of, I receiv'd from the Mouth of the chief Actor in this History, the *Hero* himself, who gave us the whole Transactions of his Youth; and though I shall omit, for Brevity's sake, a thousand little Accidents of his Life, which, however pleasant to us, where History was scarce, and Adventures very rare; yet might prove tedious and heavy to my Reader, in a World where he finds Diversions for every Minute, new and strange: But we who were perfectly charm'd with the Character of this great Man, were curious to gather every Circumstance of his Life.

The scene of the last part of his Adventures lies in a Colony in *America,* called *Surinam,*[15] in the *West Indies.*

But before I give you the Story of this *Gallant Slave,* 'tis fit I tell you the manner of bringing them to these new *Colonies;* for those they make use of there, are not *Natives* of the place; for those we live with in perfect Amity, without daring to command 'em; but on the contrary, caress 'em with all the brotherly and friendly Affection in the World; trading with 'em for their Fish, Venison, Buffilo's, Skins, and little Rarities; as Marmosets, a sort of *Monkey* as big as a Rat or Weesel, but of a marvellous and delicate shape, and has Face and Hands like an Humane Creature: and *Cousheries,*[16] a little Beast in the form and fashion of a Lion, as big as Kitten; but so exactly made in all parts like that noble Beast, that it is it in *Minature.* Then for little *Parakeetoes,* great Parrots, *Muckaws,*[17] and a thousand other Birds and Beasts of wonderful and surprizing Forms, Shapes, and Colours. For Skins of prodigious Snakes, of which there are some threescore Yards in length; as is the Skin of one that may be seen at His Majesty's *Antiquaries:*[18] Where are also some rare Flies,[19] of amazing Forms and Colours, presented to 'em by my self; some as big as my Fist, some less; and all of various Excellencies, such as Art cannot imitate. Then we trade for

(handwritten margin note: These are used for trades)

---

[15] *Surinam:* On the northern coast of South America, near the English Caribbean colonies in the West Indies. Because the colonists in Suriname focused on the production of sugar — an extremely labor-intensive process — they established large plantations and quickly began importing large numbers of slaves to work on the farms. The colony in Suriname was founded in 1651 by Francis, Lord Willoughby, governor of Barbados, who spent very little time in Suriname himself, as Behn laments at several points in *Oroonoko.* It remains unclear whether she knew Willoughby personally, but she shared his Royalist politics, and may have traveled to Suriname at his request. For further discussion of Willoughby and colonial life in Suriname, see Part Two, Chapter 4.

[16] *Cousheries:* Though various contemporary sources mention this animal, they differ in their descriptions. It probably refers to a species of marmoset, a kind of small monkey.

[17] *Muckaws:* I.e., macaws.

[18] *Antiquaries:* Antiques; Behn is probably referring to the museum of the Royal Society, which collected artefacts and oddities of natural history, both ancient and modern.

[19] *rare Flies:* Butterflies.

Feathers, which they order into all Shapes, make themselves little short Habits of 'em, and glorious Wreaths for their Heads, Necks, Arms and Legs, whose Tinctures are unconceivable. I had a Set of these presented to me, and I gave 'em to the King's Theatre, and it was the Dress of the *Indian Queen*,[20] infinitely admir'd by Persons of Quality; and were unimitable. Besides these, a thousand little Knacks, and Rarities in Nature, and some of Art; as their Baskets, Weapons, Aprons, &c. We dealt with 'em with Beads of all Colours, Knives, Axes, Pins and Needles; which they us'd only as Tools to drill Holes with in their Ears, Noses and Lips, where they hang a great many little things; as long Beads, bits of Tin, Brass, or Silver, beat thin; and any shining Trincket. The Beads they weave into Aprons about a quarter of an Ell[21] long, and of the same breadth; working them very prettily in Flowers of several Colours of Beads; which Apron they wear just before 'em, as *Adam* and *Eve* did the Fig-leaves; the Men wearing a long Stripe of Linen, which they deal with us for. They thread these Beads also on long Cotton-threads, and make Girdles to tie their Aprons to, which come twenty times, or more, about the Waste; and then cross, like a Shoulder-belt, both ways, and round their Necks, Arms and Legs. This Adornment, with their long black Hair, and the Face painted in little Specks or Flowers here and there, makes 'em a wonderful Figure to behold. Some of the Beauties which indeed are finely shap'd, as almost all are, and who have pretty Features, are very charming and novel; for they have all that is called Beauty, except the Colour, which is a reddish Yellow; or after a new Oiling, which they often use to themselves, they are of the colour of a new Brick, but smooth, soft and sleek. They are extream modest and bashful, very shy, and nice[22] of being touch'd. And though they are all thus naked, if one lives for ever among 'em, there is not to be seen an indecent Action, or Glance; and being continually us'd to see one another so unadorn'd, so like our first Parents before the Fall, it seems as if they had no Wishes; there being nothing to heighten Curiosity, but all you can see, you see at once, and every Moment see; and where there is no Novelty, there can be no Curiosity. Not but I have seen a handsom

---

[20] *Indian Queen:* A character in a play by the same name, written in 1664 by John Dryden and Sir Robert Howard. It is unclear whether Behn's feathers were used in the play's first run, or in a revival staged in 1668. For more on Dryden, see Part Two, Chapter 2.

[21] *a quarter of an Ell:* An ell was about forty-five inches, so the aprons are about one square foot.

[22] *nice:* Fastidious, shy.

young *Indian,* dying for Love of a very beautiful young *Indian* Maid; but all his Courtship was, to fold his Arms, pursue her with his Eyes, and Sighs were all his Language: While she, as if no such Lover were present; or rather, as if she desired none such, carefully guarded her Eyes from beholding him; and never approach'd him, but she look'd down with all the blushing Modesty I have seen in the most severe and cautious of our World. And these People represented to me an absolute *Idea* of the first State of Innocence, before Man knew how to sin: And 'tis most evident and plain, that simple Nature is the most harmless, inoffensive and vertuous Mistress. 'Tis she alone, if she were permitted, that better instructs the World, than all the Inventions of Man: Religion wou'd here but destroy that Tranquillity, they possess by Ignorance; and Laws wou'd but teach 'em to know, Offence, of which now they have no Notion. They once made Mourning and Fasting for the Death of the *English* Governor, who had given his Hand to come on such a Day to 'em, and neither came, nor sent; believing, when once a Man's Word was past, nothing but Death cou'd or shou'd prevent his keeping it: And when they saw he was not dead, they ask'd him, what Name they had for a Man who promis'd a thing he did not do? The Governor told them, Such a man was a *Lyar,* which was a Word of Infamy to a Gentleman. Then one of 'em reply'd, *Governor, you are a Lyar, and guilty of that Infamy.* They have a Native Justice, which knows no Fraud; and they understand no vice, or Cunning, but when they are taught by the *White Men.* They have Plurality of Wives, which, when they grow old, they serve those that succeed 'em, who are young; but with a Servitude easie and respected; and unless they take Slaves in War, they have no other Attendants.

Those on that *Continent* where I was, had no King; but the oldest War Captain was obey'd with great Resignation.

A War Captain is a Man who has lead them on to Battel with Conduct, and Success; of whom I shall have Occasion to speak more hereafter, and of some other of their Customs and Manners, as they fall in my way.

With these People, as I said, we live in perfect Tranquillity, and good Understanding, as it behooves us to do; they knowing all the places where to seek the best Food of the country, and the Means of getting it; and for very small and unvaluable Trifles, supply us with what 'tis impossible for us to get; for they do not only in the Wood, and over the *Sevana's,*[23] in Hunting, supply the parts of Hounds, by

---

[23] *Sevana's:* Savannas.

swiftly scouring through those almost impassable places; and by the meer Activity of their Feet, run down the nimblest Deer, and other eatable Beasts: But in the water, one wou'd think they were Gods of the Rivers, or Fellow-Citizens of the Deep; so rare an Art they have in Swimming, Diving, and almost Living in Water; by which they command the less swift Inhabitants of the Floods. And then for Shooting; what they cannot take, or reach with their Hands, they do with Arrows; and have so admirable an Aim, that they will split almost an Hair; and at any distance that an Arrow can reach, they will shoot down Oranges, and other Fruit, and only touch the Stalk with the Darts Points, that they may not hurt the Fruit. So that they being, on all Occasions, very useful to us, we find it absolutely necessary to caress 'em as Friends, and not to treat 'em as Slaves; nor dare we do other, their Numbers so far surpassing ours in that *Continent.*

Those then whom we make use of to work in our Plantations of Sugar, are *Negro's, Black-*Slaves altogether; which are transported thither in this manner.

Those who want Slaves, make a Bargain with a Master, or Captain of a Ship, and contract to pay him so much a-piece, a matter of twenty Pound a Head for as many as he agrees for, and to pay for 'em when they shall be deliver'd on such a Plantation: So that when there arrives a Ship laden with Slaves, they who have so contracted, go a-board, and receive their Number by Lot; and perhaps in one Lot that may be for ten, there may happen to be three or four Men; the rest, Women and Children: Or be there more or less of either Sex, you are oblig'd to be contented with your Lot.

Coramantien,[24] a Country of *Blacks* so called, was one of those places in which they found the most advantageous Trading for these Slaves; and thither most of our great Traders in that Merchandice traffick'd; for that Nation is very war-like and brave; and having a continual Campaign, being always in Hostility with one neighbouring Prince or other, they had the fortune to take a great many Captives; for all they took in Battel, were sold as Slaves; at least, those common Men who cou'd not ransom themselves. Of these Slaves so taken, the General only has all the profit; and of these Generals, our Captains and Masters of Ships buy all their Freights.

---

[24] *Coramantien:* A Gold Coast slave-trading station, located in the Fantee country just a few miles east of Annamaboe (see map on p. 211). Slaves sold there were generally referred to as "Cormantines," even though many had been brought from a considerable distance inland.

The King of *Coramantien* was himself a Man of a Hundred and odd Years old, and had no Son, though he had many beautiful *Black*-Wives; for most certainly, there are Beauties that can charm of that Colour. In his younger Years he had had many gallant Men to his Sons, thirteen of which died in Battel, conquering when they fell; and he had only left him for his Successor, one Grand-Child, Son to one of these dead Victors; who, as soon as he cou'd bear a Bow in his Hand, and a Quiver at his Back, was sent into the Field, to be trained up by one of the oldest Generals, to War; where, from his natural Inclination to Arms, and the Occasions given him, with the good Conduct of the old General, he became, at the Age of Seventeen, of the most expert Captains, and bravest Soldiers, that ever saw the Field of *Mars*:[25] So that he was ador'd as the Wonder of all that World, and the Darling of the Soldiers. Besides, he was adorn'd with a native Beauty so transcending all those of his gloomy Race, that he strook an Awe and Reverence, even in those that knew not his Quality; as he did in me, who beheld him with Surprize and Wonder, when afterwards he arriv'd in our World.

He had scarce arriv'd at his Seventeenth Year, when fighting by his Side, the General was kill'd with an Arrow in his Eye, which the Prince *Oroonoko* (for so was this gallant *Moor*[26] call'd) very narrowly avoided; nor had he, if the General, who saw the Arrow shot, and perceiving it aim'd at the Prince, had not bow'd his Head between, on purpose to receive it in his own Body rather than it shou'd touch that of the Prince, and so saved him.

'Twas then, afflicted as *Oroonoko* was, that he was proclaim'd General in the Old Man's place; and then it was, at the finishing of that War, which had continu'd for two Years, that the Prince came to Court; where he had hardly been a Month together, from the time of his fifth Year, to that of Seventeen; and 'twas amazing to imagine where it was he learn'd so much Humanity; or, to give his Accomplishments a juster Name, where 'twas he got that real Greatness of Soul, those refin'd Notions of true Honour, that absolute Generosity, and that Softness that was capable of the highest Passions of Love and Gallantry, whose Objects were almost continually fighting Men, or those mangl'd, or dead; who heard no Sounds, but those of War and Groans: Some part of it we may attribute to the Care of a *French*-Man

[25] *Field of Mars:* Battlefield (Mars was the Roman god of war).
[26] *Moor:* Used generically for Africans; the term originally applied to natives of Mauritania, a region now divided between Morocco and Algeria.

of Wit and Learning; who finding it turn to very good Account to be a sort of Royal Tutor to this young *Black,* & perceiving him very ready, apt, and quick of Apprehension, took a great pleasure to teach him Morals, Language and Science; and was for it extreamly belov'd and valu'd by him. Another Reason was, He lov'd, when he came from War, to see all the *English* Gentlemen that traded thither; and did not only learn their Language, but that of the *Spaniards* also, with whom he traded afterwards for Slaves.

I have often seen and convers'd with this great Man, and been a Witness to many of his mighty Actions; and do assure my Reader, the most Illustrious Courts cou'd not have produc'd a braver Man, both for Greatness of Courage and Mind, a Judgment more solid, a Wit more quick, and a Conversation more sweet and diverting. He knew almost as much as if he had read much: He had heard of, and admir'd the *Romans;* he had heard of the late Civil Wars in *England,*[27] and the deplorable Death of our great Monarch; and wou'd discourse of it with all the Sense, and Abhorrence of the Injustice imaginable. He had an extream good and graceful Mien, and all the Civility of a well-bred great Man. He had nothing of Barbarity in his Nature, but in all Points address'd himself, as if his Education had been in some *European* Court.

This great and just Character of *Oroonoko* gave me an extream Curiosity to see him, especially when I knew he spoke *French* and *English,* and that I cou'd talk with him. But though I had heard so much of him, I was as greatly surpriz'd when I saw him, as if I had heard nothing of him; so beyond all Report I found him. He came into the Room, and address'd himself to me, and some other Women, with the best Grace in the World. He was pretty tall, but of a Shape the most exact that can be fansy'd: The most famous Statuary[28] cou'd not form the Figure of a Man more admirably turn'd from Head to Foot. His Face was not of that brown, rusty Black which most of that Nation are, but a perfect Ebony, or polish'd Jett. His Eyes were the most awful that cou'd be seen, and very piercing; the White of 'em being like Snow, as were his Teeth. His Nose was rising and *Roman,* instead of *African* and flat. His Mouth, the finest shap'd that cou'd be seen; far from those great turn'd Lips, which are so natural to the rest

[27] *late Civil Wars in England:* The wars in the 1640s between the royalists (who supported Charles I) and the parliamentarians (who supported Oliver Cromwell). Charles I was executed in 1649, but the monarchy was restored in 1660 when Charles II took the throne.

[28] *Statuary:* Sculptor.

of the *Negroes*. The whole Proportion and Air of his Face was so noble, and exactly form'd, that, bating[29] his Colour, there cou'd be nothing in Nature more beautiful, agreeable and handsome. There was no one Grace wanting, that bears the Standard of true Beauty: His Hair came down to his Shoulders, by the Aids of Art; which was, by pulling it out with a Quill, and keeping it comb'd; of which he took particular Care. Nor did the Perfections of his Mind come short of those of his Person; for his Discourse was admirable upon almost any Subject; and who-ever had heard him speak, wou'd have been convinc'd of their Errors, that all fine Wit is confin'd to the *White* Men, especially to those of *Christendom;* and wou'd have confess'd that *Oroonoko* was as capable even of reigning well, and of governing as wisely, had as great a Soul, as politick[30] Maxims, and was as sensible of Power as any Prince civiliz'd in the most refin'd Schools of Humanity and Learning, or the most Illustrious Courts.

This Prince, such as I have describ'd him, whose Soul and Body were so admirably adorn'd, was (while yet he was in the Court of his Grandfather) as I said, as capable of Love, as 'twas possible for a brave and gallant Man to be; and in saying that, I have nam'd the highest Degree of Love; for sure, great Souls are most capable of that Passion.

I have already said, the old General was kill'd by the shot of an Arrow, by the Side of this Prince, in Battel; and that *Oroonoko* was made General. This old dead *Hero* had one only Daughter left of his Race; a Beauty that, to describe her truly, one need say only, she was Female to the noble Male; the beautiful *Black Venus*,[31] to our young *Mars;* as charming in her Person as he, and of delicate Vertues. I have seen an hundred *White* Men sighing after her, and making a thousand Vows at her Feet, all vain, and unsuccessful: And she was, indeed, too great for any, but a Prince of her own Nation to adore.

Oroonoko coming from the Wars, (which were now ended) after he had made his Court to his Grandfather, he thought in Honour he ought to make a Visit to *Imoinda,* the Daughter of his Foster-father, the dead General; and to make some Excuses to her, because his Preservation was the Occasion of her Father's Death; and to present her with those Slaves that had been taken in this last Battel, as the Trophies of her Father's Victories. When he came, attended by all the young Soldiers of any Merit, he was infinitely surpriz'd at the Beauty

[29] *bating:* Except for.
[30] *politick:* Clever, shrewd.
[31] *Venus:* Roman goddess of love.

of this fair Queen of Night, whose Face and Person was so exceeding all he had ever beheld, that lovely Modesty with which she receiv'd him, that Softness in her Look, and Sighs, upon the melancholy Occasion of this Honour that was done by so great a Man as *Oroonoko,* and a Prince of whom she had heard such admirable things; the Awfulness[32] wherewith she receiv'd him, and the Sweetness of her Words and Behaviour while he stay'd, gain'd a perfect Conquest over his fierce Heart, and made him feel, the Victor cou'd be subdu'd. So that having made his first Complements, and presented her an hundred and fifty Slaves in Fetters, he told her with his Eyes, that he was not insensible of her Charms; while *Imoinda,* who wish'd for nothing more than so glorious a Conquest, was pleas'd to believe, she understood that silent Language of new-born Love; and from that Moment, put on all her Additions to Beauty.

The Prince return'd to Court with quite another Humour than before; and though he did not speak much of the fair *Imoinda,* he had the pleasure to hear all his Followers speak of nothing but the Charms of that Maid; insomuch that, even in the Presence of the old King, they were extolling her, and heightning, if possible, the Beauties they had found in her: So that nothing else was talk'd of, no other Sound was heard in every Corner where there were Whisperers, but *Imoinda! Imoinda!*

'Twill be imagin'd *Oroonoko* stay'd not long before he made his second Visit; nor, considering his Quality, not much longer before he told her, he ador'd her. I have often heard him say, that he admir'd[33] by what strange Inspiration he came to talk things so soft, and so passionate, who never knew Love, nor was us'd to the Conversation of Women; but (to use his own Words) he said, Most happily, some new, and till then unknown Power instructed his Heart and Tongue in the Language of Love, and at the same time, in favour of him, inspir'd *Imoinda* with a Sense of his Passion. She was touch'd with what he said, and return'd it all in such Answers as went to his very Heart, with a Pleasure unknown before: Nor did he use those Obligations[34] ill, that Love had done him; but turn'd all his happy Moments to the best advantage; and as he knew no Vice, his Flame aim'd at nothing but Honour, if such a distinction may be made in Love; and especially in that Country, where Men take to themselves as many as they can

---

[32] *Awfulness:* Bashfulness (she is awestruck).
[33] *admir'd:* Marveled.
[34] *Obligations:* Favors.

maintain; and where the only Crime and Sin with Woman is, to turn her off, to abandon her to Want, Shame and Misery: Such ill Morals are only practis'd in *Christian*-Countries, where they prefer the bare Name of Religion; and, without Vertue or Morality, think that's sufficient. But *Oroonoko* was none of those Professors; but as he had right Notions of Honour, so he made her such Propositions as were not only and barely such; but, contrary to the Custom of his Country, he made her Vows, she shou'd be the only woman he wou'd possess while he liv'd; that no Age or Wrinkles shou'd incline him to change, for her Soul wou'd be always fine, and always young; and he shou'd have an eternal *Idea* in his Mind of the Charms she now bore, and shou'd look into his Heart for that *Idea,* when he cou'd find it no longer in her Face.

After a thousand Assurances of his lasting Flame, and her eternal Empire over him, she condescended to receive him for her Husband; or rather, receiv'd him, as the greatest Honour the God's cou'd do her.

There is a certain Ceremony in these Cases to be observ'd, which I forgot to ask him how perform'd; but 'twas concluded on both sides, that, in Obedience to him, the Grand-father was to be first made acquainted with the Design: for they pay a most absolute Resignation to the Monarch, especially when he is a Parent also.

On the other side, the old King, who had many Wives, and many Concubines, wanted not Court-Flatterers to insinuate in his Heart a thousand tender Thoughts for this young Beauty; and who represented her to his Fancy, as the most charming he had ever possess'd in all the long Race of his numerous Years. At this Character his old Heart, like an extinguish'd Brand, most apt to take Fire, felt new Sparks of Love, and began to kindle; and now grown to his second Childhood, long'd with Impatience to behold this gay thing, with whom, alas! he cou'd but innocently play. But how he shou'd be confirm'd she was this *Wonder,* before he us'd his Power to call her to Court (where Maidens never came, unless for the King's private Use) he was next to consider; and while he was so doing, he had Intelligence brought him, that *Imoinda* was most certainly Mistress to the Prince *Oroonoko.* This gave him some *Shagrien;*[35] however, it gave him also an Opportunity, one Day, when the Prince was a-hunting; to wait on a Man of Quality, as his Slave and Attendant, who shou'd go and make a Present to *Imoinda,* as from the Prince; he shou'd then, unknown, see this fair Maid, and have an Opportunity to hear what Message she wou'd

[35] *Shagrien:* Chagrin.

return the Prince for his Present; and from thence gather the state of her Heart, and degree of her Inclination. This was put in Execution, and the old Monarch saw, and burnt: He found her all he had heard, and wou'd not delay his Happiness, but found he shou'd have some Obstacle to overcome her Heart; for she express'd her Sense of the Present the Prince had sent her, in terms so sweet, so soft and pretty, with an Air of Love and Joy that cou'd not be dissembl'd; insomuch that 'twas past doubt whether she lov'd *Oroonoko* entirely. This gave the old King some Affliction; but he salv'd it with this, that the Obedience the People pay their King, was not at all inferior to what they pay'd their Gods: And what Love wou'd not oblige *Imoinda* to do, Duty wou'd compel her to.

He was therefore no sooner got to his Apartment, but he sent the Royal Veil to *Imoinda;* that is, the Ceremony of Invitation; he sends the Lady, he has a Mind to honour with his Bed, a Veil, with which she is cover'd, and secur'd for the King's Use; and 'tis Death to disobey; besides, held a most impious Disobedience.

'Tis not to be imagin'd the Surprize and Grief that seiz'd this lovely Maid at this News and Sight. However, as Delays in these Cases are dangerous, and Pleading worse then Treason; trembling, and almost fainting, she was oblig'd to suffer her self to be cover'd, and led away.

They brought her thus to Court; and the King, who had caus'd a very rich Bath to be prepar'd, was led into it, where he sate under a Canopy, in State, to receive this long'd for Virgin; whom he having commanded shou'd be brought to him, they (after dis-robing her) led her to the Bath, and making fast the Doors, left her to descend. The King, without more Courtship, bade her throw off her Mantle, and come to his Arms. But *Imoinda* all in Tears, threw her self on the Marble, on the Brink of the Bath, and besought him to hear her. She told him, as she was a Maid, how proud of the Divine Glory she should have been of having it in her power to oblige her King: but as by the Laws, he cou'd not; and from his Royal Goodness, wou'd not take from any Man his wedded Wife: So she believ'd she shou'd be the Occasion of making him commit a great Sin, if she did not reveal her State and Condition, and tell him, she was anothers, and cou'd not be so happy to be his.

The King, enrag'd at this Delay, hastily demanded the Name of the bold Man, that had marry'd a Woman of her Degree, without his Consent. *Imoinda,* seeing his Eyes fierce, and his Hands tremble; whether with Age, or Anger, I know not; but she fansy'd the last, almost repented she had said so much, for now she fear'd the Storm wou'd fall on the Prince; she therefore said a thousand things to appease the raging of his Flame, and to prepare him to hear who it was with Calmness; but before she spoke, he imagin'd who she meant, but wou'd not seem to do so, but commanded her to lay aside her Mantle; and suffer her self to receive his Caresses; or, by his Gods, he swore, that happy Man whom she was going to name shou'd die, though it were even *Oroonoko* himself. *Therefore* (said he) *deny this Marriage, and swear thy self a Maid. That* (reply'd *Imoinda*) *by all our Powers I do; for I am not yet known to my Husband.* 'Tis enough (said the King;) 'tis *enough to satisfie both my Conscience, and my Heart.* And rising from his Seat, he went, and led her into the Bath; it being in vain for her to resist.

In this time the Prince, who was return'd from Hunting, went to visit his *Imoinda,* but found her gone; and not only so, but heard she had receiv'd the Royal Veil. This rais'd him to a Storm; and in his Madness, they had much ado to save him from laying violent Hands on himself. Force first prevail'd, and then Reason: They urg'd all to him, that might oppose his Rage; but nothing weigh'd so greatly with him as the King's Old Age uncapable of injuring him with *Imoinda.* He wou'd give way to that Hope, because it pleas'd him most, and flatter'd best his Heart. Yet this serv'd not altogether to make him cease his different Passions, which sometimes rag'd within him, and sometimes softened into Showers. 'Twas not enough to appease him, to tell him, his Grand-father was old, and cou'd not that way injure him, while he retain'd that awful Duty which the young Men are us'd there to pay to their grave Relations. He cou'd not be convinc'd he had no Cause to sigh and mourn for the Loss of a Mistress, he cou'd not with all his Strength and Courage retrieve. And he wou'd often cry, *O my Friends! were she in wall'd Cities, or confin'd from me in Fortifications of the greatest Strength; did Inchantments or Monsters detain her from me, I wou'd venture through any Hazard to free her: But here, in the Arms of a feeble old Man, my Youth, my violent Love, my Trade in Arms, and all my vast Desire of Glory, avail me nothing: Imoinda is irrecoverably lost to me, as if she were snatch'd by the cold Arms of Death: Oh! she is never to be retriev'd. If I wou'd wait tedious Years, till Fate shou'd bow the old King to his Grave; even that wou'd not leave me Imoinda free; but still that Custom that makes it so vile a Crime for a Son to marry his Father's Wives or Mistresses, wou'd hinder my Happiness; unless I wou'd either ignobly set an ill President to my Successors, or abandon my Country, and fly with her to some unknown World, who never heard our Story.*

But it was objected to him, that his Case was not the same; for *Imoinda* being his lawful Wife, by solemn Contract, 'twas he was the injur'd Man, and might, if he so pleas'd, take *Imoinda* back, the Breach of the Law being on his Grand-father's side; and that if he cou'd circumvent him, and redeem her from the *Otan*,[36] which is the Palace of the King's Women, a sort of *Seraglio,* it was both just and lawful for him so to do.

This Reasoning had some force upon him, and he shou'd have been entirely comforted, but for the Thought that she was possess'd by his Grand-father. However, he lov'd so well, that he was resolv'd to believe what most favour'd his Hope; and to endeavour to learn from *Imoinda*'s own Mouth, what only she cou'd satisfie him in; whether she was robb'd of that Blessing, which was only due to his Faith and Love. But as it was very hard to get a Sight of the Women, for no Men ever enter'd into the *Otan,* but when the King went to entertain himself with some one of his Wives, or Mistresses; and 'twas Death at any other time, for any other to go in; so he knew not how to contrive to get a Sight of her.

While *Oroonoko* felt all the Agonies of Love, and suffer'd under a Torment the most painful in the World, the old King was not exempted from his share of Affliction. He was troubl'd for having been forc'd by an irresistable Passion, to rob his Son[37] of a Treasure, he knew, cou'd not but be extreamly dear to him, since she was the most beautiful that ever had been seen; and had besides, all the Sweetness and Innocence of Youth and Modesty, with a Charm of Wit surpassing all. He found that, however she was forc'd to expose her lovely Person to his wither'd Arms, she cou'd only sigh and weep there, and think of *Oroonoko;* and oftentimes cou'd not forbear speaking of him, though her Life were, by Custom, forfeited by owning her Passion. But she spoke not of a Lover only, but of a Prince dear to him, to whom she spoke; and of the Praises of a Man, who, till now, fill'd the old Man's Soul with Joy at every Recital of his Bravery, or even his Name. And 'twas this Dotage on our young *Hero,* that gave *Imoinda* a thousand Privileges to speak of him, without offending; and this Condescention in the old King, that made her take the Satisfaction of speaking of him so very often.

Besides, he many times enquir'd how the Prince bore himself; and those of whom he ask'd, being entirely Slaves to the Merits and

---

[36] *Otan:* Probably from the Persian *otagh,* a tent or pavilion. This derivation would be in keeping with the other "Oriental" details Behn supplies here, such as the convention of the Royal Veil, and the "rich Pavilion" on p. 57.

[37] *Son:* I.e., grandson.

Vertues of the Prince, still answer'd what they thought conduc'd best
to his Service; which was, to make the old King fansy that the Prince
had no more Interest in *Imoinda,* and had resign'd her willingly to the
Pleasure of the King; that he diverted himself with Mathematicians,
his Fortifications, his Officers, and his Hunting.

This pleas'd the old Lover, who fail'd not to report these things
again to *Imoinda,* that she might, by the Example of her young Lover,
withdraw her Heart, and rest better contented in his Arms. But however she was forc'd to receive this unwelcome News, in all Appearance, with Unconcern, and Content, her Heart was bursting within,
and she was only happy when she cou'd get alone, to vent her Griefs
and Moans with Sighs and Tears.

What Reports of the Prince's Conduct were made to the King, he
thought good to justifie as far as possibly he cou'd by his Actions; and
when he appear'd in the Presence of the King, he shew'd a Face not at
all betraying his Heart: So that in a little time the old Man, being
entirely convinc'd that he was no longer a Lover of *Imoinda,* he carry'd him with him, in his Train, to the *Otan,* often to banquet with his
Mistress. But as soon as he enter'd, one Day into the Apartment of
Imoinda, with the King, at the first Glance from her Eyes, notwithstanding all his determined Resolution, he was ready to sink in the
place where he stood; and had certainly done so, but for the Support
of *Aboan,* a young Man, who was next to him; which, with his
Change of Countenance, had betray'd him, had the King chanc'd to
look that way. And I have observ'd, 'tis a very great Error in those,
who laugh when one says, A Negro can change Colour; for I have seen
'em as frequently blush, and look pale, and that as visibly as ever I saw
in the most beautiful *White.* And 'tis certain that both these Changes
were evident, this Day, in both these Lovers. And *Imoinda,* who saw
with some Joy the Change in the Prince's Face, and found it in her
own, strove to divert the King from beholding either, by a forc'd
Caress, with which she met him; which was a new Wound in the Heart
of the poor dying Prince. But as soon as the King was busy'd in looking on some fine things of *Imoinda*'s making, she had time to tell the
Prince with her angry, but Love-darting Eyes, that she resented his
Coldness, and bemoan'd her own miserable Captivity. Nor were his
Eyes silent, but answer'd hers again, as much as Eyes cou'd do,
instructed by the most tender, and most passionate Heart that ever
lov'd: And they spoke so well, and so effectually, as *Imoinda* no longer
doubted, but she was the only Delight, and the Darling of that Soul
she found pleading in 'em its Right of Love, which none was more

willing to resign than she. And 'twas this powerful Language alone that in an Instant convey'd all the Thoughts of their Souls to each other; that they both found, there wanted but Opportunity to make them both entirely happy. But when he saw another Door open'd by *Onahal,* a former old Wife of the King's, who now had Charge of *Imoinda;* and saw the Prospect of a Bed of State made ready, with Sweets and Flowers for the Dalliance of the King; who immediately lead the trembling Victim from his Sight, into that prepar'd Repose. What Rage! what wild Frenzies seiz'd his Heart! which forcing to keep within Bounds, and to suffer without Noise, it became the more insupportable, and rent his Soul with ten thousand Pains. He was forc'd to retire, to vent his Groans; where he fell down on a Carpet, and lay struggling a long time, and only breathing now and then, — *O Imoinda!* When *Onahal* had finish'd her necessary Affair within, shutting the Door, she came forth to wait, till the King call'd; and hearing some one sighing in the other Room, she pass'd on, and found the Prince in that deplorable Condition, which she thought needed her Aid: She gave him Cordials, but all in vain; till finding the nature of his Disease, by his Sighs, and naming *Imoinda.* She told him, he had not so much Cause as he imagin'd, to afflict himself; for if he knew the King so well as she did, he wou'd not lose a Moment in Jealousie, and that she was confident that *Imoinda* bore, at this Minute, part in his Affliction. *Aboan* was of the same Opinion; and both together, perswaded him to re-assume his Courage; and all sitting down on the Carpet, the Prince said so many obliging things to *Onahal,* that he half perswaded her to be of his Party. And she promis'd him, she wou'd thus far comply with his just Desires, that she wou'd let *Imoinda* know how faithful he was, what he suffer'd, and what he said.

This Discourse lasted till the King call'd, which gave *Oroonoko* a certain Satisfaction; and with the Hope *Onahal* had made him conceive, he assum'd a Look as gay as 'twas possible a Man in his Circumstances cou'd do; and presently after, he was call'd in with the rest who waited without. This King commanded Musick to be brought, and several of his young Wives and Mistresses came all together by his Command, to dance before him; where *Imoinda* perform'd her Part with an Air and Grace so passing all the rest, as her Beauty was above 'em; and receiv'd the Present, ordain'd as a Prize. The Prince was every Moment more charm'd with the new Beauties and Graces he beheld in this fair One; And while he gaz'd, and she danc'd, *Onahal* was retir'd to a Window with *Aboan.*

This *Onahal*, as I said, was one of the Cast-Mistresses[38] of the old King; and 'twas these (now past their Beauty) that were made Guardians, or Governants[39] to the new, and the young Ones; and whose Business it was, to teach them all those wanton Arts of Love, with which they prevail'd and charm'd heretofore in their Turn; and who now treated the triumphing happy Ones with all the Severity, as to Liberty and Freedom, that was possible, in revenge of those Honours they rob them of; envying them those Satisfactions, those Gallantries and Presents, that were once made to themselves, while Youth and Beauty lasted, and which they now saw pass were regardless by, and pay'd only to the Bloomings.[40] And certainly, nothing is more afflicting to a decay'd Beauty, than to behold in it self declining Charms, that were once ador'd; and to find those Caresses paid to new Beauties, to which once she laid a Claim; to hear 'em whisper as she passes by, *That once was a delicate Woman.* These abandon'd Ladies therefore endeavour to revenge all the Despights,[41] and Decays of Time, on these flourishing happy Ones. And 'twas this Severity, that gave *Oroonoko* a thousand Fears he shou'd never prevail with *Onahal*, to see *Imoinda*. But, as I said, she was now retir'd to a Window with *Aboan*.

This young Man was not only one of the best Quality, but a Man extreamly well made, and beautiful; and coming often to attend the King to the *Otan*, he had subdu'd the Heart of the antiquated *Onahal*, which had not forgot how pleasant it was to be in Love: And though she had some Decays in her Face, she had none in her Sence and Wit; she was there agreeable still, even to *Aboan*'s Youth; so that he took pleasure in entertaining her with Discourses of Love. He knew also, that to make his Court to these She-Favourites, was the way to be great; these being the Persons that do all Affairs and Business at Court. He had also observ'd that she had given him Glances more tender and inviting, than she had done to others of his Quality: And now, when he saw that her Favour cou'd so absolutely oblige the Prince, he fail'd not to sigh in her Ear, and to look with Eyes all soft upon her, and give her Hope that she had made some Impressions on his Heart. He found her pleas'd at this, and making a thousand Advances to him; but the Ceremony ending, and the King departing, broke up the Company for that Day, and his Conversation.

[38] *Cast-Mistresses:* I.e., discarded mistresses.
[39] *Governants:* Teachers (French).
[40] *Bloomings:* Young women whose beauty is still "in bloom."
[41] *Despights:* Slights, insults.

Aboan fail'd not that Night to tell the Prince of his Success, and how advantageous the Service of *Onahal* might be to his Amour with *Imoinda*. The Prince was overjoy'd with this good News, and besought him, if it were possible, to caress her so, as to engage her entirely; which he cou'd not fail to do, if he comply'd with her Desires: *For then* (said the Prince) *Her life lying at your Mercy, she must grant you the Request you make in my Behalf.* *Aboan* understood him; and assur'd him, he would make Love so effectually, that he wou'd defie the most expert Mistresses of the Art, to find out whether he dissembl'd it, or had it really. And 'twas with Impatience they waited the next Opportunity of going to the *Otan*.

The Wars came on, the Time of taking the Field approach'd, and 'twas impossible for the Prince to delay his going at the Head of his Army, to encounter the Enemy: So that every Day seem'd a tedious Year, till he saw his *Imoinda;* for he believ'd he cou'd not live, if he were forc'd away without being so happy. 'Twas with Impatience therefore, that he expected the next Visit the King wou'd make; and, according to his Wish, it was not long.

The Parley of the Eyes of these two Lovers had not pass'd so secretly, but an old jealous Lover cou'd spy it; or rather, he wanted not Flatterers, who told him, they observ'd it: So that the Prince was hasten'd to the Camp, and this was the last Visit he found he shou'd make to the *Otan;* he therefore urg'd *Aboan* to make the best of this Last Effort, and to explain himself so to *Onahal,* that she, deferring her Enjoyment of her young Lover no longer, might make way for the Prince to speak of *Imoinda*.

The whole Affair being agreed on between the Prince and *Aboan,* they attended the King, as the Custom was, to the *Otan;* where, while the whole Company was taken up in beholding the Dancing, and antick[42] Postures the Women Royal made, to divert the King *Onahal* singl'd out *Aboan,* whom she found most pliable to her Wish. When she had him where she believ'd she cou'd not be heard, she sigh'd to him and softly cry'd. *Ah,* Aboan! *When will you be sensible of my Passion? I confess it with my Mouth, because I wou'd not give my Eyes the Lye; and you have but too much already perceiv'd they have confess'd my Flame: Nor wou'd I have you believe, that because I am the abandon'd Mistress of a King, I esteem my self altogether divested of Charms.* No, Aboan; *I have still a Rest of Beauty enough engaging, and have learn'd to please too well, not to be desirable. I can have*

---

[42] *antick:* Wild, animated.

Lovers still, but will have none but Aboan. *Madam* (reply'd the half-feigning Youth) *you have already by my Eyes, found, you can still conquer; and I believe 'tis in pity of me, you condescend to this kind Confession. But, Madam, Words are us'd to be so small a part of our Country-Courtship, that 'tis rare one can get so happy an Opportunity as to tell one's Heart; and those few Minutes we have are forc'd to be snatch'd for more certain Proofs of Love, than speaking and sighing; and such I languish for.*

He spoke this with such a Tone, that she hop'd it true, and cou'd not forbear believing it; and being wholly transported with Joy, for having subdu'd the finest of all the King's Subjects to her Desires, she took from her Ears two large Pearls, and commanded him to wear 'em in his. He wou'd have refus'd 'em, crying, *Madam, these are not the Proofs of your Love that I expect; 'tis Opportunity, 'tis a Lone-hour only, that can make me happy.* But forcing the Pearls into his Hand, she whisper'd softly to him, *Oh! Do not fear a Woman's Invention, when Love sets her a-thinking.* And pressing his Hand, she cry'd; *This Night you shall be happy. Come to the Gate of the Orange-Groves, behind the* Otan; *and I will be ready, about Mid-night, to receive you.* 'Twas thus agreed, and she left him, that no notice might be taken of their speaking together.

The Ladies were still dancing, and the King, laid on a Carpet, with a great deal of pleasure, was beholding them, especially *Imoinda;* who that Day appear'd more lovely than ever, being enliven'd with the good Tidings *Onahal* had brought her of the constant Passion the Prince had for her. The Prince was laid on another Carpet, at the other end of the Room, with his Eyes fix'd on the Object of his Soul; and as she turn'd, or mov'd, so did they; and she alone gave his Eyes and Soul their Motions: Nor did *Imoinda* employ her Eyes to any other Use, than in beholding with infinite Pleasure the Joy she produc'd in those of the Prince. But while she was more regarding him, than the Steps she took, she chanc'd to fall; and so near him, as that leaping with ex-tream force from the Carpet, he caught her in his Arms as she fell; and 'twas visible to the whole Presence, the Joy wherewith he receiv'd her: He clasp'd her close to his Bosom, and quite forgot that Reverence that was due to the Mistress of a King, and that Punishment that is the Reward of a Boldness of this nature; and had not the Presence of Mind of *Imoinda* (fonder of his Safety, than her own) befriended him, in making her spring from his Arms, and fall into her Dance again, he had, at that Instant, met his Death; for the old King, jealous to the last degree, rose up in Rage, broke all the Diversion, and led *Imoinda* to her Apartment, and sent out Word to the Prince, to go immediately to the Camp; and that if he were found another Night in Court, he shou'd suffer the Death ordain'd for disobedient Offenders.

You may imagine how welcome this News was to *Oroonoko,* whose unseasonable Transport and Caress of *Imoinda* was blam'd by all Men that lov'd him; and now he perceiv'd his Fault, yet cry'd, *That for such another Moment, he wou'd be content to die.*

All the *Otan* was in disorder about his Accident; and *Onahal* was particularly concern'd, because on the Prince's Stay depended her Happiness; for she cou'd no longer expect that of *Aboan.* So that, e'er they departed, they contriv'd it so, that the Prince and he shou'd come both that Night to the Grove of the *Otan,* which was all of Oranges and Citrons; and that there they shou'd wait her Orders.

They parted thus, with Grief enough, till Night; leaving the King in possession of the lovely Maid. But nothing cou'd appease the Jealousie of the Old Lover: He wou'd not be impos'd on, but wou'd have it, that *Imoinda* made a false Step on purpose to fall into *Oroonoko's* Bosom, and that all things look'd like a Design on both sides, and 'twas in vain she protested her Innocence; He was old and obstinate, and left her more than half assur'd that his Fear was true.

The King going to his Apartment, sent to know where the Prince was, and if he intended to obey his Command. The Messenger return'd, and told him, he found the Prince pensive, and altogether unpreparing for the Campaign; that he lay negligently on the Ground, and answer'd very little. This confirm'd the Jealousie of the King, and he commanded that they shou'd very narrowly and privately watch his Motions; and that he shou'd not stir from his Apartment, but one Spy or other shou'd be employ'd to watch him: So that the Hour approaching, wherein he was to go to the Citron-Grove; and taking only *Aboan* along with him, he leaves his Apartment, and was watch'd to the very Gate of the *Otan;* while he was seen to enter, and where they left him, to carry back the Tidings to the King.

Oroonoko and *Aboan* were no sooner enter'd, but *Onahal* led the Prince to the Apartment of *Imoinda;* who, not knowing any thing of her Happiness, was laid in Bed. But *Onahal* only left him in her Chamber, to make the best of his Opportunity, and took her dear *Aboan* to her own; where he shew'd the heighth of Complaisance[43] for his

[43] *Complaisance:* Agreeableness, willingness to please.

Prince, when, to give him an Opportunity, he suffer'd himself to be caress'd in Bed by *Onahal*.

The Prince softly waken'd *Imoinda,* who was not a little surpriz'd with Joy to find him there; and yet she trembl'd with a thousand Fears. I believe, he omitted saying nothing to this young Maid, that might perswade her to suffer him to seize his own, and take the Rights of Love; and I believe she was not long resisting those Arms, where she so long'd to be; and having Opportunity, Night and Silence, Youth, Love and Desire, he soon prevail'd; and ravish'd in a Moment, what his old Grand-father had been endeavouring for so many Months.

'Tis not to be imagin'd the Satisfaction of these two young Lovers; nor the Vows she made him, that she remain'd a spotless Maid, till that Night; and that what she did with his Grand-father, had robb'd him of no part of her Virgin-Honour, the Gods, in Mercy and Justice, having reserv'd that for her plighted Lord, to whom of Right it belong'd. And 'tis impossible to express the Transports he suffer'd, while he listen'd to a Discourse so charming, from her lov'd Lips; and clasp'd that Body in his Arms, for whom he had so long languish'd; and nothing now afflicted him, but his suddain Departure from her; for he told her the Necessity, and his Commands; but shou'd depart satisfy'd in this, That since the old King had hitherto not been able to deprive him of those Enjoyments which only belong'd to him, he believ'd for the future he wou'd be less able to injure him; so that, abating the Scandal of the Veil, which was no otherwise so, than that she was Wife to another: He believ'd her safe, even in the Arms of the King, and innocent; yet wou'd he have ventur'd at the Conquest of the World, and have given it all, to have had her avoided that Honour of receiving the *Royal Veil*. 'Twas thus, between a thousand Caresses, that both bemoan'd the hard Fate of Youth and Beauty, so liable to that cruel Promotion: 'Twas a Glory that cou'd well have been spar'd here, though desir'd, and aim'd at by all the young Females of that Kingdom.

But while they were thus fondly employ'd, forgetting how Time ran on, and that the Dawn must conduct him far away from his only Happiness, they heard a great Noise in the *Otan,* and unusual Voices of Men; at which the Prince, starting from the Arms of the frighted *Imoinda,* ran to a little Battel-Ax he us'd to wear by his Side; and having not so much leisure, as to put on his Habit, he oppos'd himself against some who were already opening the Door; which they did with so much Violence, that *Oroonoko* was not able to defend it; but was forc'd to cry out with a commanding Voice, *Whoever ye*

are that have the Boldness to attempt to approach this Apartment thus
rudely, know, that I, the Prince Oroonoko, *will revenge it with the*
certain Death of him that first enters: Therefore stand back, and know,
this place is sacred to Love, and me this Night; to Morrow 'tis the
King's.

This he spoke with a Voice so resolv'd and assur'd, that they soon
retir'd from the Door, but cry'd, *'Tis by the King's Command we are*
come; and being satisfy'd by thy Voice, O Prince, as much as if we had
enter'd, we can report to the King the Truth of all his Fears, and leave
thee to provide for thy own Safety, as thou art advis'd by thy Friends.

At these Words they departed, and left the Prince to take a short
and sad Leave of his *Imoinda;* who trusting in the strength of her
Charms, believ'd she shou'd appease the Fury of a jealous King, by
saying, She was surpriz'd, and that it was by force of Arms he got into
her Apartment. All her Concern now was for his Life, and therefore
she hasten'd him to the Camp; and with much a do, prevail'd on him
to go: Nor was it she alone that prevail'd, *Aboan* and *Onahal* both
pleaded, and both assur'd him of a Lye that shou'd be well enough
contriv'd to secure *Imoinda.* So that, at last, with a Heart sad as
Death, dying Eyes, and sighing Soul, *Oroonoko* departed, and took
his way to the Camp.

It was not long after the King in Person came to the *Otan;* where
beholding *Imoinda* with Rage in his Eyes, he upbraided her Wickedness and Perfidy, and threatening her Royal Lover, she fell on her Face
at his Feet, bedewing the Floor with her Tears, and imploring his Pardon for a Fault which she had not with her Will committed; as *Ona-*
hal, who was also prostrate with her, cou'd testifie: That, unknown to
her, he had broke into her Apartment, and ravish'd her. She spoke
this much against her Conscience; but to save her own Life, 'twas
absolutely necessary she shou'd feign this Falsity. She knew it cou'd
not injure the Prince, he being fled to an Army that wou'd stand by
him, against any Injuries that shou'd assault him. However, this last
Thought of *Imoinda*'s being ravish'd, chang'd the Measures of his
Revenge; and whereas before he design'd to be himself her Executioner, he now resolv'd she shou'd not die. But as it is the greatest
Crime in nature amongst 'em to touch a Woman, after having been
possess'd by a Son, a Father, or a Brother; so now he look'd on
Imoinda as a polluted thing, wholly unfit for his Embrace; nor wou'd
he resign her to his Grand-son, because she had receiv'd the *Royal*
Veil. He therefore removes her from the *Otan,* with *Onahal;* whom he
put into safe Hands, with Order they shou'd be both sold off, as

Slaves, to another Country, either *Christian,* or *Heathen;* 'twas no matter where.

This cruel Sentence, worse than Death, they implor'd, might be revers'd; but their Prayers were vain, and it was put in Execution accordingly, and that with so much Secrecy, that none, either without, or within the *Otan,* knew any thing of their Absence, or their Destiny.

The old King, nevertheless, executed this with a great deal of Reluctancy; but he believ'd he had made a very great Conquest over himself, when he had once resolv'd, and had perform'd what he resolv'd. He believ'd now, that his Love had been unjust; and that he cou'd not expect the Gods, or Captain of the Clouds, (as they call the unknown Power) shou'd suffer a better Consequence from so ill a Cause. He now begins to hold *Oroonoko* excus'd; and to say, he had reason for what he did: And now every Body cou'd assure the King, how passionately *Imoinda* was belov'd by the Prince; even those confess'd it now, who said the contrary before his Flame was abated. So that the King being old, and not able to defend himself in War, and having no Sons of all his Race remaining alive, but only this, to maintain him on his Throne; and looking on this as a Man disoblig'd, first by the Rape of his Mistress, or rather, Wife; and now by depriving of him wholly of her, he fear'd, might make him desperate, and do some cruel thing, either to himself, or his old Grand-father, the Offender; he began to repent him extreamly of the Contempt he had, in his Rage, put on *Imoinda.* Besides, he consider'd he ought in Honour to have kill'd her, for this Offence, if it had been one: He ought to have had so much Value and Consideration for a Maid of her Quality, as to have nobly put her to death; and not to have sold her like a common Slave, the greatest Revenge, and the most disgraceful of any; and to which they a thousand times prefer Death, and implore it; as *Imoinda* did, but cou'd not obtain that Honour. Seeing therefore it was certain that *Oroonoko* wou'd highly resent his Affront, he thought good to make some Excuse for his Rashness to him; and to that End he sent a Messenger to the Camp, with Orders to treat with him about the Matter, to gain his Pardon, and to endeavour to mitigate his Grief; but that by no means he shou'd tell him, she was sold, but secretly put to death; for he knew he shou'd never obtain his Pardon for the other.

When the Messenger came, he found the Prince upon the point of Engaging with the Enemy; but as soon as he heard of the arrival of the Messenger, he commanded him to his Tent, where he embrac'd him, and receiv'd him with Joy; which was soon abated, by the down-cast Looks of the Messenger, who was instantly demanded the Cause by

Oroonoko, who impatient of Delay, ask'd a thousand Questions in a Breath; and all concerning *Imoinda:* But there needed little Return, for he cou'd almost answer himself of all he demanded, from his Sighs and Eyes. At last, the Messenger casting himself at the Prince's Feet, and kissing them, with all the Submission of a Man that had something to implore which he dreaded to utter, he besought him to hear with Calmness what he had to deliver to him, and to call up all his noble and Heroick Courage, to encounter with his Words, and defend himself against the ungrateful[44] things he must relate. *Oroonoko* reply'd, with a deep Sigh, and a languishing Voice, — *I am arm'd against their worst Efforts* — ; *for I know they will tell me,* Imoinda; *is no more* — ; *and after that, you may spare the rest.* Then, commanding him to rise, he laid himself on a Carpet, under a rich Pavilion, and remain'd a good while silent, and was hardly heard to sigh. When he was come a little to himself, the Messenger ask'd him leave to deliver that part of his Embassy, which the Prince had not yet divin'd: And the Prince cry'd, *I permit thee* — Then he told him the Affliction the old King was in, for the Rashness he had committed in his Cruelty to *Imoinda;* and how he daign'd to ask Pardon for his Offence, and to implore the Prince wou'd not suffer that Loss to touch his Heart too sensibly, which now all the Gods cou'd not restore him, but might recompence him in Glory, which he begg'd he wou'd pursue; and that Death, that common Revenger of all Injuries, wou'd soon even the Account between him, and a feeble old Man.

Oroonoko bade him return his Duty to his Lord and Master; and to assure him, there was no Account of Revenge to be adjusted between them; if there were, 'twas he was the Agressor, and that Death wou'd be just, and, maugre[45] his Age, wou'd see him righted; and he was contented to leave his Share of Glory to Youths more fortunate, and worthy of that Favour from the Gods. That henceforth he wou'd never lift a Weapon, or draw a Bow; but abandon the small Remains of his Life to Sighs and Tears, and the continual Thoughts of what his Lord and Grand-father had thought good to send out of the World, with all that Youth, that Innocence, and Beauty.

After having spoken this, whatever his greatest Officers, and Men of the best Rank cou'd do, they cou'd not raise him from the Carpet, or perswade him to Action, and Resolutions of Life; but commanding all to retire, he shut himself into his Pavillion all that Day, while the

[44] *ungrateful:* Unpleasing, disturbing.
[45] *maugre:* Despite (from the French *malgré*)

Enemy was ready to engage; and wondring at the Delay, the whole body of the chief of the Army then address'd themselves to him, and to whom they had much a-do to get Admittance. They fell on their Faces at the Foot of his Carpet; where they lay, and besought him with earnest Prayers and Tears, to lead 'em forth to Battel, and to let the Enemy take Advantages of them; and implor'd him to have regard to his Glory, and to the World, that depended on his Courage and Conduct. But he made no other Reply to all their Supplications but this, That he had now no more Business for Glory; and for the World, it was a Trifle not worth his Care. *Go,* (continu'd he, sighing) *and divide it amongst you; and reap with Joy what you so vainly prize and leave me to my more welcome Destiny.*

They then demanded what they shou'd do, and whom he wou'd constitute in his Room, that the Confusion of ambitious Youth and Power might not ruin their Order, and make them a Prey to the Enemy. He reply'd, He wou'd not give himself the Trouble — ; but wish'd 'em to chuse the bravest Man amongst 'em, let his Quality or Birth be what it wou'd: *For, O my Friends* (said he!) *it is not Titles make Men brave, or good; or Birth that bestows Courage and Generosity, or makes the Owner happy. Believe this, when you behold Oroonoko, the most wretched, and abandon'd by Fortune, of all the Creation of the Gods.* So turning himself about, he wou'd make no more Reply to all they cou'd urge or implore.

The Army beholding their Officers return unsuccessful, with sad Faces, and ominous Looks, that presag'd no good Luck, suffer'd a thousand Fears to take Possession of their Hearts, and the Enemy to come even upon 'em, before they wou'd provide for their Safety, by any Defence; and though they were assur'd by some, who had a mind to animate 'em, that they shou'd be immediately headed by the Prince, and that in the mean time *Aboan* had Orders to command as General; yet they were so dismay'd for want of that great Example of Bravery, that they cou'd make but a very feeble Resistance; and at last, downright, fled before the Enemy, who pursu'd 'em to the very Tents, killing 'em: Nor cou'd all *Aboan*'s Courage, which the Day gain'd him immortal Glory, shame 'em into a Manly Defence of themselves. The Guards that were left behind, about the Prince's Tent, seeing the Soldiers flee before the Enemy, and scatter themselves all over the Plain, in great Disorder, made such Out-cries as rouz'd the Prince from his amorous Slumber, in which he had remain'd bury'd for two Days, without permitting any Sustenance to approach him: But, in spight of all his Resolutions, he had not the Constancy of Grief to that Degree, as to make him insensible of the Danger of his Army; and in that Instant he leap'd from his Couch, and cry'd, — *Come, if we must die, let us meet Death the noblest Way and 'twill be more like* Oroonoko *to encounter him at an Army's Head, opposing the Torrent of a conquering Foe, than lazily, on a Couch, to wait his lingering Pleasure, and die every Moment by a thousand wrecking[46] Thoughts; or be tamely taken by an Enemy, and led a whining, Love-sick Slave, to adorn the Triumphs of* Jamoan, *that young Victor, who already is enter'd beyond the Limits I had prescrib'd him.*

While he was speaking, he suffer'd his People to dress him for the Field; and sallying out of his Pavilion, with more Life and Vigour in his Countenance than ever he shew'd, he appear'd like some Divine Power descended to save his Country from Destruction, and his People had purposely put him on all things that might make him shine with most Splendor, to strike a reverend Awe into the Beholders. He flew into the thickest of those that were pursuing his Men; and being animated with Despair, he fought as if he came on purpose to die, and did such things as will not be believ'd that Humane Strength cou'd perform; and such as soon inspir'd all the rest with new Courage, and new Order: And now it was, that they began to fight indeed; and so, as if they wou'd not be out-done, even by their ador'd *Hero;* who turning the Tide of the Victory, changing absolutely the Fate of the Day, gain'd an entire Conquest; and *Oroonoko* having the good Fortune to single out *Jamoan,* he took him Prisoner with his own Hand, having wounded him almost to death.

This *Jamoan* afterwards became very dear to him, being a Man very gallant, and of excellent Graces, and fine Parts; so that he never put him amongst the Rank of Captives, as they us'd to do, without distinction, for the common Sale, or Market; but kept him in his own Court, where he retain'd nothing of the Prisoner, but the Name, and return'd no more into his own Country, so great an Affection he took for *Oroonoko;* and by a thousand Tales and Adventures of Love and Gallantry, flatter'd[47] his Disease of Melancholy and Languishment; which I have often heard him say, had certainly kill'd him, but for the Conversation of this Prince and *Aboan,* and the *French* Governor[48] he had

---

[46] *wrecking:* Racking.
[47] *flatter'd:* Assuaged.
[48] *Governor:* Tutor.

from his Childhood, of whom I have spoken before, and who was a Man of admirable Wit, great Ingenuity and Learning; all which he had infus'd into his young Pupil. This *French*-Man was banish'd out of his own Country, for some Heretical Notions he held; and though he was a Man of very little Religion, he had admirable Morals, and a brave Soul.

After the total Defeat of *Jamoan*'s Army, which all fled, or were left dead upon the Place, they spent some time in the Camp; *Oroonoko* chusing rather to remain a while there in his Tents, than enter into a Place, or live in a Court where he had so lately suffer'd so great a Loss. The Officers therefore, who saw and knew his Cause of Discontent, invented all sorts of Diversions and Sports, to entertain their Prince: So that what with those Amuzements abroad, and others at home, that is, within their Tents, with the Perswasions, Arguments and Care of his Friends and Servants that he more peculiarly priz'd,. he wore off in time a great part of that *Shagrien,* and Torture of Despair, which the first Efforts of *Imoinda*'s Death had given him: Insomuch as having receiv'd a thousand kind Embassies from the King, and Invitations to return to Court, he obey'd, though with no little Reluctancy; and when he did so, there was a visible Change in him, and for a long time he was much more melancholy than before. But Time lessens all Ex-treams, and reduces 'em to *Mediums* and Unconcern; but no Motives or Beauties, though all endeavour'd it, cou'd engage him in any sort of Amour, though he had all the Invitations to it, both from his own Youth, and others Ambitions and Designs.

Oroonoko was no sooner return'd from this last Conquest, and receiv'd at Court with all the Joy and Magnificence that cou'd be express'd to a young Victor, who was not only return'd triumphant, but belov'd like a Deity, when there arriv'd in the Port an *English* Ship.

This Person[49] had often before been in these Countries, and was very well known to *Oroonoko,* with whom he had traffick'd for Slaves, and had us'd to do the same with his Predecessors.

This Commander was a Man of a finer sort of Address, and Con-versation, better bred, and more engaging, than most of that sort of Men are; so that he seem'd rather never to have been bred out of a Court, than almost all his Life at Sea. This Captain therefore was always better receiv'd at Court, than most of the Traders to those Countries were; and especially by *Oroonoko,* who was more civiliz'd, according to the *European* Mode, than any other had been, and took

[49] *This Person:* The ship's captain.

more Delight in the *White* Nations; and, above all, Men of Parts and Wit. To this Captain he sold abundance of his Slaves; and for the Favour and Esteem he had for him, made him many Presents, and oblig'd him to stay at Court as long as possibly he could. Which the Captain seem'd to take as a very great Honour done him, entertaining the Prince every Day with Globes and Maps, and Mathematical Discourses and Instruments; eating, drinking, hunting and living with him with so much Familiarity, that it was not to be doubted, but he had gain'd very greatly upon the Heart of this gallant young Man. And the Captain, in Return of all these mighty Favours, besought the Prince to honour his Vessel with his Presence, some Day or other, to Dinner, before he shou'd set Sail: which he condescended to accept, and appointed his Day. The Captain, on his part, fail'd not to have all things in a Readiness, in the most magnificent Order he cou'd possibly: And the Day being come, the Captain, in his Boat, richly adorn'd with Carpets and Velvet-Cushions, row'd to the Shoar to receive the Prince; with another Long-Boat, where was plac'd all his Musick and Trumpets, with which *Oroonoko* was extreamly delighted; who met him on the Shoar, attended by his *French* Governor, *Jamoan, Aboan,* and about an hundred of the noblest of the Youths of the Court: And after they had first carry'd the Prince on Board, the Boats fetch'd the rest off; where they found a very splendid Treat, with all sorts of fine Wines; and were as well entertain'd, as 'twas possible in such a place to be.

The Prince having drunk hard of Punch, and several Sorts of Wine, as did all the rest (for great Care was taken, they shou'd want nothing of that part of the Entertainment) was very merry, and in great Admiration of the Ship, for he had never been in one before; so that he was curious of beholding every place, where he decently might descend. The rest, no less curious, who were not quite overcome with Drinking, rambl'd at their pleasure *Fore* and *Aft,* as their Fancies guided 'em: So that the Captain, who had well laid his Design before, gave the Word, and seiz'd on all his Guests; they clapping great Irons suddenly on the Prince, when he was leap'd down in the Hold, to view that part of the Vessel; and locking him fast down, secur'd him. The same Treachery was us'd to all the rest; and all in one Instant, in several places of the Ship, were lash'd fast in Irons, and betray'd to Slavery. That great Design over, they set all Hands to work to hoist Sail; and with as treacherous and fair a Wind, they made from the Shoar with this innocent and glorious Prize, who thought of nothing less than such an Entertainment.

Some have commended this Act, as brave, in the Captain; but I will spare my Sence of it, and leave it to my Reader, to judge as he pleases.

It may be easily guess'd, in what manner the Prince resented this Indignity, who may be best resembl'd to a Lion taken in a Toil; so he rag'd, so he struggl'd for Liberty, but all in vain; and they had so wisely manag'd his Fetters, that he cou'd not use a Hand in his Defence, to quit himself of a Life that wou'd by no Means endure Slavery; nor cou'd he move from the Place, where he was ty'd, to any solid part of the Ship, against which he might have beat his Head, and have finish'd his Disgrace that way: So that being deprived of all other means, he resolved to perish for want of Food: And pleased at last with that Thought, and toil'd and tired by Rage and Indignation, he laid himself down, and sullenly resolved upon dying, and refused all things that were brought him.

This did not a little vex the Captain, and the more so, because, he found almost all of 'em of the same Humour; so that the loss of so many brave Slaves, so tall and goodly to behold, wou'd have been very considerable: He therefore order'd one to go from him (for he wou'd not be seen himself) to *Oroonoko,* and to assure him he was afflicted for having rashly done so unhospitable a Deed, and which cou'd not be now remedied, since they were far from shore; but since he resented it in so high a nature, he assur'd him he wou'd revoke his Resolution, and set both him and his Friends a-shore on the next Land they shou'd touch at; and of this the Messenger gave him his Oath, provided he wou'd resolve to live: And *Oroonoko,* whose Honour was such as he never had violated a Word in his Life himself, much less a solemn Asseveration; believ'd in an instant what this Man said, but reply'd, He expected for a Confirmation of this, to have his shameful Fetters dismiss'd. This Demand was carried to the *Captain,* who return'd him answer, That the Offence had been so great which he had put upon the Prince, that he durst not trust him with Liberty while he remained in the Ship, for fear least by a Valour natural to him, and a Revenge that would animate that Valour, he might commit some Outrage fatal to himself and the *King* his Master, to whom his Vessel did belong. To this *Oroonoko* replied, he would engage his Honour to behave himself in all friendly Order and Manner, and obey the Command of the *Captain,* as he was Lord of the *King*'s Vessel, and General of those Men under his Command.

This was deliver'd to the still doubting *Captain,* who could not resolve to trust a *Heathen* he said, upon his Parole,[50] a Man that had

---

[50] *Parole:* Word, pledge (French).

no sence or notion of the God that he Worshipp'd. *Oroonoko* then replied, He was very sorry to hear that the *Captain* pretended to the Knowledge and Worship of any *Gods,* who had taught him no better Principles, than not to Credit as he would be Credited: but they told him the Difference of their Faith occasion'd that Distrust: For the *Captain* had protested to him upon the Word of a *Christian*, and sworn in the Name of a Great *GOD*: which if he should violate, he would expect eternal Torment in the World to come. *Is that all the Obligation he has to be Just to his Oath,* replied Oroonoko? *Let him know I Swear by my Honour, which to violate, wou'd not only render me contemptible and despised by all brave and honest Men, and so give my self perpetual pain, but it wou'd be eternally offending and diseasing all Mankind, harming, betraying, circumventing and outraging all Men; but Punishments hereafter are suffer'd by ones self; and the World takes no cognizances whether this God have revenged 'em, nor not, 'tis done so secretly, and deferr'd so long: While the Man of no Honour, suffers every moment the scorn and contempt of the honester World, and dies every day ignominiously in his Fame, which is more valuable than Life: I speak not this to move Belief, but to shew you how you mistake, when you imagine, That he who will violate his Honour, will keep his Word with his Gods.* So turning from him with a disdainful smile, he refused to answer him, when he urg'd him to know what Answer he shou'd carry back to his *Captain:* so that he departed without saying any more.

The *Captain* pondering and consulting what to do, it was concluded that nothing but *Oroonoko*'s Liberty wou'd encourage any of the rest to eat, except the *French*-man, whom the *Captain* cou'd not pretend to keep Prisoner, but only told him he was secured because he might act something in favour of the Prince, but that he shou'd be freed as soon as they came to Land. So that they concluded it wholly necessary to free the Prince from his Irons, that he might show himself to the rest; that they might have an Eye upon him, and that they cou'd not fear a single Man.

This being resolv'd, to make the Obligation the greater, the Captain himself went to *Oroonoko;* where, after many Complements, and Assurances of what he had already promis'd, he receiving from the Prince his *Parole*, and his Hand, for his good Behaviour, dismiss'd his Irons, and brought him to his own Cabin; where, after having treated and repos'd him a while, for he had neither eat or slept in four Days before, he besought him to visit those obstinate People in Chains, who refus'd all manner of Sustenance; and intreated him to oblige 'em to eat, and assure 'em of their Liberty the first Opportunity.

Oroonoko, who was too generous, not to give Credit to his Words, shew'd himself to his People, who were transported with Excess of Joy at the sight of their Darling Prince; falling at his Feet, and kissing and embracing 'em; believing, as some Divine Oracle, all he assur'd 'em. But he besought 'em to bear their Chains with that Bravery that became those whom he had seen act so nobly in Arms; and that they cou'd not give him greater Proofs of their Love and Friendship, since 'twas all the Security the Captain (his Friend) cou'd have, against the Revenge, he said, they might possibly justly take, for the Injuries sustain'd by him. And they all, with one Accord, assur'd him, they cou'd not suffer enough, when it was for his Repose and Safety.

After this they no longer refus'd to eat, but took what was brought 'em, and were pleas'd with their Captivity, since by it they hop'd to redeem the Prince, who, all the rest of the Voyage, was treated with all the Respect due to his Birth, though nothing cou'd divert his Melancholy; and he wou'd often sigh for *Imoinda,* and think this a Punishment due to his Misfortune, in having left that noble Maid behind him, that fatal Night, in the *Otan,* when he fled to the Camp.

Possess'd with a thousand Thoughts of past Joys with this fair young Person, and a thousand Griefs for her eternal Loss, he endur'd a tedious Voyage, and at last arriv'd at the Mouth of the River of *Surinam,* a Colony belonging to the King of *England,* and where they were to deliver some part of their Slaves. There the Merchants and Gentlemen of the Country going on Board, to demand those Lots of Slaves they had already agreed on; and, amongst those, the Over-seers of those Plantations where I then chanc'd to be, the Captain, who had given the Word, order'd his Men to bring up those noble Slaves in Fetters, whom I have spoken of; and having put 'em, some in one, and some in other Lots, with Women and Children (which they call *Pickaninies,*[51]) they sold 'em off, as Slaves, to several Merchants and Gentlemen; not putting any two in one Lot, because they wou'd separate 'em far from each other; not daring to trust 'em together, lest Rage and Courage shou'd put 'em upon contriving some great Action, to the Ruin of the Colony.

Oroonoko was first seiz'd on, and sold to our Over-seer, who had the first Lot, with seventeen more of all sorts and sizes, but not one of Quality with him. When he saw this, he found what they meant; for, as I said, he understood *English* pretty well; and being wholly unarm'd

---

[51] *Pickaninies:* A term used in the West Indies for children of African origin; probably a diminutive of the Spanish *pequeño* or the Portuguese *pequeno,* meaning "little."

and defenceless, so as it was in vain to make any Resistance, he only beheld the Captain with a Look all fierce and disdainful, upbraiding him with Eyes, that forc'd Blushes on his guilty Cheeks, he only cry'd, in passing over the Side of the Ship. *Farewel, Sir: 'Tis worth my Suffering to gain so true a Knowledge both of you, and your Gods by whom you swear.* And desiring those that held him to forbear their pains, and telling 'em he wou'd make no Resistance, he cry'd, *Come, my Fellow-Slaves; let us descend, and see if we can meet with more Honour and Honesty in the next World we shall touch upon.* So he nimbly leap'd into the Boat, and shewing no more Concern, suffer'd himself to be row'd up the River, with his seventeen Companions.

The Gentleman that bought him was a young *Cornish* Gentleman, whose Name was *Trefry;*[52] a Man of Great Wit, and fine Learning, and was carry'd into those Parts by the Lord —— Governor, to manage all his Affairs. He reflecting on the last Words of *Oroonoko* to the Captain, and beholding the Richness of his Vest,[53] no sooner came into the Boat, but he fix'd his Eyes on him; and finding something so extraordinary in his Face, his Shape and Mien, a Greatness of Look, and Haughtiness in his Air, and finding he spoke *English,* had a great mind to be enquiring into his Quality and Fortune; which, though *Oroonoko* endeavour'd to hide, by only confessing he was above the Rank of common Slaves, *Trefry* soon found he was yet something greater than he confess'd; and from that Moment began to conceive so vast an Esteem for him, that he ever after lov'd him as his dearest Brother, and shew'd him all the Civilities due to so great a Man.

Trefry was a very good Mathematician, and a Linguist; cou'd speak *French* and *Spanish;* and in the three Days they remain'd in the Boat (for so long were they going from the Ship, to the Plantation) he entertain'd *Oroonoko* so agreeably with his Art and Discourse, that he was no less pleas'd with *Trefry,* than he was with the Prince; and he thought himself, at least, fortunate in this, that since he was a Slave, as long as he wou'd suffer himself to remain so, he had a Man of so excellent Wit and Parts for a Master: So that before they had finish'd their Voyage up the River, he made no scruple of declaring to *Trefry* all his Fortunes, and most part of what I have here related, and put himself wholly into the Hands of his new Friend, whom he found resenting all the Injuries were done him, and was charm'd with all the Greatnesses

---

[52] *Trefry:* John Trefry, manager of Lord Willoughby's estate at Parham Hill.
[53] *Vest:* Robe.

of his Actions; which were recited with that Modesty, and delicate Sence, as wholly vanquish'd him and subdu'd him to his Interest. And he promis'd him on his Word and Honour, he wou'd find the Means to reconduct him to his own Country again; assuring him, he had a perfect Abhorrence of so dishonourable an Action; and that he wou'd sooner have dy'd, than have been the Author of such a Perfidy. He found the Prince was very much concern'd to know what became of his Friends, and how they took their Slavery; and *Trefry* promis'd to take care about the enquiring after their Condition, and that he shou'd have an Account of 'em.

Though, as *Oroonoko* afterwards said, he had little Reason to credit the Words of a *Backearary*,[54] yet he knew not why; but he saw a kind of Sincerity, and awful Truth in the Face of *Trefry*; he saw an Honesty in his Eyes, and he found him wise and witty enough to understand Honour; for it was one of his Maxims, *A Man of Wit cou'd not be a Knave or Villain.*

In their passage up the River, they put in at several Houses for Refreshment; and ever when they landed, numbers of People wou'd flock to behold this man; not but their Eyes were daily entertain'd with the sight of Slaves, but the Fame of *Oroonoko* was gone before him, and all People were in Admiration of his Beauty. Besides, he had a rich Habit on, in which he was taken, so different from the rest, and which the Captain cou'd not strip him of, because he was forc'd to surprize his Person in the Minute he sold him. When he found his Habit made him liable, as he thought, to be gaz'd at the more, he begg'd *Trefry* to give him something more befitting a Slave; which he did, and took off his Robes. Nevertheless, he shone through all; and his *Osenbrigs* (a sort of brown *Holland* Suit he had on) cou'd not conceal the Graces of his Looks and Mien; and he had no less Admirers, than when he had his dazeling Habit on: The Royal Youth appear'd in spight of the Slave, and People cou'd not help treating him after a different manner, without designing it: As soon as they approach'd him, they venerated and esteem'd him; his Eyes insensibly commanded Respect, and his Behaviour insinuated it into every Soul. So that there was nothing talk'd of but this young and gallant Slave, even by those who yet knew not that he was a Prince.

I ought to tell you, that the *Christians* never buy any Slaves but they

---

[54] *Backearary:* White person, possibly from the Ibo term *backra*, or *buckra*, meaning "master."

give 'em some Name of their own,[55] their native ones being likely very barbarous, and hard to pronounce; so that Mr *Trefry* gave *Oroonoko* that of *Cæsar;* which Name will live in that Country as long as that (scarce more) glorious one of the great *Roman;* for 'tis most evident, he wanted no part of the Personal Courage of that *Cæsar,* and acted things as memorable, had they been done in some part of the World replenish'd with People, and Historians, that might have given him his due. But his Mis-fortune was, to fall in an obscure World, that afforded only a Female Pen to celebrate his Fame; though I doubt not but it had liv'd from others Endeavours, if the *Dutch,* who, immediately after his Time, took that Country,[56] had not kill'd, banish'd and dispers'd all those that were capable of giving the World this great Man's Life, much better than I have done. And Mr *Trefry,* who design'd it, dy'd before he began it; and bemoan'd himself for not having undertook it in time.

For the future therefore, I must call *Oroonoko, Cæsar,* since by that Name only he was known in our Western World, and by that Name he was receiv'd on Shoar at *Parham-House,*[57] where he was destin'd a Slave. But if the King himself (God bless him) had come a-shore, there cou'd not have been greater Expectations by all the whole Plantation, and those neighbouring ones, than was on ours at that time; and he was receiv'd more like a Governor, than a Slave. Notwithstanding, as the Custom was, they assign'd him his Portion of Land, his House, and his Business, up in the Plantation. But as it was more for Form, than any Design, to put him to his Task, he endur'd no more of the Slave but the Name, and remain'd some Days in the House, receiving all Visits that were made him, without stirring towards that part of the Plantation where the *Negroes* were.

At last, he wou'd needs go view his Land, his House, and the Business assign'd him. But he no sooner came to the Houses of the Slaves, which are like a little Town by it self, the *Negroes* all having left Work,

---

[55] *Name of their own:* Typically a heroic name; thus Oroonoko is named for Gaius Julius Caesar, the Roman statesman and dictator who conquered Gaul and Britain, but who was ultimately betrayed and stabbed by his friend Brutus. Behn later mentions a slave called Tuscan (p. 86), presumably named for Tuscany, a major artistic and military center in the Italian Renaissance. For further discussion of the convention of renaming slaves, see the headnote to "The Royal African" in Part Two, Chapter 3.

[56] *the Dutch . . . took that Country:* After the Dutch attacked Suriname in 1667, England ceded the territory in exchange for New York (then called New Amsterdam).

[57] *Parham-House:* The house of Lord Willoughby's estate at Parham Hill, near the Suriname River.

all came forth to behold him, and found he was that Prince who had, at several times, sold most of 'em to these Parts; and, from a Veneration they pay to great Men, especially if they know 'em, and from the Surprize and Awe they had at the sight of him, they all cast themselves at his Feet, crying out, in their Language, *Live, O King! Long live, O King!* And kissing his Feet, paid him even Divine Homage.

Several *English* Gentlemen were with him; and what Mr *Trefry* had told 'em, was here confirm'd; of which he himself before had no other Witness than *Cæsar* himself: But he was infinitely glad to find his Grandure confirm'd by the Adoration of all the Slaves.

Cæsar troubl'd with their Over-joy, and Over-Ceremony, besought 'em to rise, and to receive him as their Fellow-Slave; assuring them, he was no better. At which they set up with one Accord a most terrible and hidious Mourning and condoling, which he and the *English* had much a-do to appease; but at last they prevail'd with 'em, and they prepar'd all their barbarous Musick, and every one kill'd and dress'd something of his own Stock (for every Family has their Land apart, on which, at their leisure-times, they breed all eatable things;) and clubbing it together, made a most magnificent Supper, inviting their *Grandee*[58] *Captain,* their *Prince,* to honour it with his Presence; which he did, and several *English* with him; where they all waited on him, some playing, others dancing before him all the time, according to the Manners of their several Nations; and with unwearied Industry, endeavouring to please and delight him.

While they sat at Meat Mr *Trefry* told *Cæsar,* that most of these *Slaves* were undone in Love, with a fine she *Slave,* whom they had had about Six Months on their Land; the *Prince,* who never heard the Name of *Love* without a Sigh, nor any mention of it without the Curiosity of examining further into that tale, which of all Discourses was most agreeable to him, asked, how they came to be so Unhappy, as to be all Undone for one fair *Slave? Trefry,* who was naturally Amorous, and lov'd to talk of Love as well as any body, proceeded to tell him, they had the most charming Black that ever was beheld on their *Plantation,* about Fifteen or Sixteen Years old, as he guest; that, for his part, he had done nothing but Sigh for her ever since she came; and that all the white Beautys he had seen, never charm'd him so absolutely as this fine Creature had done; and that no Man, of any Nation, ever beheld her, that did not fall in Love with her; and that she

---

[58] *Grandee:* The highest rank of Spanish and Portuguese nobility; hence, by extension, a person of high rank or eminence.

had all the *Slaves* perpetually at her Feet; and the whole Country resounded with the Fame of *Clemene*, for so said he, we have Christ'ned her: But she denys us all with such a noble Disdain, that 'tis a Miracle to see, that she, who can give such eternal Desires, shou'd herself be all Ice, and all Unconcern. She is adorn'd with the most Graceful Modesty that ever beautifyed Youth; the softest Sigher — that, if she were capable of Love, one would swear she languish'd for some absent happy Man; and so retir'd, as if she fear'd a Rape even from the God of Day;[59] or that the Breezes would steal Kisses from her delicate Mouth. Her Task of Work some sighing Lover every day makes it his Petition to perform for her, which she accepts blushing, and with reluctancy, for fear he will ask her a Look for a Recompence, which he dares not presume to hope; so great an Awe she strikes into the Hearts of her Admirers. *I do not wonder, replied the Prince, that Clemene shou'd refuse Slaves, being as you say so Beautiful, but wonder how she escapes those who can entertain her as you can do; or why, being your Slave, you do not oblige her to yield. I confess, said Trefry, when I have, against her will, entertain'd her with Love so long, as to be transported with my Passion; even above Decency, I have been ready to make use of those advantages of Strength and Force Nature has given me. But oh! she disarms me, with that Modesty and Weeping so tender and so moving, that I retire, and thank my Stars she overcame me.* The Company laught at his Civility to a *Slave*, and *Cæsar* only applauded the nobleness of his Passion and Nature; since that Slave might be Noble, or what was better, have true Notions of Honour and Vertue in her. Thus past they this Night, after having received, from the *Slaves*, all imaginable Respect and Obedience.

The next Day *Trefry* ask'd *Cæsar* to walk, when the heat was allay'd, and designedly carried him by the Cottage of the *fair Slave*; and told him, she whom he spoke of last Night liv'd there retir'd. *But, says he, I would not wish you to approach, for, I am sure, you will be in Love as soon as you behold her. Cæsar* assur'd him, he was proof against all the Charms of that Sex; and that if he imagin'd his Heart cou'd be so perfidious to Love again, after *Imoinda,* he believ'd he shou'd tear it from his Bosom: They had no sooner spoke, but a little shock Dog,[60] that *Clemene* had presented her, which she took great Delight in, ran out; and she, not knowing any body was there, ran to

---

[59] *God of Day:* Apollo, and so, by extension, the sun.
[60] *shock Dog:* Shaggy dog or poodle, a common pet among fashionable women in England.

get it in again, and bolted out on those who were just Speaking of her: When seeing them, she wou'd have run in again; but *Trefry* caught her by the Hand, and cry'd, Clemene, *However you fly a Lover, you ought to pay some Respect to this Stranger:* (pointing to *Cæsar*) But she, as if she had resolv'd never to raise her Eyes to the Face of a Man again, bent 'em the more to the Earth, when he spoke, and gave the *Prince* the Leasure to look the more at her. There needed no long Gazing, or Consideration, to examin who this fair Creature was; he soon saw *Imoinda* all over her; in a Minute he saw her Face, her Shape, her Air, her Modesty, and all that call'd forth his Soul with Joy at his Eyes, and left his Body destitute of almost Life; it stood without Motion, and, for a Minute, knew not that it had a Being; and, I believe, he had never come to himself, so opprest he was with over-Joy, if he had not met with this Allay, that he perceiv'd *Imoinda* fall dead in the Hands of *Trefry:* this awaken'd him, and he ran to her aid, and caught her in his Arms, where, by degrees, she came to herself; and 'tis needless to tell with what transports, what extasies of Joy, they both a while beheld each other, without Speaking; then Snatcht each other to their Arms; then Gaze again, as if they still doubted whether they possess'd the Blessing: They Graspt, but when they recovered their Speech, 'tis not to be imagin'd, what tender things they exprest to each other; wondering what strange Fate had brought 'em again together. They soon inform'd each other of their Fortunes, and equally bewail'd their Fate; but, at the same time, they mutually protested, that even Fetters and Slavery were Soft and Easy; and wou'd be supported with Joy and Pleasure, while they cou'd be so happy to possess each other, and to be able to make good their Vows. *Cæsar* swore he disdain'd the Empire of the World, while he cou'd behold his *Imoinda;* and she despis'd Grandure and Pomp, those Vanities of her Sex, when she cou'd Gaze on *Oroonoko.* He ador'd the very Cottage where she resided, and said, That little Inch of the World wou'd give him more Happiness than all the Universe cou'd do; and she vow'd, It was a Pallace, while adorn'd with the Presence of *Oroonoko.*

Trefry was infinitely pleas'd with this Novel,[61] and found this *Clemene* was the Fair Mistress of whom *Cæsar* had before spoke; and was not a little satisfied, that Heaven was so kind to the *Prince,* as to sweeten his Misfortunes by so lucky an Accident; and leaving the Lovers to themselves, was impatient to come down to *Parham House,* (which was on the same *Plantation)* to give me an Account of what

---

[61] *Novel:* Piece of news ("new thing").

had hapned. I was as impatient to make these Lovers a Visit, having already made a Friendship with *Cæsar;* and from his own Mouth learn'd what I have related, which was confirmed by his French-man, who was set on Shore to seek his Fortunes; and of whom they cou'd not make a Slave, because a Christian;[62] and he came daily to *Parham Hill* to see and pay his Respects to his Puple *Prince:* So that concerning and interesting my self, in all that related to *Cæsar,* whom I had assur'd of Liberty, as soon as the Governor arriv'd, I hasted presently to the Place where the Lovers were, and was infinitely glad to find this Beautiful young *Slave* (who had already gain'd all our Esteems, for her Modesty and her extraordinary Prettyness) to be the same I had heard *Cæsar* speak so much off. One may imagine then, we paid her a treble Respect; and though from her being carv'd in fine Flowers and Birds all over her Body, we took her to be of Quality before, yet, when we knew *Clemene* was *Imoinda,* we cou'd not enough admire her.

I had forgot to tell you, that those who are Nobly born of that country, are so delicately Cut and Rac'd[63] all over the fore-part of the Trunk of their Bodies, that it looks as if it were Japan'd; the Works being raised like high Poynt round the Edges of the Flowers: Some are only Carv'd with a little Flower, or Bird, at the Sides of the Temples, as was *Cæsar;* and those who are so Carv'd over the Body, resemble our Ancient *Picts,*[64] that are figur'd in the Chronicles, but these Carvings are more delicate.

From that happy Day *Cæsar* took *Clemene* for his Wife, to the general Joy of all People; and there was as much Magnificence as the Country wou'd afford at the Celebration of this Wedding: and in a very short time after she conceiv'd with Child; which made *Cæsar* even adore her, knowing he was the last of his Great Race. This new Accident made him more Impatient of Liberty, and he was every Day treating with *Trefry* for his and *Clemene*'s Liberty; and offer'd either Gold, or a vast quantity of Slaves, which shou'd be paid before they let him go, provided he cou'd have any Security that he shou'd go when his Ransom was paid: They fed him from Day to Day with Promises,

---

[62] *cou'd not . . . because a Christian:* As noted in the Introduction, beliefs about the enslavement of Christians varied widely; see, for example, Ligon and Godwyn in Part Two, chapter 4 and the legal decisions in Part Two, Chapter 4.

[63] *Rac'd:* Slit with a sharp instrument. In presenting Oroonoko's body as an aesthetic object, Behn uses several other terms drawn from handicrafts: japanning is a technique for creating a hard, black varnish, and "high Point" refers to the textured effect of needlepoint.

[64] *Picts:* An ancient people of North Britain; their name is thought to derive from *Picti,* Latin for "painted or tattooed people."

and delay'd him, till the Lord Governor shou'd come; so that he began to suspect them of falshood, and that they wou'd delay him till the time of his Wives delivery, and make a Slave of that too, For all the Breed is theirs to whom the Parents belong: This Thought made him very uneasy, and his Sullenness gave them some Jealousies[65] of him; so that I was oblig'd, by some Persons, who fear'd a Mutiny (which is very Fatal sometimes in those Colonies, that abound so with Slaves, that they exceed the Whites in vast Numbers) to discourse with *Cæsar,* and to give him all the Satisfaction I possibly cou'd; they knew he and *Clemene* were scarce an Hour in a Day from my Lodgings; that they eat with me, and that I oblig'd 'em in all things I was capable of: I entertain'd him with the Lives of the Romans,[66] and great Men, which charm'd him to my Company; and her, with teaching her all the pretty Works[67] that I was Mistress off; and telling her Stories of Nuns,[68] and endeavouring to bring her to the knowledge of the true God. But of all Discourses *Cæsar* lik'd that the worst, and wou'd never be reconcil'd to our Notions of the Trinity, of which he ever made a Jest; it was a Riddle, he said, wou'd turn his Brain to conceive, and one cou'd not make him understand what Faith was. However, these Conversations fail'd not altogether so well to divert him, that he lik'd the Company of us Women much above the Men; for he cou'd not Drink; and he is but an ill Companion in that Country that cannot: So that obliging him to love us very well, we had all the Liberty of Speech with him, especially my self, whom he call'd his *Great Mistress;* and indeed my Word wou'd go a great way with him. For these Reasons, I had Opportunity to take notice to him, that he was not well pleas'd of late, as he us'd to be; was more retir'd and thoughtful; and told him, I took it Ill he shou'd Suspect we wou'd break our words with him, and not permit both him and *Clemene* to return to his own Kingdom, which was not so long a way, but when he was once on his Voyage he wou'd quickly arrive there. He made me some Answers that shew'd a doubt in him, which made me ask him, what advantage it wou'd be to doubt? it would but give us a Fear of him, and possibly compel us to

---

[65] *Jealousies:* Suspicions.

[66] *Lives of the Romans:* By Plutarch (c. 46–c. 120). Jacob Tonson, who published several volumes of Behn's plays and poems in the late 1670s and early 1680s, also published John Dryden's translation of Plutarch in 1683.

[67] *pretty Works:* Handicrafts such as needlepoint.

[68] *Stories of Nuns:* Such as Behn herself wrote. Her novella *The Fair Jilt* (1688) features a nun as its main character, and her *History of the Nun* was published in 1689, a year after *Oroonoko.*

treat him so as I shou'd be very loath to behold: that is, it might occasion his Confinement. Perhaps this was not so Luckily spoke of me, for I perceiv'd he resented that Word, which I strove to Soften again in vain: However, he assur'd me, that whatsoever Resolutions he shou'd take, he wou'd Act nothing upon the White-People; and as for my self, and those upon that *Plantation* where he was, he wou'd sooner forfeit his eternal Liberty, and Life it self, than lift his Hand against his greatest Enemy on that Place: he besought me to suffer no Fears upon his Account, for he cou'd do nothing that Honour shou'd not dictate; but he accus'd himself for having suffer'd Slavery so long; yet he charg'd that weakness on Love alone, who was capable of making him neglect even Glory it self; and, for which, now he reproches himself every moment of the Day. Much more to this effect he spoke, with an Air impatient enough to make me know he wou'd not be long in Bondage; and though he suffer'd only the Name of a Slave, and had nothing of the Toil and Labour of one, yet that was sufficient to render him Uneasy; and he had been too long Idle, who us'd to be always in Action, and in Arms: He had a Spirit all Rough and Fierce, and that cou'd not be tam'd to lazy Rest; and though all endeavors were us'd to exercise himself in such Actions and Sports as this World afforded, as Running, Wrastling, Pitching the Bar,[69] Hunting and Fishing, Chasing and Killing *Tigers* of a monstrous Size, which this Continent affords in abundance; and wonderful *Snakes*, such as *Alexander* is reported to have incounter'd at the River of *Amazons*,[70] and which *Cæsar* took great Delight to overcome; yet these were not Actions great enough for his large Soul, which was still panting after more renown'd Action.

Before I parted that Day with him, I got, with much ado, a Promise from him to rest, yet a little longer with Patience, and wait the coming of the Lord Governor, who was every Day expected on our Shore; he assur'd me he wou'd, and this Promise he desired me to know was given perfectly in Complaisance to me, in whom he had an intire Confidence.

After this, I neither thought it convenient to trust him much out of our View, nor did the country who fear'd him; but with one accord it was advis'd to treat him Fairly, and oblige him to remain within such a compass, and that he shou'd be permitted, as seldom as cou'd be, to go up to the Plantations of the negroes; or, if he did, to be accompany'd

---

[69] *Pitching the Bar:* A game in which players compete to throw a heavy bar the farthest.

[70] *Alexander . . . at the River of Amazons:* An encounter Alexander the Great was reported to have had during one of his military campaigns.

by some that shou'd be rather in appearance Attendants than Spys. This Care was for some time taken, and *Cæsar* look'd upon it as a Mark of extraordinary Respect, and was glad his discontent had oblig'd 'em to be more observant to him; he received new assurance from the Overseer, which was confirmed to him by the Opinion of all the Gentlemen of the Country, who made their court to him: During this time that we had his Company more frequently than hitherto we had had, it may not be unpleasant to relate to you the Diversions we entertain'd him with, or rather he us.

My stay was to be short in that Country, because my Father dy'd at Sea, and never arriv'd to possess the Honour was design'd him, (which was Lieutenant-General of Six and thirty Islands, besides the Continent of *Surinam*) nor the advantages he hop'd to reap by them, so that though we were oblig'd to continue on our Voyage, we did not intend to stay upon the Place: Though, in a Word, I must say thus much of it, That certainly had his late Majesty, of sacred Memory, but seen and known what a vast and charming World he had been Master of in that Continent, he would never have parted so Easily with it to the *Dutch.* 'Tis a Continent whose vast Extent was never yet known, and may contain more Noble Earth than all the Universe besides; for, they say, it reaches from East to West; one Way as far as *China,* and another to *Peru:* It affords all things both for Beauty and Use; 'tis there Eternal Spring, always the very Months of *April, May* and *June;* the Shades are perpetual, the Trees, bearing at once all degrees of Leaves and Fruit, from blooming Buds to ripe Autumn, Groves of Oranges, Limons, Citrons, Figs, Nutmegs, and noble Aromaticks, continually bearing their Fragrancies. The Trees appearing all like Nosegays adorn'd with Flowers of different kind; some are all White, some Purple, some Scarlet, some Blew, some Yellow; bearing, at the same time, Ripe Fruit and Blooming Young, or producing every Day new. The very Wood of all these Trees have an intrinsick Value above common Timber; for they are, when cut, of different Colours, glorious to behold; and bear a Price considerable, to inlay withal. Besides this, they yield rich Balm, and Gums; so that we make our Candles of such an Aromatick Substance, as does not only give a sufficient Light, but, as they Burn, they cast their Perfumes all about. Cedar is the common Firing, and all the Houses are built with it. The very Meat we eat, when set on the Table, if it be Native, I mean of the Country perfumes the whole Room; especially a little Beast call'd an *Armadilly,*[71] a thing which I can liken to

71 *Armadilly:* Armadillo.

nothing so well as a *Rhinoceros;* 'tis all in white Armor so joynted, that it moves as well in it, as if it had nothing on; this Beast is about the bigness of a Pig of Six Weeks old. But it were endless to give an Account of all the divers Wonderfull and Strange things that Country affords, and which we took a very great Delight to go in search of; though those adventures are oftentimes Fatal and at least Dangerous: But while we had *Cæsar* in our Company on these Designs we fear'd no harm, nor suffer'd any.

As soon as I came into the Country, the best House in it was presented me, call'd St *John's Hill.*[72] It stood on a vast Rock of white Marble, at the Foot of which the River ran a vast depth down, and not to be descended on that side; the little Waves still dashing and washing the foot of this Rock, made the softest Murmurs and Purlings in the World; and the Oposite Bank was adorn'd with such vast quantities of different Flowers eternally Blowing,[73] and every Day and Hour new, fenc'd behind 'em with lofty Trees of a Thousand rare Forms and Colours, that the Prospect was the most raving[74] that Sands can create. On the Edge of this white Rock, towards the River, was a Walk or Grove of Oranges and Limon Trees, about half the length of the Marl[75] hear, whose Flowery and Fruity bare Branches meet at the top, and hinder'd the Sun, whose Rays are very fierce there, from entering a Beam into the Grove; and the cool Air that came from the River made it not only fit to entertain People in, at all the hottest Hours of the Day, but refresh'd the sweet Blossoms, and made it always Sweet and Charming; and sure the whole Globe of the World cannot show so delightful a Place as this Grove was: Not all the Gardens of boasted *Italy* can produce a Shade to outvie this, which Nature had joyn'd with Art to render so exceeding Fine; and 'tis a marvel to see how such vast Trees, as big as English Oaks, cou'd take footing on so solid a Rock, and in so little Earth, as cover'd that Rock; but all things by Nature there are Rare, Delightful and Wonderful. But to our Sports;

Sometimes we wou'd go surprizing, and in search of young *Tigers* in their Dens, watching when the old Ones went forth to forage for Prey; and oftentimes we have been in great Danger, and have fled apace for our Lives, when surpriz'd by the Dams. But once, above all

---

[72] *St John's Hill:* This estate, which belonged to Sir Robert Harley, was near Lord Willoughby's estate at Parham Hill and included what Behn herself called "the best house" in the settlement; for further discussion, see Part Two, Chapter 4.

[73] *Blowing:* Blooming.

[74] *raving:* Ravishing.

[75] *the Marl:* I.e., the tree-lined mall at St. James's Park in London.

other times, we went on this Design, and *Cæsar* was with us, who had
no sooner stol'n a young *Tiger* from her Nest, but going off, we
incounter'd the Dam, bearing a Buttock of a Cow, which he had torn
off with his mighty Paw, and going with it towards his *Den;* we had
only four Women, *Cæsar,* and an English Gentlemen, Brother to *Harry
Martin,* the great *Oliverian;*[76] we found there was no escaping this
inrag'd and ravenous Beast. However, we Women fled as fast as we
cou'd from it; but our Heels had not sav'd our Lives, if *Cæsar* had not
laid down his *Cub,* when he found the *Tiger* quit her Prey to make the
more speed towards him; and taking Mr *Martin's* Sword desir'd him
to stand aside, or follow the Ladies. He obey'd him, and *Cæsar* met
this monstrous Beast of might, size, and vast Limbs, who came with
open Jaws upon him; and fixing his Awful stern Eyes full upon those of
the Beast, and putting himself into a very steddy and good aiming posture of Defence, ran his Sword quite through his Breast down to his
very Heart, home to the Hilt of the Sword; the dying Beast stretch'd
forth her Paw, and going to grasp his Thigh, surpris'd with Death in
that very moment, did him no other harm than fixing her long Nails in
his Flesh very deep, feebly wounded him, but cou'd not grasp the Flesh
to tear off any. When he had done this, he hollow'd[77] to us to return;
which, after some assurance of his Victory, we did, and found him lug-
ging out the Sword from the Bosom of the *Tiger,* who was laid in her
Bloud on the Ground; he took up the *Cub,* and with an unconcern,
that had nothing of the Joy and Gladness of a Victory, he came and
laid the Whelp at my Feet: We all extreamly wonder'd at his Daring,
and at the Bigness of the Beast, which was about the highth of an
Heifer, but of mighty, great, and strong Limbs.

Another time, being in the Woods, he kill'd a *Tiger,* which had long
infested that part, and born away abundance of Sheep and Oxen, and
other things, that were for the support of those to whom they belong'd; abundance of People assail'd this Beast, some affirming they
had shot her with several Bullets quite through the Body, at several
times; and some swearing they shot her through the very Heart, and
they believ'd she was a Devil rather than a Mortal thing. *Cæsar,* had
often said, he had a mind to encounter this Monster, and spoke with

[76] *Oliverian:* George Marten, whom Behn later mentions by name, was the younger
brother of Henry Marten (1602–1680), who signed the warrant for the execution of
Charles I in 1649. Since he was a parliamentarian, Marten might be generally aligned
with Oliver Cromwell's faction, but Marten's relations with Cromwell in particular
were uneasy at best.

[77] *hollow'd:* Called ("hallo'd").

several Gentlemen who had attempted her; one crying, I shot her with so many poyson'd Arrows, another with his Gun in this part of her, and another in that; so that he remarking all these Places where she was shot, fancy'd still he shou'd overcome her, by giving her another sort of a Wound than any had yet done; and one day said (at the Table) *What Trophies and Garlands Ladies will you make me, if I bring you home the Heart of this Ravenous Beast, that eats up all your Lambs and Pigs?* We all promis'd he shou'd be rewarded at all our Hands. So taking a Bow, which he chus'd out of a great many, he went up in the Wood, with two Gentlemen, where he imagin'd this Devourer to be; they had not past very far in it, but they heard her Voice, growling and grumbling, as if she were pleas'd with something she was doing. When they came in view they found her muzzling in the Belly of a new ravish'd Sheep, which she had torn open; and seeing herself approach'd, she took fast hold of her Prey, with her fore Paws, and set a very fierce raging Look on *Cæsar,* without offering to approach him; for fear, at the same time, of loosing what she had in Possession. So that *Cæsar* remain'd a good while, only taking aim, and getting an opportunity to shoot her where he design'd; 'twas some time before he cou'd accomplish it, and to wound her, and not kill her, wou'd but have enrag'd her more, and indanger'd him: He had a Quiver of Arrows at his side, so that if one fail'd he cou'd be supply'd; at last, retiring a little, he gave her opportunity to eat, for he found she was Ravenous, and fell too as soon as she saw him retire; being more eager of her Prey than of doing new Mischiefs. When he going softly to one side of her, and hiding his Person behind certain Herbage that grew high and thick, he took so good aim, that, as he intended, he shot her just into the Eye, and the Arrow was sent with so good a will, and so sure a hand, that it stuck in her Brain, and made her caper, and become mad for a moment or two; but being seconded by another Arrow, he fell dead upon the Prey: *Cæsar* cut him Open with a Knife to see where those Wounds were that had been reported to him, and why he did not Die of 'em. But I shall now relate a thing that possibly will find no Credit among Men, because 'tis a Notion commonly receiv'd with us, That nothing can receive a Wound in the Heart and Live; but when the Heart of this courageous Animal was taken out, there were Seven Bullets of Lead in it, and the wounds seam'd up with great Scars, and she liv'd with the Bullets a great while, for it was long since they were shot: This Heart the Conqueror brought up to us, and 'twas a very great Curiosity, which all the Country came to see; and which gave *Cæsar* occasion of many fine Discourses; of Accidents in War, and Strange Escapes.

At other times he wou'd go a Fishing; and discoursing on that Diversion, he found we had in that Country a very Strange Fish, call'd a *Numb Eel*,[78] (an *Eel* of which I have eaten) that while it is alive, it has a quality so Cold, that those who are Angling, though with a Line of never so great a length, with a Rod at the end of it, it shall, in the same minute the Bait is touched by this *Eel,* seize him or her that holds the Rod with benumb'dness, that shall deprive 'em of Sense, for a while; and some have fall'n into the Water, and other drop'd as dead on the Banks of the Rivers where they stood, as soon as this Fish touches the Bait. *Cæsar* us'd to laugh at this, and believ'd it impossible a Man cou'd loose his Force at the touch of a Fish; and cou'd not understand that Philosophy, that a cold Quality should be of that Nature: However, he had a great Curiosity to try whether it wou'd have the same effect on him it had on others, and often try'd, but in vain; at last, the sought for Fish came to the Bait, as he stood Angling on the Bank; and instead of throwing away the Rod, or giving it a sudden twitch out of the Water, whereby he might have caught both the *Eel,* and have dismist the Rod, before it cou'd have too much Power over him; for Experiment sake, he grasp'd it but the harder, and fainting fell into the River; and being still possest of the Rod, the Tide carry'd him senseless as he was a great way, till an *Indian* Boat took him up; and perceiv'd, when they touch'd him, a Numbness seize them, and by that knew the Rod was in his Hand; which, with a Paddle (that is, a short Oar) they struck away, and snatch'd it into the Boat, *Eel* and all. If *Cæsar* were almost Dead, with the effect of this Fish, he was more so with that of the Water, where he had remain'd the space of going a League; and they found they had much a-do to bring him back to Life: But, at last, they did, and brought him home, where he was in a few Hours well Recover'd and Refresh'd; and not a little Asham'd to find he shou'd be overcome by an *Eel;* and that all the People, who heard his Defiance, wou'd Laugh at him. But we cheared him up; and he, being convinc'd, we had the *Eel* at Supper; which was a quarter of an Ell about, and most delicate Meat; and was of the more Value, since it cost so Dear, as almost the Life of so gallant a Man.

About this time we were in many mortal Fears, about some Disputes the *English* had with the *Indians;* so that we cou'd scarce trust our selves, without great Numbers, to go to any *Indian* Towns, or Place, where they abode; for fear they shou'd fall upon us, as they did immediately after my coming away; and that it was in the possession

---

[78] *Numb Eel:* Electric eel.

of the *Dutch,* who us'd 'em not so civilly as the *Englisl* cut in pieces all they cou'd take, getting into Houses, ai the Mother, and all her Children about her; and cut a I behind me, all in Joynts, and nail'd him to Trees.

This feud began while I was there; so that I lost half the satisfaction I propos'd, in not seeing and visiting the *Indian* Towns. But one Day, bemoaning of our Misfortunes upon this account, *Cæsar* told us, we need not Fear; for if we had a mind to go, he wou'd undertake to be our Guard: Some wou'd; but most wou'd not venture; about Eighteen of us resolv'd, and took Barge; and, after Eight Days, arriv'd near an *Indian* Town: But approaching it, the Hearts of some of our Company fail'd, and they wou'd not venture on Shore; so we Poll'd who wou'd, and who wou'd not: For my part, I said, If *Cæsar* wou'd, I wou'd go; he resolv'd, so did my Brother, and my Woman, a Maid of good Courage. Now none of us speaking the Language of the People, and imagining we shou'd have a half Diversion in Gazing only; and not knowing what they said, we took a Fisherman that liv'd at the Mouth of the River, who had been a long Inhabitant there, and oblig'd him to go with us: But because he was known to the *Indians,* as trading among 'em; and being, by long Living there, become a perfect *Indian* in Colour, we, who resolv'd to surprize 'em, by making 'em see something they never had seen (that is, White People) resolv'd only my self, my Brother, and woman shou'd go; so *Cæsar,* the Fisherman, and the rest, hiding behind some thick Reeds and Flowers, that grew on the Banks, let us pass on towards the Town, which was on the Bank of the River all along. A little distant from the Houses, or Hutts; we saw some Dancing, other busy'd in fetching and carrying of Water from the River: They had no sooner spy'd us, but they set up a loud Cry, that frighted us at first; we thought it had been for those that should Kill us, but it seems it was of Wonder and Amazement. They were all Naked, and we were Dress'd, so as is most comode[79] for the hot Countries, very glittering and Rich; so that we appear'd extreamly fine; my own Hair was cut short, and I had a Taffaty[80] Cap, with Black Feathers, on my Head; my Brother was in a Stuff[81] Sute, with Silver Loops and Buttons, and abundance of Green Ribon; this was all infinitely surprising to them, and because we saw them stand still, till we approach'd 'em, we took Heart and advanc'd; came up to 'em, and

[79] *comode:* Convenient, comfortable.
[80] *Taffaty:* Taffeta, a glossy, silk fabric.
[81] *Stuff:* Woolen.

offer'd 'em our Hands; which they took, and look'd on us round about, calling still for more Company; who came swarming out, all wondering, and crying out *Tepeeme;* taking their Hair up in their Hands, and spreading it wide to those they call'd out too; as if they would say (as indeed it signify'd) *Numberless Wonders,* or not to be recounted, no more than to number the Hair of their Heads. By degrees they grew more bold, and from gazing upon us round, they touch'd us; laying their Hands upon all the Features of our Faces, feeling our Breasts and Arms, taking up one Petticoat, then wondering to see another; admiring our Shoes and Stockings, but more our Garters, which we gave 'em; and they ty'd about their Legs, being Lac'd with Silver Lace at the ends, for they much Esteem any shining things: In fine, we suffer'd 'em to survey us as they pleas'd, and we thought they wou'd never have done admiring us. When *Cæsar,* and the rest, saw we were receiv'd with such wonder, they came up to us; and finding the *Indian* Trader whom they knew, (for 'tis by these Fishermen, call'd *Indian* Traders, we hold a Commerce with 'em; for they love not to go far from home, and we never go to them) when they saw him therefore they set up a new Joy; and cry'd, in their Language, *Oh! here's our* Tiguamy, *and we shall now know whether those things can speak:* So advancing to him, some of 'em gave him their Hands, and cry'd, *Amora Tiguamy,* which is as much as, *How do you,* or *Welcome Friend;* and all, with one din, began to gabble to him, and ask'd, If we had Sense, and Wit? if we cou'd talk of affairs of Life, and War, as they cou'd do? if we cou'd Hunt, Swim, and do a thousand things they use? He answer'd 'em, We cou'd. Then they invited us into their Houses, and dress'd Venison and Buffelo for us; and, going out, gathered a Leaf of a Tree, call'd a *Sarumbo* Leaf, of Six Yards long, and spread it on the Ground for a Table-Cloth; and cutting another in pieces instead of Plates, setting us on little bow *Indian* Stools, which they cut out of one intire piece of Wood, and Paint, in a sort of Japan Work: They serve every one their Mess[82] on these pieces of Leaves, and it was very good, but too high season'd with Pepper. When we had eat, my Brother, and I, took out our Flutes, and play'd to 'em, which gave 'em new Wonder; and I soon perceiv'd, by an admiration, that is natural to these People, and by the extream Ignorance and Simplicity of 'em, it were not difficult to establish any unknown or extravagant Religion among them; and to impose any Notions or Fictions upon 'em. For

---

[82] *Mess:* Meal.

seeing a Kinsman of mine set some Paper a Fire, with a Burning-glass, a Trick they had never before seen, they were like to have Ador'd him for a God; and beg'd he wou'd give them the Characters or Figures of his Name, that they might oppose it against Winds and Storms; which he did, and they held it up in those Seasons, and fancy'd it had a Charm to conquer them; and kept it like a Holy Relique. They are very Superstitious, and call'd him the Great *Peeie,* that is *Prophet.* They show'd us their *Indian Peeie,* a Youth of about Sixteen Years old, as handsom as Nature cou'd make a Man. They consecrate a beautiful Youth from his Infancy, and all Arts are us'd to compleat him in the finest manner, both in Beauty and Shape: He is bred to all the little Arts and cunning they are capable of; to all the Legerdemain Tricks, and Slight of Hand, whereby he imposes upon the Rabble; and is both a Doctor in Physick and Divinity. And by these Tricks makes the Sick believe he sometimes eases their Pains; by drawing from the afflicted part little Serpents, or odd Flies, or Worms, or any Strange thing; and though they have besides undoubted good Remedies, for almost all their Diseases, they cure the Patient more by Fancy than by Medicines; and make themselves Fear'd, Lov'd, and Reverenc'd. This young *Peeie* had a very young Wife, who seeing my Brother kiss her, came running and kiss'd me; after this, they kiss'd one another, and made it a very great Jest, it being so Novel; and new Admiration and Laughing went round the multitude, that they never will forget that Ceremony, never before us'd or known. *Cæsar* had a mind to see and talk with their War *Captains,* and we were conducted to one of their Houses; where we beheld several of the great *Captains,* who had been at Councel: But so frightful a Vision it was to see 'em no Fancy can create; no such Dreams can represent so dreadful a Spectacle. For my part I took 'em for Hobgoblins, or Fiends, rather than Men; but however their Shapes appear'd, their Souls were very Humane and Noble; but some wanted their Noses, some their Lips, some both Noses and Lips, some their Ears, and others Cut through each Cheek, with long Slashes; through which their teeth appear'd; they had other several formidable Wounds and Scars, or rather Dismemberings; they had *Comitias,* or little Aprons before 'em; and Girdles of Cotton, with their Knives naked, stuck in it; a Bow at their Backs, and a Quiver of Arrows on their Thighs; and most had Feathers on their Heads of divers Colours. They cry'd, *Amora Tigame* to us, at our entrance, and were pleas'd we said as much to 'em; they seated us, and gave us Drink of the best Sort; and wonder'd, as much as the others had done before, to see us. *Cæsar* was marvelling as much at their Faces, wondering how they shou'd all be so Wounded in War; he was impatient to know how they all came by those frightful Marks of Rage or Malice, rather than Wounds got in Noble Battel: They told us, by our Interpreter, That when any War was waging, two Men chosen out by some old *Captain,* whose Fighting was past, and who cou'd only teach the Theory of War, these two Men were to stand in Competition for the Generalship, or Great War Captain; and being brought before the old judges, now past Labour, they are ask'd, What they dare do to shew they are worthy to lead an Army? When he, who is first ask'd, making no Reply, Cuts off his Nose, and throws it contemptably[83] on the Ground; and the other does something to himself that he thinks surpasses him, and perhaps deprives himself of Lips and an Eye; so they Slash on till one gives out, and many have dy'd in this Debate. And 'tis by a passive Valour they shew and prove their Activity; a sort of Courage too Brutal to be applauded by our Black Hero; nevertheless he express'd his Esteem of 'em.

In this Voyage *Cæsar* begot so good an understanding between the *Indians* and the *English,* that there were no more Fears, or Heartburnings during our stay; but we had a perfect, open, and free Trade with 'em: Many things Remarkable, and worthy Reciting, we met with in this short Voyage; because *Cæsar* made it his Business to search out and provide for our Entertainment, especially to please his dearly Ador'd *Imoinda,* who was a sharer in all our Adventures; we being resolv'd to make her Chains as easy as we cou'd, and to Compliment the Prince in that manner that most oblig'd him.

As we were coming up again, we met with some *Indians* of strange Aspects; that is, of a larger Size, and other sort of Features, than those of our Country; Our *Indian Slaves,* that Row'd us, ask'd 'em some Questions, but they cou'd not understand us; but shew'd us a long Cotton String, with several Knots on it; and told us, they had been coming from the Mountains so many Moons as there were Knots, they were habited in Skins of a strange Beast, and brought along with 'em Bags of Gold Dust; which, as well as they cou'd give us to understand, came streaming in little small Chanels down the high Mountains, when the Rains fell; and offer'd to be the Convoy to any Body, or Persons, that wou'd go to the Mountains. We carry'd these Men up to *Parham,* where they were kept till the Lord Governour came: And because all the Country was mad to be going on this Golden Adven-

---

[83] *contemptably:* Contemptuously.

ture,[84] the Governour, by his Letters, commanded (for they sent some of the Gold to him) that a Guard shou'd be set at the Mouth of the River of *Amazons*, (a River so call'd, almost as broad as the River of *Thames*) and prohibited all People from going up that River, it conducting to those Mountains of Gold. But we going off for *England* before the Project was further prosecuted, and the Governour being drown'd in a Hurricane,[85] either the Design dy'd, or the *Dutch* have the Advantage of it: And 'tis to be bemoan'd what his Majesty lost by loosing that part of *America*.

Though this digression is a little from my Story, however since it contains some Proofs of the Curiosity and Daring of this great Man, I was content to omit nothing of his Character.

It was thus, for sometime we diverted him; but now *Imoinda* began to shew she was with Child, and did nothing but Sigh and Weep for the Captivity of her Lord, her Self, and the Infant yet Unborn, and believ'd, if it were so hard to gain the Liberty of Two, 'twou'd be more difficult to get that for Three. Her Griefs were so many Darts in the Great Heart of *Cæsar;* and taking his Opportunity one *Sunday,* when all the Whites were overtaken in Drink, as there were abundance of several Trades, and *Slaves* for Four Years,[86] that Inhabited among the *Negro* Houses; and *Sunday* was their Day of Debauch, (otherwise they were a sort of Spys upon *Cæsar;*) he went pretending out of Goodness to 'em, to Feast amongst 'em; and sent all his Musick, and order'd a great Treat for the whole Gang, about Three Hundred *Negros;* and about a Hundred and Fifty were able to bear Arms, such as they had, which were sufficient to do Execution[87] with Spirits accordingly: For the *English* had none but rusty Swords, that no Strength cou'd draw from a Scabbard; except the People of particular Quality, who took care to Oyl 'em and keep 'em in good Order: The Guns also, unless here and there one, or those newly carri'd from *England,* wou'd do no good or harm; for 'tis the Nature of that Country to Rust and Eat up Iron, or any Metals, but Gold and Silver. And

---

[84] *Golden Adventure:* Behn is alluding, somewhat mockingly, to the persistent European myth of the existence of a "city of gold" in Guiana; for more detailed versions of the myth, see the selections from Richard Jobson in Part Two, Chapter 3 and from Sir Walter Raleigh in Chapter 4.

[85] *the Governour being drown'd in a Hurricane:* During a conflict with the French over the possession of St. Kitts, another island in the West Indies, Lord Willoughby set off with a military force from Barbados and was lost at sea in July 1666.

[86] *Slaves for Four Years:* Indentured servants; for further discussion of the analogy between indentured servitude and slavery, see Part Two, Chapter 5.

[87] *to do Execution:* To fight.

they are very Unexpert at the Bow, which the *Negroes* and *Indians* are perfect Masters of.

Cæsar, having singl'd out these Men from the Women and Children, made an Harangue to 'em of the Miseries, and Ignominies of Slavery; counting up all their Toyls and Sufferings, under such Loads, Burdens, and Drudgeries, as were fitter for Beasts than Men; Senseless Brutes, than Humane Souls. He told 'em it was not for Days, Months, or Years, but for Eternity; there was no end to be of their Misfortunes: They suffer'd not like Men who might find a Glory, and Fortitude in Oppression; but like Dogs that lov'd the Whip and Bell, and fawn'd the more they were beaten: That they had lost the Divine Quality of Men, and were become insensible Asses, fit only to bear; nay worse: an Ass, or Dog, or Horse having done his Duty, cou'd lye down in Retreat, and rise to Work again, and while he did his Duty indur'd no Stripes; but Men, Villanous, Senseless Men, such as they, Toyl'd on all the tedious Week till Black *Friday,*[88] and then, whether they Work'd or not, whether they were Faulty or Meriting, they promiscuously, the Innocent with the Guilty, suffer'd the infamous Whip, the sordid Stripes, from their Fellow *Slaves* till their Blood trickled from all Parts of their Body; Blood, whose every drop ought to be Reveng'd with a Life of some of those Tyrants, that impose it: *And why,* said he, *my dear Friends and Fellow-sufferers, shou'd we be Slaves to an unknown People? Have they Vanquish'd us Nobly in Fight? Have they Won us in Honourable Battel? And are we, by the chance of War, become their Slaves? This wou'd not anger a Noble Heart, this wou'd not animate a Souldiers Soul; no, but we are Bought and Sold like Apes, or Monkeys, to be the Sport of Women, Fools and Cowards; and the Support of Rogues, Runagades, that have abandon'd their own Countries, for Rapin, Murders, Thefts and Villanies: Do you not hear every Day how they upbraid each other with infamy of Life, below the Wildest Salvages;*[89] *and shall we render Obedience to such a degenerate Race, who have no one Humane Vertue left, to distinguish 'em from the vilest Creatures? Will you, I say, suffer the Lash from such Hands?* They all Reply'd, with one accord, *No, no, no; Cæsar has spoke like a Great Captain; like a Great King.*

After this he wou'd have proceeded, but was interrupted by a tall *Negro* of some more Quality than the rest, his Name was *Tuscan;* who Bowing at the Feet of *Cæsar,* cry'd, *My Lord, we have listen'd with Joy*

---

[88] *Black Friday:* Term for a day regularly set aside for torture or punishment.
[89] *Salvages:* I.e., savages.

and Attention to what you have said; and, were we only Men, wou'd follow so great a Leader through the World: But oh! consider, we are Husbands and Parents too, and have things more dear to us than Life; our Wives and Children unfit for Travel, in these unpassable Woods, Mountains and Bogs; we have not only difficult Lands to overcome, but Rivers to Wade, and Monsters to Incounter; Ravenous Beasts of Prey — To this, *Cæsar* Reply'd, *That Honour was the First Principle in Nature, that was to be Obey'd; but as no Man wou'd pretend to that, without all the Acts of Vertue, Compassion, Charity, Love, Justice and Reason; he found it not inconsistent with that, to take an equal Care of their Wives and Children, as they wou'd of themselves; and that he did not Design, when he led them to Freedom, and Glorious Liberty, that they shou'd leave that better part of themselves to Perish by the Hand of the Tyrant's Whip: But if there were a Woman among them so degenerate from Love and Vertue to chuse Slavery before the pursuit of her Husband, and with the hazard of her Life, to share within in his Fortunes; that such an one ought to be Abandon'd, and left as a Prey to the common Enemy.*

To which they all Agreed, — and Bowed. After this, he spoke of the Impassable Woods and Rivers; and convinc'd 'em, the more Danger, the more Glory. He told them that he had heard of one *Hannibal* a great Captain, had Cut his Way through Mountains of solid Rocks;[90] and shou'd a few Shrubs oppose them; which they cou'd Fire before 'em? No, 'twas a trifling Excuse to Men resolv'd to die, or overcome. As for Bogs, they are with a little Labour fill'd and harden'd; and the Rivers cou'd be no Obstacle, since they Swam by Nature; at least by Custom, from their First Hour of their Birth: That when the Children were Weary they must carry them by turns, and the Woods and their own Industry wou'd afford them Food. To this they all assented with Joy.

Tuscan then demanded, What he wou'd do? He said, they wou'd Travel towards the Sea; Plant a New Colony, and Defend it by their Valour; and when they cou'd find a Ship, either driven by stress of Weather, or guided by Providence that way, they wou'd Sieze it, and make it a Prize, till it had Transported them to their own Countries; at least, they shou'd be made Free in his Kingdom, and be Esteem'd as his Fellow-sufferers, and Men that had the Courage, and the Bravery to

---

[90] *Hannibal . . . solid rocks:* Carthaginian general, famous for cutting his way through the Alps in 218 B.C.E. in his attempt to invade Italy.

attempt, at least, for Liberty; and if they Dy'd in the attempt it wou'd be more brave, than to Live in Perpetual Slavery.

They bow'd and kiss'd his Feet at this Resolution, and with one accord Vow'd to follow him to Death. And that Night was appointed to begin their March; they made it known to their Wives, and directed them to tie their Hamaca[91] about their Shoulder, and under their Arm like a Scarf; and to lead their Children that cou'd go, and carry those that cou'd not. The Wives who pay an intire Obedience to their Husbands obey'd and stay'd for 'em, where they were appointed: The Men stay'd but to furnish, themselves with what defensive Arms they cou'd get; and All met at the Rendezvous, where *Cæsar* made a new incouraging Speech to 'em, and led 'em out.

But, as they cou'd not march far that Night, on Monday early, when the Overseers went to call 'em all together, to go to Work, they were extreamly surpris'd, to find not one upon the Place, but all fled with what Baggage they had. You may imagine this News was not only suddenly spread all over the *Plantation*, but soon reached the Neighbouring ones; and we had by Noon about Six Hundred Men, they call the *Militia* of the County, that came to assist us in the persute of the Fugitives: But never did one see so comical an Army march forth to War. The Men, of any fashion, wou'd not concern themselves, though it were almost the common Cause; for such Revoltings are very ill Examples, and have very fatal Consequences oftentimes in many Colonies: but they had a Respect for *Cæsar,* and all hands were against the *Parhamites,* as they call'd those of *Parham Plantation*; because they did not, in the first place, love the Lord Governor; and secondly they wou'd have it, that *Cæsar* was Ill us'd, and Baffl'd with;[92] and 'tis not impossible but some of the best in the Country was of his Council in this Flight, and depriving us of all the *Slaves;* so that they of the better sort wou'd not meddle in the matter. The Deputy Governor,[93] of whom I have had no great occasion to speak, and who was the most Fawning fair-tongu'd Fellow in the World, and one that pretended the most Friendship to *Cæsar,* was now the only violent Man against him; and though he had nothing, and so need fear nothing, yet talk'd and look'd bigger than any Man: He was a Fellow, whose Character is not

---

[91] *Hamaca:* Hammock.
[92] *Baffl'd with:* Tricked.
[93] *Deputy Governor:* William Byam, whose name Behn gives on p. 89; he acted as governor in the absence of Lord Willoughby. Though Behn shared Byam's Royalist politics, she strongly disliked him; see the selections on *Colonial Life in Suriname,* in Part Two, Chapter 4.

fit to be mention'd with the worst of the *Slaves*. This Fellow wou'd lead his Army forth to meet *Cæsar*, or rather to persue him; most of their Arms were to those sort of cruel Whips they call *Cat with Nine Tayls;*[94] some had rusty useless Guns for show; others old Basket-hilts,[95] whose Blades had never seen the Light in this Age; and others had long Staffs, and Clubs. Mr *Trefry* went a long, rather to a Mediator than a Conqueror, in such a Batail; for he foresaw, and knew, if by fighting they put the *Negroes* into dispair, they were a sort of sullen Fellows, that wou'd drown, or kill themselves, before they wou'd yield; and he advis'd that fair means was best: But *Byam* was one that abounded in his own wit, and wou'd take his own Measures.

It was not hard to find these Fugitives; for as they fled they were forc'd to fire and cut the Woods before 'em, so that Night or Day they persu'd 'em by the light they made, and by the path they had clear'd: But as soon as *Cæsar* found he was persu'd, he put himself in a Posture of Defence, placing all the Women and Children in the Reer; and himself, with *Tuscan* by his side, or next to him, all promising to Dye or Conquer. Incourag'd thus, they never stood to Parley, but fell on Pell-mell upon the *English,*and kill'd some, and wounded a good many; they having recourse to their Whips, as the best of their Weapons: And as they observ'd no Order, they perplex'd the Enemy so sorely, with Lashing 'em in the Eyes; and the Women and Children, seeing their Husbands so treated, being of fearful Cowardly Dispositions, and hearing the *English* cry out, *Yield and Live, Yield and be Pardon'd;* they all run in amongst their Husbands and Fathers, and hung about 'em, crying out, *Yield, yield; and leave* Cæsar *to their Revenge;* that by degrees the *Slaves* abandon'd *Cæsar*, and left him only *Tuscan* and his Heroick *Imoinda;* who, grown big as she was, did nevertheless press near her Lord, having a Bow, and a Quiver full of poyson'd Arrows, which she manag'd with such dexterity, that she wounded several, and shot the *Governor* into the Shoulder; of which Wound he had like to have Dy'd, but that an *Indian* Woman, his Mistress, suck'd the Wound, and cleans'd it from the Venom: But however, he stir'd not from the Place till he had Parly'd with *Cæsar*, who he found was resolv'd to dy Fighting, and wou'd not be Taken; no more wou'd *Tuscan*, or *Imoinda*. But he, more thirsting after Revenge of another sort, than that of depriving him of Life, now made use of all his Art of talking, and dissembling; and besought *Cæsar* to yield himself upon

---

[94] *Cat with Nine Tayls:* A whip with nine knotted lashes.
[95] *Basket-hilts:* Swords with rounded protective hilts.

Terms, which he himself should propose, and should be Sacredly
assented to and kept by him: He told him, It was not that he any
longer fear'd him, or cou'd believe the force of Two Men, and a young
Heroine, cou'd overcome all them, with all the Slaves now on their
side also; but it was the vast Esteem he had for his Person; the desire he
had to serve so Gallant a Man, and to hinder himself from the
Reproach hereafter, of having been the occasion of the Death of a
Prince, whose Valour and Magnanimity deserv'd the Empire of the
World. He protested to him, he look'd upon this Action, as Gallant
and Brave; however tending to the prejudice of his Lord and Master,
who wou'd by it have lost so considerable a number of *Slaves;* that this
Flight of his shou'd be look'd on as a heat of Youth, and rashness of a
too forward Courage, and an unconsider'd impatience of Liberty, and
no more; and that he labour'd in vain to accomplish that which they
wou'd effectually perform, as soon as any Ship arriv'd that wou'd
touch on his Coast. *So, that if you will be pleas'd,* continued he, *to surrender your self, all imaginable Respect shall be paid you; and your
Self, your Wife, and Child, if it be here born, shall depart free out of
our Land.* But *Cæsar* wou'd hear of no Composition;[96] though *Byam*
urg'd, If he persu'd, and went on in his Design, he wou'd inevitably
Perish, either by great *Snakes,* wild Beasts, or Hunger; and he ought to
have regard to his Wife, whose Condition required ease, and not the
fatigues of tedious Travel; where she cou'd not be secur'd from being
devoured. But *Cæsar* told him, there was no Faith in the White Men,
or the Gods they Ador'd; who instructed 'em in Principles so false, that
honest Men cou'd not live amongst 'em; though no People profess'd so
much, none perform'd so little; that he knew what he had to do, when
he dealt with Men of Honour; but with them a Man ought to be eternally on his Guard, and never to Eat or Drink with *Christians* without
his Weapon of Defence in his Hand; and, for his own Security, never to
credit one word they spoke. As for the rashness and inconsiderateness
of his Action he wou'd confess the Governor is in the Right; and that
he was asham'd of what he had done, in endeavoring to make those
Free, who were by Nature *Slaves,* poor wretched Rogues, fit to be us'd
as *Christians* Tools; Dogs, treacherous and cowardly, fit for such Masters; and they wanted only but to be whipt into the knowledge of the
Christian Gods to be the vilest of all creeping things; to learn to Worship such Deities as had not Power to make 'em Just, Brave, or Honest.
In fine, after a thousand things of this Nature, not fit here to be recited,

[96] *Composition:* Compromise, agreement.

he told *Byam,* he had rather Dye than Live upon the same Earth with such Dogs. But *Trefry* and *Byam* pleaded and protested together so much, that *Trefry* believing the *Governor* to mean what he said; and speaking very cordially himself, generously put himself into *Cæsar*'s Hands, and took him aside, and perswaded him, even with Tears, to Live, by Surrendring himself, and to name his Conditions. *Cæsar* was overcome by his Wit and Reasons, and in consideration of *Imoinda;* and demanding what he desir'd, and that it shou'd be ratify'd by their Hands in Writing, because he had perceiv'd that was the common way of contract between Man and Man, amongst the Whites: All this was perform'd, and *Tuscan*'s Pardon was put in, and they Surrender to the governor, who walked peaceably down into the *Plantation* with 'em, after giving order to bury their dead. *Cæsar* was very much toyl'd with the bustle of the Day; for he had fought like a Fury, and what Mischief was done he and *Tuscan* perform'd alone; and gave their Enemies a fatal Proof that they durst do any thing, and fear'd no mortal Force.

But they were no sooner arriv'd at the Place, where all the Slaves receive their Punishments of Whipping, but they laid Hands on *Cæsar* and *Tuscan,* faint with heat and toyl; and, surprising them, Bound them to two several Stakes, and Whipt them in a most deplorable and inhumane Manner, rending the very Flesh from their Bones; especially *Cæsar,* who was not perceiv'd to make any Mone, or to alter his Face, only to roul his Eyes on the Faithless *Governor,* and those he believ'd Guilty, with Fierceness and Indignation; and, to compleat his Rage, he saw every one of those *Slaves,* who, but a few Days before, Ador'd him as something more than Mortal, now had a Whip to give him some Lashes, while he strove not to break his Fetters; though, if he had, it were impossible: But he pronounced a Woe and Revenge from his Eyes, that darted Fire, that 'twas at once both Awful and Terrible to behold.

When they thought they were sufficiently Reveng'd on him, they unty'd him, almost Fainting, with loss of Blood, from a thousand Wounds all over his Body; from which they had rent his Cloaths, and led him Bleeding and Naked as he was; and loaded him all over with Irons; and then rubbed his Wounds, to compleat their Cruelty, with *Indian Pepper,* which had like to have made him raving Mad; and, in this Condition, made him so fast to the Ground that he cou'd not stir, if his Pains and Wounds wou'd have given him leave. They spar'd *Imoinda,* and did not let her see this Barbarity committed towards her Lord, but carry'd her down to *Parham,* and shut her up; which was not in kindness to her, but for fear she shou'd Dye with the Sight, or

Miscarry; and then they shou'd loose a young *Slave,* and perhaps the Mother.

You must know, that when the News was brought on Monday Morning, that *Cæsar* had betaken himself to the Woods, and carry'd with him all the *Negroes.* We were possess'd with extream Fear, which no perswasions cou'd Dissipate, that he wou'd secure himself till Night; and then, that he wou'd come down and Cut all our Throats. This apprehension made all the Females of us fly down the River, to be secur'd; and while we were away, they acted this Cruelty: For I suppose I had Authority and Interest enough there, had I suspected any such thing, to have prevented it; but we had not gone many Leagues, but the News overtook us that *Cæsar* was taken, and Whipt like a common *Slave.* We met on the River with Colonel *Martin,* a Man of great Gallantry, Wit, and Goodness, and whom I have celebrated in a Character of my New *Comedy,*[97] by his own Name, in memory of so brave a Man: He was Wise and Eloquent; and, from the fineness of his Parts, bore a great Sway over the Hearts of all the *Colony:* He was friend to *Cæsar,* and resented this false Dealing with him very much. We carried him back to *Parham,* thinking to have made an Accommodation; when we came, the First News we heard was, that the *Governor* was Dead of a Wound *Imoinda* had given him; but it was not so well: But it seems he wou'd have the Pleasure of beholding the Revenge he took on *Cæsar;* and before the cruel Ceremony was finish'd, he drop'd down; and then they perceiv'd the Wound he had on his Shoulder, was by a venom'd Arrow; which, as I said, his *Indian* Mistress heal'd, by Sucking the Wound.

We were no sooner Arriv'd, but we went up to the *Plantation* to see *Cæsar,* whom we found in a very Miserable and Unexpressable Condition; and I have a Thousand times admired how he liv'd, in so much tormenting Pain. We said all things to him, that Trouble, Pitty, and Good Nature cou'd suggest; Protesting our Innocency of the Fact, and our Abhorance of such Cruelties. Making a Thousand Professions of Services to him, and Begging as many Pardons for the Offenders, till we said so much, that he believ'd we had no Hand in his ill Treatment; but told us, he cou'd never Pardon *Byam;* as for *Trefry,* he confess'd he saw his Grief and Sorrow, for his Suffering, which he cou'd not hinder, but was like to have been beaten down by the very *Slaves,* for Speaking

---

[97] *my New Comedy: The Younger Brother, or The Amorous Jilt;* though probably completed by 1684, the play was not performed until 1696, seven years after Behn's death. The hero is named George Marteen.

in his Defence: But for *Byam*, who was their Leader, their Head; — and shou'd, by his Justice, and Honor, have been an Example to 'em. — For him, he wish'd to Live, to take a dire Revenge of him, and said, *It had been well for him, if he had Sacrific'd me, instead of giving me the contemptable Whip.* He refus'd to Talk much, but Begging us to give him our Hands; he took 'em, and Protested never to lift up his, to do us any Harm. He had a great Respect for Colonel *Martin*, and always took his Counsel, like that of a Parent; and assur'd him, he wou'd obey him in any thing, but his Revenge on *Byam*. *Therefore,* said he, *for his own Safety, let him speedily dispatch me; for if I cou'd dispatch my self, I wou'd not, till that Justice were done to my injur'd Person, and the contempt of a Souldier: No, I wou'd not kill my self, even after a Whiping, but will be content to live with that Infamy, and be pointed at by every grinning Slave, till I have compleated my Revenge; and then you shall see that* Oroonoko *scorns to live with the Indignity that was put on* Cæsar. All we cou'd do cou'd get no more Words from him; and we took care to have him put immediately into a healing Bath, to rid him of his Pepper; and order'd a Chirurgeon[98] to anoint him with healing Balm, which he suffer'd, and in some time he began to be able to Walk and Eat; we fail'd not to visit him every Day, and, to that end, had him brought to an apartment at *Parham.*

The *Governor* was no sooner recover'd and had heard of the menaces of *Cæsar*, but he call'd his Council; who (not to disgrace them, or Burlesque the Government there) consisted of such notorious Villains as *Newgate*[99] never transported; and possibly originally were such, who understood neither the Laws of *God* or *Man*; and had no sort of Principles to make 'em worthy the Name of Men: But, at the very Council Table, wou'd Contradict and Fight with one another; and Swear so bloodily that 'twas terrible to hear, and see 'em. (Some of 'em were afterward Hang'd, when the *Dutch* took possession of the place: others sent off in Chains:) But calling these special Rulers of the Nation together, and requiring their Counsel in this weighty Affair, they all concluded, that (Damn 'em) it might be their own Cases; and that *Cæsar* ought to be made an Example to all the *Negroes*, to fright 'em from daring to threaten their Betters, their Lords and Masters; and, at this rate, no Man was safe from his own *Slaves*, and concluded, *nemine contradicente*[100] that *Cæsar*, shou'd be Hang'd.

[98] *Chirurgeon:* Surgeon.
[99] *Newgate:* Prison in London; on the practice of transporting convicts to the American colonies and the Caribbean, see the "Petitions," pp. 408–14.
[100] *nemine contradicente:* Without dissent, unanimously (Latin).

Trefry then thought it time to use his Authority; and told *Byam* his Command did not extend to his Lord's *Plantation;* and that *Parham* was as much exempt from the Law as *White-hall;*[101] and that they ought no more to touch the Servants of the Lord — (who there represented the King's Person) than they cou'd those about the King himself; and that *Parham* was a Sanctuary; and though his Lord were absent in Person, his Power was still in Being there; which he had intrusted with him, as far as the Dominions of his particular *Plantations* reach'd, and all that belong'd to it; the rest of the *Country,* as *Byam* was Lieutenant to his Lord, he might exercise his Tyrany upon. *Trefry* had others as powerful, or more, that int'rested themselves in *Cæsar's* Life, and absolutely said, he shou'd be Defended. So turning the *Governor,* and his wise Council, out of Doors (for they sate at *Parham-house)* they set a Guard upon our Landing Place, and wou'd admit none but those we call'd Friends to us and *Cæsar.*

The *Governor* having remain'd wounded at *Parham,* till his recovery was compleated, *Cæsar* did not know but he was still there; and indeed, for the most part, his time was spent there; for he was one that lov'd to Live at other Peoples Expence; and if he were a Day absent, he was Ten present there; and us'd to Play, and Walk, and Hunt, and Fish, with *Cæsar.* So that *Cæsar* did not at all doubt, if he once recover'd Strength, but he shou'd find an opportunity of being Reveng'd on him: Though, after such a Revenge, he cou'd not hope to Live; for if he escap'd the Fury of the *English* Mobile,[102] who perhaps wou'd have been glad of the occasion to have kill'd him, he was resolv'd not to survive his Whipping; yet he had, some tender Hours, a repenting Softness, which he called his fits of Coward; wherein he struggl'd with Love for the Victory of his Heart, which took part with his charming *Imoinda* there; but, for the most part, his time was past in melancholy Thought, and black Designs; he consider'd, if he shou'd do this Deed, and Dye, either in the Attempt, or after it, he left his lovely *Imoinda* a Prey, or at best a *Slave,* to the inrag'd Multitude; his great Heart cou'd not indure that Thought. *Perhaps,* said he, *she may be first Ravished by every Brute; exposed first to their nasty Lusts, and then a shameful Death.* No; he could not Live a Moment under that Apprehension too insupportable to be born. These were his Thoughts, and his silent Arguments with his Hearts, as he told us afterwards; so that now resolving not only to kill *Byam,* but all those he thought had inrag'd

---

[101] *White-hall:* The royal palace in London.
[102] *Mobile:* Rabble; mob (Latin).

him; pleasing his great Heart with the fancy'd Slaughter he shou'd
make over the whole Face of the *Plantation*. He first resolv'd on a
Deed, that (however Horrid it at first appear'd to us all) when we had
heard his Reasons, we thought it Brave and Just: Being able to Walk,
and, as he believ'd, fit for the Execution of his great Design, he beg'd
Trefry to trust him into the Air, believing a Walk wou'd do him good;
which was granted him, and taking *Imoinda* with him, as he us'd to do
in his more happy and calmer Days, he led her up into a Wood, where,
after (with a thousand Sighs, and long Gazing silently on her Face,
while Tears gust, in spight of him, from his Eyes) he told her his Design
first of Killing her, and then his Enemies, and next himself, and the
impossibility of Escaping, and therefore he told her the necessity of
Dying; he found the Heroick Wife faster pleading for Death than
he was to propose it, when she found his fix'd Resolution; and, on
her Knees, besought him, not to leave her a Prey to his Enemies. He
(griev'd to Death) yet pleased at her noble Resolution, took her up,
and imbracing her, with all the Passion and Languishment of a dying
Lover, drew his Knife to kill this Treasure of his Soul, this Pleasure of
his Eyes; while Tears trickl'd down his Cheeks, hers were Smiling with
Joy she shou'd dye by so noble a Hand, and be sent in her own Country, (for that's their Notion of the next World) by him she so tenderly
Lov'd, and so truly Ador'd in this; for Wives have a respect for their
Husbands equal to what any other People pay a Deity; and when a
Man finds any occasion to quit his Wife, if he love her, she dyes by his
Hand; if not, he sells her, or suffers some other to kill her. It being thus,
you may believe the Deed was soon resolv'd on; and 'tis not to be
doubted, but the Parting, the eternal Leave taking of Two such Lovers,
so greatly Born, so Sensible,[103] so Beautiful, so Young, and so Fond,
must be very Moving, as the Relation of it was to me afterwards.

    All that Love cou'd say in such cases, being ended; and all the inter-
mitting Irresolutions being adjusted, the Lovely, Young, and Ador'd
Victim lays her self down, before the Sacrificer; while he, with a Hand
resolv'd, and a Heart breaking within, gave the Fatal Stroke; first, cutting her Throat, and then severing her, yet Smiling, Face from the Delicate Body, pregnant as it was with Fruits of tend'rest Love. As soon as
he had done, he laid the body decently on Leaves and Flowers; of
which he made a Bed, and conceal'd it under the same cover-lid of
Nature; only her Face he left yet bare to look on: But when he found
she was Dead, and past all Retrieve, never more to bless him with her

[103] *Sensible:* Sensitive.

Eyes, and soft Language; his Grief swell'd up to Rage; he Tore, he Rav'd he Roar'd, like some Monster of the Wood, calling on the lov'd Name of *Imoinda;* a thousand times he turn'd the Fatal Knife that did the Deed, toward his own Heart, with a Resolution to go immediately after her; but dire Revenge, which now was a thousand times more fierce in his Soul than before, prevents him; and he wou'd cry out, *No; since I have sacrificed* Imoinda *to my Revenge, shall I loose that glory which I have purchas'd so dear, as at the Price of the fairest, dearest softest Creature that ever Nature made? No, no!* Then, at her Name, Grief wou'd get the ascendant of Rage, and he wou'd lye down by her side, and water her Face with showers of Tears, which never were wont to fall from those Eyes: And however bent he was on his intended Slaughter, he had not power to stir from the Sight of this dear Object, now more Belov'd, and more Ador'd than ever.

He remain'd in this deploring Condition for two Days, and never rose from the Ground where he had made his sad Sacrifice; at last, rousing from her side, and accusing himself with living too long, now *Imoinda* was dead; and that the Deaths of those barbarous Enemies were deferr'd too long, he resolv'd now to finish the great Work; but offering to rise, he found his Strength so decay'd, that he reel'd to and fro, like Boughs assail'd by contrary Winds; so that he was forced to lye down again, and try to summon all his Courage to his Aid; he found his Brains turn round, and his Eyes were dizzy; and Objects appear'd not the same to him they were wont to do; his Breath was short; and all his Limbs surprised with a Faintness he had never felt before: He had not Eat in two Days, which was one occasion of this Feebleness, but excess of Grief was the greatest; yet still he hop'd he shou'd recover Vigour to act his Design, and lay expecting it yet six Days longer; still mourning over the dead Idol of his Heart, and striving every Day to rise, but cou'd not.

In all this time you may believe we were in no little affliction for *Cæsar,* and his Wife; some were of Opinion he was escap'd never to return; other thought some Accident had hap'ned to him: But however, we fail'd not to send out a hundred People several ways to search for him; a Party, of about forty, went that way he took; among whom was *Tuscan,* who was perfectly reconcil'd to *Byam;* they had not gone very far into the Wood, but they smelt an unusual Smell, as of a dead Body; for Stinks must be very noisom[104] that can be distinguish'd among such a quantity of Natural Sweets, as every Inch of that Land

---

[104] *noisom:* Unpleasant.

produces. So that they concluded they shou'd find him dead, or some-body that was so; they past on towards it, as Loathsom as it was, and made such a rusling among the Leaves that lye thick on the Ground, by continual Falling, that *Cæsar* heard he was approach'd; and though he had, during the space of these eight Days, endeavor'd to rise, but found he wanted Strength, yet looking up, and seeing his Pursuers, he rose, and reel'd to a Neighbouring Tree, against which he fix'd his Back; and being within a dozen Yards of those that advanc'd, and saw him; he call'd out to them, and bid them approach no nearer, if they wou'd be safe: So that they stood still, and hardly believing their Eyes, that wou'd perswade them that it was *Cæsar* that spoke to 'em, so much he was alter'd; they ask'd him, What he had done with his Wife? For they smelt a Stink that almost struck them dead. He, pointing to the dead Body, sighing, cry'd *Behold her there;* they put off the Flow-ers that cover'd her with their Sticks, and found she was kill'd and cry'd out, *Oh, Monster! that hast murther'd thy Wife:* Then asking him, Why he did so cruel a Deed? He replied, he had no leasure to answer impertinent Questions; *You may go back,* continued he, *and tell the Faithless Governor, he may thank Fortune that I am breathing my last; and that my Arm is too feeble to obey my Heart, in what it had design'd him:* But his Tongue faultering, and trembling, he cou'd scarce end what he was saying. The *English* taking Advantage by his Weakness, cry'd, *Let us take him alive by all means:* He heard 'em; and, as if he had reviv'd from a Fainting, or a Dream, he cry'd out, *No, Gentlemen, you are deceiv'd; you will find no more* Cæsars *to be Whipt; no more find a Faith in me: Feeble as you think me, I have Strength yet left to secure me from a second Indignity.* They swore all a-new, and he only shook his Head, and beheld them with Scorn; then they cry'd out, *Who will venture on this single Man? Will no body?* They stood all silent while *Cæsar* replied, *Fatal will be the Attempt to the first Adventurer; let him assure himself,* and at the Word, held up his Knife in a menacing Posture, *Look ye, ye faithless Crew,* said he, *'tis not Life I seek, nor am I afraid of Dying;* and, at that Word, cut a piece of Flesh from his own Throat, and threw it at 'em, *yet still I wou'd Live if I cou'd, till I had perfected my Revenge. But oh! it can-not be; I feel Life gliding from my Eyes and Heart; and, if I make not haste, I shall yet fall a Victim to the Shameful Whip.* At that, he rip'd up his own Belly; and took his Bowels and pull'd 'em out, with what Strength he cou'd; while some, on their Knees imploring, besought him to hold his Hand. But when they saw him tottering, they cry'd out, *Will none venture on him?* A bold *English* cry'd, *Yes, if he were the Devil;* (taking Courage when he saw him almost Dead) and swearing a horrid Oath for his farewell to the World, he rush'd on *Cæsar,* with his Arm'd Hand met him so fairly, as stuck him to the Heart, and he fell Dead at his Feet. *Tuscan* seeing that, cry'd out, *I love thee, oh* Cæsar; *and therefore will not let thee Dye, if possible:* And, running to him, took him in his Arms; but, at the same time, warding a Blow that *Cæsar* made at his Bosom, he receiv'd it quite through his Arm; and *Cæsar* having not the Strength to pluck the Knife forth, though he attempted it, *Tuscan* neither pull'd it out himself, nor suffer'd it to be pull'd out; but came down with it sticking in his Arm; and the reason he gave for it was, because the Air shou'd not get into the Wound: They put their Hands a-cross, and carried *Cæsar* between Six of 'em, fainted as he was; and they thought Dead, or just Dying; and they brought him to *Parham,* and laid him on a Couch, and had the Chirurgeon immediately to him, who drest his Wounds, and sow'd up his Belly, and us'd means to bring him to Life, which they effected. We ran all to see him; and, if before we thought him so beautiful a Sight, he was now so alter'd, that his Face was like a Death's Head black'd over; nothing but Teeth, and Eyeholes: For some Days we suffer'd no body to speak to him, but caused Cordials to be poured down his Throat, which sustained his Life; and in six or seven Days he recover'd his Senses: For, you must know, that Wounds are almost to a Miracle cur'd in the *Indies;* unless Wounds in the Legs, which rarely ever cure.

When he was well enough to speak, we talk'd to him; and ask'd him some Questions about his Wife, and the Reasons why he kill'd her; and he then told us what I have related of that Resolution, and of his Parting; and he besought us, we would let him Dye, and was extreamly Afflicted to think it was possible he might Live: he assur'd us, if we did not Dispatch him, he wou'd prove very Fatal to a great many. We said all we cou'd to make him Live, and gave him new Assurances; but he begg'd we wou'd not think so poorly of him, or of his love to *Imoinda,* to imagine we cou'd Flatter him to Life again; but the Chirurgeon assur'd him, he cou'd not Live, and therefore he need not Fear. We were all (but *Cæsar*) afflicted at this News; and the Sight was ghastly; his Discourse was sad; and the earthly Smell about him so strong, that I was perswaded to leave the Place for some time; (being my self but Sickly, and very apt to fall into Fits of dangerous Illness upon any extraordinary Melancholy) the Servants, and *Trefry,* and the Chirurgeons, promis'd all to take what possible care they cou'd of the Life of *Cæsar;* and I, taking Boat, went with other company to Colonel *Mar-*

tin's, about three Days Journy down the River; but I was no sooner gone, but the *Governor* taking *Trefry,* about some pretended earnest Business, a Days Journey up the River; having communicated his Design to one *Banister,* a wild *Irish* Man,[105] and one of the Council; a Fellow of absolute Barbarity, and fit to execute any Villany, but was Rich. He came up to *Parham,* and forcibly took *Cæsar,* and had him carried to the same Post where he was Whip'd; and causing him to be ty'd to it, and a great Fire made before him, he told him, he shou'd Dye like a Dog, as he was. *Cæsar* replied, this was the first piece of Bravery that ever *Banister* did; and he never spoke Sence till he pronounc'd that Word; and, if he wou'd keep it, he wou'd declare, in the other World, that he was the only Man, of all the Whites, that ever he heard speak Truth. And turning to the Men that bound him, he said, *My Friends, am I to Dye, or to be Whip'd?* And they cry'd, *Whip'd! no; you shall not escape so well:* And then he replied, smiling, *A Blessing on thee;* and assur'd them, they need not tye him, for he wou'd stand fixt, like a Rock; and indure Death so as shou'd encourage them to Dye. *But if you Whip me,* said he, *be sure you tye me fast.*

He had learn'd to take Tobaco; and when he was assur'd he should Dye, he desir'd they would give him a Pipe in his Mouth, ready Lighted, which they did; and the Executioner came, and first cut off his Members,[106] and threw them into the Fire; after that, with an ill-favoured Knife, they cut his Ears, and his Nose, and burn'd them; he still Smoak'd on, as if nothing had touch'd him; then they hacked off one of his Arms, and still he bore up, and held his Pipe; but at the cutting of this other Arm, his Head Sunk, and his Pipe drop'd; and he gave up the Ghost, without a Groan, or a Reproach. My mother and Sister were by him all the while, but not suffer'd to save him; so rude and wild were the Rabble, and so inhumane were the Justices, who stood by to see the Execution, who after paid dearly enough for their Insolence. They cut *Cæsar* in Quarters, and sent them to several of the chief *Plantations:* One Quarter was sent to Colonel *Martin,* who refus'd it; and swore, he had rather see the Quarters of *Banister,* and the *Governor* himself, than those of *Cæsar,* on his *Plantations;* and

---

[105] *Banister, a wild Irish Man:* Major James Banister, who succeeded Byam as Deputy Governor. Behn is alluding both to the stereotype of the hotheaded Irishman and to the predominance of Irish among those transported to the colonies (see the "Petitions," pp. 408–14).

[106] *Members:* Genitals.

that he cou'd govern his *Negroes* without Terrifying and Grieving them with frightful Spectacles of a mangl'd King.

Thus Dy'd this Great Man; worthy of a better Fate, and a more sublime Wit than mine to write his Praise; yet, I hope, the Reputation of my Pen is considerable enough to make his Glorious Name to survive to all ages; with that of the Brave, the Beautiful, and the Constant *Imoinda.*

FINIS

a preservation of the plantation system

As a woman she needs to make this commitment to history.
Seperating his story from others.

— A narrative
— novel

Part Two

Oroonoko; or, The Royal Slave
Cultural Contexts

OROONOKO.

Barralet ad viv del.   Grignion sculp

MR SAVIGNY *in the Character of* **OROONOKO.**

Oro. *I'll turn my Face away, and do it so.*

Published Novr. 23. 1776 by T. Lowndes & Partners

Adaptations of *Oroonoko*

During the eighteenth century, the version of *Oroonoko* that found the widest audience was not Behn's novella but Thomas Southerne's dramatic adaptation, which was frequently performed after its successful premiere in November 1695. Southerne himself, in his introduction to the play, predicted that a dramatic retelling of the story would eclipse the prose version, remarking that Behn "had a great command of the stage, and I have often wondered that she would bury her favorite hero in a novel when she might have revived him on the scene."

In "reviving" the story, Southerne changes a number of important details. He makes Oroonoko the prince of Angola rather than "Coramantien," thus heavily revising the story's commercial geography. South of what Europeans called the Guinea coast, Angola was often excluded from their accounts of the slave trade, since in the late seventeenth century it represented a less plentiful source of slaves than the states along the Gulf of Guinea. Southerne also makes Imoinda a

≺ Thomas Southerne's stage adaptation of *Oroonoko* was popular throughout the eighteenth century. Revised by John Hawkesworth in 1759, the stage adaptation was the best-known form of Behn's story. This illustration of the play's tragic climax is the frontispiece to an edition of *Oroonoko, A Tragedy, As it is now Acted at the Theatre Royal in Drury-Lane*. It depicts one of the premier tragedians of the era, Mr. Savigny, as the royal slave turning away from the brave Imoinda as he prepares to kill her in order to save their honor. Southerne made Imoinda a European raised in Africa.

Roberts del.   Publish'd for Bells British Theatre Nov.r 1777.

M.rs HARTLEY in the Character of IMOINDA.

I fear no danger; life, or death, I will enjoy with you.

This illustration of Mrs. Hartley in the role of Imoinda preparing for battle served as frontispiece to a 1777 edition of Southerne's play "as performed at the Theatre-Royal in Covent-Garden."

European rather than an African (she is identified as the daughter of Oroonoko's mentor), and his play adds a comic subplot that tracks the adventures of two Englishwomen who travel to Suriname in search of husbands. The women's comic commercial view of the marriage market — they show no reluctance to express their demands in terms of cash — offers an ironic counterpoint to the play's more sober depiction of the slave market. Finally, in Southerne's play Oroonoko commits suicide rather than suffering the torture and dismemberment he undergoes in Behn's version. Southerne's depiction of Oroonoko owes much to the tradition of heroic tragedy, pioneered by Dryden and represented in this volume by Dryden's *The Indian Emperor* (Part Two, Chapter 2).

Southerne's version was itself revised on at least four separate occasions during the latter half of the eighteenth century by adapters who removed the comic subplot and intensified the antislavery rhetoric. The first of these, a revision by the dramatist and critic John Hawkesworth, was published and staged in 1759, and it remained extremely popular for the remainder of the century, replacing Southerne's *Oroonoko* in the theaters. In dignifying the play by cutting out those elements that detracted from its tragic and heroic elements, Hawkesworth also restricted himself entirely to blank verse, abandoning Southerne's distinction between characters who speak in prose and those who speak in more poetic language. Two more versions appeared in 1760: one by the playwright and actor Francis Gentleman, and a second, anonymous play that apparently was never performed. By the mid-eighteenth century, opportunities for the expression of tender feeling and tearful sentiment were becoming increasingly popular on the English stage, and these revisions of *Oroonoko* all followed the trend — especially the anonymous play, which is excerpted here.

In 1788, John Ferriar produced a revision of Hawkesworth's play, having accused Hawkesworth of weakening the antislavery implications of the story by adhering too closely to Southerne's original design: "Although the incidents appeared even to invite sentiments adverse to slavery," Ferriar argued, "yet Southerne . . . delivered by the medium of his Hero, a grovelling apology for slave-holders, which Hawkesworth has retained." In Ferriar's play, Oroonoko's arguments for the necessity of rebellion and escape emphasize both the arbitrary tyranny inherent in slavery and its tragic destruction of the family bond. As some of the documents included in Part Two, Chapter 4 suggest, this antislavery interpretation of Behn's story had become extremely influential by the end of the eighteenth century.

Act V.   Scene III.

BRITAIN

OROONOKO.

Oro. Death is security for all our fears.

Hamilton pinxt   A. Smith sc

London. Printed for J. Bell. British Library. Strand. Nov.r 12. 1791.

◁ As abolitionist sentiment grew stronger in the last decades of the eighteenth century, further revised versions of Oroonoko's tragedy appeared, but Hawkesworth's revision of Southerne's play held the stage. This illustration from *Oroonoko, a Tragedy*, by Thomas Southerne (London, 1791), depicts the scene in which Oroonoko shows Imoinda the body of Aboan, remarking, "Death is Security for all our Fears."

THOMAS SOUTHERNE

From *Oroonoko, a Tragedy*

Thomas Southerne (1659–1746) was a leading Restoration playwright; he produced a number of comedies and tragedies, of which *Oroonoko* was perhaps his most popular success. Southerne was personally acquainted with Behn, and his play *The Fatal Marriage, or the Innocent Adultery* (1694) was based in part on another of her tales — *The History of the Nun, or the Fair Vow-Breaker*. Despite its many revisions, Southerne's version of *Oroonoko* remained popular throughout the eighteenth century. In her abolitionist poem "The Slave Trade" (1789), Hannah More praises Southerne for precisely the sentiments that seemed especially creditable to later eighteenth-century audiences: "O, plaintive Southerne! whose impassion'd page / Can melt the soul to grief, or rouse to rage!" (Works 1:27)

The following selection is from *Oroonoko, a Tragedy*, ed. Maximillian E. Novak and David Stuart Rodes, *Regents Restoration Drama Series* (Lincoln: U of Nebraska P, 1976) I.ii:22–34; II.ii:42–46; V.v:112–24.

PERSONS REPRESENTED

Men

	By
OROONOKO	*Mr. Verbruggen*
ABOAN	*Mr. Powell*
LIEUTENANT GOVERNOR OF SURINAM	*Mr. Williams*
BLANFORD	*Mr. Harland*
STANMORE	*Mr. Horden*
JACK STANMORE	*Mr. Mills*
CAPTAIN DRIVER	*Mr. Ben. Johnson*
DANIEL, son to Widow Lackitt	*Mr. Mich. Lee*
HOTTMAN	*Mr. Sympson*
PLANTERS, INDIANS, NEGROES, MEN, WOMEN, AND CHILDREN.	

	Women		
			By
IMOINDA			*Mrs. Rogers*
WIDOW LACKITT			*Mrs. Knight*
CHARLOTTE WELLDON, in man's clothes			*Mrs. Verbruggen*
LUCY WELLDON, her sister			*Mrs. Lucas*

[At the opening of act I, scene ii of Southerne's play, the Lieutenant Governor of Suriname (based on Byam in Behn's narrative) and Blanford (based on Trefry in Behn's version) meet immediately after the arrival of the slave ship carrying Oroonoko. Note that Oroonoko speaks throughout in blank verse (unrhymed iambic pentameter), a speech pattern reserved for noble characters in Restoration drama. Blanford, who begins in regular, unmarked speech, eventually joins him. Southerne specifically calls attention to the contrast between the Captain of the slave ship, with his hypocritical professions of Christianity, and the honest slave who refuses to lie or break his word; this contrast was already a familiar one, as the selections from Sir John Mandeville and Montaigne in Part Two, Chapter 2 demonstrate. Also appearing in this scene are Widow Lackitt, Lucy Welldon, and her sister, Charlotte Welldon (who disguises herself as a man, and who is identified in the stage directions as Welldon); they form part of the play's comic subplot, in which the Welldons come to Suriname in search of husbands.]

Act I, Scene ii

[I.ii]   *An open place.*
          Enter Lieutenant Governor *and* Blanford.

GOVERNOR.
    There's no resisting your fortune, Blanford; you draw all the prizes.
BLANFORD.
    I draw for our Lord Governor, you know; his fortune favors me.
GOVERNOR.
    I grudge him nothing this time; bur if fortune had favored me in the last sale, the fair slave had been mine; Clemene had been mine.
BLANFORD.
    Are you still in love with her?
GOVERNOR.
    Every day more in love with her.

Enter Captain Driver, *teased and pulled about by* Widow Lackitt *and several* Planters. *Enter at another door* Welldon, Lucy, Stanmore [and Jack Stanmore].

WIDOW.

Here have I six slaves in my lot and not a man among 'em, all women and children; what can I do with 'em, Captain? Pray consider, I am a woman myself and can't get my own slaves as some of my neighbors do.

I PLANTER.

I have all men in mine. Pray, Captain, let the men and women be mingled together, for procreation sake, and the good of the plantation.

2 PLANTER.

Ay, ay, a man and a woman, Captain, for the good of the plantation.

CAPTAIN.

Let 'em mingle together and be damned, what care I? Would you have me pimp for the good of the plantation?

I PLANTER.

I am a constant customer, Captain.

WIDOW.

I am always ready money to you, Captain.

I PLANTER.

For that matter, mistress, my money is as ready as yours.

WIDOW.

Pray hear me, Captain.

CAPTAIN.

Look you, I have done my part by you; I have brought the number of slaves you bargained for; if your lots have not pleased you, you must draw again among yourselves.

3 PLANTER.

I am contented with my lot.

4 PLANTER.

I am very well satisfied.

3 PLANTER.

We'll have no drawing again.

CAPTAIN.

Do you hear, mistress? You may hold your tongue. For my part, I expect my money.

WIDOW.

Captain, nobody questions or scruples the payment. But I won't hold my tongue; 'tis too much to pray and pay too. One may speak for one's own, I hope.

CAPTAIN.

Well, what would you say?

WIDOW.

I say no more than I can make out.

CAPTAIN.

Out with it then.

WIDOW.

I say, things have not been so fair carried as they might have been. How do I know how you have juggled together in my absence? You drew the lots before I came, I'm sure.

CAPTAIN.

That's your own fault, mistress; you might have come sooner.

WIDOW.

Then here's a prince, as they say, among the slaves, and you set him down to go as a common man.

CAPTAIN.

Have you a mind to try what a man he is? You'll find him no more than a common man at your business.

. . . .

GOVERNOR.

Where are the slaves, Captain? They are long a-coming.

BLANFORD.

And who is this prince that's fallen to my lot for the Lord Governor? Let me know something of him that I may treat him accordingly; who is he?

CAPTAIN.

He's the devil of a fellow, I can tell you — a prince every inch of him. You have paid dear enough for him for all the good he'll do you. I was forced to clap him in irons and did not think the ship safe neither. You are in hostility with the Indians, they say; they threaten you daily. You had best have an eye upon him.

BLANFORD.

But who is he?

GOVERNOR.

And how do you know him to be a prince?

CAPTAIN.

He is son and heir to the great King of Angola, a mischievous monarch in those parts, who by his good will would never let any of his neighbors be in quiet. This son was his general, a plaguy[1] fighting fellow. I have formerly had dealings with him for slaves which he took prisoners, and have got pretty roundly[2] by him. But the wars being at an end and nothing more to be got by the trade of that country, I made bold to bring the prince along with me.

GOVERNOR.

How could you do that?

BLANFORD.

What! Steal a prince out of his own country? Impossible!

CAPTAIN.

'Twas hard indeed, but I did it. You must know, this Oroonoko —

BLANFORD.

Is that his name?

CAPTAIN.

Ay, Oroonoko.

GOVERNOR.

Oroonoko —

CAPTAIN.

Is naturally inquisitive about the men and manners of the white nations. Because I could give him some account of the other parts of the world, I grew very much into his favor. In return of so great an honor, you know I could do no less upon my coming away than invite him on board me. Never having been in a ship, he appointed his time and I prepared my entertainment. He came the next evening as privately as he could, with about some twenty along with him. The punch[3] went round, and as many of his attendants as would be dangerous I sent dead drunk on shore; the rest we secured. And so you have the Prince Oroonoko.

1 PLANTER.

Gad-a-mercy, Captain, there you were with him, i'faith.

2 PLANTER.

Such men as you are fit to be employed in public affairs. The plantation will thrive by you.

3 PLANTER.

Industry should be encouraged.

---

[1] *plaguy:* Annoying.
[2] *roundly:* Completely, absolutely; the Captain is saying that he has profited thoroughly from their trade.
[3] *punch:* A drink composed of wine or other alcohol, mixed with hot water or milk, and flavored with sugar, lemons, and spice.

CAPTAIN.
There's nothing done without it, boys. I have made my fortune this way.

BLANFORD.
Unheard-of villainy!

STANMORE.
Barbarous treachery!

BLANFORD.
They applaud him for't.

GOVERNOR.
But, Captain, methinks you have taken a great deal of pains for this Prince Oroonoko; why did you part with him at the common rate of slaves?

CAPTAIN.
Why, Lieutenant Governor, I'll tell you; I did design to carry him to England to have showed him there, but I found him troublesome upon my hands and I'm glad I'm rid of him, — O, ho, here they come.

Black slaves, men, women, and children, pass across the stage by two and two; Aboan, *and others of Oroonoko's attendants two and two;* Oroonoko *last of all in chains.*

LUCY.
Are all these wretches slaves?

STANMORE.
All sold, they and their posterity all slaves.

LUCY.
O miserable fortune!

BLANFORD.
Most of 'em know no better; they were born so and only change their masters. But a prince, born only to command, betrayed and sold! My heart drops blood for him.

CAPTAIN.
Now, Governor, here he comes, pray observe him.

OROONOKO.
So, sir, you have kept your word with me.

CAPTAIN.
I am a better Christian, I thank you, than to keep it with a heathen.

OROONOKO.
You are a Christian, be a Christian still.
If you have any god that teaches you

To break your word, I need not curse you more.
Let him cheat you, as you are false to me.
You faithful followers of my better fortune!
We have been fellow-soldiers in the field;

                    Embracing his friends.

Now we are fellow-slaves. This last farewell.
Be sure of one thing that will comfort us:
Whatever world we next are thrown upon
Cannot be worse than this.

                    All slaves go off but Oroonoko.

CAPTAIN.

You see what a bloody pagan he is, Governor; but I took care that none of his followers should be in the same lot with him for fear they should undertake some desperate action to the danger of the colony.

OROONOKO.

Live still in fear; it is the villain's curse
And will revenge my chains. Fear even me
Who have no pow'r to hurt thee. Nature abhors
And drives thee out from the society
And commerce of mankind for breach of faith.
Men live and prosper but in mutual trust,
A confidence of one another's truth.
That thou hast violated. I have done.
I know my fortune and submit to it.

GOVERNOR.

Sir, I am sorry for your fortune and would help it if I could.

BLANFORD.

Take off his chains. You know your condition, but you are fallen into honorable hands. You are the Lord Governor's slave, who will use you nobly. In his absence it shall be my care to serve you.

                    Blanford *applying to him.*

OROONOKO.

I hear you, but I can believe no more.

GOVERNOR.

Captain, I'm afraid the world won't speak so honorably of this action of yours as you would have 'em.

CAPTAIN.

I have the money. Let the world speak and be damned; I care not.

OROONOKO.

I would forget myself.

(*To* Blanford.) Be satisfied,
I am above the rank of common slaves.
Let that content you. The Christian there that knows me,
For his own sake will not discover more.

CAPTAIN.

I have other matters to mind. You have him, and much good may
do you with your prince.

The Planters *pulling and staring at* Oroonoko.

BLANFORD.

What would you have there? You stare as if you never saw a man
before. Stand further off.   *Turns 'em away.*

OROONOKO.

Let 'em stare on.
I am unfortunate, but not ashamed
Of being so. No, let the guilty blush,
The white man that betrayed me. Honest black
Disdains to change its color. I am ready.
Where must I go? Dispose me as you please.
I am not well acquainted with my fortune,
But must learn to know it better; so I know, you say:
Degrees make all things easy.

BLANFORD.

All things shall be easy.

OROONOKO.

Tear off this pomp and let me know myself.
The slavish habit best becomes me now.
Hard fare and whips and chains may overpow'r
The frailer flesh and bow my body down.
But there's another, nobler part of me,
Out of your reach, which you can never tame.

BLANFORD.

You shall find nothing of this wretchedness
You apprehend. We are not monsters all.
You seem unwilling to disclose yourself;
Therefore, for fear the mentioning your name
Should give you new disquiets, I presume
To call you Caesar.

OROONOKO.

I am myself, but call me what you please.

STANMORE.

A very good name, Caesar.

GOVERNOR.

And very fit for his great character.

OROONOKO.

Was Caesar then a slave?

GOVERNOR.

I think he was, to pirates too.[4] He was a great conqueror, but unfortunate in his friends —

OROONOKO.

His friends were Christians?

BLANFORD.

No.

OROONOKO.

No! That's strange.

GOVERNOR.

And murdered by 'em.

OROONOKO.

I would be Caesar then. Yet I will live.

BLANFORD.

Live to be happier.

OROONOKO.

Do what you will with me.

BLANFORD.

I'll wait upon you, attend, and serve you.

> *Exit with* Oroonoko.

LUCY.

Well, if the Captain had brought this prince's country along with him and would make me queen of it, I would not have him after doing so base a thing.

WELLDON.

He's a man to thrive in the world, sister. He'll make you the better jointure.

LUCY.

Hang him, nothing can prosper with him.

STANMORE.

Enquire into the great estates, and you will find most of 'em depend upon the same title of honesty. The men who raise 'em first are much of the Captain's principles.

WELLDON.

Ay, ay, as you say, let him be damned for the good of his family. Come, sister, we are invited to dinner.

---

[4] *he was, to pirates too:* Julius Caesar was said to have been captured by pirates in the Mediterranean; after being freed, he captured them and had them killed.

GOVERNOR.

Stanmore, you dine with me.

Exeunt omnes.

[In act II, scene ii, Oroonoko and Blanford meet in private for the first time, and Oroonoko recounts the story of his marriage to Imoinda and their separation. By this time, Stanmore is the only character not to speak in blank verse. The "beautiful slave" described at the end of the scene as the Lieutenant Governor's "mistress" is, of course, Imoinda, who has arrived in Suriname before Oroonoko.]

Act II, Scene ii

[*Enter*] Oroonoko *and* Blanford.

OROONOKO.

You grant I have good reason to suspect
All the professions you can make to me.

BLANFORD.

Indeed you have.

OROONOKO.

The dog that sold me did profess as much
As you can do — but yet I know not why —
Whether it is because I'm fall'n so low
And have no more to fear — that is not it:
I am a slave no longer than I please.
'Tis something nobler: being just myself,
I am inclining to think others so.
'Tis that prevails upon me to believe you.

BLANFORD.

You may believe me.

OROONOKO.   I do believe you.
From what I know of you, you are no fool.
Fools only are the knaves and live by tricks;
Wise men may thrive without 'em and be honest.

BLANFORD (*aside*).

They won't all take your counsel —

OROONOKO.

You know my story and you say you are
A friend to my misfortunes. That's a name
Will teach you what you owe yourself and me.

BLANFORD.

   I'll study to deserve to be your friend.
   When once our noble governor arrives,
   With him you will not need my interest;
   He is too generous not to feel your wrongs.
   But be assured I will employ my pow'r
   And find the means to send you home again.

OROONOKO.

   I thank you, sir — (*sighing*) my honest, wretched friends!
   Their chains are heavy. They have hardly found
   So kind a master. May I ask you, sir,
   What is become of 'em? Perhaps I should not.
   You will forgive a stranger.

BLANFORD.   I'll enquire,
   And use my best endeavors, where they are,
   To have 'em gently used.

OROONOKO.   Once more I thank you.
   You offer every cordial that can keep
   My hopes alive to wait a better day.
   What friendly care can do, you have applied.
   But, O! I have a grief admits no cure.

BLANFORD.

   You do not know, sir —

OROONOKO.   Can you raise the dead?
   Pursue and overtake the wings of time?
   And bring about again the hours, the days,
   The years that made me happy?

BLANFORD.

   That is not to be done.

OROONOKO.

   No, there is nothing to be done for me.

                          Kneeling and kissing the earth.
   Thou god-adored! Thou ever-glorious sun!
   If she be yet on earth, send me a beam
   Of thy all-seeing power to light me to her.
   Or if thy sister goddess has preferred
   Her beauty to the skies to be a star,
   O tell me where she shines, that I may stand
   Whole nights and gaze upon her.

BLANFORD.

   I am rude and interrupt you.

OROONOKO.   I am troublesome.
But pray give me your pardon. My swoll'n heart
Bursts out its passage, and I must complain.
O! Can you think of nothing dearer to me —
Dearer than liberty, my country, friends,
Much dearer than my life — that I have lost:
The tend'rest, best belov'd, and loving wife.

BLANFORD.
Alas! I pity you.

OROONOKO.   Do, pity me.
Pity's akin to love, and every thought
Of that soft kind is welcome to my soul.
I could be pitied here.

BLANFORD.   I dare not ask
More than you please to tell me, but if you
Think it convenient to let me know
Your story, I dare promise you to bear
A part in your distress, if not assist you.

OROONOKO.
Thou honest-hearted man! I wanted such,
Just such a friend as thou art, that would sit
Still as the night and let me talk whole days
Of my Imoinda. I! I'll tell thee all
From first to last, and pray observe me well.

BLANFORD.
I will most heedfully.

OROONOKO.
There was a stranger in my father's court
Valued and honored much. He was a white,
The first I ever saw of your complexion.
He changed his gods for ours and so grew great;
Of many virtues and so famed in arms
He still[5] commanded all my father's wars.
I was bred under him. One fatal day,
The armies joining, he before me stepped,
Receiving in his breast a poisoned dart
Levelled at me; he died within my arms.
I've tired you already.

_____

[5] *still*: Always.

BLANFORD.   Pray go on.

OROONOKO.

He left an only daughter, whom he brought
An infant to Angola. When I came
Back to the court a happy conqueror,
Humanity obliged me to condole
With this sad virgin for a father's loss,
Lost for my safety. I presented her
With all the slaves of battle to atone
Her father's ghost. But when I saw her face
And heard her speak, I offered up myself
To be the sacrifice. She bowed and blushed;
I wondered and adored. The sacred pow'r
That had subdued me then inspired my tongue,
Inclined her heart; and all our talk was love.

BLANFORD.

Then you were happy.

OROONOKO.   O! I was too happy.

I married her. And though my country's custom
Indulged the privilege of many wives,
I swore myself never to know but her.
She grew with child, and I grew happier still.
O my Imoinda! But it could not last.
Her fatal beauty reached my father's ears.
He sent for her to court, where, cursed court!
No woman comes but for his amorous use.
He raging to possess her, she was forced
To own herself my wife. The furious king
Started at incest. But grown desperate,
Not daring to enjoy what he desired,
In mad revenge, which I could never learn,
He poisoned her, or sent her far, far off,
Far from my hopes ever to see her more.

BLANFORD.

Most barbarous of fathers! The sad tale
Has struck me dumb with wonder.

OROONOKO.   I have done.

I'll trouble you no farther. Now and then
A sigh will have its way; that shall be all.

                    Enter Stanmore.

STANMORE.

Blanford, the Lieutenant Governor is gone to your plantation. He desires you would bring the royal slave with you. The sight of his fair mistress, he says, is an entertainment for a prince; he would have his opinion of her.

OROONOKO.

Is he a lover?

BLANFORD.

So he says himself; he flatters a beautiful slave that I have and calls her mistress.

OROONOKO.

Must he then flatter her to call her mistress?
I pity the proud man who thinks himself
Above being in love. What though she be a slave,
She may deserve him.

BLANFORD.

You shall judge of that when you see her, sir.

OROONOKO.

I go with you.   *Exeunt.*

[Act V, scene v presents the heroic conclusion of Southerne's story. By this point in the play, Oroonoko has organized an unsuccessful rebellion among the slaves — unsuccessful because the other slaves, deceived by the Lieutenant Governor's promises of forgiveness, abandon their struggle as soon as he appears. Oroonoko, Imoinda, and Aboan, more skeptical of those promises, finally yield when Blanford guarantees their safety, only to find that the Lieutenant Governor intends to separate and punish them. When Oroonoko appears next, he is stretched out in chains; Blanford and Stanmore free him and promise to reunite him with Imoinda. The Lieutenant Governor attempts to rape Imoinda, and he fails only because Blanford intercedes and defends her, as she explains to Oroonoko in this scene.]

Act V, Scene v

Oroonoko *enters.*

OROONOKO.

To honor bound! And yet a slave to love!
I am distracted by their rival powers,
And both will be obeyed. O great revenge!

Thou raiser and restorer of fall'n fame!
Let me not be unworthy of thy aid
For stopping in thy course. I still am thine,
But can't forget I am Imoinda's too;
She calls me from my wrongs to rescue her.
No man condemn me who has never felt
A woman's power or tried the force of love.
All tempers yield and soften in those fires.
Our honors, interests resolving down,
Run in the gentle current of our joys,
But not to sink and drown our memory.
We mount again to action like the sun
That rises from the bosom of the sea
To run his glorious race of light anew
And carry on the world. Love, love will be
My first ambition, and my fame the next.

> Aboan *enters bloody.*

My eyes are turned against me and combine
With my sworn enemies to represent
This spectacle of honor. Aboan!
My ever faithful friend!
ABOAN.   I have no name
That can distinguish me from the vile earth
To which I'm going: a poor, abject worm
That crawled awhile upon a bustling world
And now am trampled to my dust again.
OROONOKO.
I see thee gashed and mangled.
ABOAN.   Spare my shame
To tell how they have used me; but believe
The hangman's hand would have been merciful.
Do not you scorn me, sir, to think I can
Intend to live under this infamy.
I do not come for pity to complain.
I've spent an honorable life with you,
The earliest servant of your rising fame,
And would attend it with my latest care.
My life was yours and so shall be my death.
You must not live —
Bending and sinking, I have dragged my steps

Thus far to tell you that you cannot live,
To warn you of those ignominious wrongs,
Whips, rods, and all the instruments of death
Which I have felt and are prepared for you.
This was the duty that I had to pay.
'Tis done, and now I beg to be discharged.

OROONOKO.
What shall I do for thee?

ABOAN.   My body tires
And wonnot bear me off to liberty;
I shall again be taken, made a slave.
A sword, a dagger yet would rescue me.
I have not strength to go to find out death.
You must direct him to me.

OROONOKO.   Here he is,

Gives him a dagger.

The only present I can make thee now,
And next the honorable means of life,
I would bestow the honest means of death.

ABOAN.
I cannot stay to thank you. If there is
A being after this, I shall be yours
In the next world, your faithful slave again.
This is to try.   *Stabs himself.*
               I had a living sense
Of all your royal favors, but this last
Strikes through my heart. I wonnot say farewell,
For you must follow me.

OROONOKO.   In life and death
The guardian of my honor! Follow thee!
I should have gone before thee; then perhaps
Thy fate had been prevented. All his care
Was to preserve me from the barbarous rage
That wronged him only for being mine.
Why, why, you gods! Why am I so accurst
That it must be a reason of your wrath,
A guilt, a crime sufficient to the fate
Of anyone, but to belong to me?
My friend has found it and my wife will soon.
My wife! The very fear's too much for life;
I can't support it. Where? Imoinda! O!

Going out, she meets him, running into his arms.

Thou bosom softness! Down of all my cares!
I could recline my thoughts upon this breast
To a forgetfulness of all my griefs
And yet be happy, but it wonnot be.
Thou art disordered, pale, and out of breath!
If fate pursues thee, find a shelter here.
What is it thou wouldst tell me?

IMOINDA.   'Tis in vain
To call him villain.

OROONOKO.   Call him Governor.
Is it not so?

IMOINDA.   There's not another sure.

OROONOKO.
Villain's the common name of mankind here,
But his most properly. What! What of him?
I fear to be resolved and must enquire.
He had thee in his power.

IMOINDA.   I blush to think it.

OROONOKO.
Blush! To think what?

IMOINDA.   That I was in his power.

OROONOKO.
He could not use it?

IMOINDA.   What can't such men do?

OROONOKO.
But did he? Durst he?

IMOINDA.   What he could, he dared.

OROONOKO.
His own gods damn him then! For ours have none,
No punishment for such unheard-of crimes.

IMOINDA.
This monster, cunning in his flatteries,
When he had wearied all his useless arts,
Leapt out, fierce as a beast of prey, to seize me.
I trembled, feared.

OROONOKO.   I fear and tremble now.
What could preserve thee? What deliver thee?

IMOINDA.
That worthy man you used to call your friend —

OROONOKO.
  Blanford.
IMOINDA.   Came in and saved me from his rage.
OROONOKO.
  He was a friend indeed to rescue thee!
  And for his sake I'll think it possible
  A Christian may be yet an honest man.
IMOINDA.
  O! Did you know what I have struggled through
  To save me yours, sure you would promise me
  Never to see me forced from you again.
OROONOKO.
  To promise thee! O! Do I need to promise?
  But there is now no farther use of words.
  Death is security for all our fears.
                              Shows Aboan's body on the floor.
  And yet I cannot trust him.
IMOINDA.   Aboan!
OROONOKO.
  Mangled and torn, resolved to give me time
  To fit myself for what I must expect,
  Groaned out a warning to me and expired.
IMOINDA.
  For what you must expect?
OROONOKO.   Would that were all.
IMOINDA.
  What! To be butchered thus —
OROONOKO.   Just as thou see'st.
IMOINDA.
  By barbarous hands, to fall at last their prey!
OROONOKO.
  I have run the race with honor; shall I now
  Lag and be overtaken at the goal!
IMOINDA.   No.
OROONOKO (*tenderly*).
  I must look back to thee.
IMOINDA.   You shannot need.
  I'm always present to your purpose; say
  Which way would you dispose me?
OROONOKO.   Have a care,
  Thou'rt on a precipice and dost not see

Whither that question leads thee. O! Too soon
Thou dost enquire what the assembled gods
Have not determined and will latest doom.
Yet this I know of fate, this is most certain:
I cannot as I would dispose of thee;
And as I ought I dare not. O Imoinda!

IMOINDA.
Alas! That sigh! Why do you tremble so?
Nay, then 'tis bad indeed if you can weep.

OROONOKO.
My heart runs over; if my gushing eyes
Betray a weakness which they never knew,
Believe thou, only thou couldst cause these tears.
The gods themselves conspire with faithless men
To our destruction.

IMOINDA.   Heav'n and earth our foes!

OROONOKO.
It is not always granted to the great
To be most happy. If the angry pow'rs
Repent their favors, let 'em take 'em back.
The hopes of empire which they gave my youth
By making me a prince I here resign.
Let 'em quench in me all those glorious fires
Which kindled at their beams; that lust of fame,
That fever of ambition, restless still
And burning with the sacred thirst of sway
Which they inspired to qualify my fate
And make me fit to govern under them,
Let 'em extinguish. I submit myself
To their high pleasure and devoted bow
Yet lower to continue still a slave
Hopeless of liberty; and if I could
Live after it, would give up honor too
To satisfy their vengeance, to avert
This only curse, the curse of losing thee.

IMOINDA.
If Heav'n could be appeased, these cruel men
Are not to be entreated or believed.
O! Think on that and be no more deceived.

OROONOKO.
What can we do?

IMOINDA.   Can I do anything?

OROONOKO.
    But we were born to suffer.

IMOINDA.   Suffer both.
    Both die, and so prevent 'em.

OROONOKO.   By thy death!
    O! Let me hunt my travelled thoughts again,
    Range the wide waste of desolate despair,
    Start any hope. Alas! I lose myself;
    'Tis pathless, dark, and barren all to me.
    Thou art my only guide, my light of life,
    And thou art leaving me. Send out thy beams
    Upon the wing; let 'em fly all around,
    Discover every way. Is there a dawn,
    A glimmering of comfort? The great god
    That rises on the world must shine on us.

IMOINDA.
    And see us set before him.

OROONOKO.   Thou bespeak'st
    And go'st before me.

IMOINDA.   So I would, in love:
    In the dear unsuspected part of life,
    In death for love. Alas! What hopes for me?
    I was preserved but to acquit myself,
    To beg to die with you.

OROONOKO.   And can'st thou ask it?
    I never durst enquire into myself
    About thy fate, and thou resolv'st it all.

IMOINDA.
    Alas! My lord! My fate's resolved in yours.

OROONOKO.
    O! Keep thee there. Let not thy virtue shrink
    From my support, and I will gather strength
    Fast as I can to tell thee —

IMOINDA.   I must die.
    I know 'tis fit and I can die with you.

OROONOKO.
    O! Thou hast banished hence a thousand fears
    Which sickened at my heart and quite unmanned me.

IMOINDA.
    Your fear's for me; I know you feared my strength

And could not overcome your tenderness
To pass this sentence on me. And indeed
There you were kind, as I have always found you,
As you have ever been; for though I am
Resigned and ready to obey my doom,
Methinks it should not be pronounced by you.

OROONOKO.

O! That was all the labor of my grief.
My heart and tongue forsook me in the strife.
I never could pronounce it.

IMOINDA.

I have for you, for both of us.

OROONOKO.

Alas! For me! My death
I could regard as the last scene of life
And act it through with joy to have it done.
But then to part with thee —

IMOINDA.   'Tis hard to part.
But parting thus, as the most happy must,
Parting in death, makes it the easier.
You might have thrown me off, forsaken me
And my misfortunes. That had been a death
Indeed of terror to have trembled at.

OROONOKO.

Forsaken! Thrown thee off!

IMOINDA.

But 'tis a pleasure more than life can give,
That with unconquered passion to the last
You struggle still and fain would hold me to you.

OROONOKO.

Ever, ever, and let those stars which are my enemies
Witness against me in the other world,
If I would leave this mansion of my bliss
To be the brightest ruler of their skies.

Embracing her.

O! That we could incorporate, be one,
One body, as we have been long one mind.
That blended so, we might together mix,
And losing thus our beings to the world,
Be only found to one another's joys.

IMOINDA.
Is this the way to part?

OROONOKO.   Which is the way?

IMOINDA.
The god of love is blind and cannot find it.
But quick, make haste, our enemies have eyes
To find us out and show us the worst way
Of parting; think on them.

OROONOKO.
Why dost thou wake me?

IMOINDA.   O! No more of love.
For if I listen to you, I shall quite
Forget my dangers and desire to live.
I can't live yours.   *Takes up the dagger.*

OROONOKO.   There all the stings of death
Are shot into my heart — what shall I do?

IMOINDA.
This dagger will instruct you.   *Gives it him.*

OROONOKO.   Ha! This dagger!
Like fate it points me to the horrid deed.

IMOINDA.
Strike, strike it home and bravely save us both.
There is no other safety.

OROONOKO.   It must be —
But first a dying kiss —   *Kisses her.*
                    This last embrace —
                                        Embracing her.
And now —

IMOINDA.   I'm ready.

OROONOKO.   O! Where shall I strike?
Is there a smallest grain of that loved body
That is not dearer to me than my eyes,
My bosomed heart, and all the lifeblood there?
Bid me cut off these limbs, hew off these hands,
Dig out these eyes, though I would keep them last
To gaze upon thee. But to murder thee!
The joy and charm of every ravished sense,
My wife! Forbid it, nature.

IMOINDA.   'Tis your wife
Who on her knees conjures you. O! In time
Prevent those mischiefs that are falling on us.

You may be hurried to a shameful death,
And I too dragged to the vile Governor.
Then I may cry aloud; when you are gone
Where shall I find a friend again to save me?

OROONOKO.
It will be so. Thou unexampled virtue!
Thy resolution has recovered mine.
And now prepare thee.

IMOINDA.   Thus with open arms
I welcome you, and death.

> *He drops his dagger as he looks on her and throws himself*
> *on the ground.*

OROONOKO.   I cannot bear it.
O let me dash against this rock of fate.
Dig up this earth, tear, tear her bowels out
To make a grave deep as the center down
To swallow wide and bury us together!
It wonnot be. O! Then some pitying god
(If there be one a friend to innocence)
Find yet a way to lay her beauties down
Gently in death and save me from her blood.

IMOINDA.
O rise! 'Tis more than death to see you thus.
I'll ease your love and do the deed myself —

> *She takes up the dagger, he rises in haste to take it from her.*

OROONOKO.
O! Hold, I charge thee, hold.

IMOINDA.   Though I must own
It would be nobler for us both from you.

OROONOKO.
O! For a whirlwind's wing to hurry us
To yonder cliff which frowns upon the flood
That in embraces locked we might plunge in
And perish thus in one another's arms.   [*A shout.*]

IMOINDA.
Alas! What shout is that?

OROONOKO.   I see 'em coming.
They shannot overtake us. This last kiss.
And now farewell.

IMOINDA.   Farewell, farewell forever.
OROONOKO.
  I'll turn my face away and do it so.
  Now, are you ready?
IMOINDA.   Now. But do not grudge me
  The pleasure in my death of a last look.
  Pray look upon me — now I'm satisfied.
OROONOKO.
  So fate must be by this.

Going to stab her he stops short; she lays her hands on his in order to give the blow.

IMOINDA.
  Nay then I must assist you.
  And since it is the common cause of both,
  'Tis just that both should be employed in it.   *Stabs herself.*
  Thus, thus 'tis finished, and I bless my fate
  That where I lived, I die, in these loved arms.   *Dies.*
OROONOKO.
  She's gone. And now all's at an end with me.
  Soft, lay her down. O, we will part no more.
                              Throws himself by her.
  But let me pay the tribute of my grief,
  A few sad tears to thy loved memory,   *Weeps over her.*
  And then I follow —   *A noise again.*
              But I stay too long.
  The noise comes nearer. Hold, before I go
  There's something would be done. It shall be so.
  And then, Imoinda, I'll come all to thee.   *Rises.*

Blanford *and his party enter before the* Governor *and his party, swords drawn on both sides.*

GOVERNOR.
  You strive in vain to save him; he shall die.
BLANFORD.
  Not while we can defend him with our lives.
GOVERNOR.
  Where is he?
OROONOKO.   Here's the wretch whom you would have.
  Put up your swords and let civil broils

Engage you in the cursed cause of one
Who cannot live and now entreats to die.
This object will convince you.   *They gather about the body.*
BLANFORD.   'Tis his wife!
Alas! There was no other remedy.
GOVERNOR.
Who did the bloody deed?
OROONOKO.   The deed was mine.
Bloody I know it is and I expect
Your laws should tell me so. Thus self-condemned,
I do resign myself into your hands,
The hands of justice — but I hold the sword
For you — and for myself.

Stabs the Governor *and himself, then throws himself by Imoinda's body.*

STANMORE.
He has killed the Governor and stabbed himself.
OROONOKO.
'Tis as it should be now. I have sent his ghost
To be a witness of that happiness
In the next world which he denied us here.   *Dies.*
BLANFORD.
I hope there is a place of happiness
In the next world for such exalted virtue.
Pagan or unbeliever, yet he lived
To all he knew; and if he went astray,
There's mercy still above to set him right.
But Christians guided by the heavenly ray
Have no excuse if we mistake our way.

FINIS

From *Oroonoko, a Tragedy*

Several late writers accentuated *Oroonoko*'s potential as an antislavery story in their revisions of Southerne's play. This anonymous revision, like John Hawkesworth's version but unlike Southerne's, focuses on the story's tragic aspects; accordingly, all the characters speak in the language of blank verse. The anonymous author adds two new characters, Maria and Heartwell, precisely in order to multiply the number of sympathetic speeches about the misfortunes of Imoinda and Oroonoko. The addition of Maria also means that the dramatic version of *Oroonoko* for the first time includes an English woman who befriends Oroonoko, and it thereby adds a figure who resembles Behn's narrator. The following text is from *Oroonoko, a Tragedy, altered from the original play of that name by the late Thomas Southern* (London: Printed for A. and C. Corbett, 1760) 5–6, 32–33, 38–42.

CHARACTERS OF THE PLAY.

Men.

Oroonoko,
Aboan,
Lieutenant-Governour,
Blandford,
Heartwell, President of the Council.
Hotman,
Planters,
Slaves.

Women.

Imoinda,
Maria, Sister to the Lieut. Governour,
   and contracted to *Blandford.*

[In this selection from the play's first scene, Imoinda presents a religious critique of slavery that was already familiar to English readers from such antislavery writings as Thomas Tryon's "Discourse . . . between an Ethiopean or Negro-Slave and a Christian" (see p. 368). At the beginning of the scene, before the extract included here, we learn that Maria, sister of the Lieutenant Governor, is Imoinda's confidante, and that Maria is engaged to Blandford. His role as plantation agent for the absent Governor gives him the power to protect Imoinda from the Lieutenant Governor, who has just declared his love for her before departing to examine the newly arrived shipment of slaves, which includes Oroonoko and his followers. No sooner does he leave than Maria and Imoinda take up the subject of slavery itself.]

From Act I, Scene i

Imoi. I have heard, *Maria,* the Isle which gave thee Birth,[1]
Is mark'd for hospitable Deeds, humane
Benevolence, extended Charities —
With ev'ry social Virtue — Is't possible?
A Nation thus distinguish'd, by the Ties,
Of soft Humanity, shou'd give its Sanction,
To its *dependant* States, to exercise,
This more than savage Right, of thus disposing,
Like th' marketable Brute, their Fellow-Creatures Blood?
Whose equal Rectitude of fair Proportion —
Their Strong Intelligence — their Aptitude,
In Reason's Rules, loudly, nay, terribly pronounce,
They stand the equal Work of Reason's God.
    Mar. Too just the Charge — too closely urg'd — for one,
Unknowing in the hidden Paths of States,
T'answer, with that Energy of reas'ning.
Thou, so forcibly, hast given it — Yet —
I am well persuaded — the Justice, Equity,
With Wisdom blended, of the sage Rulers,
Of my Parent Country, cou'd furnish forth,
Fit Argument; and with Humanity,
Conjoin'd, to authorize an Act, I must with thee,
Confess, has much alarm'd, and shock'd my feeling Soul.
    But, let us wave this Subject, charg'd with Grief
Wilt thou, with me, retire, t'aid my Fancy,
In th' Ornaments, befit a Bridal State;
Which *Blandford*'s Merit, Truth, and Love, demand.
    Imoi. Alas! *my* Fancy long, has lost its Force —
As best but weak — and in the Modes which *Europe* holds,
Wholly unknowing — but, at thy Instance,
I will, a while, throw off my Fate's Distress;

---

[1] *the Isle which gave thee Birth:* i.e., England.

Renewing ev'ry Female, decorating Gift,
Nature has form'd, inherent to our sex.

[*Exeunt.*]

.   .   .   .

[Act III, scene ii includes one of the play's more pointed appeals to sentiment in a dialogue between Maria and her friend Heartwell, president of
the council in the English settlement. The previous act includes another
passionate speech from the Lieutenant Governor, who finds Imoinda
alone and offers to free her if she will reciprocate his affection; when she
struggles to escape his embrace, however, he does not pursue her. By this
time Oroonoko has recognized Imoinda, and having been apprised of the
Lieutenant Governor's passion, and of the likelihood that his own children
are doomed to become slaves, Oroonoko agrees to help lead the other
Africans to freedom in the speech immediately preceding this extract.
After the conclusion of this dialogue, Oroonoko and the other conspirators return and reaffirm their intention to organize the rebellion that
evening.]

Act III, Scene ii

Heartwell, Maria, *meeting.*

Mar. Oh! gracious *Heartwell.*
Heart. In Tears! Are these fit Preludes,
To a bridal Morn? Alas! what means these
Deep felt Throes of overwhelming Anguish?
Mar. O! if thy sympathizing Friendship's Aid,
For *Blandford's* Peace! for Virtue's fair Repose!
For th' chaste Sanction of the Marriage-Bed!
For Lovers, yet unblest with Hymeneal Rites!
If these befit — (and well I know they do)
Thy firm Integrity of Mind, to guard?
Instant find my Brother — stop the Purpose
Of the complicated Guilt, his Passion urges.
Heart. Ha! what complicated Guilt! what Purpose?
Mar. Urg'd by th' impetuous Passion, for the Slave,
We call'd *Clemene* — now *Imoinda* —
And avow'd the Consort of the Captive Prince —
Renouncing all Regards, to mine — his own —
His House's strong Pretensions to unsullied Fame —

Forgetting all the Rev'rence, Virgin Truth,
And Modesty demand — urg'd me — O Shame!
To speak! — I wou'd sollicit *Blandford* to exert
His Pow'r, as her deputed Lord, and aid
Him in his fell Intent, to perpetrate
Th' Violation of their Royal Bed.
    Heart. You much amaze me! Is it possible,
His Passion should transport him, thus,
Beyond the Bounds of Honour's nicer[2] Rules?
And of that Pride, with which we hold,
A *Sister*'s Fame, in Ballance with a *Wife*'s!
With th' same kindl'd Warmth of just Resentment,
Calling to the Field, the bold Invader,
Should, with licentious Taint, impeach its Worth.
    Mar. When, with Indignation, I refused
Th' unworthy Task, he with Rage incens'd,
Pronounc'd his firm, immoveable Resolve,
I shou'd be instantly convey'd on Board the Ship,
Now waiting for a Wind, to sail for *England.*
Anulling thus, the solemn, firm,
Engagement, ratified with *Blandford* —
With myself — and sworn before the Throne of Heaven —
Tho' yet unhallowed by the sacred Priest.
    Heart. With th' earliest, I'll remonstrate to him —
Procedures violent and base, like those,
Tho' back'd by Power, are Power's *Disease*;
And largely warrant th' Assembly's superceding,
'Till the Governour's Return, th' Man, who seated
Eminent in Place, forgets he holds it,
As th' bright Mirror, to reflect fair Virtue's Face —
Not her Destroyer, by the Lightning's Rage.

. . . .

[In Act IV, scene i, Heartwell first tries to dissuade the Lieutenant Governor from his passion for Imoinda. Failing, he asserts his authority as president of the council but manages only to extract a feigned acquiescence from the Lieutenant Governor. When they learn of the rebellion, Maria

---

[2] *nicer:* More refined.

and Blandford call for an end to slavery, reiterating their commitment to
the English principles of freedom already invoked in Act I, scene i.]

From Act IV, Scene i

Governour — Heartwell.

Gov. I Blame, with you, this Tempest of the Mind:
But Storms and Earthquakes are not *reason'd* down,
Nor will the Rules of cold Philosophy,
Adopted by Infirmity and Age,
Abate th' vig'rous Impulse Nature bids,
And Beauty, deck'd with Royalty, inspires.
    Heart. What *Nature* prompts, by *Reason's* Aid unblest,
Is the *Convulsion,* not the *Law* of Nature.
Which, still, by just and uniform Degrees,
Moves undisturb'd, and calm, thro' all her Works:
Nor owns what boist'rous Passion urges,
Veil'd beneath her specious Name.
    Gov. Why, yes! this is the pedant Preacher's Tale —
Yet, unsustained by ought, but the dark Vizor,[3]
Or subtlest Prudence — close Hypocrisy —
Or languid, dull, and unimpassion'd Souls.
But fair *Clemene*'s Eyes, more ardent Fires
Diffuse, transcending far beyond the narrow Bounds,
Discretion marks, or frozen Temp'rance knows.
    Heart. This daring Outrage is forbid, by all the Ties,
Which ev'n Savage, rude Barbarians, hold
Inviolate and pure — which Heaven
Proclaims most sacred, by its fix'd Decree
Whose gracious Eye, beholds our *parlying*[4] Passions,
With a lenient Brow — but if Presumption
Bids Defiance to its suspended Arm,
And kind Reflection's mediating Call,
We hardily denounce our own Destruction.
    Gov. The Trade of Priests — by sordid Av'rice form'd,
To alarm our Fears, and swell their Coffers.
    Heart. You are of *Britain,* Sir, whose purer Faith,

---

[3] *Vizor:* Mask.
[4] *parlying:* Speaking.

Unmix'd by Priestly Arts, sustains its Pow'r by Truth.
Where Honour has, for Ages, held its State,
And soft Humanity conjoin'd, have mark'd
The happy Natives, as their eldest born.
　　Shall, then, a Son of her's — possess'd with Pow'r,
To plant new Wreaths of Glory, round her Head,
By giving injur'd Majesty Redress,
Decline the Godlike Task? And sunk in sensual Toils,
Devote a royal, suff'ring Pair, unblest
In all, but mutual Love, and fond Endearment,
To the distracting Horrors of Despair,
By an accumulated Grief, I blush,
The Man, I've call'd my Friend, should meditate.
　　Gov. Your Blushes, *gracious* Sir, have more of Pride,
And haughty Insolence, than Virtue's Base;
Thus *piously* dissembl'd — But be sure,
It shall not fail of ample Retribution.
　　Heart. Nay then — Away with mild, dissuasive Means!
I must instruct you, Sir, the Rank I hold,
As first in th' Assembly, will not admit
My tacit Suff'rage,[5] to a Crime, which must reflect
Dishonour, Infamy, and Guilt upon the whole.
To whose most grave Determination,
I shall appeal, whether the Man, who wields
Th' Sword of Pow'r unjustly, does not, from thence,
Forfeit all Right, of longer holding it.
And they — as Agents for th' Public Welfare,
Become invested with supreme Command,
To take the Rein of Government themselves —
Stopping th' wild Career of him, wou'd, madly,
Let it loose, and trample on th' very Source
Of all the social Virtues — The first, great,
Pillars, which strengthen, and support a State.
　　Gov. I must assume the *Penitent* — This Man
Of *Virtue,* else, will foil the promis'd Hope, 　} *Aside.*
Ambition feeds — And am'rous Joy invites.
Confus'd — Abash'd — But happily convinc'd —
I stand a Convert, to the just Precepts,

---

[5] *Suff'rage:* Consent.

Your virtuous Friendship has inspired.
Th' warm impetuous Thoughts, so lately prevalent,
Subsiding cool — while Reputation's fairer Claim —
Th' nobler Calls of Honour — Religion's sacred Bond —
Banish this Female Folly, far from hence —
And light a purer Flame, within my Breast.
    Heart. Th' gen'ral Tenour of your Conduct, must be owned
Superior to th' wanton Perseverance,
E'er now maintained, ev'n t' irregular Warmth.
    Yet, give one leave, in farther Friendship, Sir,
T' observe, there *is* a Vice, yourself decry'd —
Transcending that, intemp'rate Wishes form —
The Vice of dark *Hypocrisy* — which *Man*
Disclaims, as basely, mean, and vile.
But, if to *Heav'n* — with outward Semblance,
Of Religion's sacred Name, we mask
The dark Recesses of corrupt Intention,
We close all Entrance at th' Gate of Mercy.
    Gov. Too unkindly urg'd — and —

                    Enter Messenger hastily.

    Heart. Whence this Haste?
    Mess. Th' Council, Sir, intreat your speedy Presence.
The Slaves, with *Oroonoko* at their Head;
In sudden, unforeseen Revolt, are now,
In Arms, threatening the Colony, with
Instant Devastation — If they're oppos'd,
In making Seizure of th' Ship, which brought 'em,
To reconvey 'em, to their wished for Home.
    Gov. Give Orders for th' assembling of the Troops —

                                        [*Exit Mess.*]

This Prince, you find, has not approv'd himself,
So deeply anxious for *our Safety,*
As you have been, in your adher'd Defence,
And Preservation of *his Honour.*
But let us, hence — Each in his Department,
To stop the Growth of this impending Ill —
From which, if my Prophetick Gift be just,   } *Aside.*
I shall possess an ampler Field to spring my Game.

                                        [*Exit*]

A Drum, and Shouts, heard at a Distance.

Blandford — Maria.

Mar. This dread Alarm, my dearest *Blandford,* fills
My anxious Bosom, with a thousand Fears —
Th' Number, Disposition, native Fierceness
Of these Moors,[6] led on by *Oroonoko* —
A Prince of their own Clime — Of warlike Fame;
Renown'd, 'tis said, in Arms, and Hostile Deeds,
Will spread the Face of wild Destruction,
Horror, and keenest Slaughter o'er the Land!

Blan. Be not dismay'd, my gentle Love — I know
The Prince, although impatient of the Captive State;
In which, himself, his Wife, and Friends were held;
Has Sentiments, superior to ev'ry Act,
Which carries but remotest Tendency,
To Inhumanity, and savage Barbarism.
His glorious Ardor, kindled alone,
From Principles of Heav'n born Liberty —
Th' universal Gift to Human Nature.
And shall a Prince! th' Inheritor of Crowns!
Be tamely subject, underneath a Loss,
Our *British* Peasants have, for Ages, held,
Inviolate and sacred, from oppressive Pow'r?

Mar. The Princess too, I am well persuaded,
Has, with her Weight of Influence, given
Prevailing Force to th' Enterprize — Holding
This Barter for Mankind, in just Disdain.

Blan. It were, indeed, well to be wished, some
More humane Expedient cou'd be found,
For Cultivation of our Lands — And yet,
There are, who say, this Practice carries Mercy,
Rather than Marks of an unfeeling Stamp —
Since in th' Wars, they wage, each with the other —
Were not this Channel of commercial Intercourse
Kept open, th' Pris'ners taken, would exchange
This Slavery, for cruel, and tormenting Deaths.

Mar. Reasoning will not weigh with those, who feel

---

[6] *Moors:* Though sometimes applied generally to Africans, the term referred originally to natives of Mauritania, in northern Africa, and it was often used to differentiate them from the darker-skinned peoples in the southern parts of the continent.

Th' Oppression — nor *stop* their warm Impatience
To purchase Freedom, with their Master's Blood.
    Blan. These Fears too much alarm thy trembling Heart —
Th' weak Attempt, conceiv'd by Desperation,
Rather than Hope, quickly must incline them,
To accept such Terms, th' Council will admit.
And I'll dispose th' Prince, with my best Influence,
To receive — from Motives of that feeling Impulse,
He has read, in *Nature*'s, and in *Virtue*'s
Book — more prevalent, with noble Minds,
Than those, by Schoolmen taught, in all their learn'd Harangues.
    Mar. May th' Event be prosp'rous to thy generous Wishes!

.   .   .   .

2

Literary Contexts

This section introduces other works by Aphra Behn as well as a number of *Oroonoko*'s literary antecedents and descendants. It is designed to illustrate both Behn's inventions as, arguably, the first in a long line of professional women writers, and her debt to the literary tradition of depicting exotic heroes and noble savages. Thus, it brings together two lines of literary history that meet in *Oroonoko*.

The professional woman writer was among the cultural innovations of the period of the Restoration of the English monarchy (1660–1688). Women had certainly published books before, but none had ever claimed to be making a living by her pen. Indeed, professional authors of either sex were practically unheard of before the Restoration. Shakespeare and Jonson were among the few propertyless men who wrote for a living, but most authors were either independent gentlemen or members of the learned professions. During their twenty-year rule, the Puritans had closed the London theaters, and few playwrights and actors from the first half of the century were still alive when the playhouses were reopened after 1660. The new Restoration stage allowed for an increase in the number of professional authors, and the opening of the theatrical world to women actresses (women's parts had previously been played by boys) may have encouraged women to write plays. Two plays by women seem to have been produced in the 1660s, but Behn was the first woman to sustain a substantial career. Her precedent was followed in the period by a half-dozen less successful female playwrights.

In order to sharpen our sense of how unusual Behn's works must have seemed to her contemporaries, we should note that the vast majority of women who published in the seventeenth century were the authors of religious literature. Most works by women were pious, and many were written explicitly for the instruction and spiritual improvement of other women. Even the romances that had sometimes appeared under women's names or in translations by women usually emphasized the unconquerable purity of their heroines. Behn's plays, in contrast, were full of sexual intrigue, and the poems and short romances she published in the 1680s depicted seduction, adultery, impotence, and even the sexual attraction of women to each other. This chapter contains two of Behn's "amorous" poems, both of which express longings for erotic freedom and an expanded field of sexual pleasure. Also included is part of a short romance featuring a villainous black women whose desire for the hero destroys a pair of young lovers. In this story, the "Blackamoor" is depicted as having an unruly, passionate nature, but so are many of Behn's heroines. The author seems to be using blackness in this story more as a metaphor for secretiveness, for dark and invisible designs, than as a sign of destructive sexuality.

As noted in the general introduction (p. 22), Aphra Behn liked to call attention to the unprecedented licentiousness of her works, at times even designating herself as scandalous, for it served her political interests as well as her need for celebrity. The Restoration court was bent on driving the puritanism of its political enemies out of fashion, and Behn no doubt intended her rather lascivious works to help depuritanize the prevailing atmosphere. Her works were always saturated in political meanings, and this, like their licentiousness, was a departure for a woman writer, especially for a commoner. Early in the century, a few women had published works that might have been interpreted as allegories of courtly politics, and many women were drawn into the national conflict in the years of civil war, but Behn made a public spectacle of her partisan sentiments. Political parties were only just beginning to form during the Restoration, and the number of people enfranchised in England was very small, but writers were increasingly being employed by political factions to heroize their leaders and slander their enemies. Behn loudly proclaimed her Tory partisanship, and her outspoken support of the unpopular James II in works such as the "Congratulatory Poem to the King's Most Sacred Majesty" (1688), included in this chapter, would not have won her any favor in the succeeding Court of William and Mary.

Although Behn did not live long enough to suffer the consequences of her political enthusiasm, her career nevertheless remained an important landmark in the history of English letters, and *Oroonoko,* in many ways the most chaste of her writings, stood as its primary monument. As noted in the general Introduction to this volume, *Oroonoko* partakes of two figures already well developed in European literature: the Candid Infidel and the Noble Savage. The following selections from Sir John Mandeville and Michel de Montaigne contain early instances of the use of these figures for satirical purposes. Mandeville's Sultan and Montaigne's cannibals serve to magnify the vices and hypocrisy of European Christians, thus challenging the premise of Christian superiority. In contrast, Ben Jonson's and John Dryden's depictions of the Noble Savage have few such satirical resonances. Indeed, the noble Africans and Indians in *The Masque of Blacknesse* (1605) and *The Indian Emperor* (1665) admire Europeans even as they are subjugated by them. Jonson's masque was performed at court, and it portrays James I as a great king whose fame has spread to the banks of the Niger. In reality, James I had little in the way of empire or international power; he certainly, as the documents included in Chapter 3 will demonstrate, had no power in Africa. Jonson's masque might be said to express a *desire* for foreign subjects, for rich and noble people who would be worthy vassals, by staging the willingness of exotic royals to subordinate their sovereignty to that of the English monarch. The African ladies in Jonson's masque come to pay tribute in James's court, and the concept of subordinate rule is carried as well in the recurrent imagery of tributary streams that are to be ordered by King Oceanus.

Dryden's *The Indian Emperor* concerns another exotic royal family that yields to the superior might of a European power, and his depictions of Hernán Cortés and Francisco Pizarro remind us that the English wish for wealthy and robust subordinate powers was inspired by the Spanish conquests of the Aztec and Inca empires. The English envied the Spanish not only the earliness, extent, and richness of their American conquests, but also the level of civil development of their vassals. According to the prevailing chivalrous ideas of warfare, the Aztecs were worthy foes, a nation one could win honor through conquering. The point is made repeatedly in Dryden's play by the perfect symmetry with which heroes are matched in the two camps, Aztec and Spanish, as well as by the endless pairs of speeches in which they declare their vast respect for each other.

The English were hard pressed to find such a sophisticated empire to conquer, and thus had to settle for idealizations of simplicity, such as those we find in *Oroonoko*. Behn's poem "The Golden Age," which, like *Oroonoko*, praises the innocent life of the Indians, illustrates the preferred British imperial genre of pastoral tragedy. Like Sir Walter Raleigh's depictions of guileless and innocent Indians, reproduced on pages 334–37, Behn's pastorals give us harmless, rather than heroic, natives. As for satire, although both Dryden and Behn manage to give their Indians some critical purchase on the Europeans they encounter, neither has the mordancy of Montaigne. Dryden's work is too deeply steeped in the ethos of honorable chivalric warfare, which required the mutual admiration of the combatants, and Behn's is too invested in a mythic universal past to risk the truly disorienting cultural relativism of Montaigne's essay. The contrast between Dryden's chivalric, imperialist impulse and the pastoral influence in Behn's *Oroonoko*, however, should not be overstated, for the desire for a noble captive people may be one of Behn's reasons for introducing Oroonoko into the new world. While the Caribs are too primitive and simple to constitute worthy antagonists, the African prince, like the Indian Emperor, provides the chivalric backbone of tragedy. Behn's story departs from Dryden's more conventional pattern by failing to match Oroonoko against a noble European antagonist. However, by emphasizing the distance between Oroonoko's grandeur and the brutality of his tormentors, Behn revives the critical and satiric function of the Noble Savage.

By the eighteenth century, the literature of the empire was less apt to follow the satirical tradition of Montaigne, or the neoclassical conventions of either pastoral or heroic tragedy. British power waxed while Spanish power waned, and the basic facts of the new world system came to seem ordinary. This chapter includes three eighteenth-century literary treatments of noble savages that were particularly popular and enduring. In various ways, each demonstrates the decline of the neoclassical paradigms. Richard Steele's tale of Yarico and Inkle, first published in *The Spectator* in 1711, was retold many times in the course of the century, and like *Oroonoko*, it became more antislavery with each telling. Steele uses the tale, in which a British merchant sells his dark mistress into slavery, to illustrate the cruelty of men toward women, but Yarico and Inkle soon became a parable for the inhumanity of slavery. The elements of sexual betrayal and unrequited love, as well as the triumph of mercenary motives over emotional attachments, all combined to make it a sentimental staple of the antislavery canon. Yarico may be a noble savage, but she possesses neither the defiant spirit once represented by that figure nor the stature of a conquered sovereign, which could enhance the glory of a conqueror. Her overriding virtue is loyalty, but it is made pathetic by the unworthiness of its object.

In Joseph Addison's story of two West Indian slaves who love the same woman, even the virtue of steadfastness is devalued. Addison's tale partakes of the eighteenth-century sentimental mode of depicting slaves' lives but combines sentimentality with moral didacticism. The fact that the lovers are African slaves is presented as an explanation of why they kill the woman they both love and then commit suicide. This instance of "barbarous" love and honor is attributed to the lack of "a suitable Education" and regarded as inferior to civilized ways of coping with disappointment. Addison's story may be read as part of a consistent eighteenth-century debunking of seventeenth-century heroic genres, and it seems almost a direct criticism of Dryden's and Behn's neoclassical ideals of heroic behavior, in which principled suicides were praiseworthy.

Daniel Defoe's *Robinson Crusoe* (1719) might be read as an anti-heroic tale of the adventures of a colonial merchant. Crusoe inhabits a fictional world in which slavery is a neutral fact of life, and the selections from his story included here bear comparison with the Yarico and Inkle tale, for Crusoe, like Inkle, sells his companion into slavery as soon as he himself is freed. Defoe's works, with their close attention to the physical textures of life and their matter-of-fact reporting of events, have long been thought to have inaugurated novelistic realism. In this realism, elements of the Noble Savage and the Candid Infidel seem to have been resurrected only to be exorcized. The island where Crusoe becomes stranded (in an episode too well known to be reprinted here) is off the coast of Guiana, so its position recalls Behn's Suriname and even Montaigne's more distant Tupinamba (Brazil), the land of the cannibals. However, when the cannibals appear on Crusoe's island they are easily scattered, and their victim, whom they leave behind to become Crusoe's companion Friday, resembles the earlier noble savages only in his loyalty to his rescuer and his physical prowess. He has nothing to teach Crusoe, no satirical edge or independent viewpoint on the world. His long hair and his beautiful form may remind readers of Oroonoko, but he has no authority or charisma. He is simply an empty vessel waiting to be filled up by Crusoe's civilization; as in the stories by Addison and Steele, the savage in *Robinson Crusoe* is sympathetic, but desperately in need of rescue. Defoe seems to be commenting on the literary tradition of the Noble Savage by creating a figure who conjures the previous satirical and heroic meanings and then burying such "heroism" in images of abject dependence.

APHRA BEHN

The Golden Age.
A Paraphrase on a Translation out of French.

———

To the Fair Clarinda,
Who Made Love to Me, Imagin'd More Than Woman.

———

A Congratulatory Poem to the King's Most Sacred
Majesty, on the Happy Birth of the Prince of Wales.

———

The Unfortunate Bride: or, The Blind Lady a Beauty.

———

These selections help to reveal how race, eroticism, and royalism, themes that are central to *Oroonoko,* figure elsewhere in Behn's poetry and fiction. "The Golden Age," first published in Behn's *Poems upon Several Occasions* (1684), is a translation and revision of the opening chorus in *Aminta* (1573), by the Italian poet Torquato Tasso. In expanding Tasso's poem (the original is only sixty-five lines), Behn elaborates the various harms that have not yet been introduced into the world, such as labor, war, ambition, property, and honor. The myth of an idyllic Golden Age comes from Hesiod (c. 700 B.C.E.), and Behn's account shares many features with Montaigne's in "On Cannibals." Unlike Montaigne, however, Behn emphasizes the lack of constraint on amorous impulses, describing a kind of sexual freedom far more absolute than anything that appears in *Oroonoko;* notice, for example, that she curses honor as a concept that turns all humans into slaves. Even the Suriname Indians, who are represented as embodying "an absolute *Idea* of the first State of Innocence" (p. 40), seem remarkably chaste in Behn's account, as when she describes a young Indian who courts his beloved by folding his arms, gazing at her, and sighing. The innocence of "The Golden Age," by contrast, depends on the complete absence of such notions as modesty, chastity, and impurity.

"To the Fair *Clarinda,*" first published in *Lycidus* (1688), presents an erotic figure "imagin'd" as a hermaphrodite (Hermaphroditus was the child of Hermes and Aphrodite, mentioned in the poem's last line). In her treatment of an act that is at once innocent and criminal, Behn imagines a condition that combines the blissfully unconstrained eroticism of the Golden Age with the anxious knowledge of a postlapsarian state. Her view of erotic pleasure here is significantly more complicated than in

Oroonoko, where the appeal of Oroonoko and Imoinda depends precisely on their innocence and purity.

"A Congratulatory Poem to the King's Most Sacred Majesty," published as a broadside in 1688, congratulates James II on the birth of his son, James Francis Edward Stuart; some months earlier, Behn had published a poem hoping for the birth. At a time of widespread opposition to the Stuart monarchy — motivated in large part by hostility to the king's Catholic inclinations — Behn was among the few writers willing to proclaim her support for James and to wish for a continuation of his line. The birth itself, coming after numerous miscarriages, was greeted with suspicion (skeptics alleged that the child was not the queen's, but had been smuggled into the room in a warming pan). Shortly after the birth, James was forced by the events of the "Glorious Revolution" to flee to France with his family, and William and Mary assumed the throne. Behn, whose politics would have made her unpopular with the new regime, died within the year.

"The Unfortunate Bride," published posthumously in a collection of Behn's fiction in 1698 or 1700 (its bibliographical history remains obscure), features an evil "Blackamoor Lady" whose elaborate ruses recall certain aspects of the amorous court intrigues in the African section of *Oroonoko.* Moorea, however, resembles not Onahal but Oroonoko's grandfather: like him, she nurses an illicit desire that remains doomed to frustration. Where the grandfather appears as a figure of fun, Moorea is a stock villain, condensing various stereotypes about Africans and jealous women. Notice the suggestion that any marriage between a white man and a "Blackamoor" is "unlawful" — a subject that Behn treats more ambiguously in *Oroonoko.*

These texts are taken from *The Works of Aphra Behn,* 7 vols., ed. Janet Todd (Columbus: Ohio UP, 1992–1996) 1: 30–35, 288, 297–99; 3: 325–334.

The Golden Age.
A Paraphrase on a Translation out of French.

I

Blest Age! when ev'ry Purling° Stream
   Ran undisturbed and clear,
When no scorn'd Shepherds on your Banks were seen,
Tortur'd by Love, by Jealousie, or Fear;

1. *Purling:* Flowing, whirling.

When an Eternal Spring drest ev'ry Bough,   5
And Blossoms fell, by new ones dispossest;
These their kind Shade affording all below,
And those a Bed where all below might rest.
The Groves appear'd all drest with Wreaths of Flowers,
And from their Leaves dropt Aromatick Showers,   10
Whose fragrant Heads in Mystick Twines above,
Exchang'd their Sweets, and mix'd with thousand Kisses,
    As if the willing Branches strove
    To beautifie and shade the Grove
    Where the young wanton Gods of Love   15
Offer their Noblest Sacrifice of Blisses.

II

Calm was the Air, no Winds blew fierce and loud,
The Skie was dark'ned with no sullen Cloud;
But all the Heav'ns laugh'd with continued Light,
And scatter'd round their Rays serenely bright.   20
    No other Murmurs fill'd the Ear
    But what the Streams and Rivers purl'd,
When Silver Waves o'er Shining Pebbles curl'd; .
  Or when young *Zephirs*° fan'd the Gentle Breez,
  Gath'ring fresh Sweets from Balmy Flow'rs and Trees,   25
Then bore 'em on their Wings to perfume all the Air:
    While to their soft and tender Play,
    The Gray-Plum'd Natives of the Shades
Unwearied sing till Love invades,
Then Bill,° then sing agen, while Love and Musick makes the Day.   30

III

    The stubborn Plough had then,
  Made no rude Rapes upon the Virgin Earth;
Who yeilded of her own accord her plentious Birth;
    Without the Aids of men;
    As if within her Teeming° Womb,   35
    All Nature, and all Sexes lay,
    Whence new Creations every day
    Into the happy World did come:
    The Roses fill'd with Morning Dew;

24. *Zephirs:* Zephyrus is the Greek god of the west wind.
30. *Bill:* Kiss or touch beaks together.
35. *Teeming:* Fertile.

Bent down their loaded heads,   40
T' Adorn the careless Shepherds Grassy Beds
While still young opening Buds each moment grew
And as those withered, drest his shaded Couch a new;
　　Beneath who's boughs the Snakes securely dwelt,
　　Not doing harm, nor harm from others felt;   45
　　With whom the Nymphs did Innocently play,
　　No spightful Venom in the wantons° lay;
But to the touch were Soft, and to the sight were Gay.

IV

　　Then no rough sound of Wars Alarms,
　　Had taught the World the needless use of Arms: 50
　　　　Monarchs were uncreated then,
　　　　Those Arbitrary Rulers over men;
　　Kings that made Laws, first broke 'em, and the Gods
By teaching us Religion first, first set the World at Odds:
　　　　Till then Ambition was not known,   55
　　　　That Poyson to Content, Bane to Repose;
　　Each Swain° was Lord o'er his own will alone,
　　His Innocence Religion was, and Laws.
　　Nor needed any troublesome defence
　　　　Against his Neighbours Insolence.   60
　　Flocks, Herds, and every necessary good
　　Which bounteous Nature had design'd for Food,
　　　　Whose kind increase o'er-spread the Meads and Plaines,
Was then a common Sacrifice to all th'agreeing Swaines.

V

　　Right and Property were words since made,   65
　　　　When Power taught Mankind to invade:
　　When Pride and Avarice became a Trade;
　　　　Carri'd on by discord, noise and wars,
　　　　For which they barter'd wounds and scarrs;
And to Inhaunce the Merchandize, miscall'd it, Fame,   70
　　　　And Rapes, Invasions, Tyrannies,
　　　　Was gaining of a Glorious Name:
　　Stiling their salvage° slaughters, Victories;
　　　　Honour, the Error and the Cheat

47. *wantons:* Sportive, unrestrained lovers.
57. *Swain:* Shepherd.
73. *salvage:* Savage.

Of the Ill-natur'd Bus'ey Great,   75
Nonsense, invented by the Proud,
Fond Idol of the slavish Crowd,
Thou wert not known in those blest days
Thy Poyson was not mixt with our unbounded Joyes;
    Then it was glory to pursue delight,   80
And that was lawful all, that Pleasure did invite,
    Then 'twas the Amorous world injoy'd its Reign;
And Tyrant Honour strove t' usurp in Vain.

                              VI
The flowry Meads the Rivers and the Groves,
Were fill'd with little Gay-wing'd Loves: 85
    That ever smil'd and danc'd and Play'd,
And now the woods, and now the streames invade,
And where they came all things were gay and glad:
When in the Myrtle Groves the Lovers sat
    Opprest with a too fervent heat;   90
A Thousand Cupids fann'd their wings aloft,
And through the Boughs the yielded Ayre would waft:
Whose parting Leaves discovered all below,
And every God his own soft power admir'd,
And smil'd and fann'd, and sometimes bent his Bow;   95
Where e'er he saw a Shepherd uninspir'd.
The Nymphs were free, no nice,° no coy disdain,
Deny'd their Joyes, or gave the Lover pain;
The yielding Maid but kind Resistance makes;
Trembling and blushing are not marks of shame,   100
    But the Effect of kindling Flame:
Which from the sighing burning Swain she takes,
While she with tears all soft, and down-cast eyes,
Permits the Charming Conqueror to win the Prize.

                             VII
The Lovers thus, thus uncontroul'd did meet,   105
Thus all their Joyes and Vows of Love repeat:
    Joyes which were everlasting, ever new
    And every Vow inviolably true;
Not kept in fear of Gods, no fond Religious cause,

97. *nice:* Fastidious.

Nor in Obedience to the duller Laws.   110
Those Fopperies of the Gown° were then not known,
Those vain, those Politick Curbs to keep man in,
Who by a fond° mistake Created that a Sin;
Which freeborn we, by right of Nature claim our own.
    Who but the Learned and dull moral Fool   115
Could gravely have forseen, man ought to live by Rule?

VIII

Oh cursed Honour! thou who first didst damn,
    A Woman to the Sin of shame;
    Honour! that rob'st us of our Gust,°
    Honour! that hindred mankind first,   120
At Loves Eternal Spring to squench° his amorous thirst.
    Honour! who first taught lovely Eyes the art,
    To wound, and not to cure the heart:
With Love to invite, but to forbid with Awe,
    And to themselves prescribe a Cruel Law;   125
    To Veil 'em from the Lookers on,
    When they are sure the slave's undone,
And all the Charmingst part of Beauty hid;
Soft Looks, consenting Wishes, all deny'd.
    It gathers up the flowing Hair,   130
    That loosely plaid with wanton Air.
The Envious Net, and stinted order hold,
The lovely Curls of Jet and shining Gold,
No more neglected on the Shoulders hurl'd:
Now drest to Tempt, not gratify the World,   135
Thou Miser Honour hord'st the sacred store,
And starv'st thy self to keep thy Votaries° poor.

IX

Honour! that put'st our words that should be free
    Into a set Formality.
Thou base Debaucher of the generous heart,   140
That teachest all our Looks and Actions Art;

111. *Fopperies of the Gown:* Legal complexities.
113. *fond:* Foolish.
119. *Gust:* Taste.
121. *squench:* Quench.
137. *Votaries:* Worshipers.

What Love design'd a sacred Gift,
What Nature made to be possest,
Mistaken Honour, made a Theft,
For Glorious Love should be confest: 145
For when confin'd, all the poor Lover gains,
Is broken Sighs, pale Looks, Complaints, & Pains.
Thou Foe to Pleasure, Nature's worst Disease,
    Thou Tyrant over mighty Kings,
What mak'st thou here in Shepheards Cottages;   150
Why troublest thou, the quiet Shades & Springs?
    Be gone, and make thy Fam'd resort
        To Princes Pallaces;
Go Deal and Chaffer° in the Trading Court,
That busie Market for Phantastick Things;   155
Be gone and interrupt the short Retreat,
    Of the Illustrious and the Great;
    Go break the Politicians sleep,
    Disturb the Gay Ambitious Fool,
        That longs for Scepters, Crowns, and Rule,   160
Which not his Title, nor his Wit can keep;
But let the humble honest *Swain* go on,
In the blest Paths of the first rate of man;
    That nearest were to Gods Alli'd,
And form'd for love alone, disdain'd all other Pride.   165

                        X
Be gone! and let the Golden age again,
    Assume its Glorious Reign;
  Let the young wishing Maid confess,
  What all your Arts would keep conceal'd:
    The Mystery will be reveal'd,   170
And she in vain denies, whilst we can guess,
She only shows° the Jilt to teach man how,
To turn the false Artillery on the Cunning Foe.
    Thou empty Vision hence, be gone,
        And let the peaceful *Swain* love on;   175
The swift pac'd hours of life soon steal away:
    Stint not yee Gods his short liv'd Joy.
The Spring decays, but when the Winter's gone,

154. *Chaffer:* Bargain, haggle.
172. *shows:* Acts.

The Trees and Flowers a new comes on.
The Sun may set, but when the night is fled,   180
    And gloomy darkness does retire,
    He rises from his Watry Bed:
All Glorious, Gay, all drest in Amorous Fire.
    But *Sylvia* when your Beauties fade,
When the fresh Roses on your Cheeks shall die,   185
    Like Flowers that wither in the Shade,
Eternally they will forgotten lye,
And no kind Spring their sweetness will supply.
When Snow shall on those lovely Tresses lye
And your fair Eyes no more shall give us pain,   190
    But shoot their pointless Darts in vain.
What will your duller honour signifie?
Go boast it then! and see what numerous Store
Of Lovers, will your Ruin'd Shrine Adore.
    Then let us *Sylvia* yet be wise,   195
    And the Gay hasty minutes prize:
The Sun and Spring receive but our short Light,
Once sett, a sleep brings an Eternal Night.

To the Fair Clarinda, *Who Made Love to Me,*
Imagin'd More Than Woman.

Fair lovely Maid, or if that Title be
Too weak, too Feminine for Nobler thee,
Permit a Name that more Approaches Truth:
And let me call thee, Lovely Charming Youth.⁴
This last will justifie my soft complaint,   5
While that may serve to lessen my constraint;
And without Blushes I the Youth persue,
When so much beauteous Woman is in view,
Against thy Charms we struggle but in vain
With thy deluding Form thou giv'st us pain,   10
While the bright Nymph betrays us to the Swain.
In pity to our Sex sure thou wer't sent,
That we might Love, and yet be Innocent:
For sure no Crime with thee we can commit;
Or if we shou'd — thy Form excuses it.   15

4. *Youth:* A young person of either gender.

For who, that gathers fairest Flowers believes
A Snake lies hid beneath the Fragrant Leaves.

   Thou beauteous Wonder of a different kind,
Soft *Cloris* with the dear *Alexis°* join'd;
When e'r the Manly part of thee, wou'd plead   20
Thou tempts us with the Image of the Maid,
While we the noblest Passions do extend
The Love to *Hermes, Aphrodite°* the Friend.

   19. *Cloris . . . Alexis:* Conventional names for female and male lovers, respectively,
in pastoral poetry.
   23. *Hermes, Aphrodite:* Hermes was the Greek messenger of the gods and god of
eloquence; Aphrodite was the Greek goddess of love, corresponding to the Roman
Venus. Here they are presumably also introduced as the male and female aspects of Hermaphroditus.

A CONGRATULATORY POEM TO THE
King's Most Sacred Majesty, On the Happy BIRTH
of the PRINCE of WALES.

Joy to the *Greatest MONARCH* of the Earth!
As many Joys as this *Illustrious BIRTH*
Has Elevated Hearts! As Endless too,
As are the VOWS we Offer up for You.
"Oh Happy *KING!* to whom a *SON* is Born!   5
"What more cou'd *Heaven* for this Bless'd Land perform?

   Long with *Prophetick Fire,* Resolv'd and Bold,
Your *Glorious FATE* and *FORTUNE* I foretold.°
I saw the *Stars* that did attend Your *REIGN,*
And how they Triumph'd o'er Great *Charles's Wain.°*   10
Far off I saw this *HAPPY DAY* Appear;
This *Jubilee,* not known this *Fifty Year.*
This Day, foretold, (*Great SIR!*) that gives you more
Than even Your *Glorious Virtues* did before.

   8. *I foretold:* Behn had specifically predicted the birth of a prince in her "Congratulatory Poem to Her Most Sacred Majesty, on the Universal Hopes . . . for a Prince of
Wales," published just a few months earlier; lines 5–6 quote directly from this earlier
poem.
   10. *Great Charles's Wain:* The constellation called the Great Bear, which resembles
a rustic Wagon (from the Anglo-Saxon *ceor les wan,* "farmer's wagon").

No *MONARCH's Birth* was ever Usher'd in   15
With Signs so Fortunate as this has been.
The *Holy Trinity*° his *BIRTH-DAY* claims,
Who to the World their best *Lov'd Blessings* sends.
Guarded he comes, in Triumph over *FATE,*
And all the *Shining HOST* around him wait.   20
Angels and *Saints,* that do this *Train* Adorn,
In Hallelujahs Sing, *A KING IS BORN!*
Blest *MARGARET,*° *Scotlands* Royal *Saint* and *Queen,*
The last *Great Branch* of all the *Saxon Line,*
Waits on this *HAPPY BIRTH,* and does Declare   25
He, in her Right to *Saxons,* is the *HEIR.*
In the *Fam'd* Room, by happy Fate brought forth,
Where Two *Illustrious KINGS*° receiv'd their *Birth.*
   The *LESSONS* for *This Day,* by Chance *Divine,*
Appear'd as they were Order'd by Design.   30
The *First,* the *Holy PROPHET* did Unfold
When he the *Birth* of the *MESSIAH* told.
The Words are These; *His Fan is in his Hand,*
And he shall throughly purge the Floor or Land,
Gathering the Wheat into the Granary:°   35
Then all *One FAITH,* at least *One SOUL* shall be.

"The *ANGEL* next the *PATRIARCH* did Inform,
"That *ISAAC,* Chosen *ISAAC,* shou'd be *Born.*°

ASTROLOGERS Divine! that when the *Sun*
Is Mounted to his Full Meridian,   40
'Tis Lucky to be *Born;* and does Portend
Long Life, that can by no Misfortune end.
Thus, in his Summer-*Solstice* views the Light,
Breaks out, and makes our *Longest Day* more *Bright.*

17. *Holy Trinity:* Trinity Sunday. [Behn's note]. The date of the prince's birth, June 10, 1688, fell on Trinity Sunday, the first Sunday after Whitsun.
   23. *Margaret:* St. Margaret's Day [Behn's note].
   28. *Two Illustrious KINGS:* Charles II, James II. [Behn's note].
   35. *His Fan . . . Granary:* Math. 3.12. [Behn's note.] These lines from the book of Matthew announce the coming of the Holy Ghost: "Whose fan is in his hand, and he will thoroughly purge his floor, and gather his wheat into the garner."
   38. *The ANGEL . . . Born:* The Evening Lesson, Gen. 18.10. [Behn's note.] Behn refers to God's promise to Abraham ("the patriarch"): "Sarah thy wife shall bring thee a son indeed; and thou shalt call his name Isaac" (Gen. 17.19).

Methinks I hear the *Belgick LION*° Roar,   45
And Lash his *Angry Tail* against the Shore.
Inrag'd to hear a *PRINCE OF WALES* is *Born:*
Whose *BROWS* his *Boasted Laurels* shall Adorn.
Whose *Angel FACE* already does express
His *Foreign CONQUESTS*, and *Domestick PEACE*.   50
While in his *Awful little EYES* we Find
He's of the *Brave*, and the *Forgiving KIND*.

All Joy *Great QUEEN!* — if to your *Happy Store*
Our Grateful Pray'rs, and *Wishes* can add more.
Your *Blest DELIVERANCE* to Congratulate,   55
The *Adoring World* is Prostrate at your *Feet*.
Where *TEARS* of *Joy*, and *Humble VERSE* I lay
Too mean a *Trophy* for this *GLORIOUS DAY:*
Inspir'd by Nothing but *Prophetick Truth*,
They Boast no other *Fire*, no other *Worth*.   60
Full of the *JOY*, no *LINES Correct* can write,
My *Pleasure's* too Extream for *Thought* or Wit.
Charm'd to Excess, alas! I strive in *Vain*,
In *Scanty VERSE* my Transports to Explain
Too *Vast* for *Narrow NUMBERS*° to Contain.   65

45. *Belgick LION:* A lion appeared on the crest of the house of Nassau; William of
Orange, Count of Nassau, was next in line for the English throne if James II died without an heir.
65. *Numbers:* Verse, metrical units.

The Unfortunate Bride:
or, The Blind Lady a Beauty.

Frankwit and *Wildvill* were two young Gentlemen of very considerable Fortunes, both born in *Staffordshire*,[1] and during their minority,
both educated together, by which opportunity they contracted a very
inviolable Friendship, a Friendship which grew up with them; and
though it was remarkably known to every body else, they knew it not
themselves; they never made profession of it in words, but actions; so
true a warmth their fires could boast, as needed not the effusion of
their breath to make it live. *Wildvill* was of the richest Family, but

[1] *Staffordshire:* A county in midwest England, presumably chosen as an area in the
country, distant from London.

Frankwit of the noblest; *Wildvill* was admired for outward qualifications, as strength, and manly proportions, *Frankwit* for a much softer beauty, for his inward endowments, pleasing in his conversation, of a free, and moving air, humble in his behaviour, and if he had any pride, it was but just enough to shew that he did not affect humility, his mind bowed with a motion as unconstrained as his body, nor did he force this virtue in the least, but he allowed it only; so amiable he was, that every Virgin that had Eyes, knew too she had a Heart, and knew as surely she should lose it. His *Cupid*[2] could not be reputed blind, he never shot for him, but he was sure to wound. As every other Nymph admired him, so he was dear to all the Tuneful Sisters, the Muses[3] were fired with him as much as their own radiant God *Apollo*,[4] not their loved Springs and Fountains were so grateful to their eyes as he, him they esteemed their *Helicon* and *Parnassus*[5] too; in short, when ever he pleased, he could enjoy them all. Thus he enamour'd the whole Female Sex, but amongst all the sighing captives of his Eyes, *Belvira* only boasted charms to move him, her parents lived near his, and even from their Childhood they felt mutual Love, as if their Eyes at their first meeting had struck out such glances as had kindled into am'rous flame. And now *Belvira* in her fourteenth year, (when the first spring of young virginity began to cast more lively bloomings in her Cheeks, and softer longings in her Eyes) by her indulgent Father's care was sent to *London* to a Friend, her Mother being lately dead: When, as if fortune ordered it so, *Frankwit*'s Father took a journey to the other World, to let his Son the better enjoy the pleasures and delights of this: the young Lover now with all imaginable haste interred his Father, nor did he shed so many Tears for his loss as might in the least quench the Fires, which he received from his *Belvira*'s Eyes, but (master of seventeen hundred pounds a year, which his Father left him) with all the Wings of Love he flys to *London,* and sollicits *Belvira* with such fervency, that it might be thought he meant Deaths Torch should kindle *Hymen*'s:[6] and now as soon as he arrives at his Journeys end, he goes to pay a visit to the fair Mistress of his Soul, and assures her, that tho he was absent from her, yet she was still with him; and that all the

---

[2] *Cupid:* The Roman god of love, son of Venus, the goddess of love.
[3] *Muses:* The nine daughters of Zeus and Mnemosyne, who preside over poetry, song, and the various arts and sciences.
[4] *Apollo:* Greek god of the sun, poetry, and music.
[5] *Helicon and Parnassus:* Two mountains in Greece, both portrayed in classical literature as sacred to Apollo and the nine Muses.
[6] *Hymen's:* Hymen was the Greek god of marriage.

Road he Travell'd her beauteous Image danced before him, and like
the ravished Prophet, he saw his Deity in every Bush; in short, he paid
her constant visits, the Sun ne're rose, or set, but still he saw it in her
company, and every minute of the day he counted by his sighs so inces-
santly he importuned her that she could no longer hold out, and was
pleased in the surrender of her heart, since it was he was Conqueror,
and therefore felt a triumph in her yielding; their Flames now joyned,
grew more and more, glowed in their Cheeks, and lightened in their
glances; eager they looked, as there were pulses beating in their Eyes;
and all endearing, at last she vowed, that *Frankwit* living she would
ne're be any other mans; thus they past on some time, while every day
rowled over fair. Heaven showed an aspect all serene, and the Sun
seemed to smile at what was done; he still caressed his charmer with
an innocence becoming his sincerity, he lived upon her tender breath,
and basked in the bright lustre of her Eyes, with pride, and secret joy.
     He saw his Rivals languish for that bliss, those charms, those raptu-
ous and extatick transports which he engrossed alone. But now some
eighteen months (some ages in a lovers Kalendar) winged with delights,
and fair *Belvira* now grown fit for riper joys, knows hardly how she
can deny her pressing lover and herself to crown their vows, and joyn
their hands as well as hearts. All this while the young Gallant wash'd
himself clean of that shining dirt, his Gold; he fancied little of Heaven
dwelt in his yellow Angels, but let them fly away as it were on their
own Golden wings, he only valued the smiling Babies in *Belvira*'s Eyes.
His generosity was boundless as his Love, for no man every truly loved
that was not generous. He thought his Estate like his passion, was a
sort of a Pontick Ocean,[7] it could never know an Ebb: but now he
found it could be fathom'd, and that the Tide was turning, therefore
he sollicits with more impatience, the consumation of their joys, that
both might go like Martyrs from their flames immediately to Heaven;
and now at last it was agreed between them that they should both be
one, but not without some reluctancy on the female side, for 'tis the
humour of our Sex, to deny most eagerly those grants to Lovers, for
which most tenderly we sigh; so contradictory are we to our selves, as
if the Deity had made us with a seeming reluctancy to his own designs,
placing as much discords in our minds, as there is harmony in our
faces. We are a sort of airy Clouds, whose Lightning flash out one way,
and the Thunder another. Our words and thoughts can ne're agree. So,
this young charming Lady thought her desires could live in their own

[7] *Pontick Ocean:* The Black Sea.

longings, like Misers wealth-devouring Eyes; and e're she consented to her Lover, preparing him first with speaking looks, and then with a fore-running sigh, applyed to the dear charmer thus: *Frankwit, I am afraid to venture the Matrimonial bondage, it may make you think your self too much confined, in being only free to one.* Ah! my dear *Belvira,* he replyed, that one, like Manna,[8] has the taste of all, why should I be displeased to be confined to Paradice, when it was the curse of our fore-fathers to be set at large, tho they had the whole World to roam in: You have, my Love, ubiquitary[9] charms, and you are all in all, in every part. *Ay but,* reply'd *Belvira, we are all like perfumes, and too continual smelling makes us seem to have lost our Sweets, I'll be judged by my Cousin* Celesia *here, if it be not better to live still in mutual love, without the last Enjoyment.* (I had forgot to tell my Reader that *Celesia* was an heiress, the only child of a rich *Turkey* Merchant, who when he dyed left her fifty thousand pound in Money, and some Estate in land; but, poor creature, she was blind to all these riches, having been born without the use of sight, though in all other respects charming to a wonder.) *Indeed, says* Celesia, (for she saw clearly in her mind) *I admire you should ask my judgment in such a case, where I have never had the least experience; but I believe it is but a sickly soul which cannot nourish its Off-spring of desires without preying upon the body.* Believe me, reply'd *Frankwit,* I bewail you want of sight, and I could almost wish you my own eyes for a moment, to view your charming Cousin, where you would see such Beauties as are too dazzling to be long beheld; and if too daringly you gazed, you would feel the misfortune of the loss of sight, much greater than the want on't; and you would acknowledge, that in too presumptuously seeing, you would be blinder then, than now unhappily you are.

Ah! I most confess, reply'd Belvira, *my poor dear Cousin is blind, for I fancy she bears too great an esteem for* Frankwit, *and only longs for sight to look on him.* Indeed, reply'd *Celesia,* I could be glad to see *Frankwit,* for I fancy he's as dazzling as he but now describ'd his Mistress, and if I fancy I see him, sure I do see him, for sight is fancy, is it not? or do you feel my Cousin with your Eyes? *This is indeed, a charming blindness, reply'd* Frankwit, *and the fancy of your sight excels the certainty of ours; strange, that there should be such glances even in blindness? You, fair Maid, require not Eyes to conquer, if your night has such Stars, what Sunshine would your day of sight have, if*

---

[8] *Manna:* Divine nourishment.
[9] *ubiquitary:* Universal, capable of being everywhere at once.

ever you should see? I fear those Stars you talk of, said *Belvira,* have some influence on you, and by the compass you sail by now, I guess you are steering to my Cousin. She is indeed charming enough to have been another Off-spring of bright *Venus,* blind like her Brother *Cupid. That* Cupid, *reply'd* Celesia, *I am afraid has shot me, for methinks I could not have you marry* Frankwit, *but rather live as you do without the least Enjoyment, for methinks if he were marry'd, he would be more out of my sight than he already is.* Ah! Madam, return'd *Frankwit,* love is no Camelion, it cannot feed on Air alone. *No but, rejoyn'd* Celesia, *you Lovers that are not blind like love itself, have am'rous looks to feed on.* Ah! believe it, said *Belvira,* 'tis better *Frankwit,* not to lose Paradice by too much knowledge; Marriage enjoyment does but wake you from your sweet golden Dreams: Pleasure is but a Dream, dear *Frankwit,* but a Dream and to be waken'd. *Ah! Dearest, but unkind* Belvira, *answer'd* Frankwit, *sure there's no waking from delight, in being lull'd on those soft Breasts of thine.* Alas! (reply'd the Bride to be) it is that very lulling wakes you; Women enjoy'd, are like Romances read, or Raree-shows[10] once seen, meer tricks of the slight of hand, which, when found out, you only wonder at your selves for wondering so before at them. 'Tis expectation endears the blessing; heaven would not be heaven, could we tell what 'tis. When the Plot's out you have done with the Play, and when the last Act's done, you see the Curtain drawn with great indifferency. O *my* Belvira, *answered* Frankwit, *that expectation were indeed a Monster which enjoyment could not satisfy; I should take no pleasure* he rejoin'd, *running from hill to hill, like Children chasing that Sun which I could never catch.* O thou shalt have it then, that Sun of Love, reply'd *Belvira,* fir'd by this complaint, and gently rush'd into his Arms, (rejoyning,) so *Phœbus*[11] rushes radiant, and unsullied into a gilded Cloud. *Well then, my dear* Belvira, answer'd Frankwit, *be assured I shall be ever yours, as you are mine; fear not you shall never draw Bills of Love upon me so fast as I shall wait in readiness to pay them; but now I talk of Bills, I must retire into* Cambridgeshire,[12] *where I have a small concern as yet unmortgaged, I will return thence with a brace of thousand pounds within a week at farthest, with which our Nuptials by their celebration shall be worthy of our love. And then, my Life, my Soul, we shall be joyn'd, never to part again.* This

---

[10] *Raree-shows:* Peep shows, carried around in a box.

[11] *Phœbus:* Another name for Apollo.

[12] *Cambridgeshire:* A county near the eastern coast of England, not far from London.

tender expression mov'd *Belvira* to shed some few tears, and poor *Celesia* thought herself most unhappy that she had not eyes to weep with too; but if she had, such was the greatness of her grief, that sure she would have soon grown blind with weeping. In short, after a great many soft vows, and promises of an inviolable faith, they parted with a pompous sort of pleasing woe; their concern was of such a mixture of joy and sadness, as the weather seems, when it both rains and shines. And now the last, the very last of last adieu's was over, for the farewels of Lovers hardly ever end, and *Frankwit* (the time being Summer) reach'd *Cambridge* that night, about nine a clock; (strange! that he should have made such haste to fly from what so much he lov'd!) and now, tir'd with the fatigue of his Journey, he thought fit to refresh himself by writing some few lines to his belov'd *Belvira;* for a little Verse after the dull prose company of his servant, was as great an ease to him, (from which it flow'd as naturally and unartificially, as his love or his breath) as a pace or hand-gallop,[13] after a hard, uncouth, and rugged trot. He therefore, finding his *Pegasus*[14] was no way tir'd with his land travel, takes a short journey thro the air, and writes as follows.

> *My dearest dear* Belvira,
> You knew my soul, you knew it yours before,
> I told it all, and now can tell no more;
> Your presence never wants fresh charms to move,
> But now more strange, and unknown pow'r you prove,
> For now your very absence 'tis I love.
> Something there is which strikes my wandring view,
> And still before my eyes I fancy you.
> Charming you seem, all charming, heavenly fair,
> Bright as a Goddess does my love appear,
> You seem, *Belvira,* what indeed you are.
> Like the Angelick off-spring of the skies,
> With beatifick glorie in your eyes.
> Sparkling with radiant lustre all Divine,
> Angels, and Gods! oh heavens! how bright they shine!
> Are you *Belvira?* can I think you mine!
> Beyond ev'n thought, I do thy beauties see,

---

[13] *hand-gallop:* An easy gallop, which allows control of the horse by preventing excess speed.
[14] *Pegasus:* A winged horse from Greek mythology.

Can such a heaven of heavens be kept for me!
O be assur'd, I shall be ever true,
I must —
For if I would, I can't be false to you.
Oh! how I wish I might no longer stay,
Tho I resolve I will no time delay,
One tedious week, and then I'll fleet away.
Tho love be blind, he shall conduct my road,
Wing'd with almighty love to your abode,
I'll fly, and grow immortal as a God.
Short is my stay, yet my impatience strong,
Short tho it is, alas! I think it long.
I'll come, my life, new blessings to pursue,
Love then shall fly a flight, he never flew,
I'll stretch his balmy wings; I'm your, . . . *Adieu.*

                                                    Frankwit.

This Letter *Belvira* receiv'd with unspeakable joy, and laid it up safely in her bosom, laid it, where the dear Author of it lay before, and wonderfully pleas'd with his humour of writing in Verse, resolv'd not to be at all behind hand with him, and so writ as follows.

My dear Charmer,
You knew before what power your love could boast,
But now your constant faith confirms me most.
Absent sincerity the best assures,
Love may do much, but faith much more allures,
For now your constancy has bound me yours.
I find, methinks, in Verse some pleasure too,
I cannot want a Muse, who write to you.
Ah! soon return, return, my charming dear,
Heav'n knows how much we mourn your absence here:
My poor *Celesia* now would charm your soul,
Her eyes, once blind, do now divinely rowl.
An aged Matron has by charms unknown,
Given her clear sight as perfect as thy own.
And yet, beyond her eyes, she values thee,
'Tis for thy sake alone she's glad to see.
She begg'd me, pray remember her to you,
That is a task, which now I gladly do.
Gladly, since so I only recommend

A dear relation, and a dearer friend,
Ne're shall my love — but here my note must end.

> *Your ever true* Belvira.

When this Letter was written, it was strait shown to *Celesia,* who lookt upon any thing that belong'd to *Frankwit* with rejoycing glances; so eagerly she perus'd it, that her tender eyes beginning to water, she cry'd out, (fancying she saw the words dance before her view) Ah! Cousin, Cousin, your Letter is running away, sure it can't go itself to *Frankwit?* A great deal of other pleasing innocent things she said, but still her eyes flow'd more bright with the lustrous beams, as if they were to shine out; now all that glancing, radiancy which had been so long kept secret, and as if, as soon as the cloud of blindness once was broke, nothing but lightnings were to flash for ever after. Thus in mutual discourse they spent their hours, while *Frankwit* was now ravished with the receipt of this charming answer of *Belvira*'s, and blest his own eyes which discovered to him the much welcome news of fair *Celesia*'s. Often he reads the Letter o're and o're, but there his fate lay hid, for 'twas that very fondness proved his ruin. He lodg'd at a Cousin's House of his, and there, (it being a private family) lodged likewise a Blackamoor[15] Lady, then a Widow; a whimsical Knight had taken a fancy to enjoy her; *enjoy her did I say? enjoy the Devil in the flesh at once?* I know not how it was, but he would fain have been a bed with her, but she not consenting on unlawful terms, (*but sure all terms with her unlawful*) the Knight soon marry'd her, as if there were not hell enough in Matrimony, but he must wed the Devil too. The Knight a little after died, and left this Lady of his (whom I shall call *Moorea*) an Estate of six thousand pounds *per Ann.* Now this *Moorea* observed the joyous *Frankwit* with an eager look, her Eyes seemed like Stars of the first magnitude glaring in the night; she greatly importuned him to discover the occasion of his transport, but he denying it, (as 'tis the humour of our Sex) made her the more inquisitive; and being jealous that it was from a Mistress, employ'd her Maid to steal it, and if she found it such to bring it her; accordingly it succeeded, for *Frankwit* having drank hard with some of the Gentlemen of that Shire, found himself indisposed, and soon went to Bed, having put the Letter in his pocket: The Maid therefore to *Moorea* contrived that all the other Servants should be out of the way, that she might plausibly

---

[15] *Blackamoor:* A black African (by contrast, for example, with "tawny Moor," sometimes used during this period for the lighter-skinned Moors of northern Africa).

officiate in the warming the bed of the indisposed Lover, but likely, had it not been so, she had warmed it by his intreaties in a more natural manner; he being in bed in an inner Room, she slips out the Letter from his pocket, carries it to her Mistress to read, and so restores it whence she had it; in the morning the poor Lover wakened in a violent Fever, burning with a fire more hot than that of Love. In short, he continued sick a considerable while, all which time the Lady *Moorea* constantly visited him, and he as unwillingly saw her (poor Gentleman) as he would have seen a Parson; for as the latter would have perswaded, so the former scared him to Repentance. In the mean while, during his sickness, several Letters were sent to him by his Dear *Belvira,* and *Celesia* too, (then learning to write) had made a shift to give him a line or two in Postscript with her Cousin, but all was intercepted by the jealousy of the Black *Moorea,* black in her mind, and dark, as well as in her body. *Frankwit* too writ several Letters as he was able, complaining of her unkindness, those likewise were all stopt by the same Blackmoor Devil. At last, it happened that *Wildvill,* (who I told my Reader was *Frankwit's* friend) came to *London,* his Father likewise dead, and now Master of a very plentiful fortune, he resolves to marry, and paying a visit to *Belvira,* enquires of her, concerning *Frankwit,* she all in mourning for the loss, told him his friend was dead. Ah! *Wildvill,* he is dead, said she, and died not mine, a Blackmoor Lady had bewitched him from me; I received a Letter lately which informed me all; there was no name subscribed to it, but it intimated, that it was written at the request of dying *Frankwit.* Oh! I am sorry at my soul, said *Wildvill,* for I loved him with the best, the dearest friendship; no doubt then, rejoyned he, 'tis Witchcraft indeed that could make him false to you; what delight could he take in a Blackmoor Lady, tho she had received him at once with a soul as open as her longing arms, and with her Petticoat put off her modesty. Gods! How could he change a whole *Field argent* into downright *Sables.*[16] 'Twas done, returned *Celesia,* with no small blot, I fancy to the Female Scutcheon.[17] In short, after some more discourse, but very sorrowful, *Wildvill* takes his leave, extreamly taken with the fair *Belvira,* more beauteous in her cloud of woe; he paid her afterwards frequent visits, and found her wonder for the odd inconstancy of *Frankwit,* greater than her sorrow, since he dy'd so unworthy of her. *Wildvill* attack'd her with all the force of

---

[16] *Field argent into downright Sables:* A silver background, turned to black (in a heraldic coat of arms).

[17] *with no small blot . . . to the Female Scutcheon:* A blot on the escutcheon is a disgrace to the family (literally, a stain on the family coat of arms).

vig'rous love, and she (as she thought) fully convinc'd of *Frankwit*'s death, urg'd by the fury and impatience of her new ardent Lover, soon surrender'd, and the day of their Nuptials now arriv'd, their hands were joyn'd. In the mean time *Frankwit*, (for he still liv'd) knew nothing of the injury the base *Moorea* practic'd, knew not that 'twas thro her private order, that the fore-mention'd account of his falshood and his death was sent; but impatient to see his Dear *Belvira,* tho yet extreamly weak, rid post[18] to *London,* and that very day arriv'd there, immediately after the Nuptials of his Mistress and his Friend were celebrated. I was at this time in *Cambridge,* and having some small acquaintance with this Blackmoor Lady, and sitting in her Room that evening, after *Frankwit*'s departure thence, in *Moorea*'s absence, saw inadvertently a bundle of Papers which she had gathered up, as I suppose, to burn, since now they grew but useless, she having no further hopes of him; I fancy'd I knew the hand, and thence my curiosity only led me to see the name, and finding *Belvira* subscrib'd, I began to guess there was some foul play in hand, *Belvira* being my particularly intimate acquaintance: I read one of them, and finding the contents convey'd them all secretly out with me, as I thought, in point of justice I was bound, and sent them to *Belvira* by that night's Post; so that they came to her hands soon after the minute of her Marriage, with an account how, and by what means I came to light on them. No doubt but they exceedingly surpriz'd her: but Oh! Much more she grew amaz'd immediately after to see the poor, and now unhappy *Frankwit,* who privately had enquir'd for her below, being received as a stranger, who said he had some urgent business with her in a back Chamber below stairs. What Tongue, what Pen can express the mournful sorrow of this Scene: At first they both stood dumb, and almost senseless; she took him for the Ghost of *Frankwit*; he looked so pale, new risen from his sickness, he (for he had heard at his entrance in the House, that his *Belvira* marry'd *Wildvill*) stood in a maze, and like a Ghost indeed, wanted the power to speak, till spoken to the first. At last, he draws his Sword, designing there to fall upon it in her presence; she then imagining it his Ghost too sure, and come to kill her, shrieks out and swoons; he ran immediately to her, and catch'd her in his arms, and while he strove to revive and bring her to herself tho that he thought could never now be done, since she was marry'd, *Wildvill* missing his Bride, and hearing the loud shriek, came running down, and entring the Room, sees his Bride lye claspt in *Frankwit*'s arms, Ha!

[18] *post:* Speedily.

Traytor! He crys out, drawing his Sword with an impatient fury, have you kept that Strumpet[19] all this while, curst *Frankwit,* and now think fit to put your damn'd cast Mistress upon me; could not you forbear her neither ev'n on my wedding day? Abominable Wretch! Thus saying, he made a full pass at *Frankwit,* and run him thro the left arm, and quite thro the Body of the poor *Belvira;* that thrust immediately made her start, tho *Frankwit's* endeavours all before were useless. Strange! that her death reviv'd her! for ah! she felt that now she only liv'd to dye! striving thro wild amazement to run from such a Scene of horror, as her apprehensions shew'd her; down she dropt, and *Frankwit* seeing her fall, (all friendship disannull'd by such a chain of injuries) draws, fights with, and stabs his own lov'd *Wildvill.* Ah! who can express the horror and distraction of this fatal misunderstanding! the House was alarm'd, and in came poor *Celesia,* running in confusion just as *Frankwit* was off'ring to kill himself, to dye with a false friend, and perjur'd Mistress, for he suppos'd them such. Poor *Celesia* now bemoan'd her unhappiness of sight, and wish'd she again were blind. *Wildvill* dy'd immediately, and *Belvira* only surviv'd him long enough to unfold[20] all their most unhappy fate, desiring *Frankwit* with her dying breath, if ever he lov'd her, (and now she said that she deserv'd his love, since she had convinc'd him that she was not false) to marry her poor dear *Celesia,* and love her tenderly for her *Belvira's* sake; leaving her, being her nearest Relation, all her fortune, and he, much dearer than it all, to be added to her own; so joyning his and *Celesia's* Hands, she pour'd her last breath upon his Lips, and said, Dear *Frankwit, Frankwit,* I dye yours. With tears and wondrous sorrow he promis'd to obey her Will, and in some months after her interrment, he perform'd his promise.

[19]*strumpet:* Prostitute.
[20]*unfold:* Disclose.

SIR JOHN MANDEVILLE

From *Dialogue between the Pagan and the Christian*

As the introduction to this volume explains, the Sultan in *The Travels of Sir John Mandeville* represents one of the first instances of the truth-telling infidel. The *Travels* were probably written in French in the late 1350s; the earliest dated version was produced in 1371, and the first English translation is thought to date from the 1390s. In his prologue, the author purports to be an English gentleman ("Johan Maundeville, chevaler") who began his journey in 1322 and returned to England in 1356; however, his identity and voyage now appear to be equally fictitious. The language of the *Travels*' composition and the pattern of sources on which the author relied suggest that the book was probably written by a French ecclesiastic who had access to a major European library, most likely in northern France or Flanders. He almost certainly never undertook any journey even vaguely resembling the one he describes, the itinerary of which was evidently patched together from a variety of other travel narratives and encyclopedias, creatively combined and supplemented with historical and religious lore that the author gleaned from his wide reading. His account, however, was generally credited, and by 1500 the *Travels* were available in translation all over Europe. Its exotic descriptions — and the author's witty critique of his own culture — continued to influence European thinking until the seventeenth century, when explorers who traveled to the regions it describes came to recognize the text's fabrications.

The dialogue excerpted here takes place during the author's stay with the Sultan of Egypt. The episode has been shown to derive from Caesarius of Heisterbach's *Dialogus Miraculorum* ("the dialogue of miracles"), written c. 1220–35. In book 4, chapter 15, Caesarius recounts a conversation between an Englishman and a Saracen nobleman who, like Mandeville's Sultan, quizzes his acquaintance about the piousness of his countrymen; when the Englishman lies to protect their reputation, the Saracen indicts Christians for many of the sins mentioned here — gluttony, pride, lechery, and the forcing of daughters and wives into prostitution. Through the retelling of this episode, Mandeville helped to give it a much wider circulation.

The text is taken from C. W. R. D. Moseley's modern translation of the *Travels* (Harmondsworth, Middlesex: Penguin, 1983), 107–08.

Now I shall tell you what the Sultan told me one day in his chamber. He made everyone else leave his chamber, lords as well as others who were there, for he wanted to have a private talk between ourselves alone. And when they had all gone out, he asked me how Christians governed themselves in our countries. And I said, 'Lord, well enough — thanks be to God.' And he answered and said, 'Truly, no. It is not so. For your priests do not serve God properly by righteous living, as they should do. For they ought to give less learned men an example of how to live well, and they do the very opposite, giving examples of all manner of wickedness. And as a result, on holy days, when people should go to church to serve God, they go to the tavern and spend all the day — and perhaps all the night — in drinking and gluttony, like beasts without reason which do not know when they have had enough. And afterwards through drunkenness they fall to proud speeches, fighting and quarrelling, till someone kills somebody. Christian men commonly deceive one another, and swear the most important oaths falsely. And they are, moreover, so swollen with pride and vainglory that they never know how to dress themselves — sometimes they wear short fashions of clothing, sometimes long, sometimes cut full, sometimes figure-fitting. You ought to be simple, meek and truthful, and ready to give charity and alms, as Christ was, in whom you say you believe. But it is quite otherwise. For Christians are so proud, so envious, such great gluttons, so lecherous, and moreover so full of covetousness, that for a little silver they will sell their daughters, their sisters, even their own wives to men who want to lie with them. And everyone takes another's wife, and no one keeps his faith to another: and you so wickedly and evilly despite and break the Law that Christ gave you. Certainly it is because of your sinfulness that you have lost all this land which we hold and keep.

MICHEL DE MONTAIGNE

From *On Cannibals*

The following passages from Michel de Montaigne's essay "On Cannibals," first published in French in 1580, further demonstrate the satirical potential of the Noble Savage, whose adherence to Nature's laws provides a foil against which Christian "civilization" looks decadent. The essay refers to the Tupinamba, natives of what is now Brazil, where the explorer Nicolas Durand de Villegaignon landed in 1557. Though Montaigne never traveled to Brazil, he did meet some Tupinamba in Rouen in 1563, and he queried them extensively about their perceptions of French society. He also relied heavily on two travel narratives that discussed their customs at length: *Les Singularités de la France Antarctique, autrement nommée Amérique* (1557), by the cosmographer André Thévet, and *Histoire d'un voyage fait en la terre du Brésil, autrement dite Amérique* (1578), by the missionary Jean de Léry. Léry, in particular, emphasized

that the Tupinamba practiced cannibalism not because of a primal and
primitive impulse to satisfy their hunger, but because it functioned as a
cultural ritual, a means of reaffirming group identity, and Montaigne
adopts and elaborates on this interpretation. He describes a world in
which food is plentiful, language is direct and unmediated, and there are
no corrupting influences to vitiate such basic passions as courage and its
cousin, revenge. In short, he represents this Edenic paradise as a place
where the noblest virtues of human nature may be observed, accompanied
by a kind of brutality seen as entirely consistent with those traits; Behn's
characterizations of both Oroonoko and the natives of Suriname are
deeply indebted to this essay.

   Montaigne (1533–1592) was a pioneer of the essay as a literary form,
and his massively influential works were first published in English in
1603, in the translation by John Florio used here. They were next translated in 1685 by Charles Cotton, who published a commendatory poem
the following year in praise of Behn's play *La Montre: or The Lover's
Watch,* itself a translation from the French.

   The text is excerpted from the Everyman's edition of Montaigne's
Essays (London: Dent, 1910) 219–21, 221–22, 223, 223–25, 227–28,
229.

   I finde (as farre as I have beene informed) there is nothing in that
nation, that is either barbarous or savage, unless men call that barbarisme which is not common to them. As indeed, we have no other
ayme of truth and reason, than the example and *Idea* of the opinions
and customes of the countrie we live in. There is ever perfect religion,
perfect policie,[1] perfect and compleat use of all things. They are even
savage, as we call those fruits wilde, which nature of her selfe, and of
her ordinarie progresse hath produced: whereas indeed they are those
which our selves have altered by our artificiall devices, and diverted
from their common order, we should rather terme savage. In those
are the true and most profitable vertues, and naturall properties most
lively and vigorous, which in these we have bastardized, applying
them to the pleasure of our corrupted taste. And if notwithstanding, in
divers fruits of those countries that were never tilled, we shall finde,
that in respect of ours they are most excellent, and as delicate unto our
taste; there is no reason art should gaine the point of honour of our

---

[1] *policie:* Political management.

great and puissant mother Nature. We have so much by our inventions surcharged[2] the beauties and riches of her workes, that we have altogether overchoaked her: yet where ever her puritie shineth, she makes our vaine and frivolous enterprises wonderfully ashamed.

All our endevour or wit, cannot so much as reach to represent the nest of the least birdlet, it's contexture, beautie, profit and use, no nor the web of a seely[3] spider. *All things* (saith *Plato) are produced, either by nature, by fortune, or by art. The greatest and fairest by one or other of the two first, the least and imperfect by the last.* Those nations seeme therefore so barbarous unto me, because they have received very little fashion from humane wit, and are yet neere their originall naturalitie. The lawes of nature doe yet command them, which are but little bastardized by ours; And that with such puritie, as I am sometimes grieved the knowledge of it came no sooner to light, at what time there were men, that better than we could have judged of it. I am sorie, *Lycurgus* and *Plato*[4] had it not: for me seemeth that what in those nations we see by experience, doth not only exceed all the pictures wherewith licentious Poesie hath proudly imbellished the golden age, and all her quaint inventions to faine[5] a happy condition of man, but also the conception and desire of Philosophy. They could not imagine a genuitie[6] so pure and simple, as we see it by experience; nor ever beleeve our societie might be maintained with so little art and humane combination. It is a nation, would I answer *Plato,* that hath no kinde of traffike, no knowledge of Letters, no intelligence of numbers, no name of magistrate, nor of politike superioritie; no use of service, of riches or of povertie; no contracts, no successions, no partitions, no occupation but idle; no respect of kinred,[7] but common, no apparrell but naturall, no manuring[8] of lands, no use of wine, corne, or mettle.[9] The very words that import lying, falshood, treason, dissimulations, covetousnes, envie, detraction, and pardon, were never heard of amongst them. How dissonant would hee finde his imaginarie commonwealth from this perfection!

---

[2] *surcharged:* Overloaded.

[3] *seely:* Insignificant.

[4] *Lycurgus and Plato:* Ancient Greek thinkers who created legal codes rather than relying on what Montaigne presents as the laws of nature.

[5] *faine:* Feign, imitate.

[6] *genuitie:* Genuineness.

[7] *kinred:* Kindred, family.

[8] *manuring:* Cultivation, tillage.

[9] *mettle:* I.e., metal.

Furthermore, they live in a country of so exceeding pleasant and temperate situation, that as my testimonies have told me, it is verie rare to see a sicke body amongst them; and they have further assured me, they never saw any man there, either shaking with the palsie,[10] toothlesse, with eies dropping, or crooked and stooping through age. They are seated alongst the sea-coast, encompassed toward the land with huge and steepie mountaines, having betweene both, a hundred leagues or thereabout of open and champaine[11] ground. They have great abundance of fish and flesh, that have no resemblance at all with ours, and eat them without any sawces, or skill of Cookerie, but plaine boiled or broiled. The first man that brought a horse thither, although he had in many other voyages conversed with them, bred so great a horror in the land, that before they could take notice of him, they slew him with arrowes. They spend the whole day in dancing. Their young men goe a hunting after wilde beasts with bowes and arrowes. Their women busie themselves therewhil'st with warming of their drinke, which is their chiefest office. Some of their old men, in the morning before they goe to eating, preach in common to all the houshold, walking from one end of the house to the other, repeating one selfe-same sentence many times, till he have ended his turne (for their buildings are a hundred paces in length) he commends but two things unto his auditorie, *First, valour against their enemies, then lovingnesse unto their wives.* They never misse (for their restraint) to put men in minde of this dutie, that it is their wives which keepe their drinke luke-warme and well-seasoned. The forme of their beds, cords, swords, blades, and woodden bracelets, wherewith they cover their hand wrists, when they fight, and great Canes open at one end, by the sound of which they keepe time and cadence in their dancing, are in many places to be seene, and namely in mine owne house. . . .

They warre against the nations, that lie beyond their mountaines, to which they go naked, having no other weapons than bowes, or woodden swords, sharpe at one end, as our broaches[12] are. It is an admirable thing to see the constant resolution of their combats, which never end but by effusion of bloud and murther: for they know not what feare or rowts[13] are. Every Victor brings home the head of the enemie he hath slaine as a Trophey of his victorie, and fastneth the

---

[10] *palsie:* An irresistible tremor.
[11] *champaine:* Unenclosed land.
[12] *broaches:* Pointed rods or spits.
[13] *rowts:* Routs, forced retreats in battle.

same at the entrance of his dwelling place. After they have long time used and entreated their prisoners well, and with all commodities they can devise, he that is the Master of them; sommoning a great assembly of his acquaintance; tieth a corde to one of the prisoners armes, by the end whereof he holds him fast, with some distance from him, for fear he might offend him, and giveth the other arme, bound in like manner, to the dearest friend he hath, and both in the presence of all the assembly kill him with swords: which done, they roast, and then eat him in common, and send some slices of him to such of their friends as are absent. It is not as some imagine, to nourish themselves with it, (as anciently the Scithians[14] wont to doe,) but to represent an extreme, and inexpiable revenge.

I am not sorie we note the barbarous horror of such an action, but grieved, that prying so narrowly[15] into their faults we are so blinded in ours. I thinke there is more barbarisme in eating men alive, than to feed upon them being dead; to mangle by tortures and torments a body full of lively sense, to roast him in peeces, to make dogges and swine to gnaw and teare him in mammockes[16] (as wee have not only read, but seene very lately, yea and in our owne memorie, not amongst ancient enemies, but our neighbours and fellow-citizens; and which is worse, under pretence of pietie and religion) than to roast and eat him after he is dead. *Chrysippus* and *Zeno,*[17] arch-pillers of the Stoicke sect, have supposed that it was no hurt at all, in time of need, and to what ever soever, to make use of our carrion bodies, and to feed upon them, as did our fore-fathers, who being besieged by *Cæsar* in the Citie of *Alexia,* resolved to sustaine the famine of the siege, with the bodies of old men, women, and other persons unserviceable and unfit to fight.[18]

> *Vascones (fama est) alimentis talibus usi*
> *Produxere animas.* — JUVEN. *Sat.* xv. 93.
>
> *Gascoynes* (as fame reports)
> Liv'd with meats of such sorts.

---

[14] *the Scithians:* A people who lived around what is now the Crimea between the eighth century B.C.E. and the second century C.E.; feared because of their military prowess, they were also accused of cannibalism.

[15] *narrowly:* With careful scrutiny.

[16] *mammockes:* Shreds, pieces.

[17] *Chrysippus and Zeno:* Stoic philosophers of ancient Greece.

[18] *Cæsar . . . unfit to fight:* During Julius Caesar's siege of Alesia (discussed in *Caesar's Gallic Wars,* 7.77), a Gaul chieftain named Critognatus proposed that his followers resort to cannibalism if they ran out of food.

And Physitians feare not, in all kindes of compositions availefull to our health, to make use of it, be it for outward or inward applications: But there was never any opinion found so unnaturall and immodest, that would excuse treason, treacherie, disloyaltie, tyrannie, crueltie, and such like, which are our ordinarie faults. We may then well call them barbarous, in regard to reasons rules, but not in respect of us that exceed them in all kinde of barbarisme. Their warres are noble and generous, and have as much excuse and beautie, as this humane infirmitie may admit: they ayme at nought so much, and have no other foundation amongst them, but the meere jelousie of vertue. They contend not for the gaining of new lands; for to this day they yet enjoy the natural ubertie[19] and fruitfulnesse, which without labouring toyle, doth in such plenteous abundance furnish them with all necessary things, that they need not enlarge their limits. They are yet in that happy estate as they desire no more, than what their naturall necessities direct them: whatsoever is beyond it, is to them superfluous. Those that are much about one age, doe generally enter-call one another brethren, and such as are younger they call children, and the aged are esteemed as fathers to all the rest. These leave this full possession of goods in common, and without division to their heires, without other claime or title, but that which doth plainely impart unto all creatures, even as shee brings them into the world. If their neighbours chance to come over the mountaines to assaile or invade them, and that they get the victorie over them, the Victors conquest is glorie, and the advantage to be and remaine superior in valour and vertue: else have they nothing to doe with the goods and spoyles of the vanquished, and so returne into their countrie, where they neither want any necessarie thing, nor lacke this great portion, to know how to enjoy their condition happily, and are contented with what nature affoordeth them. So doe these when their turne commeth. They require no other ransome of their prisoners, but an acknowledgement and confession that they are vanquished. And in a whole age, a man shall not finde one, that doth not rather embrace death, than either by word or countenance remissely to yeeld one jot of an invincible courage. There is none seene that would not rather be slaine and devoured, than sue[20] for life, or shew any feare. . . .

Surely, in respect of us these are very savage men: for either they must be so in good sooth,[21] or we must be so indeed: There is a wondrous

[19] *ubertie:* Fertility.
[20] *sue:* Beg.
[21] *sooth:* Truth.

distance betweene their forme and ours. Their men have many wives; and by how much more they are reputed valiant, so much the greater is their number. The manner and beautie in their marriages is wondrous strange and remarkable: For, the same jealousie our wives have to keepe us from the love and affection of other women, the same have theirs to procure it. Being more carefull for their husbands honour and content, then of any thing else: They endevour and apply all their industrie, to have as many rivals as possibly they can, forasmuch as it is a testimonie of their husbands vertue. Our women would count it a wonder, but it is not so: It is vertue properly Matrimoniall; but of the highest kinde. . . . Three of that nation . . . were at *Roane*[22] in the time of our late King *Charles* the ninth, who talked with them a great while. They were shewed our fashions, our pompe, and the forme of a faire Citie; afterward some demanded their advise, and would needs know of them what things of note and admirable they had observed amongst us: they answered three things, the last of which I have forgotten, and am very sorie for it, the other two I yet remember. They said, *First, they found it very strange, that so many tall men with long beards, strong and well armed, as it were about the King's person (it is very likely they meant the Switzers of his guard) would submit themselves to obey a beardlesse childe, and that we did not rather chuse one amongst them to command the rest.* Secondly (they have a manner of phrase whereby they call men but a moytie[23] one of another.) *They had perceived, there were men amongst us full gorged with all sortes of commodities, and others which hunger-starved, and bare with need and povertie, begged at their gates: and found it strange, these moyties so needy could endure such an injustice, and that they tooke not the other by the throte, or set fire on their houses. . . .*

[22] *Roane:* I.e., Rouen, a city in northern France, on the Seine.
[23] *moytie:* Moiety, part.

BEN JONSON

From *The Masque of Blacknesse*

The lines from Ben Jonson's 1605 court masque attest both to early-seventeenth-century English ideas about the causes of "blacknesse" and to its exotic attraction. Jonson's masque, his first collaboration with the set designer Inigo Jones for the court of King James I, also represents the first theatrical use of blackface; *Othello* had been staged at court some two months earlier, and the queen specifically requested that Jonson provide a masque whose players would appear as Moors. In the performance, the queen (six months pregnant) and several great ladies of her court were cast as Niger's fertile daughters. They colored their faces with burnt cork to impersonate "Ethiopian" ladies journeying to England so that they might bask in the light of the king, whose rays, unlike those of the sun, would turn them white. (The effect was not universally approved: one spectator complained that the women's "black faces, and hands which were painted and bare up to the elbowes, was a very lothsome sight, and I am sory that strangers should see owr court so strangely disguised." [10: 449]) Nobility in this masque, as in *Oroonoko*, transcends color difference; modern notions of race, as well as seventeenth- and eighteenth-century ideas that dark skin resulted from God's curse, are altogether absent. Although the "Ethiopian" ladies long to be "fair," Niger takes their desire to be evidence of women's credulity (they believe the infectious "fictions" of mere poets). At the same time, Jonson differentiates this "beautious race" from its Western counterpart in notably polarized terms, imagining an unruly "floud" that has come to mix with — and submit to — the "fixed" and orderly streams of King Oceanus. Jonson's Ethiopia is part of the "Orient" and his sources of information about it are classical — in the marginal glosses (reprinted here as footnotes), he cites such authorities as Diodorus Siculus, Herodotus, and Pliny.

Jonson (1573–1637) was an important playwright and poet as well as an author of court masques. His classicism, insistence that Greek and Latin works should serve as models for English literature, and satirical tone resonated loudly throughout the literature of the next two centuries and can be clearly heard in *Oroonoko*.

The text is taken from *Ben Jonson*, 11 vols., ed. C. H. Herford, Percy Simpson, and Evelyn Simpson (Oxford: Clarendon, 1925–52) 7: 172–75.

SONG.

Sound, sound aloud
The welcome of the *Orient* floud,
Into the *West;*
Fayre NIGER, sonne to OCEANUS,°   100
Now honord, thus,
With all his beautious race:
Who, though but blacke in face,
Yet, are they bright,
And full of life, and light.   105
To prove that beauty best,
Which not the colour, but the feature
Assures unto the creature.

OCEANUS.

Be silent, now the ceremonie's done,   110
And NIGER, say, how comes it, lovely sonne,
That thou, the ÆTHIOPES river, so farre *East,*
Art seene to fall into th'extremest *West*
Of me, the king of flouds, OCEANUS,
And, in mine empires heart, salute me thus?   115
My ceaselesse current, now, amazed stands!
To see thy labour, through so many lands,
Mixe thy fresh billow, with my brackish streame;°

100. *sonne to OCEANUS:* All rivers are said to be the sons of the *Ocean:* for, as the Ancients thought, out of the vapours, exhaled by the heat of the *Sunne,* rivers, and fountaines were begotten. And both by *Orph. in Hymn & Homer Iliad.* ε *Oceanus* is celebrated *tanquam pater, & origo, dijs, & rebus, quia nihil sine humectatione nascitur, aut putrescit.* [Jonson's note.] Jonson refers to *Orphic Hymns* 83, "To Oceanus," where the sea is called "father and begetter of immortal gods." The *Orphic Hymns,* however, were written in Greek, and Jonson's Latin quotation, which continues by explaining that "nothing is born or decays without water," comes from a critical gloss on the text supplied by a later commentator. In his reference to Homer, Jonson cites book 5 of the *Iliad,* but he is evidently referring to *Iliad* 21.195–96, which describes "the great might of deep-flowing Oceanus, from whom all rivers flow and every sea, and all the springs and deep wells."

118. *Mixe thy fresh billow . . . stream:* There wants not inough, in nature, to authorize this part of our fiction, in separating *Niger,* from the *Ocean* (besides the fable of *Alpheus,* and that, to which *Virgil* alludes of *Arethusa* in his 10. *Eclog. Sic tibi, cum fluctus subterlabere Sicanos, Doris amara suam non intermisceat undam*) examples of *Nilus, Iordan,* and others, whereof see *Nican. lib.* I. *de flumin.* & *Plut. in vita Syllæ,* even of this our river (as some thinke) by the name of Melas. [Jonson's note.] According to Greek myth the wood nymph Arethusa, in order to escape from the river Alpheus, threw herself into the sea and was transformed into an underwater spring, but Alpheus reached her and mingled its own waters with hers. In his reference to Virgil, Jonson

And, in thy sweetnesse, stretch thy diademe,
To these farre distant, and un-equall'd skies,   120
This squared Circle of cœlestiall bodies.

NIGER.

Divine OCEANUS, 'tis not strange at all
That (since the immortall soules of creatures mortall,
Mixe with their bodies, yet reserve for ever   125
A power of separation) I should sever
My fresh streames, from thy brackish (like things fixed)
Though, with thy powerfull saltnesse, thus far mixed.
Vertue, though chain'd to earth, will still live free;
And hell it selfe must yeeld to industrie.   130

OCEANUS.

But, what's the end of thy *Herculean* labors,
Extended to these calme, and blessed shores?

NIGER.

To do a kind, and carefull fathers part,   135
In satisfying every pensive heart
Of these my *Daughters,* my most loved birth:
Who though they were the first form'd dames of earth,°
And in whose sparckling, and refulgent° eyes,
The glorious *Sunne* did still delight to rise;   140
Though he (the best judge, and most formall cause
Of all dames beauties) in their firme hiewes, drawes
Signes of his fervent'st love; and thereby shewes

---

quotes from *Eclogues,* X.4–5, in which the poet calls on Arethusa for inspiration; he asks her to aid him "If, when thou glidest beneath Sicilian waves, thou wouldst not have briny Doris blend her stream with thine." Jonson's other citations are to Nicander of Colophon's *Theracia,* 686, and Plutarch's life of Sulla, xx.4, both of which mention the river Melas.

138. *the first form'd dames of earth:* Read *Diod. Sicul. lib.* 3. It is a conjecture of the old *Ethnicks,* that they, which dwell under the *South,* were the first begotten of the earth. [Jonson's note.] Diodorus of Sicily wrote that the Ethiopians, who "dwell beneath the noon-day sun" (because of their proximity to the Equator) "were, in all likelihood, the first to be generated by the earth," reasoning that since "the warmth of the sun . . . dried up the earth when it was still wet and impregnated it with life, it is reasonable to suppose that the region which was nearest the sun was the first to bring forth living creatures" (III.2.1). By "the old *Ethnicks,*" Jonson means pagans or heathens generally.

139. *refulgent:* Radiant, resplendent.

That, in their black, the perfectst beauty growes;
Since the fix't colour of their curled haire,   145
(Which is the highest grace of dames most faire)
No cares, no age can change; or there display
The fearefull tincture of abhorred *Gray;*
Since *Death* her selfe (her selfe being pale and blue)
Can never alter their most faithfull hiew;   150
All which are arguments, to prove, how far
Their beauties conquer, in great beauties warre;
And more, how neere *Divinitie* they be,
That stand from passion, or decay so free.
Yet, since the fabulous voices of some few   155
Poore brain-sicke men, stil'd *Poets,* here with you,
Have, with such envie of their graces, sung
The painted *Beauties,* other *Empires* sprung;
Letting their loose, and winged fictions flie
To infect all clymates, yea our puritie;   160
As of one PHAET(H)ON, that fir'd the world,°
And, that, before his heedlesse flames were hurld
About the *Globe,* the *Æthiopes* were as faire,
As others *Dames;* now blacke, with blacke dispaire:
And in respect of their complections chang'd,   165
Are eachwhere, since, for lucklesse creatures rang'd.°
Which, when my *Daughters* heard, (as women are
Most jelous of their beauties) feare, and care
Possess'd them whole; yea, and beleeving *them,*°
They wept such ceaselesse teares, into my streame,   170
That it hath, thus far, overflow'd his shore
To seeke them patience: who have since, e'remore
As the *Sunne* riseth, chardg'd his burning throne

---

161. *PHAET(H)ON, that fir'd the world: Notissima fabula.* Ovid. *Met. lib.* 2. [Jon-
son's note.] Jonson refers to the "famous story" recounted in Ovid, *Metamorphoses,*
2.1–366. Phaethon, son of Apollo, foolishly insisted on driving his father's chariot of the
sun. His failure to stay on course threatened to destroy the earth and heavens with fire.
    166. *lucklesse creatures rang'd:* Alluding to that of *Juvenal, Satir.* 5. *Et cui per
mediam nolis occurrere noctem.* [Jonson's note.] Jonson cites part of Juvenal, *Satires,*
5.54, which describes a guest who is handed a cup by a Moor "whom you would rather
not meet at midnight" when out driving past the monuments in the hills.
    169. *them:* The *Poets.* [Jonson's note.]

With volleys of revilings;° 'cause he shone
On their scorch'd cheekes, with such intemperate fires,   175
And other *Dames*, made queenes of all desires.
To frustrate which strange error, oft, I sought,
(Though most in vaine, against a setled thought
As womens are) till they confirm'd at length
By miracle, what I, with so much strength   180
Of argument resisted; els they fain'd:
For in the *Lake*, where their first spring they gain'd,
As they sate, cooling their soft Limmes, one night,
Appear'd a face, all circumfus'd with light;
(And sure they saw't, for *Æthiopes* never dreame)°   185
Wherein they might decipher through the streame,
These words.

> *That they a* Land *must forthwith seeke,*
> *Whose termination (of the* Greeke)
> *Sounds* TANIA°; *where bright* Sol, *that heat*   190
> *Their blouds, doth never rise, or set,°*
> *But in his Journey passeth by,*
> *And leaves that* Clymat *of the sky,*
> *To comfort of a greater* Light,
> *Who formes all beauty, with his sight.*

173–74. *chardg'd . . .* With *volleys of revilings:* A custome of the *Aethiopes*, notable in *Herod.* and *Diod. Sic.* See *Plinie. Nat. Hist. lib.* 5, *cap.* 8. [Jonson's note.] The references are to Herodotus, II.22, Diodorus Siculus, III.ix.2m, and Pliny's *Natural History*, V.8.45, which describe "the Atlas tribe," an Ethiopian people, asserting that "when they behold the rising and setting sun, they utter awful curses against it as the cause of disaster to themselves and their fields, and when they are asleep they do not have dreams like the rest of mankind."

185. *Æthiopes never dreame: Plin.* ibid. [Jonson's note.] See previous note.

190. *Sounds TANIA:* I.c., Britannia.

190–91. *Sol . . . doth never rise, or set:* Consult with *Tacitus, in vita Agric.* and the *Paneg. ad Constant.* [Jonson's note.] Jonson's citation of Tacitus refers to *Agricola* 12, which says that in the distant parts of Britain, "the sun's brilliance . . . is visible throughout the night: it neither sets or rises, but simply passes over." The same idea appears in the anonymous "Panegyric of Constantine" *(Panegyrici Latini* VI.9.3), which celebrates life in Britain, where "the sun itself, which to us seems to set, . . . appears to pass overhead."

JOHN DRYDEN

From *The Indian Emperor*

The Indian Emperor portrays the New World at the moment of its first contact with Europe, and the play abounds in images that were already familiar from earlier travel narratives, depicting a land richly endowed with gold, and a noble Indian who goes to his death fearlessly. Notice that John Dryden (1631–1700) explicitly rejects the imputation that the Aztecs are savage or uncivilized, pointing instead to the relativity of such notions. Like Oroonoko, Montezuma displays a sincerity and heroism that shames his European persecutors.

First performed in 1665, *The Indian Emperor* was an early contribution to a genre that became extremely popular on the Restoration stage — the heroic tragedy, which Dryden had pioneered the previous year with *The Indian Queen,* written in collaboration with his brother-in-law, Sir Robert Howard. One of the costumes for that play included a set of feather trappings that Behn brought back from Suriname, as she explains early in *Oroonoko*; they were probably used again in *The Indian Emperor,* since the sequel used many of the same props. The play was immediately successful, and had a regular place in the theatrical repertory for more than seventy years. Usually revolving around conflicts in which love and honor are the primary motives, heroic tragedies typically feature characters who specialize in self-immolating fortitude, elaborated in highly stylized proclamations that exhibit the speaker's noble and rarefied ideals. Behn, herself a playwright, draws on that model at the end of *Oroonoko.*

Dryden, the leading dramatist and poet of his day, was also England's first poet laureate; appointed in 1670, he was removed from the post after the Glorious Revolution of 1688. Dryden, like Behn a Catholic supporter of James II, refused to swear allegiance to the new Protestant monarch, William III, and accordingly was dismissed from the laureateship. Dryden knew Behn personally, though not well, and in 1679 he invited her to participate in a collaborative translation of Ovid's *Heroides,* along with several other writers.

The text is excerpted from *The Dramatic Works of John Dryden,* 8 vols., ed. George Saintsbury (Edinburgh: Paterson, 1882) 2:321–27, 338–39, 395–400, 409–10.

Connection
of
The Indian Emperor
to
The Indian Queen

The conclusion of the Indian Queen (part of which poem was writ by me) left little matter for another story to be built on, there remaining but two of the considerable characters alive, viz. Montezuma and Orazia. Thereupon the author of this thought it necessary to produce new persons from the old ones: and considering the late Indian Queen, before she loved Montezuma, lived in clandestine marriage with her general Traxalla, from those two he has raised a son and two daughters, supposed to be left young orphans at their death. On the other side, he has given to Montezuma and Orazia, two sons and a daughter; all now supposed to be grown up to men's and women's estate; and their mother, Orazia (for whom there was no further use in the story), lately dead.

So that you are to imagine about twenty years elapsed since the coronation of Montezuma; who, in the truth of the history, was a great and glorious prince; and in whose time happened the discovery and invasion of Mexico, by the Spaniards, under the conduct of Hernando Cortez, who joining with the Traxallan Indians, the inveterate enemies of Montezuma, wholly subverted that flourishing empire; — the conquest of which is the subject of this dramatic poem.

I have neither wholly followed the story, nor varied from it; and, as near as I could, have traced the native simplicity and ignorance of the Indians, in relation to European customs; — the shipping, armour, horses, swords, and guns of the Spaniards, being as new to them, as their habits and their language were to the Christians.

The difference of their religion from ours, I have taken from the story itself; and that which you find of it in the first and fifth acts, touching the sufferings and constancy of Montezuma in his opinions, I have only illustrated, not altered, from those who have written of it.

DRAMATIS PERSONÆ

INDIAN MEN.

MONTEZUMA, *Emperor of Mexico.*
ODMAR, *his eldest son.*
GUYOMAR, *his younger son.*
ORBELLAN, *son of the late Indian Queen by* TRAXALLA.
High Priest of the Sun.

WOMEN.

CYDARIA, MONTEZUMA's daughter.
ALMERIA, } *Sisters; and daughters to the late Indian Queen.*
ALIBECH, }

SPANIARDS.

CORTEZ, *the Spanish General.*
VASQUEZ, } *Commanders under him.*
PIZZARO, }

SCENE — *Mexico, and two leagues about it.*

The Indian Emperor.

Act I. Scene I. — *A pleasant Indian country.*

Enter CORTEZ, VASQUEZ, PIZZARO, *with
Spaniards and Indians in their party.*

Cort. On what new happy climate are we thrown,
So long kept secret, and so lately known;
As if our old world modestly withdrew.
And here in private had brought forth a new?
    Vasq. Corn, wine, and oil, are wanting to this ground,
In which our countries fruitfully abound;
As if this infant world, yet unarrayed,
Naked and bare in Nature's lap were laid.
No useful arts have yet found footing here.
But all untaught and savage does appear.
    Cort. Wild and untaught are terms which we alone
Invent, for fashions differing from our own;
For all their customs are by nature wrought,
But we, by art, unteach what nature taught.
    Piz. In Spain, our springs, like old men's children, be
Decayed and withered from the infancy;
No kindly showers fall on our barren earth,
To hatch the season in a timely birth;

Our summer such a russet livery wears,
As in a garment often dyed appears.
   Cort. Here nature spreads her fruitful sweetness round,
Breathes on the air, and broods upon the ground;
Here days and nights the only seasons be;
The sun no climate does so gladly see;
When forced from hence, to view our parts, he mourns,
Takes little journeys, and makes quick returns.
   Vasq. Methinks, we walk in dreams on Fairyland,
Where golden ore lies mixt with common sand;
Each downfall of a flood, the mountains pour
From their rich bowels, rolls a silver shower.
   Cort. Heaven from all ages wisely did provide
This wealth, and for the bravest nation hide,
Who, with four hundred foot and forty horse,[1]
Dare boldly go a new-found world to force.
   Piz. Our men, though valiant, we should find too few,
But Indians join the Indians to subdue;
Traxallan, shook by Montezuma's powers,
Has, to resist his forces, called in ours.
   Vasq. Rashly to arm against so great a king.
I hold not safe; nor is it just to bring
A war without a fair defiance made.
   Piz. Declare we first our quarrel; then invade.
   Cort. Myself, my king's ambassador will go;
Speak, Indian guide, how far to Mexico?
   Ind. Your eyes can scarce so far a prospect make,
As to discern the city on the lake;
But that broad causeway will direct your way,
And you may reach the town by noon of day.
   Cort. Command a party of our Indians out,
With a strict charge, not to engage, but scout;
By noble ways we conquest will prepare;
First, offer peace, and, that refused, make war.

[Exeunt.]

Act I. Scene II. — A Temple.

   Vasq. His power must needs unquestioned be below,
For he in heaven an empire can bestow.
   Mont. Empires in heaven he with more ease may give,

---

[1] *foot . . . horse:* I.e., foot soldiers and horsemen.

And you, perhaps, would with less thanks receive:
But heaven has need of no such viceroy here,
Itself bestows the crowns that monarchs wear.

   Piz. You wrong his power, as you mistake our end,
Who came thus far religion to extend.

   Mont. He, who religion truly understands,
Knows its extent must be in men, not lands.

   Odm. But who are those that truth must propagate
Within the confines of my father's state?

   Vasq. Religious men, who hither must be sent
As awful guides of heavenly government;
To teach you penance, fasts, and abstinence,
To punish bodies for the soul's offence.

   Mont. Cheaply you sin, and punish crimes with ease,
Not as the offended, but the offenders please;
First injure heaven, and, when its wrath is due,
Yourselves prescribe it how to punish you.

   Odm. What numbers of these holy men must come?

   Piz. You shall not want, each village shall have some;
Who, though the royal dignity they own,
Are equal to it, and depend on none.

   Guy. Depend on none! you treat them sure in state,
For 'tis their plenty does their pride create.

. . . .

   Mont. Those ghostly kings would parcel out my power,
And all the fatness of my land devour.
That monarch sits not safely on his throne
Who bears, within, a power that shocks his own.
They teach obedience to imperial sway,
But think it sin if they themselves obey.

   Vasq. It seems, then, our religion you accuse.
And peaceful homage to our king refuse?

   Mont. Your Gods I slight not, but will keep my own;
My crown is absolute, and holds of none.
I cannot in a base subjection live.
Nor suffer you to take, though I would give.

   Cort. Is this your answer, sir?

   Mont. —— This, as a prince,
Bound to my people's and my crown's defence.
I must return; but, as a man, by you
Redeemed from death, all gratitude is due.

Cort. It was an act my honour bound me to:
But what I did, were I again to do,
I could not do it on my honour's score,
For love would now oblige me to do more.
Is no way left that we may yet agree?
Must I have war, yet have no enemy?
  Vasq. He has refused all terms of peace to take.
  Mont. Since we must fight, hear, heavens, what prayers I make!
First, to preserve this ancient state and me.
But if your doom the fall of both decree,
Grant only he, who has such honour shown,
When I am dust, may fill my empty throne!
  Cort. To make me happier than that wish can do,
Lies not in all your Gods to grant, but you

· · · · · · · · · · · · · · · ·

Act V. Scene II. — *A Prison.*

MONTEZUMA, *Indian High Priest, bound:*
PIZARRO, *Spaniards with swords drawn, a Christian Priest.*

  Piz. Thou hast not yet discovered[2] all thy store.
  Mont. I neither can nor will discover more;
The gods will punish you, if they be just;
The gods will plague your sacrilegious lust.
  Chr. Priest. Mark how this impious heathen justifies
His own false gods, and our true God denies;
How wickedly he has refused his wealth,
And hid his gold, from Christian hands, by stealth;
Down with him, kill him, merit heaven thereby.
  Ind. High Pr. Can heaven be author of such cruelty?
  Piz. Since neither threats nor kindness will prevail,
We must by other means your minds assail;
Fasten the engines[3]: stretch 'em at their length,
And pull the straightened cords with all your strength.
                [*They fasten them to the rack, and then pull them.*]
  Mont. The gods, who made me once a king, shall know,
I still am worthy to continue so:
Though now the subject of your tyranny,

---

[2] *discovered:* Revealed.
[3] *engines:* Implements of torture.

I'll plague you worse than you can punish me.
Know, I have gold, which you shall never find;
No pains, no tortures, shall unlock my mind.
  Chr. Pr. Pull harder yet; he does not feel the rack.
  Mont. Pull till my veins break, and my sinews crack.
  Ind. High Pr. When will you end your barbarous cruelty?
I beg not to escape, I beg to die.
  Mont. Shame on thy priesthood, that such prayers can bring!
Is it not brave, to suffer with thy king?
When monarchs suffer, gods themselves bear part;
Then well mayest thou, who but my vassal art:
I charge thee, dare not groan, nor show one sign,
Thou at thy torments dost the least repine.
  Ind. High Pr. You took an oath, when you received the crown,
The heavens should pour their usual blessings down;
The sun should shine, the earth its fruits produce,
And nought be wanting to your subjects' use;
Yet we with famine were opprest, and now
Must to the yoke of cruel masters bow.
  Mont. If those above, who made the world, could be
Forgetful of it, why then blamest thou me?
  Chr. Pr. Those pains, O prince, thou sufferest now, are light
Compared to those, which, when thy soul takes flight,
Immortal, endless, thou must then endure,
Which death begins, and time can never cure.
  Mont. Thou art deceived; for whensoe'er I die,
The Sun, my father, bears my soul on high;
He lets me down a beam, and mounted there,
He draws it back, and pulls me through the air;
I in the eastern parts, and rising sky,
You in heaven's downfall, and the west must lie.
  Chr. Pr. Fond man, by heathen ignorance misled,
Thy soul destroying when thy body's dead;
Change yet thy faith, and buy eternal rest.
  Ind. High Pr. Die in your own, for our belief is best.
  Mont. In seeking happiness you both agree;
But in the search, the paths so different be,
That all religions with each other fight,
While only one can lead us in the right.
But till that one hath some more certain mark,

Poor human-kind must wander in the dark;
And suffer pain eternally below,
For that, which here we cannot come to know.
    Chr. Pr. That, which we worship, and which you believe,
From nature's common hand we both receive;
All, under various names, adore and love
One Power immense, which ever rules above.
Vice to abhor, and virtue to pursue,
Is both believed and taught by us and you;
But here our worship takes another way —
    Mont. Where both agree, 'tis there most safe to stay:
For what's more vain than public light to shun,
And set up tapers,[4] while we see the sun?
    Chr. Pr. Though nature teaches whom we should adore,
By heavenly beams we still discover more.
    Mont. Or this must be enough, or to mankind
One equal way to bliss is not designed;
For though some more may know, and some know less,
Yet all must know enough for happiness.
    Chr. Pr. If in this middle way you still pretend[5]
To stay, your journey never will have end.
    Mont. Howe'er, 'tis better in the midst to stay,
Than wander farther in uncertain way.
    Chr. Pr. But we by martyrdom our faith avow.
    Mont. You do no more than I for ours do now.
To prove religion true —
If either wit or sufferings would suffice,
All faiths afford the constant and the wise;
And yet even they, by education swayed,
In age defend what infancy obeyed.
    Chr. Pr. Since age by erring childhood is misled,
Refer yourself to our unerring head.
    Mont. Man, and not err! what reason can you give?
    Chr. Pr. Renounce that carnal reason, and believe.
    Mont. The light of nature should I thus betray,
'Twere to wink[6] hard, that I might see the day.

[4] *tapers:* Candles.
[5] *pretend:* Attempt.
[6] *wink:* Squint.

Chr. Pr. Condemn not yet the way you do not know;
I'll make your reason judge what way to go.
      Mont. 'Tis much too late for me new ways to take,
Who have but one short step of life to make.
      Piz. Increase their pains, the cords are yet too slack.
      Chr. Pr. I must by force convert him on the rack.
      Ind. High Pr. I faint away, and find I can no more:
Give leave, O king, I may reveal thy store.
And free myself from pains, I cannot bear.
      Mont. Think'st thou I lie on beds of roses here,
Or in a wanton bath stretched at my ease?
Die, slave, and with thee die such thoughts as these.

                              [*High Priest turns aside, and dies.*]

      Enter CORTEZ *attended by Spainards, he speaks entering.*

      Cort. On pain of death, kill none but those who fight;
I must repent me of this bloody night;
Slaughter grows murder when it goes too far,
And makes a massacre what was a war;
Sheathe all your weapons, and in silence move.
'Tis sacred here to beauty, and to love.
Ha —   [*Sees* MONT.]
What dismal sight is this, which takes from me
All the delight, that waits on victory!

                              [*Runs to take him off the rack.*]

Make haste: How now, religion, do you frown?
Haste, holy avarice, and help him down,
Ah, father, father, what do I endure

                              [*Embracing* MONT.]

To see these wounds my pity cannot cure!
      Mont. Am I so low that you should pity bring,
And give an infant's comfort to a king?
Ask these, if I have once unmanly groaned;
Or aught have done deserving to be moaned.
      Cort. Did I not charge, thou shouldst not stir from hence?

                                              [*To* PIZ.]

But martial law shall punish thy offence.
And you,   [*To the Christian Priest.*]
Who saucily teach monarchs to obey,
And the wide world in narrow cloisters sway;
Set up by kings as humble aids of power,

You that which bred you, viper-like, devour,
You enemies of crowns —
   Chr. Pr. Come, let's away,
We but provoke his fury by our stay.
   Cort. If this go free, farewell that discipline,
Which did in Spanish camps severely shine;
Accursed gold, 'tis thou hast caused these crimes;
Thou turn'st our steel against thy parent climes!
And into Spain wilt fatally be brought,
Since with the price of blood thou here art bought.

                        [*Exeunt Priest and* PIZARRO.]
             [CORTEZ *kneels by* MONTEZUMA, *and weeps.*]
   Cort. Can you forget those crimes they did commit?
   Mont. I'll do what for my dignity is fit:
Rise, sir, I'm satisfied the fault was theirs;
Trust me, you make me weep to see your tears;
Must I cheer you?
   Cort. Ah heavens!
   Mont. You're much to blame;
Your grief is cruel, for it shows my shame,
Does my lost crown to my remembrance bring;
But weep not you, and I'll be still a king.

. . . .

   Cort. Live, and enjoy more than your conqueror;   [*To* GUYOMAR.]
Take all my love, and share in all my power.
   Guy. Think me not proudly rude, if I forsake
Those gifts I cannot with my honour take;
I for my country fought, and would again,
Had I yet left a country to maintain;
But since the gods decreed it otherwise,
I never will on its dear ruins rise.
   Alib. Of all your goodness leaves to our dispose,
Our liberty's the only gift we choose;
Absence alone can make our sorrows less;
And not to see what we can ne'er redress.
   Guy. Northward, beyond the mountains, we will go,
Where rocks lie covered with eternal snow,
Thin herbage in the plains and fruitless fields,
The sand no gold, the mine no silver yields;
There love and freedom we'll in peace enjoy;
No Spaniards will that colony destroy.

We to ourselves will all our wishes grant;
And, nothing coveting, can nothing want.
   Cort. First your great father's funeral pomp provide;
That done, in peace your generous exiles guide;
While I loud thanks pay to the powers above,
Thus doubly blest, with conquest and with love.

[Exeunt.]

RICHARD STEELE

On Inkle and Yarico (The Spectator, No. 11)

JOSEPH ADDISON

On a Slave Love-Triangle (The Spectator, No. 215)

   Richard Steele's retelling of the story of Inkle and Yarico in *The Spectator* (1711) is, like *Oroonoko*, a tale of betrayal. It is used by Steele to illustrate, not the injustices of slavery, but the mistreatment of women by men. The earliest version of the story seems to be the one narrated in Jean Mocquet's *Voyages* (1616), which was translated into English in 1696. Steele's source, however, as he acknowledges, was the version narrated by Richard Ligon in his history of Barbados, published in 1657 (see pp. 355–65). Steele adds several new elements to the story, naming the Englishman Inkle (a kind of linen tape used for trimming fabric), and elaborating a romantic relationship that remains implicit, at best, in Ligon's account.

   Alongside the enormous growth of the British slave trade, the eighteenth century saw the inception and slow advance of antislavery sentiment in England, and the abolitionist potential of the Inkle and Yarico story was fully realized as it underwent various poetic and dramatic retellings in the course of the century. Versions of the story appeared with increasing frequency beginning in the mid-1730s, but Weddell's play *Incle and Yarico* (printed in 1742 but probably not performed) represents the first effort to use the tale as a vehicle for protesting against slavery; the author acknowledges a debt to Steele in the preface. The century's most popular dramatization was *Inkle and Yarico* (1787), a comic opera by George Colman the younger. This version supplies the main characters with a pair of farcical attendants — Wowski ("an angel of a rather darker sort") and Trudge; their courtship stands as a model of fidelity against the faithless behavior of Inkle, who attempts to sell Yarico to the Governor of Barbados and to marry the Governor's daughter. Wowski and Trudge condemn the institution of slavery, and all ends well when Inkle reforms and marries Yarico in the last scene.

Joseph Addison's story of a love triangle among slaves is meant to illustrate the dangers of unregulated passion, and the value of moral education. Addison describes a combination of sincerity and "Barbarity" that resembles, in some respects, the condition that Montaigne describes in his essay on cannibals. However, Addison emphasizes the tragic aspect of unrestrained emotion; rather than striving to illustrate the uncorrupted nobility of Montaigne's Indians, or the romantic purity that Behn ascribes to Oroonoko, Addison tells a story of "savage" love that serves, by contrast, to celebrate the blessings of civilization. Addison's tale, far less amenable to an antislavery interpretation than Steele's, also had fewer imitators, and it never gained the currency of the Yarico and Inkle story. Steele, however, later wrote of a similar love triangle in which one of the men sleeps with his friend's wife and then commits suicide (see *The Lover* 36, 1714).

Steele (1672–1729) and Addison (1672–1719) had both engaged in political writing before collaborating on *The Tatler* (1709–11) and *The Spectator* (1711–12; 1714), two periodicals that are generally credited with reforming prose writing in England, simplifying its style, softening its satire, and promoting "common sense." As Whigs, Steele and Addison supported the developing commercial interests against the Tories' more traditional model of governance and authority organized around the monarchy. The two writers' essays, often didactic in tone, promoted social intercourse, frequently examining problems of love and marriage. Though noted for their condescending treatment of women as "the fair sex," Addison and Steele were among the first periodical writers to treat women as a significant part of their readership and to print a substantial number of letters from women subscribers.

The texts are taken from *The Spectator,* no. 11 (March 13, 1711), and no. 215 (Nov. 6, 1711), in *The Spectator,* 3 vols., ed. Donald F. Bond (Oxford: Clarendon, 1965) 1: 47–51, 2: 339–41.

On Inkle and Yarico

No. 11.   *Tuesday, March* 13, 1711

Dat veniam corvis, vexat censura columbas.[1]
Juv.

Arietta is visited by all Persons of both Sexes, who have any Pretence[2] to Wit and Gallantry. She is in that time of Life which is neither affected with the Follies of Youth, or Infirmities of Age; and her Conversation is so mixed with Gaiety and Prudence, that she is agreeable both to the Young and the Old. Her Behaviour is very frank, without being in the least blameable; and as she is out of the Tract of any amorous or ambitious Pursuits of her own, her Visitants entertain her with Accounts of themselves very freely, whether they concern their Passions or their Interests. I made her a Visit this Afternoon, having been formerly introduced to the Honour of her Acquaintance, by my Friend *Will. Honeycomb,* who has prevailed upon her to admit me sometimes into her Assembly, as a civil, inoffensive Man. I found her accompanied with one Person only, a Common-Place Talker, who, upon my Entrance, rose, and after a very slight Civility sat down again; then turning to *Arietta,* pursued his Discourse, which I found was upon the old Topick, of Constancy in Love. He went on with great Facility in repeating what he talks every Day of his Life; and, with the Ornaments of insignificant Laughs and Gestures, enforced his Arguments by Quotations out of Plays and Songs, which allude to the Perjuries of the Fair, and the general Levity of Women. Methought he strove to shine more than ordinarily in his Talkative Way, that he might insult my Silence, and distinguish himself before a Woman of *Arietta*'s Taste and Understanding. She had often an Inclination to interrupt him, but could find no Opportunity, 'till the Larum[3] ceased of its self; which it did not 'till he had repeated and murdered the celebrated Story of the *Ephesian* Matron.[4]

---

[1] *Dat veniam corvis, vexat censurat columbas:* "He tolerates the crows and censures the doves." Juvenal, *Satires,* 2.63.

[2] *Pretence:* Claim.

[3] *Larum:* Hubbub, tumultuous noise.

[4] *the celebrated Story of the Ephesian Matron:* A story about the fickleness of women, from Petronius Arbiter's first-century C.E. *Satyricon.* It tells how a woman of Ephesus mourned her husband's death, and nearly starved herself to death, until a soldier persuaded her to put an end to her fast and to her chaste behavior.

Arietta seemed to regard this Piece of Railery as an Outrage done to her Sex, as indeed I have always observed that Women, whether out of a nicer[5] Regard to their Honour, or what other Reason I cannot tell, are more sensibly touched with those general Aspersions, which are cast upon their Sex, than Men are by what is said of theirs.

When she had a little recovered her self from the serious Anger she was in, she replied in the following manner.

Sir, When I consider, how perfectly new all you have said on this Subject is, and that the Story you have given us is not quite two thousand Years Old, I cannot but think it a Piece of Presumption to dispute with you: But your Quotations put me in Mind of the Fable of the Lion and the Man. The Man walking with that noble Animal, showed him, in the Ostentation of Human Superiority, a Sign of a Man killing a Lion. Upon which the Lion said very justly, *We Lions are none of us Painters, else we could show a hundred Men killed by Lions, for one Lion killed by a Man.* You Men are Writers, and can represent us Women as Unbecoming as you please in your Works, while we are unable to return the Injury. You have twice or thrice observed in your Discourse, that Hipocrisy is the very Foundation of our Education; and that an Ability to dissemble our Affections, is a professed Part of our Breeding. These, and such other Reflections, are sprinkled up and down the Writings of all Ages, by Authors, who leave behind them Memorials of their Resentment against the Scorn of particular Women, in Invectives against the whole Sex. Such a Writer, I doubt not, was the celebrated *Petronius,* who invented the pleasant Aggravations of the Frailty of the *Ephesian* Lady; but when we consider this Question between the Sexes, which has been either a Point of Dispute or Raillery ever since there were Men and Women, let us take Facts from plain People, and from such as have not either Ambition or Capacity to embellish their Narrations with any Beauties of Imagination. I was the other Day amusing my self with *Ligon*'s Account of *Barbadoes;*[6] and, in Answer to your well-wrought Tale, I will give (as it dwells upon my Memory) out of that honest Traveller, in his fifty fifth Page, the History of *Inkle* and *Yarico.*

Mr. *Thomas Inkle* of *London,* aged 20 Years, embarked in the *Downs* on the good Ship called the *Achilles,* bound for the *West-Indies,* on the 16th of *June* 1647, in order to improve his Fortune by

---

[5] *nicer:* More delicate.

[6] *Ligon's Account of Barbadoes:* Richard Ligon's *True and Exact History of the Island of Barbados* (1657); see pp. 355–65.

Trade and Merchandize. Our Adventurer was the third Son of an eminent Citizen, who had taken particular Care to instill into his Mind an
early Love of Gain, by making him a perfect Master of Numbers, and
consequently giving him a quick View of Loss and Advantage, and
preventing the natural Impulses of his Passions, by Prepossession
toward his Interests. With a Mind thus turned, young *Inkle* had a Person every way agreeable, a ruddy Vigour in his Countenance, Strength
in his Limbs, with Ringlets of fair Hair loosely flowing on his Shoulders. It happened, in the Course of the Voyage, that the *Achilles,* in
some Distress, put into a Creek on the Main of *America,* in Search of
Provisions: The Youth, who is the Hero of my Story, among others,
went ashore on this Occasion. From their first Landing they were
observed by a Party of *Indians,* who hid themselves in the Woods for
that Purpose. The *English* unadvisedly marched a great distance from
the Shore into the Country, and were intercepted by the Natives, who
slew the greatest Number of them. Our Adventurer escaped among
others, by flying into a Forest. Upon his coming into a remote and
pathless Part of the Wood, he threw himself, tired and breathless, on a
little Hillock, when an *Indian* Maid rushed from a Thicket behind
him: After the first Surprize, they appeared mutually agreeable to each
other. If the *European* was highly Charmed with the Limbs, Features,
and wild Graces of the Naked *American;* the *American* was no less
taken with the Dress, Complexion and Shape of an *European,* covered
from Head to Foot. The *Indian* grew immediately enamoured of him,
and consequently sollicitous for his Preservation: She therefore conveyed him to a Cave, where she gave him a Delicious Repast of Fruits,
and led him to a Stream to slake his Thirst. In the midst of these
good Offices, she would sometimes play with his Hair, and delight in
the Opposition of its Colour, to that of her Fingers: Then open his
Bosome, then laugh at him for covering it. She was, it seems, a Person
of Distinction, for she every day came to him in a different Dress, of
the most beautiful Shells, Bugles and Bredes.[7] She likewise brought
him a great many Spoils, which her other Lovers had presented to her;
so that his Cave was richly adorned with all the spotted Skins of
Beasts, and most Party-coloured[8] Feathers of Fowls, which that World
afforded. To make his Confinement more tolerable, she would carry
him in the Dusk of the Evening, or by the favour of Moon-light, to

[7] *Bugles and Bredes:* Beads and braid.
[8] *Party-coloured:* Multicolored.

unfrequented Groves and Solitudes, and show him where to lye down in Safety, and sleep amidst the Falls of Waters, and Melody of Nightingales. Her Part was to watch and hold him in her Arms, for fear of her Country-men, and wake him on Occasions to consult his Safety. In this manner did the Lovers pass away their Time, till they had learn'd a Language of their own, in which the Voyager communicated to his Mistress, how happy he should be to have her in his Country, where she should be Cloathed in such Silks as his Wastecoat was made of, and be carried in Houses drawn by Horses, without being exposed to Wind or Weather. All this he promised her the Enjoyment of, without such Fears and Alarms as they were there Tormented with. In this tender Correspondence these Lovers lived for several Months, when *Yarico,* instructed by her Lover, discovered a Vessel on the Coast, to which she made Signals, and in the Night, with the utmost Joy and Satisfaction accompanied him to a Ships-Crew of his Country-Men, bound for *Barbadoes.* When a Vessel from the Main arrives in that Island, it seems the Planters come down to the Shoar, where there is an immediate Market of the *Indians* and other Slaves, as with us of Horses and Oxen.

To be short, Mr. *Thomas Inkle,* now coming into *English* Territories, began seriously to reflect upon his loss of Time, and to weigh with himself how many Days Interest of his Mony he had lost during his Stay with *Yarico.* This Thought made the Young Man very pensive, and careful what Account he should be able to give his Friends of his Voyage. Upon which Considerations, the prudent and frugal young Man sold *Yarico* to a *Barbadian* Merchant; notwithstanding that the poor Girl, to incline him to commiserate her condition, told him that she was with Child by him: But he only made use of that Information, to rise in his Demands upon the Purchaser.

I was so touch'd with this Story, (which I think should be always a Counterpart to the *Ephesian* Matron) that I left the Room with Tears in my Eyes; which a Woman of *Arietta*'s good Sense, did, I am sure, take for greater Applause, than any Compliments I could make her.

On a Slave Love-Triangle

No. 215   *Tuesday, November 6, 1711*

> . . . *Ingenuas didicisse fideliter artes*
> *Emollit mores, nec sinit esse feros.*[1]
>   Ov.

I consider an Human Soul without Education like Marble in the
Quarry, which shews none of its inherent Beauties, till the Skill of the
Polisher fetches out the Colours, makes the Surface shine, and discovers
every ornamental Cloud, Spot and Vein that runs through the Body
of it. Education, after the same manner, when it works upon a noble
Mind, draws out to View every latent Vertue and Perfection, which
without such Helps are never able to make their Appearance.

If my Reader will give me leave to change the Allusion so soon upon
him, I shall make use of the same Instance to illustrate the Force of
Education, which *Aristotle* has brought to explain his Doctrine of
Substantial Forms, when he tells us, that a Statue lies hid in a Block
of Marble; and that the Art of the Statuary only clears away the superfluous Matter, and removes the Rubbish.[2] The Figure is in the Stone,
the Sculptor only finds it. What Sculpture is to a Block of Marble, Education is to an Human Soul. The Philosopher, the Saint, or the Hero,
the Wise, the Good, or the Great Man, very often lie hid and concealed
in a Plebean,[3] which a proper Education might have disenterred, and
have brought to Light. I am therefore much delighted with Reading
the Accounts of Savage Nations, and with contemplating those
Vertues which are wild and uncultivated; to see Courage exerting it
self in Fierceness, Resolution in Obstinacy, Wisdom in Cunning,
Patience in Sullenness and Despair.

Mens Passions operate variously, and appear in different kinds of
Actions, according as they are more or less rectified and swayed by
Reason. When one hears of Negroes, who upon the Death of their
Masters, or upon changing their Service, hang themselves upon the
next Tree, as it frequently happens in our *American* Plantations, who
can forbear admiring their Fidelity, though it expresses it self in so

---

[1] *Ingenus . . . feros:* "Faithful study of the liberal arts softens the manners and prevents cruelty." Ovid, *Ex Ponto,* 2.9.47–48.

[2] *Aristotle . . . removes the Rubbish:* Aristotle is credited with this theory in Dio-
genes Laertius, *Vitam Philosophorum,* 5.33.

[3] *Plebean:* Someone of low rank or birth.

dreadful a manner? What might not that Savage Greatness of Soul, which appears in these poor Wretches on many Occasions, be raised to, were it rightly cultivated? And what Colour of Excuse can there be for the Contempt with which we treat this Part of our Species; That we should not put them upon the common foot of Humanity, that we should only set an insignificant Fine upon the Man who murders them; nay, that we should, as much as in us lies, cut them off from the Prospects of Happiness in another World as well as in this, and deny them that which we look upon as the proper Means for attaining it?

Since I am engaged on this Subject, I cannot forbear mentioning a Story which I have lately heard, and which is so well attested, that I have no manner of reason to suspect the Truth of it. I may call it a kind of wild Tragedy that passed about twelve Years ago at St. *Christophers,* one of our *British* Leeward Islands. The Negroes who were concern'd in it, were all of them the Slaves of a Gentleman who is now in *England.*

This Gentlemen among his Negroes had a young Woman, who was looked upon as a most extraordinary Beauty by those of her own Complexion. He had at the same time two young Fellows who were likewise Negroes and Slaves, remarkable for the Comeliness of their Persons, and for the Friendship which they bore to one another. It unfortunately happened that both of them fell in Love with the Female Negro abovementioned, who would have been very glad to have taken either of them for her Husband, provided they could agree between themselves which should be the Man. But they were both so passionately in Love with her, that neither of them could think of giving her up to his Rival; and at the same time were so true to one another, that neither of them would think of gaining her without his Friend's Consent. The Torments of these two Lovers were the Discourse of the Family to which they belonged, who could not forbear observing the strange Complication of Passions which perplexed the Hearts of the poor Negroes, that often dropped Expressions of the Uneasiness they underwent, and how impossible it was for either of them ever to be happy.

After a long Struggle between Love and Friendship, Truth and Jealousy, they one Day took a Walk together into a Wood, carrying their Mistress along with them: Where, after abundance of Lamentations, they stabbed her to the Heart, of which she immediately died. A Slave who was at his Work not far from the Place where this astonishing piece of Cruelty was committed, hearing the Shrieks of the dying Person, ran to see what was the Occasion of them. He there discovered the Woman lying dead upon the Ground, with the two Negroes on each side of her, kissing the dead Corps, weeping over it, and beating their Breasts in the utmost Agonies of Grief and Despair. He immediately ran to the *English* Family with the News of what he had seen; who upon coming to the Place saw the Woman dead, and the two Negroes expiring by her with Wounds they had given themselves.

We see, in this amazing Instance of Barbarity, what strange Disorders are bred in the Minds of those Men whose Passions are not regulated by Virtue, and disciplined by Reason. Though the Action which I have recited is in it self full of Guilt and Horror, it proceeded from a Temper of Mind which might have produced very noble Fruits, had it been informed and guided by a suitable Education.

It is therefore an unspeakable Blessing to be born in those Parts of the World where Wisdom and Knowledge flourish; though it must be confest, there are, even in these Parts, several poor uninstructed Persons, who are but little above the Inhabitants of those Nations of which I have been here speaking; as those who have had the Advantages of a more liberal Education rise above one another, by several different degrees of Perfection. For to return to our Statue in the Block of Marble, we see it sometimes only begun to be chipped, sometimes rough-hewn and but just sketched into an human Figure, sometimes we see the Man appearing distinctly in all his Limbs and Features, sometimes we find the Figure wrought up to a great Elegancy, but seldom meet with any to which the Hand of a *Phidias* or a *Praxiteles*[4] could not give several nice touches and Finishings.

Discourses of Morality, and Reflections upon human Nature, are the best Means we can make use of to improve our Minds, and gain a true Knowledge of our selves, and consequently to recover our Souls out of the Vice, Ignorance and Prejudice which naturally cleave to them. I have all along profest my self in this Paper a Promoter of these great Ends, and I flatter my self that I do from Day to Day contribute something to the polishing of Mens Minds; at least my Design is laudable, whatever the Execution may be. I must confess that I am not a little encouraged in it by many Letters, which I receive from unknown Hands, in Approbation of my Endeavours, and must take this Opportunity of returning my Thanks to those who write them, and excusing my self for not inserting several of them in my Papers, which I am sensible would be a very great Ornament to them. Should I publish the Praises which are so well penned, they would do Honour to the Persons who write them; but my publishing of them would I fear be a sufficient Instance to the World that I did not deserve them.

[4] *a Phidias or a Praxitiles:* Ancient Greek sculptors.

DANIEL DEFOE

From *Robinson Crusoe*

Daniel Defoe (1659–1731), best known as the author of *Robinson Crusoe* (1719) and *Moll Flanders* (1724), devoted most of his career to political journalism and social commentary, publishing periodical essays and scores (possibly hundreds) of books and pamphlets (many of them anonymous) before he began writing the narratives for which he is now remembered. The first three passages reprinted here occur early in the novel, before the shipwreck that leaves Crusoe stranded on an island. At this point in his narrative, Crusoe has escaped with his life after a disastrous first journey at the age of nineteen, and has completed his only entirely successful voyage — a trip to Guinea, where he has traded £40 worth of "Toys and Trifles" for £300 worth of gold dust. It is the success of that transaction that has convinced him to "set up for a *Guiney* Trader" — a profession that typically would also include the buying and selling of slaves. The last passage occurs immediately after Crusoe's attack on a group of cannibals and his rescue of their would-be victim, Friday.

Defoe himself defended the slave trade in his periodical essays in the *Review* and in several pamphlets, including *An Essay upon the Trade to Africa* (1711) and *A Brief Account of the Present State of the African Trade* (1713); he also owned stock in the Royal African Company. While he supported the company's ventures on mercantilist grounds, endorsing the growth of English commerce, he also lamented the decline of an imperialist model of expansion that might bring glory and even greater wealth. In a 1720 essay in *The Manufacturer*, after trivializing the "*Exchange-Alley* Discoveries" encouraged by the financiers behind such joint stock ventures as the Royal African Company, Defoe asks, "Why has no bold Undertaker follow'd the glorious Sir *Walter Raleigh* up the River of *Amazon*, the *Rio Parano*, and the Great *Oroonoque* [i.e., the Orinoko], where thousands of Nations remain undiscover'd, and where the Wealth . . . exceeds all that has ever been conquer'd or discover'd in the *American* World?" Published only a year after *Crusoe*, the essay suggests that in placing his island "near the mouth of the great river of Oroonoque," Defoe meant to identify his hero as someone who might, in another age, have shared not only Raleigh's enterprising spirit but also, perhaps, his valor as a "conqueror."

The text is taken from *The Life and Strange Surprizing Adventures of Robinson Crusoe, of York, Mariner, Who lived Eight and Twenty years,*

all alone in an un-inhabited Island on the Coast of America, near the
Mouth of the Great River of Oroonoque; having been cast on Shore by
Shipwreck, wherein all the men perished but himself. With An Account
how he was at last strangely deliver'd by Pyrates, ed. Donald J. Crowley
(London: Oxford UP, 1972) 18–19, 21–23, 32—34, 205–6.

I was now set up for a *Guiney*[1] Trader; and my Friend, to my great
Misfortune, dying soon after his Arrival, I resolved to go the same
Voyage again, and I embark'd in the same Vessel with one who was his
Mate in the former Voyage, and had now got the Command of the
Ship. This was the unhappiest Voyage that ever Man made; for tho' I
did not carry quite 100 *l*. of my new gain'd Wealth, so that I had 200
left, and which I lodg'd with my Friend's Widow, who was very just to
me, yet I fell into terrible Misfortunes in this Voyage; and the first was
this, *viz*. Our Ship making her Course towards the *Canary* Islands, or
rather between those Islands and the *African* Shore, was surprised in
the Grey of the Morning, by a *Turkish* Rover of *Sallee*,[2] who gave
Chase to us with all the Sail she could make. We crowded also as much
Canvas as our Yards would spread, or our Masts carry, to have got
clear; but finding the Pirate gain'd upon us, and would certainly come
up with us in a few Hours, we prepar'd to fight; our Ship having 12
Guns, and the Rogue 18. About three in the Afternoon he came up
with us, and bringing to by Mistake, just athwart our Quarter, instead
of athwart our Stern, as he intended, we brought 8 of our Guns to bear
on that Side, and pour'd in a Broadside upon him, which made him
sheer off again, after returning our Fire, and pouring in also his small
Shot from near 200 men which he had on Board. However, we had not
a Man touch'd, all our Men keeping close. He prepar'd to attack us
again, and we to defend our selves; but laying us on Board the next
time upon our other Quarter, he entred 60 Men upon our Decks, who
immediately fell to cutting and hacking the Decks and Rigging. We
ply'd them with Small-shot, Half-Pikes, Powder-Chests, and such like,
and clear'd our Deck of them twice. However, to cut short this melan-
cholly Part of our Story, our Ship being disabled, and three of our Men

---

[1] *Guiney:* On the geographical range encompassed by this term, see the introduction
to Part Two, Chapter 3.
[2] *a Turkish Rover of Sallee:* The Moroccan seaport of Sallee was known for har-
bouring pirates. "Turkish" is used here generically for Muslim.

kill'd, and eight wounded, we were obliged to yield, and were carry'd all Prisoners into *Sallee,* a Port belonging to the *Moors.*

The Usage I had there was not so dreadful as at first I apprehended, nor was I carried up the Country to the Emperor's Court, as the rest of our Men were, but was kept by the Captain of the Rover, as his proper Prize, and made his Slave, being young and nimble, and fit for his Business. At this surprising Change of my Circumstances from a Merchant to a miserable Slave, I was perfectly overwhelmed; and now I look'd back upon my Father's prophetick Discourse to me, that I should be miserable, and have none to relieve me, which I thought was now so effectually brought to pass, that it could not be worse; that now the Hand of Heaven had overtaken me, and I was undone without Redemption. But alas! this was but a Taste of the Misery I was to go thro', as will appear in the Sequel of this Story.

As my new Patron or Master had taken me Home to his House, so I was in hopes that he would take me with him when he went to Sea again, believing that it would some time or other be his Fate to be taken by a *Spanish* or *Portugal* Man of War; and that then I should be set at Liberty. But this Hope of mine was soon taken away; for when he went to sea, he left me on Shoar to look after his little Garden, and do the common Drudgery of Slaves about his House; and when he came home again from his Cruise, he order'd me to lye in the Cabbin to look after the Ship.

Here I meditated nothing but my Escape; and what Method I might take to effect it, but found no Way that had the least Probability in it: Nothing presented to make the Supposition of it rational; for I had no Body to communicate it to, that would embark with me; no Fellow-Slave, no *Englishman, Irishman,* or *Scotsman* there but my self; so that for two Years, tho' I often pleased my self with the Imagination, yet I never had the least encouraging Prospect of putting it in Practice. . . .

We went frequently out with this Boat a fishing, and as I was most dextrous to catch fish for him, he never went without me: It happen'd that he had appointed to go out in this Boat, either for Pleasure or for Fish, with two or three *Moors* of some Distinction in that Place, and for whom he had provided extraordinarily; and had therefore sent on board the Boat over Night, a larger Store of Provisions than ordinary; and had order'd me to get ready three Fuzees[3] with Powder and Shot, which were on board his Ship; for that they design'd some Sport of Fowling as well as Fishing.

[3] *Fuzees:* Light guns.

I got all things ready as he had directed, and waited the next Morning with the Boat, washed clean, her Antient and Pendants[4] out, and every thing to accomodate his Guests; when by and by my Patroon came on board alone, and told me his Guests had put off going, upon some Business that fell out, and order'd me with the Man and Boy, as usual, to go out with the Boat and catch them some Fish, for that his Friends were to sup at his House; and commanded that as soon as I had got some Fish I should bring it home to his House; all which I prepar'd to do.

This Moment my former Notions of Deliverance darted into my Thoughts, for now I found I was like to have a little Ship at my Command; and my Master being gone, I prepar'd to furnish my self, not for a fishing Business but for a Voyage; tho' I knew not, neither did I so much as consider whither I should steer; for any where to get out of that Place was my Way.

My first Contrivance was to make a Pretence to speak to this *Moor,* to get something for our Subsistance on board; for I told him we must not presume to eat of our Patroon's Bread, he said that was true; so he brought a large Basket of Rusk[5] or Bisket of their kind, and three Jarrs with fresh Water into the Boat; I knew where my Patroon's Case of Bottles stood, which it was evident by the make were taken out of some *English* Prize; and I convey'd them into the Boat while the *Moor* was on Shoar, as if they had been there before, for our Master: I convey'd also a great Lump of Bees-Wax into the Boat, which weighed above half a Hundred Weight, with a Parcel of Twine or Thread, a Hatchet, a Saw and a Hammer, all which were of great Use to us afterwards; especially the Wax to make Candles. Another Trick I try'd upon him, which he innocently came into also; his Name was *Ismael,* who they call *Muly* or *Moely,* so I call'd to him, *Moely* said I, our Patroon's Guns are on board the Boat, can you not get a little Powder and Shot, it may be we may kill some *Alcamies* (a Fowl like our *Curlieus)*[6] for our selves, for I know he keeps the Gunner's Stores in the Ship? Yes, *says he,* I'll bring some, and accordingly he brought a great Leather Pouch which held about a Pound and half of Powder, or rather more; and another with Shot, that had five or six Pound, with some Bullets; and put all into the Boat: At the same time I had found some Powder of my Master's in the Great Cabbin, with which I fill'd one of the large Bottles in the Case, which was almost empty;

---

[4] *Antient and Pendants:* Flag and pennants.
[5] *Rusk:* Bread broken into small pieces and refired to make it hard and crisp.
[6] *Curlieus:* I.e., curlews, long-legged wading birds with slender, curved bills.

pouring what was in it into another: and thus furnished with every thing needful, we sail'd out of the Port to fish: The Castle which is at the Entrance of the Port knew who we were, and took no Notice of us; and we were not above a Mile out of the Port before we hal'd in our Sail, and set us down to fish: The wind blew from the N.NE. which was contrary to my Desire; for had it blown southerly I had been sure to have made the Coast of *Spain,* and at least reacht to the Bay of *Cadiz;*[7] but my Resolutions were, blow which way it would, I would be gone from that horrid Place where I was, and leave the rest to Fate.

After we had fisht some time and catcht nothing, for when I had Fish on my Hook, I would not pull them up, that he might not see them; I said to the *Moor,* this will not do, our Master will not be thus serv'd, we must stand farther off: he thinking no harm agreed, and being in the head of the Boat set the Sails; and as I had the Helm I run the Boat out near a League farther, and then brought her too as if I would fish; when giving the Boy the Helm, I stept forward to where the *Moor* was, and making as if I stoopt for something behind him, I took him by Surprize with my Arm under his Twist,[8] and tost him clear over-board into the Sea; he rise[9] immediately, for he swam like a Cork, and call'd to me, begg'd to be taken in, told me he would go all over the World with me; he swam so strong after the Boat that he would have reacht me very quickly, there being but little Wind; upon which I stept into the Cabbin and fetching one of the Fowling-pieces,[10] I presented it at him, and told him, I had done him no hurt, and if he would be quiet I would do him none; but said I, you swim well enough to reach to the Shoar, and the Sea is calm, make the best of your Way to Shoar and I will do you no harm, but if you come near the Boat I'll shoot you thro' the Head; for I am resolved to have my Liberty; so he turn'd himself about and swam for the Shoar, and I make no doubt but he reacht it with Ease, for he was an Excellent Swimmer.

I could ha' been content to ha' taken this *Moor* with me, and ha' drown'd the Boy, but there was no venturing to trust him: When he was gone I turn'd to the Boy, who they call'd *Xury,* and said to him, *Xury,* if you will be faithful to me I'll make you a great Man, but if you will not stroak your Face to be true to me, *that is, swear by* Mahomet *and his Father's Beard,* I must throw you into the Sea too; the Boy smil'd

[7] *Cadiz:* A seaport in southwestern Spain.
[8] *Twist:* The groin.
[9] *Rise:* Rose.
[10] *Fowling-pieces:* A kind of gun.

in my Face and spoke so innocently that I could not mistrust him; and swore to be faithful to me, and go all over the World with me. . . .

In this Dilemma, as I was very pensive, I stept into the Cabbin and sat me down, *Xury* having the Helm, when on a suddain the Boy cry'd out, *Master, Master, a Ship with a Sail,* and the foolish Boy was frighted out of his Wits, thinking it must needs be some of his Master's Ships sent to pursue us, when, I knew we were gotten far enough out of their reach. I jump'd out of the Cabbin, and immediately saw not only the Ship, but what she was, *(viz.)* that it was a *Portuguese* Ship, and as I thought was bound to the Coast of *Guinea* for *Negroes.* But when I observ'd the Course she steer'd, I was soon convinc'd they were bound some other way, and did not design to come any nearer to the Shoar; upon which I stretch'd out to Sea as much as I could, resolving to speak with them if possible.

With all the Sail I could make, I found I should not be able to come in their Way, but that they would be gone by, before I could make any Signal to them; but after I had crowded to the utmost,[11] and began to despair, they it seems saw me by the help of their Perspective-Glasses,[12] and that it was some *European* Boat, which as they supposed must belong to some Ship that was lost, so they shortned Sail to let me come up. I was encouraged with this, and as I had my Patroon's Antient on Board, I made a Waft[13] of it to them for a Signal of Distress, and fir'd a Gun, both which they saw, for they told me they saw the Smoke, tho' they did not hear the Gun; upon these Signals they very kindly brought too, and lay by for me, and in about three Hours time I came up with them.

They ask'd me what I was, in *Portuguese,* and in *Spanish,* and in *French,* but I understood none of them; but at last a *Scots* Sailor who was on board, call'd to me, and I answer'd him, and told him I was an *Englishman,* that I had made my escape out of Slavery from the *Moors* at *Sallee;* then they bad me come on board, and very kindly took me in, and all my Goods.

It was an inexpressible Joy to me, that any one will believe, that I was thus deliver'd, as I exteem'd it, from such a miserable and almost hopeless Condition as I was in, and I immediately offered all I had to the Captain of the Ship, as a Return for my Deliverance; but he gener-

[11] *crowded to the utmost:* Set off at full speed.
[12] *Perspective-Glasses:* Telescopes.
[13] *Waft:* A signal made by waving.

ously told me, he would take nothing from me, but that all I had should be deliver'd safe to me when I came to the *Brasils,* for says he, *I have sav'd your Life on no other Terms than I would be glad to be saved my self, and it may one time or other be my Lot to be taken up in the same Condition; besides,* said he, *when I carry you to the* Brasils, *so great a way from your own Country, if I should take from you what you have, you will be starved there, and then I only take away that Life I have given. No, no, Seignor* Inglese, says he, *Mr.* Englishman, *I will carry you thither in Charity, and those things will help you to buy your Subsistance there and your Passage home again.*

As he was Charitable in his Proposal, so he was Just in the Performance to a tittle, for he ordered the Seamen that none should offer to touch any thing I had; then he took every thing into his own Possession, and gave me back an exact Inventory of them, that I might have them, even so much as my three Earthen Jarrs.

As to my Boat it was a very good one, and that he saw, and told me he would buy it of me for the Ship's use, and ask'd me what I would have for it? I told him he had been so generous to me in every thing, that I could not offer to make any Price of the Boat, but left it entirely to him, upon which he told me he would give me a Note of his Hand to pay me 80 Pieces of Eight[14] for it at *Brasil,* and when it came there, if any one offer'd to give more he would make it up; he offer'd me also 60 Pieces of Eight more for the Boy *Xury,* which I was loath to take, not that I was not willing to let the Captain have him, but I was very loath to sell the poor Boy's Liberty, who had assisted me so faithfully in procuring my own. However when I let him know my Reason, he own'd it to be just, and offer'd me this Medium, that he would give the Boy an Obligation[15] to set him free in ten Years, if he turn'd Christian; upon this, and *Xury* saying he was willing to go to him, I let the Captain have him.

We had a very good Voyage to the *Brasils,* and arrived in the *Bay de Todos los Santos,* or *All-Saints Bay,*[16] in about Twenty-two Days after. And now I was once more deliver'd from the most miserable of all Conditions of Life, and what to do next with my self I was now to consider.

---

[14] *Pieces of Eight:* Spanish silver dollars, or *pesos,* so called because they were worth eight *reals.*
[15] *Obligation:* Contract.
[16] *All-Saints Bay:* A harbor on the coast of Brazil.

The generous Treatment the Captain gave me, I can never enough remember; he would take nothing of me for my Passage, gave me twenty Ducats[17] for the Leopard's Skin, and forty for the Lyon's Skin which I had in my Boat, and caused every thing I had in the Ship to be punctually deliver'd me, and what I was willing to sell he bought, such as the Case of Bottles, two of my Guns, and a Piece of the Lump of Bees-wax, for I had made Candles of the rest; in a word, I made about 220 Pieces of Eight of all my Cargo, and with this Stock I went on Shoar in the *Brasils*. . . .

[While stranded on a desert island, Crusoe rescues a young man about to be killed by cannibals and describes him in the following passage.]

He was a comely handsome Fellow, perfectly well made; with straight strong Limbs, not too large; tall and well shap'd, and as I reckon, about twenty six Years of Age. He had a very good Countenance, not a fierce and surly Aspect; but seem'd to have something very manly in his Face, and yet he had all the Sweetness and Softness of an *European* in his Countenance too, especially when he smil'd. His Hair was long and black, not curl'd like Wool; his Forehead very high, and large, and a great Vivacity and sparking Sharpness in his Eyes. The colour of his Skin was not quite black, but very tawny; and yet not of an ugly yellow nauseous tawny, as the *Brasilians*, and *Virginians*, and other Natives of *America* are; but of a bright kind of a dun olive Colour, that had in it something very agreeable; tho' not very easy to describe. His Face was round, and plump; his Nose small, not flat like the Negroes, a very good Mouth, thin Lips, and his fine Teeth well set, and white as Ivory. After he had slumber'd, rather than slept, about half an Hour, he wak'd again, and comes out of the Cave to me; for I had been milking my Goats, which I had in the Enclosure just by: When he espy'd me, he came running to me, laying himself down again upon the Ground, with all the possible Signs of an humble thankful Disposition, making a many antick[18] Gestures to show it: At last he lays his Head flat upon the Ground, close to my Foot, and sets my other Foot upon his Head, as he had done before; and after this, made all the Signs to me of Subjection, Servitude, and Submission imaginable, to let me know, how he would serve me as long as he liv'd; I understood him in many Things, and let him know, I was very well

---

[17] *Ducats:* The ducat was a gold or silver coin, of varying value depending on its composition.
[18] *antick:* Grotesque, fantastic

pleas'd with him; in a little Time I began to speak to him, and teach him to speak to me; and first, I made him know his Name should be *Friday*, which was the Day I sav'd his Life; I call'd him so for the Memory of the Time; I likewise taught him to say *Master*, and then let him know, that was to be my Name; I likewise taught him to say, YES, and No, and to know the Meaning of them; I gave him some Milk, in an earthen Pot, and let him see me Drink it before him, and sop my Bread in it; and I gave him a Cake of Bread, to do the like, which he quickly comply'd with, and made Signs that it was very good for him.

3

West Africa
in the Triangular Trade

To the seventeenth- and eighteenth-century Englishmen who plied the triangular trade, Africa was more of a coast than a continent.[1] Cruising the periphery of what they called "Guinea" — an area extending approximately from the Senegal River to the Congo — their contacts with Africans were almost exclusively commercial. Most Europeans had very limited designs on Africa, in marked contrast to their ambitions in both North and South America. They indicated little desire to explore the interior of Guinea, to annex its territory, or to establish settlements. While the Guinea coast, especially the southward-facing shore of the Gulf of Guinea, bristled with the forts of the European strangers by the late seventeenth century, they were established at the sufferance of African rulers, who severely restricted the Europeans' movements, could cut off their supplies of commodities, and were expert at playing the different nationalities against one another. With the exception of Portugal, European governments positively forbade their representatives to alter any part of the land, and, in 1678, an agent of the British Royal African Company even expressed a preference for staying afloat and conducting all trade from ships,

---

[1] In addition to sources quoted in the text, information for this chapter comes from Acholonu; Blackburn, *Making;* Curtin, *Africa;* Curtin, *Atlantic;* Daaku; Davidson; K. Davies; Grant; Hewett; Inikori and Engerman; Jones; Kea; Law, *Slave Coast;* Lovejoy; Makepeace; Manning; Meredith; Thomas; and Uchendu.

explaining that, "Once settled ashore, a factor [agent] is absolutely under the command of the king where he lives, and is liable for the least displeasure to lose all the goods he has in his possession, with danger also to his life" (quoted in Thomas 226). A late seventeenth-century map of the southward-facing coast (see pp. 210 and 211) shows the heavy concentration of European "factories," or warehouses, for keeping and shipping commodities, including, increasingly, slaves, and indicates the limited knowledge Europeans then possessed about the interior of the country.

On the coastal map, just east of "Cabo Corso," (Cabo Cors on the map on page 211), you can see the name "Coromantyn" (Cormantyn), which designates the depot from which Oroonoko was supposedly taken in the early 1660s. The English established a stronghold at that spot shortly before 1630, and, although the fort was taken from them by the Dutch in 1661, they continued referring to the slaves from the Gold Coast (approximately the coast of modern Ghana) as "Coromantines" or "Cormantines." Arriving late, the English were not a truly significant European power in the region until the very end of the century. The Portuguese had been the first Europeans to sail the Guinea coast, and they were trading for slaves there as early as 1445. They sold captive Africans in Southern Europe and the Mediterranean basin before Columbus pointed the way toward new continents. Holding the islands of Madeira and the Azores, which gave them strategic advantages, the Portuguese also began working large plantations with slaves much farther south, at São Tomé. When the Spanish began conquering, mining, and planting Mexico and Peru, the Portuguese supplied them with slaves, and by 1530, they were shipping Africans to their own colony of Brazil, the country that would eventually absorb over one third of the approximately eleven million[2] Africans taken across the Atlantic between 1500 and 1870. Pope Nicholas V approved the Portuguese monopoly on the trade in 1454, but Genoan and Spanish interlopers competed with the Portuguese throughout the fifteenth century, and later in the sixteenth century the trade was increasingly carried on by Spanish merchants.

A few Englishmen briefly attempted to cut into the Spanish and Portugese control of the slave trade in the sixteenth century. In the

---

[2] Estimates of the number of enslaved Africans brought to America differ, with Curtin (1969) placing the figure between nine and ten million and Inikori placing it at fifteen-and-a-half million. We are using the figures provided by Thomas: approximately thirteen million taken from Africa and eleven million delivered alive to America (804–05).

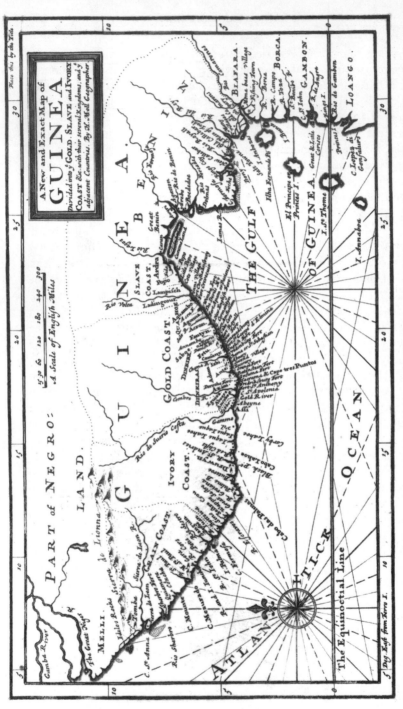

The map of Guinea was published in the English translation of Willem Bosman's *A New and Accurate Description of the Coast of Guinea*, London, 1705. It shows the coast of the Gulf of Guinea in the late seventeenth century, identifying the places where European nations had established forts from which slaves were shipped to the Americas. Courtesy of the John Carter Brown Library at Brown University.

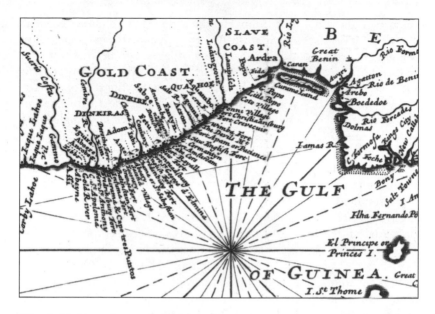

The Gold Coast (here enlarged from the map on page 210) bristles with the names of numerous European forts, testifying to the briskness of the traffic there. The map shows many names that appear either in *Oroonoko* or in this chapter's selections: "Cormantyn" (identified as Oroonoko's "kingdom"), "Annamaboe" (homeland of the "Young Prince of Annamaboe"), and "Cabo Corso" (or "Cape Coast" from which Cugoano embarked) are all within a few miles of one another on the Gold Coast; "Commendo" (shown as "Comany," described by the anonymous French writer) is farther west, and Why-daw (here "Fida," where Phillips traded for slaves and the correspondents of the Royal African Company were stationed) is farther east on the Slave Coast. The Gambia River (site of Jobson's travels and Job Ben Solomon's abduction) is in the top left-hand corner of the full map on page 210. Just under it, the mapmaker wrongly identifies what is probably the Gêba River as "The Great Niger River," a common mistake before 1798, for it was not until that year that the Niger was proved to flow from west to east, dividing into a fan shaped delta where it empties into the Gulf of Guinea in the region labeled "C. Formosa" on this map. This is the region from which Equiano was shipped. Courtesy of the John Carter Brown Library at Brown University.

reign of Elizabeth I, one John Hawkins raided the Guinea coast in search of slaves to sell in Spanish America, stealing the cargoes of Portuguese slavers and decimating some villages on the Sierra Leone River; but he was soon imprisoned by the Spanish, and his countrymen were largely inactive in the African trade for the rest of the sixteenth and the early years of the seventeenth centuries. Moreover, as the first of the selections in this chapter indicates, the few Englishmen who did sail to Africa in the opening decades of the seventeenth century were single-mindedly intent on finding an advantageous trade in gold: Richard Jobson's account of his journey on the Gambia in 1620, recounts an incident in which slaves were explicitly rejected as legitimate commodities. Jobson's narrative is also one of the few describing travel into the continent, for the Gambia River was virtually the only African waterway that the British explored until the nineteenth century; further expeditions were made in 1661, 1681, and 1723–27. British traders on that river, though, remained largely indifferent to the slaves offered in the seventeenth century, who were few and expensive. Gold and gum (from acacia trees) were the lucrative commodities sought by both the French and the English in the Senegambia (the region between the Senegal and Gambia rivers).

However, less than a decade after Jobson's declaration on the shores of the Gambia that the British did not deal in human commodities, England officially entered the slave trade in the Gulf of Guinea. In 1630, King Charles I granted a syndicate of traders a license to transport slaves from Guinea; that syndicate was headed by a man named Nicholas Crisp, who had already built the factory at Coromantine. The beheading of Charles I and the establishment of a Commonwealth did not entirely halt the slow growth of the British presence on the African Coast. A new, and not very prosperous, Guinea Company was founded in 1651, and, with the Restoration of the monarchy, came royal monopolies, granted first to the Royal Adventurers in 1660, and then to the Royal African Company (hereafter referred to as the RAC) in 1672. In 1665, the Royal Adventurers estimated that its income from gold (from which the British coin called the "guinea" took its name) was two hundred thousand pounds, its income from slaves one hundred thousand, and its income from all other commodities one hundred thousand. The succeeding monopoly, the RAC, devoted even more of its resources to the slave trade. Royal support allowed the construction or reconstruction of British forts, and the RAC built factories on the Gold Coast at Cormantine (which they had taken back from the Dutch), Anashan, Commenda, Aga, and Accra, as well as a

headquarters at Cape Coast that housed a garrison of fifty English soldiers and thirty slaves. In the first seventeen years of its existence,
between 1672 and the Glorious Revolution that ended James II's reign
in 1688, the RAC shipped ninety thousand slaves from its forts.

And yet, with all of its activity during the Restoration, the RAC did
not keep up with the growing demand for slaves; "separate" traders
and interlopers became common features of the British trade. The
RAC agents, or "factors," as they were called, were also continually
vexed by the Dutch, who sought control of the Guinea coast in the
wake of the declining power of Spain and Portugal (see the selection
from Willem Bosman), and by the rivalry of assorted French, Danish,
and Brandenburgher companies. As the selections from the RAC correspondence show, the factors mainly concentrated on outmaneu-
vering other national monopolies who were vying for the favor and
exclusive trading privileges of African rulers, and on trying to control
British interlopers. The letters included here are from a fort on the
Slave Coast, to the east of the Gold Coast, where, as the name of the
territory indicates, the RAC's trade was primarily for slaves. The selection from Thomas Phillips's journal describes a short journey along
the Slave Coast from one of the RAC forts to the village where the
king resided in order to pay both homage and "customs" (a royal tax
on the privilege of trading). Phillips records the common experience of
learning that he would have to buy the slaves offered for sale by the
king before purchasing others. In 1698, the RAC lost its royal monopoly, but it continued to be responsible for maintaining British forts,
and a new act of Parliament required all British traders on the West
Coast of Africa to contribute a ten-percent tax to their support. By
1700, the British presence there was still only half that of the Dutch:
four hundred Dutchmen, two hundred Englishmen, eighty-five Danes,
and eighty-five Brandenburgers made up the European population on
the Gold Coast, where it was most heavily concentrated.

This was to change in the eighteenth century, after the Treaty of
Utrecht (1713) awarded the British a monopoly known as the *asiento*
on providing slaves to Spanish America, an event that was crucial to
the eventual British domination of the triangular trade. The French,
who had unsuccessfully tried to supply Spanish America, became the
main British rivals, and British operations were expanded both up and
down the coast. Several of the selections in this section were written
during this period of expansion, and they document the continued
attempts by British traders to gain competitive advantage over the
French, to control the trade, and, increasingly, to convince British

readers of its humanity. In his 1734 story of a slave mutiny, for example, William Snelgrave carefully justifies the trade, indicating his awareness of the early stirrings of abolitionist sentiment. But the basic conditions of the West African trade remained stable: despite the fact that the British had become the dominant Europeans, their power was confined, by common agreement with their African trading partners, to their own forts. The land around them, indeed even the land under them, belonged to the local rulers, and the British government continued to warn against intrusion onto the land or attempts at cultivation (even of gardens) by factors on the Gold Coast, who were to consider themselves "only tenants of the soil which we hold at the good will of the natives" (British Board of Trade, quoted in Thomas 226).

Isolated as they were in their ships and factories, what could the British traders have known of the "natives," or their wills, beyond the narrow strip of coast to which they had such limited access? The Atlantic trade had been shaping that coast, as well as some of the adjacent inland societies, for centuries. It had introduced crops from the Americas, especially American corn, and cloth from Europe and India. The woolen cloth was often unraveled and used in the local textile production, which, like mining and metallurgy, was probably stimulated by the trade. European trade also spread local commodities and currency from one end of the coast to the other. Gold was bought on the Gold Coast in the seventeenth century and sold on the Slave Coast, for example, and cowrie shells became a widespread money. Fishing villages were developed into trading towns, and some independent city-states were established on the coast. In the early eighteenth century, the trade's impact became much wider, as it armed the rulers with guns and changed the structure of African warfare. In some places, such as Congo, it furthered the decay of an indigenous monarchy, while in others, such as Ashanti and Dahomey, it helped bring powerful new polities into being. Early in the eighteenth century, Bambara, on the Middle Niger, arose as a slave-making "machine" (Thomas 227) that cheapened and increased the supply of slaves in the region of Senegambia. Our selection from the story of Ayuba Suleiman Diallo (called "Job Ben Solomon" by the British) illustrates some of the political destabilization that resulted from this change, as well as the British response to the new availability of slaves in a region where they had previously traded (still on the Gambia River) mainly for gold and gum.

Thomas Bluett's and Francis Moore's narratives of Ayuba (called Job) are the first of five selections in this chapter that focus on the experiences of Africans in the slave trade. The stories of both Ayuba and the "Prince of Annamaboe" concern the unusual destinies of young men who were enslaved and then returned to their African homes from captivity in America when the Royal African Company realized the strategic advantages of their repatriation. These young men were, like the fictional Oroonoko, slave traders themselves, and their return to Africa served to confirm the solidarity between their families and the British. Indeed, Ayuba later helped to extend British interests in Senegambia. These stories were written by Englishmen, but they nevertheless give us an inkling of how the slave trade looked from the vantage point of the African suppliers. They also provide insight into the cultures of the Muslim clerical merchants in Senegambia and the domestic relations in the small slave-trading city-states of the Gold Coast.

The other two narratives were written late in the eighteenth century by Africans who had been taken from the Guinea Coast in childhood and eventually became part of the community of freedmen living in London. Their stories are more informative than the other two, not only about the typical experiences of most Africans in the Atlantic slave trade, but also about the world behind the West African coast. Certainly that world, too, was various and dynamic, and we should recall that, before the seventeenth century brought a sizable concentration of European traders to the coast, the inland peoples considered the coast to be isolated, peripheral, and insignificant. The powerful states of Guinea were in the interior, and they looked north and east for foreign trade and contact, especially to the trading empires of the Sudanese grasslands. During the course of the seventeenth and eighteenth centuries, the Atlantic trade inverted their orientation, turning them to face what had previously been the ends of the earth. In the inland areas affected by the Atlantic slave trade, there were dozens of languages and ethnic groups arranged in numerous political configurations, with widely divergent cultural practices, so generalizations about these cultures are difficult to make. The two slave memoirs in this chapter illustrate contrasting modes by which the inland societies of the forest belts adapted to the trade.

The best eighteenth-century memoir of life in a West African village is Olaudah Equiano's short description of his childhood, but the culture it depicts is in many ways specific to its particular place and time. Equiano was an Ibo, born in what is now Nigeria, above the Niger Delta and east of both the Gold Coast and the Slave Coast. The Ibo were under the titular dominion of Benin City, a relation Equiano describes as "nominal" subjection to its "king." The chief men of

Equiano's village were titled, but there was no single local leader, and the small villages lived in a state of armed and unstable neutrality, which intermittently broke down into hostility. The Oba of Benin was not a very active slave trader, and Equiano was probably brought to the coast by those supplying the independent Ibo city-states of the Niger Delta, and then sold to a British slaver at one of the eastern delta ports: Brass, New Calabar, or Bonny. Those states were products of the European trade; they had not existed before its onset, but their new prosperity allowed them to develop a system for milking people out of the inland Ibo communities. In this Ibo system, slaves from the relatively isolated villages of the forest belt were often demanded by the religious confederations on the coast. Although there was no centralized, controlling political power, religious imperatives, along with raids, wars, and kidnapping, kept up a strong supply.

Ottobah Cugoano was born into a contrasting polity, in the forest belt behind the Gold Coast, where the Fante and the Ashanti were in the process of becoming rival imperial powers through the use of new mass armies to which European firepower was crucial. He was taken from the borderlands of the Fante, which was itself an important slave-trading power, at a time of general hostilities, when the Ashanti were consolidating under a central inland administrative town and trying to extend their control over the entire region, including the coast. The Ashanti resisted selling their own kind, but they needed slaves to buy guns, and so their military dominance of the region depended on controlling the slave routes that extended from markets farther north to the sea. Hence, although some economic historians have held that the basic agrarian West African economy was too separate from the slave trade to have felt its impact deeply, others contend that it helped change the political administration of the countryside and, thereby, the daily lives of the peasantry.

Despite the opposite natures of these two polities — the inland Ibo were influenced by the little independent city-states of the Niger Delta, whereas the towns directly on the shores of the Gold Coast were increasingly under the centralized dominance of the inland imperial powers, especially the Ashanti — their cultures certainly had much in common. They lived by agriculture, which combined male and female labor; they grew cotton and manufactured fast-dyed textiles; they smelted iron and worked other metals (the Ashanti smiths had gold; the Ibo only brass and silver); they made palm wine. They both practiced polygamy when they could afford it, and they were parts of wide-ranging and sophisticated social, commercial, and political networks.

Both cultures originated in regions that included villages and various-sized towns, where markets were held and crafts were practiced, and both Equiano and Cugoano report that their fathers owned many slaves.

Equiano's narrative is a particularly rare memoir of eighteenth-century African domestic slavery, for the child was repeatedly sold on his way to the coast. In one of the households in which he served, he was treated as the equal of the son and heir, leading a modern historian to suggest that Equiano was unwittingly involved in "a widespread African practice, that of ritual association of two persons for the purpose, in this case, of diverting or transferring evil influences, intended to harm the son, to his associate who was then removed from the community" (Jones 68). His experiences with African slavery seem not to have lessened his horror at the prospect of being shipped out into the vast nothingness of the ocean's watery horizon. The mingled terror and childish wonder in his account of being taken from Africa make Equiano's autobiography the most compelling description in English of the almost unutterable strangeness of that experience. Imagine it duplicated, centuries before and a century afterwards, thirteen million[3] times.

---

[3]Thomas estimates that thirteen million people were taken from Africa as slaves, while some eleven million landed alive in the Americas (804–05).

RICHARD JOBSON

From *The Golden Trade*

Richard Jobson tells us most of what we need to know about his book's history and goal in the title: *The Golden Trade, or a Discovery of the River Gambra and the Golden Trade of the Aethiopeans; also the Commerce with a great blacke merchant called Buckor Sano, and his report of the houses covered with gold, and other strange observations for the good of our owne countrey, set downe as they were collected in travelling part of the yeares 1620 and 1621.* Jobson's expedition, like Raleigh's to Guiana (see pp. 334–37), was aimed at gold. The Europeans' search for gold had become especially intense in Gambia after Leo Africanus described the fabulous wealth of Timbuktu in his *Description of Africa* (1526), fueling competition between French and Portuguese merchants and prompting English merchants to establish an ongoing trade for gold and ivory in the region. Jobson's employers, the Company of Adventurers to "Gynny and Bynny" (Guinea and Benin), were chartered by James I in 1618, and lost nearly £2,000 worth of cargo later that year when their first ship was captured by the Portuguese. Part of Jobson's task in recounting his expedition was to restore the investors' faltering confidence in the enterprise. Thus, he stresses the commercial possibilities of African exploration in spite of his failure to locate the gold mines he sought. Jobson made two further journeys to the Gambia region, but these, too, were commercial disasters, and after losing £5,000 on the venture, the Company of Adventurers closed down its operations. The preferential treatment they had enjoyed, but had failed to capitalize on, provoked bitter criticism from other colonial merchants, who attacked the 1618 monopoly grant as an indefensible drain on their own businesses.

Jobson characterizes the Africans he met and dealt with as friendly, literate, and trustworthy. His belief in a tribe of people who would gladly give away their superabundant gold for the salt they treasure parallels Raleigh's assurance that his Indian allies only want women, not gold. Both Jobson's and Raleigh's accounts express a wish for a peaceful, symmetrical trade in which each party gets more than it spends because of differing needs and values. Jobson's assertion that Englishmen would not trade in slaves appears to have been sincere, for he betrays no knowledge of the short-lived British slave trade of the previous century, which had been suppressed by the Spanish. After Jobson's expedition, English trading companies obtained charters to found settlements along the Gambia, in what is now Senegal. For a glimpse of the later slave trade on this river, see the selections on Job Ben Solomon on pages 259–73.

The text is excerpted from the first edition (London: Printed by Nicholas Okes, 1623) 107, 109–15, 117–18.

George Thompson, in his diligence, while hee lived, hearing of diverse Caravans, that past in the country, and went downe to the King of *Bursals*[1] dominions for salt, had learned, that the onely and principallest man that maintained the greatest Trade, was that *Buckor*

---

[1] *King of Bursals:* This king's dominion lay on the north side of the Gambia River, in what is now Senegal; the name *Bursal* comes from the Wolof term *Bur* ("king") and the Salum River, north of the Gambia, which also formed part of the king's dominion.

Sano,[2] whose dwelling was at *Tinda,*[3] who maintained and kept 300. Asses following that tedious travell. *Tompsons* desire led him forthwith, to goe finde this Marchant, and in a paire of Oares, as I spake in the beginning, went up the River, and travelling some way by land recovered[4] *Tinda,* but found not his blacke Merchant, in regard he was travelled higher into the Country, in the sale and uttering[5] of his salt Commodity: *Thompson* returned, but found his expectation so satisfied, in that he had hard[6] of the Moores of *Barbary,*[7] and was come so neere where they frequented, that hee talkt of nothing, but how to settle habitations, and fortefie the River to defende themselves, and keepe out other nations; but these his desires died in his unhappy end, and this was all our acquaintance; which now I came to second, by sending unto this *Buckor Sano* to come downe unto the River to us, as the onely man we were willing to sell, and commend our commodities unto.

The next day about noone, came *Buckor Sano* with his musicke playing before him, with great solemnity, and his best clothes on, and about some 40. more, armed with their bows and arrowes with him, hee shewed no more at first, howbeit within two houres after, there were two hundred men and women come thither: he sat downe upon the banke under a shady tree: after a little stay, I went a shore to him, and our salutations being past, I desired him to go aboord, whereof he kindly accepted; and withall shewed me a beefe he had brought to give me for the present I had sent him, diverse goates the people had likewise brought, and corne, and cockes, and hens, so as there was no neede to doubt any more want of victuall: He carried no more aboord with him, but two: after he was in the boate, I shot off three such guns as I had to welcome him, at the noyse whereof he seemed much to rejoyce, calling the report of the powder, by the name of the white mens thunder, and taking notice of the head, and the hide of the Deare which we had killed, which we shewed him was slaine by one of our

---

[2] *Buckor Sano:* "Buckor" is probably an abbreviation of Abubakar, Mohammed's successor as leader of Islam.

[3] *Tinda:* A town on the upper Gambia River, near the eastern border of the modern state of Gambia.

[4] *recovered:* Found.

[5] *uttering:* Vending.

[6] *hard:* I.e., heard.

[7] *Moores of Barbary:* The Barbary Coast was on the northern shore of Africa; Europeans often characterized the northern African Moors as having lighter skin than the peoples of Equitorial and southern Africa.

guns, they sent, with admiration,[8] from one place to another, and cer-
tified, that there was a people come, who with thunder killed the wild
beasts in the wood, and the fowles in the ayre: Which for it was our
dayly use to kill one sort of fowle called a Stalker, which is as high as a
man, and hath as much meate of his body, as is in a Lambe, which
diverse times[9] we used to kill, and eate, more especiall we desired to
have his feathers, which grew on his tayle, which are of use, and such
as are worne, and esteemed of here at home amongst us: I had of my
owne provision good Rosa-solis,[10] taking forth a glasse, I dranke unto
him, after he had dranke he tooke off his sword and gave it me to lay
up, saying defend me here in your boate, and I will secure you on
shore, he liked our drinke so well, he suckt it in, and as it seems not
knowing the strength of it, took more then he would have done, insomuch as he fell asleepe, the people that came with him, in the meane
time cutting of reedes, made them houses, others fetching in wood,
made fires every where about them, so as it seemed a little towne;
Buckor Sano slept soundly upon my bed by me in the boate, and in the
morning complained of his head, and this much I must justifie in his
behalfe, that during the time we were together, he was never overtaken
by drinking after, but observed the course he saw we used, to take a
small cup before meate, and another after, and this ever gave him satisfaction: He desired to see all the Commodities we had, which he liked
very well of, and whereas we thought our Iron would have beene
greedily desired, we found it not so, for they told us, there was a
people neighbours unto them who had knowledge to make it, howbeit
they were diverse times in wars together, but some of our Iron we put
away, at better rates then below, by one third, and might have done
away all we had, if we would have accepted of hides, which for the
reason I shall presently shew was refused; howsomever this was the
maine businesse, that after they saw our salt, no other thing was
esteemed amongst them, which at first seemed strange unto them,
forasmuch as they had never seene any of that fashion before: the salt
we had, was onely bay salt,[11] which after they put in their mouthes,
and tasted, they would looke up and cry, *Alle,* in token of the good
esteeme they had of it; After two houres of the morning spent, my
Merchant went on shore, keeping my gowne about him, which when

[8] *admiration:* Wonder.
[9] *diverse times:* Often.
[10] *Rosa-solis:* A liquor made with brandy, sugar, and various spices (Latin, "rose of
the sun").
[11] *bay salt:* Salt in large crystals, made by evaporating salt water.

the evening shut in, the night before I had put upon him, and in a manner of state, he went one shore withall,[12] wearing of it in that manner, it might well appeare, they were not used to such kind of ornaments.

The first thing he did, after he came on shore, he caused on to make a lowed[13] outcry, in manner of a proclamation prohibiting any of the people, to buy or barter with us, but as he bargaind.

All that day hee found himselfe so sicke, after his drinking, that hee told me hee could tend no businesse, onely hee shewed unto mee, certaine young blacke women, who were standing by themselves, and had white strings crosse their bodies, which hee told me were slaves, brought for me to buy, I made answer, We were a people, who did not deale in any such commodities, neither did wee buy or sell one another, or any that had our owne shapes; he seemed to marvell much at it, and told us, it was the only marchandize, they carried downe into the countrey, where they fetcht all their salt, and that they were solde there to white men, who earnestly desired them, especially such young women, as hee had brought for us: we answered, They were another kinde of people different from us, but for our part, if they had no other commodities, we would returne againe: he made reply, that they had hides and Elephants teeth, cotton yarne, and the clothes of the countrey, which in our trade we call Negroes clothes; he was answerd, for their hides, we would not buy, in regard our boate was little, and wee could not conveniently carry them, but if they would bring them lower downe the River, where our bigger vessels could come, we would buy them all, but for their teeth, cotton, and clothes, wee would deale for them: so against the next morning, being Satterday, we had a house built by the water side, open round about, and covered with reeds on the toppe, to shadow us from the Sunne: and this was our market house; when we came to trade, we asked which should be the Staple commoditie, to pitch the price upon, to value other things by, they shewed us one of their clothes, and for that they onely desired our salt, wee fell to loveing and bidding upon the proportion,[14] wherein we had such difference, and held so long, that many of them seemed to dislike, and made shew, that they would goe away, but after we concluded, there was no more difference, every man bringing his commodities, our salt went away, and as they dispatcht, they likewise returned in companies together, and still others came, that we had the place

---

[12] *withall:* Therewith.
[13] *lowed:* I.e., loud.
[14] *loveing and bidding upon the proportion:* Haggling over the proper standard of value.

continually furnished: We never talked unto them of golde, the princi-pall we came for, but wayted opportunitie, and notwithstanding we saw it worne in their womens eares, warning was given, none of our people, should take any great notice of it, as a thing wee should greatly desire, untill occasion was given, by *Buckor Sano* himselfe, who tak-ing note of our guilt swords, and some other things wee had, although but poorely set out, with some shew of gold trimming, did aske if that were gold: hee was answered, Yes: it should seeme sayth he, you have much of this in your Countrey: Wee affirmed the same, and that it was a thing our men did all use to weare, and therefore if they had any, wee would buy it of them, because wee had more use then they for it, you shall have sayd he, what is amongst our women here; but if I did know you would esteeme of that, I would be provided, to bring you such quantitie, as should buy all things you brought: and if you would be sure to come still unto us, I would not faile to meete you. And pro-ceeding further hee sayd: This Countrey above doth abound there-with, insomuch as these eyes of mine (poynting two of his fingers to his eyes, as the Countrey manner in speaking is,) hath beene foure sever-all[15] times, at a great Towne above, the houses whereof are covered onely with gold: wee demaunded of him, how long he was going, and comming thither: he answered foure Moones; we asked him, if hee would carry some of us thither, hee answered: Yes, but they had ene-mies by the way, somtimes to fight with them, wee shewed him presently our gunnes, and tolde him wee would carry them with us, and kill them all, at which he seemed to take a great deale of content. . . .

I tooke some speciall note of the blade of his sword, and a paire of brasse bracelts one of his wives had upon her armes, both which things did appeare to me, to be such as might very well be brought in their beginnings, either from London, or some other part of this our native Country, I demanded of him where he had them, he made answere there was a people used to come amongst them, whom they called *Arabecks,* who brought them these, and diverse other commodities; we askt what manner of people, he described the Tawny Moore[16] unto us, and sayde they came in great companies together, and with many Cammels: How acceptable this report was unto me, may be conjec-tured by any such, who are seriously enclined, to give a faire and just

---

[15] *severall:* Different, separate.
[16] *Tawny Moore:* This phrase was used formulaically to describe the people of North Africa.

accompt[17] of any such imployments they are interest in, and whose desires, with affection, labours the full satisfaction of the trust imposed upon them;

This his relation made it certaine, that these were the Moores of *Barbary*, the discovery of whose trade and trafficke, was the ground of this our being so high in the river: we grew to question him, how neare those people came to the place we were now at; he answered, within 6 dayes journey there is a towne called *Mumbarre*, unto which towne, the next Moone, these *Arabeckes* will come: we askt againe, what commodities they brought with them, hee answered much salt and divers other things, wee desired then to know what they exchange for, and carryed backe: he answered nothing but gold, and that they onely desired to have, and returned nothing else; wee questioned him farther, whether hee would undertake to carry any of us safe to see those *Arabeckes*, and that wee might returne without danger; hee stopt his nose betweene his finger and thumbe: and cryed *Hore, Hore,* which is the greatest oath they use amongst them that he would performe it . . .

[17]*accompt:* I.e., account.

From *Rélation du voyage fait sur les costes d'Afrique, 1670–1671*

This passage, by an anonymous French trader on the Gold Coast in 1671, illustrates the common European sentiment that Gold Coast natives were superior to other Africans. The writer is much taken by the people he encounters at the port of Commendo (whose king was actively courting alliances with both the French and the English) and he singles out a local governor for special praise in language very close to Behn's description of Oroonoko. Throughout this account, the Africans are represented as shrewd traders, deceiving the French officers with copper powder gilded to look like gold, exercising their soldiers in a show of military force, and carefully watching over their visitors and inquiring into their motives. But while he describes the Africans as cunning and intimidating, the author remains fully confident in his men; warned of threats from the Dutch, he deliberately advances to their fortress. Moreover, he never criticizes or condemns the Africans for their cautious and suspicious behavior; indeed, his respectful comments about his hosts, and his detailed descriptions of their fruits and animals, seem designed to stimulate the interest of his readers and to assure them that the journey is safe and pleasurable.

Commendo, some thirty miles west of Annamaboe on the Gold Coast, became a site of conflict between the English, the French, and the Dutch in the later 1670s. While the Dutch believed they had the right to control European trading in the area, they had largely neglected the commercial opportunities there, provoking the king of Commendo to invite other European traders to build forts. The second port of call described in this selection, the "Château de la Minne," probably refers to the area known to the English as the Elmina Castle, about ten miles east of Commendo (while the latitude specified in this report is fairly accurate, the longitude given for both ports is entirely incorrect, as indicated in the footnotes). Elmina was settled in 1481 by the Portuguese, who built the "older" fortress mentioned on p. 228; the Dutch seized control in 1637, and, as the writer suggests, in the later seventeenth century they sought to monopolize the local slave trade, maintaining a newer and more imposing fortress in the mountains in an effort to intimidate their competitors.

The translation, made specifically for this edition by Laura Schattschneider, is from *Rélation du voyage fait sur les costes d'Afrique, aux mois de Novembre & Decembre de l'année 1670, Janvier & Février 1671, commençat au Cap Verd,* 15–20; the *Rélation* is one of several travel narratives, each printed with separate pagination, in Henri Justel, ed., *Recueil de divers voyages faits en Afrique et en l'Amerique, qui n'ont point esté encore publiez* (Paris: Billaine, 1674).

While we were ashore, there were many Blacks who came aboard to get brandy, and the Officers who were there traded it to them, in which they were deceived, for instead of gold powder, they were given copper: because they were shrewd enough to gild it so well, that those who are not accustomed to that sort of commodity, and not having anything with which to test it, are thereby infallibly taken in: they will give openwork[1] for a thousand ecus, which one would have had great difficulty to have for 100 sols.[2] Also on that day the Negroes of the

---

[1] *openwork:* Handiwork in a grid or lattice pattern, with visible interstices, usually metal or fabric.

[2] *ecus . . . sols:* Ecus were a French silver coin named for the shield motif stamped on the front; sols were the smallest unit of French currency (also called *sous*), worth one-twentieth of a livre. Fluctuations make it difficult to determine the coins' relative values, but at one point the ecu was worth more than 150 sols.

little Commendo[3] came, asking us to come see them, and telling us they had a French heart,[4] and on the following day, we dropped anchor before their city, which is situated at five degrees six minutes of latitude, and at twenty-one degrees forty minutes of longitude.[5]

We found on setting foot ashore, that the inhabitants were armed, in order to better receive us, with the Commander of the region in the absence of the Governor, they saluted us with three musket salvos,[6] and then we were accompanied by a great troop of men and women, who danced to the music of diverse instruments made of ivory, and some guitars in their style. All those people were like those which I have depicted, except the women, who were adorned with those Levantine[7] scarves, and with many keys hanging from their sashes, and this is among them a great ornament, for there is nothing in their houses upon which there is no lock. We walked thus through the city, meeting in every section a crush of people, many of them dancers, and passing through a grand square, found it was filled with men and women, who danced also, crying, "Long live France!" In short, they all appeared to us to be quite contented to see us, and led us to a house that the French had built in bygone days, telling us that it was ours, and that we were the Masters of it. We stayed there two hours watching them dance: there were men who had tiger skins for shawls, and around the loins a sort of mail coat, which they also take when they go to war, not having anything but that to cover them, the rest of the body being nude.

When we exited that house to go embark, a Black came to tell us that the Governor had come from the Court, which is not four leagues from that place, called the great Commendo,[8] where the King usually resides. We decided thus to go visit this Governor, and I must say that I was surprised to find in him nothing of the barbarian, but instead, much humanity, and he received us quite differently from all the others we had seen. I had noticed well upon entering the Gold Coast, that the peoples were more humanized there than in other places: in truth,

[3] *little Commendo:* On the coast of the kingdom of Kommendo, in what is now Ghana (called "Comany" on the Gold Coast map on p. 211). Kommendo was an extremely fertile area and was also located near several important slave-trading centers; in consequence, it was the object of intense conflict between the English, the Dutch, and the French.

[4] *had a French heart:* Loved the French.

[5] *latitude . . . longitude:* The latitude specified here is correct, but the proper longitude is forty minutes west.

[6] *salvos:* Military salutes, produced by firing artillery.

[7] *Levantine:* From the Levant, the eastern Mediterranean.

[8] *great Commendo:* See Comany in the Gold Coast map on p. 211.

when I saw him I had a good opinion of him, and if those persons have an engaging physiognomy, this one had it more than all Negroes put together. He is tall and well-proportioned, all his limbs are striking for their strength, not having that ugly pug nose, nor that large mouth, that the other Blacks have: his eyes were at the front of his face, quite open, brilliant and full of fire. In all, one noted that his features were regular and that therein was pride, and much gentleness. He attested to us that the King was pleased when he was told that a French ship had arrived at that coast, and he had forthwith ordered him to depart to assure us that we were welcome, and that he in particular[9] wished to be able to be of service to us, telling us many things of good sense. Then he gave audience to us and to all those who wished to speak and without confusion, not having any in his chamber, which we found furnished with benches, tables, and coffers, but us other Frenchmen, and the people of that country were in a kind of antechamber, in which he had them enter one by one, and upon entering, they threw themselves to their knees, and spoke to him from that posture. And after having been received by him as a sort of benediction, they departed: the principals came to kneel at his feet, to them he extended his hand. He was visited thus by all the musicians, who came in their turn to revere him, accompanied by dancers male and female. He had them dance outside while he gave us something to eat, and quite properly. He proposed that we go see the King his Master and told us that if we planned to do so, he would furnish us with as many slaves as we wanted for carrying us there in cotton swings, this is their transport which is very comfortable and very soft, and which even goes quite fast. Monsieur le Chevalier d'Hailly thanked him, and told him that he was in a hurry to make our voyage, and that if he had not arrived he would have already set sail, but that nevertheless he asked him to come aboard, and that he would try to feast him. He accepted the offer that was made him, saying that he had great confidence in Frenchmen, and that he did not see our equal among other nations. He had us exit his chamber first, and at his door there were three slaves, who marched before him: there were two of them who each carried a musket, and the other carried his coat of arms and his sword, which is of iron, and very sharp, as they have found the secret of tempering that metal: they make them into sabers, but these are as large as butchers' knives: there are at the hilt, which is made of a very solid/heavy wood,

---

[9] *he in particular:* He himself, privately and independently of the king's orders.

two lions' heads which he had killed with his own hands. We came thus up to the coast, and on passing through the place again where we had found so many dancers, I was surprised to see it full of merchants who sold fruits of the country, namely, pineapples, oranges, lemons, bananas, and many others of which I do not know the names. There is the fat grain of Turkey, of which one makes a bread that one finds there already cooked, and also wheat, millet, rice, many tubers, fish, palm nuts, from which they make an oil which is used all along that coast. One found woolen cloth, and everything that Europeans bring them. The markets are open continually every day. Having thus led him to our ship, we endeavored to get him to drink, but he did not have the wherewithal,[10] appearing to us very sober. He found that he was known to a Portuguese man from the island of St. Thomas, who had been shipwrecked in departing from Europe, and since our plan was to pass by that island, Monsieur le Chevalier d'Hailly had taken him aboard in order to return him to his home. This Portuguese man assured us that this was the most resolute Negro of all Guinea, and that he had taken by force the fort of Cabo Carlo which belonged to the Dutch, and had then sold it to the English, who still possessed it. In speaking thus of war, he appeared completely animated to us, and showed us seven musket shots which he had received upon his body. After having stayed with us for three hours, he attested that he wished to retire, and the rowboat was readied for him, and when he took leave of us, he asked us to believe that he did not have a heart as black as his body, and that we must be assured of all the offers that he had made us. When he had embarked, and as the rowboat was let down from the ship five shots of cannon were let off, which strongly flattered[11] his martial humor. The following day, as we were under sail, he sent word to us that the Dutch were set upon arresting us as soon as we were at the Château de la Minne: we told his messenger that we were grateful to him for his advice, and that we could assure him that the Dutch would not dare undertake anything against us, as they feared insulting our king. What obliged them to give us that advice was that the Dutch had in their city an Assistant to Men of State,[12] and another from England, each of which carried on their business, and in all of the festivities they had held for us, the Dutchman did not want to

---

[10] *wherewithal:* In either the physical or monetary sense.

[11] *flattered:* Pleased.

[12] *Assistant to Men of State:* A translator appointed to deal with traders from the various European nations doing business there.

not appear at all, and even showed chagrin at the joy the people demonstrated for us, and perhaps also, said something approaching all that, so much so that we left our good friends of Commendo thus, and despite the threats that had been made toward us, we dropped anchor under the Château de la Minne, at five degrees fifteen minutes latitude, and at 21 degrees 55 minutes longitude.[13] There are two fortresses, one on the coast, which was the older one that had been built by the Portuguese; the other is upon a mountain which commands over[14] the first, and that one was built by the Dutchmen. The place is one of very great commerce, the General of State resides there, and gives orders to the Governors of the places along the Coast. He received us very courteously and hosted us "à l'Allemande"[15] for four days, giving us a great deal to drink. And yet, he appeared to mistrust us, for when we had first entered into the fortress, the doors had been barred to us when we wanted to leave, and it was not even permitted to us to enter into another chamber without being followed by several slaves. He asked us many times what our intentions were along the Coast, and even though we told him that our orders were to escort Merchants and serve the allies of the Crown, he always conjectured some other thing in it, not having been accustomed to see the vessels of the King in those countries: in short, everything took place in great secrecy. Monsieur d'Hailly gave presents to him and received the same from him, among other things a very strange bird, named the crowned bird. It was four feet high, with a fat body like an Indian cock, and black and white plumage, a very long neck, and long and pointed feathers. Its crown made a great tower like the bristles of a wild boar, of a yellow color mixed with a bit of black. Between its crown and its beak it had something like a velvet toque,[16] and its eyes verged on lemon-colored, and each was the size of a thirty-sol piece. It had a very fine skin whiter than snow, and its ears were of the most beautiful flesh color in the world that came to just under the throat. In truth, that is the most remarkable bird I have ever seen, I also saw a turtledove which had something special about it, because it was extremely green, and had red eyes, feet, and beak.

---

[13] *latitude . . . longitude:* Again, while the latitude specified here is nearly accurate, the correct longitude is approximate thirty minutes west.

[14] *commands over:* Probably meaning not that it controls the operations of the coastal fortress, but only that the Dutch fort, with its vantage point on the mountain, towers over the Portuguese one.

[15] *à l'Allemande:* In the German style.

[16] *toque:* Cap or bonnet.

During our debauches,[17] the Negroes who are in the village that is below the fortresses took arms and came in numbers of three hundred or four hundred, with their flags unfurled, to exercise at the bottom of the square. I believe that they did this on his orders, but he told us that it was done by themselves alone, and that they were crazy, assembling at every hour, day and night. It is true that that nation appeared to me to have great joy, being always dancing. They diverted us with their exercise, as we watched them charge as if they had wanted to shoot at ducks through bushes. They always battle like that, by surprise, never attacking all at the same time, but rather splitting to the right and left, and when they have crawled well, close to the ground, and shot from their muskets (which never miss, having a better fuse than ours, made from tree bark) they jump back three times, and then run with such great speed that they are back among their ensign[18] in a moment. I believe that if they had their enemy at the rear, rallying would not be without confusion, although in the time that the Dutch chased the Portuguese out of that country, they fought very vigorously, and were a great deal of trouble to vanquish.

After the Negro Commander had finished his exercise, he came to see the Chevalier d'Hailly, who was inside the fortress with the Dutch General, of whom he requested permission to entertain us with the music he had with him, being composed of diverse ivory trumpets, which made a furious noise: but nevertheless, one noticed a kind of symphony, because each had a different pitch. Sieur d'Hailly invited him on the following day to come and dine aboard his ship, and also invited the Dutch Officers, and that as a guarantee for their safety, there would be Officers of the ship who would remain ashore; they would have clearance from the General, and everyone on one side and on the other performed his duty well.

---

[17] *debauches:* Indulgences, here in eating or drinking; not an indication of moral degeneracy.

[18] *ensign:* A company of men serving under one banner.

JOHN CARTER AND JOSEPH BLYTH

Correspondence of Slave Traders in the Royal African Company

Two letters from agents of the Royal African Company at Whydah (spelled "Fida" on the seventeenth-century map on p. 210) give us a sense of the daily business of trading slaves in the late seventeenth century, especially the complex maneuvering for trade and military alliances with African kings and generals, and the ruses practiced to avoid paying custom to African trading partners. The Africans rented land to the Europeans to build forts and agreed to restrict their trading to a particular European nation in exchange for that nation's military assistance in the event of war with a neighbor. Such alliances, as these letters demonstrate, shifted ceaselessly, especially in the last decades of the century.

Whydah was a major center for European slave traffic on the Slave Coast, east of the Gold Coast, and in 1687, when these letters were written, the English were consolidating their position as the dominant traders in the area. The Royal African Company had begun trading in Whydah in 1681, and probably exported between 1,400 and 3,000 slaves annually during the late 1680s; in the 1690s, their exports rose to more than 5,000 slaves per year. By the end of the decade, however, Dutch and French traders had returned to the area. John Carter, author of the first letter printed here, was chief agent for the Royal African Company at Whydah from 1684 to 1688; Joseph Blyth was commander of the *George*, a slave-trading ship.

The text is taken from Robin Law, ed., *Further Correspondence of the Royal African Company of England, Relating to the 'Slave Coast', 1681–1699* (Madison: African Studies Program, U of Wisconsin-Madison, 1992), 47–48.

John Carter, Whiddah, 10 May 1687:

Since my last to you by Occammy[1] I have been at little Poppo[2] and the Towne where the Canoes used to depart from is called Attome

---

[1] *Occammy:* The title for a linguist or spokesman; here Carter seems to be referring to Annomah, whom he mentions several lines later, and who had carried other letters for him.

[2] *little Poppo:* Also spelled Popo; located just west of the border between the modern states of Togo and Benin; since 1683, it had been the site of an English slave-trading post. In the later 1680s, the area was appropriated by Ofori, the king of Accra (see n. 7 on p. 231).

being a few houses (or rather beehives only larger) standing on the sand by the seaside, there I saw Annomah the Canooman which[3] gave me my letters which I have now sent, At this Towne of Attome[4] I with Monsieur Couerden the French Chiefe who went with me were Received by Monsieur John Poeselwitt factor for the Branderburgh,[5] who hath dispatcht two of their Shipps thence, but will no more I suppose,[6] Monsieur Poeselwitt, in respect to us, put up his flagg, Intending to make us welcome as he could and that day we went up to see Oferry Grandy the king of Accraa[7] who recides about half a myle from thence and while we were there the blacks at the said towne [i.e. Attome] took down Mr Poeselwitts flagg and put up a dutch flagg at which affront to our friend we returned immediately to the Towne and pulled down the Dutch flagg intending[8] the branderburghs flagg up again but soon after another Dutch flagg was up noe Dutch men were reciding there only [we] now perceive them all Mine people[9] or at least the Rulers, while we were arguing the reason with the Captain of the Towne Dutch flaggs were put up at severall Houses to the Number of six, we had no pretence to the place but Immediately tooke our things and departed with our Canoes to Oferye's, the King and I lay their that Night, the Next day we went to Soferyes or Oferye Occamyes that is about 2 or 3 Myles more windwards we Generally call him Sofery Pickaninnee who is the Generall of the Accraes and lives in much more Grandeiur than the King having always good strength of soldiers at his command . . . and [he] lives in the Midway between the Sea and the river and the whole distance between the River and the Sea is about a quarter of a Myle, he Profered me [that] I would send the Canoes to take their departure at his place, he will hall [=haul] over the Canoes to the sea and furnish them with all necessaryes for the voyage and

---

[3] *which:* I.e., who.

[4] *Attome:* This port has not been located.

[5] *factor for the Branderburgh:* Trading agent for the Brandenburgh Company. Brandenburgh is a state in what is now northern Germany. As this passage suggests, the Brandenburgers engaged in intense competition with their European rivals; however, by the 1720s, they had abandoned the slave trade.

[6] *will no more I suppose:* Presumably Carter thinks the Brandenburgh Company will do no further trade at Attome because of the dispute he goes on to describe.

[7] *Oferry Grandy the king of Accraa:* The king of Accra, on the coast of Ghana, was named Ofori; "Oferry Grandy" means "Great Ofori," by contrast with the king's general, also named Ofori, whom Carter calls "Soferey Pickaninnee," meaning "little warrior Ofori." (Though "pickaninny" typically refers to children, and is used in that sense in *Oroonoko,* here it simply means "little.") The general eventually succeeded his namesake as king.

[8] *intending:* I.e., intending to put.

[9] *Mine people:* I.e., from Elmina.

always speed them away, he is a person much afore the King for wisdom, valour etc. very solid and very honest by all report, I thought him a fitt person to secure and have now sent a Canoe to fetch him down to take Fetish[10] to serve the Company only and shall give him a Companyes flagg and a letter to any of the Companyes ships that shall have occasion to stop there and they shall apply themselves to him and not to the Mine people, they always abuse the english, twas these Attome people that got all the Chareletoon sloops Gold[11] or else we had gott some of that againe. If I Can Secure this Sofery Pickaninny he is a More than all the people of those parts and can doe as he pleases, he shews a respect to the King of Accraa but the king is nothing without him and they are as brothers the rest I leave the canoomen to Informe [you of]. Just after I had wrote this I was told that the Generall of the Mine has sent the said Sofery a letter about 3 weeks ago and that the letter was sent by Sofery to the [Dutch] Chiefe at Ofrah[12] who Invited Sofery down to him, the truth of which I have now sent up my boy Cufee to know and whether he will be true to our Company, if soe I will engage him as firme as I can for we stand in need of him (I now perceive) on account of our Canoomen, for if the dutch gett him there is no passage out of the River but by this Man and the Attome people, and the pride and Insolency of the Dutch is not pleasant and the Mine blacks take after the Dutch, they have all along stopped our Canoes and our canoomen will not or dare not complaine.

Honoured Sirs I herewith send 5 Bills of Lading of the last shipps that went away all having quick dispatch some 14 days some 15 and the longest 20 days.

The succeeding Commander of the Lucitania (Notwithstanding I furnished him with a canoe to slave him by reason his canoe was too long and not so ready to goe of here) at his going away sold his canoe to the Interloper without speaking the least word to me of selling itt. When I heard of it I told him twas unkind not to offer me the refusall, since I had lent him a Canoe to Slave his shipp Gratis,[13] so at last he sold her to me, and now the Canoomen having no canoo fitting to

---

[10] *Fetish:* An object believed to have magic powers or to be animated by a spirit (from Portuguese *feitiço,* meaning "charm, sorcery").

[11] *got all the Chareletoon sloops Gold:* Late in 1685, the sloop *Charlton* had been attacked at Great Popo, east of Little Popo.

[12] *Ofrah:* A trading post on the coast of what is now Benin, east of Little Popo and near the Ouémé River.

[13] *Gratis:* Free (Latin).

carry them up I lent them this 9 hand Canoe to carry them up and request your Honour will please to order her downe againe by the first Conveyance she being mightily convenient for the river here. Quavoo[14] hath promised me to take care of her but I cannot depend on that. Here is few Canoomen here and no Canoes to depend upon, We have now no goods in the Factory of the Companys however I will not be wanting to discharge my Duty to them.

If it be possible that the Canooman Say hath spoke words to that high degree of Mischeife[15] I Request so much Christian Justice (If heathanism doth not predominate at Cabo Corso Castle[16] above Christianity for ought I can hear great creditt is given to the single Report or Whisper of a heathen Rascall) I request the said Say may be punished according to his Deserts and sent off or down here the villany is to[o] bad for me to bear that such report shall be forged and I cannot come to Give better satisfaction, how many times have I requested a vessell down here to come up and [it] cannot be granted and [I] will not be a boy[17] to come up in a Canoe. God bless all people from such hard fate.

Joseph Blyth, On board the George Sloope, Whidah, 7 Aug. 1687:

These may give you to understand that I doe intend (if God willing) to sett saile from Whydah this day in Company with Captain Thompson having now on board Sixty one Negroes vizt[18] Fortye six Males and Fifteen Females, having Fifty of them at Little Paw Paw,[19] where I found I could Purchase noe more. [I] Came here wanting onety five [=fifteen], the King threatning to make me pay the usuall Customes, but I denied that I wanted noe Slaves, [and] gott them a board Captain Thompson where taking my opertunity [I] got them on board the Sloope, having Signed to the Bills of Lading and taken Three Receipts of Mr Carter, for these following Remaining goods, vizt Four hundred

---

[14] *Quavoo:* Apparently an African employee of the RAC; another letter refers to him as "Captain Quow."

[15] *Say . . . Mischeife:* In a letter dated two months earlier, Carter has accused Say, a Whidah canoeman, of spreading a "strange ill report" about a disagreement between Carter and another captain in the RAC.

[16] *Cabo Corso Castle:* An English trading post in the Fetu kingdom (see the map on p. 210).

[17] *be a boy:* Be treated as an inferior.

[18] *vizt:* An abbreviation for *videlicit,* meaning "that is to say."

[19] *little Paw Paw:* Presumably a variant spelling of little Popo.

Forty Six Pounds of Bouges,[20] Twelve Sallampores,[21] Thirty two Ounces of Corall,[22] Twenty Five Iron Bars, soe having little more to trouble you withall at Present only telling you, that I shall have not have Four Chests of Corne, of the last Ten, which came on board, it being so wett that I could not, with all my Endeavours, save it.

[20] *Bouges:* Cowries, a kind of shell used as currency (see the selection from Equiano later in this chapter).
[21] *Sallampores:* Salempore was a blue cotton cloth, imported from India and often used to clothe slaves.
[22] *Corall:* Certain kinds of coral were used as precious stones.

THOMAS PHILLIPS

From *A Journal of a Voyage Made in the* Hannibal

Like the previous selection, the passages from Thomas Phillips's "A Journal of a Voyage Made in the *Hannibal* of London, 1693–94" describe a visit to Whydah (spelled "Fida" on the seventeenth-century map on p. 211), on the Slave Coast. The "Captain Tom" whom he praises on p. 242 was an official translator for the English at Whydah, and a former employee of the Royal African Company. By the time of Phillips's visit, the slave trade in the region was busy enough to require a local translator for each of the European countries doing business there.

Phillips's attitudes and behavior toward the king and his court seem fairly typical for this period. Although he is frequently contemptuous of the manners and hygiene of his hosts — especially the king — he conceals his disdain by means of a strict compliance with court etiquette and a respectful adherence to local customs. While he complains about the expensive conditions imposed on him, Phillips represents the commerce in slaves as a process of mutual deception and manipulation, in which both buyers and sellers strive to take advantage of each other. His narrative evinces conflicting feelings about his task. When obliged to spend three hours in the buildings where the slaves are kept for days, he mainly feels sorry for himself, and though he mentions the horrific conditions in the hold of his slave ship, where venereal disease is rampant, his main object is to complain, once again, about the losses he suffers. However, he later launches into a passionate declaration of the equal humanity of Africans. Phillips's journal is further evidence that racism is the result rather than

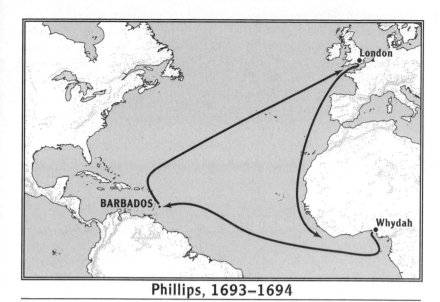

Phillips, 1693–1694

Phillips's triangular route, shown on this map, was typical of the trade.

the cause of slavery, and that belief in the full humanity of slaves did not necessarily lead to antislavery conclusions in the seventeenth century.

The text is excerpted from the fourth edition of *A Collection of Voyages and Travels,* 8 vols., ed. Awnsham Churchill (London: Printed for J. Walthoe, 1752) 6: 232–36, 250, 251.

As soon as the king understood of our landing, he sent two of his cappasheirs,[1] or noblemen, to compliment us at our factory, where we design'd to continue that night, and pay our devoirs[2] to his majesty the next day, which we signify'd to them, and they, by a foot-express, to their monarch; whereupon he sent two more of his grandees[3] to invite

---

[1] *cappasheirs:* From Portuguese *cabaceiro,* meaning "head man," usually applied to subordinate chiefs (see also Willem Bosman's use of this term, which he spells "Cabacero's," on p. 251).

[2] *devoirs:* Dutiful respects.

[3] *grandees:* The highest rank of Spanish and Portuguese nobility; hence, by extension, a person of high rank or eminence.

us there that night, saying he waited for us, and that all former captains used to attend him the first night: whereupon, being unwilling
to infringe the custom, or give his majesty any offence, we took
our hamocks, and Mr. *Peirson,* myself, captain *Clay,* our surgeons,
pursers,[4] and about twelve men armed for our guard, were carry'd
to the king's town,[5] which contains about fifty houses. When we came
to the palace (which was the meanest I ever saw, being low mud walls,
the roof thatched, the floor the bare ground, with some pools of water
and dirt in it) we were met at the entrance by several cappasheirs, with
the usual ceremony of clapping their hands, and taking and shaking
us by ours, with great demonstration of affection: when we entered
the palace-yard they all fell on their knees near the door of the
room where the king was, clapping their hands, knocking the ground
with their foreheads, and kissing it, which they repeated three
times, being their usual ceremony when they approached his majesty,
we standing and observing till they had done; then rising, they led
us to the room where the king was, which we found cover'd with
his nobility upon their knees, and those that introduced us fell on
theirs, and crawled to their several stations, and so they continued
all the time we were with the king then, and all other times when we
saw him.

When we were entered, the king peep'd upon us from behind a curtain, and beckoned us to him; whereupon we approached close to his
throne, which was of clay, raised about two foot from the ground, and
about six foot square, surrounded with old dirty curtains, always
drawn betwixt him and his cappasheirs, whom he will not allow the
sight of his handsome phiz.[6] He had two or three little black children with him, and was smoking tobacco in a long wooden pipe, the
bole of which, I dare say, would hold an ounce, and rested upon his
throne, with a bottle of brandy and a little dirty silver cup by his side;
his head was tied about with a roll of coarse callico,[7] and he had a
loose gown of red damask[8] to cover him; he has gowns and mantles of
rich silver and gold brocaded silks, trimm'd with flowers of small

---

[4] *pursers:* The officers of the ship who keep accounts and oversee the provisions.
[5] *were carry'd to the king's town:* From the factory to the king's town is about four
miles, thro' very pleasant fields, full of India and Guiney corn, potatoes, yams in great
plenty, of which they have two harvests yearly. [Phillips's note.]
[6] *phiz:* Physiognomy, face.
[7] *callico:* A coarse cotton cloth, often decorated with bright colors.
[8] *damask:* An ornately decorated fabric, especially of silk or linen, originally produced in Damascus.

party-coloured[9] beads, which were presents made him, as he told us, by white captains, who traded there, and his variety of which he often shewed us; but he never wore shirt, shoe, nor stocking, in his life.

We saluted him with our hats, and he took us by the hands, snapt our fingers, and told us we were very welcome, that he was glad to see us, that he long'd for it, and that he lov'd *Englishmen* dearly, that we were his brothers, and that he would do us all the good offices he could; we returned him thanks by his interpreter, and assured him how great affection our masters, the royal *African* company of *England,* bore to him, for his civility and fair and just dealing with their captains; and that notwithstanding there were many other places, more plenty of negro slaves that begg'd their custom,[10] yet they had rejected all the advantageous offers made them out of their good will to him, and therefore had sent us to trade with him, to supply his country with necessaries, and that we hoped he would endeavour to continue their favour by his kind usage and fair dealing with us in our trade, that we may have our slaves with all expedition, which was the making of our voyage; that he would oblige his cappasheirs to do us justice, and not impose upon us in their prices; all which we should faithfully relate to our masters, the royal *African* company, when we came to *England.* He answered, that the *African* company was a very good brave[11] man; that he lov'd him; that we should be fairly dealt with, and not imposed upon: But he did not prove as good as his word; nor indeed (tho' his cappasheirs shew him so much respect) dare he do any thing but what they please.

He desired us to sit down upon a bench close by him, which we did; then he drank to us his brother the king of *England's* health, the *African* company's, our welcome, *&c.* in brandy and pitto, which is a pleasant liquor made of *Indian* corn soak'd in water, some so strong that it will keep three months, and two quarts will fuddle a man; it drinks much like new ale. We had not staid long before there came a repast on a little square table, with an old sheet for a cloth, old battered pewter plates and spoons, with a large pewter bason of the same hue with his majesty's complexion, fill'd with stew'd fowls and broth, and a wooden bowl of boil'd potatoes to serve instead of bread; we had no napkins, knives, nor forks laid us, nor do they ever use any, but always tear their meat; and indeed we had no occasion for any, for our

---

[9] *party-coloured:* Particolored, variously colored.
[10] *begg'd their custom:* Sought to trade with the RAC.
[11] *brave:* Fine, excellent.

fowls were boil'd to such mash, that they would not bear carving. We had no great stomach to our dainties, however, in complaisance to his majesty, we supp'd two or three spoonfuls of the broth, which was very well relish'd with malagetta[12] and red pepper; we often drank to the king out of a cup made of a cocoa-nut shell, which was all the plate I saw he had, except a little silver dram[13] cup. He would bow to us, kiss his hand, and burst out often in loud screaming laughter. When we had signify'd to his majesty that we had satisfy'd our stomachs with his dainties, he gave some of the fowls out of the broth, with his own hands, to the little children that were with him, and the rest among his nobles, who scrambled for it on their bellies like so many dogs, making spoons of their hands, which they would dip into the broth, and then lick'd them, which sight did affect my stomach so much, (tho' it is not very nice)[14] that I had much ado to refrain making them an addition of what I had eaten.

When they had done, the king ask'd for Capt. *Shurley,* and we acquainted him that he died upon the *Gold Coast* at *Acra,*[15] when of a sudden his note was changed from laughing to a loud howling and crying, wringing his hands and often wiping his eyes, (tho' no tears came out) saying that *Shurley* was his great friend; that he was exceedingly troubled for his death, and that the *Gold Coast* negroes had given him something to drink which killed him; then he told us of mortar pieces, pictures, silks, and many other things, Capt. *Shurley* promised to bring him for presents; when Mr. *Clay* told him there were no such things on board, he seemed to be angry, and told *Clay* that he was sure they were brought, but because *Shurley* was dead he would keep them for himself; but to appease him we promised to present him with blunderbusses,[16] silks, *&c.* which we had from the royal *African* company for that purpose; so after having examined us about our cargo, what sort of goods we had, and what quantity of slaves we wanted, &c. we took our leaves and returned to the factory having promised to come in the morning to make our palavera or

---

[12] *malagetta:* A spice, also used medicinally, made from a West African plant, Amomum Meliguetta.

[13] *dram:* A small amount of liquid.

[14] *nice:* Delicate, fastidious.

[15] *Acra:* A major trading center on the coast of Ghana; between 1650 and 1680, trading posts were established here by the English (Fort James), the French (Fort Crevecoeur), and the Danish (Christiansborg Castle). See the detail of the Bosman map on p. 211.

[16] *blunderbusses:* Short, wide-barreled guns, used to fire scatter shot at close range (as the name suggests, they do not allow for precise targeting).

agreement with him about prices, how much of each sort of our goods for a slave.

According to promise we attended his majesty with samples of our goods, and made our agreement about the prices, tho' not without much difficulty; he and his cappasheirs exacted very high, but at length we concluded as *per* the latter end; then we had warehouses, a kitchen, and lodgings assigned us, but none of our rooms had doors till we made them, and put on locks and keys; next day we paid our customs to the king and cappasheirs, as will appear hereafter; then the bell was ordered to go about to give notice to all people to bring their slaves to the trunk to sell us; this bell is a hollow piece of iron in shape of a sugar loaf, the cavity of which would contain about 50 lb. of cowries: This a man carry'd about and beat with a stick, which made a small dead sound.

We were every morning, during our stay here, invited to breakfast with the king, where we always found the same dish of stew'd fowls and potatoes; he also would send us a hog, goat, sheep, or pot of pitto every day for our table, and we usually return'd his civility with three or four bottles of brandy, which is his *summum bonum*:[17] We had our cook ashore, and eat as well as we could, provisions being plenty and cheap; but we soon lost our stomachs by sickness, most of my men having fevers, and myself such convulsions and aches in my head, that I could hardly stand or go to the trunk without assistance, and there often fainted with the horrid stink of the negroes, it being an old house where all the slaves are kept together, and evacuate nature where they lie, so that no jakes[18] can stink worse; there being forced to sit three or four hours at a time, quite ruin'd my health, but there was no help.

Capt. Clay and I had agreed to go to the trunk to buy the slaves by turns, each his day, that we might have no distraction or disagreement in our trade, as often happens when there are here more ships than one, and the commanders can't set their horses together, and go hand in hand in their traffick, whereby they have a check upon the blacks, whereas their disagreements create animosities, underminings, and out-bidding each other, whereby they enhance the prices to their general loss and detriment, the blacks well knowing how to make the best use of such opportunities, and, as we found, make it their business, and endeavour to create and foment misunderstandings and jealousies

---

[17] *summum bonum:* Greatest good (Latin).
[18] *jakes:* Latrines.

between commanders, it turning to their great account in the disposal of their slaves.

When we were at the trunk, the king's slaves, if he had any, were the first offer'd to sale, which the cappasheirs would be very urgent with us to buy, and would in a manner force us to it ere they would shew us any other, saying . . . we must not refuse them, tho' as I observ'd they were generally the worst slaves in the trunk, and we paid more for them than any others, which we could not remedy, it being one of his majesty's prerogatives; then the cappasheirs each brought out his slaves according to his degree and quality, the greatest first, &c., and our surgeon examined them well in all kinds, to see that they were sound wind[19] and limb, making them jump, stretch out their arms swiftly, looking in their mouths to judge of their age; for the cappasheirs are so cunning, that they shave them all close before we see them, so that let them be never so old we can see no grey hairs in their heads or beards; and then having liquor'd[20] them well and sleek with palm oil, 'tis no easy matter to know an old one from a middle-aged one, but by the teeths decay; but our greatest care of all is to buy none that are pox'd,[21] lest they should infect the rest aboard; for tho' we separate the men and women aboard by partitions and bulk-heads, to prevent quarrels and wranglings among them, yet do what we can they will come together, and that distemper which they call the yaws,[22] is very common here, and discovers itself by almost the same symptoms as the *Lues Venerea*[23] or clap does with us; therefore our surgeon is forc'd to examine the privities of both men and women with the nicest scrutiny, which is a great slavery, but what can't be omitted: When we had selected from the rest such as we liked, we agreed in what goods to pay for them, the prices being already stated before the king, how much of each sort of merchandize we were to give for a man, woman, and child, which gave us much ease, and saved abundance of disputes and wranglings, and gave the owner a note, signifying our agreement of the sorts of goods; upon delivery of which the next day he receiv'd them; then we mark'd the slaves we had bought in the breast, or shoulder, with a hot iron, having the letter of the ship's name on it, the place

---

[19] *wind:* Respiratory health, capacity for normal breathing.
[20] *liquor'd:* Greased.
[21] *pox'd:* Infected with syphilis (from the pockmarks, or pocks, left by the disease).
[22] *yaws:* A disease characterized by raspberry-like swellings on the skin.
[23] *Lues Venerea:* Syphilis (Latin, "plague of Venus" or "plague of love"); "the clap" is another term for the disease.

being before anointed with a little palm oil, which caused but little pain, the mark being usually well in four or five days, appearing very plain and white after.

When we had purchased to the number of 50 or 60, we would send them aboard, there being a cappasheir, intitled[24] the captain of the slaves, whose care it was to secure them to the water-side, and see them all off; and if in carrying to the marine any were lost, he was bound to make them good to us, the captain of the trunk being oblig'd to do the like, if any run away while under his care, for after we buy them we give him charge of them till the captain of the slaves comes to carry them away: These are two officers appointed by the king for this purpose, to each of which every ship pays the value of a slave in what goods they like best for their trouble, when they have done trading; and indeed they discharg'd their duty to us very faithfully, we not having lost one slave thro' their neglect in 1300 we bought here.

There is likewise a captain of the sand, who is appointed to take care of the merchandize we have come ashore to trade with, that the negroes do not plunder them, we being often forced to leave goods a whole night on the sea shore, for want[25] of porters to bring them up; but notwithstanding his care and authority, we often came by the loss, and could have no redress.

When our slaves were come to the seaside, our canoos were ready to carry them off to the longboat, if the sea permitted, and she convey'd them aboard ship, where the men were all put in irons, two and two shackled together, to prevent their mutiny, or swimming ashore.

The negroes are so wilful and loth to leave their own country, that they have often leap'd out of the canoos, boat and ship, into the sea, and kept under water till they were drowned, to avoid being taken up and saved by our boats, which pursued them; they having a more dreadful apprehension of *Barbadoes* than we can have of hell, tho' in reality they live much better there than in their own country; but home is home, &c. we have likewise seen divers of them eaten by the sharks, of which a prodigious number kept about the ships in this place, and I have been told will follow her hence to *Barbadoes*, for the dead negroes that are thrown over-board in the passage. I am certain in our voyage there we did not want the sight of some every day, but that they were the same I can't affirm.

[24] *intitled:* Designated.
[25] *want:* Lack.

We had about 12 negroes did wilfully drown themselves, and other starv'd themselves to death; for 'tis their belief that when they die they return home to their own country and friends again.

I have been inform'd that some commanders have cut off the legs or arms of the most wilful, to terrify the rest, for they believe if they lose a member, they cannot return home again: I was advised by some of my officers to do the same, but I could not be perswaded to entertain the least thoughts of it, much less to put in practice such barbarity and cruelty to poor creatures, who, excepting their want of christianity and true religion, (their misfortune more than fault) are as much the works of God's hands, and no doubt as dear to him as ourselves; nor can I imagine why they should be despised for their colour, being what they cannot help, and the effect of the climate it has pleased God to appoint them. I can't think there is any intrinsick value in one colour more than another, nor that white is better than black, only we think it so because we are so, and are prone to judge favourably in our own case, as well as the blacks, who in odium[26] of the colour, say, the devil is white, and so paint him.

Near the king's palace on one side is a town, consisting of about 40 houses wall'd round, in which are kept the king's wives, to whom none are admitted but an old cappasheir, who is captain of them; and the king himself. I have been assur'd by the interpreter here, Capt. *Tom*, (who is a sensible *Gold Coast* negro, and lived a long time with one of our factors, as his boy, and thereby learnt the *English* language, and is now one of the greatest men in the king of *Whidaw's* court) that the number of the king's wives are near 3000; and considering the custom of that country, it's very probable, for each cappasheir has from 10 to 20 wives, more or less, as he pleases, and can maintain; all which, together with his goods, fall to the king at his death, there being no regard had to his children, they having nothing but what is privately convey'd away by stealth during their father's sickness; nor do the king's sons after grown to any stature come near him but in private, for fear of giving umbrage to the great cappasheirs, who expect next to be elected king, and to them the king's sons give as much respect as the meanest subject: When the king dies all his wives and estate fall to the next king by election. The present king often, when ships are in a great strait for[27] slaves, and cannot be supply'd otherwise, will sell 3 or 400 of his wives to compleat their number, but we always pay dearer for

[26] *odium:* Contempt, aversion.
[27] *strait for:* Shortage of.

his slaves than those bought of the cappasheirs, his measure for booges[28] being much larger than theirs, and he was allow'd accordingly in all other goods we had.

For every slave the cappasheirs sold us publickly, they were oblig'd to pay part of the goods they receiv'd for it to the king, as toll or custom, especially the booges, of which he would take a small dish-full out of each measure; to avoid this they would privately send for us to their houses in the night, and dispose of two or three slaves at a time, and we as privately would send them the goods agreed upon for them; but this they did not much practice for fear of offending the king, should he come to know it, who injoyns[29] them to carry all their slaves to be sold publickly at the trunk with his own; sometimes, after he had sold one of his wives or subjects, he would relent, and desire us to exchange for another, which we freely did often, and he took very kindly.

Their marriages are as in the primitive times. When a man fancies a young woman he applies himself to her father, and desires her for a wife, which is seldom refused; then he gives her a fine cloth, and bracelets and necklaces of rangoes mix'd with coral for her arms and neck; invites her friends and his to a treat of pitto, and the ceremony is over, never having a farthing[30] portion with her.

Their women are most employ'd in making *Whidaw* cloths, mats, baskets, canchy, pitto, and in planting and sowing their corn, yams, potatoes, &c. The *Whidaw* cloth is about two yards long, and about a quarter of a yard broad, three such being commonly joyn'd together. It is of divers colours, but generally white and blue. For a pound of leaf tobacco, be it never so rotten and bad, we could buy one of these cloths, which would yield a crown in *Barbadoes;* also one for eight knives, value prime cost eighteen pence. To make these cloths, especially the blue streaks, they unravel most of the sayes and perpetuanoes[31] we sell them. . . .

We spent in our passage from St. Thomas to Barbadoes two months eleven days, from the 25th of August to the 4th of November following: in which time there happen'd much sickness and mortality among my poor men and negroes, that of the first we buried 14, and of the

---

[28] *booges:* See n. 20 on p. 234.
[29] *injoyns:* Enjoins, commands.
[30] *farthing:* A quarter of a penny, the smallest unit in English currency.
[31] *sayes and perpetuanoes:* Kinds of woolen cloth. Say was more finely textured, while perpetuano (or perpetuana) was designed for greater durability.

last 320, which was a great detriment to our voyage, the royal African company losing ten pounds by every slave that dies, and the owners of the ship ten pounds ten shillings. . . .

But what the small-pox spar'd, the flux[32] swept off, to our great regret, after all our pains and care to give them their messes[33] in due order and season, keeping their lodgings as clean and sweet as possible, and enduring so much misery and stench so long among a parcel of creatures nastier than swine; and after all our expectations to be defeated by their mortality. No gold-finders[34] can endure so much noisome[35] slavery as they do who carry negroes; for those have some respite and satisfaction, but we endure twice the misery; and yet by their mortality our voyages are ruin'd, and we pine and fret our selves to death, to think that we should undergo so much misery, and take so much pains to so little purpose.

I deliver'd alive to Barbadoes to the company's factors 372, which being sold, came out at about nineteen pounds per head one with another.

[32] *the flux:* Dysentery.
[33] *messes:* Meals.
[34] *gold-finders:* A slang term for cleaners of latrines; hence, by implication, people engaged in dirty, difficult work.
[35] *noisome:* Unpleasant.

WILLEM BOSMAN

From *A New and Accurate Description of the Coast of Guinea*

Willem Bosman (1672–?), a Dutchman, wrote his description of the coast of Guinea in 1701–02, having resided there as an agent of the Dutch West India Company for fourteen years. His is the fullest European account of the Gold Coast at the end of the seventeenth century. By that time, the Dutch had ceased to be the world's supreme naval power, and their dominance on the Guinea Coast was over. The 1690s was an especially unstable decade in the area, for competing European traders fomented African wars, and some inland kingdoms were extending their power. Like the agents of the English Royal African Company, the Dutch traders who were licensed to do business in Africa were perennially confronted by the problem of private interlopers who disregarded the official monopoly, trading with Africans at advantageous rates. Bosman admits that the private traders offer more attractive terms, and he makes no effort to justify his employer's policy. In his account of warfare in the region, Bosman stresses its affordability, seemingly with an eye on the possibility of more aggressive European intervention, and this probably helps to explain why his book was translated so quickly into French and English. Bosman also devotes a good deal of attention to the geography and the social arrangements of the countries he visits, seeking to correct common misperceptions about the size and wealth of these kingdoms. He emphasizes the lack of poverty among citizens, describing a work-for-hire program reminiscent, in some respects, of Thomas More's proposal for a form of slavery in *Utopia* (see pp. 401–05).

Bosman, who arrived in Guinea in 1688 at the age of sixteen, rose within ten years to the rank of Chief Merchant in the Dutch West India Company, a position subordinate only to that of the company's governor on the coast. He returned to Holland in 1701 after having failed to be promoted to governor because of political rivalries, and his *New and Accurate Description of the Coast of Guinea* was motivated in part by a desire to expose the shortcomings of the organization he had left. In his dedication he informs the directors of the Dutch West India Company that he seeks to describe "the true condition of the coast," which has been "hidden from you in order that some evil-doers could better serve their selfish interests." His book, written in the form of letters to a friend, was first published in Dutch in 1703, and it quickly became a best-seller, going through four editions in the next fifteen years. It was translated into French in 1705, and that same year, an anonymous writer used the French text as the basis for an English translation. This selection is excerpted from the first English edition, titled *A New and Accurate Description of the Coast of Guinea: Divided into the Gold, the Slave, and the Ivory Coasts* (London: Knapton, 1705) 4–7, 11–13, 128–29, 130–31, 132–33, 140–41, 178–81, 183.

Guinea[1] is a large Country, extended several Hundred Miles, abounding with innumerable Kingdoms, and several Commonwealths.

Several Authors have presented *Guinea* as a Mighty Kingdom, whose Prince by his Victoriousness had subdued numerous Countries,

---

[1] *Guinea:* As the introduction to this chapter explains, Guinea was often used to describe a long stretch of the coast of western Africa, from the Senegambia region down to the Congo in central Africa; as his description makes clear, however, Bosman uses this name to describe a much more restricted area, covering most of the south-facing coast of western Africa. (See also Equiano's account of Guinea, at the beginning of the selection from his autobiography, later in this chapter.)

and erected their whole extent of Land into one Mighty Kingdom, which he called *Guinea:* How great this mistake is, I hope to evince to you; since the very Name of *Guinea,* is not so much as known to the Natives here, nor the imaginary *Guinea* Monarchy yet to be found in the World.

The Gold-Coast being a part of *Guinea,* is extended about Sixty Miles, beginning with the Gold River three Miles *West* of *Assine,* or twelve above *Axim,* and ending with the Village *Ponni* seven or eight Miles *East* of *Acra.*[2]

I am unwilling to detain you with a Description of the Tract of Land betwixt *Assine* and *Rio,* or the River *Cobre,* about a Mile above our Fort; since the Trade of that Place is at present so inconsiderable that it is very little frequented, tho' nine or ten Years ago its Commerce was in a Flourishing state; But since the Golden Country of *Assine* (from whence Gold was brought thither) was Conquer'd, and almost Devastated, the *Dinckin-rase*[3] Traffick has run at a low Ebb, and the little Gold-Dust which is brought thither is either Sophisticated[4] or of very small Value: wherefore I shall steer my Course along the Gold-Coast, and without considering the Rank of Precedence, take them fairly as they lie my way, and describe them as well as the compass of a Letter will permit.

The Countries from the *Ancobersian* River to the Village *Ponni,* are Eleven in Number, *viz. Axim, Ante, Adom, Jabi, Commani, Fetu, Saboe, Fantyn, Acron, Agonna,*and *Aquamboe;*[5] each containing one, two, or three Towns or Villages, lying upon the Sea-shore, as well under, as betwixt the Forts of the *Europeans;* their greatest and most Populous Towns being generally farther on Land. Seven of these are Kingdoms, Governed by their respective Kings; and the rest being Govern'd by some of the Principal Men amongst them, seem to approach nearer to Commonwealths: But I shall give you a more particular Account of them hereafter, and in order thereto at present begin with *Axim;* which, as the Notion of Power runs here, was formerly a Potent Monarchy,[6] but the Arrival of the *Brandenburghers*[7] divided

---

[2] *Assine . . . Axim . . . Ponni . . . Acra:* See the detail of Bosman's map on p. 211. Assine, or "Assi," Axim, and Acra appear at the far west, while Ponni, or "Bony," appears at the far east.

[3] *Dinckin-rase:* I.e., Denkyirans, natives of Denkyira, or "Dinkine" (see p. 211).

[4] *Sophisticated:* Adulterated.

[5] *Ancobersian . . . Aquamboe:* These areas appear sequentially, with some spelling variations, on the map on p. 211.

[6] *which, as the Notion of Power runs here . . . Monarchy:* Bosman's original text says nothing about a monarchy, and would be more accurately translated: "it [i.e.,

This engraving of Fort Amsterdam at Cormentyn is taken from Jean Barbot's *A Description of the Coasts of North and South-Guinea, and of Ethiopia Inferior, Vulgarly Angola . . . Now First Printed from His Original Manuscript.* In *A Collection of Voyages and Travels,* ed. Awnsham Churchill (5:177) (London: Walthoe, 1752). According to Willem Bosman, this fortress was "The chief Residence of the English, till they were driven from thence by Admiral De Ryters, An. 1665." Fort Amsterdam must, therefore, have been the "Coromantine" from which Africans were shipped to Suriname during the period portrayed in *Oroonoko.*

the Inhabitants, one part of them putting themselves under the Protection of the New-comers, in expectation of an easier Government and looser Reins, in which they were not mistaken, as the Consequence evinced; but the other part, which were the most Honest and least Changeable, staid under our Government.

The *Negro* Inhabitants are generally very Rich, driving a great Trade with the *Europeans* for Gold, which they chiefly Vend to the *English* and *Zealand* Interlopers,[8] notwithstanding the severe Penalty they incurr thereby; for if we catch them, their so bought Goods are

Axim] was formerly considerable in size and power (as the notion of power runs here)." This alternate translation, as well as the others in the notes for this section, comes from a series of articles by Albert Van Dantzig entitled "English Bosman and Dutch Bosman: A Comparison of Texts." Part I was published in *History in Africa* 2 (1975): 185–216; part II in *History in Africa* 3 (1976): 91–126; and part III in *History in Africa* 4 (1977): 247–73.

[7] *Brandenburghers:* See n. 5 on p. 231.

[8] *The Negro Inhabitants . . . Interlopers:* A more accurate translation would read: "The blacks *(Negroes)* or Inhabitants of this *Country* are generally rich and live luxuriously and carry on a great trade with *Merchants* coming from the *Interior;* but their Gold they spend mostly on Board Ships coming to trade here on the *Coast,* such as *English* and *Zealand* Interlopers." Zealand was a province of the Netherlands.

not only Forfeited, but a heavy Fine is laid upom 'em: Not deterr'd I say by this, they all hope to escape; to effect which, they Bribe our Slaves, (who are set as Watches and Spies over them) to let them pass by Night; by which means we are hindred from having much above an Hundredth part of the Gold of this Land:[9] And the plain Reason why the Natives run this Risque of Trading with the Interlopers, is, that their Goods are sometimes better than ours, and always to be had one third part cheaper; whereby they are encouraged against the danger, very well knowing, that a successful Correspondence will soon enrich them. . . .

The Inhabitants of *Axim*, [whom] we find industriously employ'd either in Trade, Fishing, or agriculture, and that is chiefly exercised in the Culture of *Rice*, which grows here above all other places in an incredible abundance, and is Transported hence all the Gold-Coast over. The Inhabitants in lieu returning full Fraught with *Millet, Jammes,*[10] *Potatoes,* and *Palm Oyl*; all which are very rare here, for the Soil is naturally moist, and tho' fit to produce *Rice,* and Fruit-Trees, doth not kindly yield other Fruits. . . .

This River[11] is too pleasant to be slightly passed over, and as I have already told you, is a Mile above our Fort St. *Anthony;*[12] its Mouth is very wide, with so shallow Water, that I question whether 'tis passable with a Boat, but a little farther it grows deeper and narrower; after which, in several Miles no observable alteration appears. How far its inland Course extends I cannot inform you, tho' I have travelled above three small days Voyage upon it, and found it as pleasant as any part of the *Guinea* Coast, not excepting *Fida* it self:[13] each of its Banks being adorned with fine lofty Trees, which afford the most agreeable shade in the World, defending the Traveller from the scorching Beams of the Sun. 'Tis also not unpleasant to observe the beautiful variegated Birds, and the sportive Apes, diverting themselves on the verdant Boughs all the way. To render it yet more Charming, having Sailed

---

[9] *by which means . . . Gold of this Land:* A more accurate translation would read: "by which means we are hindered from intercepting more than one-hundredth of these Goods."

[10] *Jammes:* I.e., yams.

[11] *This River:* I.e., the Ancobra.

[12] *Fort St. Anthony:* Near the Ancobra (or Combre River) in the map on p. 210.

[13] *not excepting Fida it self:* Mistranslated; this should read: "perhaps excepting Fida." Fida is the Dutch name for Whydah; cf. the selection from *The Royal African,* p. 284.

about a Mile up,[14] you are entertain'd with the view of a fine populous Village, extending about a quarter of a Mile on its *Western* Shore: Of such Villages hereabouts are a great number, which together make up three several Countries, of which the First situate next the Sea is called *Ancober;* (whether the River be obliged to the Country or the Country to the River for its Name I shall not determine;) the Second next occuring Land is *Abocroe,* and the Last *Eguira.*[15] The first I observed was a Monarchy, and the other two Common-wealths. Several Years past we had a Fort in the Country of *Eguira,* and drove a very considerable Trade there; for besides the Afflux[16] of Gold thither from all foreign Parts, the Country it self affords some Gold Mines; and I remember when I had the Government of *Axim;* a very Rich one was discovered; but we lost our Footing there in a very Tragical manner: For the Commander in Chief of the *Negroes,* being closely Besieged by our Men, (as Fame Reports) shot Gold instead of Bullets, hinting by Signs that he was ready to Treat, and afterwards Trade with the Besiegers, but in the midst of their Negotiation he blew up himself and all his Enemies at once, as Unfortunately as Bravely, putting an end to our Siege and his Life, and like *Sampson* revenging his Death upon his Enemies.[17] To compass his Design, he had encouraged a Slave by promising him new Cloaths, to stand ready with a lighted Match, with which he was to touch the Powder when he saw him stamp with his Foot, which the silly Wretch but too punctually perform'd undiscover'd by any but one of our Companies Slaves, who observing it, withdrew as silently as timely, being only left alive to bring us the News; and since we could get no better Account, we were obliged to believe this; it being but too certain that our Fort to the cost of our Director and some of our Enemies was Blown up. . . .

In the beginning of this Letter I told you the *Negroes* were very idle and not easily prevailed on to work, as well as that they had very few Manual Arts: All which indeed are employed chiefly in the making of Wooden or Earthen Cups, Troughs, matting of Chairs, making of

---

[14] *having Sailed about a Mile up:* Mistranslated; this should read: "you meet every quarter of an hour, sailing past the West bank of the river, a fine, populous Village, whose houses are nicely built on the water-front."

[15] *Ancober . . . Abocroe . . . Eguira:* With some variations in spelling, these areas appear near the western end of the map on p. 210.

[16] *Afflux:* Flowing toward a point.

[17] *Sampson . . . Enemies:* In Judg. 16.23–30, Samson avenges himself on his captors by pulling down two great pillars, killing both his enemies and himself.

Copper Ointment Boxes,[18] and Arm-Rings of Gold, Silver or Ivory, with some other Trash.[19] Their chief Handicraft, with which they are best acquainted being the Smithery; for with their sorry Tools they can make all sorts of War-Arms that they want, Guns only excepted: as well as whatever is required in their Agriculture and House-keeping. They have no Notion of Steel and yet they make their Sables and all cutting Instruments: Their principal tools are a kind of hard Stone instead of an Anvil, a pair of Tongues, and a small pair of Bellows,[20] with three or more Pipes; which blow very strong and are an Invention of their own. These are most of their Arts, besides that of making of *Fetiche's*;[21] which I have before informed you of: But their most artful Works are the fine Gold and Silver Hat-bands which they make for us; the Thread and Contexture of which is so fine, that I question whether our *European* Artists[22] would not be put to it to imitate them: And indeed if they could, and were no better paid than the *Negroes,* they would be obliged to live on dry Bread.

Though the Gold Coast is not extended above sixty Miles in length, yet we find there seven or eight several Languages, so different that three or four of them are interchangeably unintelligible to any but the respective Natives: The *Negroes* of *Junmore,* ten Miles above *Axim,* cannot understand[23] those of *Egira, Abocroe, Ancober* and *Axim:* There is indeed a vast difference in their Languages. That of *Axim* is a very disagreeable brutal Sound; that of *Ante* very different from it, though not much more beautiful: But more shocking is that of *Acra,* not having the least Similitude with any of the rest. The other Coast *Negroes,* those of *Aquamboe* only excepted, generally understand one

[18] *matting of Chairs . . . Boxes:* Mistranslated; this should read: "Stools, Mats, Copper Ointment Boxes."

[19] *Trash:* I.e., Trifles.

[20] *they make their Sables . . . pair of Bellows:* Mistranslated; this should read: "they make their *Swords* and *Cutlasses hard* and *sharp* enough, and similarly their *Pick*-axes and the other agricultural *ware* they may need. Their principal tools consist of a large, hard stone, which serves them as an *Anvil,* two or three *sledge-hammers,* and a small pair of Bellows . . . "

[21] *Fetiche's:* Mistranslated; this should read: "*Gold Fetiches.*" Though typically used to describe charms (see p. 232), the term "fetish" evidently also applied to certain items of commerce; elsewhere in his book, Bosman defines "fetish" as "a sort of artificial Gold composed of several ingredients."

[22] *Artists:* Mistranslated; this should read: "*Goldsmiths.*"

[23] *cannot understand:* Mistranslated; this should read: "manage to make themselves understood to."

another: But the In-land *Negroes* is by much the pleasant and most agreeable; I mean those of *Dinkira, Akim, Acanny* and *Adom;* this difference is easily discernable to a Person but the least acquainted with their Languages, and appears as that betwixt *Brabanders* and Foreigners:[24] And if the *Negroes,* which we daily converse with, who live about our Forts, expressed themselves as agreeably as the others, 'twould be no difficult matter to learn their Language in two or three Years, which we find at present we can scarce do in ten, at least not in any sort of Perfection. Some of us, amongst which I dare reckon my self, have made such a Progress, that we understand the greatest part of it, though we can hardly hit the Pronunciation. The Sound of some Words is so strange, that though we have often endeavoured to express them with our *European* Letters, yet we have never been able to do it; and the *Negroes* can neither write nor read, and consequently have no use of Letters; which renders it impossible for us to trace their Faults. . . .

I have observed five Degrees of men amongst the *Negroes;* the first of which are their Kings or Captains, for the Word is here *Synonymous.*

The second, their *Cabocero's,* or Chief Men; which reducing to our manner of Expression, we should be apt to call them Civil Fathers;[25] whose Province is only to take care of the Welfare of the City or Village, and to appease any Tumult.[26]

The third sort are those who have acquired a great Reputation by their Riches, either devolved on them by Inheritance or gotten by Trade. And these are the Persons which some Authors have represented as Noblemen; but whether they are in the right or not,[27] shall hereafter plainly appear.

The fourth are the common People imployed in the Tillage of Wines, Agriculture and Fishing.

---

[24] *But the In-land Negroes:* This should read: "But the *Language* of the inland *Negroes";* *"appears as that betwixt Brabanders and Foreigners"*: A more literal translation would be: "appears as great as that betwixt Brabanders and the *Overseas People."* Brabant was a Flemish duchy in an area now divided between the Netherlands and Belgium.

[25] *Civil Fathers:* Bosman actually uses the Dutch term for "Burgomasters" ("bourough masters" or "city fathers" of a Dutch town).

[26] *appease any Tumult:* A more literal translation would be "settle any disputes."

[27] *some Authors . . . in the right or not:* Bosman's text uses the singular rather than plural, to indicate that he is continuing a critique, begun earlier in the book, of Olfert Dapper's *Accurate Description of the African Regions,* published in Amsterdam in 1668.

The fifth and last are the Slaves, either sold by their Relations, taken in War, or come so by Poverty.

These five being the only Degrees which are to be found amongst the *Negroes;* let us enquire by what means they arrive at any of the three first.

First, The Dignity of King or Captain in most of these Countries, descends Hereditarily from Father to Son, and in defect of Issue to the next Male-Heir; though sometimes so much regard is had to his Riches in Slaves and Money,[28] that he who is plentifully stored with these, is often preferred to the Right Heir. . . .

What is most commendable amongst the *Negroes,* is, that we find no poor amongst them who beg; for though they are never so wretchedly poor they never beg: The Reason of which is, that when a *Negroe* finds he cannot subsist, he binds[29] himself for a certain Summ of Money, or his Friends do it for him; and the Master to whom he hath obliged himself keeps him in all Necessaries, setting him a sort of Task, which is not in the least slavish, being chiefly to defend his Master on occasion, and in sowing time to work as much as he himself pleases. So that, as I have before told you, here are no Beggars obliged to be so by Poverty; But shameless Beggars without the least necessity, are so plentiful that they all undistinguishably deserve that Name: A King himself is not ashamed to beg; and that for such mean things as he might buy for one penny or two pence; they are so scandalous importunate, that 'tis impossible to get from them without giving them something. . . .

Common Prisoners who cannot raise their Ransom, are kept and sold for Slaves at pleasure:[30] If they take any considerable Person, he is very well guarded and a very high Ransom put upon him: But if the Person who occasioned the beginning of the War be taken, they will not easily admit him to Ransom, though his weight in Gold were offered, for fear he should for the future form some new design against their repose.

The most Potent *Negroe* can't pretend[31] to be insured from Slavery; for if he ever ventures himself in the Wars it may easily become his Lot; he is consequently obliged to remain in that State till the Summ

---

[28] *though sometimes . . . Slaves and Money:* A more accurate translation would read: "Sometimes, too, the Ability of such an heir is taken into consideration, as well as his wealth in slaves and money . . . "

[29] *binds:* More accurately translated: "pawns."

[30] *at pleasure:* At will, at the choice of the capturer.

[31] *pretend:* Claim, allege.

demanded for his Redemption is fully paid; which withal[32] is frequently set so high, that he, his Friends, and all his Interest are not sufficient to raise it: on which account he is forced to a perpetual Slavery, and the most contemptible Offices. Some amongst them are so barbarous, that finding their hopes of a high Ransom frustrated, they pay themselves by cruelly murthering the wretched Prisoner.

Wars betwixt two Despotical Kings, who have their Subjects intirely at their Command, are of a long Duration, and frequently last several Years successively, or till the utter Ruine of one of 'em ends the dispute. They frequently lye a whole Year incampt[33] against each other without attempting any thing, a few diverting Skirmishes excepted: only against rainy Weather they each return home without molesting one another.

[32] *withal:* Moreover.
[33] *incampt:* Encamped, lodged in tents.

WILLIAM SNELGRAVE

From *A New Account of Guinea, and the Slave Trade*

Captain William Snelgrave was involved in the slave trade for some thirty years, undertaking his first voyage to Africa in 1704 and traveling to Sierra Leone, the Gold Coast, and the Slave Coast on later journeys. His account of mutiny on board a slaving vessel in 1721 gives us another glimpse of the "stout stubborn . . . Cormantines" who feature in Behn's story. Snelgrave's careful presentation of his actions as reasoned, necessary, and humane reveals a newly felt need to defend the trade against accusations of cruelty. In passages of his book not reprinted here, Snelgrave undertakes a full-blown justification of the British slave trade, arguing that African rulers would put their prisoners of war to death if they could not sell them. Such "humanitarian" arguments for the slave trade indicate Snelgrave's awareness of the rise of philanthropic sentiment within an important section of the English educated classes, a sentiment that would ripen into the abolitionist movement

In persuading the captured Africans not to rebel, Snelgrave disclaims any responsibility for their enslavement, and his description of how they have "forfeited their Freedom" is partially accurate, at least in a technical sense. In some African kingdoms, such crimes as theft, adultery, and gambling could be punished legally by enslavement; nevertheless, while clear statistical evidence is unavailable, capture in war appears to have been a much more common source of slaves. What evidence we do have suggests that both judicial slavery and the taking of war prisoners increased dramatically in response to the growing market for slaves.

Snelgrave's narrative is a repository of the professional knowledge he acquired in the course of his career. His account of his ability to persuade the captured Africans not to rebel, and his familiarity with their beliefs about the monetary value of human life and about the dismemberment of dead bodies, help to demonstrate the skills that a successful trader depended on. Even as Snelgrave boasts about his talents, he emphasizes his need for a native translator. His travel narrative probably served as a kind of instruction manual for those entering the slaving trade, indicating both the skills necessary to maintain peace shipboard and the ideological claims necessary to justify one's activities. First published in 1734, the book was quickly translated into French and German.

The text is excerpted from the second edition of *A New Account of Guinea, and the Slave Trade, Containing . . . The Manner How the Negroes Become Slaves* (London: Printed for J. Wren, 1754) 168–74, 174–75, 177, 178–80, 181–85.

Sometimes we meet with stout stubborn People amongst them, who are never to be made easy; and these are generally some of the *Cormantines,* a Nation of the *Gold Coast.* I went in the year 1721, in the *Henry* of *London,* a Voyage to that part of the *Coast,* and bought a good many of these People. We were obliged to secure them very well in Irons, and watch them narrowly: Yet they nevertheless mutinied, tho' they had little prospect of succeeding. I lay at that time near a place called *Mumfort*[1] on the *Gold-Coast,* having near five hundred Negroes on board, three hundred of which were Men. Our Ship's Company consisted of fifty white People, all in health: And I had very good Officers; so that I was very easy in all respects.

This Mutiny began at Midnight (the Moon then shining very bright) in this manner. Two Men that stood Centry[2] at the Fore-hatch[3]

---

[1] *Mumfort:* Probably Montfort, at the east end of the coast of Fantin, near the border with Akron (see p. 210).

[2] *Centry:* I.e., sentry.

[3] *Fore-hatch:* A framework at the front of the ship, covering the openings to the deck (hatchways).

way, where the Men Slaves came up to go to the house of Office,[4] permitted four to go to that place; but neglected to lay the Gratings[5] again, as they should have done: Whereupon four more Negroes came on Deck, who had got their Irons off, and the four in the house of Office having done the same, all the eight fell on the two Centries, who immediately called out for help. The Negroes endeavoured to get their Cutlaces from them, but the Lineyards (that is the Lines by which the handles of the Cutlaces were fastned to the Mens Wrists) were so twisted in the Scuffle, that they could not get them off before we came to their Assistance. The Negroes perceiving several white Men coming towards them, with Arms in their hands, quitted the Centries, and jumped over the Ship's side into the Sea.

I being by this time come forward on the Deck, my first care was to secure the Gratings, to prevent any more Negroes from coming up; and then I ordered People to get into the Boat, and save those that had jumped over-board, which they luckily did: For they found them all clinging to the Cables the Ship was moored by.

After we had secured these People, I called the Linguists, and ordered them to bid the Men-Negroes between Decks be quiet (for there was a great noise amongst them). On their being silent, I asked, "What had induced them to mutiny? They answered, I was a great Rogue to buy them, in order to carry them away from their own Country and that they were resolved to regain their Liberty if possible." I replied, "That they had forfeited their Freedom before I bought them, either by Crimes, or by being taken in War, according to the Custom of their Country; and they being now my Property, I was resolved to let them feel my Resentment, if they abused my Kindness: Asking at the same time, Whether they had been ill used by the white Men, or had wanted for any thing the Ship afforded?" To this they replied, "They had nothing to complain of." Then I observed to them, "That if they should gain their Point and escape to the Shore, it would be no Advantage to them, because their Countrymen would catch them, and sell them to other Ships." This served my purpose, and they seemed to be convinced of their Fault, begging, "I would forgive them, and promising for the future to be obedient, and never mutiny again, if I would not punish them this time." This I readily granted, and so they went to sleep. When Day-light came we called the Men Negroes up on Deck, and examining their Irons, found them all secure. So this Affair

---

[4] *house of Office:* Bathroom, latrine.
[5] *lay the Gratings:* Fasten the bars in the entryway.

happily ended, which I was very glad of; for these People are the stoutest and most sensible *Negroes* on the Coast: Neither are they so weak as to imagine as others do, that we buy them to eat them; being satisfied we carry them to work in our Plantations, as they do in their own Country.

However, a few days after this, we discovered they were plotting again, and preparing to mutiny. For some of the Ringleaders proposed to one of our Linguists, If he could procure them an Ax, they would cut the Cables the Ship rid by in the night; and so on her driving (as they imagined) ashore, they should get out of our hands, and then would become his Servants as long as they lived.

For the better understanding of this I must observe here, that these Linguists are Natives and Freemen of the Country, whom we hire on account of their speaking good *English,* during the time we remain trading on the Coast; and they are likewise Brokers between us and the black Merchants.

This Linguist was so honest as to acquaint me with what had been proposed to him; and advised me to keep strict Watch over the Slaves: For tho' he had represented to them the same as I had done on their mutinying before, That they would be all catch'd again, and sold to other Ships, in case they could carry their Point, and get on Shore; yet it had no effect upon them.

This gave me a good deal of Uneasiness. For I knew several Voyages had proved unsuccessful by Mutinies; as they occasioned either the total loss of the Ship and the white Mens Lives; or at least by rendring it absolutely necessary to kill or wound a great number of the Slaves, in order to prevent a total Destruction. Moreover, I knew many of these *Cormantine* Negroes despised[6] Punishment, and even Death it self: It having often happened at *Barbadoes* and other Islands, that on their being any ways hardly dealt with, to break them of their Stubbornness in refusing to work, twenty or more have hang'd themselves at a time in a Plantation. However, about a Month after this, a sad Accident happened, that brought our Slaves to be more orderly, and put them in a better Temper: And it was this. On our going from *Mumfort* to *Annamaboe,* which is the principal part on the *Gold Coast,* I met there with another of my Owner's Ships, called the *Elizabeth.* One Captain *Thompson* that commanded her was dead; as also his chief Mate. . . .

---

[6] *despised:* Had no concern about.

When I met with this Vessel I had almost disposed of my Ship's Cargoe; and the *Elizabeth* being under my Direction, I acquainted the second Mate, who then commanded her, That I thought it for our Owner's Interest, to take the Slaves from on board him, being about 120, into my ship; and then go off the Coast; and that I would deliver him at the same time the Remains of my Cargoe, for him to dispose of with his own after I was sailed . . .

But that very Night, which was near a month after the Mutiny on board of us at *Mumfort,* the Moon shining now very bright, as it did then, we heard, about ten a Clock, two or three Musquets fired on board the *Elizabeth.* Upon that I ordered all our Boats to be manned, and having secured every thing in our Ship, to prevent our Slaves from mutinying, I went my self. . . . to the fore-part of the Ship with some of my People, and there we found the Cooper[7] lying on his back quite dead, his Scull being cleft asunder with a Hatchet that lay by him. At the sight of this I called for the Linguist, and bid him ask the *Negroes* between Decks, "Who had killed the white Man?" They answered, "They knew nothing of the matter; for there had been no design of mutinying amongst them:" Which upon Examination we found true; for above one hundred of the Negroes then on board, being bought to Windward, did not understand a word of the *Gold-Coast* Language, and so had not been in the Plot. But this Mutiny was contrived by a few *Cormantee-Negroes,* who had been purchased about two or three days before. At last, one of the two Men-Negroes we had taken up along the Ship side, impeached his Companion, and he readily confessed he had kill'd the Cooper, with no other View, but that he and his Countrymen might escape undiscovered by swimming on Shore. For on their coming upon Deck, they observed, that all the white Men set to watch were asleep; and having found the Cook's Hatchet by the Fire-place, he took it up, not designing then to do any Mischief with it; but passing by the Cooper, who was centry, and he beginning to awake, the Negroe rashly struck him on the head with it, and then jump'd overboard. Upon this frank Confession, the white Men would have cut him to Pieces; but I prevented it, and carried him to my own Ship. Early the next morning, I went on board the *Elizabeth* with my Boats, and sent away all the Negroes then in her, into my own Ship. . . .

After having sent the Slaves out of the *Elizabeth,* as I have just now mentioned, I went on board my own Ship; and there being then in the

---

[7] *the Cooper:* The person who fixes casks, buckets, tubs, etc. on the ship.

Road of *Anamaboe,* eight sail of Ships besides us, I sent an Officer in my Boat to the Commanders of them, "To desire their Company on board my Ship, because I had an Affair of great Consequence to communicate to them." Soon after, most of them were pleased to come; and I having acquainted them with the whole Matter, and they having also heard the Negroe's Confession, "That he had killed the white Man;" They unanimously advised me to put him to death; arguing, "That Blood required Blood, by all Laws both divine and human; especially as there was in this Case the clearest Proof, namely the Murderer's Confession: Moreover this would in all probability prevent future Mischiefs; for by publickly executing this Person at the Ship's Fore-yard Arm,[8] the Negroes on board their Ships would see it; and as they were very much disposed to mutiny, it might prevent them from attempting it." These Reasons, with my being in the same Circumstances, made me comply.

Accordingly we acquainted the Negroe, that he was to die in an hour's time for murdering the white Man. He answered, "He must confess it was a rash Action in him to kill him; but he desired me to consider, that if I put him to death, I should lose all the Money I had paid for him." To this I bid the Interpreter reply, "That tho' I knew it was customary in his Country to commute for Murder by a Sum of Money, yet it was not so with us; and he should find that I had no regard to my Profit in this respect: For as soon as an Hour-Glass, just then turned, was run out, he should be put to death;" At which I observed he shewed no Concern.

Hereupon the other Commanders went on board their respective Ships, in order to have all their Negroes upon deck at the time of Execution, and to inform them of the occasion of it. The Hour-Glass being run out, the Murderer was carried on the Ship's Forecastle,[9] where he had a Rope fastened under his Arms, in order to be hoisted up to the Fore-yard Arm, to be shot to death. This some of his Countrymen observing, told him, (as the Linguist informed me afterwards) "That they would not have him be frightened; for it was plain I did not design to put him to death, otherwise the Rope would have been put about his neck, to hang him." For it seems they had no thought of his being shot; judging he was only to be hoisted up to the Yard-arm, in order to scare him: But they immediately saw the contrary; for as soon as he was hoisted up, ten white Men who were placed behind the

---

[8] *Fore-yard Arm:* The arm of the lowest rod supporting the sail on the foremast.
[9] *Forecastle:* A short raised deck at the front of the ship.

Barricado[10] on the Quarter-deck, fired their Musquets, and instantly killed him. This struck a sudden Damp[11] upon our Negroe-Men, who thought, that, on account of my Profit, I would not have executed him.

The Body being let down upon the Deck, the Head was cut off, and thrown overboard. This last part was done, to let our Negroes see, that all who offended thus, should be served in the same manner. For many of the Blacks believe, that if they are put to death and not dismembred, they shall return again to their own Country, after they are thrown overboard. But neither the Person that was executed, nor his Countrymen of *Cormantee* (as I understood afterwards,) were so weak as to believe any such thing; tho' many I had on board from other Countries had that Opinion.

When the Execution was over, I ordered the Linguist to acquaint the Men-Negroes, "That now they might judge, no one that killed a white Man should be spared:" And I thought proper now to acquaint them once for all, "That if they attempted to mutiny again, I should be obliged to punish the Ringleaders with death, in order to prevent further Mischief." Upon this they all promised to be obedient, and I assured them they should be kindly used, if they kept their Promise: which they faithfully did. For we sailed, two days after, from *Anamaboe* for *Jamaica;* and tho' they were on board near four Months, from our going off the Coast, till they were sold at that Island, they never gave us the least reason to be jealous of them; which doubtless was owing to the Execution of the white Man's Murderer.

[10] *Barricado:* Boundary.
[11] *struck a sudden Damp:* Discouraged.

THOMAS BLUETT

From *Some Memoirs of the Life of Job, the Son of Solomon*

This selection and the next one offer two perspectives on the story of Ayuba Suleiman Diallo (c. 1720–1773) of Bondu, a literate young Muslim merchant known to the Europeans as Job Ben Solomon. Thomas Bluett, a clergyman from Maryland, provides a brief account of Ben Solomon's experiences, explaining how he was captured and then freed. During a trip along the Gambia in 1731, Ben Solomon was abducted by non-Muslims,

An engraving of Ayuba Suleiman Diallo (Job Ben Solomon), from *The Gentleman's Magazine* 20 (1750): 272. Photo courtesy of The New York Public Library.

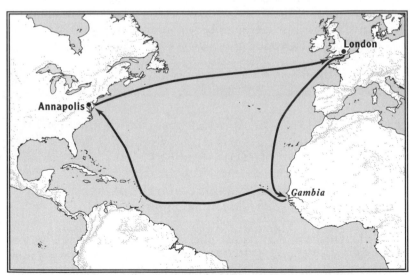

Suleiman Diallo ben Solomon, 1731–1734

Suleiman Diallo's route across the Atlantic to North America, then to England, and finally back to the banks of the Gambia.

sold into slavery, and shipped to Maryland, where he met Bluett. When Ben Solomon wrote a letter in Arabic to his father, sent via London, it came to the attention of James Oglethorpe, the director of the Royal African Company, who in turn sent it to Oxford to be translated. Oglethorpe and Bluett then assisted in securing Ben Solomon's emancipation and in arranging a fourteen-month tour of England for him prior to his return to Bondu.

Bluett represents Ben Solomon as inherently noble and physically graceful. He is already persuaded, on their first meeting, that Ben Solomon is "no common Slave" (p. 264). Like Behn, Bluett describes a brave, strong, and quick-witted African whose abilities are taken to demonstrate his incapacity for slavery. Bluett does not use Ben Solomon's story to argue against the inhumanity of slavery as an institution. Rather, he tacitly assumes that he has met with an isolated exception, remarking indifferently, for example, that Ben Solomon's interpreter, captured along with him, "is a Slave in *Maryland* still" (p. 262).

Though Bluett's pamphlet was printed only once, in 1734, his narrative reached a wider audience when it was reprinted in Thomas Astley's very popular compendium of travel literature, *A New General Collection of Voyages and Travels* (4 vols., 1743–47), which also included Francis Moore's account of Ben Solomon and Thomas Phillips's account of the Slave Coast in the 1690s.

The text is excerpted from the first edition of *Some memoirs of the life of Job, the Son of Solomon, the high priest of Boonda in Africa; who was a slave about two years in Maryland; and afterwards being brought to England, was set free, and sent to his native Land in the Year 1734* (London: Printed for Richard Ford, 1734) iii–viii, 9–10, 12–33, 46–55, 58–63.

SECT. II.

Of the Manner of his being taken Captive; and what followed upon it, till his Return.

In *February*, 1730. JOB's Father hearing of an *English* Ship at *Gambia* River,[1] sent him, with two Servants to attend him, to sell two Negroes, and to buy Paper, and some other Necessaries; but desired

---

[1] *Gambia River:* In what is now Senegal; the same river that Richard Jobson traveled along in his search for gold more than a century earlier.

him not to venture over the River, because the Country of the *Mandingoes,* who are Enemies to the People of *Futa,* lies on the other side. JOB not agreeing with Captain *Pike* (who commanded the Ship, lying then at *Gambia,* in the Service of Captain *Henry Hunt,* Brother to Mr. *William Hunt,* Merchant, in *Little Tower-Street, London)* sent back the two Servants to acquaint his Father with it, and to let him know that he intended to go farther. Accordingly, having agreed with another Man, named *Loumein Taoi,* who understood the *Mandingoe*[2] Language, to go with him as his Interpreter, he crossed the River *Gambia,* and disposed of his Negroes for some Cows. As he was returning Home, he stopp'd for some Refreshment at the House of an old Acquaintance; and the Weather being hot, he hung up his Arms in the House, while he refresh'd himself. Those Arms were very valuable; consisting of a Gold-hilted Sword, a Gold Knife, which they wear by their Side, and a rich Quiver of Arrows, which King *Sambo*[3] had made him a Present of. It happened that a Company of the *Mandingoes,* who live upon Plunder, passing by at that Time, and observing him unarmed, rush'd in, to the Number of seven or eight at once, at a back Door, and pinioned JOB, before he could get to his Arms, together with his Interpreter, who is a Slave in *Maryland* still. They then shaved their Heads and Beards, which JOB and his Man resented as the highest Indignity; tho' the *Mandingoes* meant no more by it, than to make them appear like Slaves taken in War. On the 27th of *February,* 1730, they carried them to Captain *Pike* at *Gambia,* who purchased them; and on the first of *March* they were put on Board. Soon after JOB found means to acquaint Captain *Pike* that he was the same Person that came to trade with him a few Days before, and after what Manner he had been taken. Upon this Captain *Pike* gave him leave to redeem himself and his Man; and JOB sent to an Acquaintance of his Father's, near *Gambia,* who promised to send to JOB's Father, to inform him what had happened, that he might take some Course to have him set at Liberty. But it being a Fortnight's Journey between that Friend's House and his Father's, and the Ship sailing in about a Week after, JOB was brought with the rest of the Slaves to *Annapolis* in *Maryland,* and delivered to Mr. *Vachell Denton,* Factor to Mr. *Hunt,* before men-

---

[2] *Mandingoe:* A people living in the region south of the Gambia; they were often represented in contemporary sources as warlike. They were among the earliest converts to Islam in Africa, and so their capture of Ben Solomon, if accurately reported, indicates that religious convictions had little significance for their participation in the slave trade.
[3] *King Sambo:* According to this narrative, Sambo was king of Futa and had been a companion of Job Ben Solomon's when they were young.

tioned. JOB heard since, by Vessels that came from *Gambia,* that his Father sent down several Slaves, a little after Captain *Pike* sailed, in order to procure his Redemption; and that *Sambo,* King of *Futa,* had made War upon the *Mandingoes,* and cut off great Numbers of them, upon account of the Injury they had done to his Schoolfellow.

Mr. *Vachell Denton* sold JOB to one Mr. *Tolsey* in *Kent* Island[4] in *Maryland,* who put him to work in making Tobacco; but he was soon convinced that JOB had never been used to such Labour. He every Day shewed more and more Uneasiness under this Exercise, and at last grew sick, being no way able to bear it; so that his Master was obliged to find easier Work for him, and therefore put him to tend the Cattle. JOB would often leave the Cattle, and withdraw into the Woods to pray; but a white Boy frequently watched him, and whilst he was at his Devotion would mock him, and throw Dirt in his Face. This very much disturbed JOB, and added considerably to his other Misfortunes; all which were increased by his Ignorance of the *English* Language, which prevented his complaining, or telling his Case to any Person about him. Grown in some measure desperate, by reason of his present Hardships, he resolved to travel at a Venture; thinking he might possibly be taken up by some Master, who would use[5] him better, or otherwise meet with some lucky Accident, to divert or abate his Grief. Accordingly, he travelled thro' the Woods, till he came to the Country of *Kent,* upon *Delaware Bay,* now esteemed Part of *Pensilvania;* altho' it is properly a Part of *Maryland,* and belongs to my Lord *Baltimore.* There is a Law in force, throughout the Colonies of *Virginia, Maryland, Pensilvania,* &c. as far as *Boston* in *New England,* viz. That any Negroe, or white Servant who is not known in the Country, or has no Pass, may be secured by any Person, and kept in the common Goal, till the Master of such Servant shall fetch him. Therefore JOB being able to give no Account of himself, was put in Prison there.

This happened about the Beginning of *June,* 1731, when I, who was attending the Courts there, and had heard of JOB, went with several Gentlemen to the Goaler's[6] House, being a Tavern, and desired to see him. He was brought into the Tavern to us, but could not speak one Word of *English.* Upon our Talking and making Signs to him, he

---

[4] *Kent Island:* In the Chesapeake Bay.
[5] *use:* Treat.
[6] *Goaler's:* I.e., jailer's.

wrote a Line or two before us, and when he read it, pronounced the Words *Allah* and *Mahommed;*[7] by which, and his refusing a Glass of Wine we offered him, we perceived he was a *Mahometan,* but could not imagine of what Country he was, or how he got thither; for by his affable[8] Carriage, and the easy Composure of his Countenance, we could perceive he was no common Slave.

When Job had been some time confined, an old Negroe Man, who lived in that Neighbourhood, and could speak the *Jalloff*[9] Language, which Job also understood, went to him, and conversed with him. By this Negroe the Keeper was informed to whom Job belonged, and what was the Cause of his leaving his Master. The Keeper thereupon wrote to his Master, who soon after fetch'd him home, and was much kinder to him than before; allowing him a Place to pray in, and some other Conveniencies, in order to make his Slavery as easy as possible. Yet Slavery and Confinement was by no means agreeable to Job, who had never been used to it; he therefore wrote a Letter in *Arabick* to his Father, acquainting him with his Misfortunes, hoping he might yet find Means to redeem him. This Letter he sent to Mr. *Vachell Denton,* desiring it might be sent to *Africa* by Captain *Pike;* but he being gone to *England,* Mr. *Denton* sent the Letter inclosed to Mr. *Hunt,* in order to be sent to *Africa* by Captain *Pike* from *England;* but Captain *Pike* had sailed for *Africa* before the Letter came to Mr. *Hunt,* who therefore kept it in his own Hands, till he should have a proper Opportunity of sending it. It happened that this Letter was seen by *James Oglethorpe,* Esq; who, according to his usual Goodness and Generosity, took Compassion on Job, and gave his Bond to Mr. *Hunt* for the Payment of a certain Sum, upon the Delivery of Job here in *England.* Mr. *Hunt* upon this sent to Mr. *Denton,* who purchas'd him again of his Master for the same Money which Mr. *Denton* had formerly received for him; his Master being very willing to part with him, as finding him no ways fit for his Business.

He lived some time with Mr. *Denton* at *Annapolis,* before any Ship could stir out, upon account of the Ice that lay in all the Rivers of *Maryland* at that Time. In this Interval he became acquainted with the

---

[7] *Allah and Mahommed:* Respectively the deity and founder of the Muslim religion (also called "Mohametanism" in the eighteenth century).

[8] *affable:* Pleasing.

[9] *Jalloff:* A people living in an area between the Gambia and Senegal rivers.

Reverend Mr. *Henderson,* a Gentleman of great Learning, Minister of *Annapolis,* and Commissary to the Bishop of *London,* who gave JOB the Character of a Person of great Piety and Learning; and indeed his good Nature and Affability gain'd him many Friends besides in that Place.

In *March,* 1733, he set sail in the *William,* Captain *George Uriel* Commander; in which Ship I was also a Passenger. The Character which the Captain and I had of him at *Annapolis,* induced us to teach him as much of the *English* Language as we could, he being then able to speak but few Words of it, and those hardly intelligible. This we set about as soon as we were out at Sea, and in about a Fortnight's Time taught him all his Letters, and to spell almost any single Syllable, when distinctly pronounced to him; but JOB and my self falling sick, we were hindered from making any greater Progress at that Time. However, by the Time that we arrived in *England,* which was the latter End of *April,* 1733, he had learned so much of our Language, that he was able to understand most of what we said in common Conversation; and we that were used to his Manner of Speaking, could make shift to understand him tolerably well.

During the Voyage, he was very constant in his Devotions; which he never omitted, on any Pretence, notwithstanding we had exceeding bad Weather all the time we were at Sea. We often permitted him to kill our fresh Stock, that he might eat of it himself; for he eats no Flesh, unless he has killed the Animal with his own Hands, or knows that it has been killed by some *Mussulman.*[10] He has no Scruple about Fish; but won't touch a bit of Pork, it being expresly forbidden by their Law. By his good Nature and Affability he gained the good Will of all the Sailors, who (not to mention other kind Offices) all the way up the Channel shewed him the Head Lands and remarkable Places; the Names of which JOB wrote down carefully, together with the Accounts that were given him about them. His Reason for so doing, he told me, was, that if he met with any *Englishman* in his Country, he might by these Marks be able to convince him that he had been in *England.*

On our Arrival in *England,* we heard that Mr. *Oglethorpe* was gone to *Georgia,* and that Mr. *Hunt* had provided a Lodging for JOB at

---

[10] *Musselman:* Muslim.

Limehouse.[11] After I had visited my Friends in the Country, I went up on purpose to see JOB. He was very sorrowful, and told me, that Mr. *Hunt* had been applied to by some Persons to sell him, who pretended they would send him home; but he feared they would either sell him again as a Slave, or if they sent him home would expect an unreasonable Ransom for him. I took him to *London* with me, and waited on Mr. *Hunt*, to desire leave to carry him to *Cheshunt* in *Hartfordshire*;[12] which Mr. *Hunt* comply'd with. He told me he had been apply'd to, as JOB had suggested, but did not intend to part with him without his own Consent; but as Mr. *Oglethorpe* was out of *England*, if any of JOB's Friends would pay the Money, he would accept of it, provided they would undertake to send him home safely to his own Country. I also obtained his Promise that he would not dispose of him till he heard farther from me.

JOB, while he was at *Cheshunt*, had the Honour to be sent for by most of the Gentry of that Place, who were mightily pleased with his Company, and concerned for his Misfortunes. They made him several handsome Presents, and proposed that a Subscription should be made for the Payment of the Money to Mr. *Hunt*. The Night before we set out for *London* from *Cheshunt*, a Footman belonging to *Samuel Holden*, Esq; brought a Letter to JOB, which was, I think, directed to Sir *Byby Lake*. The Letter was delivered at the *African* House;[13] upon which the House was pleased to order that Mr. *Hunt* should bring in a Bill of the whole Charges which he had been at about JOB, and be there paid; which was accordingly done, and the Sum amounted to Fifty-nine Pounds, Six Shillings, and eleven Pence Half-penny. This Sum being paid, Mr. *Oglethorpe's* Bond was deliver'd up to the Company. JOB's Fears were now over, with respect to his being sold again as a Slave; yet he could not be persuaded but that he must pay an extravagant Ransom, when he got home. I confess, I doubted much of the Success of a Subscription, the Sum being great, and JOB's Acquaintance in *England* being so small; therefore, to ease JOB's Mind, I spoke to a Gentleman about the Affair, who has all along been JOB's Friend in a very remarkable Manner. This Gentleman was so far from discouraging the Thing, that he began the Subscription himself with a

[11] *Limehouse:* A docking area in what is now east-central London, but was at that time in the eastern half of the city.

[12] *Cheshunt in Hartfordshire:* Cheshunt is located just north of London, in the country of Hartfordshire.

[13] *African House:* The office of the RAC in London.

handsome Sum, and promised his further Assistance at a dead List. Not to be tedious:[14] Several Friends, both in *London* and in the Country, gave in their charitable Contributions very readily; yet the Sum was so large, that the Subscription was about twenty Pounds short of it; but that generous and worthy Gentleman before mentioned, was pleased to make up the Defect, and the whole Sum was compleated.

I went (being desired) to propose the Matter to the *African* Company; who, after having heard what I had to say, shew'd me the Orders that the House had made; which were, that JOB should be accommodated at the *African* House at the Company's Expence, till one of the Company's Ships should go to *Gambia,* in which he should be sent back to his Friends without any Ransom. The Company then ask'd me, if they could do any Thing more to make JOB easy; and upon my Desire, they order'd, that Mr. *Oglethorpe's* Bond should be cancelled, which was presently done, and that JOB should have his Freedom in Form, which he received handsomely engross'd, with the Company's Seal affixed; after which the full Sum of the whole Charges *(viz.* Fifty-nine Pounds, Six Shillings; and eleven Pence Half-penny) was paid in to their Clerk, as was before proposed.

JOB's Mind being now perfectly easy, and being himself more known, he went chearfully among his Friends to several Places, both in Town and Country. One Day being at Sir *Hans Sloan's,*[15] he expressed his great Desire to see the Royal Family. Sir *Hans* promised to get him introduced, when he had Clothes proper to go in. JOB knew how kind a Friend he had to apply to upon occasion; and he was soon cloathed in a rich silk Dress, made up after his own Country Fashion, and introduced to their Majesties, and the rest of the Royal Family. Her Majesty was pleased to present him with a rich Gold Watch; and the same Day he had the Honour to dine with his Grace the Duke of *Mountague;*[16] and some others of the Nobility, who were pleased to make him a handsome Present after Dinner. His Grace, after that, was

[14] *tedious:* Overly circumstantial.

[15] *Sir Hans Sloan's:* A physician and member of the Royal Society, Sloane (1660–1753) had traveled to Jamaica, Barbados, and other islands in the West Indies in the 1680s, and he published a natural history of Jamaica in two volumes (1707, 1725).

[16] *the Duke of Mountague:* John Montagu, second Duke of Montagu (1688?–1749), who was well-known as a patron of visiting Africans and African-Americans, and who reappears in Moore's account, on pp. 275 and 276. Montagu was the dedicatee of Bluett's book. He also took an interest in the young Ignatius Sancho, who became his widow's butler (see p. 451).

pleased to take JOB often into the Country with him, and shew him the Tools that are necessary for Tilling the Ground, both in Gardens and Fields, and made his Servants shew him how to use them; and afterwards his Grace furnished JOB with all Sorts of such Instruments, and several other rich Presents, which he ordered to be carefully done up in Chests, and put on Board for his Use. 'Tis not possible for me to recollect the many Favours he received from his Grace, and several other Noblemen and Gentlemen, who shewed a singular Generosity towards him; only, I may say in general, that the Goods which were given him, and which he carried over with him, were worth upwards of 500 Pounds; besides which, he was well furnished with Money, in case any Accident should oblige him to go on Shore, or occasion particular Charges at Sea. About the latter End of *July* last he embark'd on Board one of the *African* Company's Ships, bound for *Gambia;* where we hope he is safely arrived, to the great Joy of his Friends, and the Honour of the *English* Nation. . . .

SECT. IV.

Of JOB's Person *and* Character.

JOB was about five Feet ten Inches high, strait limb'd, and naturally of a good Constitution; altho' the religious Abstinence which he observed, and the Fatigues he lately underwent, made him appear something lean and weakly. His Countenance was exceeding pleasant, yet grave and composed; his Hair long, black, and curled, being very different from that of the Negroes commonly brought from *Africa*.

His natural Parts[17] were remarkably good; and I believe most of the Gentlemen that conversed with him frequently, will remember many Instances of his Ingenuity. On all Occasions he discovered a solid Judgment, a ready Memory, and a clear Head. And, notwithstanding the Prejudices which it was natural for him to have in favour of his own religious Principles, it was very observable with how much Temper and Impartiality he would reason in Conversation upon any Question of that kind, while at the same Time he would frame such Replies, as were calculated at once to support his own Opinion, and to oblige or please his Opponent. In his Reasonings there appeared nothing trifling, nothing hypocritical or over-strained; but, on the con-

---

[17] *Parts:* Talents, abilities.

trary, strong Sense, joined with an innocent Simplicity, a strict Regard to Truth, and a hearty Desire to find it. Tho' it was a considerable Disadvantage to him in Company, that he was not sufficient Master of our Language; yet those who were used to his Way, by making proper Allowances, always found themselves agreeably entertained by him.

The Acuteness of his Genius appear'd upon many Occasions. He very readily conceived the Mechanism and Use of most of the ordinary Instruments which were shewed to him here; and particularly, upon seeing a Plow, a Grist Mill, and a Clock taken to pieces, he was able to put them together again himself, without any farther Direction.

His Memory was extraordinary; for when he was fifteen Years old he could say the whole *Alcoran*[18] by heart, and while he was here in *England* he wrote three Copies of it without the Assistance of any other Copy, and without so much as looking to one of those three when he wrote the others. He would often laugh at me when he heard me say I had forgot any Thing, and told me he hardly ever forgot any Thing in his Life, and wondered that any other body should.

In his natural Temper there appeared a happy Mixture of the Grave and the Chearful, a gentle Mildness, guarded by a proper Warmth, and a kind of compassionate Disposition towards all that were in Distress. In Conversation he was commonly very pleasant; and would every now and then divert the Company with some witty Turn, or pretty Story, but never to the Prejudice[19] of Religion, or good Manners. I could perceive, by several slight Occurrences, that, notwithstanding his usual Mildness, he had Courage enough, when there was occasion for it: And I remember a Story which he told me of himself, that is some Proof of it. As he was passing one Day thro' the Country of the *Arabs,* on his way home, with four Servants, and several Negroes which he had bought, he was attacked by fifteen of the wild *Arabs,* who are known to be common *Bandetti,* or Robbers in those Parts. JOB, upon the first Sight of this Gang, prepared for a Defence; and setting one of his Servants to watch the Negroes, he, with the other three, stood on his Guard. In the Fight one of JOB's Men was killed, and JOB himself was run thro' the Leg with a Spear. However,

[18] *Alcoran:* The Koran.
[19] *Prejudice:* Disadvantage.

having killed two of the *Arabs,* together with their Captain and two Horses, the rest fled, and JOB brought off his Negroes safe.

JOB's Aversion to Pictures of all Sorts, was exceeding great; insomuch, that it was with great Difficulty that he could be brought to sit for his own. We assured him that we never worshipped any Picture,[20] and that we wanted his for no other End but to keep us in mind of him. He at last consented to have it drawn; which was done by Mr. *Hoare.*[21] When the Face was finished, Mr. *Hoare* ask'd what Dress would be most proper to draw him in; and, upon JOB's desiring to be drawn in his own Country Dress,[22] told him he could not draw it, unless he had seen it, or had it described to him by one who had: Upon which JOB answered, If you can't draw a Dress you never saw, why do some of you Painters presume to draw God, whom no one ever saw? I might mention several more of his smart Repartees in Company, which shewed him to be a Man of Wit and Humour, as well as good Sense: But that I may not be tedious, what I have said shall suffice for this Head.

As to his Religion, 'tis known he was a *Mahometan,* but more moderate in his Sentiments than most of that Religion are. He did not believe a sensual Paradise,[23] nor many other ridiculous and vain Traditions, which pass current among the Generality of the *Turks.*[24] He was very constant in his Devotion to God; but said, he never pray'd to *Mahommed,* nor did he think it lawful to address any but God himself in Prayer. He was so fixed in the Belief of one God, that it was not possible, at least during the Time he was here, to give him any Notion of the Trinity;[25] so that having had a new Testament given him in his own Language, when he had read it, he told me he had perused it with a great deal of Care, but could not find one Word in it of three Gods, as some People talk: I did not care to puzzle him, and therefore answered in general, that the *English* believed only in one God. He shewed upon

---

[20] *never worshipped any Picture:* The Koran does not specifically forbid any representation of the human form, but it does forbid the worship of idols (see, e.g., V.4.116). However, the Mosaic prohibition against pictures as idolatrous was very influential (see Exod. 20.4).

[21] *Mr. Hoare:* Probably William Hoare (1707?–1792), who was just beginning his career at this point; he went on to become a prominent portrait painter.

[22] *his own Country Dress:* I.e., his native garb.

[23] *sensual Paradise:* The luxurious afterlife that would be promised to Ben Solomon as a faithful Muslim.

[24] *Turks:* Here used as a generic term for Muslims.

[25] *Trinity:* The unity of three figures in one deity (the Father, the Son, and the Holy Spirit).

all Occasions a singular Veneration for the Name of God, and never pronounced the Word *Allah* without a peculiar Accent, and a remarkable Pause: And indeed his Notions of God, Providence, and a future State, were in the main very just and reasonable.

His Learning, considering the Disadvantages of the Place he came from, was far from being contemptible. The Books in his Country are all in Manuscript, all upon Religion; and are not, as I remember, more than Thirty in Number. They are all in *Arabick;* but the *Alcoran,* he says, was originally wrote by God himself, not in *Arabick,* and God sent it by the Angel *Gabriel* to *Ababuker,* some time before *Mahommed* was born; the Angel taught *Ababuker* to read it, and no one can read it but those who are instructed after a different Manner from that in which the *Arabick* is commonly taught. However, I am apt to think that the Difference depends only upon the Pointing[26] of the *Arabick,* which is of later Date. JOB was well acquainted with the historical Part of our Bible, and spoke very respectfully of the good Men mentioned in Scripture; particularly of JESUS CHRIST, who, he said, was a very great Prophet, and would have done much more Good in the World, if he had not been cut off so soon by the wicked *Jews;* which made it necessary for God to send *Mahomet* to confirm and improve his Doctrine.

CONCLUSION;

Containing Some REFLECTIONS *upon the whole.*

One can't but take Notice of a very remarkable Series of Providence, from the Beginning of JOB's Captivity, till his Return to his own Country. When we reflect upon the Occasion and Manner of his being taken at first, and the Variety of Incidents during his Slavery, which, from slight and unlikely Beginnings, gradually brought about his Redemption, together with the singular Kindness he met with in this Country after he was ransomed, and the valuable Presents which he carried over with him; I say, when all these Things are duly considered, if we believe that the wise Providence of the great Author of Nature governs the World, 'tis natural for us to conclude that this Process, in the divine Oeconomy[27] of Things, is not for nought, but that there is some important End to be served by it. . . .

[26] *Pointing:* Punctuation.
[27] *Oeconomy:* Economy, here in the sense of divinely ordained dispensation.

With some such Reflections as these JOB used to comfort himself in his Captivity; and upon proper Occasions, in Conversation, would speak very justly and devoutly of the Care of God over his Creatures, and particularly of the remarkable Changes of his own Circumstances; all which he piously ascribed to an unseen Hand. He frequently compared himself to *Joseph*;[28] and when he was informed that the King of *Futa* had killed a great many of the *Mandingoes* upon his Account, he said, with a good deal of Concern, if he had been there he would have prevented it; for it was not the *Mandingoes*, but God, who brought him into a strange Land.

It would be Presumption in us to affirm positively what God is about to do at any Time; but may we not be allowed humbly to hope that one End of JOB's Captivity, and happy Deliverance, was the Benefit and Improvement of himself and his People? His Knowledge is now extended to a Degree which he could never have arrived at in his own Country; and the Instruments which he carried over, are well adjusted to the Exigencies of his Countrymen. Who can tell, but that thro' him a whole Nation may be made happy? The Figure which he makes in those Parts, as Presumptive High-priest, and the Interest which he has with the King of the Country, considering the singular Obligations he is under to the *English*, may possibly, in good time, be of considerable Service to us also; and we have reason to hope this, from the repeated Assurances we had from JOB, that he would, upon all Occasions, use his best Endeavours to promote the *English* Trade before any other. But whatever be the consequences, we cannot but please our selves with the Thoughts of having acted so good and generous a Part to a distressed Stranger. And as this gives me occasion to recommend Hospitality, I cannot conclude, without saying something in favour of it.

Among the various Branches of Friendship and Beneficence, there is none of a more noble and disinterested Nature, or that tends more directly to the Union, and consequently the Subsistence of the human Species, than that of Hospitality and Kindness to Strangers. In many Instances of private Friendship, we are apt to be guided by our own private Interest; and very often the Exchange of good Offices among Friends, is little better than mere Barter, where an Equivalent is expected on both Sides. In most Acts of Charity and Compassion too, we may be, and very often are wrought upon by the undue Influence of

---

[28] *Joseph:* In the book of Genesis, Joseph undergoes a series of trials, but God protects him throughout (see Gen. 37.1–50.26).

some selfish View, and thereby we destroy in good measure the Merit of them: But in shewing Pity to Strangers, as such, and kindly relieving them in their Distress, there is not such Danger of being influenced by private Regards; nor is it likely that we are so. Here we act for God's sake, and for the sake of human Nature; and we seem to have no Inducement superior to the Will of Heaven, and the Pleasure that results from the Consciousness of a generous Respect for our common Humanity.

There is something singularly sublime, and even God-like, in this benevolent Disposition towards Strangers. The common Parent of the Universe pours out his Blessings daily upon all Mankind, in all Places of the Earth; the Just and the Unjust, the Rich and the Poor, all the classes, all the Families of human Creatures, subsist by his Bounty, and have their Share of his universal Favours. The good hospitable Man, in his low Sphere, imitates his Maker, and deals about him to his Fellow Mortals with great Chearfulness. He considers his Species in one complex View, and wishes that his Abilities were as extensive as his Inclinations. He does not confine his Benevolence to his Relations, or any particular Party of Men; his Affections are too warm, too general to be thus circumscribed; they must range round the whole Globe, and exert themselves in all Places, where an Opportunity offers.

Such a happy Temper of Mind appeared eminently in those worthy Gentlemen, that promoted and encouraged a Subscription for the Relief of Job; and we hope there are many more such Instances of Hospitality among us, which is one very honourable Part of the Character of the *English*.

FRANCIS MOORE

From *Travels into the Inland Parts of Africa*

The author of this selection, Francis Moore, worked for the Royal African Company on the Gambia in the 1730s. When Job Ben Solomon returned to Africa in 1734, Moore escorted him up the Gambia to his home, and the following passage describes their experiences along the way.

The Royal African Company, which by the turn of the eighteenth century had lost the power to monopolize the slave trade, tried to carve out a role for itself by regulating the trade. Moore presents the company as a friend of the Africans, dedicated to wiping out the abuses of the slave trade. It should be noted, however, that the 1730s marked an especially profitable time for the company's ventures in the Gambia, which had not previously been an important source of slaves for European merchants, and the company hoped to use Ben Solomon's friendship as a means of exploiting all the commercial possibilities available around Bondu — slaves, gold, and gum. Ben Solomon remained in contact with the company through the 1740s, and after the company failed, in the early 1750s, he maintained some connections with its successor, the Company of Merchants Trading to Africa, until his death in 1773. The last reference to Ben Solomon in the Royal African Company's records, dating from 1746, involves a dispute over two slaves he claimed were owed to him. Like Oroonoko, he evidently did not regard his own enslavement as a basis for opposing the institution of slavery.

The text is excerpted from the first edition (London: Printed by Edward Cave for the author, 1738) 202–09.

[On August 8, 1734] about Noon came up the *Dolphin* Snow,[1] which saluted the Fort with nine Guns, and had the same Number returned; after which came on Shore the Captain, four Writers,[2] one Apprentice to the Company, and one Black Man, by Name *Job Ben Solomon*. . . who in the Year 1731, as he was travelling in *Jagra*,[3] and driving his Herds of Cattle across the Countries, was robbed and carried to *Joar*,[4] where he was sold to Captain *Pyke*, Commander of the Ship *Arabella*, who was then trading there. By him he was carried to *Maryland*, and sold to a Planter, with whom *Job* lived about a Twelvemonth without being once beat by his Master; at the End of which time he had the good Fortune to have a Letter of his own writing in the *Arabic* Tongue convey'd to *England*. This Letter coming to the Hand of Mr. *Oglethorpe*,[5] he sent the same to *Oxford* to be translated; which, when done, gave him so much Satisfaction, and so good an

---

[1] *Dolphin Snow:* A snow was a small ship, often a warship; this one, owned by the RAC, was called the *Dolphin*.

[2] *Writers:* Clerks.

[3] *Jagra:* A point along the Gambia, about forty miles inland from Fort James.

[4] *Joar:* Site of a trading post of the RAC, fifty miles inland along the Gambia, about ten miles north of Jagra.

[5] *Mr Oglethorpe:* Cf. p. 261.

Opinion of the Man, that he directly order'd him to be bought from his Master, he soon after setting out for *Georgia*. Before he returned from thence, *Job* came to *England;* where being brought to the Acquaintance of the Learned Sir *Hans Sloane,*[6] he was by him found a perfect Master of the *Arabic* Tongue, by translating several Manuscripts and Inscriptions upon Medals: He was by him recommended to his Grace the Duke of *Montague,* who being pleased with the Sweetness of Humour, and Mildness of Temper, as well as Genius and Capacity of the Man, introduced him to Court, where he was graciously received by the Royal Family, and most of the Nobility, from whom he received distinguishing Marks of Favour. After he had continued in *England* about fourteen Months, he wanted much to return to his Native Country, which is *Bundo,* (a Place about a Week's Travel over Land from the Royal *African* Company's Factory at *Joar,* on the River *Gambia)* of which Place his Father was High-Priest, and to whom he sent Letters from *England.* Upon his setting out from *England* he received a good many noble Presents from her most Gracious Majesty Queen *Caroline,* his Highness the Duke of *Cumberland,* his Grace the Duke of *Montague,* the Earl of *Pembroke,* several Ladies of Quality, Mr. *Holden,* and the Royal *African* Company, who have order'd their Agents to show him the greatest Respect. . . .

JOB Ben Solomon having a Mind to go up to *Cower*[7] to talk with some of his Countrymen, went along with me. In the Evening we weighed Anchor, saluting the Fort with five Guns, which return'd the same Number.

On the 26th we arrived at the Creek of *Damasensa,*[8] and having some old Acquaintances at the Town of *Damasensa, Job* and I went up in the Yawl;[9] in the Way, going up a very narrow Place for about half a Mile, we saw several Monkeys of a beautiful Blue and Red,[10] which the Natives tell me never set their Feet on the Ground, but live entirely amongst the Trees, leaping from one to another at so great Distances, as any one, were they not to see it, would think improbable.

---

[6] *Sir Hans Sloane:* See n. 15, p. 267.
[7] *Cower:* A town on the coast, near the Gambia.
[8] *Damasensa:* Another town along the Gambia.
[9] *Yawl:* A small boat.
[10] *Monkeys of a beautiful Blue and Red:* Mandrills, native to the jungles of equatorial West Africa.

IN the Evening, as my Friend *Job* and I were sitting under a great Tree at *Damasensa,* there came by us six or seven of the very People who robb'd and made a Slave of *Job,* about thirty Miles from hence, about three Years ago; *Job,* tho' a very even-temper'd Man at other times, could not contain himself when he saw them, but fell into a most terrible Passion, and was for killing them with his broad Sword and Pistols, which he always took care to have about him. I had much ado to dissuade him from falling upon the six Men; but at last, by representing to him the ill Consequences that would infallibly attend such a rash Action, and the Impossibility of mine or his own escaping alive, if he should attempt it, I made him lay aside the Thoughts of it, and persuaded him to sit down and pretend not to know them, but ask them Questions about himself; which he accordingly did, and they answer'd nothing but the Truth. At last he ask'd them how the King their Master did; they told him he was dead, and by further Enquiry we found, that amongst the Goods for which he sold *Job* to Captain *Pyke* there was a Pistol, which the King used commonly to wear slung about his Neck with a string; and as they never carry Arms without being loaded, one Day this accidentally went off, and the Balls lodging in his Throat, he died presently. At the Closing of this Story *Job* was so very much transported, that he immediately fell on his Knees, and returned Thanks to *Mahomet* for making this Man die by the very Goods for which he sold him into Slavery; and then turning to me, he said, 'Mr. *Moore,* you see now God Almighty was displeas'd at this Man's making me a Slave, and therefore made him die by the very Pistol for which he sold me; yet I ought to forgive him, *says he,* because had I not been sold, I should neither have known any thing of the *English* Tongue, nor have had any of the fine, useful and valuable Things I now carry over, nor have known that in the World there is such a Place as *England,* nor such noble, good and generous People as Queen *Caroline,* Prince *William,* the Duke of *Montague,* the Earl of *Pembroke,* Mr *Holden,* Mr *Oglethorpe,* and the Royal *African* Company.

ON the 1st of *September* we arrived at *Joar,* the Freshes[11] being very strong against us. I immediately took an Inventory of the Company's Effects, and gave Receipts to Mr *Gill* for the same. After which we unloaded the Sloop, and then I sent her up to *Yanimarew* for a Load of

---

[11] *Freshes:* Fresh streams.

Corn for *James* Fort,[12] where he stayed till the 25th, and then came back to *Joar,* during which time I made some Trade with the Merchants, though at a pretty high Price.

On *Job's* first Arrival here, he desired I would send a Messenger up to his own Country to acquaint his Friends of his Arrival. I spoke to one of the *Blacks* which we usually employ upon those Occasions, to procure me a Messenger, who brought to me a *Pholey,* who knew the High Priest his Father, and *Job* himself, and express'd great Joy at seeing him in safety returned from Slavery, he being the only Man (except one) that was ever known to come back to this Country, after having been once carried a Slave out of it by White Men. *Job* gave him the Message himself, and desired his Father should not come down to him, for it was too far for him to travel; and that it was fit for the Young to go to the Old, and not for the Old to come to the Young. He also sent some Presents by him to his Wives, and desired him to bring his little one, which was his best beloved, down to him. After the Messenger was gone, *Job* went frequently along with me to *Cower,* and several other Places about the Country; he spoke always very handsome of the *English,* and what he said, took away a great deal of the Horror of the *Pholeys* for the State of Slavery amongst the *English;* for they before generally imagined, that all who were sold for Slaves, were generally either eaten or murdered, since none ever returned. His Description of the *English* gave them also a great notion of the Power of *England,* and a Veneration for those who traded amongst them. He sold some of the Presents he brought with him from *England* for Trading-Goods, with which he bought a Woman-Slave and two Horses, which were very useful to him there, and which he designed to carry with him to *Bundo,* whenever he should set out thither. He used to give his Country People a good deal of Writing-Paper, which is a very useful Commodity amongst them, and of which the Company had presented him with several Reams. He used to pray frequently, and behaved himself with great Mildness and Affability to all, so that he was very popular and well-beloved. The Messenger not being thought to return soon, *Job* desired to go down to *James* Fort to take care of his Goods, I promising to send him word when the Messenger came

---

[12] *Yanimarew . . . James Fort:* Yanimarew was a port on the Gambia River; Fort James was a port near the river's mouth (not to be confused with the Fort James at Accra, on the Gold Coast).

back, and also to send some other Messengers, for fear the first should miscarry.

ON the 26th I send down the *Fame* Sloop to *James* Fort, and *Job* going along with her, I gave the Master Orders to shew him all the Respect he could.

From *The Royal African: Or,*
Memoirs of the Young Prince of Annamaboe

The Royal African, first published in 1749, is based on the experiences of William Ansah Sessarakoo, son of the ruling family at Annamaboe, just west of Coromantine on the Gold Coast. Sold into slavery in Barbados in 1744, Sessarakoo was eventually freed, and he visited England in 1749 (see p. 445). His experiences recall the story of Oroonoko in several particulars, and indeed, *The Royal African* specifically invokes Behn's model on its title page: "In *Oroonoko* shines the Hero's Mind, / With native Lustre by no Art refin'd." This story, however, offers a conclusion radically different from Behn's, ending (like the narrative of Job Ben Solomon) with the restoration of the young prince to his African home. It is prefaced by a polemic against contemptuous racist attitudes toward Africans, the anonymous writer arguing that a lack of respect for African rulers will damage the reputation of the British in Africa and will impair their trade.

The story of Sessarakoo remained current in the English press for several years after his return to Annamaboe. In 1751, *The Gentleman's Magazine* reported that "the Kings of *Anisham* and *Faetu,* two great trading nations in the south of *Africa,* are preparing to send their eldest sons to *England,* to be educated in the manner as the prince *Annamaboa,* who arrived safe there in *December* last, to the joy of his royal father" (p. 331). Four years later, the same magazine announced the baptism in London of "[t]wo Africans, one of them son to the King of *Annamaboe*" (p. 184); this report evidently refers to a different son, sent to England after the return of the prince whose story is told here.

Narratives of kidnapped African nobility had already enjoyed some currency by the time of Sessarakoo's story: Adomo Oroonoko Tomo, a visitor to London in the late 1720s, was said to be a member of the nobility, though William Snelgrave questioned this claim. The anonymous *Histoire de Louis Anniaba, roi d'Essénie en Afrique sur la cote de Guinée,* published in Paris in the 1740s, narrates the fictionalized memoirs of

An engraving of William Ansah Sessarakoo ("Prince of Annamaboe"), the subject of *The Royal African*, from *The Gentlemen's Magazine* 20 (1750): 272. Photo courtesy of The New York Public Library.

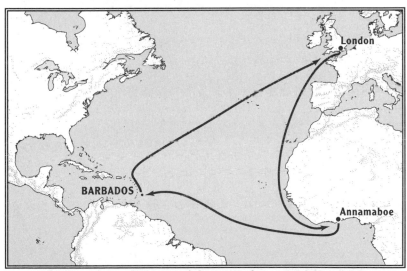

Sessarakoo, Prince of Annamaboe, 1744–1748

Map of the travels of Sessarakoo.

"Prince Anniaba," supposedly a king from Assini on the present-day Ivory Coast, who appeared at the courts of England and France.

The text is excerpted from the first edition (London: Printed for W. Reeve, G. Woodfall, and J. Barnes, 1749) i–v, 11–53. For the quotations from *The Gentleman's Magazine*, see vol. 21 (1751): 331, and vol. 25 (1755): 184.

To the HONOURABLE

**** ****** of ******, in Essex, Esq;

It is very natural, Sir, that you should be surprized at the Accounts which our News-Papers have given you, of the Appearance of an African Prince in England *under Circumstances of Distress and Ill-usage, which reflect very highly upon us as a People. The deep Concern which you so pathetically express for his Misfortunes, is suitable to the Goodness and Generosity of your Heart; and as to your Apprehensions that this Story will not be confined within the Bounds of the* British *Dominions, wherever situated, it is certainly very just; for upon reading your Letter, I made it my Business to examine the foreign Prints[1] at the Coffee-Houses about the* Royal-Exchange, *where they are taken in, and found the Story very circumstantially related from* Hamburgh.[2] *But if this, Sir, raises your Resentment, that all* Europe *should be informed of a Fact that does us so little Honour, be pleased at the same Time to reflect, that those who read it must at the same Time read the general Abhorrence with which the News of this Piece of Treachery was received here; and how effectually as well as honourably, the Mischief has been repaired by the Interposition of the Government.*

What my Friend told you, with respect to the Pains taken by me, to come as near as possible at the Truth of this Affair, was very well founded, as indeed was every thing else which he said upon that Occasion; excepting the high Commendations he was pleased to bestow

---

[1] *Prints:* Newspapers.

[2] *Hamburgh:* While this detail suggests that the news of the prince's story was circulating so widely as to be known in Germany, it should also be noted that Hamburg was a prominent rival of Britain's in the slave trade at this time (see p. 437, in the selection from Sir Dalby Thomas in Part Two, Chapter 5).

upon the short Account that I have committed to writing of the Mis-fortunes of the Young African. *The plain and naked Truth is, that not being perfectly satisfied with the Narrative in the News-Papers, and having had always a Curiosity to learn, with as much Exactness as may be, the Circumstances that attend such extraordinary Events as happen in our own Times, I have been, perhaps, more diligent and nice in my Enquiries into the Matter of Fact, and whatever relates to it, than many People, and finding my Pains rewarded by some Acquisi-tions of Knowledge, which I thought considerable, it appeared to me worth employing a few leisure Hours, in reducing what I have learned into some Kind of Order, that the Facts and Observations might not escape my Memory. This gave Rise to the following* Memoirs, *which are heartily at your Service; nor am I at all sollicitous[3] about the Fate of them. You may, if you please, shew them to the Persons you men-tion, or to any of your Acquaintance who desire to peruse them; and you may likewise assure them, that to the best of my Power, there is not a Syllable inserted which I do not firmly believe to be true.*

I must not however dissemble, that there are many People in the World who affect to treat this Affair in another Light; some from that strange Principle of Incredulity, which induces them to question the Veracity of every thing that does not fall immediately within the Com-pass[4] of their own Observation, or does not exactly tally with the Notions they have formed of Persons or Things, tho' the former may be of no great Extent, and the latter none of the most accurate. Some again have an Interest in the representing this Affair in an opposite Point of View, which you will very easily conceive; for after so flagrant a Breach of Trust, as selling a Free-Man, *and a Person of Considera-tion, whatever his Complexion may be, for a* Slave; *it is no great Won-der that such as have had any Connection with the Persons concerned in such a Transaction, should use all their Industry and Skill to lessen his Character and Consideration, and endeavour to screen so flagrant an Act of Injustice, not to give it a harsher Name; by circulating Sto-ries, which if true, would be far from disculpating[5] them; and which, from the visible Absurdities and Contradictions they are loaded with, all who have not as much Interest in believing, as the Authors of them had for inventing, consider as groundless and false. No Man breathing who betrays and sells a* Prince, *unless judicially convicted of it, will*

---

[3] *sollicitous:* Concerned.
[4] *Compass:* Scope.
[5] *disculpating:* Excusing.

acknowledge the Crime; especially when he has an Excuse so ready at Hand, as denying that the Person so treated is a Prince, *tho' that should be only a Quibble upon the* Word.

There is, without doubt, a great Propensity in many of our own People, who have lied and traded in these Parts, to magnify such as were possessed of the Government with whom they traded, with whom they had an intimate Acquaintance, and from whom they received great Favours. It is very likely that such Gentlemen may use the Terms Emperor, King, and Prince, with visible Impropriety upon some Occasions, and upon all with a Liberality[6] that may not admit of a strict Justification. But on the other Hand, some other Travellers, and those too commonly of the meanest Sort, take an unaccountable and a very unwarrantable Liberty of treating such Negro Governors with a ludicrous Contempt. For by this Means they lose themselves, and teach the Seamen with whom they converse, to forget not only all Decency and Respect, but (as bad Morals often accompany ill Manners) all Distinction of Right and Wrong; which leads them into Practices equally base in their Nature, and destructive in their Consequences; so that while, from a Vanity and Insolence (which are the usual Effects of Ignorance) they look down upon the poor black People as infinitely beneath them, they really degrade themselves, and which is much worse, draw a Scandal upon their Countrymen by their barbarous, iniquitous, and profligate Behavior.

One may be easily extricated out of any Difficulty that arises as to the just Claim of the Young African *now in* England *to a Title of Distinction, notwithstanding all the Sophisms[7] of those, who either from Prejudice or Interest[8] pretend to dispute it.* Things *are in all Countries the same, however the* Names *by which they are called may differ. As for Instance,* Rice *brought from* Guinea *remains* Rice *when it is brought here; tho' the* Negroes *know nothing of that* Word, *and we know as little of theirs for that Kind of Corn. A Person who has the Supreme Authority in any District, let it be of a larger or lesser Extent, is in the common Acceptation of Speech, a* Prince; *and if from his Influence our Trade may be either advanced or hindered, he deserves a proportionable Respect from us, tho' he would be certainly entitled to strict Justice, whether he had that Influence or not. It is no Matter therefore what his* Title *be in* Africa, *or what the Nature of that Gov-*

---

[6] *Liberality:* Freedom, looseness.
[7] *Sophisms:* Specious excuses.
[8] *Interest:* Bias.

ernment which he administers; for if he be at the Head *of it, and in consequence of his being at the Head of it, can assist, or injure us in our* Trade, *he is strictly speaking a* Prince; *and his Children may be so stiled by Courtesey without any Solecism. If at any Time heretofore we have treated Persons of the like Rank with his Sons, or even if we had treated other Sons of his ever so rudely or indifferently, this is nothing to the Purpose; for we never could have treated them so if they had not been in our* Power; *and our having used it* ill *either then or now, does not reflect upon* him *or* them, *but upon* us; *and this Aspersion could only be wiped off by the Conduct that has been lately pursued, which is just in itself, and therefore honourable to us as a Nation. . . .*

. . . Amongst other Places that have of late Years mended their Condition, we may reckon the Town of *Annamaboe,* which commands all that Coast, and is the Center of Trade for the *Fantin*[9] Country. The *Brasso,* Head *Caboceiro,* or *Negroe* Chief, values himself upon his *English* Name, which is *John Corrente;* he has enjoyed that Post long, is a Man, who to very good natural Parts having joined much Experience, is regarded even by the *Europeans,* as a very sensible Person; and as he directs all Things in a Place that is absolutely independent, and in Right of that directs the Commerce of the whole Coast, he has been all along courted, and caressed by such as have found it their Interest to deal with him.

He is a very considerable Trader himself in Gold, Slaves, and whatever else the Country affords, and lived always upon very good Terms with the Servants of the *African* Company, who have on their Side taken care to pay him his Rent very exactly for the Fort, and that too since they found it no longer in their Power to keep it. For it is to be observed, that though they slighted that Fort, yet they have always had a great Attention to the Trade of *Annamaboe,* and have laboured as much as in them lay to preserve it; in order to which it was necessary to maintain and to depend upon the Friendship and good Faith of this potent Negroe, which is now the only Security they have for it. This sufficiently shews the Nature of his Office, and the Extent of his Power, and yet there are some other Instances which may here be very properly mentioned as plainly proving the Necessity of their living well with him, and even of having some degree of Complaisance[10] for

[9] *Fantin:* See "Fantyn" in the map on p. 211.
[10] *Complaisance:* Willingness to please.

a Person of his Character, whether we bestow upon it a Negro, or an *English* Title, that is, whether we call him *Caboceiro,* Prince, or plain *John Corrente.*

Now it must be observed, that the *French,* who are very established at *Whydaw,*[11] have been for many Years desirous of having a Share in the Trade of *Annamaboe,* and for that Purpose took extraordinary Pains to gain the good-will of the *Caboceir John,* as knowing no better, indeed no other Way to procure it. Neither will it appear at all strange or unbecoming in him, that he accepted of these Addresses, or entered into a Correspondence with them; for the *Fantinians,* as before observed, were never under any kind of subjection to the Company, even in its most prosperous Condition, but held themselves at full liberty to deal with whom they pleased, and to vend their Commodities how, when, where, and to whom they thought proper.

What without doubt induced him the more readily to enter into Dealings with them, was not barely the superior Civilities, but the strict Justice and generous Way of trading that he met with amongst them; for it must be allowed, that the Negroes find all these Qualities in the Subjects of that Crown, who are employed in the Management of Affairs in *Africa.* Yet no Argument must be drawn from hence in favour of that People, as if their Virtue, Piety or Honour, exceeded those of other Nations, since nothing like that is the Case; they are not a Grain better, but only a little wiser than their Neighbours. As yet they are very far from being powerful in these Parts, for the Establishment that they have at *Whydaw,* which they call *Juda,* and the *Dutch Fida,* is almost the only one at least of any Importance that they have upon the Coast of *Guinea,* and therefore to supply the want of Force they have recourse to Condescension, Affability, Fair-dealing, and giving a good Price.

Now from whatever Motives Men are led to behave in this manner, it is certain that let them be of what Colour they will, or come from where they will, they must be regarded as honest Traders, and good Customers; indeed of late Years this Trade is grown of very high Consequence to that Nation, because of the present Demand of Negroes from their *American* Colonies, which is the Reason of their being so attentive to whatever may promote and extend their Commerce on the Coast of *Guinea;* and this it is that engages them to act in the manner they do, and to neglect no Opportunity of ingratiating themselves with the black Chiefs, or of supplanting their Rivals in Trade, who were

---

[11] *Whydaw:* See "Fida," on the slave coast, in the map on p. 210.

settled here long before them. In this, without question, they act wisely and worthily, nor with any Reason can we blame them; but at the same time it ought to put us upon our guard, and excite us to be very active and vigilant in an Affair which so nearly concerns our Honour and Interest, and in which, notwithstanding all their Arts and Influence, they can never hurt us, unless by Negligence or Inattention, we concur to prejudice ourselves.

But tho' the great Assiduity and constant Civility of these new Traders made some Impression upon the Negro *Caboceiro,* and induced him so far to gratify their Inclinations as to take off considerable Quantities of their Goods, and to furnish them in return with Gold and Slaves: He notwithstanding continued to keep up a fair Correspondence with our *African* Company, and shewed them it was not a mere Compliment when He valued himself upon being an *Englishman.* The *French* saw and were piqued at this, because it hurt their national Vanity, at the same Time that it was prejudicial to their Interest, they redoubled their Attacks therefore in order to engage him entirely; for tho' they could have no Hopes of engrossing the Trade, yet they were excessively desirous of being the most favoured Nation at *Annamaboe.* To carry this to its utmost Extent they boasted mightily of the great Power of their King, the Magnificence of his Court, the Extent of his Dominions, the Number, Wealth, and Politeness of his Subjects. Honest *John Corrente,* who had imbibed a Tincture of the *English* Spirit, would now and then cross them a little, and seemed to doubt whether all they said was true; upon which they took Occasion to propose his sending one of his Sons over to *France,* who might not only see that Matters were really as they had stated them, but might himself feel the good Effects of the clear Light, in which they had represented the Power, the Probity, and the kind Behaviour of the Caboceiro of *Annamaboe.*

At first this made little or no Impression, but being earnestly pushed[12] and often repeated, the Negro Chief began to reflect within himself upon the Consequences that might attend it, and the Advantage that must arise from having one of his Children more knowing, and by far better bred than any of his Countrymen ever were; and by running this over in his Mind, he saw, or at least he thought he saw, so fair a Prospect, attended with so few Difficulties or Inconveniencies, that in the End he consented to their Proposition, and declared his Resolution, that when the next *French* Ships came to *Whydaw,* he

---

[12] *pushed:* Urged.

would send one of his Sons on board them, to be carried by them to *France* at their Return, which gave those who had negotiated this Matter vast Satisfaction.

It is a vulgar,[13] and at the same Time a most erroneous Opinion, that the Negroes upon the Coast of *Guinea* have little or no Tenderness for their Children, but sell them frequently for Slaves without Concern. This is so far from being true, that no People in the World, generally speaking, express greater Kindness for their Offspring than they do, allowing for the Manners of the Country, and the Hardiness with which they are brought up. On some Parts of the Coast indeed, if Children are undutiful, upon Complaint to the King or Magistrates, they are thrice admonished: and at length the Father has a Power given him, to prevent worse Consequences, to sell them in case they will not be reclaimed; but this very Practice directly refutes that Notion. It must however be granted, that Instances there are of Negroes selling their Children; but in Times only of excessive Famine, when they part with them to preserve the Childrens Lives and their own.

This was the Case about twenty Years ago amongst the People of *Whydaw,* when the King of *Dahome*[14] drove them out of their Country, and obliged them to take Shelter upon several barren Islands not far from the Coast, where, for want of Canoes, it was impossible for his Troops to follow them. The Distress to which People are driven in such Cases of Necessity, exempts their Actions from turning to the Prejudice of their general Characters. Hunger and the Sword are very pressing Arguments with white People as well as black; and therefore, what they compel Men to, can never be taken for the Custom of any Nation. In the present Instance, the Precaution of the Negro Chief shews him not to have been at all destitute, either of sound Sense or paternal Affection; he thought it for his own Interest, and for that of his Family, to send one of his Sons to *France;* but that Son was born of a Slave, which is a Circumstance among the Negroes that creates a kind of Illegitimacy; and we shall see that he was not altogether so cautious, when he thought fit to trust another Child in *English* Hands.

The young Negro was sent over to *France* with proper Recommendations to the Company; and these made not only a strong Impression on those to whom they were addressed, but also upon the Court, to which they were immediately communicated. The Son of the *African* Chief was received with all the Honours due to a Prince; he was not

---

[13] *vulgar:* Common.
[14] *Dahome:* An inland country, north of Whydah; now Benin.

only cloathed, lodged, maintained, and attended, but educated in all Respects in a Manner suitable to one of that Dignity; and as such was received and treated at Court, where he appeared on all Occasions in a splendid Dress, and was allowed to wear a Knot[15] upon his right Shoulder, which as now we are so well acquainted with *French* Customs needs no Explanation.

Due Care was taken to inform the Father of his Son's Reception and Situation; and after he had remained in *France* a proper Time, and all imaginable Care had been taken to shew him every thing that might give him high Ideas of the King and People, he was sent home in one of the Company's Ships, in a very handsome Manner, and with fine laced Cloaths to dazzle the Eyes of the Negroes, and to draw the Father over entirely to the *French* Interest. There is no doubt to be made that he was very welcome to the old Caboceiro, who was highly pleased to see his Son safe returned to *Africa*, and to hear what mighty Honours had been paid him in *Europe*; he expressed himself in very full Terms upon this Subject to the *French* Agents, with whom he dealt more largely than formerly, but without estranging himself from the *English*.

This Conduct of the *French* Nation will appear more laudable the more it is weighed, the more it is sifted[16] and considered; for undoubtedly nothing could contribute more to the spreading a general good Opinion of the *French* Nation amongst the Negroes, or produce a stronger Effect upon the particular Person it was meant to gain. All the Inland Traders coming from the most distant Part of *Africk* to bring their Gold and Slaves to *Annamaboe*, had an Opportunity of seeing the young *African* in all his *French* Finery, and to hear from his own Mouth, not only the Testimonies of Respect paid him, and the high Civilities shewn him by Persons of the first Quality, and such as were nearest in Power and Blood to the Throne; but also the vast Extent of the Dominions, the Number and Discipline of the Forces, the Affluence and Prosperity of the People subject to the *French* King. The Credit due to his Accounts were doubly inforced by his being an Eyewitness, relating what he saw, what he had an Opportunity of examining, and what it was impossible for him to be deceived in; and by his being himself a Negro, their Countryman, one whom they had no Cause to suspect, and whose Appearance, joined to the concurring Testimonies of his Father, and the *French* Traders, delivered them from any Apprehensions of his meaning to deceive them.

---

[15] *Knot:* Epaulet or decorative braid signifying superior status.
[16] *sifted:* Examined.

So high a Character to be spread amongst so many Thousands of People was very cheaply purchased by two or three Years Board to a single Man, and the Present of a few fine Cloaths when he was sent home. It ought also to be considered as a convincing Proof of the Abilities and Integrity of the Company's Agents in *Africa,* who both formed and executed a Scheme of such Consequence to their Nation, with so great Dexterity, and who were seconded so thoroughly by the Company and the Court. We are apt enough to copy *French* Customs, *French* Fashion, and *French* Taste in Trifles; in this Respect it would not be amiss to copy their Policy, since it is very certain that the Trade of *France* is very much the Care of the Court, by which, to say the Truth, it principally thrives; for wanting the Advantages that we possess, an extensive Freedom, and a Number of wealthy Merchants, nothing could contribute to fix and establish their Trade here, in the *East Indies,* or in the *West,* if the Court did not lend its Influence and Assistance.

It was not only with the *English* and *French* Companies that the Caboceiro of *Annamaboe* maintained a close Correspondence, but with the separate Traders of the former Nation also, who in modern Times have much improved and extended their Commerce in those Parts, not only by the Advantage they have of trading without the Incumbrances of Forts, Garrisons, and regular Establishments, of all which however they enjoy the Protection, but by their keeping a Kind of settled Magazines[17] or floating Factories almost constantly on the Coasts, from whence they are enabled to supply the Negroes continually with a Variety of Goods; and that too at a very cheap Rate, which, tho' a Convenience and an Advantage to those People, sinks the Value of *British* Commodities and Manufactures in *Guinea,* and raises the Price of Slaves in our Colonies in the *West Indies.*

With these Traders the Caboceiro had a constant Intercourse, took off vast Quantities of their Effects, and afforded them in return the Prime of every Thing that came to his Hands. For Interest is a universal Deity, the *Fettish,*[18] as these People call it, of the Negroes, as much as of the *Europeans;* and notwithstanding any Ties of Friendship and old Acquaintance with the *African* Company's Servants, towards whom he always carried himself with Civility and Respect, his Visits, for the Reasons beforementioned, were very frequent to the separate

[17] *Magazines:* Storehouses.
[18] *Fettish:* See n. 10, p. 232.

Traders,[19] and from the very same Motives, those who were entrusted with the Management of their Concerns, paid him all the Marks of extraordinary Complaisance that the highest Pitch of Negroe Vanity could expect or desire; they knew his Influence, which made them ready to court him, tho', when out of the Reach of it (as is natural enough) they may affect to ridicule and despise it.

A certain Captain, who was one of the principal Directors of this Kind of Commerce, and more especially of the new Scheme, laboured with all the Address of which he was Master, to render himself a Favourite with the Caboceiro of *Annamaboe;* in order to which,[20] he neglected nothing that might either contribute to promote his Interest, or gratify his Inclinations; he was remarkably punctual in all Transactions with him, and very willing to give him Credit (which is often necessary) for as much and as long as his Occasions required. In short, he not only sought to acquire his Confidence as a Trader, but took every Step that he could possibly devise to live with him upon the familiar Footing of a Friend; and the better to accomplish this, he put on a seeming Affection for the Negroes, and a Degree of Complaisance for their Manners; which, however little to their Honour, it must be confessed is not very unusual amongst the *Europeans* of every Nation, who have for a Course of Years frequented the Coast of *Guinea.*

By the Practice of Arts like these, it is not at all strange that he fully accomplished his Design; and grew not only into such Credit, but into such Intimacy with *John Corrente,* that he was scarce more Master on board than ashore, which answered all his Purposes perfectly, as well with Regard to Ease and Conveniency in living, as procuring unusual Advantages in his Dealings; which turned, or might have turned very much to his Account. For there is nothing that gains more upon the Negroes, more especially in their own Country, and where they are not at all in Danger of feeling the Effects of a sudden Change of Temper than this familiar Manner of associating with them, which proceeds from their natural Deference for white Men, and the Pleasure as well as Pride they have in living upon a Level and an Equality with them; which at the same Time contributes not a little to heighten the Reverence and Respect paid them by those of their own Complexion, who are naturally apt to fancy that there must be Qualities peculiarly great

---

[19] *separate Traders:* Interloping traders, by contrast with those authorized by the RAC.

[20] *in order to which:* I.e., in order to do which.

and noble, in Persons, who are thus admitted into Friendship, and a close Correspondence with Captains and others of superior Rank among the *Whites*. Besides, it affords them many Opportunities of prying into, and discovering what otherwise they could never any Way reach, as the Negroes are a cunning and subtle[21] People, in common with other barbarous Nations; for this Turn of Mind is chiefly owing to want of Education, and a Power of thinking extensively, that forces Men to aim at compassing[22] what they want by the Strength of their own narrow Abilities, which drives them into crooked Paths, just as Workmen perform Things but rudely and imperfectly who have the Use only of a few, and those, it may be, but coarse and unhandy Tools.

It was to this Captain particularly, that the Caboceiro of *Annamaboe* opened himself frequently upon the Head of his Son's Voyage to *France,* and the Sense he had of the great Honours that were done him during his Residence in that Country; asking at the same Time, what Difference there was between *France* and *England?* whether the latter was as good a Country, the King as powerful, or his Subjects as rich? to which the Captain gave such Answers as he judged convenient, not apprehending perhaps at first, to what these Inquiries tended. When Opportunities offered, the Caboceiro, proposed the same Question to such of the Company's Servants as he had Occasion to transact Business with, from whom he received more clear and explicit Answers, and who told him plainly that the *French* were a Nation that delighted in Pomp and Splendour; but that the *English* were much superior to them in Naval Power, and in the extent of their Trade; of which the Negroe was easily convinced, on comparing the Number of Ships sent by the two Nations on the Coast of *Guinea.* From these Conversations, he picked up Hints that were very serviceable to him in many Respects, and enabled him to sift even out of the *French* Traders themselves Matters of Fact, that left him no Room to doubt of the Truth of what the *Englishmen* had told him.

This dwelt very much upon his Mind, and finding how useful the Knowledge which one of his Sons had acquired by Travel was, by the serving as an Interpreter with one Set of People, he had a Mind to procure the like Advantages, by employing another Son to enter as thoroughly into the Affairs of another Nation; which from their Superiority in Trade, and much greater Variety of Commodities and Manufactures in which they dealt, promised still greater Advantages.

[21] *subtle:* Shrewd, adroit.
[22] *compassing:* Achieving.

Several Accidents concurred to fortify him in this Opinion; but particularly his observing that the *English* separate Traders were much keener, and more expert in the Management of their Business than the *French;* that they frequently formed Schemes of outwitting them in their Commerce, and, generally speaking, succeeded in it; and in respect to this, he was the more confirmed by conferring with the most experienced of his own Nation, whose Observations concurred in this Particular, as likewise did those of the Inland Merchants, whose Demands were chiefly for *British* Goods and Manufactures.

The Son he intended to send to *England,* and who is actually here at present, was his greatest Favourite; his Mother was not only a free Woman and his chief Wife, but also the Daughter of one of the principal Persons in the Country. The Youth had been always distinguished by the quickness of his Parts, and the Affability of his Behaviour, as well as by a graceful Deportment, and a very agreeable Person.[23] He had lived for a Time, when a perfect Child, in the Fort with one of the *African* Company's principal Officers, where he had learned to speak *English,* and had acquired a great Confidence in as well as a sincere Affection for the Nation. The old Caboceiro encouraged this Disposition in him all he could, told him frequently that himself was an *Englishman,* and that he ought to think himself so too; that the *English* were their best Friends, and treated them with the most Kindness, that they were a great and powerful Nation, as appeared from the Number of Ships that arrived annually in the Road of *Annamaboe,* and their rich Cargoes; that their dominions in other Parts must be very large and productive of vast Riches, since they bought yearly such a Number of Blacks, who were employed in their Tillage and Cultivation, and that therefore he could not do better than to improve that Kindness and Esteem they had for him, by endeavouring every Day to merit more and more their Favour and Friendship.

As these Rules suited exactly with his Inclination, the Lad pursued them with all the Spirit and Diligence imaginable, attached himself entirely to the *English* who frequented the Port, and from thence was taken Notice of and caressed by them in a very extraordinary Manner. The *French* Traders easily perceiving how much this Son was beloved of his Father and respected in the Family, as well as pleased with the Modesty of his Carriage, and his superior Abilities, were not wanting in their Applications, which however had very little Effect; for tho' he was never deficient in Civility, yet his Humour of piquing himself upon

[23] *Person:* Physical appearance.

being an *Englishman,* and the strong Impressions he had received in the Fort, gave him a Distaste to that Nation, which it was not possible for him to conceal. He was besides very little struck with Finery, and had accustomed himself to a frank and open Manner of expressing his Sentiments, without the Gloss of Compliments or any dark Reserves.

Amongst all the People that had Business with the Caboceiro of *Annamaboe,* the Captain beforementioned had not only the greatest Credit with him, but was the freest and most intimate with his Family; and seeing his Father's Affection for him, professed always a peculiar Regard and a singular Tenderness for this Youth; who on his Part loved him with the sincerity natural to his Years, and testified as much Duty towards him as if he had been his Father. When therefore the old Caboceiro expressed in general Terms his Wish, that some Opportunity might offer of sending him to *England* that he might be educated there, and acquire that Knowledge which rendered white Men so much superior to themselves, and to the rest of the Negroe Nations; it was very agreeable News both to the Lad and to the Captain.

The former, to whom the *English* had given the Name of Cupid,[24] as most expressive of his sweet and amiable Temper, shewed the greatest Willingness imaginable to enter into his Father's Scheme, and to make a Voyage to *Europe;* as on the other Hand the Captain seemed to be ravish'd[25] with the Proposal, which at once shewed the Confidence of the old Man, and afforded him an Opportunity of adding to the Marks of Kindness and Good-will, that he had formerly given to his Son. Their Voyage to *England* was thenceforward the sole Topick of their Conversation; the Father was settled in his Resolution, the Boy was delighted with it, and the Captain spoke to him in a Language that was perfectly paternal. He was continually forecasting what Advantages he might draw from this Adventure, and without knowing it, was a very true Prophet of the Respect and Esteem which the young Man would certainly attract by his good Qualities, when in *England.* In a word, this Project was the great Topick of Discourse in the Family, and they delighted themselves with the Expectation of seeing with what mighty Improvements their young *Englishman* would return to *Annamaboe.*

As the Season was at a Distance in which the Captain proposed to depart, all Parties had sufficient Leisure to contemplate their respective Schemes in every Light, of which they were capable, and to flatter their

---

[24] Cupid: The Roman god of love.
[25] *ravish'd:* Overjoyed.

Imaginations with any Circumstances that might set off and adorn them. The *Caboceiro* might probably propose the preserving in his Family that Post of Honour, tho' in its Nature elective, by rendering his Children so much superior in Knowledge to his Countrymen; and at the same time qualifying them to serve the Community with such extraordinary Advantages. His darling Son ran over in his Mind all the strange Things he had heard in the *English* Fort, or among the Traders and Sailors of that Nation: He pleased himself with the Hopes of seeing these, and of comprehending perfectly a Multitude of Subjects, of which in spite of all his Inquiries he had only dark and confused Ideas. In respect to the Captain, it may be presumed from his future Conduct, that he looked upon his young Pupil as an Acquisition of so much Wealth as he would sell for, and applied himself besides to make all the Uses in his Power of the *Caboceiro's* Interest and Influence, while he remained in the Country.

Indeed this had been all along of very great Benefit to him, and tho' the *Caboceiro* did not enter in every Respect into his Views, he had made him subservient to his carrying into Execution most of his Projects, by which himself and his Associates had gained the Reputation of being among the Number of the most clear-sighted and adroit Traders that ever visited the Coast of *Guinea*. What Returns both the old *Caboceiro* and his Son have met with for their Friendships, Hospitality and Favours, the World is not unacquainted with; and what Right they have to treat with the most ignominious and contemptible Language the Negroes in general, Mankind will likewise judge. But supposing them as low and mean as those who hate and despise them most can represent them; this can afford no Justification for deceiving or maltreating them. There is certainly no Credit to be acquired by outwitting the Ignorant, nor will it prove a Recommendation in any Country under the Cope of Heaven, for Men who have had a good Education, to compass their own Ends by imposing false Colours upon such as they look upon as beneath them in every Respect. What Grounds there is for this Opinion, or how Man can differ from Man, but by the Superior Virtues of the Mind, the best Judges will find it hard to distinguish, since as to all other Advantages they are meerly accidental, and he who makes the best use of them is the best Man, let his Complexion be *black* or *white*.

At length the Time came that the Captain had finish'd his Affairs upon the Coast, and was to leave it, which gave great Pleasure to all Parties; the old Man was desirous that his Son should go speedily, that he might have the better Chance of living to see him return Home. The sprightly[26] Youth, full of the fond Hopes of seeing the World, was impatient to depart; the Captain gave not the least Check to their Hopes, but on the contrary, continued to inspire his Pupil with a passionate Desire of viewing all the Beauties of an Island the most celebrated in the known World. His Conduct was in every respect as kind as it had ever been; and indeed the noble Youth does him even now the Justice to acknowledge, that he had no Hardships to complain of in the Passage, and that on the contrary, he treated him with all the Tenderness, all the Attention of a Father.

This no doubt confirmed him entirely in those Sentiments of Respect and Veneration, which he had been so long accustomed to have for his Father's Friend, and kept even the slightest Suspicion from entering into his Thoughts. Under this happy Delusion he compleated his Voyage from the Road of *Annamaboe,* to *Bridge-Town*[27] in *Barbadoes;* nor was he undeceived even there. The very same Behaviour was kept up to the last, and the unfortunate Youth had not the least Foresight of the impending Evil, till like a Torrent it came pouring upon him all at once; and but for the Interposition of Providence, had irretrievably buried him in Misery and Despair.

When the Captain had sold him, and he was put into a Boat to be carried to his Master, he thought he was going on board the Ship that was to carry him to *England.* But what Language can express his Surprize, when from the rough Usage that he met with from two Slaves that were in the Boat, he had no Room left him to doubt that his Condition was the same with theirs? It must be left to the Reader's Imagination to frame a Notion of his Distress, which will be so much the harder, as the Freedom and Happiness of our Situation hinders us from ever beholding a Sight that any way resembles it. It must assuredly have struck him with a Horror, for white Men in general; have filled his Mind at once with as black Thoughts of them, and with better Foundation than some of these, affect to have for those of his Country with very little Cause.

But whatever his Thoughts, whatever his Reflections might be, they left him scarce a glimmering of Hope, distant from Home, far from Father, Family, or Friends, betrayed and abandoned by him whom he had always esteemed his Protector; and this in the very Dawn of Life. He had before him a Prospect so gloomy, that he stood in need of superior Greatness of Mind to bear the Shock without sinking under

---

[26] *sprightly:* Lively, animated.
[27] *Bridge-Town:* The capital of Barbadoes, on the island's southwestern coast.

it, or taking some desperate Method to remove the Load. It was some Relief to him that he fell into the Hands of a Gentleman of distinguished Character, where he was treated with much Humanity, which abated somewhat of the Bitterness of that sudden and undeserved Reverse of Fortune, revived him a little, and encouraged him to breathe and live. This by Degrees gave him Leisure to look round him, to compare his past and present Condition, and to furnish himself with the best Helps that Reflection and Experience could suggest towards his Amusement and Relief.

He saw numbers in the like Condition, from a Variety of Accidents, but none of them in any Degree comparable to that which had brought this heavy Lot upon him. He was ashamed however to shew less Courage than the rest, or not to oppose Misfortune with equal Steadiness of Mind; he resolved therefore to bear, tho' he could not be reconciled to his Fate, and to sustain without complaining a Calamity it was out of his Power to remove. In this sad State his Innocence afforded him the only Consolation; it was a Satisfaction that he had not drawn this upon himself, and by Degrees the Fairness and Mildness of his Behavior, procured other Alleviations of that galling Yoke. But neither Time nor these transient Comforts, could so far dissipate the Sense of his Condition, as to remove that Melancholy which followed his first Consternation; but as this was not attended with any Tincture of Sullenness or Obstinacy, it rather heightened than abated his other good Qualities, which gained him universal Esteem, while in the low State of a Slave.

The Captain, to cover this Matter in the best Manner possible; either about the Time, or soon after his selling his Pupil, transmitted to the Caboceiro of *Annamaboe,* an Account current, upon the Foot of which he was considerably in his Debt; the Justice of this however he has since controverted.[28] But be the Matter how it will, it seems very clear, that both Parties knew one another well enough to give Credit at other Times; so that there could be no Cause for proceeding with that amazing Severity at this Juncture: it is also apparent, that if procuring Satisfaction for his Debt was all the Captain had in View, he might as well have obtained it by keeping the young Man in his Custody, till the Father had satisfied his Agents; but to proceed in so abrupt, so strange, and so clandestine a Manner, affords sufficient Light for the World to judge of the Nature of this Transaction. However, not long after this the Captain died; and left the young *African* in Circumstances

---

[28] *controverted:* Disputed.

as miserable, and as desperate as could be imagined; for he was not only a Slave, but a Slave at such a Distance from his Country, Father, and Friends, and so totally deprived of the Means of communicating to them his Condition, that if his Relief had in any degree depended upon his own Abilities to promote it, there is no doubt that he had lived and died in that deplorable Condition.

Yet if the Author of his Misfortune had been so pleased, he might have prevented this, by giving the old Caboceiro such Lights as would have put it in his Power to have redeemed his Son; or it may be, if he had acted ingenuously[29] with the Gentleman to whom he sold him at *Barbadoes,* the same might have been brought to pass; but by doing neither, he plainly shewed, that, in his Opinion, all Blacks were destined to be Slaves; and this therefore satisfied him, that he had only left the Youth, for whom he professed so much Friendship, in his proper Situation. But it is now Time to leave the young Man for the present, and return to *Africa,* in order to observe by what strange and secret Steps divine Providence provided for the extricating out of his Misfortunes an innocent Youth, unable to help himself.

The *French* continued to keep up their Intimacy and close Correspondence with the Caboceiro of *Annamaboe,* in which they had all along so much found their Account; and as, after the Departure of the Captain, the separate Traders did not so much frequent the Coast, the Commerce of *Annamaboe* fell almost wholly into the Hands of the *French;* which, as it was very natural, gave great Distaste to the Servants of the Royal *African* Company, who considering the then Situation of Things, very reasonably expected their Affairs should have taken rather a better than a worse Turn. They did not spare either Endeavours or Expostulations with the Caboceiro, but to very little Purpose. At first, indeed, he gave them good Words, but by Degrees all Ceremonies were dropped, and he told them very plainly, that he did no more than he had a Right to do; and that he meant for the future to deal not only on what Terms, and in what Manner, but with whom he pleased.

This Declaration needed no Commentary; and therefore those who were intrusted with the *African* Company's Concerns, resolved, as the News of the War between the two Nations was arrived, and one of his *Britannick* Majesty's Ships actually upon the Coast, to recur to the only Means now left to set Affairs to rights, which was Force. Accordingly, at the Request of one of the Company's principal Agents, the

---

[29] *ingenuously:* Frankly, honestly.

King's Frigate stood in as near the Town of *Annamaboe,* as could be done with Safety, and began to fire upon it. This had the desired Effect, at least in Appearance; for the Caboceiro complied with the Terms prescribed; and, as he said, sent all the *French* Traders out of the Place; which however was afterwards discovered to be no more than a temporary Expedient, since he only concealed their Persons and Effects till such Time as the Man of War went off the Coast, and then they appeared and traded again as openly as ever, from a full Persuasion that the Danger was over; and that for the future they had nothing farther to fear.

It was not long, however, before another of his Majesty's Ships arrived upon the Coast, to the Captain of which the like Application was made on the *African* Company's Behalf, and as readily complied with. The Company's Agent at this time embarked on board the Vessel, and after a brisk cannonading had put the Place into much Confusion, he took an Opportunity of sending a Servant on shore in whom he could confide, with a Message to the *Caboceiro,* importing, that as he had always valued himself upon being an *Englishman,* and that the Nation was now at War with the *French,* it was not only improper but unlawful for him to correspond with them. At the same time he put him in mind of his former good Correspondence with the Company, the sincere Regard they had always shewn for him, and the great readiness on their Part to forget what was past, and to renew their old Friendship.

The Negroe *Caboceiro* received their Message with great chearfulness and satisfaction; he acknowledged the Case was very fairly stated, but insisted upon the kind Usage his Son had met with in *France,* and the Outrage and Insult that had been offered him by the Captain, who, under Colour of carrying his Child to be educated in *England,* had sold him for a Slave, which Fact he looked upon as sufficient to release him from all former Obligations. However, in regard he was still an *Englishman,* he was highly pleased to find that he was treated as such; and that, provided satisfaction was made for the Injustice that had been done him, he was very willing that Things between them should be once more set upon their former Foot, and that there was no need of Force to compel him to a Measure, which was of all others the most suitable to his natural Inclination. It is easy to see that this was a satisfactory Answer, and gave Grounds sufficient to enter into a Negotiation.

The Terms of the new Agreement were not long in settling; for old Friendships are sometimes like old China, when the Pieces are properly applied and well rivetted they are stronger than at first. It was promised to the Caboceiro *John,* that the Company would enquire after and recover his Son, that he should be carried to *England* and taken care of there, after which he should be also sent safely home. All other Disputes were likewise regulated to the mutual Satisfaction of the Parties, the Caboceiro only insisting that no Violence should be offered to the Persons of the *French* Traders, whom, under Colour of being forced to it by the *English,* he cut off from all Commerce, and thereby compelled them to surrender to the Company's Servants, by whom they were sent, as had been stipulated, in great safety down to *Whydaw.*

Thus this Affair terminated much to the Advantage of the Company, but so that they were obliged to take upon them the satisfaction of an Injury in which they had not the least Concern; and to this the Company will be always liable, because in *Africa,* as well as in *England,* they are considered as a corporate Body, to which Application may be always made, and who are at all Times answerable to the several *Negroe* Governments upon the Coast for the Conduct and Behaviour of the *British* Nation, which is a Point highly deserving Notice.

Before we come to mention the finding and redeeming the Son of the *Caboceiro* of *Annamaboe,* it may not be amiss to give a signal Instance of Generosity of Mind, and a truly great Spirit, in the Father of the sprightly *Negroe,* who lives with our young *Hero* as his Companion. This Man in his own Country is stiled the *English Caboceiro;* for it is to be observed, that tho' *John Corrente* is stiled the *Caboceiro,* by way of Excellence or Distinction, the old Term of *Brasso* not being now much in use; yet he governs his little Territory by the Advice of the other *Heads* of Families, who are also stiled *Caboceiros,* and who form a Council, that, in a politer State, would be called a *Senate* or *Regency.*

Amongst these some are particularly appointed for the managing and transacting Affairs with different Nations, and hence the Title of the *English Caboceiro* is bestowed upon him who manages with the *English* Company and confers, as Occasion requires, with their Agents and Servants. This Man having always professed a sincere and hearty Regard for our Nation, applied himself to the Gentleman who negotiated and concluded the Agreement that has been just mentioned; and after previously observing how much Credit the *French* had obtained by their good Usage of one of his Countrymen, and what an Odium had been thrown upon the *English,* on the score of selling that young Man's Brother, he told him, he had a Proposal to make, which was this; That as it was impossible to foresee what Difficulties would arise in executing literally what had been promised to *John Corrente,* he voluntarily offered his own Son to accompany him to *England,* that it might appear they had still a Confidence in the Nation, and the Company; nor did he give himself any Concern about the manner of his Treatment, which he left entirely to the good Pleasure of the Person to whom he recommended him. "But, *said he,* when he comes back, be sure to afford him a *Lace Coat,* at least as fine as that which was bestowed by the *French,* that our People here may be undeceived, and freed from their Prejudices in favour of the one, and to the discredit of the other Nation. This, *continued he,* is the only Method I can contrive for the Service of those to whom I have always professed a Friendship, and shall esteem it my greatest Happiness if one of my Family can in any Degree contribute to restore the good Opinion, that I could always wish my Countrymen might entertain of the People of *England.*"

This was certainly as clear and signal a Proof of Gratitude and Respect, as it was in the Power of Man to give, and is a sufficient Demonstration of the important Consequences that attend a judicious and humane Behaviour towards distant and barbarous Nations; a Thing long ago observed, and strongly recommended by the best Writers upon Trade, and more especially by Sir *Josiah Child,*[30] than whom no Man ever understood the Subject better. We may therefore very readily imagine that the Offer was willingly embraced, and the strongest Assurances given to the *English* Caboceiro, that his Son should be well treated, sent home safe, and that the Point of the laced Coat, should also be properly attended to.

To some indeed these will appear very trivial Things, and by them small Regard will be had to a People capable of being influenced, even in the most important Affairs, by Circumstances of so little Moment. But Persons of stronger Heads will see it in another Light; and find no Difficulty in discovering, that with all the Advantages of Sagacity and Politeness, other Nations are as much affected by Things which are at the bottom of as little Significance; for what are those great Points, of Stile, Rank, and Ceremony in all publick Negotiations, but *laced Coats,* if beheld in a critical and impartial View?

---

[30] *Sir Josiah Child:* Child (1630–1699), a member of the Court of Assistants in the RAC, wrote numerous treatises on international trade and the commerce between England and the East Indies, including *The Great Honor and Advantage of the East-India Trade to the Kingdom, Asserted* (1697) and *A New Discourse of Trade* (1693), which was frequently reprinted in the eighteenth century.

When the Season come in which this Agent of the *Royal* African *Company* was to return to the *West-Indies,* and from thence to take his Passage home; the *English* Caboceiro, in strict Compliance with his Promise, sent his Son along with him, who was treated in the Voyage, as he has been ever since, with all the Kindness and Regard possible. Upon their Arrival at *Barbadoes,* the Son of the Caboceiro of *Annamaboe* was without much Difficulty found, and a valuable Consideration being given to the Gentleman who bought him, he was happily restored to Liberty, and to his former good Opinion of the Candour of the *British* Nation. For the Pains taken on his Behalf, and the great Zeal expressed to wipe off the Aspersion occasioned by his ill Usage, satisfied him fully that his Misfortune befel him from the Disposition of a single Person, and was entirely disapproved by *Englishmen* of every Denomination; those even of the lowest Rank expressing a just Disdain of such iniquitous Practices; not more incompatible with the Doctrines of Religion, or the Principles of Morality, than with the natural Candour and Generosity of a true *English* Soul; to which, the young Prince has been clearly convinced that the Usage he met with was no just Exception.

After he was once restored to his Freedom, and the Nature of his Case became publick, every body expressed an Inclination to see him, and all who saw him were charmed with his Behaviour and Address. He was continually expatiating on the Justice, Kindness, and Goodness of those who had taken so much Pains to find him out in his low Condition, and to deliver him from the Load of his Misfortunes; but he rather affected Silence with Respect to the Author of them, and whenever he was obliged to mention him; did it not only without any Marks of an outragious Resentment, but with a Decency that could scarce be expected, and as if he was conscious that no Exaggeration could make a more lasting Impression, than the simple and naked Relation of the Fact itself; in this without doubt he has thoroughly succeeded; for all Men of good Sense, and good Nature, which takes in all who feel the Weight of what others have unjustly suffered, are more affected by their own Reflections, than by the passionate Expressions, even of the most justifiable Resentment.

Upon his coming to *England* his Case was properly represented, and the Facts relating to it justified by all the necessary Testimonies that the singular and extraordinary Nature of them, and the various Circumstances that attended them, required, and which have entitled him to that high Protection, that generous and kind Notice which has been taken of him, by those who have a becoming Concern for natural

Equity and Justice, as well as for the Reputation and Honour of the *British* People. This, as every Measure of the Kind will be, has been received with a Voice of universal Applause; the Nation has ratified and confirmed the Rectitude of this Attention shewn by the Government, and have taken a just Share in that wise and well-judged Compassion, which the Case of this noble and unfortunate Stranger so apparently deserved.

It is indeed true, that a Conduct so rational in itself is not without a Precedent even in the present Reign, tho' in favour of a Person of less Consequence. When the King of *Dahome* conquered *Whydaw* and carried away not only Multitudes of the Natives, but also an *Englishman,* whom they had very unjustly made Prisoner, one Capt. *Lamb,*[31] then in the *African* Company's Service, he treated him very kindly, and after a long Captivity dismissed him freely with considerable Presents; and upon his Promise of returning to him, allowed him to take one of his Negroe Subjects called *Tomo,* as his Servant. It seems the Captain did not care to run the Hazard of putting himself once more into the Hands of a Conqueror, whose Temper was none of the mildest; and who was apt to commit great Cruelties from Caprice; but however he ought certainly to have sent back *Tomo;* and his not doing it, gave just Reason to the Negroe Monarch to be very much offended, as he really was. It was some Years before this Matter was clearly understood in *England;* but as soon as it was understood, and *Tomo* brought by his Master to *London,* due Enquiry was made, the Negro discharged from his Service, proper Care taken of him while he remained here; and as soon as it could be conveniently done, he was sent home again, at the Expence of the Government, as it was highly fitting that he should.

These are Matters that will always claim a suitable Regard, not only for the Sake of those to whom such Civilities are done, but for our own. And as there is no Country to which the Fame of the *British* Nation has not been carried by the Power of our Naval Force, or by the Industry of our Merchants, it imports us not a little, that our

[31] *Capt. Lamb:* Captain Bulfinch Lambe, an employee of the RAC; in 1722 he was captured by the king of Allada, who claimed that the RAC had not paid its debts, and who threatened to enslave Lambe. When Agaja, the king of Dahomey, conquered Allada in 1724, he took Lambe as well and treated him as a guest. Lambe left in 1726 with an interpreter, Adomo Oroonoko Tomo, and though he had promised to return soon, Lambe eventually left his interpreter in Maryland, apparently having sold him as a slave. Lambe returned to London in 1731, and when the details of his story emerged, Tomo was also brought to London where he was feted and then finally returned to Dahomey.

Humanity and Justice should be as extensive, as either the Terror of our Navies, or the Attention we have to Trade. It is of as great Consequence to be esteemed, and to be loved, as to be dreaded or revered; the former is, and ought to be the natural Effects of our own Inclinations; the latter can only be right when it is justified by the Disrespect or Injuries we receive from others.

All singular and surprising Accidents have a general Influence, for the present; they employ every Tongue, they affect every Mind when they happen; yet Sensations of this Sort are momentary, and universal Oblivion, in a short Space of Time, succeeds to universal Admiration: But this is sometimes not at all expedient; for in many Cases it is very requisite that such Phænomena should be cautiously examined, and sincerely and circumstantially recorded. At least, these Things appear in this Light to those Minds that recollect the Disturbance it has frequently given them to meet only with broken Hints, and irreconcileable Circumstances of Matters that have happened in past Times, which they would be willing to comprehend more fully. This inclines People of such a Disposition to provide against the Disappointment of Men of the same Turn in succeeding Times; which it is presumed will appear not only a rational, but a laudable Species of industrious Curiosity.

The Subject of this short Discourse is as good an Instance as can be given of the Kind, in as much as in its Certainty and Importance it is to the full as considerable as in Singularity. The greatest and the best People in the Kingdom have thought it worthy of their Enquiry, and their Enquiries have been constantly succeeded by an entire Satisfaction; their Eyes, their Ears, their Senses, and their Understanding have been equally gratified; and our *African* Prince has appeared such from the Gracefulness of his Person, the Nobleness of his Sentiments, the Modesty of his Deportment, and the grateful Acknowledgments he continually expresses for the Justice that has been done him, and the Favours that he has received: Circumstances that amount to a kind of natural Demonstration; and which, without exceeding the Bounds of Truth, may be said to have spread universal Conviction amongst all who are not wilfully blind and deaf; and who lie open only to Conviction of another Kind.

OTTOBAH CUGOANO

From *Thoughts and Sentiments on the Evil and Wicked Traffic of the Slavery and Commerce of the Human Species*

Ottobah Cugoano was probably born in 1757 in the Fanti country of the Gold Coast, in what is now Ghana. He was captured in 1770 and taken to Grenada, where he worked as a slave, probably on a sugar plantation, before being taken to England as a servant in 1772. As Cugoano explains in a brief set of autobiographical remarks prefixed to some copies of his *Thoughts and Sentiments,* "I was advised by some good people to get myself baptized, that I might not be carried away and sold again." At his baptism in 1773, Cugoano took the name John Steuart, but when he came to publish his book, he used only his African name. In his short reminiscence, he claims descent from the "chief men in the kingdom of Agimaque and Assinee" — seemingly affiliating himself with the nobility. It is not clear how Cugoano became a free man, but records show that he was a leader and spokesman for black men and women in London in the 1780s. He was a friend of the abolitionist leader Granville Sharp, and of Olaudah Equiano, with whom he campaigned as a member of the Sons of Africa to secure human rights for Africans living in Britain. In the early 1790s, Cugoano worked with the Sierra Leone Company, a project designed to help former slaves resettle in Africa, but he seems to have had little faith in the practical value of such efforts.

Thoughts and Sentiments was first published in 1787, and it was followed by a second edition later that year. A French translation appeared in 1788, and in 1791 Cugoano published a condensed version.

The text is excerpted from the first edition (London: 1787) 6–13, 92–93.

I was born in the city of Agimaque,[1] on the coast of Fantyn; my father was a companion to the chief in that part of the country of Fantee, and when the old king died I was left in his house with his family; soon after I was sent for by his nephew, Ambro Accasa, who succeeded the old king in the chiefdom of that part of Fantee known by

---

[1] *Agimaque:* A town in the Fantyn country, slightly east of Annamabo and approximately fifteen miles inland from the coast (now spelled Ajumako).

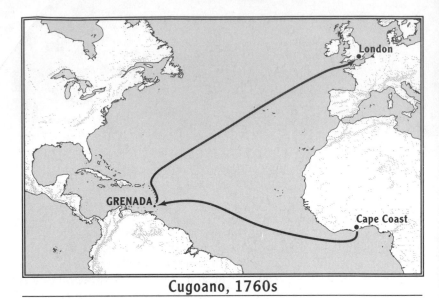

Cugoano, 1760s

Map of the route of Cugoano.

the name of Agimaque and Assinee.[2] I lived with his children, enjoying peace and tranquillity, about twenty moons, which, according to their way of reckoning time, is two years. I was sent for to visit an uncle, who lived at a considerable distance from Agimaque. The first day after we set out we arrived at Assinee, and the third day at my uncle's habitation, where I lived about three months, and was then thinking of returning to my father and young companion at Agimaque; but by this time I had got well acquainted with some of the children of my uncle's hundreds of relations, and we were some days too ventursome in going into the woods to gather fruit and catch birds, and such amusements as pleased us. One day I refused to go with the rest, being rather apprehensive that something might happen to us; till one of my playfellows said to me, because you belong to the great men, you are afraid to venture your carcase, or else of the *bounsam,* which is the devil. This enraged me so much, that I set a resolution to join the rest, and we went into the woods as usual; but we had not been above two

<hr />

[2] *Assinee:* A kingdom near the eastern end of the Guinea coast.

hours before our troubles began, when several great ruffians came upon us suddenly, and said we had committed a fault against their lord, and we must go and answer for it ourselves before him.

Some of us attempted in vain to run away, but pistols and cutlasses were soon introduced, threatening, that if we offered to stir we should all lie dead on the spot. One of them pretended to be more friendly than the rest, and said, that he would speak to their lord to get us clear, and desired that we should follow him: we were then immediately divided into different parties, and drove after him. We were soon led out of the way which we knew, and towards the evening, as we came in sight of a town, they told us that this great man of theirs lived there, but pretended it was too late to go and see him that night. Next morning there came three other men, whose language differed from ours, and spoke to some of those who watched us all the night, but he that pretended to be our friend with the great man, and some others, were gone away. We asked our keepers what these men had been saying to them, and they answered, that they had been asking them, and us together, to go and feast with them that day, and that we must put off seeing the great man till after; little thinking that our doom was so nigh, or that these villains meant to feast on us as their prey. We went with them again about half a day's journey, and came to a great multitude of people, having different music playing; and all the day after we got there, we were very merry with the music, dancing and singing. Towards the evening, we were again persuaded that we could not get back to where the great man lived till next day; and when bedtime came, we were separated into different houses with different people. When the next morning came, I asked for the men that brought me there, and for the rest of my companions; and I was told that they were gone to the sea side to bring home some rum, guns and powder, and that some of my companions were gone with them, and that some were gone to the fields to do something or other. This gave me strong suspicion that there was some treachery in the case, and I began to think that my hopes of returning home again were all over. I soon became very uneasy, not knowing what to do, and refused to eat or drink for whole days together, till the man of the house told me that he would do all in his power to get me back to my uncle; then I eat a little fruit with him, and had some thoughts that I should be sought after, as I would be then missing at home about five or six days. I enquired every day if the men had come back, and for the rest of my companions, but could get no answer of any satisfaction. I was kept about six days at this man's house, and in the evening there was another man came and talked with him a good while, and I heard the one say to the other he must go, and the other said the sooner the better; that man came out and told me that he knew my relations at Agimaque, and that we must set out to-morrow morning, and he would convey me there. Accordingly we set out next day, and travelled till dark, when we came to a place where we had some supper and slept. He carried a large bag with some gold dust, which he said he had to buy some goods at the sea side to take with him to Agimaque. Next day we travelled on, and in the evening came to a town, where I saw several white people, which made me afraid that they would eat me, according to our notion as children in the inland parts of the country. This made me rest very uneasy all the night, and next morning I had some victuals brought; desiring me to eat and make haste, as my guide and kidnapper told me that he had to go to the castle with some company that were going there, as he had told me before, to get some goods. After I was ordered out, the horrors I soon saw and felt, cannot be well described; I saw many of my miserable countrymen chained two and two, some hand-cuffed, and some with their hands tied behind. We were conducted along by a guard, and when we arrived at the castle, I asked my guide what I was brought there for, he told me to learn the ways of the *browsow,* that is the white faced people. I saw him take a gun, a piece of cloth, and some lead for me, and then he told me that he must now leave me there, and went off. This made me cry bitterly, but I was soon conducted to a prison, for three days, where I heard the groans and cries of many, and saw some of my fellow-captives. But when a vessel arrived to conduct us away to the ship, it was a most horrible scene; there was nothing to be heard but rattling of chains, smacking of whips, and the groans and cries of our fellow-men. Some would not stir from the ground, when they were lashed and beat in the most horrible manner. I have forgot the name of this infernal fort; but we were taken in the ship that came for us, to another that was ready to sail from Cape Coast.[3] When we were put into the ship, we saw several black merchants coming on board, but we were all drove into our holes, and not suffered to speak to any of them. In this situation we continued several days in sight of our native land; but I could find no good person to give any information of my situation to Accasa at Agimaque. And when we found ourselves at last taken away, death was more preferable than life, and a plan was concerted amongst us, that we might burn and blow up the ship, and to perish all together in the flames; but we were betrayed by one of our own countrywomen, who

---

[3] *Cape Coast:* Also known as Cabo Corso; see p. 233.

slept with some of the head men of the ship, for it was common for the dirty filthy sailors to take the African women and lie upon their bodies; but the men were chained and pent up in holes. It was the women and boys which were to burn the ship, with the approbation and groans of the rest; though that was prevented, the discovery was likewise a cruel bloody scene.

But it would be needless to give a description of all the horrible scenes which we saw, and the base treatment which we met with in this dreadful captive situation, as the familiar cases of thousands, which suffer by this infernal traffic, are well known. Let it suffice to say, that I was thus lost to my dear indulgent parents and relations, and they to me. All my help was cries and tears, and these could not avail; nor suffered long, till one succeeding woe, and dread, swelled up another. Brought from a state of innocence and freedom, and, in a barbarous and cruel manner, conveyed to a state of horror and slavery: This abandoned situation may be easier conceived than described. From the time that I was kid-napped and conducted to a factory, and from thence in the brutish, base, but fashionable way of traffic, consigned to Grenada,[4] the grievous thoughts which I then felt, still pant in my heart; though my fears and tears have long since subsided. And yet it is still grievous to think that thousands more have suffered in similar and greater distress, under the hands of barbarous robbers, and merciless taskmasters; and that many even now are suffering in all the extreme bitterness of grief and woe, that no language can describe. The cries of some, and the sight of their misery, may be seen and heard afar; but the deep sounding groans of thousands, and the great sadness of their misery and woe, under the heavy load of oppressions and calamities inflicted upon them, are such as can only be distinctly known to the ears of Jehovah Sabaoth.[5]

This Lord of Hosts, in his great Providence, and in great mercy to me, made a way for my deliverance from Grenada. — Being in this dreadful captivity and horrible slavery, without any hope of deliverance, for about eight or nine months, beholding the most dreadful scenes of misery and cruelty, and seeing my miserable companions often cruelly lashed, and as it were cut to pieces, for the most trifling faults; this made me often tremble and weep, but I escaped better than many of them. For eating a piece of sugar-cane, some were cruelly lashed, or struck over the face to knock their teeth out. Some of the

---

[4] *Grenada:* An island in the West Indies, off the coast of Venezuela.

[5] *Jehovah Sabaoth:* God, or "the Lord of Hosts," as Cugoano translates the phrase in the next sentence. Cf. Romans 9.29 and James 5.4, both of which use the phrase "Lord of Saboath."

stouter ones, I suppose often reproved, and grown hardened and stupid with many cruel beatings and lashings, or perhaps faint and pressed with hunger and hard labour, were often committing trespasses of this kind, and when detected, they met with exemplary punishment. Some told they had their teeth pulled out to deter others, and to prevent them from eating any cane in future. Thus seeing my miserable companions and countrymen in this pitiful, distressed and horrible situation, with all the brutish baseness and barbarity attending it, could not but fill my little mind with horror and indignation. But I must own, to the shame of my own countrymen, that I was first kidnapped and betrayed by some of my own complexion, who were the first cause of my exile and slavery; but if there were no buyers there would be no sellers. So far as I can remember, some of the Africans in my country keep slaves, which they take in war, or for debt; but those which they keep are well fed, and good care taken of them, and treated well; and, as to their cloathing, they differ according to the custom of the country. But I may safely say, that all the poverty and misery that any of the inhabitants of Africa meet with among themselves, is far inferior to those inhospitable regions of misery which they meet with in the West-Indies, where their hard-hearted overseers have neither regard to the laws of God, nor the life of their fellow-men.

Thanks be to God, I was delivered from Grenada, and that horrid brutal slavery. — A gentleman coming to England, took me for his servant, and brought me away, where I soon found my situation become more agreeable. After coming to England, and seeing others write and read, I had a strong desire to learn, and getting what assistance I could, I applied myself to learn reading and writing, which soon became my recreation, pleasure, and delight; and when my master perceived that I could write some, he sent me to a proper school for that purpose to learn. Since, I have endeavoured to improve my mind in reading, and have sought to get all the intelligence I could, in my situation of life, towards the state of my brethren and countrymen in complexion, and of the miserable situation of those who are barbarously sold into captivity, and unlawfully held in slavery. . . .

The Spaniards began their settlements in the West Indies and America, by depredations of rapine, injustice, treachery and murder; and they have continued in the barbarous practice of devastation, cruelty, and oppression ever since: and their principles and maxims in planting colonies have been adopted, in some measure, by every other nation in Europe. This guiltful method of colonization must undoubtedly and imperceptibly have hardened men's hearts, and led them on from

one degree of barbarity and cruelty to another: f
destroyed, wasted and desolated the native inha
many of their own people, enriched with plund
returned home to enjoy their ill-gotten wealth, othe
to labour and cultivate the ground, and such other
ments were wanted. Vast territories and large po___
getting inhabitants to labour for them, were of no use. A general part
of what remained of the wretched fugitives, who had the best native
right to those possessions, were obliged to make their escape to places
more remote, and such as could not, were obliged to submit to the
hard labour and bondage of their invaders; but as they had not been
used to such harsh treatment and laborious employment as they were
then subjected to, they were soon wasted away and became few. Their
proud invaders found the advantage of having their labour done for
nothing, and it became their general practice to pick up the unfortunate strangers that fell in their way, when they thought they could
make use of them in their service. That base traffic of kidnapping and
stealing men was begun by the Portuguese on the coast of Africa, and
as they found the benefit of it for their own wicked purposes, they
soon went on to commit greater depredations. The Spaniards followed
their infamous example, and the African slave-trade was thought most
advantageous for them, to enable themselves to live in ease and affluence by the cruel subjection and slavery of others. The French and
English, and some other nations in Europe, as they founded settlements and colonies in the West Indies, or in America, went on in the
same manner, and joined hand in hand with the Portuguese and
Spaniards, to rob and pillage Africa, as well as to waste and desolate
the inhabitants of the western continent. But the European depredators and pirates have not only robbed and pillaged the people of Africa
themselves; but, by their instigation, they have infested the inhabitants
with some of the vilest combinations of fraudulent and treacherous
villains, even among their own people; and have set up their forts and
factories as a reservoir of public and abandoned thieves, and as a den
of desperadoes, where they may ensnare, entrap and catch men. So
that Africa has been robbed of its inhabitants; its free-born sons and
daughters have been stole, and kidnapped, and violently taken away,
and carried into captivity and cruel bondage. And it may be said, in
respect to that diabolical traffic which is still carried on by the European depredators, that Africa has suffered as much and more than any
other quarter of the globe. O merciful God when will the wickedness
of man have an end?

OLAUDAH EQUIANO

From *The Interesting Narrative of the Life of Olaudah Equiano, or Gustavus Vassa, the African*

Olaudah Equiano's *Interesting Narrative* is the first full-length autobiography by an African who had been a slave in British territory. Besides portraying village and family life in the mid-eighteenth century with extraordinary vibrancy, its African sections give views of indigenous slavery, stressing the differences between that institution and slavery in the British colonies. The vivid narrative of the "middle passage" across the Atlantic (probably made by Equiano in 1756) is the first published by a former African slave.

Notice that Equiano, like Ottobah Cugoano, emphasizes the nobility of his family, describing his father as one of the "chief men" in his society, a powerful figure occupying a place of the "highest distinction." Later in his *Narrative,* in the course of an episode in which he and his companions are shipwrecked on an island, Equiano returns to his sense of natural nobility, explaining that the others made him "a kind of chieftan amongst them" during the time that they were stranded.

Scholars believe Equiano (c. 1745–1797) was an Ibo, from the village of Isseke in what is now Nigeria. After being taken from Africa, Equiano spent many years as a slave shipboard, fighting in the Seven Years' War between Britain and France. An English naval officer, following the convention of naming slaves after European heroes, called him Gustavus Vassa after King Gustavus I, the sixteenth-century leader who won independence for Sweden; Equiano chose this name himself when he was baptized in 1759. In 1762, he was resold and taken to the West Indies. He bought his own freedom there in 1766, but had trouble maintaining it, and consequently moved in 1777 to England, where he worked with Cugoano and other abolitionists. Equiano's *Narrative* was a best-seller in the 1790s; following its initial publication in 1789 it went through eight editions in five years, and was quickly translated into Dutch, German, and Russian. A later, revised edition appeared in 1814.

The text is excerpted from the first edition (London: Printed for and sold by the author, 1789) 1: 4–7, 20–27, 46–75, 78–82.

This engraving of Olaudah Equiano was the frontispiece to *The Interesting Narrative of the Life of Olaudah Equiano, or Gustavus Vassa, the African* (London: Printed for the Author, 1789).

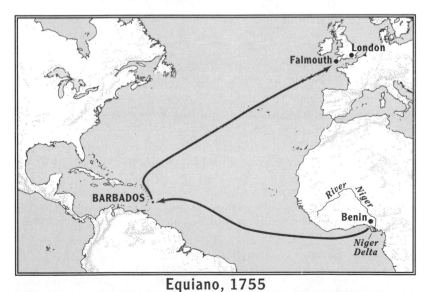

Equiano, 1755

This map shows Equiano's travels during the first year of his enslavement.

That part of Africa, known by the name of Guinea, to which the trade for slaves is carried on, extends along the coast above 3400 miles, from Senegal to Angola, and includes a variety of kingdoms. Of these the most considerable is the kingdom of Benin,[1] both as to extent and wealth, the richness and cultivation of the soil, the power of its king, and the number and warlike disposition of the inhabitants. It is situated nearly under the line,[2] and extends along the coast about 170 miles, but runs back into the interior part of Africa to a distance hitherto I believe unexplored by any traveller; and seems only terminated at length by the empire of Abyssinia,[3] near 1500 miles from its beginning. This kingdom is divided into many provinces or districts: in one of the most remote and fertile of which, I was born, in the year 1745, situated in a charming fruitful vale, named Essaka.[4] The distance of this province from the capital of Benin and the sea coast must be very considerable; for I had never heard of white men or Europeans, nor of the sea; and our subjection to the king of Benin was little more than nominal; for every transaction of the government, as far as my slender observation extended, was conducted by the chiefs or elders of the place. The manners and government of a people who have little commerce with other countries are generally very simple; and the history of what passes in one family or village, may serve as a specimen of the whole nation. My father was one of those elders or chiefs I have spoken of, and was styled Embrenché;[5] a term, as I remember, importing the highest distinction, and signifying in our language a *mark* of grandeur. This mark is conferred on the person entitled to it, by cutting the skin across at the top of the forehead, and drawing it down to the eye-brows; and while it is in this situation applying a warm hand, and rubbing it until it shrinks up into a thick *weal* across the lower part of the forehead. Most of the judges and senators were thus marked; my father had long borne it: I had seen it conferred on one of my brothers, and I also was *destined* to receive it by my parents. Those Embrenché or chief men, decided disputes and punished crimes; for which purpose they always assembled together. The proceedings were generally short; and in most cases the law of retaliation prevailed. I

---

[1] *Benin:* This kingdom covered a vast expanse at the easternmost end of the Guinea coast.

[2] *the line:* I.e., the equator.

[3] *Abyssinia:* The ancient name for Ethiopia.

[4] *Essaka:* Located in northwest Nigeria; now spelled Isseke.

[5] *Embrenché:* Equiano's rendering of the Ibo term *mgburichi,* meaning "men who bear scars on the face."

remember a man was brought before my father, and the other judges, for kidnapping a boy; and, although he was the son of a chief or senator, he was condemned to make recompense by a man or woman slave. Adultery, however, was sometimes punished with slavery or death; a punishment which I believe is inflicted on it throughout most of the nations of Africa:[6] so sacred among them is the honour of the marriage bed, and so jealous are they of the fidelity of their wives. . . .

Our land is uncommonly rich and fruitful, and produces all kinds of vegetables in great abundance. We have plenty of Indian corn, and vast quantities of cotton and tobacco. Our pine apples grow without culture; they are about the size of the largest sugar-loaf, and finely flavoured. We have also spices of different kinds, particularly pepper; and a variety of delicious fruits which I have never seen in Europe; together with gums of various kinds, and honey in abundance. All our industry is exerted to improve those blessings of nature. Agriculture is our chief employment; and every one, even the children and women, are engaged in it. Thus we are all habituated to labour from our earliest years. Every one contributes something to the common stock; and as we are unacquainted with idleness, we have no beggars. The benefits of such a mode of living are obvious. The West India planters prefer the slaves of Benin or Eboe[7] to those of any other part of Guinea, for their hardiness, intelligence, integrity, and zeal. Those benefits are felt by us in the general healthiness of the people, and in their vigour and activity; I might have added too in their comeliness. Deformity is indeed unknown amongst us, I mean that of shape. Numbers of the natives of Eboe now in London might be brought in support of this assertion: for, in regard to complexion, ideas of beauty are wholly relative. I remember while in Africa to have seen three negro children, who were tawny, and another quite white, who were universally regarded by myself, and the natives in general, as far as related to their complexions, as deformed. Our women too were in my eyes at least uncommonly graceful, alert, and modest to a degree of bashfulness; nor do I remember to have ever heard of an instance of incontinence amongst them before marriage. They are also remarkably cheerful.

---

[6] *a punishment . . . throughout most of the nations of Africa:* See Benezet's Account of Guinea throughout. [Equiano's note.] This note refers to Anthony Benezet's *Some Historical Account of Guinea, Its Situation, Produce, and the General Disposition of its Inhabitants, with an Inquiry into the Rise and Progress of the Slave Trade, Its Nature and Effects,* which was first published in Philadelphia in 1771. Benezet (1713–1784) was a vocal critic of slavery, and wrote a number of treatises advocating abolition.

[7] *Eboe:* I.e., Ibo or Igbo.

Indeed cheerfulness and affability are two of the leading characteristics of our nation.

Our tillage is exercised in a large plain or common, some hours walk from our dwellings, and all the neighbours resort thither in a body. They use no beasts of husbandry; and their only instruments are hoes, axes, shovels, and beaks, or pointed iron to dig with. Sometimes we are visited by locusts, which come in large clouds, so as to darken the air, and destroy our harvest. This however happens rarely, but when it does, a famine is produced by it. I remember an instance or two wherein this happened. This common is often the theatre of war; and therefore when our people go out to till their land, they not only go in a body, but generally take their arms with them for fear of a surprise; and when they apprehend an invasion they guard the avenues to their dwellings, by driving sticks into the ground, which are so sharp at one end as to pierce the foot, and are generally dipt in poison. From what I can recollect of these battles, they appear to have been irruptions of one little state or district on the other, to obtain prisoners or booty. Perhaps they were incited to this by those traders who brought the European goods I mentioned amongst us. Such a mode of obtaining slaves in Africa is common; and I believe more are procured this way, and by kidnaping, than by any other.[8] When a trader wants slaves, he applies to a chief for them, and tempts him with his wares. It is not extraordinary, if on this occasion he yields to the temptation with as little firmness, and accepts the price of his fellow creatures liberty with as little reluctance as the enlightened merchant. Accordingly he falls on his neighbours, and a desperate battle ensues. If he prevails and takes prisoners, he gratifies his avarice by selling them; but, if his party be vanquished, and he falls into the hands of the enemy, he is put to death: for, as he has been known to foment their quarrels, it is thought dangerous to let him survive, and no ransom can save him, though all other prisoners may be redeemed. We have firearms, bows and arrows, broad two-edged swords and javelins: we have shields also which cover a man from head to foot. All are taught the use of these weapons; even our women are warriors, and march boldly out to fight along with the men. Our whole district is a kind of militia: on a certain signal given, such as the firing of a gun at night, they all rise in

---

[8] *more . . . by kidnaping, than by any other:* See Benezet's Account of Africa throughout. [Equiano's note.] Equiano refers to Anthony Benezet's *A Short Account of that Part of Africa, Inhabited by the Negroes, with Respect to the Fertility of the Country, the Good Disposition of Many of the Natives, and the Manner by Which the Slave Trade is Carried on,* which was published in Philadelphia in 1762.

arms and rush upon their enemy. It is perhaps something remarkable, that when our people march to the field a red flag or banner is borne before them. I was once a witness to a battle in our common. We had been all at work in it one day as usual, when our people were suddenly attacked. I climbed a tree at some distance, from which I beheld the fight. There were many women as well as men on both sides; among others my mother was there, and armed with a broad sword. After fighting for a considerable time with great fury, and after many had been killed our people obtained the victory, and took their enemy's Chief prisoner. He was carried off in great triumph, and, though he offered a large ransom for his life, he was put to death. A virgin of note among our enemies had been slain in the battle, and her arm was exposed in our market-place, where our trophies were always exhibited. The spoils were divided according to the merit of the warriors. Those prisoners which were not sold or redeemed we kept as slaves: but how different was their condition from that of the slaves in the West Indies! With us they do no more work than other members of the community, even their masters; their food, clothing and lodging were nearly the same as theirs, (except that they were not permitted to eat with those who were free-born); and there was scarce any other difference between them, than a superior degree of importance which the head of a family possesses in our state, and that authority which, as such, he exercises over every part of his household. Some of these slaves have even slaves under them as their own property, and for their own use. . . .

My father, besides many slaves, had a numerous family, of which seven lived to grow up, including myself and a sister, who was the only daughter. As I was the youngest of the sons, I became, of course, the greatest favourite with my mother, and was always with her; and she used to take particular pains to form my mind. I was trained up from my earliest years in the art of war; my daily exercise was shooting and throwing javelins; and my mother adorned me with emblems, after the manner of our greatest warriors. In this way I grew up till I was turned the age of eleven, when an end was put to my happiness in the following manner: — Generally when the grown people in the neighbourhood were gone far in the fields to labour, the children assembled together in some of the neighbours' premises to play; and commonly some of us used to get up a tree to look out for any assailant, or kidnapper, that might come upon us; for they sometimes took those opportunities of our parents' absence to attack and carry off as many as they could seize. One day, as I was watching at the top of a tree in our yard, I saw one of those people come into the yard of our next neighbour but one, to kidnap, there being many stout young people in it. Immediately on this I gave the alarm of the rogue, and he was surrounded by the stoutest of them, who entangled him with cords, so that he could not escape till some of the grown people came and secured him. But alas! ere long it was my fate to be thus attacked, and to be carried off, when none of the grown people were nigh. One day, when all our people were gone out to their works as usual, and only I and my dear sister were left to mind the house, two men and a woman got over our walls, and in a moment seized us both, and, without giving us time to cry out, or make resistance, they stopped our mouths, and ran off with us into the nearest wood. Here they tied our hands, and continued to carry us as far as they could, till night came on, when we reached a small house, where the robbers halted for refreshment, and spent the night. We were then unbound, but were unable to take any food; and, being quite overpowered by fatigue and grief, our only relief was some sleep, which allayed our misfortune for a short time. The next morning we left the house, and continued travelling all the day. For a long time we had kept the woods, but at last we came into a road which I believed I knew. I had now some hopes of being delivered; for we had advanced but a little way before I discovered some people at a distance, on which I began to cry out for their assistance: but my cries had no other effect than to make them tie me faster and stop my mouth, and then they put me into a large sack. They also stopped my sister's mouth, and tied her hands; and in this manner we proceeded till we were out of the sight of these people. When we went to rest the following night they offered us some victuals; but we refused it; and the only comfort we had was in being in one another's arms all that night, and bathing each other with our tears. But alas! we were soon deprived of even the small comfort of weeping together. The next day proved a day of greater sorrow than I had yet experienced; for my sister and I were then separated, while we lay clasped in each other's arms. It was in vain that we besought them not to part us; she was torn from me, and immediately carried away, while I was left in a state of distraction not to be described. I cried and grieved continually; and for several days I did not eat any thing but what they forced into my mouth. At length, after many days travelling, during which I had often changed masters, I got into the hands of a chieftain, in a very pleasant country. This man had two wives and some children, and they all used me extremely well, and did all they could to comfort me; particularly the first wife, who was something like my mother.

Although I was a great many days journey from my father's house, yet these people spoke exactly the same language with us. This first master of mine, as I may call him, was a smith, and my principal employment was working his bellows, which were the same kind as I had seen in my vicinity. They were in some respects not unlike the stoves here in gentlemen's kitchens; and were covered over with leather; and in the middle of that leather a stick was fixed, and a person stood up, and worked it, in the same manner as is done to pump water out of a cask with a hand pump. I believe it was gold he worked, for it was of a lovely bright yellow colour, and was worn by the women on their wrists and ankles. I was there I suppose about a month, and they at last used to trust me some little distance from the house. This liberty I used in embracing every opportunity to inquire the way to my own home: and I also sometimes, for the same purpose, went with the maidens, in the cool of the evenings, to bring pitchers of water from the springs for the use of the house. I had also remarked where the sun rose in the morning, and set in the evening, as I had travelled along; and I had observed that my father's house was towards the rising of the sun. I therefore determined to seize the first opportunity of making my escape, and to shape my course for that quarter; for I was quite oppressed and weighed down by grief after my mother and friends; and my love of liberty, ever great, was strengthened by the mortifying circumstance of not daring to eat with the free-born children, although I was mostly their companion. While I was projecting my escape, one day an unlucky event happened, which quite disconcerted my plan, and put an end to my hopes. I used to be sometimes employed in assisting an elderly woman slave to cook and take care of the poultry; and one morning, while I was feeding some chickens, I happened to toss a small pebble at one of them, which hit it on the middle and directly killed it. The old slave, having soon after missed the chicken, inquired after it; and on my relating the accident (for I told her the truth, because my mother would never suffer me to tell a lie) she flew into a violent passion, threatened that I should suffer for it; and, my master being out, she immediately went and told her mistress what I had done. This alarmed me very much, and I expected an instant flogging, which to me was uncommonly dreadful; for I had seldom been beaten at home. I therefore resolved to fly; and accordingly I ran into a thicket that was hard by, and hid myself in the bushes. Soon afterwards my mistress and the slave returned, and, not seeing me, they searched all the house, but not finding me, and I not making answer when they called to me, they thought I had run away, and the whole neighbourhood was raised in the pursuit of me. In that part of the country (as in ours) the houses and villages were skirted with woods, or shrubberies, and the bushes were so thick that a man could readily conceal himself in them, so as to elude the strictest search. The neighbours continued the whole day looking for me, and several times many of them came within a few yards of the place where I lay hid. I then gave myself up for lost entirely, and expected every moment, when I heard a rustling among the trees, to be found out, and punished by my master: but they never discovered me, though they were often so near that I even heard their conjectures as they were looking about for me; and I now learned from then, that any attempt to return home would be hopeless. Most of them supposed I had fled towards home; but the distance was so great, and the way so intricate, that they thought I could never reach it, and that I should be lost in the woods. When I heard this I was seized with a violent panic, and abandoned myself to despair. Night too began to approach, and aggravated all my fears. I had before entertained hopes of getting home, and I had determined when it should be dark to make the attempt; but I was now convinced it was fruitless, and I began to consider that, if possibly I could escape all other animals, I could not those of the human kind; and that, not knowing the way, I must perish in the woods. Thus was I like the hunted deer:

> — "Ev'ry leaf and ev'ry whisp'ring breath,
> "Convey'd a foe, and ev'ry foe a death."[9]

I heard frequent rustlings among the leaves; and being pretty sure they were snakes I expected every instant to be stung by them. This increased my anguish, and the horror of my situation became now quite insupportable. I at length quitted the thicket, very faint and hungry, for I had not eaten or drank any thing all the day; and crept to my master's kitchen, from whence I set out at first, and which was an open shed, and laid myself down in the ashes with an anxious wish for death to relieve me from all my pains. I was scarcely awake in the morning when the old woman slave, who was the first up, came to light the fire, and saw me in the fire place. She was very much surprised to see me, and could scarcely believe her own eyes. She now promised to intercede for me, and went for her master, who soon after came,

---

[9] *Ev'ry leaf . . . ev'ry foe a death:* Sir John Denham, *Cooper's Hill* (1642), 287–88, slightly misquoted; the poem actually reads: "Now ev'ry leaf, and ev'ry moving breath / Presents a foe, and ev'ry foe a death."

and, having slightly reprimanded me, ordered me to be taken care of, and not to be ill-treated.

Soon after this my master's only daughter, and child by his first wife, sickened and died, which affected him so much that for some time he was almost frantic, and really would have killed himself, had he not been watched and prevented. However, in a small time afterwards he recovered, and I was again sold. I was now carried to the left of the sun's rising, through many different countries, and a number of large woods. The people I was sold to used to carry me very often, when I was tired, either on their shoulders or on their backs. I saw many convenient well-built sheds along the roads, at proper distances, to accommodate the merchants and travellers, who lay in those buildings along with their wives, who often accompany them; and they always go well armed.

From the time I left my own nation I always found somebody that understood me till I came to the sea coast. The languages of different nations did not totally differ, nor were they so copious as those of the Europeans, particularly the English. They were therefore easily learned; and, while I was journeying thus through Africa, I acquired two or three different tongues. In this manner I had been travelling for a considerable time, when one evening, to my great surprise, whom should I see brought to the house where I was but my dear sister! As soon as she saw me she gave a loud shriek, and ran into my arms — I was quite overpowered: neither of us could speak; but, for a considerable time, clung to each other in mutual embraces, unable to do any thing but weep. Our meeting affected all who saw us; and indeed I must acknowledge, in honour of those sable destroyers of human rights, that I never met with any ill treatment, or saw any offered to their slaves, except tying them, when necessary, to keep them from running away. When these people knew we were brother and sister they indulged us together; and the man, to whom I supposed we belonged, lay with us, he in the middle, while she and I held one another by the hands across his breast all night; and thus for a while we forgot our misfortunes in the joy of being together: but even this small comfort was soon to have an end; for scarcely had the fatal morning appeared, when she was again torn from me for ever! I was now more miserable, if possible, than before. The small relief which her presence gave me from pain was gone, and the wretchedness of my situation was redoubled by my anxiety after her fate, and my apprehensions lest her sufferings should be greater than mine, when I could not be with her to alleviate them. Yes, thou dear partner of all my childish sports! thou sharer of my joys and sorrows! happy should I have ever esteemed myself to encounter every misery for you, and to procure your freedom by the sacrifice of my own. Though you were early forced from my arms, your image has been always rivetted in my heart, from which neither *time nor fortune* have been able to remove it; so that, while the thoughts of your sufferings have damped my prosperity, they have mingled with adversity and increased its bitterness. To that Heaven which protects the weak from the strong, I commit the care of your innocence and virtues; if they have not already received their full reward, and if your youth and delicacy have not long since fallen victims to the violence of the African trader, the pestilential stench of a Guinea ship, the seasoning in the European colonies, or the lash and lust of a brutal and unrelenting overseer.

I did not long remain after my sister. I was again sold, and carried through a number of places, till, after travelling a considerable time, I came to a town called Tinmah,[10] in the most beautiful country I had yet seen in Africa. It was extremely rich, and there were many rivulets which flowed through it, and supplied a large pond in the centre of the town, where the people washed. Here I first saw and tasted cocoa-nuts, which I thought superior to any nuts I had ever tasted before; and the trees, which were loaded, were also interspersed amongst the houses, which had commodious shades adjoining, and were in the same manner as ours, the insides being neatly plastered and white-washed. Here I also saw and tasted for the first time sugar-cane. Their money consisted of little white shells,[11] the size of the finger nail. I was sold here for one hundred and seventy-two of them by a merchant who lived and brought me there. I had been about two or three days at his house, when a wealthy widow, a neighbour of his, came there one evening, and brought with her an only son, a young gentleman about my own age and size. Here they saw me; and, having taken a fancy to me, I was bought of the merchant, and went home with them. Her house and premises were situated close to one of those rivulets I have mentioned, and were the finest I ever saw in Africa: they were very extensive, and she had a number of slaves to attend her. The next day I was washed and perfumed, and when meal-time came I was led into the presence of my mistress, and ate and drank before her with her

[10] *Tinmah:* This name may refer to Tinam, Utuma, or Uto Etim, villages near the eastern border of Ibo.

[11] *little white shells:* Cowries, used as currency in West Africa. Though Equiano goes on to say he was traded for 172 shells, he presumably means 172 pounds, since this is how slave prices were calculated (see Joseph Blyth's letter on p. 233).

son. This filled me with astonishment; and I could scarce help expressing my surprise that the young gentleman should suffer me, who was bound, to eat with him who was free; and not only so, but that he would not at any time either eat or drink till I had taken first, because I was the eldest, which was agreeable to our custom. Indeed every thing here, and all their treatment of me, made me forget that I was a slave. The language of these people resembled ours so nearly, that we understood each other perfectly. They had also the very same customs as we. There were likewise slaves daily to attend us, while my young master and I with other boys sported our darts and bows and arrows, as I had been used to do at home. In this resemblance to my former happy state I passed about two months; and I now began to think I was to be adopted into the family, and was beginning to be reconciled to my situation, and to forget by degrees my misfortunes, when all at once the delusion vanished; for, without the least previous knowledge, one morning early, while my dear master and companion was still asleep, I was wakened out of my reverie to fresh sorrow, and hurried away even amongst the uncircumcised.

Thus, at the very moment I dreamed of the greatest happiness, I found myself most miserable; and it seemed as if fortune wished to give me this taste of joy, only to render the reverse more poignant. The change I now experienced was as painful as it was sudden and unexpected. It was a change indeed from a state of bliss to a scene which is inexpressible by me, as it discovered to me an element I had never before beheld, and till then had no idea of, and wherein such instances of hardship and cruelty continually occurred as I can never reflect on but with horror.

All the nations and people I had hitherto passed through resembled our own in their manners, customs, and language: but I came at length to a country, the inhabitants of which differed from us in all those particulars. I was very much struck with this difference, especially when I came among a people who did not circumcise, and ate without washing their hands. They cooked also in iron pots, and had European cutlasses and cross bows, which were unknown to us, and fought with their fists amongst themselves. Their women were not so modest as ours, for they ate, and drank, and slept, with their men. But, above all, I was amazed to see no sacrifices or offerings among them. In some of those places the people ornamented themselves with scars, and likewise filed their teeth very sharp. They wanted sometimes to ornament me in the same manner, but I would not suffer them; hoping that I might some time be among a people who did not thus disfigure themselves, as I thought they did. At last I came to the banks of a large river, which was covered with canoes, in which the people appeared to live with their household utensils and provisions of all kinds. I was beyond measure astonished at this, as I had never before seen any water larger than a pond or a rivulet: and my surprise was mingled with no small fear when I was put into one of these canoes, and we began to paddle and move along the river. We continued going on thus till night; and when we came to land, and made fires on the banks, each family by themselves, some dragged their canoes on shore, others stayed and cooked in theirs, and laid in them all night. Those on the land had mats, of which they made tents, some in the shape of little houses: in these we slept; and after the morning meal we embarked again and proceeded as before. I was often very much astonished to see some of the women, as well as the men, jump into the water, dive to the bottom, come up again, and swim about. Thus I continued to travel, sometimes by land, sometimes by water, through different countries and various nations, till, at the end of six or seven months after I had been kidnapped, I arrived at the sea coast. It would be tedious and uninteresting to relate all the incidents which befell me during this journey, and which I have not yet forgotten; of the various hands I passed through, and the manners and customs of all the different people among whom I lived: I shall therefore only observe, that in all the places where I was the soil was exceedingly rich; the pomkins, eadas,[12] plantains, yams, &c. &c. were in great abundance, and of incredible size. There were also vast quantities of different gums, though not used for any purpose; and every where a great deal of tobacco. The cotton even grew quite wild; and there was plenty of redwood. I saw no mechanics[13] whatever in all the way, except such as I have mentioned. The chief employment in all these countries was agriculture, and both the males and females, as with us, were brought up to it, and trained in the arts of war.

The first object which saluted my eyes when I arrived on the coast was the sea, and a slave ship, which was then riding at anchor, and waiting for its cargo. These filled me with astonishment, which was soon converted into terror when I was carried on board. I was immediately handled and tossed up to see if I were sound by some of the crew; and I was now persuaded that I had gotten into a world of bad spirits, and that they were going to kill me. Their complexions too differing so

---

[12] *pomkins, eadas:* Pumpkins and cocoa yams *(eddo* in Ibo).
[13] *mechanics:* Manual laborers or craftsmen.

much from ours, their long hair, and the language they spoke, (which was very different from any I had ever heard) united to confirm me in this belief. Indeed such were the horrors of my views and fears at the moment, that, if ten thousand worlds had been my own, I would have freely parted with them all to have exchanged my condition with that of the meanest slave in my own country. When I looked round the ship too and saw a large furnace or copper boiling, and a multitude of black people of every description chained together, every one of their countenances expressing dejection and sorrow, I no longer doubted of my fate; and, quite overpowered with horror and anguish, I fell motionless on the deck and fainted. When I recovered a little I found some black people about me, who I believed were some of those who brought me on board, and had been receiving their pay; they talked to me in order to cheer me, but all in vain. I asked them if we were not to be eaten by those white men with horrible looks, red faces, and loose hair. They told me I was not; and one of the crew brought me a small portion of spirituous liquor in a wine glass; but, being afraid of him, I would not take it out of his hand. One of the blacks therefore took it from him and gave it to me, and I took a little down my palate, which, instead of reviving me, as they thought it would, threw me into the greatest consternation at the strange feeling it produced, having never tasted such liquor before. Soon after this the blacks who brought me on board went off, and left me abandoned to despair. I now saw myself deprived of all chance of returning to my native country, or even the least glimpse of hope of gaining the shore, which I now considered as friendly; and I even wished for my former slavery in preference to my present situation, which was filled with horrors of every kind, still heightened by my ignorance of what I was to undergo. I was not long suffered to indulge my grief; I was soon put down under the decks, and there I received such a salutation in my nostrils as I had never experienced in my life: so that, with the loathsomeness of the stench, and crying together, I became so sick and low that I was not able to eat, nor had I the least desire to taste any thing. I now wished for the last friend, death, to relieve me; but soon, to my grief, two of the white men offered me eatables; and, on my refusing to eat, one of them held me fast by the hands, and laid me across I think the windlass,[14] and tied my feet, while the other flogged me severely. I had never experienced any thing of this kind before; and although, not

---

[14] *windlass:* A horizontal barrel, turned with a crank to wind up and let out a hoisting rope.

being used to the water, I naturally feared that element the first time I saw it, yet nevertheless, could I have got over the nettings, I would have jumped over the side, but I could not; and, besides, the crew used to watch us very closely who were not chained down to the decks, lest we should leap into the water: and I have seen some of these poor African prisoners most severely cut for attempting to do so, and hourly whipped for not eating. This indeed was often the case with myself. In a little time after, amongst the poor chained men, I found some of my own nation, which in a small degree gave ease to my mind. I inquired of these what was to be done with us; they gave me to understand we were to be carried to these white people's country to work for them. I then was a little revived, and thought, if it were no worse than working, my situation was not so desperate: but still I feared I should be put to death, the white people looked and acted, as I thought, in so savage a manner; for I had never seen among any people such instances of brutal cruelty; and this not only shewn towards us blacks, but also to some of the whites themselves. . . .

At last, when the ship we were in had got in all her cargo, they made ready with many fearful noises, and we were all put under deck, so that we could not see how they managed the vessel. But this disappointment was the least of my sorrow. The stench of the hold while we were on the coast was so intolerably loathsome, that it was dangerous to remain there for any time, and some of us had been permitted to stay on the deck for the fresh air; but now that the whole ship's cargo were confined together, it became absolutely pestilential. The closeness of the place, and the heat of the climate, added to the number in the ship, which was so crowded that each had scarcely room to turn himself, almost suffocated us. This produced copious perspirations, so that the air soon became unfit for respiration, from a variety of loathsome smells, and brought on a sickness among the slaves, of which many died, thus falling victims to the improvident avarice, as I may call it, of their purchasers. This wretched situation was again aggravated by the galling[15] of the chains, now become insupportable; and the filth of the necessary tubs,[16] into which the children often fell, and were almost suffocated. The shrieks of the women, and the groans of the dying, rendered the whole a scene of horror almost inconceivable. Happily perhaps for myself I was soon reduced so low here that it was thought necessary to keep me almost always on deck; and from my

[15] *galling:* Chafing.
[16] *necessary tubs:* Latrines.

extreme youth I was not put in fetters. In this situation I expected every hour to share the fate of my companions, some of whom were almost daily brought upon deck at the point of death, which I began to hope would soon put an end to my miseries. Often did I think many of the inhabitants of the deep much more happy than myself. I envied them the freedom they enjoyed, and as often wished I could change my condition for theirs. Every circumstance I met with served only to render my state more painful, and heighten my apprehensions, and my opinion of the cruelty of the whites. One day they had taken a number of fishes; and when they had killed and satisfied themselves with as many as they thought fit, to our astonishment who were on the deck, rather than give any of them to us to eat as we expected, they tossed the remaining fish into the sea again, although we begged and prayed for some as well as we could, but in vain; and some of my countrymen, being pressed by hunger, took an opportunity, when they thought no one saw them, of trying to get a little privately; but they were discovered, and the attempt procured them some very severe floggings. One day, when we had a smooth sea and moderate wind, two of my wearied countrymen who were chained together (I was near them at the time), preferring death to such a life of misery, somehow made through the nettings and jumped into the sea: immediately another quite dejected fellow, who, on account of his illness, was suffered to be out of irons, also followed their example; and I believe many more would very soon have done the same if they had not been prevented by the ship's crew, who were instantly alarmed. Those of us that were the most active were in a moment put down under the deck, and there was such a noise and confusion amongst the people of the ship as I never heard before, to stop her, and get the boat out to go after the slaves. However two of the wretches were drowned, but they got the other, and afterwards flogged him unmercifully for thus attempting to prefer death to slavery. In this manner we continued to undergo more hardships than I can now relate, hardships which are inseparable from this accursed trade. Many a time we were near suffocation from want of fresh air, which we were often without for whole days together. This, and the stench of the necessary tubs, carried off many.

4

The Caribbean
in the Triangular Trade

Suriname, Oroonoko's destination, is on the north coast of South America, in a region called Guiana, which lies between the mouths of the rivers Orinoco and Amazon, on the shores of the Caribbean Sea.[1] If the continents were once part of one large land mass, as geologists tell us they were, the northeast shoulder of South America would have fit into Africa at the Gulf of Guinea. As if in testimony to their primeval adjacency, Guinea and Guiana share many natural features, such as vast tropical forests and navigable rivers. It would have taken some forty-four days to sail from Guinea to Guiana in a British ship in the 1670s.

Despite the geographic similarities between the two coasts, relations with the indigenous inhabitants were quite dissimilar. Whereas in Guinea Europeans were confined to the coast, they met no interference from the coastal inhabitants when they sailed into the waterways of Guiana. By the time English ships arrived, Amerindians living on those coastal rivers had been harried and dislodged for generations by Spanish and Portuguese slave raiders, and they were open to English offers to protect them from the established empires. Since it was impossible to keep Europeans out of their territory, they looked on the newcom-

---

[1] In addition to sources quoted in the text, information in this chapter comes from Allen; Astley; Aykroyd; Beckles; Beckles and Shepherd; Beer; Blackburn, *Making;* Bridenbaugh and Bridenbaugh; Goveia; Harlow; Lorimer; Nicholl; Panday; Price; Sheridan; Thomas; Williams, E.; and Williamson.

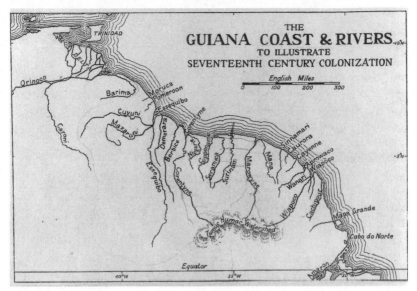

The "wild coast" of Guiana lay between the mouths of the Orinoco River, which formed the eastern frontier of the Spanish empire, and the Amazon River, which marked the northern boundary of the Portuguese empire. The English colony in which *Oroonoko* is set lay along the banks of the Suriname River. The map is the frontispiece of James A. Williamson, *English Colonies in Guiana and on the Amazon, 1604–1668* (Oxford: Clarendon, 1923).

ers from northern Europe (who also included the French and the Dutch) as possible allies. Of course, there was some friction — the Caribs were anxious to maintain their dominance among the indigenous people and misunderstandings led to the disappearance of a few small European settlements — but in general Aphra Behn's picture of amicable relations between the English and Irish settlers and the Amerindians on this "wild coast," as the Portuguese called it, is fairly accurate.

The Portuguese called the coast of Guiana "wild" because neither they (who had colonized neighboring Brazil) nor the Spanish (who had their hands full with Mexico, Central America, and all of South America west of Brazil) had been able to occupy it. This did not keep the Portuguese and Spanish from claiming Guiana, only from enforcing their claim. Indeed, by the time the English arrived in the Caribbean to stay, there was not much prime territory left. The Spanish held the four large islands of Cuba, Hispaniola, Jamaica, and

Puerto Rico, and the region known as the "Spanish Main" (the Isthmus of Panama east as far as Margarita, which is off the coast of what is now Venezuela); the Portuguese had the northeast corner of South America as part of Brazil, and were slowly making their way, in a northwesterly direction, up the slanting coastline. That meant that the late-coming northern Europeans — the French, the British, the Dutch, and the Danes — had either to poach on their predecessors' property or to take the leftovers. The British took some islands the Spanish had passed up as unpromising, among them Barbados, and in the 1650s took Jamaica. They also sailed into the undefended rivers of Guiana.

Most of the Britons setting sail for Guiana in the early seventeenth century, however, were no more interested in colonial territory than were the Britons on the West African coast: they were looking for any trade they could pick up in the periphery of the Spanish Empire, and their profits often came from illegal traffic, forbidden by the imperial power, with the Spanish colonists themselves. The earlier desire to found a rival empire in South America that Sir Walter Raleigh expresses in the selection that opens this chapter had always been somewhat unusual and would soon be altogether obsolete. Raleigh was convinced of the rightness of engaging in a holy Protestant war against the Catholic Spanish in the new world, and he thought that reaching a golden city, the El Dorado of Spanish legends, deep in the interior of Guiana would give him the power to fight such a war. But when James I ascended the English throne in 1603, such ambitions were officially discouraged. James I was by no means the Protestant crusader that his predecessor Queen Elizabeth I had been. He pursued a foreign policy designed to lessen religious animosities in Europe, ending the long Spanish war and recognizing the Spanish right to territories in the Americas that were actually in the possession of Philip III. While James insisted that territories not in fact possessed but only claimed by the Spanish monarch, such as Guiana, might be settled by anyone, he was unwilling to risk alienating the Spanish and ruining his foreign policy by aggressive colonization of the region.

The British enterprises on the Guiana rivers in the early decades of the seventeenth century were, therefore, modest and hesitant; investors were reluctant to put up capital for projects that the crown would not vigorously defend. Any Englishmen who sailed to Guiana in the grip of fantasies like Raleigh's were soon disappointed: Raleigh himself made a second, disastrous, voyage in 1617, with a fleet of fourteen ships, but was sent home in defeat by the Spanish and executed by King James. Various privately organized British expeditions nevertheless tried to plant small outposts in Guiana, for the profits were good, but they were unable to get a secure foothold. Some did temporarily prosper, especially those on the Amazon, but they were wiped out by the Portuguese in 1625. In the second selection included here, Major John Scott enumerates various attempts by French, Dutch, Irish, and English groups to settle in the region.

The only expedition to establish a colony of any permanence in Guiana came not from northern Europe but from an already established English colony in the Caribbean, the island of Barbados, under the direction of Francis, Lord Willoughby. Willoughby was a Royalist who managed to obtain a twenty-one years' lease of proprietary rights to the "Caribbee" islands in 1647. After the defeat of the Royalist cause in 1649, he went to Barbados, and from there he sent a party to explore Guiana and negotiate with the Caribs: "I have had return of my discovery of Guiana," he wrote to his wife in 1651, "and the gentleman which I sent hath brought with him to me two of the Indian kings, having spoke with divers of them, who are all willing to receive our nation, and that we shall settle amongst them" (qtd. in Williamson 153). These seasoned colonials, not green immigrants from northern Europe, knew how to stay on good terms with the Caribs as well as how to farm the land, and they immediately began importing African slaves and planting tobacco and sugar.

As the description of Suriname given by George Warren in this chapter indicates, it was not a large colony even at its height. Willoughby had placed approximately 300 settlers there in 1651–52, and by 1662 the colony contained some 2,000 freeholders and freemen. In comparison, Barbados was overflowing with at least 23,000 settlers by the mid-1650s. Warren tells us there were approximately 500 plantations in Suriname, each with its own landing dock and boats. These were spread out along the Suriname River in a relaxed manner that reflected the confidence the settlers had in their compact with the Caribs. The river provided a broad, convenient, and navigable highway for the planters and their commodities, which made overland traffic largely unnecessary. When Behn describes Oroonoko's progress through the colony, we should realize that he travels by boat and is viewed by the slaves at various plantations from the shoreline. The map of Suriname on p. 338 shows the layout of the colony in Behn's time. On entering the Suriname River from the Caribbean Sea, a ship would have passed a small village called Paramoribo, where a fort was under construction in the early 1660s, and traveled another sixty miles into the interior before reaching the capital town of Torarica, which had a church and a hundred houses. Ships of three hundred tons could reach Torarica, and the river was navigable for another thirty miles beyond.

Barbados had switched from subsistence and tobacco farming to sugar production in the late 1630s, so the colonists who settled Suriname arrived with the knowledge that sugar was the key to prosperity in the Caribbean. And sugar production, they knew, required backbreaking toil in the tropical sun, which few European servants were willing to perform. With the Portuguese, Dutch, and a growing number of English and French already supplying the area with West African slaves, the solution to the labor problem seemed readily available, and Suriname planters began a brisk trade on the triangular route, taking slaves off of ships coming from Africa and reloading the ships' holds with sugar to be eaten in Europe. A letter from a colonist in 1663 attests to the success of this system: "The colony begins to be populous partly with supplies [of slaves] that arrive weekly, and partly with a succeeding generation, for the women are very prolific and have lusty children. . . The chiefest commodity is sugar and better cannot be made. . . " (qtd. in Panday 11).

As the still unfinished state of the fort at Paramoribo in 1665 indicates, the growing little colony no more feared aggression from other seagoing Europeans than they feared it from the Amerindians. They were, after all, too far to the northwest to meet with the Portuguese and too far to the southeast to encounter the Spanish; as for the Dutch and French, they had tended to cooperate amicably with the English on the Guiana Coast. But that friendliness ended when hostilities broke out between the Dutch and English on the Guinea Coast, in their rivalry over the slave trade, that ricocheted throughout the Atlantic triangle. As a result of the ensuing combat, Suriname was lost as an *English* colony in 1667, when the Dutch (who had first taken it and then lost it in battle) acquired it securely in the Peace of Breda, trading it for an equally obscure bit of property in North America then called New Amsterdam and soon to be rechristened New York.

Thus ended the English possession of any part of the South American mainland until the late eighteenth century, but the history of their African captives in that part of the world is more dramatic and extensive. Oroonoko's rebelliousness might be said to represent that of the numerous slave revolt leaders who repeatedly unsettled Suriname in the seventeenth and eighteenth centuries and guided thousands of enslaved Africans into the forests of Guiana, where they established autonomous agricultural communities that closely resembled those of their homeland. The selection from John Gabriel Stedman's *Narrative of a Five Years Expedition against the Revolted Negroes of Surinam* (1796) describes the resulting political and military configuration of the country in the late eighteenth century, with a European colony on the river, and numerous West African settlements in the interior (sometimes making peace and sometimes engaging in warfare with their former captors). The topography of Guiana was conducive to the success of slave rebellions and the maintenance of independent African communities, for the hinterland was enormous, and inaccessible to most European fighting forces. Suriname thus, in spite of the designs of its European colonists, became a cradle of self-governing African settlement in the new world.

Most of the Africans brought to the *British* Caribbean, however, were taken to the islands, where it was virtually impossible to rebel piecemeal or to escape into the forest and join independent communities. To get a sense of what was typical in the Caribbean corner of the Atlantic triangle, therefore, we have to push off of the mainland and into the sea. After the Peace of Breda, England had the islands of Barbados, Jamaica, and a score of less important windward and leeward islands. The colonial societies that developed on these islands were a product of the triangular trade. In the last section, we saw that Guinea was affected by the trade, but its fundamental agrarian economy and way of life remained relatively stable throughout the seventeenth and much of the eighteenth centuries. The West Indian colonies, in contrast, belonged wholly to the trade. They were populated by it, their laws were invented for it, and their economies were completely dedicated to it. The European appetite for a single foodstuff, sugar, came to shape every aspect of the British West Indies.

The island of Barbados led the way in this development. Unpopulated when a small group of English settlers arrived in 1627, it grew slowly until the Dutch taught the colonists how to grow and process sugar cane in 1637, after which it soon became a strong competitor with the Dutch and Portuguese for the European sugar market. The British were probably the most productive sugar producers in the Americas between 1680 and 1720, and almost half of their sugar came from Barbados, although Jamaica, a much larger island, was later to become more productive. The amount of sugar shipped from Barbados quadrupled between 1650 and 1700, and the planters were constantly in need of more slaves. Plantations grew in size, small farmers were crowded out, and the white population decreased while the number of African and African-descended slaves increased. Between 1655 and 1700, the white population dropped from 23,000 to approximately 15,000, while the slave population rose from 20,000 to over 50,000.

In the mid-seventeenth century, there were numbers of European indentured servants and political prisoners working on plantations, as the political instability in England made Barbados a convenient place to deposit one's enemies. As late as 1685, as a result of the trials that prosecuted the enemies of the newly crowned James II, eight hundred Englishmen were sentenced to toil their lives away in the West Indies, and one rumored slave revolt in 1686 was said to involve Creole slaves and members of the "Irish nation." But gradually an almost absolute racialization of the economy developed, in which a relatively small group of white planters extracted the labor of West Africans who vastly outnumbered them. And the racialization of labor and property was bolstered by legal and cultural institutions that defined people according to race. There were, to be sure, exceptions to the general rule: pockets of poor whites in the countryside and, in the eighteenth century, free "colored" people with considerable property in the towns. But racial categorization and subordination were the dominant processes of the society, and institutions were organized to increase racial difference. First, there was the basic fact of perpetual slavery beginning at birth for the offspring of any African slave woman, which seemed quite strange to early English visitors: "Thay sell them one to the other as we done shepe," marveled one contemporary (qtd. in Tree 16). And a system of local laws built up a formidable edifice of differential treatment, reinforced by custom. Until well into the eighteenth century, educating slaves and converting them to Christianity were either forbidden or discouraged. Three selections in this chapter, those of Richard Ligon, Morgan Godwyn, and Thomas Tryon, refer to the cultural gap that the planters purposely maintained between Europeans and Africans.

Certainly, the conditions of enslavement were just as oppressive on the island of Barbados as they were in Suriname, and the slaves of Barbados were also rebellious in the seventeenth century. There were aborted revolts in 1649, 1675, and 1692, and ongoing, small-scale subversion is indicated by the continuous complaints about runaway slaves and the repeated issuing of orders to the militia "to make search and find out or discover such negroes as do stand forth in rebellion" (qtd. in Beckles and Shepherd 37). Richard Ligon's *True and Exact History of the Island of Barbados,* written in 1653, notes that the planters' very construction of their houses seemed to anticipate rebellion since they were fortified and built with elevated cisterns to "throw down hot water upon the naked bodies of their negroes" (qtd. in Beckles and Shepherd 35). Unlike the rebellions in Suriname, however, the well-planned Barbados plots of 1675 and 1692 were all-or-nothing actions in which the slaves projected taking the island in its entirety and then defending it against reconquest by the British. The rebels in Barbados were less successful than those in Suriname because the densely populated island had no hinterland that could support a network of free African communities.

Olaudah Equiano, who was both a slave and a freedman in Barbados, testifies to the demoralizing effects of slavery there. Even after buying his freedom and amassing property in the late eighteenth century, he had to struggle to assert his rights in the pervasively racist climate and was repeatedly robbed, cheated, and denied recourse to justice. The creolization of the island, the process by which the majority of its population became native to it rather than imported from either Europe or Africa, certainly produced greater commonality between the races, but racism saturated and defined the shared culture. To an African-born cosmopolitan like Equiano, the British West Indies seemed barbarous. His account allows us to gauge not only the gap between the races but also that which separated the sugar colonies from the British homeland.

Members of the Barbadian white plantocracy were keenly aware of the latter gap. They were often described as culturally and morally inferior to their distant cousins in northern Europe. Moreover, like eighteenth-century North American colonials, they believed themselves to be the victims of various economic injustices perpetrated by the mother country. Proud as they proclaimed themselves to be of their Britishness, they longed for free trade and nursed their grievances against the English government. Toward the end of the eighteenth century, as antislavery sentiment began to grow in Britain, the planters were increasingly depicted as lazy, tyrannical, drunken, and sadistic — the products and leaders of an intrinsically corrupt society. Equiano's memoirs certainly reinforce these images by presenting London as the cosmopolitan center of enlightened humanity, and the West Indies as the contrasting territory of brutality and ignorance.

Far from uncovering a monolithic "British" ideology of race and colonial conquest, therefore, these documents relating to the West Indies, like those from West Africa in the previous chapter, demonstrate that perceptions were adapted to local power relations and immediate interests. The three "worlds" identified at the outset of

Behn's *Oronooko* had been connected by the triangular trade for 150 years by the time that Equiano inhabited them, but he nevertheless portrays them as utterly distinct.

SIR WALTER RALEIGH

From *The Discovery of the Large, Rich, and Beautiful Empire of Guiana*

These passages from Raleigh's account of his travels, first published in 1596, illustrate the extent to which sixteenth-century English exploration of the region was driven by a desire to discover a source of gold that would make England as important a world power as Spain. This selection should be compared with Jobson's account of his African expedition (see p. 217), which also assures the reader that there is a city of gold just beyond the point where the explorer had to turn back, but accessible to a future, properly funded expedition. The myth promoted by Raleigh of "Manoa" or "El Dorado," the golden city, is gently mocked in *Oroonoko*. Note that Raleigh imagines a noncompetitive relation between the English and their Indian allies, claiming that the Indians seek only the restoration of their women and would be happy to let the English have their gold. This dream of peaceful coexistence, however, is shattered by the rhetoric of rape that ends the book.

Raleigh (1554–1618) was an Elizabethan courtier who undertook his voyage in the hope of regaining the queen's favor; in 1591, he had impregnated and then secretly married one of the queen's maids of honor, and when Elizabeth learned of the events, she expelled the couple from court. In the mid-1580s, Raleigh had sponsored a pair of voyages that led to a short-lived colony at Roanoke, Virginia (though he did not accompany the travelers himself), and he regarded the Guiana voyage as an opportunity to surpass his earlier efforts. He set off in February 1595, and arrived at the Orinoco Delta some three months later. In mid-June, after traveling more than 150 miles up the river, Raleigh turned back when he was confronted with waterfalls that presented an insurmountable barrier. Nevertheless, he remained convinced of the immense wealth to be found in the region, and undertook another trip in 1617. The Spanish had established their own settlements there in the intervening years, and Raleigh's men attacked them in spite of explicit orders to leave them in peace. As a result of this infraction, Raleigh was beheaded in 1618.

The text is excerpted from *The Works of Sir Walter Raleigh, Kt.* (Oxford: Oxford UP, 1829) 8: 447–48, 450–51, 464.

The next day following we left the mouth of Caroli,[1] and arrived again at the port of Morequito,[2] where we were before; (for passing down the stream we went without labour, and against the wind, little less than one hundred miles a day;) as soon as I came to anchor, I sent away one for old Topiawari,[3] with whom I much desired to have further conference; and also to deal with him for some one of his country to bring with us into England, as well to learn the language, as to confer withal by the way, (the time being now spent of any longer stay there.) Within three hours after my messenger came to him he arrived also, and with him such a rabble of all sorts of people, and every one laden with somewhat,[4] as if it had been a great market or fair in England: and our hungry companies clustered thick and threefold among their baskets, every one laying hand on what he liked. After he had rested a while in my tent, I shut out all but ourselves and my interpreter; and told him, that I knew that both the Epuremei[5] and the Spaniards were enemies to him, his country, and nations: that the one had conquered Guiana already, and that the other sought to regain the same from them both: and therefore I desired him to instruct me what he could both of the passage into the golden parts of Guiana, and to the civil towns and apparelled people of Inga.[6] . . . he gave me this good counsel, and advised me to hold it in mind, (as for himself, he knew he could not live till my return,) that I should not offer by any means hereafter to invade the strong parts of Guiana, without the help of all those nations which were also their enemies: for that it was impossible, without those, either to be conducted, to be victualled,[7] or to have ought carried with us, our people not being able to endure the march in so great heat and travel, unless the borderers gave them help,

[1] *Caroli:* The Caroni River, the principal tributary of the lower Orinoco; it marks the farthest point of Raleigh's advance into the South American continent.

[2] *the port of Morequito:* At the mouth of the Orinoco.

[3] *Topiawari:* Chief of the Orenoqueponi (meaning "the tribe on the Orinoco"), and a powerful ruler in the area near the coast.

[4] *somewhat:* I.e., something.

[5] *Epuremei:* People inhabiting an area near the western border of what is now Venezuela, close to modern-day El Dorado.

[6] *Inga:* I.e., Inca.

[7] *victualled:* Fed.

to carry with them both their meat and furniture: for he remembered, that in the plains of Macureguarai[8] three hundred Spaniards were overthrown, who were tired out, and had none of the borderers to their friends; but meeting their enemies as they passed the frontier, were environed of all sides, and the people setting the long dry grass on fire, smothered them, so as they had no breath to fight, nor could discern their enemies for the great smoke. He told me further, that four days' journey from his town was Macureguarai, and that those were the next and nearest of the subjects of Inga and of the Epuremei, and the first town of apparelled and rich people; and that all those plates of gold which were scattered among the borderers, and carried to other nations far and near, came from the said Macureguarai, and were there made; but that those of the land within were far finer, and were fashioned after the image of men, beasts, birds, and fishes. . . . He further told me, that I could not desire so much to invade Macureguarai, and the rest of Guiana, but that the borderers would be more vehement than I; for he yielded for a chief cause, that in the wars with the Epuremei, they were spoiled of their women, and that their wives and daughters were taken from them; so as for their own parts they desired nothing of the gold or treasure for their labours, but only to recover women from the Epuremei: for he further complained very sadly, (as if it had been a matter of great consequence,) that whereas they were wont to have ten or twelve wives, they were now enforced to content themselves with three or four, and that the lords of the Epuremei had fifty or one hundred. And in truth they were more for women than either for gold or dominion: for the lords of countries desire many children of their own bodies, to increase their races and kindreds; for in those consist their greatest trust and strength. Divers of his followers afterwards desired me to make haste again, that they might sack the Epuremei; and I asked them of what? they answered, Of their women for us, and their gold for you: for the hope of many of those women they more desire the war, than either for gold or for the recovery of their ancient territories. For what between the subjects of Inga and the Spaniards those frontiers are grown thin of people, and also great numbers are fled to other nations further off, for fear of the Spaniards.

---

[8] *Macureguarai:* This area, which Raleigh believed to mark the outer border of the golden land he sought, appears on his map on a spot some twenty or thirty miles northwest of modern-day El Dorado, in Venezuela.

To conclude; Guiana is a country that hath yet her maidenhead,[9] never sacked, turned, nor wrought; the face of the earth hath not been torn, nor the virtue and salt of the soil spent by manurance,[10] the graves have not been opened for gold, the mines not broken with sledges, nor their images pulled down out of their temples. It hath never been entered by any army of strength, and never conquered or possessed by any Christian prince. It is besides so defensible, that, if two forts be built in one of the provinces which I have seen, the flood setteth in so near the bank, where the channel also lieth, that no ship can pass up but within a pike's length of the artillery, first of the one, and afterwards of the other: which two forts will be a sufficient guard both to the empire of Inga, and to an hundred other several kingdoms, lying within the said river, even to the city of Quito[11] in Peru.

[9] *maidenhead:* Virginity.
[10] *manurance:* Plowing or other means of cultivation.
[11] *Quito:* Now the capital of Ecuador, in the north-central part of the country.

Colonial Life in Suriname

The following documents give us a sense of the nature of colonial life in Suriname around the time that Behn lived there. In particular, they underscore the remoteness of the plantations, and their dependence on a constant influx of slave labor. In 1647, Francis, Lord Willoughby of Parham (1613?–1666) had received a twenty-one year lease of property rights in Barbados, Suriname, and Antigua. He became governor of Barbados in 1650, but was removed from office by Parliament two years later because of his Royalist politics. In 1651, Willoughby had sent men to found a settlement in Suriname, but rather than going there himself, he returned to England leaving William Byam, one of his political associates, to serve as deputy governor of Suriname in his absence. In 1663, several years after Charles II had been restored to the throne, Willoughby reassumed control in Barbados, and he died three years later during a territorial conflict with the French. At the time of Behn's stay in Suriname, then, Willoughby would have been resident in Barbados — hence her reference to the "Lord" whose absence permits Byam to abuse his authority (see p. 94).

Barbados had begun as a tobacco colony, and it shifted toward sugar production only in the 1640s. In Suriname, by contrast, it was clear from

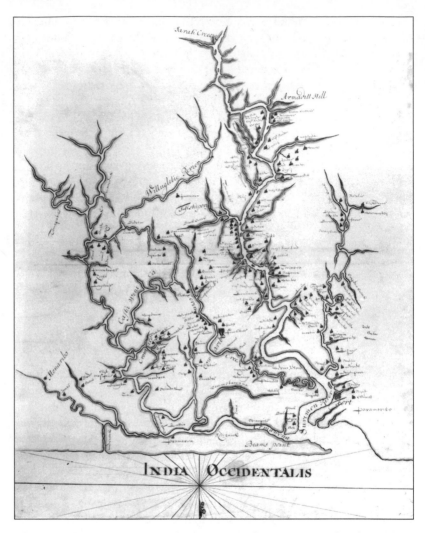

This map shows Suriname in the last years of its possession by the English, in the same period as events depicted in *Oroonoko*. It is a Dutch copy of an English map, which accounts for the odd spelling of place names (see detail, p. 339). Oriented with the south at the top, and the northern coast at the bottom, it shows the plantations along the Suriname River, the tributary Commewigne ("Comawena") paralleling the coast toward the mouth, and several smaller creeks. Courtesy of the John Carter Brown Library at Brown University.

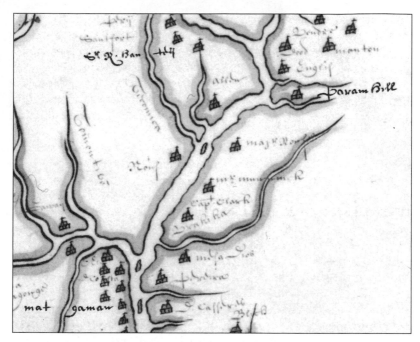

This detail of the map on page 338 includes a number of the places referred to in *Oroonoko,* including Sir Robert Harley's plantation, Morganam (or "Morgoename"), spelled "Matgamaw" on this map, and Lord Willoughby's Parram (or Parham) Hill. Courtesy of the John Carter Brown Library at Brown University.

the outset that sugar would be the most profitable crop to cultivate. Willoughby was already familiar with the economics and the daily requirements of sugar farming, and when he established the English settlement in 1651, he recognized the imperative demand for huge numbers of laborers if the Suriname plantations were to thrive. The amount of space required for a successful plantation meant that the average sugar estate included more than two hundred slaves at a time when the tobacco plantations of Virginia typically included fewer than fifteen.

The first document reprinted here is by Major John Scott (fl. 1650–1696), an adventurer, who gives an overview of the many colonizing efforts in Suriname in the years preceding the English settlement in 1651. His account emphasizes the conflicts between Europeans and Indians, and also between Europeans of different nations. Scott was a notorious liar, but recent historians have argued for the accuracy of his record, which remained in manuscript until published by the Hakluyt Society in 1925. Note how Scott's description of the diversity of Indian cultures and interests contrasts with Behn's simplified presentation in *Oroonoko*.

The second document, which probably dates from the mid-1650s, is Willoughby's advertisement for colonists, which welcomes single women, as well as men, to become planters, although it offers them slightly less advantageous terms. Economic problems in England in the 1640s had induced many of the poor to emigrate to the colonies, but increasing stability in the 1650s made it difficult to attract new settlers.

Next is a group of letters to Sir Robert Harley, an old friend and political ally of Willoughby's. When Willoughby returned to Barbados in 1663, he appointed Harley chancellor, and Harley acquired several major plantations in Suriname, including the property at St. John's Hill mentioned in *Oroonoko*, which he purchased from Byam and hired Trefry to manage. It has been suggested that the reference to "Ladeyes . . . att St Johnes hill" in Yearworth's letter may refer to Behn and her party. Byam's letter uses coded names to describe a flirtation between Behn ("Astrea") and William Scot (the "Grand Sheapheard Celedon"). Scot and his father, apparently no relation to the John Scott mentioned above, had been involved in international espionage on behalf of Cromwell's government during the interregnum (the period between 1649 and 1660). When the monarchy was reinstated in 1660, Scot's father was executed and Scot himself fled from England in order to escape arrest and avoid a £1000 debt. We do not know exactly when he arrived in Suriname, but presumably he hoped its remoteness would shield him from his pursuers. There, he aroused the suspicions of Deputy Governor Byam, who kept him under surveillance, and whose choice of code names for Behn and Scot suggests his hostility toward both of them. Byam draws on Honore D'Urfé's long romance *L'Astrée*, published in four parts in 1607–1625 but still widely read at the end of the century; "Astrea" refers to D'Urfé's noble and virginal heroine, and "Celeadon" to the sincere and passionate hero. The names, of course, sit incongruously with the notoriously provocative Behn and her disreputable friend. Moreover, Byam's letter suggests that when Scot followed Behn back to England, he feigned the part of the romantic lover rather than acknowledge that he was trying once again to escape the £1000 warrant, which had finally caught up with him. It has been speculated that Behn herself was sent to Suriname as a spy, possibly for Willoughby, who may have wanted to know something about Byam's actions besides the information Byam himself provided in his letters. Whether or not this accounts for Behn's presence in Suriname, we do know that she traveled to Antwerp as an intelligence agent in 1666–67, where she tried unsuccessfully to persuade Scot (then working for the Dutch) to trade his knowledge about Dutch military secrets in exchange for a pardon from Charles II. In their correspondence, Behn herself used the code name "Astrea" and Scot signed himself "Celadon." She also later used "Astrea" as a pen name.

All of these texts are taken from V. T. Harlow, ed., *Colonising Expeditions to the West Indies and Guiana, 1621–1667* (London: Hakluyt Society, 1925) 136–44, 174–77, 189–91.

Major John Scott

Numbers, and the Habitations of ye[1] Natives.

The most numerous nacion of Indians in Guiana are ye Careebs, and these are Inhabited in Aricare[2] about 6000 Careeb Families.

✓ In Wiapoca, Macoria, & Abrewaco,[3] Eleven thousand Careebe Families.

✓ In the River Marrawina,[4] about 800 Careeb Families.

And up the same River, and towards the head of Sinnamar lives about 1400 Paricoates,[5] the great Masters of Poyson in America, they pretend[6] to poyson Fountaines. (They) are a people very formall, marry ever within their owne Nation, have little Commerce but for their Poyson, which they sell to other nacions. The Careebs have some Judgment in ye art of Poisoning their Arrowes, and are great Masters in the cure but short of these people.

---

[1] *ye:* The.

[2] *Aricare:* (Now spelled Araguari) a river in the northeast of Brazil, south of the mouth of the Amazon.

[3] *Wiapoca, Macoria, & Abrewaco:* The Wiapoco (now spelled Oyapock) and the Abrewaco (now spelled Approuague) appear in the eastern part of the map on p. 327. The Macoria (now spelled Macouria), is too small to be included on the map, but it would appear slightly east of the Caurora.

[4] *Marrawina:* Marowyne (now spelled Marowjne) see map on p. 327.

[5] *Sinnamar . . . Paricoates:* The Sinnamari (now spelled Sinnamary) appears in the eastern part of the map on p. 327; the Paricoates lived in Paracou (not represented on the map), near the coast and slightly east of the Sinnamary.

[6] *pretend:* Claim.

In Suranam, Commowina, Suramaco, Copenham, & Currianteen[7] are about 5000 Carreeb Families, and there lives in Suramaco, and the upper parts of Suranam, about 1400 Turroomacs, And up Curianteen about 1200 Sapoyes.[8]

From the West side of Curianteen to Wina,[9] there lives about 8000 Families of Arawagoes, the best humoured Indians of America being both very just and generous minded people; and in little villages by the Sea side lives about 400 Families of Warooes in Moroca[10] and Wina. And in the Islands of Oranoque River[11] and neare the mouth of that River lives about 5000 Families of Warooes, the only Ship-wrights of those parts, for all the great Periagoes[12] are made by them. They make their vessells, their Cordage,[13] Sayles, Hammocks, Bread and Drinke all of one tree, they likewise make great Periagoes of an other wood called white wood. They differ from all other Indians in Life and manners (have nothing for delight whilst all other Indians are great Lovers of fine Gardens, Drinking, Danceing, and divers other pleasures), are a people bloody and Trecherous, and not to be Conversed with. And therefore I advise all people that Sayle into those parts, to discource with the Warooes nation with their Armes in their hands.

From Wina to the utmost part of Awarabish,[14] on the west syde of Oranoque, and the Rivers Oranoque, Poraema, and Amacora,[15] are about 20000 Careebs Families. The Occowyes, Shawhouns, and Semi-corals,[16] are great powerfull Nacions, that Live in the uplands of

---

[7] *Commowina . . . Currianteen:* The Commowina (now spelled Commewigne) is on the northern coast of Suriname; the Suramaco (now spelled Saramacca), the Copenham (now spelled Coppename), and the Currianteen (now spelled Corentyne) appear along the central coastal section of the map on p. 327.

[8] *Sapoyes:* A tribe living in the central forest region of Guiana, between the coastal plains and the mountains in the west.

[9] *Wina:* Possibly the Cuyuni in the map on p. 327.

[10] *Moroca:* I.e., Moruca, in the western part of the map on p. 327.

[11] *Oranoque River:* I.e., the Orinoco.

[12] *Periagoes:* I.e., canoes.

[13] *Cordage:* Cords, ropes.

[14] *Awarabish:* I.e., Point Araguapiche, north of the mouth of the Orinoco, on the northwest coast of the delta.

[15] *Poraema, and Amacora:* I.e., Barima, near the western end of the coast on the map on p. 327, and the Amacuro, which is located too far west to be represented there; it flows along what is now the border between Venezuela and Guiana.

[16] *Occowyes, Shawhouns, and Semicorals:* The Occowyes lived in the central forest region of Guiana, between the coastal plains and the mountains in the west, and the Shawhouns lived in the area between the Amazon and Negro rivers. "Semicorals" may be a misspelling of "Kenicurus," a tribe on the shores of Lake Barima noted for their fine clothing.

Guiana, either under the Line[17] or in South Lattitude, and there hath none soe converced with them, as to make a judgment of them as to their Numbers. But its most Certaine they are setled in a most Fertile Countrey, and Cover a vast Tract of Land beginning at ye mountaines of the Sun on the West and north, and extending them selfes to Rio Negroe[18] 500 miles south, and East, a famous River there (which) emties itselfe into the great Amazone. They have a Constant Warr with some nations on the Islands in the Amazones, and are often gauld[19] by the Willey Careebs, who often when they are Ingaged abroad visett their Townes to their noe small prejudice. And thus much of the Natives.

When first made knowne to the Europeans and what fortune they Successively have had.

The first Christian that ever attempted to sett footeing on Guiana, to the Southward of Oranoque, was Pedro de Acosta, a Spaniard, (who) with . . . 300 men Anno 1530 setled in Parema,[20] (&) was drave[21] thence by the Indians the same yeare, many slaine and their Goods and Chattles become a booty to the Careebs.

The second Colonie was setled at Cayan by Gasper de Sotelle being one hundred & 26 Families, from Spaine Anno 1568, but were expelled by the Careebs and Paracoates Anno 1573.

The third setlement was by three ships from France at Wiapoca Anno 1607 and being 400 men, began to plant Tobacco, and to thinke themselves secure, and too franckly to Converse with the natives. They were all cut off[22] Anno 1609 except a few Marriners.

The fourth Colonie was of 160 Families, from France Landed at Cayan,[23] and Fortified themselves Anno 1613. The Parecoates begun to offer them Freindship; they were in few months many distroyed, and the rest forct to quitt the place and retire for France.

The fift Colonie consisted of two hundred and eighty Zealanders[24] with two small ships, (who) Landed theire men at Cayan, Anno 1615, but could not bring the Natives to a Trade, were often Gauled by the

---

[17] *the Line:* The equator.
[18] *Rio Negroe:* A major tributary of the Amazon, in northwest Brazil.
[19] *gauld:* I.e., galled, harassed.
[20] *Parema:* Cf. Barima on p. 327.
[21] *drave:* Driven, forced to flee.
[22] *cut off:* Killed.
[23] *Cayan:* I.e., Cayenne; see the map on p. 327.
[24] *Zealanders:* Zealand was a province of the Netherlands.

Indians, and were at Lenth forced to quit their Poste Returned to Zealand the same yeare.

The sixth Colonie was undertaken by one Capt. Gromweagle[25] a Dutchman that had served the Spaniard in Oranoque. But understanding a Companie of Merchants of Zealand had before undertaken a voyage to Guiana, and attempted a Settlement there, he deserted the Spanish Service, and tendred himselfe to his owne Countrey; which was excepted[26] and he dispatched from Zealand Anno 1616 with two ships and a Galliote,[27] and was the first man that tooke firme footeing on Guiana by the good likeing of the natives, whose humours the Gent. perfectly understood. He erect(ed) a Fort on a Smal Island 30 Leagues up the River Disseekeeb,[28] which looked into two great branches of that Famous River. All his time the Colonie flourished. He managed a great Trade with the Spaniards by the Indians with great Secrecy. He was a great freind of all new Colonies of Christians of what nacion soever, And Barbados oweth its first assistance both for Foode and Trade to this mans speciall kindness Anno 1627, at what time they were in a misserable Condition. He dyed Anno 1664 and in the 83[d] yeare of his Age, a welthy man; haveing been Governor of that Colonie Forty 8 yeares. In this Colonie the Authour had the good Fortune to meet with some Injenious Observacions of the former Governors of what had been Transacted in Guiana in his time, to whome the word is obliged for many particulars of this Story.

The seaventh was a small factory at Berbishus[29] about ye yeare 1624, (which) is now a Strong Garrison and belongeth to two Merchants of Flushing,[30] Myn heer van Ree, and Myn heer van Pear, a place that abounds with excellent horses & Chattle and is a good factory for Annotta,[31] Dye, and Druggs.

Sir Walter Raleighs first Voyage 1598 and his last unfortunate Voyage 1618, and the business of Mr harcourt[32] at Wiapoca, being writt

---

[25] *Gromweagle:* Aert Adriaensz Groenewegen (d. 1664).

[26] *excepted:* I.e., accepted.

[27] *Galliote:* A small ship or galley used for swift navigation.

[28] *Disseekeeb:* See Essequibo in the map on p. 327.

[29] *Berbishus:* See Berbice in the map on p. 327.

[30] *Flushing:* A port on the southwest coast of the Netherlands (now spelled Vlissinger).

[31] *Annotta:* I.e., anatta. The waxy pulp (or "cod") around the plant's seeds is used to make a red-orange dye; see the remarks on Anotta in the selection from George Warren, p. 354.

[32] *harcourt:* Sir Robert Harcourt, who undertook a journey to Guiana in 1609, which he described in his *Relation of a Voyage to Guiana* (1613).

with their owne penns I shall say nothing of them, onely that If Sr Walter Raleigh had lived he would have left matter for a Gratefull[33] story. He left soe good and so great a name behind him with the Native Indians in those parts, that the English have often been Obliged to Remember with Honour.

The eight Colonie was a ship and a Barque from France which landed their people at Meriwina,[34] Anno 1625. The next vessell that came could heare noe news of their Collonie, and were without all dout distroyed by the Natives.

The ninth Collonie was 3 Ships from Rochell[35] Anno 1626 with 534 men some Women and Children. They setled at Suramaca lived 3 yeares in peace, but sicknesse falling amongst them and the Indians being Troublesome (Those few that were left) deserted the Collonie and went to St. Christophers.[36]

The tenth Collonie was two ships and a small vessell from France Anno 1639 with 370 men settled at Suramaca, and the yeare after came to theme from France many Famillies. They lived peaceably untill the yeare 1642 at what time they had great Supplies of men Ammunicion & provision from France. (They) grew carelesse, spred themselves to Suranam, and Curanteen, had differance with ye Indians, and were all cut of in one Day.

The elleaventh Collonie was one Mr. Marshall with 300 Families of England Imployed by the Earle of Warwick, &c^r, who settled Suranam, Suramaca & Curanteen[37] Anno 1643, lived peaceably untill the yeare 1645 at which time they espoused the Quarrell of ye French and were cut of by the natives.

The twelfth Collonie was of Dutch setled by the Zealanders in the Rivers, Borowma,[38] Wacopon, & Moroca, haveing been drave of(f) from Tobago[39] Anno 1650. And ye yeare following a great Collonie of Dutch, and Jewes, drave of from Brazile, by the Portugaize setled there and being Experienced Planters, that soone grew a Flourishing Colonie.

The thirteenth Collonie was of French at Suramaca and at Chyan,[40] were the greatest part cut of by the Careebs and Saepoyes[41] Anno 1649.

---

[33] *Gratefull:* Gratifying, enjoyable.
[34] *Meriwina:* Cf. Marrawina on p. 341.
[35] *Rochell:* I.e., La Rochelle, a port on the western coast of France.
[36] *St. Christophers:* One of the Leeward Islands; also called "St. Kitts."
[37] *Curanteen:* Cf. Currianteen on p. 342.
[38] *Borowma:* I.e., Pomeroon; see the map on p. 327.
[39] *Tobago:* An island in the West Indies, off the coast of Venezuela.
[40] *Chyan:* I.e., Cayenne.
[41] *Saepoyes:* Cf. Sapoyes, p. 342.

The fourteenth Collonie was at Suranam, Anno 1650, about 300 people of the English Nacion from ye Island of Barbados under the Collonie of one Lieut. Collonel Anthony Rowse,[42] a Gentleman of great Gallantrie and Prudence and of Long Experience in ye West Indies. His makeing a firme peace with the Indians, soone after his Landing, and Reviveing the name of Sr Walter Raleigh, have the English firme footeing in those parts, and it soone became a hopefull Collonie.

These people had the Accomodacion of a Ship from Francis Lord Willoughby of Parham (then at the Barbados) and the Loane of a parcell of Indian Trade. The Lord Willoughby settled a Plantacion amongst them at Suranam, another at Comonina upon which he Disburst at least 26000 Pownd.

Anno 1654 Lieutenant Coll. Rowse haveing established this Collonie, left it in a flourishing Condicion, and in perfect Peace with the Indians, & one Major William Byam was Chosen Governor, A Judicious Gentleman. And in that Condicion it Stood dayly increaseing untill the yeare 1660, at which time his Majestie[43] being happily restored to his Just Rights, Francis Lord Willoughby (amongst other pretences in the West Indies) layd Claime to Suranam by vertue of a Compact with ye first Setlers. And in Consideracion of his great Disburstments in those parts, And although there was some difference in that point between the Inhabitants and his Lordship, it passed in favour of his Lordship and Laurence Hide, Esq,[44] second Sonn to the Earle of Clarendon, as Lord Proprietors of that Province under the Appellacion of Willoughby Land. But Major Byam was Continued Deputy Governor to the Proprietors, and was Commissionated Lieut. Generall of Guiana.

Lord Willoughby

CERTAINE OVERTURES MADE BY YE LORD WILLOUGHBY OF PARHAM UNTO ALL SUCH AS SHALL INCLINE TO PLANT IN YE COLONYE OF SARANAM ON YE CONTINENT OF GUAIANA.

---

[42] *Lieut. Collonel Anthony Rowse:* Also spelled Rous or Rouse. He was a Barbados planter.

[43] *his Majestie:* King Charles II

[44] *Laurence Hide, Esq:* Usually spelled Hyde; in 1663, he and Willoughby were jointly awarded a grant giving them proprietary rights to "all that part of the mainland of Guiana called Surinam."

1. Such as are able & willing to transport themselves at their own charge shall have a shippe or shippes provided for them, according to their number in 3 moneths or lesse after they signifye their resolucions & the number of persons and quantitye of goods; & in ye sayde vessels they shall have accommodation according to ther qualitye. They shall pay for ther passage but 5£ a head, & in this also ther wilbe an abatement for children under 10 yeeres old, for 2 of them shalbe accompted but for one passenger in pay & allowance (provided alwayes that they never any messe[45] above 7 in number), sucking children to goe free. Every passenger also, according to ye manner to have his sea chest or trunk to goe free, & to pay but 50 shill. per tunn for fraight of other goods.

2. Upon ther arriveall in ye Countrye ther shal be allotted to every single person, man or woman that payes for ther own passage, 50 Acres of Land of inheritance. And a married man to have so much for himself & 50 more for his wife, 30 for every child, 20 for every man or mayd servant, & as ther familyes increase in children or servants, so to increase in ther lot of land. This land to be layd out as shalbe most convenient for situation & goodness, according to ye choyce of the person concerned. And if any shall thinck fit to depart from ye Countrye, they shall have liberty to sell ther lands & goods to whom they please, or on other occasion to dispose thereof by deed will or Contract.

3. When any of ther children grow up to a distinct familye, then to have 50 Acres of other land of inheritance, & when any of ther servants are set free to have 30 Acres.

4. Such single persons, men or women (as being serviceable & of good report), are willing but not able to goe may be entertained into service by ye Lord Willoughby, & at his alone charge transported, serving ther but foure yeers, in all which time to be fully provided with sufficient meat, drinck, lodging & apparrell, & at ye end of the sayd terme, shall have ten pounds sterling payd them in mony or Country Commodityes, & 30 Acres of good land alotted them for them & ther heires for ever. And ye servant that is an Artificer[46] shall have further incouragement in his Art. Likewise ther wil be entertainment for boyes & girles for 7 yeers or such other time as is fit for their age, & at ye end of ther time, they shall have 30 Acres & some reward in Tooles clothes or other materialls.

5. For the transport & support of industrious & well disposed persons & familyes which are not able to doe this of themselves, as in ye

---

[45] *messe*: Feed, require food for.
[46] *Artificer*: Skilled craftsman.

first Artickle, neither are so fit to pay for it by service, as in ye 4th Article, ther is a desire to propound or finde out & accept such a way as may glue just encouragement to ye transporter & transported. That which is at present thought on & practised is, That such persons & familyes shall have their passage at ye alone charge of ye Lord Willoughby, or anye other Patron, & upon their arriveall, every person if single, shall have 40 Acres of good land allotted to him, & if married as much also for his wife & 15 for each child or servant, & when a child of such a familye, shall goe forth to finde a new on, to have 40 Acres & when a servant is free 30.

Those persons so transported to be true debtors to ye Lord Willoughby or any other patron, for ther passage & therefore to hold ther land on condition of paying after the 2^d yeere a tenth part of the proffits thereof either in kinde as it riseth, or at a rate compounded for. Good order is to be taken to prevent fraud or neglect by appointing a proportion of land to be planted with provision & Commodityes, & if any such person or familyes, as being in Townes shall desire wholy to employ themselves in some Arts or misterye[47] rather then in planting, then to pay ye Patron some lesser part of ther true gaine be it a 20th, or any other part which shalbe agreed upon.

The Lord Willoughby is willing for ye first 8 moneths (in which time & before, they may hav[e] a croppe of their own) to furnish such poore familyes with provision to be payd for at ye 2^d yeere in kinde: otherwise also to trust them with tooles & other necessaryes out of his Store: likewise to furnish them at ye countrye rates with cattell & servants, English or Negroes: for which if not payd for in 3 moneths after the delivery, the Planter is to allow wages for so much of the price as is unpayd at 6 per centum.

Incouragement is considered of for all considerable persons & ingenuous Artists or Students, as able preachers, schoolmasters, Physitians, Chyrurgions,[48] midwives, Surveyors, Architectors, Chymists[49] & other persons singularly improveable for ye good of ye Colonye; ther books instruments or tooles needfull in ye exercise of their ingenuity, shalbe fraight free, & any other reasonable foods indulged.

---

[47] *misterye:* Art, handicraft.
[48] *Chyrurgions:* Surgeons.
[49] *Chymists:* Dealers in medicinal drugs.

To Sir Robert Harley from the Stewards
of His Plantations in Surinam (1663–1664).

(Addressed:)
> ffor ye wriht Hon'ble Sr Roberte Harloe Lo. Chanseler
> of Barbadus The(se) Deliver with Truste.

Honoured Sr,

These are toe Acquainte yowr ho[n]re That Cap. George Straing is
verey sik, more like toe Dey then toe live. These are allsoe toe Aquante
yowre hoñre That According as yow weere Pleased toe order mee, I
Did looke ffor A Plase upone yowre land att ye Cotten Tree toe Buld
mee Ane House. Butt ye ffreshese[50] Being varey High in ye river, Itt is
All Drouned upone ye ffase of ye river. Theareffore I made Choyse of
A Plase 3 leages Above Sand Poynt Called Morgoename[51]; it is verey
neare ye Guese.[52] I Doe live in hopes that I shall have good Imployment Theare; and According toe my Judgment this Coloney is like toe
bee verey hopefull. Iff yowre Hoñre bee soe Pleased toe send a yong
nigroe of 16 or 18 yeares of Age, I will Instruckte him in my *Trad:* ffor
yowre Honres servis in as short a time as hee will bee Capable toe
learne. And Iff yowre Hoñre will bee Pleased toe Healpe mee toe one
yong negroe, I will in A shorte tim sattisfy yow god willing. Theare is
A genney man[53] Arived heare in This river of ye 24th of This Instant att
Sande poynt. Shee hase 130 nigroes one Borde; ye Comanders name
Joseph John Woode; shee has lost 54 negroes in y[o] viage. The Ladeyes
that are heare live att St Johnes hill.[54] Itt is reported heare that yowre
Honoure have sould that Plantation toe my Lord Willughby. Soe with
my Humbell servis toe yowre Honr[e] I remaine yow[re] Hoñres servant
WILLI. YEARWORTH.

Morgoname this 27th of Jaunarey 1663
   in Surranam River.

---

[50] *ffreshese:* I.e., freshes, fresh streams.
[51] *Morgoename:* (Spelled "Matgamaw" on the map of Suriname on p. 339) an area
roughly ten miles inland from the coast.
[52] *Guese:* I.e., geyser.
[53] *genney man:* I.e., "Guinea man," a slave ship from the Guinea coast.
[54] *St Johnes hill:* The estate appears in the map on p. 339, where it is marked as
"Sr R. Harley."

(Addressed:)
> These ffor the Right Hon^able Sr Robert Harley Knight
> at St Michaells Towne In Barbados,
>   with my most humble service.

HONORED S^R

my humble respects & service salute you. S^r, the fouerty Acres of land the Lieute Gen^ll and my selfe weare to fell and plant for you, wee have performed according to our agreement, and have had it run out by a sworne Surveyour whose sertificate you will receive from the Lieute Gen^ll. M^r. Rowland Stibben have seen yor plantation, whoe can informe you the Condition of it. S^r, I humbly request you to supply it with negroes by the first opportunity and those other necessaries I formerly writt to yor Honor for. S^r, be confident I shall use my utmost Ceare & endeavor in the management of it. S^r, for all things else I refer you to the Lieute Gen^ll Letter. Thus with my humble respects & service to yor Honour I Rest

> Yo^r Most Humble Servant

Surinam   GEO^r STRAUNGE.
     March 4th 1663.

To Sir Robert Harley from friend William Byam

(Addressed:)
> Th(ese) ffor ye Honble S^r, Robert Harley K^t Barbados.

> Surynam. March the 14th 63.

HON^BLE S^R,

Haveing by severall Conveyances given you a full accompt of all yor busines here and since y^t Mr Rowland will give you a perfect relation of all, I need not enlarge But to advise you of the sympatheticall passion of ye Grand Sheapheard Celedon who is fled after Astrea,[55] beeing resolvd to espouse all distresse or felicities of fortune wth her. But the more Certaine cause of his flight (waveing the Arrow & services he had for the Lodger)[56] was a Regiment of protests to the number of 1000 of pounds sterlin drawne up against him. And he beeing a Tender Gentlemen & unable to keepe the feild hath betaken himselfe to

---

[55] *ye Grand Sheapheard Celedon . . . Astrea:* John Scot and Aphra Behn; see the introduction to this selection.

[56] *waveing the Arrow & services he had for the Lodger:* Putting aside his romantic motive (Cupid's arrow) and his attention to Behn, the lodger at St. John's Hill.

the other element as fletting[57] as himselfe, but whether for certain I cannot yett resolve you. Truly the Brethren[58] are much startled that the Governor of the Reformation should Turne Tayle on the day of battle. S^r, I have mett with a choice sumattse(?) wch I present you by Rowland, desiring yor acceptance. I desire yor favour to Mr. Chester, Master of the Ketch wherein I am interested, and to furder[59] him with freight or passengers in what you may. All here salute you with their hūble service.

I am S^r, Yo^r very faithfull friend & hūble servt

W^M BYAM.

Maior Banister & Lady present their
   hūble service to you.

---

[57] *fletting:* I.e., fleeing — Byam is saying that Scot has taken an ocean voyage.
[58] *Brethren:* Parliamentarians, who shared Scot's political sympathies.
[59] *furder:* I.e., further, assist.

GEORGE WARREN

From *An Impartial Description of Surinam*

George Warren's *An Impartial Description of Surinam*, published in 1667, is often cited as a possible source for *Oroonoko*. Many of Warren's descriptions, such as his references to the slaves' belief in the transmigration of souls and the Indians' ignorance of "that innocent and warm delight of Kissing," (354) are echoed in *Oroonoko*, and his account of Indian warriors demonstrating their courage by undergoing scourging finds a parallel in Behn's description of Indian self-mutilation. Nevertheless, Warren has little interest in noble savages or new gardens of Eden. On the one hand, he describes the Indians as blessed with a perfect sufficiency of food, and comments on the women's innocence, and yet he quickly attributes to them a lasciviousness worthy of the female Yahoos of Jonathan Swift's *Gulliver's Travels*. Like Littleton, Warren documents the brutal treatment of African slaves without suggesting that slavery should be outlawed.

Little is known about the author besides what he tells us in his book, which reports that he spent three years in Suriname and that he met the deputy governor, William Byam, who evidently left a much more favorable impression on Warren than on Behn. Warren assures his readers that

Byam "is too much of a Gentleman to be the Author of a Lye," while in Behn's story Byam figures as a deceitful and hypocritical villain. In its accounts of the flora and fauna of Suriname, Warren's book has rarely been questioned; in twenty-eight pages, it provides a concise and useful guide to the geography and climate of the region. The book was translated into Dutch in 1669, and it was reprinted in 1745 in Thomas Osborne's popular anthology *A Collection of Voyages and Travels.*

The text is excerpted from the first edition of *An Impartial Description of Surinam upon the Continent of Guiana in America* (London: Printed by William Godbid for Nathaniel Brooke, 1667) 17–20, 23–25.

Of the Plantations,

Which are in all about five hundred, whereof Forty or Fifty have *sugar-works,* yielding no small profit to the Owners, for a slight Disbursement, considering how brave[1] a Revenue, if prudently manag'd, may be rais'd from it in a few years: far larger (if no Contingency divert the ordinary Course of things) than is usually produc'd from a greater foundation, and more Continu'd Industry in *England.*

The Seasons for Felling down the Wood are between *April* and *August,* it being left upon the Ground to drye till about the latter end of *September,* when; 'tis burnt, and the Soil enrich'd with its Ashes. *Indian*-Corn and Canes are planted upon the Lower-Grounds. *Yames* and other Provisions upon that which is higher. The Corn grows upon a Stalk like a *Reed,* commonly six or seven foot high, and two Ears upon a Stalk: The Grain is about the bigness of a *Pea,* which becomes ripe in four Months. They have two Crops in a year, and the Increase is at least five hundred for one. *Canes* become fit to break in Twelve Months when they are about six foot high, and as thick as a Man's Wrist: They bear a Top like a Flag, which being cut off, and the Canes squeesed through a Mill, the Juice is boyl'd in Coppers to a competent thickness, and then pour'd into Wooden Pots made broad and square at the top, and taper'd to the compass of a Sixpence at the Bottome with a Hole thorough, which is stopp'd with a little stick, till the Sugar begins to be cold, and stiffen'd; when 'tis pull'd out, and by that Passage, the *Molasses* drains from it; and being Cur'd a while after this manner, is knock'd out into Hogsheads, and so shipp'd off.

---

[1] *brave:* Fine, excellent.

Of the Negroes or Slaves,

Who are most brought out of *Guiny* in *Africa* to those parts, where they are sold like *Dogs,* and no better esteem'd but for their Work sake, which they perform all the Week with the severest usages for the slightest fault, till *Saturday* afternoon, when, they are allowed to dress their own Gardens or Plantations, having nothing but what they can produce from thence to live upon; unless perhaps once or twice a year, their Masters vouchsafe them, as a great favour, a little rotten Salt-fish: Or if a *Cow* or *Horse* die of itself, they get Roast-meat: Their Lodging is a hard Board, and their black Skins their Covering. These wretched miseries not seldome drive them to desperate attempts for the Recovery of their Liberty, endevouring to escape, and, if like to be re-taken, sometimes lay violent hands upon themselves; or if the hope of Pardon brings them again alive into their Masters power, they'l manifest their fortitude, or rather obstinacy in suffering the most exquisite tortures can be inflicted upon them, for a terrour and example to others without shrinking. They are there a mixture of several Nations, which are always Clashing with one another, so that no Conspiracy can be hatching, but 'tis presently detected by some party amongst themselves disaffected to the Plot, because their Enemies have a share in't: They are naturally treacherous and bloody, and practice no Religion there, though many of them are Circumcis'd: But they believe the Ancient *Pythagorean* Errour of the Soul's Transmigration out of one body into another,[2] that when they dye, they shall return into their own Countries and be Regenerated, so live in the World by a Constant Revolution; which Conceit makes many of them over-fondly wooe their Deaths, not otherwise hoping to be freed from that indeed un-equall'd Slavery. . . .

Of the Indians,

Who are a People Cowardly and Treacherous, qualities inseparable: there are several Nations which Trade and familiarly Converse with the People of the Colony, but those they live amongst are the *Charibes,* or *Caniballs,*[3] who are more numerous than any of the rest, and are

---

[2] *Pythagorean Errour . . . into another:* Pythagoras believed that souls traveled between human bodies, animals, and vegetables.

[3] *Charibes, or Caniballs:* The Caribs were reputed to be cannibals and were also called by that name; for further discussion, see the selection from Montaigne and the introduction to the selection from Defoe in Part Two, Chapter 2). It should be noted that numerous African and South American tribes were described as cannibals; seventeenth-century maps are filled with such descriptions.

setled upon all the Islands, & in most of the Rivers, from the famous one of *Amazones*, to that of *Oronoque:* They go wholly naked, save a Flap for Modesty, which the Women, after having had a Child or two, throw off. Their Skins are of an Orange Tawny Colour, and their Hair black, without Curles: A happy people as to this World, if they were sensible of their own hap: Nature with little toyl providing all things which may serve her own necessities. The Women are generally lascivious, and some so truly handsom, as to Features and Proportion, that if the most Curious Symetrian[4] had been there, he could not but subscribe to my opinion: and their pretty Bashfulness (especially while Virgins) in the presence of a Stranger, adds such a Charming grace to their perfections (too nakedly expos'd to every wanton Eye) that who ever lives amongst them had need be owner of no less than *Joseph's* Continency,[5] not at least to Covet their embraces: They have been yet so unfortunately ignorant, not to enrich their amorous Caresses with that innocent and warm delight of Kissing, but Conversing so frequently with Christians, and being naturally docile and ingenious, we have Reason to believe, they will in time be taught it. Their Houses for the night, are low thatch'd Cottages, with the Eves close to the ground; for the day, they have higher, and open on every side, to defend them from the violence of the Sun's Raies, yet letting in the grateful Coolness of the Air. Their Houshold Utensils are curiously painted Earthen Pots and Platters, and their Napery[6] is the Leaves of Trees. Their Beds or Hamackoes (which are also used amongst the *English*) are made of *Cotton*, square like a Blanket, and so ordered with strings at each end, that being tyed a Convenient distance from one another, it opens the full breadth. For Bread and Drink, they plant Gardens of *Cassader*,[7] and the Woods and Rivers are their constant Suppeditories[8] of Flesh and Fish. For ornament they Colour themselves all over into neat works, with a red Paint called *Anotta*,[9] which grows in Cods upon small Trees, and the Juice of certain Weeds; they bore holes also through their Noses, Lips, and Ears, whereat they hang glass Pendants, Peices of Brass, or any such like Bawbles their Service can procure from the *English;* they Load their Legs, Necks, and Arms too,

---

[4] *Symetrian:* Expert in symmetry.
[5] *Joseph's Continency:* In Genesis 39.11–12, Joseph rejects the sexual advances of Potiphar's wife.
[6] *Napery:* Table linen.
[7] *Cassader:* I.e., cassava; see n. 10, p. 364.
[8] *Suppeditories:* Suppliers.
[9] *Anotta:* See p. 344.

with Beads, Shels of Fishes, & almost any trumpery[10] they can get; they have no Law nor Government but Oeconomical,[11] living like the Patriarchs of old, the whole Kindred in a Family, where the eldest Son always succeeds his Father as the greatest; yet they have some more than ordinary persons, who are their Captains, and lead them out to Wars, whose Courage they first prove, by sharply Whipping them with Rods, which if they endure bravely without Crying, or any considerable motion, they are acknowledg'd gallant fellows and honour'd by the less hardy. These Chiefs or Heads of Families, have commonly three or four Wives a piece, other but one, who may indeed more properly be term'd their Vassals than Companions, being no less subjected to their Husbands than the meanest Servants amongst us are to their Masters, the Men rarely oppress their Shoulders with a Burthen, the Women carry all, and are so very humble and observant in their Houses, that at Meals, they alwayes wait upon their Husbands, and never eat till they have done; when a Woman is delivered of her first Child; she presently goes about her business as before, and the Husband fains himself distemper'd, and is hang'd up to the Ridge of the House in his Homacko, where he continues certain dayes dieted with the Bread and Water of Affliction, then, being taken down is stung with *Ants* (a punishment they usually inflict upon their Women, Dogs, or Children, when they are foolish, for that's the term they usually put upon any misdemeanours) and a lusty drinking Bout is made at the Conclusion of the Ceremony. Their Language sounds well in the expression, but is not very easie to be learn'd, because many single Words admit of divers Senses, to be distinguish'd only by the tone or alteration of the voice.

[10] *trumpery:* Trifles.
[11] *Oeconomical:* Conforming to the divine government delineated in scripture.

RICHARD LIGON

From *A True and Exact History of the Island of Barbados*

The English lost Suriname to the Dutch in 1667, but they maintained and extended their control in the Caribbean islands. This selection and the next three take us to those islands, delineating English views on life in the West Indies during the second half of the seventeenth century. Richard

This 1671 engraving of sugar-making in the French Antilles shows the process used throughout the Caribbean in the late seventeenth century. The engraving is from Jean-Baptiste Du Tetre, *Histoire générale des Antilles habitées par les Francois*, II (Paris, 1671) 122.

Ligon wrote his *True and Exact History of the Island of Barbados* while in prison for debt in London in 1653. He had gone to Barbados in 1647, during the very early years of the sugar revolution, to seek his fortune. Prior to the 1640s, English colonists had been growing tobacco in Barbados, but their economy collapsed when tobacco production increased elsewhere in the British American colonies, leading to a drop in prices. While tobacco farmers required only small holdings to raise their crops, sugar farming required large tracts of land, expensive machinery, and a massive labor force (the illustration above gives some idea of the equipment involved). As a result of these demands, the import of slaves rose dramatically after the onset of the sugar revolution, and the total population grew from 10,000 in 1640 to more than 50,000 in 1667. Ligon, who was in his late fifties when he moved to Barbados, was significantly older than most other farmers. On his arrival, he purchased half of a plantation, which he lived on for three years as he learned how to manage a sugar estate. Many planters on the island were passing from poverty to prosperity, but Ligon's enterprise ultimately failed, like those of many small holders, and he was imprisoned for debt on his return to England. He was a victim of the transition from small holdings to large plantations, and he records the plight of other victims, especially indentured servants from Britain and African slaves. Although a slaveholder himself, he made contributions to the later antislavery cause by first telling the story of Yarico and Inkle (see Chapter 2) and by praising the honor and fidelity of African slaves. His remarks about the incompatibility between Christianity and slavery recall the legal arguments over this point raised in the court cases in Chapter 5.

Ligon's book was first published in 1657; the text is excerpted from the second edition (London: Printed by Peter Parker, 1673) 45–46, 46–50, 53–54, 59.

Description of a Barely Averted Rebellion of White Indentured Servants

A little before I came from thence,[1] there was such a combination amongst them, as the like was never seen there before. Their sufferings being grown to a great height, and their daily complainings to one another (of the intolerable burdens they labour'd under) being spread throughout the Island; at the last, some amongst them, whose spirits were not able to endure such slavery, resolved to break through it, or dye in the act; and so conspired with some others of their acquaintance, whose sufferings were equal, if not above theirs; and their spirits no way inferiour, resolved to draw as many of the discontented party into this plot, as possibly they could; and those of this perswasion, were the greatest numbers of Servants in the Island. So that a day was appointed to fall upon their Masters, and cut all their throats, and by that means, to make themselves only freemen, but Masters of the Island. And so closely was this plot carried, as no discovery was made, till the day before they were to put it in act: And then one of them, either by the failing of his courage, or some new obligation from the love of his Master, revealed this long plotted conspiracy; and so by this timely advertisement, the Masters were saved: Justice *Hethersall*[2] (whose servant this was) sending Letters to all his friends, and they to theirs, and so one to another, till they were all secured; and, by examination, found out the greatest part of them; whereof eighteen of the

---

[1] *thence:* I.e., Barbados.
[2] *Justice Hethersall:* Probably Thomas Hothersall, who was also captain of a militia.

..cipal men in the conspiracy, and they the first leaders and contrivers of the plot, were put to death, for example to the rest. And the reason why they made examples of so many, was, they found these so haughty in their resolutions, and so incorrigible, as they were like enough to become Actors in a second plot, and so they thought good to secure them; and for the rest, to have a special eye over them. . . .

Description of the Slaves

It has been accounted a strange thing, that the *Negroes*, being more than double the numbers of the Christians that are there, and they accounted a bloody people, where they think they have power or advantages; and the more bloody, by how much they are more fearful than others: that these should not commit some horrid massacre upon the Christians, thereby to enfranchise themselves, and become Masters of the Island. But there are three reasons that take away this wonder; the one is, They are not suffered to touch or handle any weapons: The other, That they are held in such awe and slavery, as they are fearful to appear in any daring act; and seeing the mustering of our men, and hearing their Gun-shot, (than which nothing is more terrible to them) their spirits are subjugated to so low a condition, as they dare not look up to any bold attempt. Besides these, there is a third reason, which stops all designs of that kind, and that is, They are fetch'd from several parts of *Africa*, who speak several languages, and by that means, one of them understands not another. For, some of them are fetch'd from *Guinny* and *Binny*, some from *Cutchew*,[3] some from *Angola*, and some from the River of *Gambia*. And in some of these places where petty Kingdomes are, they sell their Subjects, and such as they take in Battle, whom they make slaves; and some mean men sell their Servants, their Children, and sometimes their Wives; and think all good traffick, for such commodities as our Merchants send them.

When they are brought to us, the Planters buy them out of the Ship, where they find them stark naked, and therefore cannot be deceived in any outward infirmity. They choose them as they do Horses in a Market; the strongest, youthfullest, and most beautiful, yield the greatest prices. Thirty pound sterling is a price for the best man *Negroe;* and twenty five, twenty six, or twenty seven pound for a Woman; the Children are at easier rates. And we buy them so as the sexes may be equal; for, if they have more Men than Women, the men who are unmarried

---

[3] *Binny . . . Cutchew:* I.e., Benin and Cachou, an area on the west coast of Africa, slightly south of the Gambia River.

will come to their Masters, and complain, that they cannot live without Wives, and desire him they may have Wives. And he tells them, that the next ship that comes, he will buy them Wives, which satisfies them for the present; and so they expect the good time: which the Master performing with them, the bravest[4] fellow is to choose first, and so in order, as they are in place, and every one of them knows his better, and gives him the precedence, as Cows do one another, in passing through a narrow gate; for, the most of them are as near beasts as may be, setting their souls aside. Religion they know none; yet most of them acknowledge a God, as appears by their motions and gestures: For, if one of them do another wrong, and he cannot revenge himself, he looks up to Heaven for vengeance, and holds up both his hands, as if the power must come from thence, that must do him right. Chast they are as any people under the Sun; for, when the men and women are together naked, they never cast their eyes towards the parts that ought to be covered; and those amongst us, that have Breeches and Petticoats, I never saw so much as a kiss, or embrace, or a wanton glance with their eyes between them. Jealous they are of their Wives, and hold it for a great injury and scorn, if another man make the least courtship to his Wife. And if any of their Wives have two Children at a birth, they conclude her false to his Bed, and so no more adoe but hang her. We had an excellent *Negro* in the Plantation, whose name was *Macow,* and was our chief Musician; a very valiant man, and was keeper of our Plantine-Grove. This *Negroe's* Wife was brought to bed of two Children, and her Husband, as their manner is, had provided a cord to hang her. But the Overseer finding what he was about to do, enformed the Master of it, who sent for *Macow,* to disswade him from this cruel act, of murdering his Wife, and used all perswasions that possibly he could, to let him see, that such double births are in Nature, and that divers presidents were to be found amongst us of the like; so that we rather praised our Wives, for their fertility, than blamed them for their falseness. But this prevailed little with him, upon whom custom had taken so deep an impression; but resolved, the next thing he did, should be to hang her. Which when the Master perceived, and that the ignorance of the man, should take away the life of the woman, who was innocent of the crime her Husband condemned her for, told him plainly, that if he hang'd her, he himself should be hang'd by her, upon the same bough; and therefore wish'd him to consider what he did. This threatning wrought more with him than all the reasons of

---

[4] *bravest:* Best.

Philosophy that could be given him; and so let her alone; but he never car'd much for her afterward, but chose another which he lik'd better. For the Planters there deny not a slave, that is a brave fellow, and one that has extraordinary qualities, two or three Wives, and above that number they seldom go: But no woman is allowed above one Husband.

At the time the wife is to be brought a bed, her Husband removes his board, (which is his bed) to another room (for many several divisions they have, in their little houses,) and none above six foot square) And leaves his wife to God, and her good fortune, in the room, and upon the board alone, and calls a neighbour to come to her, who gives little help to her delivery, but when the child is born, (which she calls her Pickaninny)[5] she helps to make a little fire near her feet, and that serves instead of Possets, Broaths, and Caudles.[6] In a fortnight, this woman is at work with her Pickaninny at her back, as merry a soul as any is there. If the Overseer be discreet, she is suffer'd to rest her self a little more than ordinary; but if not, she is compelled to do as others do. Times they have of suckling their Children in the fields, and refreshing themselves; and good reason, for they carry burthens on their backs; and yet work too. Some women, whose Pickaninnies are three years old, will, as they work at weeding, which is a stooping work, suffer the hee Pickaninny, to sit a stride upon their backs, like St. *George* a Horse-back;[7] and there Spur his mother with his heels, and sings and crows on her back, clapping his hands, as if he meant to flye; which the mother is so pleas'd with, as she continues her painful stooping posture, longer than she would do, rather than discompose her Jovial Pickaninny of his pleasure, so glad she is to see him merry. The work which the women do, is most of it weeding, a stooping and painful work; at noon and night they are call'd home by the ring of a Bell, where they have two hours time for their repast at noon; and at night, they rest from six, till six a Clock next morning.

On *Sunday* they rest, and have the whole day at their pleasure; and the most of them use it as a day of rest and pleasure; but some of them

---

[5] *Pickaninny:* A term used in the West Indies for children of African origin.

[6] *Possets . . . Caudles:* Drinks used as remedies for the ill. Posset consists of hot milk curdled with wine or other liquor, usually with sugar and spices added; caudle, used specifically for women in childbed, had largely the same ingredients, but with warm, thin gruel rather than milk.

[7] *St. George a Horse-back:* St. George was the patron saint of England, famous for capturing and killing the dragon that required human sacrifices. He is often portrayed on horseback.

who will make benefit of that dayes liberty, go where the Mangrave trees[8] grow, and gather the bark, of which they make ropes, which they truck away for other Commodities, as Shirts and Drawers.

In the afternoons on *Sundayes,* they have their Musick, which is of kettle drums, and those of several sizes; upon the smallest the best Musitian playes, and the other come in as Chorasses: the drum all men know, has but one tone; and therefore variety of tunes have little to do in this musick; and yet so strangely they varie their time, as 'tis a pleasure to the most curious ears, and it was to me one of the strangest noises that ever I heard made of one tone; and if they had the variety of tune, which gives the greater scope in Musick, as they have of time, they would do wonders in that Art. And if I had not faln sick before my coming away, at least seven months in one sickness, I had given them some hints of tunes, which being understood, would have serv'd as a great addition to their harmony, for time without tune, is not an eighth part of the Science of Musick.

I found *Macow* very apt for it of himself, and one day coming into the house, (which none of the *Negroes* use to do, unless an Officer, as he was,) he found me playing on a Theorbo,[9] and singing to it, which he hearkened very attentively to; and when I had done, he took the Theorbo in his hand, and strook one string, stopping it by degrees upon every fret, and finding the notes to varie, till it came to the body of the instrument; and that the nearer the body of the instrument he stopt, the smaller or higher the sound was, which he found was by the shortning of the string, considered with himself, how he might make some tryal of this experiment upon such an instrument as he could come by; having no hope ever to have any instrument of this kind to practice on. In a day or two after, walking in the Plantine grove, to refresh me in that cool shade, and to delight my self with the sight of those plants, which are so beautiful, as though they left a fresh impression in me when I parted with them, yet upon a review, something is discern'd in their beauty more than I remembred at parting: which caused me to make often repair thither, I found this *Negro* (whose office it was to attend there) being the keeper of that grove, sitting on the ground, and before him a piece of large timber, upon which he had laid cross, six Billets, having a handsaw and a hatchet by him, would

[8] *Mangrave trees:* I.e., mangroves, a tree or large shrub whose roots grow together to form a thick, impenetrable mass; however, it has been suggested that Ligon is actually referring to the mahoe, another tree that grows in the West Indies.

[9] *Theorbo:* A large lute with a double neck and two sets of tuning pegs.

cut the billets by little and little, till he had brought them to the tunes, he would fit them to; for the shorter they were, the higher the Notes, which he tryed by knocking upon the ends of them with a stick, which he had in his hand. When I found him at it, I took the stick out of his hand, and tryed the sound, finding the six billets to have six distinct notes, one above another, which put me in a wonder, how he of himself, should without teaching do so much. I then shewed him the difference between flats and sharps, which he presently apprehended, as between *Fa*, and *Mi*: and he would have cut two more billets to those tunes, but I had then no time to see it done, and so left him to his own enquiries. I say thus much to let you see that some of these people are capable of learning Arts.

Another, of another kind of speculation I found; but more ingenious than he: and this man with three or four more, were to attend me into the woods, to cut Church wayes, for I was employed sometimes upon publick works; and those men were excellent Axe-men, and because there were many gullies in the way, which were impassable, and by that means I was compell'd to make traverses, up and down in the wood; and was by that in danger to miss of the point, to which I was to make my passage to the Church, and therefore was fain to take a Compass with me, which was a Circumferenter, to make my traverses the more exact, and indeed without which, it could not be done, setting up the Circumferenter, and observing the Needle: This *Negre Sambo* comes to me, and seeing the needle wag, desired to know the reason of its stirring, and whether it were alive: I told him no, but it stood upon a point, and for a while it would stir, but by and by stand still, which he observ'd and found it to be true.

The next question was, why it stood one way, and would not remove to any other point, I told him that it would stand no way but North and South, and upon that shew'd him the four Cardinal points of the compass, East, West, North, South, which he presently learnt by heart, and promis'd me never to forget it. His last question was, why it would stand North, I gave this reason, because of the huge Rocks of Loadstone that were in the North part of the world, which had a quality to draw Iron to it; and this Needle being of Iron, and touch'd with a Loadstone, it would always stand that way.

This point of philosophy was a little too hard for him, and so he stood in a strange muse; which to put him out of, I bad him reach his axe, and put it near to the Compass, and remove it about; and as he did so, the Needle turned with it, which put him in the greatest admiration that ever I saw a man, and so quite gave over his questions, and desired me, that he might be made a Christian; for, he thought to be a Christian, was to be endued with all those knowledges he wanted.

I promised to do my best endeavour; and when I came home, spoke to the Master of the Plantation, and told him, that poor *Sambo* desired much to be a Christian. But his answer was, That the people of that Island were governed by the Lawes of *England,* and by those Lawes, we could not make a Christian a Slave. I told him, my request was far different from that, for I desired him to make a Slave a Christian. His answer was, That it was true, there was a great difference in that: But, being once a Christian, he could no more account him a Slave, and so lose the hold they had of them as Slaves, by making them Christians; and by that means should open such a gap, as all the Planters in the Island would curse him. So I was struck mute, and poor *Sambo* kept out of the Church; as ingenious, as honest, and as good natur'd poor soul, as ever wore black, or eat green. . . .

Though there be a mark set upon these people, which will hardly ever be wip'd off, as of their cruelties when they have advantages, and of their fearfulness and falseness; yet no rule so general but hath his acception: for I believe, and I have strong motives to cause me to be of that perswasion, that there are as honest, faithful, and conscionable people amongst them, as amongst those of *Europe,* or any other part of the world.

A hint of this, I will give you in a lively example; and it was in a time when Victuals were scarce, and Plantins were not then so frequently planted, as to afford them enough. So that some of the high spirited and turbulent amongst them, began to mutiny, and had a plot, secretly to be reveng'd on their Master; and one or two of these were Firemen that made the fires in the furnaces, who were never without store of dry wood by them. These villains, were resolved to make fire to such part of the boyling-house, as they were sure would fire the rest, and so burn all, and yet seem ignorant of the fact, as a thing done by accident. But this plot was discovered, by some of the others who hated mischief, as much as they lov'd it; and so traduc'd them to their Master, and brought in so many witnesses against them, as they were forc'd to confess, what they meant should have been put in act the next night: So giving them condign punishment, the Master gave order to the overseer that the rest should have a dayes liberty to themselves and their wives, to do what they would; and withall to allow them a double proportion of victual for three dayes, both which they refus'd: which we all wonder'd at, knowing well how much they lov'd their liberties and their meat, having been lately pinch'd of the one, and not having overmuch of the other; and therefore being doubtful what their meaning was in this, suspecting some discontent amongst them, sent for three or four of the best of them, and desir'd to know why they refus'd this favour that was offer'd them, but received such an answer: as we little expected; for they told us, it was not sullenness, or slighting the gratuity their Master bestow'd on them, but they would not accept any thing as a recompence for doing that which became them in their duties to do, nor would they have him think, it was hope of reward, that made them to accuse their fellow servants, but an act of Justice, which they thought themselves bound in duty to do, and they thought themselves sufficiently rewarded in the Act. The substance of this, in such language as they had, they delivered, and poor *Sambo* was the Orator; by whose example the others were led both in the discovery of the Plot, and refusal of the gratuity. And withall they said, that if it pleas'd their Master, at any time, to bestow a voluntary boon upon them, be it never so sleight, they would willingly and thankfully accept it: and this act might have beseem'd the best Christians, though some of them were denied Christianity, when they earnestly sought it. Let others have what opinion they please, yet I am of this belief; that there are to be found amongst them, some who are as morally honest, as Conscionable, as humble, as loving to their friends, and as loyal to their Masters, as any that live under the Sun; and one reason they have to be so, is, they set no great value upon their lives: And this is all I can remember concerning the *Negroes,* except of their games, which I could never learn, because they wanted language to teach me.

As for the *Indians,* we have but few, and those fetcht from other Countries; some from the neighboaring Islands, some from the Main, which we make slaves: the women who are better vers'd in ordering the Cassavie[10] and making bread., then the *Negroes,* we imploy for that purpose, as also for making Mobbie:[11] the men we use for footmen, and killing of fish, which they are good at; with their own bowes and arrows they will go out; and in a dayes time, kill as much fish, as will serve a family of a dozen persons, two or three dayes, if you can keep the fish so long. . . .

Description of the Barter of an English Indentured Servant

There was a Planter in the Island, that came to his neighbour, and said to him, neighbour I hear you have lately bought good store of ser-

---

[10] *Cassavie:* A bread whose flour is made from the cassava plant, which grows in the West Indies.
[11] *Mobbie:* A liquor made from sweet potatoes.

vants, out of the last ship that came from *England,* and I hear withall, that you want provisions, I have great want of a woman servant; and would be glad to make an exchange; If you will let me have some of your womans flesh, you shall have some of my hogsflesh; so the price was set a groat a pound for the hogsflesh, and six-pence for the Womans flesh. The scales were set up, and the Planter had a Maid that was extream fat, lasie, and good for nothing, her name was *Honor;* The man brought a great fat sow, and put it in one scale, and *Honor* was put in the other; but when he saw how much the maid outweighed his Sow, he broke off the bargain, and would not go on: though such a case as this, may seldom happen, yet 'tis an ordinary thing there, to sell their servants to one another for the time they have to serve; and in exchange, receive any commodities that are in the Island . . .

MORGAN GODWYN

From *The Negro's and Indians Advocate, Suing for Their Admission into the Church*

   Morgan Godwyn, like Richard Ligon, stresses the hypocrisy of denying African slaves Christian religion. However, it is important to note that Godwyn sees the model of Christian submission as the ideal means of enforcing authority over slaves, remarking elsewhere in his book that "far . . . from encouraging Resistance," religious teaching "allows them not the *liberty* of *Gainsaying,* or making undutiful replies to their Masters." The possibility that his countrymen might be cajoled into such perfect obedience, of course, is one of Oroonoko's greatest fears.

   Godwyn, who had spent some time in Virginia and Barbados, concludes his book with an elaborate scheme for settling Anglican ministers in the American colonies in order to give religious instruction to Africans and to suppress their heathen customs. Under his plan, ministers would have the power to ensure that no slaves were required to work on Sunday — a suggestion that was obviously unlikely to meet with support among the planters. Godwyn was one of only a few seventeenth-century proponents of Christianization for slaves; Richard Baxter, who challenged the slave trade more directly in *Chapters from a Christian Directory* (1673), was another. In the course of the eighteenth century, their views would gain much broader support, providing the basis for a wide array of missionary programs and figuring prominently in the burgeoning abolitionist movement.

The text is excerpted from the first edition of *The Negro's and Indians Advocate, Suing for Their Admission into the Church* (London: Printed for the author by J. D., 1680) 106, 143–46.

The *absolute* necessity of a *Christian's* promoting *Christianity*, even in despite of the greatest Difficulties and Inconveniencies being shewed, I come now in the last place to examin those very *Inconveniencies*, and to try whether they are indeed such, as they are *pretended*; or whether the continuance of those practices for whose *Justification* this Plea was invented, will not upon a due trial be found more *inconvenient* and prejudicial to our *Interest:* At least whether *Christianity*, notwithstanding these *pretences* (whether true or false) may not, upon the score of its *innocent* deportment, and unquestionable *blamelessness* in all Ages, without the least hazard to any Man's *just Right and Interest*, be afforded a free course, and find entertainment amongst *all* Conditions and Degrees without *prejudice* or *offence* to any. . . .

And thus our dangers from the *Privileges* being cleared, I proceed to do the like by the *Prohibitions, viz.* Of their *Polygamy*, their *Sunday-Labour;* frequent *repudiating* and changing their Wives, usual amongst most *Heathens.* As also their Idolatrous Dances and Revels, permitted and practised by them (so often as they can steal any time from their Work) *even upon that Day*, whose *Morality* (to the danger of straining it to the height of a *Jewish Sabbath*) hath been so much, for these many Years, insisted on amongst the *English*, with other such *Recreations* and *Customs*, by them brought out of *Africa*, and here connived at, because either *gainful to their Owners*, (such as the first) or grateful to the *poor Slave* (such as the latter) *without prejudice to their Masters Business.* None of which yet are heard of amongst the *Virginia Negro's*, tho alike *Gentiles* with these: And there not laid aside or forbidden, but forgotten by disuse.

Now might not this cause one to stand still and to admire, how such things should come to be, I do not say, *justified*, but even permitted, or endured by Christians: Who, as before they were not ashamed to begrudge the poor Wretches *thus spending their strength and days in their Service*, even a miserable Subsistence, for they expect no more: So here they alledge things palpably wicked, as a pretence for a worse and more dangerous *Frugality*, if I may so call it, *viz. The starving of their Souls.* Contenting themselves to give a free course to *Turkish* and

Heathenish Licentiousness, and even to all *Irreligion* and *Atheism*, for a wretched false Gain; but in the mean time *blindly overlooking the many greater Advantages, which are the undoubted fruit of true Christianity.*

For can it be believed that the small trouble of *Christenings*, to be had without *Fees*; as also of *Catechizing, Marrying, Churching*, and *Burying* of them (the consenting to *which* will one Day, like *Nehemiah's* good deeds for *Jerusalem*, or *Tobit's* charity for the Dead,[1] be our greatest comfort;) can equal, or any way be compared with the solid benefit and satisfaction arising from the unquestionable *Fidelity* and *Integrity of a vertuous Servant?* Can a few hours *Sunday-Work* (for I plead not the other *Holy-days*) be alike beneficial to us, as the same spent in learning them their Duty, or *as the blessing of God* upon us for it in the ensuing *Week?* Can *starving, or working them to Death,* (for it cannot be denied but that these are too frequent) be equally *profitable with keeping them alive* for our future Service? Or can we believe it alike *expedient;* or conducive to our *Interest,* to be put each Year to purchase and train up *Raw, Ignorant,* and *unhandy Barbarians,* with preserving for our *occasions,* the tried and more experienced, by good *usage* of them? 'Tis true, you may alledg the temptation and *certainty of the present Profit,* with the uncertainty of *future Contingencies,* the possibility of their out-living those *hardships,* and of their dying also under *better usage;* yet surely this is but a *brutish Plea,* and at best not a little savouring of their *Providence,* who *devour all at one Meal, as uncertain whether ever they should live to enjoy another.*

As for the charge of *Instructing* them, if they think it too much to undertake themselves, (which the *holy Patriarchs* did not) they cannot but know the same Person who attends this work upon *Sundays* or *Saturdays Afternoon,* (which last was formerly allowed to both Slaves and Servants, when this *Island* was less Wealthy and Populous, than now it is) may be further useful in the rest of the Week particularly in teaching their *own,* and the neighbouring *Youth,* (or possibly in keeping their *Accounts,* &c.) which would prevent a greater Charge, together with the hazard of transporting them to *Europe* for *Education:*

---

[1] *Nehemiah's good deeds for Jerusalem, or Tobit's charity for the Dead:* Nehemiah organized the Jews and directed them in the rebuilding of the walls of Jerusalem as a defense against their enemies (see Neh. 3.1–4.23). At a time when most of the Israelites in Ninevah were not following the laws prescribed by Moses, Tobit attended to the proper burial of Jews left exposed by the king (see Tob. 1.17–18). The book of Tobit is considered apocryphal by some churches.

Not omitting that so much (beyond the *dangers* of the *Sea,* and of different *Climes*) worse mischief of their being betimes *Debauched;* scarce to be avoided at so great a distance from their *Parents care and inspection,* as in many Instances is too apparent. And this also might be a means in some measure to put a stop to that *Barbarism,* which through the want of *Schools,* do threaten the irrecoverable *Ruine* of all our *Hopes in them.*

As for the danger of our *Slaves release from Servitude* thereby, to what I have said before, I shall only add, That if they suspect the *Validity* of their own *Laws,* the contrary to which I have always found; no doubt but his *Majesty,* and the Honourable houses of *Parliament,* will have their Ears open to their just Fears and Complaints, thus arising from a pious sense of their *Duty,* and the safety of their Peoples *Souls,* no less than of their own; so as to fortifie their *Interest* with as good Laws and Fences, as themselves shall in *Reason* propose, on their *Omnipotencie* (pardon the expression, *Rulers* can do much within their proper *Spheres*) can *create,* or give life to. Nor let that over-proud fear of thereby acknowledging (*what they cannot possibly avoid*) their dependence upon *England,* nor that of rendring the rest of their Laws, with their *Legislative Power* (which, I confess, some would fain extend beyond its *due bounds*) questionable, be any impediment thereto, since neither the one nor the other are more *secured* without it: And these two being known to be *different things* in Law, *viz.* To corroborate *an old,* and *create a new Title.*

THOMAS TRYON

From *A Discourse in Way of Dialogue, between an Ethiopean or Negro-Slave and a Christian*

Thomas Tryon (1634–1703) was a genuine seventeenth-century eccentric — a pacifist, vegetarian, and mystic — who had a strong influence on Benjamin Franklin, among others. An autodidact who worked as a shepherd before moving to London and apprenticing himself to a hatter, Tryon went on several trips to Barbados in the 1660s, mainly to explore new avenues in the hatting trade. Though he took up writing late in life — he was forty-eight when his first book was published — Tryon wrote widely and voluminously, addressing such issues as dietetics, Pythagorean philosophy, domestic economy and medicine, and the psychology of dreams and insanity. His economic defense of the sugar trade is printed in Chapter 5. Aphra Behn would almost certainly have read Tryon's work, and she was probably friendly with him, since in 1685 she wrote a prefatory poem to his temperance tract, *The Way to Health, Long Life, and Happiness.*

Here, Tryon takes up the issue of Christian hypocrisy. Like Ligon, he implies that the so-called pagan leads a more Christian way of life than his master by following Nature's dictates.

The text is excerpted from "A Discourse in Way of Dialogue, between an Ethiopean or Negro-Slave and a Christian, that was his Master in America," in the first edition of Tryon's *Friendly Advice to the Gentleman-Farmers of the East and West Indies* (London: Printed by Andrew Sowle, 1684) 159–63, 164–65, 167, 168, 169–70, 175–76, 177–78, 181–83, 183–84, 187–90, 193–94, 194–96, 221.

Negr. First, I admire the *Excellency of your Doctrine,* and the *wonderful Mystery* contained therein; it undoubtedly surpasseth all other Religions in the World, as much as the Sun's Light doth that of a *Glow-Worm:* It seems to me to be an *open Gate* into *Paradise,* and a *Leaf* of the *Tree of Life;* so agreeable to the Nature and Glory of the *great God,* so suitable to the condition of *weak Man;* no wise Person can make any scruple of the things you have delivered, they command assent; for they proceed from a *true Root.*

But then I cannot but also much wonder and admire that you *Christians* live and walk so wide from, and *contrary* unto all those undeniable Truths, and holy Rules, so that what you preach with your *Tongues,* you pull down with your *Hands,* and your daily Conversation gives the Lye to your Profession.

Mast. You now grow *Sawcy* thus, to upbraid us; we have indeed *our Failings,* but I hope we do not walk to *Retrograde* as you talk of: What instances can you produce to maintain so general a Charge?

Negr. I intended not to *upbraid* you, but to satisfie my self, for perhaps you may have *some Reason* that I do not know of, why you *act contrary* to what you teach; nor do I say that all, and *every Christian* does so there may be Hundreds and Thousands that *I* am not acquainted with and there are some that I know, of whom I cannot say, but that in a very great measure they live according to that righteous Doctrine; but for the generality or major part, I must say, That in all, and every of the aforesaid Points by you mentioned, the whole

Tenour of their Ways, and the continual Practice of their Lives, is directly contrary to the same: And since you command me to instance Particulars, I shall endeavour it in some of the chief.

1: You say, that Christian Religion teacheth *to Fear the Lord,* that created Heaven and Earth: The truth of this we make no doubt of; but how can we believe, that *very many* who go under the Name of *Christians* do obey this Voice of Wisdom, since they so lightly and vainly use the *Name of God* in their Triffling; and wicked Talk; and boldly Swear by it (and that for the most part falsly too) in their ordinary Conversation, contrary to his express Commands; nay, not a few, will commonly challenge the great God to *Damn* or *Confound* them, with divers other Blasphemies; And do you call this *Fearing the Lord?*

2. To *be Merciful,* and *do as you would be done by,* you in the next place assign, as a grand and important point of *Christianity;* but where shall we find it? We cannot perceive any thing of *Mercy* to dwell in your Hearts; for you commit *Oppression* with Violence; and that which you call *Trade* or *Traffick* (as 'tis manag'd amongst you) is little better than an Art of *Circumventing* one another; and you practise all sorts of *Cruelty,* not only on the inferior Creatures, but also on those of your *own Kind,* else what makes us your *Slaves,* and to be thus Lorded and Tyrannized over by you? In a word, not only *We,* but the whole Creation groans under your heavy Burthens; & yet you tell us of your *Mercy* and *good Nature* and boast of your Christian *Charity.*

3. You acknowledge, this divine Religion requires of you to be *Sober* in Meats and Drinks; *&c.* and not to indulge Nature with things Superfluous: But does it not appear by your Conversation, that you never regard its Counsel, since your Wayes are directly opposite? Do not we see it a common Practice amongst the *Christians,* to drink to *Drunkenness,* and eat to *Superfluity* and *Gluttony?* . . .

And thus in defiance to the Laws of your Religion, and to his own Personal hurt, one great *over grown Christian* shall spend as much in *one* Day, to gratifie his Lusts or Vanity, as an *Hundred or Two* of his poor *Slaves* can get by their sore Labour and Sweat. And as for *Exercises,* there is rarely here in this Island any of the *Christians* that will labour, except pure Necessity constrain them to it but you *lay heavy Burthens* on us. . . . So that you make it a *Genteel* Quality, and honourable, to break and violate that great Command of the Creator in the beginning, which I have heard is recorded by a most famous Prophet of the *Jews,* and whom you also receive, viz. *That Man should*

---

[1] *Man . . . Sweat of his Brows:* Cf. Genesis 3.19 ("By the sweat of your face you shall eat bread").

get his Bread by the Sweat of his Brows;[1] which yet amongst the more *Noble Christians,* as you call your selves, is counted a *poor, low, Base* and *shameful* thing.

What *Heathen People* (as you call them) are there in the whole World, that more *pamper their Carcasses,* and indulge themselves like you, with things that are not needful, nor convenient? Do you not invent an hundred Superfluities and needless *Toys,* to gratifie your own, and your Childrens Pallates and Sensuality? the Wind, forsooth! must not blow upon them; and as if the Earth were not good enough to bear them, nor their Legs made to carry them, you provide *Horses* and *Coaches* for them, or we poor *Slaves,* must lugg them about, who are as well able to go as we. . . .

4. You mention that avoidance of *Evil Communications,*[2] as another duty of your Religion, which we *Heathens* do acknowledge, and therefore we have a Proverb amongst us; when any use lewd Discourse, to bid them, *Wash their Mouthes with Water;* but we have observed, that amongst the *Christians* there is nothing more frequent than *Evil Communications,* whensoever any Number meet together, are not your Discourses *vain, idle* and *frothy;* and oft-times such as no *modest Ear* can hear without tingling forth Horror and Indignation? Most of it tending to Debauchery, or injuring the good Name of Persons absent, *Jesting, Lying, Vapouring.*[3] . . .

5. You say, *You are required to observe Purity, and the natural Rules of Cleanness, and to avoid all appearance of Evil:* Which indeed is no inconsiderable point in Nature and Religion, but as far as we have been able to observe, you practise the quite contrary; For do not you appoint *set Meetings,* and make great Feasts? to which you invite the Rich, that will invite you again, where you drink to Drunkenness, and eat to Gluttony, roaring all the while like *mad Bulls,* and mixing your Food with horrid Oaths, and vain Discourses, the fear of the great Creator being banisht from your Hearts, nor any pity shewn to us your poor Vassals, that endure the heat of the day, and are ready to fall and faint under those heavy Burthens laid upon us, and would rejoyce to partake of *the Crumbs* that fall from your Tables, which you will not afford & yet spend *our Sweat,* and the Labours of our Hands, in all kinds of Wantonness and Superfluity, by which many of you contract such grievous Diseases' both to Body and Mind, that they become themselves more miserable then us their poor Slaves. . . .

---

[2] *Evil Communications:* See 1 Corinthians 15.33 ("evil communications corrupt good manners").

[3] *Vapouring:* Bragging, blustering.

On the contrary, to *believe* and know (as you say) *That the Lord will Retaliate every man according to his Work,* is a most true and necessary Principle; but if *Christians* did so, surely they could not, nor would do as they do; For what kind of *Rewards* and *Returns* do or can you expect for all your Oppressions to us your poor Vassals? For do not you oppress us at your pleasure, *beat, whip, over-labour,* and *half-starve* us, and many of you scruple not to *Kill us* for a small Offence, and possibly for none at all, but in your Drunkenness to satiate your fierce devilish Passions? Nor do our tender *Children,* and dear *Wives* escape your Violence. Now if Retaliation be one point of your Christian Doctrine, and every man shall be rewarded according to his Works, then what a *sad Reckoning* will you have to make, when God shall arise to visit for these things? And you would not certainly adventure upon those things, which you must pay *so dear* for, either in this World, or that which is to come, if you were sufficiently sensible of the Compensation that must be made for the same. . . .

11. How well you regulate your *Passions* (which is another thing you say Christian Doctrine teaches you) all the World sees, and we often *feel*; the Sea when agitated with contrary Winds; it throws up *Dirt* and *Sand* from the bottom of the Deep, and spits its *froth* up towards Heaven, is not more disorderly or dangerous to come near, than you are, when the least thing happens contrary to your Minds. . . .

Lastly, Whereas you say, your Christian Doctrine enjoyns you to be *merciful to all the Inferior Creatures,* and to *use them with Compassion,* and *avoid all kind of Oppression and Violence* to those of your own kind: How contrary most *Christians* act hereunto, our own *woful Experience* has too sadly informed us, that there is little or no Mercy or Compassion dwells in your Hearts; for on every small occasion you will not only *beat* and *oppress* us, but some of you count it no more Sin in their drunken fits to *Murther us,* than to kill their *Horse,* or their *Dog;* but let them know, we are humane *rational Souls,* and as much the *Image of God* as themselves, and want none of the noble Faculties, therefore our *innocent Blood* will equally call for *Vengeance,* and as powerfully as if you had killed one of the pretended *Christians.* The Voice of God in Nature is the same; and it is not your custom of *Killing* will make it the more *lawful* or excusable in that day, when Accounts and Retaliation must be made, every Principle then apprehends and comprehends its own Children; those that have immers'd, or precipitated themselves through Violence, into the fierce Anger and wrathful Principle, shall be therein captivated even to Eternity: It is not good Words, long Prayers, and fair Speeches, that will break or untye the wrathful Net, which men all their Lives have been tying; but look what Principle has carried the upper Dominion in the Heart, to that Kingdom you belong. . . .

Thus, Master *Christian* have I briefly shewed, that in all the particulars by you mentioned, the generality of you *Christians* do act the clean contrary; what then do you boast of, and wherein are you better than we? Only that you pretend to understand more, and *do* less, and so deserve the greater Condemnation. Will you make us believe, that those men have *any Religion,* who have *no God?* or have they indeed *a God,* who prefer their *Lusts,* or *Wealth,* or *Honour,* or any thing in the World before him, and his holy Commands; Can we think that you know what it is to *believe* that there is a God, and a Life to come. . . .

Mast. I have given you, *Sambo,* a large liberty of Prating' and you have used it very confidently. How come you so *wonderous Wise?* How dare you upbraid us that have the Light of the Gospel? Or indeed why should we mind any thing such *Heathens* as you can say or talk of?

Negr. We boast not of *Wisdom* what I have said, arises from plain *matter of Fact,* which no Person whom our Creator hath endued with a rational Soul, can be ignorant of if he do not wilfully quench and extinguish in himself that Light which enlightneth every man that cometh into the World, and which one of your own Prophets calls, *The Candle of the Lord.*[4] Nor are we altogether such ignorant *dark Heathens* as you call and suppose us; for many of the *Christians* do not esteem, nor look on us any otherwise, or better than *Dogs;* for tell me, I pray *boon Master!* what difference has our Creator made between you and us? Hath he endued you with any particular Quality or Property more then we are furnished with? The Members of our Bodies, the Faculties of our Minds, our *senses* and all the Furniture of Nature, are equal, and the same in us as in you: We are not *Beasts,* as you count, and use us, but *rational Souls,* and in us is contained the true Nature and Properties of all Elements, and created things; Nor do we contemn or slight the *Light of the Gospel,* as you call it, but we wonder at you that so much *talk* of it and so *little practise* the good Rules of Life contained therein. Besides, since you are pleased to grant us the Liberty to plead our own Cause, we might tell you, that we have the *same Gospel* that you so much talk of, written in our Hearts, and doing by Nature the things that are written in the Law, being without

---

[4] *The Candle of the Lord:* See Proverbs 20.23 ("The spirit of man is the candle of the Lord").

the Law, are a Law unto our selves,[5] as one of your illuminated Prophets speaks: And if we do the things that are right in the sight of God, and walk in his innocent Law in Nature, according to *our measure* and *understanding,* we have so far discharged our Duty. . . .

As for our *Complexion,* 'tis the Livery of our Creator, the property of the Climate and Soil, wherein his good Providence disposed of us to be born and bred; we made not our selves *Black,* nor do you make your selves *White;* wherein then have you any thing to brag of above us? If for this cause you despise us, you at the same time despise that *adorable Power,* which is the Maker both of us and you: And though *White* be an Emblem of *Innocence,* yet there are *whited Walls* filled within with Filth and Rottenness; what is only *outward,* will stand you in no stead, it is the *inward Candor* that our Creator is well-pleased with, and not the outward; have a care therefore that you be not found as *black within,* as we are externally.

You upbraid us with eating *unclean Foods,* Carrion, Vermine, *&c.* But I pray, is it not your *Cruelty,* in not affording us what is sufficient to support Nature otherwise, that makes us do it? This is first to make us *Cripples,* and then beat us with our *Crutches* for being Lame. As for our poor Coverings or going Naked, as long as Man remained in the innocent State, he wanted no Garments; and you are forced to *Rob* several sorts of Creatures to cover your *Shame;* nor do you bring into the World any greater *Wardrobe* with you, than we do; nor have you occasion to carry out any more.

As for Order in *Marriages,* we have as much as you; for though Plurality of *Wives* is contrary to your Custom, it is not to *ours;* and he is no wise man that admires or contemns the various Customs of different Regions, any further than they contradict Nature: Now this Custom of *ours,* as it is be-friended with Examples amongst the antient *Patriarchs,* and the Laws of many Nations so renowned for Civility, as to esteem all others *Barbarians,* so it seems somewhat to agree with the Law of *Nature,* and to prevent Out-rage against Nature, it being not fit, nor *natural* for Men to meddle with their Wives when they are *Breeding;* or great with-child: However, these things are more of *Custom,* than any thing else, and we our selves esteem that man most *happy* that contents himself with *one Wife:* But you, although your Customs and Laws forbid *Poligamy,* and *Adultery,* yet whilst you

---

[5] *doing by Nature . . . a Law unto our selves:* Cf. Romans 2.14 ("when the Gentiles, which have not the law, do by nature the things contained in the law, these, having not the law, are a law unto themselves").

comply somewhat in the former, do make nothing, many of you, to violate the *latter,* as often as you can meet with an opportunity.

When you say, You hardly esteem of us so well as *Beasts;* we have Reason to believe you, from your cruel Usages, and not allowing us what is necessary for Food and Rest, which yet is to be wondred at, since if we are not worthy (forsooth!) to be your *Brethren,* we are however your *Money.* So that — this Cruelty towards us, doth savour more of *Envy,* than of *Christianity* or *Frugality.* . . .

Mast. Sambo! I have hearkened attentively, and well considered your Discourse, which carries with it such Evidence and Reason; that I must acknowledge I am convinced that our former Conduct towards you, has not been agreeable to our Religion, or common Equity; therefore for my own part, you shall see by *future Usage,* what *Impression* your Words have made upon me, nor shall I be wanting to acquaint *others* with what you have offered — It grows late, therefore you were best be gone, and betake your self *to Rest.*

EDWARD LITTLETON

From *The Groans of the Plantations*

Edward Littleton (1626–c.1696) went to Barbados in 1666 as secretary to William, Lord Willoughby, who became governor following the death of his brother Francis. Within seven years, Littleton had acquired six hundred acres of land, and he served in a number of official capacities, sitting on a commission to investigate the laws of the colony, holding office as an elected representative, and acting as a judge from 1670 until 1683. He then returned to London, where he worked as an agent on behalf of the colony. Besides his treatise on the economics of the sugar trade, first published in 1689 and reprinted in 1698, Littleton wrote books on public transportation, military operations, and other, broader aspects of finance and economic regulation.

Littleton's pamphlet, written to garner sympathy for the planters, nevertheless gives frightful details of the suffering and danger endured by "Our Negroes, which cost us so dear" (376). Judging from these contemporary writings on the West Indies, the horrors of plantation life depicted at the end of *Oroonoko* do not seem exaggerated. Moreover, Behn can be seen as typical of her seventeenth-century contemporaries in noting such misery and brutality without drawing the conclusion that slavery should be abolished.

The text is taken from the first edition of *The Groans of the Plantations, or, a True Account of their Grievous and Extreme Sufferings by the Heavy Impositions upon Sugar and other Hardships. Relating more particularly to the Island of Barbados* (London: Printed by M. Clark, 1689) 19–20.

If the constant Charge of a Plantation is terrible, the Casualties do not come behind. For let a Planter be never so careful, he must ly open to many and various Accidents: and like *Job's* Messengers, one in the neck of another,[1] his People will bring him Tidings of continual Losses and Disasters.

We cannot say that Horses and Cattle are much more casual with us, then they are in other places. Only our loss is the greater, in regard they cost us much dearer. But our Canes, on which we rely and which are our Estate, are too often burnt down before our faces when they are ready to cut. They are then like Tinder: and if a Fire get amongst them, a whole Field of them is consumed in a few Minutes. Also our Boyling-houses and Still-houses are very subject to Fire.

Sometimes we suffer by extreme Droughts, and sometimes by continual violent Rains. And a sudden Gust will tear or maim our Windmills. But if a *Hurricane* come, it makes a desolation: and puts us to begin the World anew. The damage it does the Planter is sometimes so great, that the profit of divers years must go to repair it.

Our Negroes, which cost us so dear, are also extremely casual. When a man hath bought a parcel of the best and ablest he can get for money; let him take all the care he can, he shall lose a full third part of them, before they ever come to do him service. When they are season'd, and used to the Country, they stand much better, but to how many Mischances are they still subject? If a Stiller[2] slip into a Rum-Cistern, it is sudden death: for it stifles in a moment. If a Mill-feeder be catch't by the finger, his whole body is drawn in, and he is squeez'd to pieces. If a Boyler get any part into the scalding Sugar, it sticks like Glew, or Birdlime, and 'tis hard to save either Limb or Life. They will

---

[1] *Job's Messengers, one in the neck of another:* In quick succession, Job's messengers bring him news about the loss of his herds, his servants, and his sons (see Job 1.13–8).

[2] *Stiller:* I.e., a distiller; in this case, one who makes rum.

quarrell, and kill one another, upon small occasions: by many Accidents they are disabled, and become a burden: they will run away, and perhaps be never seen more: or they will hang themselves, no creature knows why. And sometimes there comes a Mortality amongst them, which sweeps a great part of them away.

When this happens, the poor Planter is in a hard condition: especially if he be still indebted for them. He must have more Negroes, or his Works must stand, and he must be ruin'd at once. And he cannot procure them without contracting new Debts; which perhaps he shall never be able to work out.

These are some of the Charges and Casualties that attend Plantations. It would be too tedious to number them all; and they are hardly to be numbered.

JOHN GABRIEL STEDMAN

From *Narrative of a Five Years Expedition against the Revolted Negroes of Surinam*

This selection, excerpted from John Gabriel Stedman's *Narrative of a Five Years Expedition against the Revolted Negroes of Surinam,* first published in 1796, takes us back to Suriname approximately 110 years after the events of *Oroonoko.* The Dutch colony still has a number of English plantations, but it is besieged by former slaves and their descendants, who have escaped into the "bush" and established large settlements of their own. The government of the colony had made many treaties with these communities, but after one treaty too many was broken, an alliance of "revolted negroes" undertook a concerted campaign against the plantations, leading the Estates General of Holland to send a military expedition against them in 1772. Stedman (1744–1797) was in that expedition, and he records its progress, or lack thereof, with an odd blend of admiration for the enemy, contempt for his officers, horror at the brutality of his job, and devotion to his "duty." Stedman was well read and had a taste for the aesthetics of the sublime and a pride in his "sensibility" that imbue his narrative of warfare and descriptions of the country with the romanticism of his age. He lived with a mixed-race slave, who bore him a son, and much of his book recounts his attempts to emancipate his wife and child.

Stedman's book was extraordinarily successful, quickly undergoing translations into Dutch, German, French, and Swedish. The text is excerpted from Richard and Sally Price's edition, based on Stedman's 1790 manuscript (Baltimore: Johns Hopkins UP, 1988) 389, 390–92, 394–95, 397–98, 400, 404, 405–06, 407–10, 411. The editors retained Stedman's unusual punctuation, for example, his use of dashes and slashes in place of commas.

The *Rebels* Flush'd with their Late Victory over Capt *Meyland* And his Party, Whether to Dare Fourgeoud,[1] or to intimidate his Troops, being Well Apprised by their Spies that he was at Barbacoeba, had the Assurance lately to set fire to all the huts in two Different Camps Which had been left Standing by his Circumbulating Padrols — and While they were Shouting and Hallowing all the night, but this however proved rather a Spur to Rouze him than otherwise, and enraged the Old man so much that he now Swore he would be revenged of them *Coute qui Coute.*[2] . . .

Having frequently Mentioned the *Rebel* Negro's, With whom we were now Certain to Have a Recounter, I here Present the Reader With the figure of one of these People upon his Guard, /As Alarmed by Supposing to hear a Rusling Amongst the Bushes, And a Couple of rangers at a Distance Ready to take him by Surprise — The first is Armed With a firelock; and a Hatchet, his hair /though Woolly/ may be Observ'd to be Plaited Close to his head, by way of Distinction from the *Rangers* or any other Stragling Negroes, who are not Accepted yet Amongst them, And his beard is Grown to a Point, like that of All the Africans when they have no opportunity to Shave — The Whole dress of this Man Consists in a Cotton Sheet Negligently tied Across his Shoulders, Which Protects him against the Rayn, And Serves him as a Bed to lay Down and Sleep, in the most Obscure Places he Can find;

[1] *Whether to Dare Fourgeoud:* Whether to threaten Col. Fourgeoud, who was in charge of Stedman's regiment of marines.
[2] *Coute qui coute:* At any cost; literally "cost what it costs" (French).

The frontispiece to John Gabriel Stedman's *Narrative of a Five Years Expedition against the Revolted Negroes of Surinam,* first published in 1796, expresses the author's typical uncertainty about the justness of the cause he served. The engraving was executed by Francesco Bartolozzi, a Royal Academician and one of four well-known engravers to work on Stedman's book.

"From different Parents, different Climes we came?
At different Periods;" Fate still rules the same.
Unhappy Youth while bleeding on the ground;
'Twas Yours to fall__ but Mine to feel the wound!

London, Published Decr 1st 1794, by J.Johnson, St Pauls Church Yard.

the Rest are his Camisa,[3] his Pouch which is made of Some Animals Skin — A few Cotton Strings for Ornament Around his Ancles and Wrists, and a Superstitious *Obia*[4] or *Amulet* tied About his Neck, in Which case he Places all his hope and Confidence — The Scull and Ribbs are Supposed to be Some of his enemies Scattered upon a Sandy Savannah.

The two *Rangers* Who make theyr Appearance at a Distance may be Distinguished by their *Red* Caps, While I must Observe that the Rebels many times have Avail'd themselves of Capturing one of these Scarlet Distinctions, Which by Clapping on their own heads, in an Engagement, has not only saved their lives, but given them an Opportunity to Shoot their Enemies —

Another Stratagem of theirs has Sometimes been Discovered, Viz that Fire Arms being Scarce Amongst them Numbers have intermix'd in the Crow'd, With only a *Crooked Stick* Shaped Something like a Musket to Supply it in Appearance, Which has even more than once had the Effect of Preventing a proper Defence by The Plantation Slaves, When they Came to Ransack the Estates, who were thus Struck With a Panick, And Whose Courage Dampt, with the Show of Such Superiors in Number, Allow'd the Rebels Calmly /after Burning the Houses/ to Carry Away even their Own Wives, and their daughters — ...

I now turned into my Hammock! Where Reflecting on all the Wonders and Wonderful Bussel of this World, while the Silver moon Glittering through the Verdure of the Trees, Added Beauty to the Quietness, and Solemnity of the Scene. I fell most perfoundly Asleep; but not Longer than till About Midnight when we All awaked in hells Darkness, and a heavy Shower of Rayn, by the Hallooing, and Shouting of the Rebel Negroes, who also Discharged Several Musket shot, but not any at our Camp, at Which we were Extremely Astonish'd, but Could not in the Least understand the Meaning — This Disturbance Continued till near Day Break having Expected ev'ry Moment to be Surrounded When we unlask'd [unlashed] our Hammocks and Proceeded on our March Due N toward the Place, where by Conjecture the Hallooing noise had Come from, While we were Extremely fatigued for want of Sleep, Especially Colonel Fourgeoud who Could hardly Support himself by the Ague[5] — We had not Marched 2 Miles

---

[3] *Camisa:* A kind of shirt.

[4] *Obia:* I.e., obeah, an amulet or charm held to possess magical powers (like the fetishes mentioned in the letter by John Carter in Part Two, Chapter 3).

[5] *Ague:* A fever accompanied by shivering and sweating.

when I having the Van Guard, a Rebel Negro Sprung up at my feet, from under a Shrub, Where he had been Conceal'd Asleep, But who /while we were forbid to fire upon Straglers, and Without he firing at me/ Disappeared like a Stag Amongst the Underwood — of this I no Sooner made Report to the Old Hero, than Swearing he was a Spy, Which I Believe was true, he Shook off his illness and Redoubled his Pace with Double Vigour. /Col: *Seibourgh*[6] Damning me for Marching too fast/ but our Pursuit was to no Purpose at least this day, Since About 1 OClock we were Led in a Bogue, that we Could hardly get out of, And thus obliged to return back to our Last nights Lodgings. . . . Hanibal,[7] Who Observeing that we Should Certainly see the Enemy to morrow Asked me, if I knew in What Manner Negroe Engaged Against Negroe, having Answered in the Negative he gave me the following Relation —

> Massera /Said he/ Both Parties are Divided in small Companys of 8 or 10 Men & Commanded by one Captain With a horn Such as this /he showing me his/ By that they do every Thing I Want, and either fight or Run Away, but if they go to fight they Seperate immediately, lay down on the Ground, And keep firing at The flash of each others Pans through the Green — While each Warrior is Supported by two Negroes *unarm'd,* the one to fill in his Place if he is kill'd, And the other to Carry Away the Dead Body, And Prevent it from falling in the hands of the Adversary — . . .

Capt: Hanibal having Mention'd to me Also, that *Bony*[8] was Supposed to be Present in Person Amongst the Adjoining Rebels, Who was born in the forrest amongst them, Notwithstanding his being a Mullato, but Which was Occasion'd by his Mother Escaping to the Woods from the ill treatment of her Master, by whom she was Pregnant — . . .

This Sable Warrior[9] further made me Acquainted With the names of Several Rebel Commanders, besides bony, And Against whom he had frequently Battled for the Europeans Such as *Quammy* Who was the Chief of a Seperate Gang, and had no Connection with any Others —

---

[6] *Col: Seibourgh:* Commander of another regiment of marines accompanying Stedman's regiment; Stedman strongly disliked him.

[7] *Hanibal:* Presumably named after the Carthaginian general (247–c. 183 B.C.E.), a masterful strategist probably best known for leading his troops through the Alps (see p. 231).

[8] *Bony:* Boni was the leader of one of the groups of "revolted negroes" that Stedman's regiment was attempting to suppress.

[9] *This Sable Warrior:* I.e., Captain Hanibal.

Coro-Mantyn Cojo–Arico–And *Joly Coeur*–the two Last being Celebrated Captains, Whose revenge was insatiable Against the Christians,
Particularly *Joly Coeur* & who had great reason indeed–he Also mention'd the noted rebel Negroe Chief *Baron* Whom he Believed was
now Serving under the great Bony —

The names of the Captain Rebel Settlements he Said were the fol-
lowing, Viz Some Already Destroyed, some in View, And some of
Which only the Appellation was Discovered, but all which I thought
so verry *Sentimental* that /as helping to illusidate our ideas of the
Negro Nation/ I have thought Proper to give them a Place in this
Narrative together with their translations and Meaning into English
Viz —

> Boucoo — It shall moulder before it Shall be taken,
> Gado Saby — God alone knows it & no Person else —
> Cofaay — Come try me–if you be men —
> Tessee See — Take a tasting–if you have a liking —
> Mele me — Do disturb me–if you Dare —
> Boosy Cray — The Woods Lament —
> Me Salasy — I Shall be Taken —
> Kebree me — Hide me O ye Surrounding Verdure —

The others were —

> Quami Condre — From the name of the Chief
> Pinenburgh — From the Pins [palisades?] which formerly Surrounded it
> Caro Condre — From the indian Corn or Maiz it Produced
> Reisee Condre — From the Quantity of Rice it afforded

Such were the names of the African Warriors And their Settlements,
And now in the hopes of a Glorious Victory — viz to do good without
Committing Cruelties I Shaked hands with the Black Captain Hanibal,
and fell most Profoundly Asleep by fatigue, /as I have said/ in a Dark
Gloomy night. With heavy Rayn, during Which Time I Dreamt of
nothing but blood and Goare[10] fire and Smoak &c — . . .

We now Vigorously redoubled our Pace till About 12, OClock
when two more Musquet Shot were Fired by an Advance Guard of the
Enemy as a Signal to *Bony* of our Approach — & A Little again after
which we Came to a fine field with Rice india Corn &c — Viz. Major
Medler, and Myself, with the Van Guard, and a Party of the Rangers;
We here made a Halt for the *two* Colonels, And to Let up the Long
rear some of Whom were at Least 2 Miles Behind us; However in

[10] *Goare:* I.e., gore.

A Negro hung alive by the Ribs to a Gallows.

One of sixteen plates engraved by William Blake for Stedman's book, three of which show tortured slaves. Although Stedman was not an abolitionist, his disgust at Suriname slave society and his depictions of its excessive brutality made his work useful for the antislavery cause.

About half an hour we all got together, and we on[c]e more Proceeded by Cutting through a Small Defile of Wood, into Which we no sooner had Entered, than /Ding Dang/ the firing at last Commenced from every Side, the Rebels retiring and we Advancing till finally we Arrived, in the most beautiful Oblong Square field with Rice in full ripeness that ever I saw in my Life. And in Which Appear'd to our View the Rebel Town at a Distance in the form of an Amphitheatre Sheltered by the foliage of a few Ranks of Lofty Trees, Which they had left Standing, the whole Presenting a truly Romantick and Enchanting *Coup Doeuil*[11] to the Unconcerned Spectator — In this field the firing now lasted like one Continued Peal of Thunder for near 40 minutes, During Which time the Rangers Acted with Wonderful Skills, and Gallantry, While the White Soldiers were too much Animated — the one firing over the other at Random, Yet a few of Which I Saw with the Greatest Deliberation imitate the Blacks. . . .

I Received myself a Ball through between the Shirt And the Skin, And my Lieutenant M^r. *Decabanes* had the Sling of his Fusee Shot Away, While Severals were Wounded, some Mortally, but I Saw not a Single man Drop *dead* at my Feet to my Great Astonishment, And for Which I Will Presently Account — The Stratagem of the Enemy in Surrounding and interspearcing the field by the Large Trunks, and the Roots of Fallen Trees we met with made our Advancing verry Different and Dangerous & at the Back of Which Fortifications they lay Lurking, and firing upon us Without themselves Could be Materially hurted, And over Numbers of which Timbers we had to Scramble before we Could Come to the Town; However we kept Advancing, and While I thought this excellent Generalship in them their Superstitious Simplicity Surprised me much of Which I'l only Relate one instance — A poor Fellow trusting in his *Amulet* or *Charm,* by Which he thought himself invulnerable Advanced frequently on one of these trees, till very near us, And having Discharg'd his Piece Walk'd off the Way he Came, to Reload With the Greatest Confidence and Deliberation, till at Last one of my men — /an intrepid Walloon[12] named *Valet*/ With a Ball Broke the bone of his Thigh, And down he Came, now Crawling for Shelter Under the Same Tree which had Supported him but the Soldier Went up to him instantly and Placing the Muzzle of his Musket in his Mouth, blew out his Brains & in Which manner Severals of his Countrymen were Knock'd Down — So much for *Priest*

---

[11] *Coup Deouil:* Vision; literally, "strike of the eye" (French).
[12] *Walloon:* A member of a people living in an area now divided between southern Belgium and northern France.

Craft in every Country, While I honestly Acknowledge that in Place of like M^r. *Sparman* who kill'd 5 or 6 Hottentots at one Shot — Even at this Moment my Sensibility Got so much the Better of my Duty, And my Pity for these poor miserable, illtreated People Was such, that I Was rather induced to fire with Eyes Shut, like *Gill Blas* when he was amongst the Robbers,[13] than to take a Proper Aim, of Which I had Frequent Opportunities —

In Short being now about to Enter the Town, a Rebel Captain wearing a Tarnish'd Gold Laced hat, & Carrying a Wisp of flaming Straw in his hand Seeing Their Ruin inevitable, frustrated the Storm in our Presence by Setting the town on fire, And which by the Dryness of the Houses instantly Occasion'd One General Conflagration, When the Popping from the Wood immediately Seized [ceased]; And Which *Masterly Manocuvre* not only Prevented that Carnage to Which the Common Soldier is too Prone in the heat of Victory, but gave them The Opportunity of Retreating With their Wives & Children, and Carrying off the Best Lumber; While our Pursuit, And even our Falling of any of the Spoil, was at once also frustrated by the Ascending flames, And the Unfathomable Marsh Which we soon found to Surround them — Upon the Whole, to Draw this Picture Were a fruitless attempt, thus I Shall only say that the incessant Noise of the Firing, Mixed With a Confused Roaring, Hallooing, Damming and Sinking, the Shrill Sound of the Negro Horns, the Crackling of the Burning houses, the Dead & Wounded all Weltering in Blood, the Clowd of Dust in Which we were involved — And flames and Smoak Assending; Were such a Scene of Beautiful Horror /if I may use the Expression/ as would not be unworthy of the Pencil of Hogarth[14] — And Which I faintly tried to Represent in the Frontispiece.[15] Where I may be seen After the Heat of the Action Dejectedly Looking on the Body of an Unfortunate Rebel Negro Stretch'd at my feet — . . .

It was now About 3 OClock PM And we as I said Were Busied Slinging our Hammocks, When we were Suddenly Surprised by an Attack from the Enemy but Who After Exchanging a few Shot Were soon Repulsed — This unexpected Visit however Put us upon our

[13] *like Gill Blas . . . amongst the Robbers:* In book 1, chapter 9 of Alain-René Lesage's *Histoire de Gil Blas de Santillane* (4 vols., 1715–35), the hero is forced by a gang of robbers to participate in a gun fight; in order to avoid responsibility for murder, he looks away while firing.

[14] *Hogarth:* William Hogarth (1697–1764), English painter and engraver, famous for his "line of beauty," an S-like curve designed to represent the human form naturally and gracefully.

[15] *the Frontispiece:* Reproduced here on p. 379.

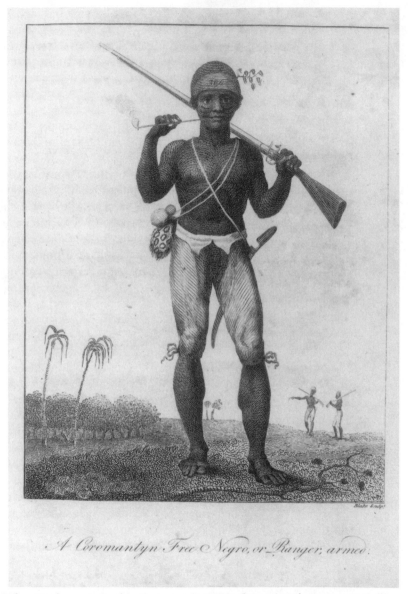

A Coromantyn Free Negro, or Ranger, armed.

When Stedman arrived in Suriname in 1773, the corps of "Rangers" — slave volunteers who were promised their freedom, a house and garden, and military pay to fight for the Dutch against the rebellious Maroons — had been in existence for one year.

Guard During the Whole night, by Allowing no fires to be Lighted and Doubling the Sentinels All around the Camp — Thus Situated I being Excessively fatigued /besides Several Others/ Ventured in my hammock, Where I soon fell asleep; but no Longer than the Space of an Hour; When my Faithful black Boy Qwacco Awaked me in pitch Darkness Crying, *Massera Massera Boosee Negro, Boosee Negro,* And hearing at the Same time a brisk firing, While the Balls Russled through the Branches About me, I imagined no other than that the Enemy was in The Middle of our Camp — in this Surprise, and not perfectly Awaked, I Started up With my fusee Cock'd, and /I not knowing where I Run/ Overset Qwacco, And next fell myself over two or three Bodies that lay on the Ground & Which I took to be Shot, but one of Which Damming me for a Son of a Bitch, told me if *I moved I was a Dead Man;* Col: Fourgeound with all his Troops laying flat on their Bellies, & Who had issued orders no more to fire, the Men having Spent most of theyr Ammonition the Preceeding Day — I took his Advice and soon Discovered him to be one of our Granadeers, Call'd Thompson — In this Situation we Continued to Lay Prostrate on our Arms till next morning, When the Sun Rose and During Which time a Most Abusive Dialogue Ensued, between the Rebels, and the Rangers, both Parties Cursing and Menacing each other at a Terrible Rate, the *first* Reproaching the others as being Poltroons,[16] and Betrayers of their Countrimen, Whom they Challenged the Next Day to Single Combat, Swearing they only Wanted to Wash their hands in the Blood of Such Scoundrels Who had been the Capital hands in Destroying their fine Settlement, While the *Rangers* Dam'd the Rebels for a Parcel of Pityful Skulking Rascals Whom they Would fight one to two in the Open field, if they Dared to Show theyr Ugly faces, that they had Deserted theyr Masters being too Lazy to Do theyr Work, while they /the Rangers/ Would Stand by the Europeans till they Died; After which they insulted each other by a kind of War hoop, then Sung Victorious Songs, And Sounded their Horns in Defiance; After Which once more the Popping Begun, And thus *Add Perpetuem*[17] the Whole night till Break of Day, the Musick of their Manly Voices &ᶜ resounding Amidst the Echoing Solitude and Surrounding woods with Redoubled force; And Which being Already dark and Gloomy Added Much to an Awful Scene of Pleasing dreadfulness; While According to

---

[16] *Poltroons:* Spiritless cowards.
[17] *Add Perpetuem:* "Endlessly" (Latin).

me the *tout ensemble*[18] Could not but inspire the Brave With thoughts of Fortitude and Heroism And Stamp the Trembling Coward for What he is —

At last Poor Fourgeoud Entered in The Conversation, by the help of myself, And Sergeant Fowler, Who spoke the Language, as his interpreters but Which Created more Mirth than I before heard in the Colony —

He Promised them Life, Liberty, Meat, Drink, and All they Wanted, but they Replied With a Loud Laugh, that they Wanted Nothing from him Who seemed a Half Starved Frenchman, Already Run Away from his own Country, that if he Would Venture to give them a Visit in Person, he should not be Hurted, And might Depend on not Returning With an Empty Belly — They Call'd to us that we were more to be Pitied than themselves, Who were only a Parcel of White Slaves, hired to be shot at, & Starved for 4 Pence a Day, And that they Scorned to Expend much of theyr Powder Upon such Scarcrows, Who had not been the Agressors by Driving them in the Forest & Only Obeying the Command of their Masters; but if the Planters and Overseers Dared to Enter the Woods themselves not a Soul of such Scoundrels should ever Return, no more than the *Rangers,* Some of Whom Might Depend on being Massacred that Very Day, or the Next, And Concluded by Swearing that *Bony* Should soon be the Governor of All the Colony — After this they Tinkled their Billhooks,[19] fired a Volly gave three Cheers Which were Answered by the Rangers, And all Dispearsed With the Rising Sun, to our great Satisfaction, being heartily tired of Such Company — Whatever small our Loss, While our Fatigues were Such that only The Hardships suffered since by the British Troops at Gibraltar,[20] could be Compared to them, Where Also /Notwithstanding the Contest Lasted such a Length of Time/ the Loss of Men by the Enemies fire was but verry inconsiderate; However the Mysterie of our Escape /Which Gibraltar was Owing to fortification/ was this Morning unrevel'd by the Surgeons, Who Dressing the Wounded Extracted in Place of Lead Bullets only *Pebbles* Coat *Buttons,* and *Silver* Coin, Which Could do us Little harm, Penetrating Scarce more than Skin Deep, While even Gold Could do themselves as Little Good in a Wild Forrest where they had nothing to buy for it — We Also Observed that Several of the Poor Rebel Negroes who had been shot, had their Pieces

---

[18] *tout ensemble:* "Whole combination" (French).

[19] *Billhooks:* Heavy, thick knives with a hooked end.

[20] *British Troops at Gibraltar:* They suffered serious losses while resisting an extended siege by the Spanish in 1779–83.

Supplied, only with the *Shard* of a Spa Watter Can in Place of a Flint Which Could not so Well answer the Effect &c — And this must Account for theyr Little Execution on the Bodies of their Cruel Beseigers, who never the Less were Pretty well Pepper'd with small Scars, and Contusions — Inconceivable are the many Shifts Which these People make in the Woods —

Inventas qui Vitam Excoluere Per Artes;
Who by invented arts have Life improved[21]

& Where in a State of *Tranquility* they Seemed as they had Said to us Want for Nothing — Being Plump and Fat at least Such we found those that had been Shot — For Instance *Game* and *fish* they Catch in Great Abundance by Artificial Traps and Springs, And Which they Preserve by Barbacuing, While with *Rice, Cassava,*[22] *Yams, Plantains,* and so on, theyr fields are ever over Stoked — *Salt* they make with the Ashes of the Palm trees like the *Gentoos* in the East Indies[23] — Or Use Red Pepper. We even Discovered Concealed near the Trunk of an Old Tree a Case *Bottle* With Excellent *Butter* Which they the Rangers told me they Made by melting and Clarifying the fat of the Palm tree Worms And Which fully Supplied the Above ingredient While I absolutely found it more Delicious — The *Pistachio* or pinda nuts they Also Convert in Butter, by their Oily Substance & Frequently use them in their Broths — The *Palm tree Wine* they are never in Want of, And which they make by Cutting Deep insitions of a Foot Over Square in the fallen trunk, where the Joice being Gathered it soon ferments by the Heat of the Sun, When it is not only a Cool and Agreeable Beveridge but Strong Sufficient to intoxicate — and Soap they have from the dwarf[?] aloes. To Build their *Houses* the Manicole or Pinda Tree Answers the Purpose, theyr *Pots* they Fabricate with Clay found near their Dwellings While the *Gourd* or Calebas[24] tree give them Cups &c the Silk Grass Plant and Maureecee tree[25] Provides them in *Hammocks* And even a kind of *Caps* Grow Natural upon the Palm trees as

[21] *Inventas . . . improved:* Virgil, *Aeneid,* vi.663 (slightly misquoted).

[22] *Cassava:* See p. 364.

[23] *the Gentoos in the East Indies:* See Guthry Page 685. [Stedman's note.] Stedman is referring to natives of India (Guthrie uses "Gentoo" as a synonym for "Hindu"). The citation is to William Guthrie's *New Geographical, Historical, and Commercial Grammar,* first published in London in 1770 and frequently reprinted; the pagination corresponds to the tenth edition (1787).

[24] *Calebas:* I.e., calabash, a kind of gourd or pumpkin; the shells were hollowed out and used as containers.

[25] *Maureecee tree:* A kind of palm tree.

Well as *Brooms* — The Various kinds of Nebees[26] Supply the Want of *Ropes, fuel* for fire they have for the Cutting, While a Wood call'd *Bee Bee*[27] Serves for Tinder to Light it by Rubbing two Pieces on each Other, And Which by its Elasticity Makes *Excellent* Corks — Neyther Do they Want *Candles,* being well Provided with Fat and Oil While the Bees Also Afford them *Wax,* And a Great Deal of Excellent *Honey,* as for Cloaths they Scorn to Wear them Preferring to go naked in a Climate Where the Mildness of The Weather Protects them from that Cursed incumbrance — ...

Our Commander order'd the next Morning a Detachment to Cross the bridge on Discovery at all Hazards — Of this Party I Led the Van, When we took the Pass without Oposition, and having All marched or rather Scrambled over this Defile of Floating trees We found ourselves in a Very Large field of Cassava and Yams, And in Which were About 30 Houses but Forsaken, being the Remains of the Old Settlement Call'd *Cofaay*[28] — In this field we Seperated in 3 Divisions to Reconnoitre Viz one Marching N one NW, And the Other W, When the Mystery Again Was Unrevell'd, Why the Rebels had Kept Shouting Singing, and Firing Round us the whole night of 20th, Viz, Not only to Cover the Retreat of their Friends by Cutting of[f] the Pass, but by theyr Unintermitting *Noise* to Prevent us from hearing them, Who were the Whole night imployed men, Women, and Children, in Preparing Hampers or Warimboes With the Finest Rice, Yams, Cassava, &[c] for theyr Subsistance During their Escape & of Which they had only Left us the Chaff, and Dregs for our Contemplation And to our Great And inconceivable Astonishment — And which most Certainly was Such a piece of Generalship in a Savage People Whom we Affect to Despise as must have Done Honour to an European Prince & Even *Frederick the Great*[29] himself Needed not to have been Ashamed of, With which Remark I beg Leave to end this Long Chapter —

[26] *Nebees:* Stedman uses this term generally for vines.
[27] *Bee Bee:* The corkwood tree.
[28] *Cofaay:* See Stedman's translation, on p. 382.
[29] *Frederick the Great:* Frederick II of Prussia (1712–1786), who achieved numerous military victories during the War of the Austrian Succession (1740–48) and the Seven Years' War (1756–63).

OLAUDAH EQUIANO

From *The Interesting Narrative of the Life of Olaudah Equiano, Gustavus Vassa, the African*

Olaudah Equiano (introduced on p. 310) here describes his arrival in Barbados as an enslaved child. Equiano was probably born in 1745 and was captured at the age of eleven, so this passage describes a Barbados slave market c. 1756. It is one of the few eighteenth-century accounts of a slave market written from the slave's point of view. Equiano's description of the child's response to his surroundings combines curiosity, surprise, fear, and horror. While he strives to recapture his initial reaction — his thoughts and emotions at the time of his arrival — Equiano also uses a highly stylized tone to reflect on the injustice he has seen. His impassioned address to the "nominal Christians" who separate brother and sister, parent and child, plays on the "truth-telling infidel" trope we have observed in the selections from Mandeville and Montaigne in Chapter 2.

The text is taken from the first edition (London: Printed for and sold by the author, 1789) 1: 83–88.

At last we came in sight of the island of Barbadoes, at which the whites on board gave a great shout, and made many signs of joy to us. We did not know what to think of this; but as the vessel drew nearer we plainly saw the harbour, and other ships of different kinds and sizes; and we soon anchored amongst them off Bridge Town.[1] Many merchants and planters now came on board, though it was in the evening. They put us in separate parcels, and examined us attentively. They also made us jump, and pointed to the land, signifying we were to go there. We thought by this we should be eaten by these ugly men, as they appeared to us; and, when soon after we were all put down under the deck again, there was much dread and trembling among us, and nothing but bitter cries to be heard all the night from these apprehensions insomuch that at last the white people got some old slaves from land to pacify us. They told us we were not to be eaten, but to work, and were soon to go on land, where we should see many of our country people. This report eased us much; and sure enough, soon

---

[1] *Bridge Town:* The capital of Barbados, on the island's southwest coast.

after we were landed, there came to us Africans of all languages. We were conducted immediately to the merchant's yard, where we were all pent up together like so many sheep in a fold, without regard to sex or age. As every object was new to me every thing I saw filled me with surprise. What struck me first was that the houses were built with stories, and in every other respect different from those in Africa: but I was still more astonished on seeing people on horseback. I did not know what this could mean; and indeed I thought these people were full of nothing but magical arts. While I was in this astonishment one of my fellow prisoners spoke to a countryman of his about the horses, who said they were the same kind they had in their country. I understood them, though they were from a distant part of Africa, and I thought it odd I had not seen any horses there; but afterwards, when I came to converse with different Africans, I found they had many horses amongst them, and much larger than those I then saw. We were not many days in the merchant's custody before we were sold after their usual manner, which is this: — On a signal given, (as the beat of a drum) the buyers rush at once into the yard where the slaves are confined, and make choice of that parcel they like best. The noise and clamour with which this is attended, and the eagerness visible in the countenances of the buyers, serve not a little to increase the apprehensions of the terrified Africans, who may well be supposed to consider them as the ministers of the destruction to which they think themselves devoted. In this manner, without scruple, are relations and friends separated, most of them never to see each other again. I remember in the vessel in which I was brought over, in the men's apartment, there were several brothers, who, in the sale, were sold in different lots; and it was very moving on this occasion to see and hear their cries at parting. O, ye nominal Christians! might not an African ask you, learned you this from your God, who says unto you, Do unto all men as you would men should do unto you? Is it not enough that we are torn from our country and friends to toil for your luxury and lust of gain? Must every tender feeling be likewise sacrificed to your avarice? Are the dearest friends and relations, now rendered more dear by their separation from their kindred, still to be parted from each other, and thus prevented from cheering the gloom of slavery with the small comfort of being together and mingling their sufferings and sorrows? Why are parents to lose their children, brothers their sisters, or husbands their wives? Surely this is a new refinement in cruelty, which, while it has no advantage to atone for it, thus aggravates distress, and adds fresh horrors even to the wretchedness of slavery.

5

Britain in the Triangular Trade

The triangular trade had an incalculable effect on Britain itself.[1] In addition to transforming that nation into a major world power within a century, the trade reshaped England's internal economy, challenged its laws, changed its daily diet, and created a new category of people in the metropolis — the black Britons. The documents in this section concentrate on the domestic effects of the Atlantic trade, especially those topics that generated the most contemporary comment: the question of how the mother country should best profit from its colonies; the transformation of sugar from a rare delicacy available only to the wealthy into a common food; the appearance of Africans in the cities; the consequent debates over the status of slavery in the mother country; and the growth of the first widespread, grassroots political movement in Britain — the movement to abolish the slave trade.

Although the British West Indian sugar plantations had been importing several thousand slaves annually from West Africa for over forty-eight years when *Oroonoko* was composed, Behn writes as though the practice will be news to some of her readers. The English were, indeed, unused to the idea of what we now call chattel slavery,

---

[1] In addition to the sources quoted in the text, information for this chapter comes from Aykroyd; Blackburn, *Making* and *Overthrow;* Bush; Carlos and Kruse; Dabydeen; Davies, C.S.L; Davies, K.; Ellis; Ferguson, M.W.; Fiddes; Gerzina; Keirn; King; Mintz; Oldham; Pagden; and Wiecek.

or personal property in another human being that allows him to be bought and sold at his master's will. While giving her consent to John Hawkins's African voyage of 1562, for example, Queen Elizabeth I cautioned that the slaves should not be forcibly taken away, for that "would be detestable and call down the vengeance of Heaven upon the undertakers" (qtd. in Thomas 156). Lest the queen's remarks should mislead us to think that early modern England was a bastion of human rights, we should note at the outset that most English people thought social and political inequality was natural, and consistent notions of the superiority of "free labor" were not developed until the late eighteenth century. There was as yet no established presumption that each individual had a right to his or her own labor, let alone a more general right to self-determination. Indeed, much in English law and custom would have contradicted the idea of such rights. The queen's warning derived not from any particularly advanced egalitarian thought, but rather from an unwillingness to abduct the subjects of a foreign realm as well as uncertainty about the exact nature and legal basis of chattel slavery and its conformity to native English institutions. Such uncertainty continued into the next two centuries.

Some small amount of attention had been paid to the topic of slavery even before the triangular trade developed, as the earliest documents in this section demonstrate. The 1547 "Act for the Punishing of Vagabonds," which was only in effect for a few years, made "slavery" for a limited period a punishment for living "idly and loiteringly," and may have been inspired by Sir Thomas More's *Utopia* (1516), which seems to recommend such a penal use of perpetual servitude. Both documents express the belief that a life of involuntary servitude will reform the lazy and dishonest, and perhaps we can discern in this notion the anticipation of a persistent argument in later pro-slavery writings that forced labor provides salutary discipline for those who are naturally unable to control themselves. Both documents stipulate that the slave should be marked indelibly to make him instantly recognizable if he tries to run away, and this desire for a permanent physical sign of slavery may help us to understand how the visible physical difference of a dark complexion could come to be seen as a kind of "natural" ineradicable mark.

However, neither the 1547 statute nor More anticipates the institution of chattel slavery, in which a man may be sold from person to person, nor does either suggest that anyone might be born into slavery. "Slavery," or "bondage," is seen as an individual punishment for individual transgressions. The punitive use of forced labor continued in the seventeenth century, and several thousand British prisoners were sent to the West Indies to toil their lives away. Significantly, the "Petitions Protesting Enslavement of Political Prisoners" included here express objections not to transportation or coerced labor as punishment, but to the treatment of prisoners as chattel slaves. The Royalists Marcellus Rivers and Oxenbridge Foyle, who petitioned Parliament toward the end of the Commonwealth period to redress their grievances, objected to being *sold*, rather than just sentenced to labor, and to being transported below decks, with horses.

Another context for early discussions of slavery sheds some light both on Queen Elizabeth's misunderstanding and on *Oroonoko's* manner of linking kingship and slavery. Elizabeth might have thought that Africans were slaves *by contract* and therefore not subject to forcible removal from their native land. In early modern times that would not have been an unreasonable assumption, for the meaning and legitimacy of a slave contract was a topic of legal discussion. Moreover, as the debate over absolute government heated up in the seventeenth century, Hugo Grotius's remarks on the slave contract were enlisted to justify the sort of monarchy coveted by the Stuarts. A Dutch jurist and humanist, Grotius in 1625 had instanced the slave contract to argue for the legitimacy of absolute government: "To every man it is permitted to enslave himself to anyone he pleases for private ownership, as is evident both from the Hebraic and from the Roman law. Why, then, would it not be permitted to a people having legal competence to submit itself to some one person, or to several persons, in such a way as plainly to transfer to him the legal right to govern, retaining no vestige of that right for himself?" (103). As we noted in the introduction, discussions of slavery were also closely linked to those of monarchical power in the works of Robert Filmer and John Locke, as well. Hence, when Aphra Behn imagines a country in Africa where the subjects seem virtually indistinguishable from slaves, and when she conceives of her hero's destiny as an absolute choice between slavery and kingship, she seems to be drawing more heavily on this European political debate over the right relations of monarchs and subjects than on the realities of chattel slavery as she had witnessed them in Suriname.

Contests over the nature of chattel slavery and its legal status had reached the London courts prior to the composition of *Oroonoko,* as the "Legal Decisions Concerning Slavery in England" included here indicate. Chattel slaves, unlike the kinds of "bond" laborers that English law had previously allowed, were commodities that could be exchanged between private individuals. Unlike villeins, they were not

attached to estates; unlike indentured servants, they were exchangeable, perpetually bound, and not contracted; and unlike prisoners,
they were not guilty of anything. Our documents show the courts taking a variety of positions on the issue of chattel slavery until 1772,
when Lord Mansfield made a decision that was interpreted to hold
that one could not claim a slave as property in the United Kingdom,
notwithstanding the local laws of the British colonies.

No one thought that a person could be made a slave in Britain itself;
the cases turn on the status of a slave purchased elsewhere when that
slave is brought to England. And this issue became pressing as more
and more West Indian planters visited the home country with their
black "servants" or took up residency there. Lord Mansfield's 1772
decision was said to affect an estimated 14,000 to 15,000 black "servants" in Britain. Although their actual situations had seldom been
very different from those of white servants — they were almost all
domestic laborers — their unusual status seemed increasingly incompatible with notions of British liberty. Many of them had been exotic,
fashionable accessories in trains of servants that accompanied aristo-
cratic ladies; black page boys dressed in white satin, with little locked
metal collars symbolizing their separate status as actual possessions,
can be seen in eighteenth-century portraits. Others had been treated
no differently from a household's white servants, so the ambiguous
legality of their servitude was submerged. Almost all stayed in their
places after Mansfield's decision, and their conditions changed little.

We should remember that many servants in England were "bound"
by apprenticeships or indentures, that the navy routinely impressed
young men into service, and that paupers were often assigned work by
the parishes that supported them, so involuntary servitude was seen as
routine. Moreover, there had been few visible signs of the differences
between the status of black slaves in England and that of other unfree
laborers: there were no slave markets, and the small traffic in "black
servants" had been casual and discreet. In 1709, a notice in *The Tatler*
advertised "A black boy, twelve years of age, fit to wait on a gentleman, to be disposed of at Denis's Coffee House in Finch Lane" (qtd. in
Gerzina 7), but advertisements for young white servants (parish children, for example) were nearly identical. Another newspaper notice
from 1696 more explicitly asserts the master's rights as the servant's
owner: "Run away from Captain John Brooke of Barford near Salisbury, about the middle of August last, a middle-sized Negro Man,
named Humphrey" (qtd. in Gerzina 7), and yet a master at the time
could also ask for the return of a runaway apprentice. We should not,

therefore, be surprised that it required a century of legal dispute to sort out the differences between chattel slavery and other forms of unfree labor.

The boyhoods of two Africans carried to England as slaves in the eighteenth century, both of whose writings are included in this section, illustrate the variety of experiences that a slave might have undergone in Britain. Ignatius Sancho was born on a slave ship in about 1729 and served in the household of three sisters in Greenwich. When they obstructed his education, he ran away and sought refuge with the widow of an aristocrat who had earlier shown an interest in him, the Duke of Montagu. The duchess eventually took Sancho into her service as a butler and left him a small independence in her will, and he ultimately managed to better his condition, in spite of having been deprived of an early education. In contrast, Olaudah Equiano, although always at the beck and call of his master as a boy, recalls the kindness of a humble English family, with whom he boarded briefly when a child; the mistress of the house taught him alongside her daughter. On shipboard, while serving with the British navy, where all hands were subject to strict discipline, Equiano claims that he did not often feel less free than the other boys. Throughout his memoirs, he expresses a preference for Britain, where he claims he experienced little racial discrimination, over the West Indies, where everything was organized to accentuate the gap between freemen and black slaves, and where the harassment against black freedmen threatened the autonomy they had supposedly acquired. Equiano certainly does not proclaim the complete absence of racial prejudice in Britain, but his desire to live in London as a freedman points once again to the differences in race relations at the three corners of the Atlantic triangle.

By the end of the eighteenth century, both Sancho and Equiano belonged to the educated elite of black London. They had relatively powerful patrons and were considered to be among the most articulate spokesmen for emancipation. Most blacks in Britain, however, were still domestic servants, and a growing number, often those who had refused to return to the West Indies with the families who had brought them to England, were sinking into the large class of city paupers. Some, even less fortunate, were driven back to the West Indies by masters who defied the new legal presumption of freedom created by Mansfield's decision. The writer Hannah More reported in 1790 that she had seen a black woman "dragged out from a hole in the top of a house [in Bristol] and forced on board ship" (qtd. in Gerzina 75). Thomas Day's poem "The Dying Negro," included here, is based on this

1773 newspaper report of a forcible attempt to return a black servant living in London to the West Indies: "a Black, who a few days before, ran away from his master, and got himself christened, with intent to marry his fellow-servant, a white woman, being taken, and sent on board the Captain's ship, in the Thames; took an opportunity of shooting himself through the head" (qtd. in the introduction to Day's poem vi). Stories like these brought the issue of colonial slavery home to Britain and inspired the abolitionist sentiment that burgeoned in the last two decades of the eighteenth century.

The seventeenth-century legal cases included here seem not to have garnered much publicity, and before abolitionists began publicizing the cases of individual slaves in Britain in the 1760s, Britons did not consider slavery the most controversial aspect of the Atlantic trade. Questions concerning the proper economic relations between the colonies and the mother country were far more likely to be the subject of heated debate in the years when *Oroonoko* was first finding an audience. Indeed, many seventeenth-century Britons were very skeptical about the desirability of colonies, fearing that such possessions would depopulate England, compete with home industries, and serve as pawns in the international operations of other European nations. Colonies were expensive to protect and police, and it was frequently claimed that they attracted the dregs of England, Scotland, and Ireland, and gave them dangerous and unearned power. Although Aphra Behn explicitly laments the loss of Suriname in *Oroonoko*, we can detect many negative attitudes toward colonies and colonists in her portrayal of Suriname officials; moreover, in her contemporaneous play *The Widdow Ranter* (published posthumously in 1690), she portrays the leading lights of colonial Virginia as a pack of hooligans.

Under the pressure of such perceptions and objections, the British government tried to ensure the immediate profitability of the colonies to the home country as well as to investors in the Atlantic trade and to the colonists themselves. They extracted revenues through a series of Navigation Acts, which specified that the colonies had to ship their produce in English vessels to English ports and imposed import duties on colonial goods. London investors in the African and West Indian trades, as well as the colonists themselves, disputed many of these economic policies. They wanted greater freedom to choose how they would trade and with whom, and they claimed that import duties on sugar shipped to England had a ruinous effect on their plantations. We have chosen two pamphlets from the late seventeenth century, one by Edward Littleton voicing West Indian interests and one by an anonymous merchant giving the government's position, that illustrate these divergent views of the usefulness of the colonies to the home country.

A third pamphleteer, Sir Dalby Thomas, emphasizes the economic importance of colonial consumption to British industries. The Atlantic trade, it should be noted, created a market for English manufactured goods in two continents; both the African and the West Indian corners of the triangle greatly stimulated industrial production at home. Shipbuilding, a hugely important component of the British economy, boomed as a result of the trade, and smaller industries prospered as well. The historian Hugh Thomas lists "gun makers, cutlers, dyers, sailmakers, weavers, and tuckers, manufacturers of wrought iron from Birmingham, serge makers, merchants from Edinburgh and from Chester, not to speak of manufacturers of Welsh flannel" (231) as among those who petitioned Parliament in the early eighteenth century to expand the African slave trade. In short, the Atlantic circuit was central, rather than peripheral, to the metropolitan economy, and it extended itself into all the corners of the new United Kingdom after England and Scotland were officially joined in 1707.

Even if the importance of that circuit to the home economy was disputed during the seventeenth, and early eighteenth centuries, no one seriously questioned its effect on the British diet. The demand for sugar rose as increased imports from the West Indian colonies caused the price to fall. At the opening of the seventeenth century, sugar was a luxury consumed only by the rich; by the end of the century, it was considered a common necessity, and the change revolutionized British eating habits. The selections by Sir Dalby Thomas and Thomas Tryon, in explaining the advantages of cheap sugar, remind us of the novelty of sugar's new availability in the seventeenth century. Sugar not only changed the consumption patterns of fruits and transformed bakers into confectioners, it also made two other colonial commodities, chocolate and coffee, palatable to the European taste. The British diet became even more dependent on exotic commodities as tea became favored over chocolate and coffee in the eighteenth century, and the sugar habit spread with the popularity of this Asian import and the elaboration of its consumption into a national ritual. The new beverages conformed to a change in manners, as well. Chocolate houses, coffeehouses, and tea tables became centers for new forms of socializing — informal meeting places where issues of the day could be critically discussed. Hence, although the new drinks were dependent on a brutal colonial system, they were associated with cosmopolitan sophistication and enlightenment.

Eventually, people became more aware of the relationship between their patterns of consumption and the continuance of the Atlantic slave trade, and abolitionists stressed the connection. Although the movement to abolish the slave trade lies largely outside the scope of this volume, even the most superficial overview of the Atlantic trade's impact on Britain must mention that the abolitionists invented a new form of political action — indeed, a new form of political consciousness — that organized those who had no political rights, such as women and disenfranchised men, and linked daily, personal behavior with the destiny of remote nations. Through petition campaigns, public meetings, and sugar boycotts, black and white abolitionists instilled in their constituency the unprecedented idea that ordinary people should take some responsibility for faraway injustices perpetrated by their nation. The breakfast table became a political issue, as this quotation from the writer Horace Walpole satirically indicates:

> The friends of government, who have thought on nothing but reducing us to our islandhood and bringing us back to the simplicity of ancient times, when we were the frugal, temperate, virtuous old England, ask how we did before tea and sugar were known. Better, no doubt; but as I did not happen to be born two or three hundred years ago, I cannot recall precisely whether diluted acorns, and barley bread spread with honey, made a very luxurious breakfast. (qtd. in Mintz 119)

Whether one agreed or disagreed with their position, the abolitionists made one aware of the distant consequences of private behavior and recommended that one might modify one's consumption in accordance with a political principle. This was an immense breakthrough in popular political consciousness, which had formerly assumed that a special class of governors would make the decisions that were in the best interests of the nation, and that the opinions of the governed would be of little moment. The fact that the abolitionists managed to create political organizations among those who were officially powerless, which were based on an issue that did not involve the participants' immediate self-interest, announced a whole new world of political possibilities, and long into the nineteenth century, reform movements of all kinds took the British campaign to abolish the slave trade as their model.

By the time that British participation in the slave trade became illegal (1807), most of the luster had worn off of Britain's American experience: it had lost its most prosperous North American colonies in the American Revolution and its Caribbean holdings were fast losing their profitability. Along with and reinforcing the humanitarian critique of the slave trade, a practical skepticism about the kind of colonial endeavors Britain had undertaken in America began to emerge. It was thought that colonies like those in North America that could produce all of their own commodities would soon want to become independent, while those on the Caribbean model, which were more specialized, would produce distorted societies and exhaustible, rigid economies. One of the most important legacies of the Atlantic trade may, therefore, have been the negative lesson it taught Britain. Putting this lesson in international perspective, historian Anthony Pagden explains that

> the real intellectual significance for Europeans of their several experiences in America was that these had demonstrated what successful empires should *not* attempt to be. By 1800 most of enlightened Europe had been persuaded that large-scale overseas settlement of the kind pursued, in their different ways, by Spain, Britain and France in the Americas could ultimately be only destructive to the metropolis itself. (6)

The next stage of British imperialism would largely eschew settlement in favor of administrative control and the exploitation of populations already in place. Instead of hauling people across the ocean to grow crops for them, the British in Bengal, for example, employed the abundant local population to grow sugar. Hence, the cessation of the triangular trade did not constitute a defeat for the British Empire; it merely stimulated its metamorphosis into a new form.

SIR THOMAS MORE

From *Utopia*

Sir Thomas More (1478–1535), statesman, humanist, and author, was one of the leading political thinkers of the English Renaissance. He was elected to Parliament in 1504, became a member of King Henry VIII's Privy Council in 1518, and was knighted in 1521. In 1523, More became speaker of the House of Commons, and in 1529, he became the first layman to be appointed lord chancellor. He resigned, however, in 1532, and was imprisoned two years later in the Tower of London for refusing to acknowledge Henry VIII as supreme head of the Church of England. Found guilty of treason, More was beheaded in 1535. Throughout his life,

More was a prolific writer, producing poetry, essays, histories, and philosophical dialogues. His *Utopia*, published in Latin in 1516 and translated into English in 1551, satirizes English politics and society by depicting an imaginary island whose laws and mores are presented as the basis of a perfectly rational and equitable paradigm, a model against which the flaws of the English system become glaringly obvious. In the preface, More identifies the book's narrator as a friend of Amerigo Vespucci (who reached the coast of what is now Venezuela in the late 1490s), and in a letter to his friend Peter Giles, More hints that the island itself is located in the Americas.

As the introduction to this volume notes, in More's time the notion that any particular group was naturally qualified for slavery had barely been articulated. In the selection from *Utopia* reprinted here, More treats slavery as a punishment best suited for thieves and appropriate only as a means of moral education, by which the slave is finally rendered capable of self-government. More uses the Latin word *servitus,* which, because of the context in which he applies it, is sometimes translated as "bondsman" or "serving man"; however, the term's commonest and most literal meaning is "slave," and elsewhere in *Utopia,* More broadens the scope of the term's application while accentuating the sense of abject submission to a master. For example, he uses the same term and its cognates to describe the fate of prisoners of war, though he specifies that in Utopia, such prisoners are taken only if they were personally engaged in combat, or were captured in retaliation for unjustified injury of Utopians traveling abroad (II.viii).

The text is excerpted from *More's* Utopia *and A Dialogue of Comfort,* introduced, with spelling modernized, by John Warrington (London: Dent, 1951) 32–35.

They that in this land be attainted[1] and convict of felony, make restitution of that which they stole to the right owner, and not (as they do in other lands) to the king, whom they think to have no more right of the thief-stolen thing than the thief himself hath. But if the thing be lost or made away, then the value of it is paid of the goods of such offenders, which else remaineth all whole to their wives and children. And they themselves be condemned to be common labourers; and, unless the theft be very heinous, they be neither locked in prison nor

[1] *attainted:* Accused.

fettered in gyves,[2] but be untied and go at large, labouring in the common works. They that refuse labour, or go slowly and slackly to their work, be not only tied in chains, but also pricked[3] forward with stripes; but being diligent about their work they live without check or rebuke. Every night they be called in by name, and be locked in their chambers. Besides their daily labour, their life is nothing hard or incommodious.[4] Their fare is indifferent good, borne at the charges of the weal-public,[5] because they be common servants to the commonwealth. But their charges in all places of the land are not borne alike, for in some parts that which is bestowed upon them is gathered of alms. And though that way be uncertain, yet the people be so full of mercy and pity, that none is found more profitable or plentiful. In some places certain lands be appointed hereunto, of the revenues whereof they be maintained; and in some places every man giveth a certain tribute for the same use and purpose.

Again, in some parts of the land these serving-men (for so be these damned persons called) do no common work, but as every private man needeth labourers, so he cometh into the market-place and there hireth some of them for meat and drink and a certain limited wages by the day, somewhat cheaper than he should hire a free man. It is also lawful for them to chastise the sloth of these serving-men with stripes. By this means they never lack work, and besides the gaining of their meat and drink, every one of them bringeth daily something into the common treasury. All and every one of them be apparelled in one colour. Their heads be not polled[6] or shaven, but rounded a little above the ears, and the tip of the one ear is cut off.[7] Every one of them may take meat and drink of their friends, and also a coat of their own colour; but to receive money is death, as well to the giver as to the receiver. And no less jeopardy it is for a free man to receive money of a serving-man for any manner of cause, and likewise for serving men to touch weapons. The serving-men of every several shire be distinct and known from other by their several and distinct badges which to cast away is death, as it is also to be seen out of the precinct of their own shire, or to talk with a serving-man of another shire. And it is no less danger to them for to intend to run away than to do it indeed. Yea,

---

[2] *gyves:* Shackles.
[3] *pricked:* Goaded, driven.
[4] *incommodious:* Inconvenient, disagreeable.
[5] *weal-public:* Public welfare.
[6] *polled:* Cropped.
[7] *the tip of the one ear is cut off:* Cropping or notching the ears of criminals was a common punishment in More's time.

and to conceal such an enterprise in a serving-man it is death, in a free man servitude. Of the contrary part, to him that openeth and uttereth such counsels be decreed large gifts, to a free man a great sum of money, to a serving-man freedom, and, to them both, forgiveness and pardon of that they were of counsel in that pretence. So that it can never be so good for them to go forward in their evil purpose as, by repentance, to turn back.

This is the law and order in this behalf, as I have shewed you. Wherein what humanity is used, how far it is from cruelty, and how commodious it is, you do plainly perceive, forasmuch as the end of their wrath and punishment intendeth nothing else but the destruction of vices and saving of men, with so using and ordering them that they cannot choose but be good, and what harm soever they did before, in the residue to their life to make amends for the same. Moreover it is so little feared that they should turn again to their vicious conditions, that wayfaring men will for their safeguard choose them to their guides before any other, in every shire changing and taking new; for if they would commit robbery they have nothing about them meet for that purpose. They may touch no weapons; money found about them should betray the robbery. They should be no sooner taken with the manner, but forthwith they should be punished. Neither they can have any hope at all to scape away by fleeing. For how should a man that in no part of his apparel is like other men fly privily[8] and unknown, unless he would run away naked? Howbeit, so also fleeing he should be descried by the rounding of his head and his ear mark. But it is a thing to be doubted that they will lay their heads together and conspire against the weal-public. No, no, I warrant you. For the serving-men of one shire alone could never hope to bring to pass such an enterprise without soliciting, enticing, and alluring the serving-men of many other shires to take their parts. Which thing is to them so impossible, that they may not as much as speak or talk together or salute[9] one another. No, it is not to be thought that they would make their own countrymen and companions of their counsel in such a matter, which they know well should be jeopardy to the concealer thereof and great commodity and goodness to the opener and detector of the same. Whereas, on the other part, there is none of them all hopeless or in despair to recover again his former state of freedom by humble obedience, by patient suffering, and by giving good tokens and likelihood of

[8] *privily:* Secretly.
[9] *salute:* Greet.

himself, that he will ever after that live like a true and an honest man. For every year divers of them be restored to their freedom through the commendation of their patience.

When I had thus spoken, saying moreover that I could see no cause why this order might not be had in England with much more profit than the justice which the lawyer so highly praised, Nay, quoth the lawyer, this could never be so stablished in England but that it must needs bring the weal-public into great jeopardy and hazard. And, as he was thus saying, he shaked his head and made a wry mouth, and so he held his peace. And all that were there present with one assent agreed to his saying.

Well, quoth the cardinal, yet it were hard to judge without a proof whether this order would do well here or no. But when the sentence of death is given, if then the king should command execution to be deferred and spared, and would prove this order and fashion, taking away the privileges of all sanctuaries, if then the proof should declare the thing to be good and profitable, then it were well done that it were stablished. . . .

An Act for the Punishing of Vagabonds, and for the Reliefe of the Poore and Impotent Persons

Though legal thinkers opposed to slavery often insisted that it was simply inimical to English traditions, this 1547 act shows that the concept of slavery — whether for a limited or indefinite period of time — was not unthinkable in English law. The statute passed with little opposition, perhaps because its conditions seemed only slightly harsher than those already familiar in such well-established practices as apprenticeship and indentured servitude. Moreover, just as many apprentices and servants were forced to labor under punitive conditions, a series of vagrancy statutes passed during the previous forty years had taken it for granted that the idle could be set to work for low wages, and that policy would remain in force for hundreds of years. The institution of villenage, too, which dated back to the eleventh century and was still extant at the time of the 1547 statute, treated peasants as the property of the lord on whose land they lived; villenage faded away during the course of the next century (during the same period in which the English began to increase their activity in the slave trade), but was often invoked in eighteenth-century legal arguments as a precedent that demonstrated the legitimacy of slavery. What differentiates the 1547 statute from these other instances, of course, is its willingness to speak explicitly about slavery and its encouragement of brutal treatment by the slave's master. It should be noted that the act remained on the books for only two years, and we have no evidence of any case in which it was actually enforced.

The text is from John Cay, ed., *The Statutes at Large, from Magna Charta, to the Thirtieth Year of King George the Second, Inclusive*, 6 vols. (London: Baskett, 1758) 2: 194.

Forasmuch as Idlenesse and Vagabondrie is the Mother and Roote of all Thefts, Robberies, and all evill Actes, and other Mischiefs, and the Multitude of People given thereto hath always bene heere within this Realme very great, and more in Number (as it may appear) than in other Regions, to the great Impoverishment of the Realme, and Danger of the Kings Highness Subjects; the which Idlenesse and Vagabondry all the Kings Highness noble Progenitours, Kings of this Realme, and this high Court of Parliament hath often and with great travel[1] gone about and assayed with godly Acts and Statutes to represse; yet untill this our Time it hath not had that successe which hath beene wished, but partly by foolish pitie and mercie of them which should have seene the said godly Lawes executed, partly by the perverse Nature and long accustomed Idleness of the Persons given to Loytering, the said godly Statutes hitherto have had small Effect, and idle and vagabond Persons being unprofitable Members, or rather Enemies of the Common Wealth, have been suffered to remaine and increase, and yet so doe, whom if they should be punished by Death, Whipping, Imprisonment, and with other corporall Paine, it were not without their Deserts, for the Example of others, and to the Benefite of the Common Wealth, yet if they could be brought to be made profitable, and do service, it were much to be wished and desired: Be it, *&c.*[2]

A Repeal of all Statutes heretofore made for the Punishment of Vagabonds, and of all Articles comprised in the same. (2) If any Person shall bring to two Justices of Peace, any Runnagate[3] Servant, or any

---

[1] *travel:* I.e., travail, difficulty.
[2] *Be it, &c:* I.e., "be it, etcetera"; the conventional phrase for summarizing the legal formula putting a statue in effect ("Be it enacted, by the king's most excellent majesty . . . ").
[3] *Runnagate:* Runaway

other which liveth idly and loiteringly; by the Space of three Days, the said Justices shall cause the said idle and loitering Servant or Vagabond, to be marked with an hot Iron on the Breast, with the Mark of *V*. (3) and adjudge him to be Slave to the same Person that brought or presented him, to have to him, his Executors or Assigns,[4] for two Years after, who shall take the said Slave, and give him Bread, Water or small Drink, and reffuse[5] Meat, and cause him to work, by beating, chaining or otherwise, in such Work and Labour as he shall put him unto, be it never to vile: (4) And if such Slave absent himself for his said Master, within the said Term of two Years, by the Space of Fourteen Days, then he shall be adjudged by two Justices of Peace to be marked on the Forehead, or the Ball of the Cheek, with an hot Iron, with the Sign of an *S*. and further shall be adjudged to be Slave to his said Master for ever: (5) And if the said Slave shall run away the Second Time, he shall be adjudged a Felon. (6) No Clerk[6] convict shall make his Purgation,[7] but shall be a Slave for one Year to him who will become bound with two Sureties,[8] in twenty Pounds to the Ordinary, to the King's Use, to take him into Service: And he shall be used in all Respects, as is aforesaid, like to a Vagabond. (7) A Clerk attainted[9] or convict, which by the Law cannot make his Purgation, may by the Ordinary[10] be delivered to any Man, who will become bound with two sufficient Sureties, to keep him as his Slave five Years: And then he shall be used in all Respects as is aforesaid for a Vagabond, saving for burning in the Breast. (8) It shall be lawful to every Person to whom any shall be adjudged a Slave, to put a Ring of Iron about his Neck, Arm or Leg. (9) A Justice of Peace and Constable may bind a Beggar's Man-child Apprentice to the Age of fourteen Years, and a Woman-child to the Age of twenty Years, to any that will require them. (10) And if the said Child run away, then his Master may retain and use him for the Term aforesaid, as his Slave. (11) All impotent, maimed and aged Persons, who cannot be taken for Vagabonds, shall have convenient Houses provided for them, and otherwise be relieved in the Cities, Boroughs or Towns where they were born, or were most conversant by the Space of three Years, by the willing and charitable Dispositions of the Parishioners: And none other shall be suffered to beg there.

---

[4] *Executors or Assigns:* People to whom the owner's property has been transferred.
[5] *reffuse:* Stale, left over.
[6] *Clerk:* A clergyman, or someone else who could read and write. At this time, convicted criminals who could demonstrate their ability to read qualified for "benefit of clergy," which usually involved a reduced sentence; here, the term of servitude is reduced by one year.
[7] *make his Purgation:* Clear himself.
[8] *Sureties:* Pledges, bonds.
[9] *attainted:* Accused.
[10] *Ordinary:* Judge or prison chaplain.

Petitions Protesting the Enslavement
of Political Prisoners

The petitions to Parliament of Marcellus Rivers and Oxenbridge Foyle, two men accused of fomenting Royalist uprisings in the last years of the interregnum, claim that they were sold into slavery and sent to the island of Barbados. This record of the petitions and the debate they excited dates from 1659, and is taken from the diary of one Thomas Burton, a member in the parliaments of Oliver and Richard Cromwell, for records of parliamentary debates were not yet officially kept. The debate indicates that thousands of other European prisoners, especially Scots and Irish, were sold into involuntary lifelong servitude in the Caribbean — a precedent that seems to have troubled the disputants not because they wished to prohibit such treatment, but because of their need to distinguish it from the case at hand. The objections to the treatment of Rivers and Foyle are based on their status as Englishmen rather than on any general opposition to slavery.

The practice of sending British subjects to Barbados involuntarily reached its height between 1649 and 1690, and probably involved between 4,000 and 5,000 people. The Victorian Thomas Carlyle claimed that the practice became so familiar during the interregnum that the verb "to transport" was replaced in popular usage by its more specific synonym, "to Barbados." This form of punishment was clearly widespread under Cromwell's government, but the single largest export of political prisoners occurred at the Bloody Assizes in 1685, during the reign of King James II, when more than 800 rebels were convicted of treason and sentenced to be transported by Chief Justice George Jeffreys (Behn, who shared Jeffreys' Royalist sympathies, praised his actions later that year in the dedication to her *Love Letters Between a Nobleman and His Sister*). In other words, the policy was not specific to any particular political faction, but was adopted by whoever happened to be in power.

Political prisoners accounted for a sizable portion of those forced into servitude, but that population also comprised numerous other convicts, including members of unpopular religious sects such as Quakers, and those deemed socially undesirable, such as drunks and prostitutes. The shipping of prisoners to Barbados should be seen as part of a more general pattern, beginning in the early seventeenth century, by which the English disposed of their criminals by exporting them to the new world, whether the Caribbean or North America. The practice continued into the nineteenth century, with the location shifting to Botany Bay, on the eastern coast of Australia, where the first shipload of transported convicts arrived in 1788.

In their petition, Rivers and Foyle explain that they were imprisoned in the course of a mass arrest after a Royalist rising against Cromwell's government at Salisbury in 1654; though not involved in the rebellion themselves, they were kept in jail for a year, and then suddenly shipped off to Barbados. Typically, authorities accused of "Barbadosing" their enemies would defend themselves by distinguishing between punitive servitude on the one hand and slavery on the other, but in the parliamentary debate reprinted here, there is little effort to invoke such distinctions. Instead speakers discuss the general issue of the forced transportation and labor of political dissenters. One speaker, Sir Henry Vane, specifically links the arbitrary victimization of English subjects with the tyranny of absolute monarchy associated with King Charles I, but several of the other disputants are careful to point out that any party might avail itself of such tactics, if given the opportunity. Rather than attempting to rationalize the practice as a developing institution, even its defenders present it as an exceptional, expedient remedy in a time of civil unrest.

The text is excerpted from *Proceedings and Debates of the British Parliaments Respecting North America*, ed. Leo Francis Stock (Washington, D.C.: Carnegie Institute, 1924) 1: 248–50, 253, 256, 257.

The petition of one Marcellus Rivers, and Oxenbridge Foyle, as well on the behalf of themselves as of three score and ten more freeborn people of this nation now in slavery in the Barbadoes; setting forth most unchristian and barbarous usage of them.

To the Honourable the Knights, Citizens, and Burgesses, assembled in Parliament, the representative of the freeborn people of England.

The humble petition of Marcellus Rivers and Oxenbridge Foyle, as well on the behalf of themselves as of three score and ten more freeborn people of this nation now in slavery,

Humbly sheweth,

That you distressed petitioners and the others, became prisoners at Exeter and Ilchester,[1] in the west, upon pretence of Salisbury rising,[2] in

---

[1] *Exeter and Ilchester:* Towns in southwest England.

[2] *upon pretence of Salisbury rising:* Upon accusation that they had participated in the Salisbury Rising, a Royalist rebellion against Cromwell's government in 1654.

the end of the year 1654, although many of them never saw Salisbury, nor bore arms in their lives. Your petitioners, and divers of the others, were picked up as they travelled upon their lawful occasions.

Afterwards, upon an indictment preferred[3] against your petitioner Rivers, *ignoramus*[4] was found; your petitioner Foyle never being indicted: and all the rest were either quitted by the jury of life and death, or never so much as tried or examined. Yet your petitioners, and the others, were all kept prisoners by the space of one whole year, and then on a sudden, (without the least provocation,) snatched out of their prisons; the greatest number by the command and pleasure of the then high-sheriff, Coplestone, and others in power in the county of Devon, and driven through the streets of the city of Exon,[5] (which is witness to his truth,) by a guard of horse and foot,[6] (none being suffered to take leave of them,) and so hurried to Plymouth,[7] aboard the ship *John*, of London, Captain John Cole, master, where, after they had lain aboard fourteen days, the captain hoisted sail; and at the end of five weeks and four days more, anchored at the isle of Barbadoes, in the West Indies, being (in sailing) four thousand and five hundred miles distant from their native country, wives, children, parents, friends, and whatever is near and dear unto them; the captive prisoners being all the way locked up under decks, (and guards,) amongst horses, that their souls, through heat and steam, under the tropic, fainted in them; and they never till they came to the island knew whither they were going.

Being sadly arrived there on the May 7, 1656, the master of the ship sold your miserable petitioners, and the others; the generality of them to most inhuman and barbarous persons, for one thousand five hundred and fifty pound weight of sugar a-piece, more or less, according to their working faculties, as the goods and chattels of Martin Noell and Major Thomas, aldermen of London, and Captain H. Hatsell, of Plymouth; neither sparing the aged of seventy-six years old, nor divines, nor officers, nor gentlemen, nor any age or condition of men, but rendering all alike in this inseparable captivity, they now generally grinding at the mills and attending at the furnaces, or digging in this scorching island; having nought to feed on (notwithstanding their

---

[3] *preferred*: Brought, submitted.

[4] *ignoramus*: The instruction to quash a bill of indictment because there is insufficient evidence to prosecute (from Latin, "we do not know").

[5] *Devon . . . Exon*: Exon is the Latin abbreviation for Exeter, the county seat of Devon.

[6] *a guard of horse and foot*: I.e., soldiers on horse and foot.

[7] *Plymouth*: A port in the county of Devon, southwest of Exeter.

hard labour) but potatoe roots, nor to drink, but water with such roots washed in it, besides the bread and tears of their own afflictions;[8] being bought and sold still from one planter to another, or attached as horses and beasts for the debts of their masters, being whipped at the whipping-posts (as rogues,) for their masters' pleasure, and sleeping in sties worse than hogs in England, and many other ways made miserable, beyond expression or Christian imagination.

Humbly your petitioners do remonstrate on behalf of themselves and others, their most deplorable, and (as to Englishmen) their unparalleled condition; and earnestly beg that this high court, since they are not under any pretended conviction of law, will be pleased to examine this arbitrary power and to question by what authority so great a breach is made upon the free people of England, they having never seen the faces of these their pretended owners, merchants that deal in slaves and souls of men, nor ever heard of their names before Mr. Cole made affidavit in the office of Barbadoes, that he sold them as their goods; but whence they derived their authority for the sale and slavery of your poor petitioners, and the rest, they are wholly ignorant to this very day. That this high court will be farther pleased to interest their power for the redemption and reparation of your distressed petitioners, and the rest; or if the names of your petitioners, and the number of the rest, be so inconsiderable as not to be worthy of relief or your tender compassion, yet, at least, that this court would be pleased on the behalf of themselves and all the free-born people of England, by whose suffrages[9] they sit in Parliament, any of whose cases it may be next, whenever a like force shall be laid on them, to take course to curb the unlimited power under which the petitioners and others suffer; that neither you nor any of their brethren, upon these miserable terms, may come into this miserable place of torment. A thing not known amongst the cruel Turks, to sell and enslave those of their own country and religion, much less the innocent. . . .

Sir Henry Vane: I do not look on this business as a Cavalierish business[10]; but as a matter that concerns the liberty of the free-born people of England.

---

[8] *the bread and tears of their own afflictions:* Cf. 2 Samuel 22.27 ("Feed him with bread of affliction, and with water of affliction").

[9] *suffrages:* Votes.

[10] *a Cavalierish business:* A concern unique to the Cavaliers, or Royalists, the political party opposed to the parliamentarians during this period. Vane is arguing that the issue is nonpartisan, even though Foyle and Rivers were accused of participating in a Royalist rebellion.

To be used in this barbarous manner, put under hatches, to see no light till they came thither, and sold there for 100*l.*: such was the case of this Thomas.

I am glad to hear the old cause[11] so well resented; that we have a sense and loathing of the tyranny of the late king, and of all that tread in his steps, to impose on liberty and property. As I should be glad to see any discouragement upon the Cavaliers, so I should be glad to see any discouragement and indignation of yours against such person as tread in Charles Stuart's steps, whoever they be. The end of the major-generals was good as to keeping down that party, but the precedent was dangerous.

Let us not be led away, that whenever the tables turn, the same will be imposed upon your best men, that is now designed to the worst. There is a fallacy and subtilty on both hands. I would have you be as vigilant against that party as you can; but if you find the liberty and property of the people of England thus violated, take occasion from these ill precedents to make good laws. . . .

Mr. Boscawen: I am as much against the Cavalier party as any man in these walls, and shall as zealously assert the old cause; but you have Paul's case before you. A Roman ought not to be beaten.[12] We are miserable slaves, if we may not have this liberty secured to us.

I am not against the ministers of state in intervals of Parliament securing men that are dangerous; but I would have it represented to the next Parliament, with the cause of their imprisonment.

These persons come to justify themselves. If you pass[13] this, our lives will be as cheap as those negroes. They look upon them as their goods, horses, etc. and rack them only to make their time out of them, and cherish them to perform their work. It may be my case. I would have you consider the trade of buying and selling men.

Sir John Lenthall: I hope it is not the effect of our war to make merchandize of men. I consider them as Englishmen. I so much love my own liberty as to part with aught to redeem these people out of captivity. We are the freest people in the world. Let us remember when we go out of these doors, we know not what may become of us if we omit this. They are put to such hardships, to heats and colds, and converse

[11] *the old cause:* The opposition to Charles Stuart, King Charles I, who was executed in 1649.

[12] *Paul's case . . . beaten:* See Acts 22.25 ("and as they bound him with thongs, Paul said to the centurion that stood by, Is it lawful for you to scourge a man that is a Roman, and uncondemned?").

[13] *pass:* Overlook, ignore.

with horses. If my zeal carry me beyond its bounds, it is to plead for the liberty of an Englishman, which I cannot hear mentioned but I must defend it

Major Knight: I move to reject the petition; for if you sit twelve months you will not have time to hear all petitions from Cavaliers. What will you do with the Scots taken at Dunbar, and at Dunham and Worcester?[14] Many of them were sent to Barbadoes. Will you hear all their petitions?

Sir Arthur Haslerigge went on, and said, by the law of the land, no Englishman ought to be imprisoned but in order to a trial. We have assizes, commissions of oyer and terminer,[15] that any Englishman may have death or liberty, which he deserves. Our ancestors have ever been tender of the liberties of Englishmen. If after a man be condemned, his keeper kill him, he shall be hanged for it. The keeper cannot, ought not, to abuse him in any kind. Nor can any man, by the law of the land, banish any man. Some of these had sentence of death. So might the rest have had, and not be kept in prison twelve months after, and then sent to banishment. The time of war and the time of peace are different.

We have had no war these seven years. True, a little rebellion, and some suffered. Blessed be God, we have had none since.

These men deny that they were ever sentenced, charged, or in arms. Some were acquitted by *ignoramus*. These men are now sold into slavery amongst beasts. I could hardly hold weeping when I heard the petition.

That which is the Cavalier's case, to-day, may be the Roundhead's[16] a year hence. I desire not to live if they prevail. I never sought them, but we must be careful of suffering such precedents. We are likely to be governed by an army. When the army went to the Isle of Rhee,[17] one

---

[14] *Dunbar, and at Durham and Worcester:* In the final phase (1650–51) of the Civil Wars, Cromwell's parliamentarian army suppressed a Scottish rebellion that made some inway into northern England before finally being halted at Worcester; many of those captured at the battles listed here were deported, and Knight is concerned to differentiate their punishment from the case at hand.

[15] *assizes, commissions of oyer and terminer:* Courts; the assizes (meaning "sittings") were held periodically in each county in England, while the commissions of oyer and terminer ("hearing and determining") were special commissions directed to hear indictments on particular offenses.

[16] *Roundhead's:* "Roundhead" was another name for the parliamentarians.

[17] *Isle of Rhee:* I.e., Ré (French Île de Ré), an island in the Bay of Biscay, opposite La Rochelle on the western coast of France; in 1627, George Villiers, Duke of Buckingham, unsuccessfully attempted a siege of the island, and following heavy losses (and in the face of heavy opposition), proposed the creation of a standing army to continue the war against France.

was hanged up by martial law. The Parliament so abhorred it, that, if it had sat, he that caused it to be done had lost his head.

I would have every man be careful how he acts any man's commands against law. If there be thirty in a crowd, ten may be guilty; the rest innocent: and haply but one innocent, and forty guilty. Were not divers of them hanged? Was not that an argument that the rest are clear?

I have never yet done aught, nor I hope shall, to give a suspicion that I have any countenance for the Cavaliers in this business. If our liberties be come to this, we have fought fair and caught a frog.

I would have this business referred back to the grand committee. I hope the gentlemen will be clear, and that they will be warier hereafter. Our ancestors left us free men. If we have fought our sons into slavery, we are of all men most miserable.

Legal Decisions Concerning Slavery in England

Like the preceding selection, these law cases reveal some of the problems the English encountered when attempting to treat slavery as a logical corollary of their established conventions — in this case, their rules for analyzing and classifying property. The decisions included here contradict one another on almost every issue they address — most saliently, the questions of whether a person can be property in England, what kind of property he or she can be, and whether baptism affects that status. Complicating these questions further is the problem that before the nineteenth century, legal decisions were not consistently reported (i.e., published in a collection of rulings); the unreported decisions, which had to be located and read in manuscript, were cited in some instances and ignored or overlooked in others. It should be noted that the factual background of the lawsuits reprinted here remains obscure; some of them might have been motivated by opposition to slavery, but in all likelihood they began as private property disputes that happened to raise the issue of slavery. Not until the last half of the eighteenth century was there any concerted abolitionist effort to make the legitimacy of slavery itself a subject of litigation.

In *Butts v. Penny* (1677), the first reported decision on slavery in English law, the plaintiff relied on two arguments that would be rehearsed frequently in later cases, arguing that Africans were "infidels" (417) and that they were customarily treated as merchandise. The judge, however, refused to rule on the legality of slavery; his *"nisi causa"* (417) judgment means that, in effect, he made no judgment at all, and so the decision had no value as a precedent. *Butts* was followed by two unreported decisions, neither of which is reprinted here: in *Sir Thomas Grantham's Case* (1687), the judge ruled that there could be property in a "monster" imported from the Indies, even though the man in question had "turned Christian and was baptized"; conversely, the ruling in *Gelly v. Cleve* (1694) seemed to treat baptism as a bar to slavery, announcing that "trover [recovery of a lost object] will lic for a Negro boy; for they are heathens, and therefore a man may have property in them" (421). The next officially reported decision, *Chamberline v. Harvey* (1697), holds that slaves were not a form of merchandise — were not so unfree as to be mere chattel property — but should instead be seen as potential sources of labor. In effect, slaves were characterized as a kind of servant, a person whose freedom was limited but not completely annihilated. Included here are two different versions of the *Chamberline* decision: the first report summarizes the plaintiff's efforts to justify his property claim, concluding with the policy arguments against regarding baptism as a bar to slavery ("it would very much endanger the trade" [420]), while the second report presents the judge's distinctions among different modes of property, hinging in this instance on the distinction between trover (recovery of a lost object) and trespass (unlawful interference with another's property). In this view, a plaintiff could succeed in a suit for the misappropriation of a slave only by specifying a particular kind of trespass (a *per quod servitium amisit*) which involved the loss of another's service, and which would also apply to the labor of an apprentice or monk. Since the plaintiff failed to bring suit on those grounds, he lost ("it will not lie in this case," the judge explains).

The next set of cases leads to further contradictions. *Smith v. Brown and Cooper* (1701), with its assertion that "as soon as a negro comes into England, he becomes free" (421) was understood by many to abolish slavery within Britain, but in fact Justice Holt's ruling carefully created a legal fiction under the law of contract (the *indebitatus assumpsit* mentioned in the first line) by which Africans, though not labeled as slaves, could still be bought and sold. Again, *Smith v. Gould* (1705) explicitly rejected *Butts* but upheld the plaintiff's action of trespass, ruling that Smith was entitled to the value of the slave he had paid for. Also included here is an unofficial manuscript report of the ruling, which further elaborates the nature of the "Speciall Property" (422) right adduced in this case — likened by the judge to a captive's ransom. Two opposite rulings were handed down in a pair of midcentury cases that went unreported, and the question finally seemed to be resolved in *Somerset v. Stewart* (1772), which William Cowper celebrated in "The Task" (1785), declaring that when slaves "touch our country . . . their shackles fall." The ruling, however, was significantly narrower, dictating only that once imported into England, slaves could not be compelled to leave the country.

In the course of the arguments in *Somerset,* the lawyers referred to the very first pronouncement on the legality of slavery in England, itself a telling indication of the legal ambiguities that would follow. *Cartwright's Case* (1569) was an unreported decision that involved a slave imported not from Africa but Russia; the master was challenged for whipping his slave, and the court ruled that "England was too pure an Air for Slaves to breathe in," a dictum that evidently influenced both the 1701 *Smith* decision and Cowper's paean to English liberty. Even in its own day, however, the *Cartwright* principle was hardly self-evident, as the 1547 statute reprinted in this chapter suggests.

Notice that the frequently invoked (and much disputed) distinction between heathens and Christians operates in the absence of any racially based definition of slavery, because no such understanding of slavery was available in English law. In the British West Indies, however, the slave owners themselves enacted the statutes they conceived to be necessary for their own safety and prosperity, and those regulations frequently relied on racial distinctions. Hence, for example, as noted in the introduction to this volume, the Barbados slave act of 1661 characterized Africans as "heathenish, brutish, and . . . dangerous" (11); the law went on to specify the kinds of physical abuse permissible for slaves but not for servants, and similarly, the act specified much harsher penalties for crimes when committed by slaves rather than by servants. Later amendments prohibited Africans from taking up such occupations as tailor or carpenter, and instituted stricter controls over the movements of Africans (for these statutes served in large part as policing measures). Following the same model, an Antigua act of 1702 ("An Act for the better Government of Slaves and Free Negroes") forbade anyone of African descent from striking or even insulting a white person.

The cases reprinted here are taken from the following volumes of the *English Reports: Butts v. Penny* appears in 83:518 and 84:1011; *Chamberline v. Harvey* appears in 87:598–600 and 91:594; and the two *Smith* decisions appear in 91:566–67. The manuscript report of *Smith v. Gould* is taken from Joseph Davy's law notes, during Michaelmas term 1705–1706, fol. 22, in his manuscript "Cases in King's Bench." The original manuscript is at Harvard Law School.

Butts v. Penny, *English Reports* 83:518 (King's Bench, 1677)

Trover for 100 *negroes,* and upon *non culp.*[1] it was found by special verdict, that the *negroes* were infidels, and the *subjects of an infidel prince,* and are usually bought and sold in America as merchandise, by the custom of merchants, and that the plaintiff bought these, and was in possession of them until the defendant took them. And Thompson argued, there could be no property in the person of a man sufficient to maintain trover. . . . That no property could be in villains[2] but by compact and conquest. But the Court held, that *negroes* being usually bought and sold among merchants, as merchandise, and also being infidels, there might be a property in them sufficient to maintain trover, and gave judgment for the plaintiff, *nisi causa,*[3] this term; and at the end of the term, upon the prayer of the Attorney-General to be heard as to this matter, day was given until next term.

Butts v. Penny, *ER* 84:1011

Special verdict in trover of 10 negroes and a half find them usually bought and sold in India, and if this were sufficient property, or conversion, was the question. And Thomson, for the defendant, said here could be no property in the plaintiff more than in villains; but per Curiam,[4] they are by usage tanquam bona,[5] and go to administrator untill they become Christians; and thereby they are infranchised[6]: and judgment for the plaintiff, nisi, and it lieth of moety[7] or third part against any stranger, albeit not against the other copartners.

Chamberline v. Harvey, *ER* 87:598–600

Trespass will not lie[8] for "taking and carrying away one *negro slave* of the price of, &c. so that the plaintiff was totally without, and lost

---

[1] *non culp:* I.e., *non culpabilis,* a pleading of "not guilty."

[2] *villains:* I.e., villeins. Villenage was a medieval English institution by which serfs, or unfree peasants, were attached to the manor of a feudal lord and were required to perform servile work, usually agricultural labor. Because of their relation to the estate, villeins were often considered a kind of property; if the lord sold his land, for example, the villeins would be included in the sale. Villenage began to disappear in the fourteenth century, and was almost extinct by the end of the sixteenth century.

[3] *nisi causa:* A decree that the judgment stands unless the losing party can show cause to have it revoked.

[4] *per Curiam:* According to the court.

[5] *tanquam bona:* Such a good, sufficient to count as property.

[6] *infranchised:* Set free.

[7] *moety:* Half.

[8] *will not lie:* Will not apply legally.

the use and benefit of, the said *negro, &c.*" for by the laws of England one man cannot have an *absolute property* in *the person* of another man; but, as under certain circumstances a man may have a *qualified property* in another, in the character of *servant, &c.* an action for taking him away, will, in such case, lie *per quod servitium amisit.*[9]

Trespass for taking a negro slave of the value of one hundred pounds; upon *not guilty* pleaded, the jury found a special verdict[10] at the Guildhall[11] in London. . . .

A case like this never happened before.

Three questions were made upon this verdict:

First, whether, upon this finding, there was any legal property vested in the plaintiff?

Secondly, if any such property be vested in him, then whether the bringing this negro into England be not a *manumission,* and the property thereby divested?

Thirdly, whether an action of *trespass* will lie for taking *a man* of the price of one hundred pounds?

As to the first, though the word "*slave*" has but a very harsh sound in a free and Christian country, yet perfect bondage has been allowed in such places. The power which naturally arises to the lord over such bondmen or slaves, is by reason of his supplying them with food and raiment during their lives, as a recompence for their labour: such is the usage of the island of Barbadoes. The jury have found a law there, which makes these slaves part of the real estate, and this negro was born of negro parents there. Now the children of such parents are slaves as well as they. So it was amongst the Romans; where both parents were aliens,[12] the children were so too. This ordinance made in Barbadoes, being subject to the Crown of England, has the same force there as an Act of Parliament has here. Now if this had been the case of *a villein* here, the jury have found enough to make him *regardant to a manor*[13] in which, by the law of this land, the lord had so absolute a property, that if he were taken away, the party detaining him gained

---

[9] *per quod servitium amasit:* Whereby he lost the service (of his servant).

[10] *special verdict:* The jury's verdict had entirely to do with the facts of the case; they agreed to accept the account of the slave's background, recounted on p. 417 (where the phrase "special verdict" appears again), but they deferred to a judge for a ruling on whether those facts could support a legal action of trespass.

[11] *the Guildhall:* The hall of the Corporation of the City of London.

[12] *aliens:* Noncitizens.

[13] *regardant to a manor:* Attached to the estate and hence inseparable from it (by contrast with personal property that the owner could sell at will).

no property in him; for then the writ *de nativo habendo*[14] must be brought against him, but it is only directed to the sheriff to take him wherever he may be found, &c. An action of *trover* will not lie, except where the plaintiff has a property in the thing demanded. Now it cannot be denied but that *trover* will lie for a *negro;* for so was the case *Butts* v. *Penny.* It is true, there is no judgment entered in that case; that may be the fault of the attorney in not bringing in the *postea.*[15]

Secondly, nothing here found amounts to a manumission or enfranchisement. Manumission is defined by Littleton[16] to be, when the lord makes a deed to his *villein* to enfranchise him, this is one kind of manumission; the other is, when the lord does some act which, in judgment of law, amounts to make his *villein* free, as by making a feoffment in fee to him, and delivering seisin[17] accordingly, &c. It is true, he may have several temporary privileges whereby he may be exempted from the seisin of the lord, as entering into religion, &c. but can in no case be enfranchised but where the lord is an actor; and even in such case, if the lord himself had enfranchised him by deed, . . . this was not a sufficient manumission of such children which he had before the execution of the deed without special words, because they were *villeins* in possession at the time. But here is nothing of the lord's consent found in this verdict; but the contrary. Then the bringing of him into England by Sir John Witham will not make him free, because he was a trespasser in so doing; for he ought not to have removed him from the plantation to which he was *regardant.* If, therefore, taking him from the plantation was *tortious,*[18] then the finding that he continued in his service, and that he was afterwards turned away, will not amount to a manumission. The chief question then is, whether *baptism* without the privity of the lord will amount to a manumission? Now if a bare consent, without any other act of the lord, will not be sufficient to make his *villein* free, so as to divest himself of that property which he had in him; then *à fortiori,*[19] what the *villein* does without the consent of the lord, cannot acquire a manumission. That a bare consent alone is not

[14] *de nativo habendo:* A writ authorizing the capture of a fugitive villein, and ordering him to be restored to his lord.

[15] *postea:* A formal record of the trial proceedings.

[16] *Littleton:* Sir Thomas Littleton (c. 1415–1481), whose *Tenures* (c. 1481), written in Law French, offered the first authoritative account of the laws relating to landholding.

[17] *feoffment in fee . . . delivering seisin:* The formal legal process for transferring property in land from one owner to another.

[18] *tortious:* Wrongful.

[19] *à fortiori:* Still more conclusively.

sufficient, appears by my Lord Coke's Commentary on Littleton,[20] and the authorities there cited in the margin, that if a *neif*[21] *regardant* to a manor marry a freeman without the license of the lord, who afterwards makes a feoffment of the manor, and then her husband dies, the lord shall still have *the neif,* and not the feoffee.[22] If baptism should be accounted a manumission, it would very much endanger the trade of the plantations, which cannot be carried on without the help and labour of these slaves; for the parsons are bound to baptize them as soon as they can give a reasonable account of the Christian faith; and if that would make them free, then few would be slaves.

Chamberline v. Harvey, *ER* 91:594

No man can have property in the person of another while in England. Therefore trespass will not lie, unless with a per quod, for taking a negro slave in England. Trespass lies for the taking an apprentice.

Trespass for taking of a negro pretii[23] 100l. The jury find a special verdict; that the father of the plaintiff was possessed of this negro, and of such a manor in Barbadoes, and that there is a law in that country, which makes the negro part of the real estate: that the father died seised,[24] whereby the manor descended to the plaintiff as son and heir, and that he endowed his mother of this negro and of a third part of the manor; that the mother married Watkins, who brought the negro into England, where he was baptized without the knowledge of the mother; that Watkins and his wife are dead, and that the negro continued several years in England; that the defendant seized him, &c. . . . This term it was adjudged, that his action will not lie. Trespass will lie for taking of an apprentice. . . . An abbot might maintain trespass for his monk; and any man may maintain trespass for another, if he declares with a per quod servitium amisit: but it will not lie in this case. And per Holt Chief Justice, trover will not lie for a negro, contra to *Butts* v. *Penny.* . . .

Gelly and Cleve, adjudged that trover will lie for a negro boy; for

---

[20] *Coke's Commentary on Littleton:* Sir Edward Coke (1552–1634) published an extremely influential commentary on Littleton's *Tenures* in 1628.

[21] *neif:* A villein.

[22] *feoffee:* The person who receives an estate through feoffment.

[23] *pretii:* Of the value of.

[24] *seised:* In possession of the estate.

they are heathens, and therefore a man may have property in them, and that the Court, without averment made, will take notice that they are heathens. . . .

Smith v. *Gould,* adjudged that it lies not.

Smith v. Brown and Cooper, ER 91:566–67

The plaintiff declared in an *indebitatus assumpsit*[25] for 20l. for a negro sold by the plaintiff to the defendant. . . . and verdict for the plaintiff; and, on motion in arrest of judgment, Holt, C.J. held, that as soon as a negro comes into England, he becomes free: one may be a villein in England, but not a slave. *Et per Powell, J.* In a villein the owner has a property, but it is an inheritance; in a ward he has a property, but it is a chattel real[26]; the law took no notice of a negro. Holt, C.J. You should have averred in the declaration, that the sale was in Virginia, and, by the laws of that country, negroes are saleable; for the laws of England do not extend to Virginia, being a conquered country their law is what the King pleases; and we cannot take notice of it but as set forth; therefore he directed the plaintiff should amend, and the declaration should be made, that the defendant was indebted to the plaintiff for a negro sold here at London, but that the said negro at the time of sale was in Virginia, and that negroes, by the laws and statues of Virginia, are saleable as chattels. Then the Attorney-General coming in, said, they were inheritances, and transferrable by deed, and not without: and nothing was done.

Smith v. Gould, ER 91:567

Trover for several things, and among the rest *de uno Æthiope vocat.* a negro[27]; and, on not guilty pleaded, verdict was for the plaintiff, and several damages; and as to the negro 30l. And it was moved in arrest of judgment, that trover lay not for a negro, for that the owner had not an absolute property in him; he could not kill him as he could an ox. *Contra,*[28] it was said property implies the right of having

---

[25] *indebitatus assumpsit:* A claim that another has undertaken a debt and has failed to pay (literally, "being indebted, he promised").

[26] *chattel real:* A right or claim to property in real estate (as opposed to outright possession). Powell's view is that humans cannot be the object of such outright possession in English law.

[27] *de uno Æthiope vocat. a negro:* An Ethiopean called a negro.

[28] *Contra:* Against, on the other side.

and enjoying, and disposing; but it does not always imply a power to destroy; that his power holds in beasts, fowl, and fish, which were made the property of mankind by the act of God, and have a natural existence, but not in things incorporeal, which consist *in jure tantum*[29]; for this being a property *ex instituto*[30] only, the owner has only a power according to the measure of this instituted right: and it was instanced in the case of a common, a way, and a ward. On a *ca. sa.*[31] the plaintiff has an interest in the body of the prisoner as a pledge not to sell, but to keep, and it goes to the executors. In a servant to work him; in a captive to sell him. That the writ *de nativo habendo* must lay the explees[32] of a villein in working and taxing him at will. That by the law of Moses a man may be a slave, and a slave was a chattel, *his master's money,* Exod. 20, 21. That by the same reason there may be a *servus prædialis,*[33] *i.e.* a villein. One may be a *servus personalis,*[34] and that first a captive and afterwards a villein. A villein in gross is a chattel, for his is of a perishable nature, and cannot endure for ever. . . . As villeins are regardant to land it is a different thing, and in that respect they are inheritances, and so are the charters. Every villein is intended in law regardant; . . . but before he was a villein he was a captive, and then a chattel. Lastly, it was insisted, that the Court ought to take notice that they were merchandize. If I imprison my negro, a *habeas corpus*[35] will not lie to deliver him, for by *Magna Charta*[36] he must be *liber homo.*[37] *Sed Curia contra,*[38] Men may be the owners, and therefore cannot be the subject of property.

Smith v. Gould, Joseph Davy's Manuscript Notes

A Man may have a Speciall Property in his Captive to Get his Ransom. So a Man may have the Like in his Villein. But he Can't either

[29] *in jure tantum:* Only in law.

[30] *ex instituto:* By convention, by a legal institution.

[31] *ca. sa.: Capias ad satisfaciendum,* a writ authorizing someone to be taken and required to appear in court in order to pay for debts or damages.

[32] *explees:* Products of an estate, including both agricultural output and rent and services.

[33] *servus prædialis:* A slave attached to a particular estate.

[34] *servus personalis:* A slave attached to a person, and therefore capable of being sold by the owner.

[35] *habeas corpus:* A writ allowing someone to appear before a court and a judge, guaranteeing the right to a legal hearing.

[36] *Magna Charta:* The "Great Charter" of personal and political liberty in England, signed by King John in 1215.

[37] *liber homo:* A free man.

[38] *Sed Curia contra:* But the court said, against this.

Wound or Mahame[39] him & of this our Law takes Notice. But our Law takes no notice of Negroes nor knows Such Slaves as you mean — And it Looks on Negroes & Polacks[40] as on the rest of mankind — Negroes are Inheritances in Barbadoes. And Bringing 'em into England don't make Chattles. — No doubt You may have an Action on the Speciall Property for them. But no Such Action as this is.

[39] *Mahame:* I.e., maim.
[40] *Polacks:* I.e., Polish serfs; the term *slave* itself came into currency because the Slavs in parts of central Europe (and especially Poland) had historically been forced into serfdom.

EDWARD LITTLETON

From *The Groans of the Plantations*

This selection and the three that follow examine the benefits of the colonial system for the English domestic economy. Littleton's 1689 pamphlet (introduced on p. 375) concentrates on the employment opportunities created in England by the need to manufacture supplies for the plantations in Barbados. It also points to the importance of England's achieving a competitive position vis-à-vis other European colonial nations. Like Sir Dalby Thomas and Thomas Tryon, Littleton undertakes to defend the sugar colonies and to promote their product as part of a late seventeenth-century campaign designed to accomplish two objectives: the reduction of English import taxes (which had been doubled in 1685 by James II's Parliament), and the dissolution of the Royal African Company's monopoly on the supply of slaves (which the planters thought artificially inflated their price). The Company's monopoly was formally terminated in 1698, but the price of slaves, far from decreasing, doubled within ten years. Littleton probably wrote his pamphlet directly after the Glorious Revolution that unseated James II in 1688. In the new political climate, royal monopolistic privileges were thought to be null and void, and Littleton seized the moment to assert the planters' interest. Moreover, the RAC in particular had counted among its managers a number of James's close associates, untouchable during his reign but now presumably ripe for criticism. Although the RAC persisted after 1688, it no longer suppressed private traders, who were responsible for the huge increase in the slave trade that characterized British colonial commerce during the next century. In this instance, Littleton's effort met with a heated rebuttal from a proponent of the duties on sugar, whose response is reprinted in the next selection.

The text is taken from the first edition of *The Groans of the Plantations: Or a True Account of Their Grievous and Extreme Sufferings by the Heavy Impositions upon Sugar, and other Hardships, Relating more particularly to the Island of Barbados* (London: Printed by M. Clark, 1689) 28–32.

We have yearly from *England* an infinite Quantity of Iron Wares ready wrought. Thousands of Dozens of Howes,[1] and great numbers of Bills[2] to cut our Canes. many Barrels of Nails; many Sets of Smiths, Carpenters, and Coopers[3] Tools; all our Locks and Hinges; with Swords, Pistols, Carbines, Muskets, and Fowling Pieces.

We have also from *England* all sorts of Tin-ware, Earthen-ware, and Wooden-ware: and all our Brass and Pewter. And many a Serne of Sope,[4] many a Quoyle[5] of Rope, and of Lead many a Fodder,[6] do the Plantations take from *England*.

Even *English* Cloth is much worn amongst us; but we have of Stuffs far greater Quantities. From *England* come all the Hats we weare; and of Shoos, thousands of Dozens yearly. The white Broad cloth that we use for Strainers,[7] comes also to a great deal of Money. Our very *Negro* Caps, of Woollen-yarn knit, (of which also we have yearly thousands of Dozens) may pass for a Manufacture.[8]

How many Spinners, Knitters, and Weavers are kept at work here in *England*, to make all the Stockings we wear? Woollen Stockings for the ordinary People, Silk Stockings when we could go to the price, Worsted Stockings in abundance, and Thread Stockings without number.

As we have our Horses from *England*; So all our Saddles and Bridles come from *England* likewise. which we desire should be good ones, and are not sparing in the price.

---

[1] *Howes:* I.e., hoes.

[2] *Bills:* Tools for pruning, cutting wood, etc.

[3] *Coopers:* Craftsmen who make casks, buckets, tubs, etc.

[4] *Serne of sope:* Possibly a variant spelling of *cerne,* meaning "circle;" hence, in this context, a cake of soap.

[5] *Quoyle:* I.e., coil.

[6] *Fodder:* I.e., fother, a large quantity.

[7] *Broad cloth . . . Strainers:* Broadcloth is a fine, plain-woven cloth, used in this case as a filter for liquid.

[8] *may pass for a Manufacture:* May be counted among the exports from England.

The Bread we eat, is of *English* Flower[9]: we take great Quantity of *English* Beer, and of *English* Cheese and Butter: we sit by the light of *English* Candles; and the Wine we drink, is bought for the most part with *English* Commodities. Ships bound for the Plantations touch at *Madera*,[10] and there sell their Goods, and invest the Produce in Wines.

Moreover we take yearly thousands of Barrels of *Irish* Beef: with the price whereof those people pay their Rents, to their Landlords that live and spend their Estates in *England*.

'Tis strange we should be thought to diminish the People of *England*, when we do so much increase the Employments. Where there are Employments, there will be People: you cannot keep them out, nor drive them away, with Pitchforks. On the other side, where the Employments faile or are wanting, the People will be gone. They will never stay there to starve, or to eat up one another. Great numbers of *French* Protestants that came lately to *England*,[11] left us again upon this account. It was their Saying; We have been received with great Kindness and Charity, but here is no Imployment.

However it is charged upon the Plantations (and we can be charged with nothing else), that they take People from *England*. But doth not *Ireland* do the same? It may be truly said, that if the *American* Colonies have taken thousands, *Ireland* hath taken ten thousands. Yet we cannot find, that people were ever stopp'd from going thither, or that ever it was thought an Inconvenience. You will say the Cases are different: in regard the *Plantations* are remote; whereas *Ireland* is neer at hand. and our people that are in *Ireland* can give us ready Assistance. In answer hereunto it is confess'd, that where Colonies are neer, the Power is more united. But it must be confess'd likewise, that where the Colonies are remote, the Power is farther extended. So that These may be as useful one way, as Those are another way. It concerns a Generall to have his Army united. but may he not detach part of it, to possess a Post at some distance, though it be of never so great advantage? It is plainly an advantage, to have a Command and Influence upon remote Parts of the World. Moreover the remote Colonies of *America* are much more advantageous to *England* in point of Trade,

---

[9] *Flower:* I.e., flour.

[10] *Madera:* An island in the North Atlantic, approximately 500 miles off the coast of Morocco. A possession of Portugal, its main exports at this time were sugar and Madeira wine.

[11] *French Protestants that came lately to England:* The Huguenots, who emigrated from France in 1685, when the revocation of the Edict of Nantes would have required them to convert to Catholicism.

then is the neer one of *Ireland*. For Ireland producing the same things, takes little from us, and also spoiles our Markets in other places. Nor doth it furnish us with any thing, which before we bought of Forrainers. But the *American* Plantations do both take off from *England* abundance of Commodities; and do likewise furnish *England* with divers Commodities of value, which formerly were imported from forrain Parts. which things are now become our owne: and are made Native. For you must know, and may please to consider, That the Sugar we make in the *American Plantations* (to instance only in that) is as much a native *English* Commodity, as if it were made and produced in *England*.

But still you will say, that we draw People from *England*. We confess we do, as a Man draws Water from a good Well. Who the more he draws in reason, the more he may: the Well being continually supplied. *Anglia puteus inexhaustus*,[12] said a Pope of old in another sense, that is, in matter of Money. But in matter of People it is likewise true; That *England* is a Well or Spring inexhausted, which hath never the less Water in it, for having some drawn from it.

You will say yet further, that the Plantations dis-people *England*. But this we utterly deny. Why may not you say as well, that the *Roman* Colonies dispeopled *Rome*? which yet was never pretended[13] or imagined. That wise and glorious State, when ever there was a convenience of settling a Colony, thought fit to send out thousands of people at a time, at the Publick Charge. And wise Men are of opinion, That as the *Roman* Empire was the greatest that the World hath yet seen; so it chiefly owed its Grandeur to its free emission of Colonies.

And whereas the Kingdoms of *Spain* may seem dispeopled and exhausted by their *American* Colonies; if the thing be well examin'd, their Sloth and not their Colonies hath been the true Cause. To which may be added the Rigour of their Government, and their many Arts and Waies of destroying Trade.

But what will you say to the *Dutch*? for They, we know, have Colonies in the *East-Indies*. Do these exhaust and depopulate *Holland*, or at least are they a Burden and an Inconvenience? The *Dutch* themselves are so far from thinking so, that they justly esteem them the chief and main foundation of their Wealth and Trade. Their *East-Indy* Trade depends upon their *East-Indy* Colonies; and their whole State in effect, that is, the Greatness and Glory of it, depends upon their *East-*

---

[12] *Anglia puteus inexhaustus:* England is an inexhaustible well.
[13] *pretended:* Alleged.

Indy Trade. Moreover as their Wealth and Trade increases, their People increase likewise.

They have also some Places in the *West-Indies:* which they prize not a little. How do they cherish *Suranam,* though it be one of the basest Countries in the World? And their Island of *Quaracoa*[14] (*Carisaw* we pronounce it) they are as tender of, as any man can be of the apple of his Eye. Also their repeated Endeavours to settle *Tabago*[15] do sufficiently evince, that they would very willingly spare some of their People, to increase their share in the Sugar Trade. But for a further proof of their Sentiment in these Matters; we may remember, that in the heat of their last War with *France,* they sent their Admiral *De Ruyter* with a great Force, to attempt the *French* Sugar Islands in *America.* which they would not have done, had they not thought them highly valuable. But the *French* King was as mindful to keep his Islands, as they were to get them: and he took such order and had such Force to defend them, as render'd the *Dutch* Attempts ineffectual. Thus the *French* and *Dutch,* while all lay at stake at home, were contending in the *West-Indies* for Plantations; which our Politicians count worth nothing, or worse then nothing. You'll say, this same French Court, and these Dutch States, are meer ignorant Novices, and do not know the World. Perhaps not so well as our Politicians: But however something they know.

Many have observed that *France* is much dispeopled by Tyranny and Oppression. But that their Plantations have in the least dispeopled it, was never yet said nor thought. And That King sets such a value upon his Plantations, and is so far from thinking his People lost that are in his Plantations; that he payes a good part of the Fraight, of all those that will go to them to settle: giving them all fair Encouragements besides.

If Colonies be so pernicious to their Mother Country, it was a great happiness to *Portugall,* that the *Dutch* stripp'd them of their *East-India* Colonies. And surely they feel the difference: but it is much for the worse. *Lisbon* is not that *Lisbon* now, which it was in those days. And did not the recovery of *Brasile* (though that Trade be now low) in some measure support them, with the help of *Madera,* the *Western Islands,* and some other Colonies; *Portugall* would be one of the poorest places upon Earth.

[14] *Quaracoa:* Curaçoa, an island of the Netherlands Antilles, off the coast of Venezuela; it was a major trading center for the Dutch West India Company in the later seventeenth century.

[15] *Tabago:* Tobago, a British colony in the West Indies.

From *A Discourse of the Duties on Merchandize, More Particularly of that on Sugars*

This pamphlet, by an anonymous "merchant," responds point by point to *The Groans of the Plantations,* claiming that many of Littleton's complaints are properly the concern of import and export merchants rather than sugar farmers, and that the taxes to which he objects do not, in any case, have an appreciable effect on the Barbados farmers' profits. The author begins by criticizing the farmers for their extravagant habits; common sense, he suggests, should warn them to live more frugally, because constantly increasing productivity means that prices cannot remain high indefinitely. The English Barbadians' manner of living, in fact, scandalized many visitors, who frequently returned home with descriptions of an utterly dissipated society, shamelessly devoted to drink and sexual pleasure. Turning to the argument over taxes on refined sugar, the writer calculates the cost of shipping "Fine Sugars" from Barbados without the export duty, and argues that sugar refiners in England were at a significant disadvantage until the duty was imposed in 1685. Moreover, he proposes that the laws of supply and demand will prevent the tax from having any effect at all on sugar consumption, claiming that any drop in prices can be ascribed entirely to a market glut. While his views on the fixity of demand are questionable, this last assessment appears to be accurate: sugar production had more than doubled between 1660 and 1690, and during the same period the price of sugar in London dropped by fifty percent. Finally, the writer closes by recommending an increase in the tax on raw sugar and a decrease in the rate on refined sugar, hoping that this concession will boost English participation in the international sugar trade.

The text is excerpted from *A Discourse of the Duties on Merchandize, More Particularly of that on Sugars, Occasionally Offer'd, In Answer to a Pamphlet, Intituled, The Groans of the Plantations, &c. By a Merchant* (London: 1695) 7, 11–13, 19, 20–21, 26–28.

Indeed what he mentions of the Management of the *Guinea* Trade, seems to me to be the first Grievance that he instances, which properly affects the Planter; but as he proposes the laying a Tax on Negro's sold, as a better way to support the Forts and Garisons in *Africa*, than the erecting a Monopoly: as that Tax must have been considerable enough to answer the end; so I doubt if it had been so manag'd, this Gentleman would now have complain'd against it as a burden as heavy upon them as any of the rest. But what he tells of the undue practices and severities of the Government there, in Seizing and condemning the Interlopers, no doubt is a great Grievance, but still it lies chiefly on the Merchant, not the Planter. . . .

No People in the World have been more remarkable for a Luxuriant way of Living, so it may be more proper to ask, Whether they have, in any measure, retrench'd those Extravagant Excesses that were wont to[1] abound amongst them, or have yet learn'd what Providence and Good Husbandry is? But as we have yet heard nothing less, so we have no reason to believe that things have been quite so bad with them, as this Gentlemen hath studied to represent.

But if this should be taken as too great a Reflection on the Planters, it could not well be avoided, because the Gentleman hath endeavoured to represent them as a poor, starv'd, undone People, when the contrary is so evident to all that are acquainted with the manner of Living in those Parts. Besides those that are Sober and Discreet among them, (of which doubtless there are many) will not blame me for a gentle Reproof of Vice, where there is so much Reason and Truth. Moreover, it may not be an unseasonable Occasion to put those Gentlemen in mind, that as they have had the Opportunity of those vast Improvements, to raise to themselves, by their own Industry, Estates of 500, some 1000, 2000l. Sterling per *Annum;* so 'tis a Wonder that Sugars should continue to hold up their price so well, when by the Settlement of so many other Plantations, there hath been so great an Encrease of that Commodity; which (and not Impositions) will probably be the means whereby the price of their Sugars must come in time to be lower'd: it would therefore very well become them, to exercise a greater Care to save and lay up against such a time; as many Prudent Men among them have done, whom (notwithstanding the great Discouragements this Gentleman would perswade us they have all along layn under) we have seen to bring very considerable Estates to *England*. But I offer not this out of Envy or Emulation (for I heartily wish them all the Prosperity and Encouragement they can reasonably desire) but meerly to excite them to affect a more Frugal and Provident way of Living.

I come now to Remark his Talking so much of the Hardship put upon them, in laying so high a Duty on White Sugars, and telling us that others can Live by Making Plain Sugar, they must Live by the Improv'd: And herein lies Ingenuity in making his Discourse relate

---

[1] *were wont to:* Used to.

more particularly to *Barbadoes,* (as he says in his Title Page) for no other of our Plantations do any thing considerable in Refining Sugars: But this let me tell him, that howsoever it may be their Interest to make White Sugars, I'm sure it's our Interest to keep such a Balance upon them, that they shall not too much Undersel our Refiners in *England,* and that they could very considerably, when those Sugars are but 5 *s. per* Hundred Duty.

Let us then state the Account between the *Barbadoes* and the *English* Refiner, that we may see on whose side the Ballance then lay: To take the usual way of computing Two hundred and an half of Raw sugar to make One hundred of Refin'd . . . this costs us in *England* 3 *s.* 9 *d.* for the Duty; next, if the Freight of his costs him but 3 *s.* our Two hundred and an half costs us 7 *s.* 6 *d.* that's 4 *s.* 6 *d.* more than his; then he loses nothing by Weight, but we may very well allow 18*d. per* Hundred for our Loss by the Running of the Sugar and Loss of Weight; Lastly, in the charge of Cask and other Expences, he saves at least 2 *s. per* Hundred, all which makes up 11 *s.* 9 *d.* that was then sav'd in Refining One hundred of Refin'd Sugar in *Barbadoes,* by Anticipating so much Charge that must be contracted upon it before it comes into the Sugar-bakers Hands here, which wants but 3 *d.* to make up the 12 *s.* which the last Additional Duty reduc'd them to pay.

At that time then they could afford their Fine Sugars in *England* about 7 *s.* and ship them for Foreign Markets about 9 *s.* 6 *d. per* Hundred cheaper than our *English* Refiners, which certainly gave them too great an Advantage, and did too much Discourage our Home Trade. And now since this last Impost of 7 *s.* more on Whites, and 2 *s.* 4 *d.* on Brown, they had 5 *s.* 10 *d. per* Hundred at the home Market, and 15 *s. per* Hundred on shipping off, more Advantage than our Refiners. All which being considered, How imprudent is it in this Gentleman, to make so great a Complaint of Oppression, in a Matter wherein they were so much favoured beyond the Traders of *England,* and which (if it should so continue) they might improve to their great Advantage? . . .

But now I'll shew him how this great Loss to the Revenue would not yet ease the Planter One Farthing: In order to which, I'll take a Maxim of his own (though indeed it overthrows his own Argument) which I'll Allow as a great Truth, *viz.* That 'tis only Plenty or Scarcity (which is really according to the demand of a Commodity) is that which Rules the Market; and Commodities of constant Use and Necessity will and do Rise in spight of the greatest Impositions that were ever laid on them, while they continue in good Demand: And 'twas the Plenty or Glut of Sugars occasion'd, not by the Imposition, but by an Accident resulting therefrom, (as I have already shewn) that was the Cause of the Fall of Sugars at that time: And I Challenge any Man to shew me any other Instance of a Commodities not Rising according to the Impost[2] laid on it. . . .

If we should Allow, that the laying an Imposition on a Commodity, might at the first put it under some Discouragement; yet 'tis but the struggling with the Alteration, for the first Year or two that makes the Difficulty: For if it be a Commodity of Consumption, its Demand will Continue, and the Trade must and will Revert, and Establish it self in the same Course it was before; so that this Difficulty will come to be lost: as it appears in the present Case of Sugars, which now bears this last Duty as current as it did the former.

But now after the Trade is come to bear it, if this Imposition, or the whole Duties (as he desires) should come to be taken off this Commodity, won't all Men expect that it will immediately Fall proportionably? It is not so long since the Temporary Impost on Wines fell away in King *Charles* the Seconds time, but that we can very well remember, that the Price of Wines did Fall answerably; and when the same came again to be laid on, in the beginning of the late King *James,*[3] they equally Rose again: And yet all this while, neither the *Frenchman* nor the *Spaniard,* did Advance or Fall the Price of their Wines at any of these Alterations. Nor is there a Jot of Reason to imagine that the Planter will be able to Advance One Farthing[4] on the Price of Sugars, if the Duties were wholly taken off. What then would be the Consequence of such a piece of Business? Why truly Their Majesties must lose a great Branch of the Revenue; all the Merchants and Traders having Sugar on their Hands, must lose prodigiously by the Fall; the Planters get nothing; only the Expenders should have their Sugars a Farthing or a Half-penny *per* Pound Cheaper, and so this Gentleman should have the Honour to Ease those that will neither thank him, nor think on him. . . .

I think there cannot be an easier way of Tax upon a People, than that of Customs, because it lies for the most part on Superfluities, and 'tis in every Mans Power to ease himself of the Charge as he pleases. And as our Nation is fallen into so great an Expense of Spice, Fruit, Wines, Brandy, Sugar, Tobacco, Silk, and many other things, which we

[2] *Impost:* Tax, imposition.
[3] *King Charles the Seconds time . . . King James:* Charles II ruled from 1660 to 1685; his brother, James II, ruled from 1685 to 1688.
[4] *Farthing:* A quarter of a penny.

see are wont to Rise and Fall very Considerably, and yet the Expence and Demand Continue, there is no doubt of their Bearing Duties; for 'tis an Infallible Rule to me, That a small Advance of Duty, cannot baulk those Commodities that are capable of so great Advances in Price so that I cannot see how our Trade can be hereby in the least Lessened or Injured.

However there ought to be certain Able and Understanding Merchants concerned in the Composing the said New Rates, for that there are divers things will occur, that ought not to be done at Adventures, but with a great deal of Scrutiny and Discretion, that no such Errors may be Committed, as was in the forementioned Imposition on Sugars, by which we beat our selves out of the Trade of Transporting Refined Sugars.

And now, since that Commodity hath given occasion to this Discourse, I shall here take the Opportunity to offer my Opinion, how the same may be yet Advanced to a higher Duty, and yet Trade not Injured thereby; Suppose then there were 5 s. *per* Hundred Duty set on Raw Sugars, which is but half a Farthing *per* Pound more than it now Pays, and comes to a Farthing and Quarter more *per* Pound in Refined; Can any one think that the Good Woman will put a Scruple the less in her Apple-Pyes for so inconsiderable an Advance? Nay, we know that when Sugar hath Risen One Peny *per* Pound, all the odds is, that they content themselves to take Sugar 1 *d. per* Pound Courser than what they used before; and so they lay out the same Money still, and the Commodity continues its Vent,[5] but this is to be understood of the Meaner People, for the Rich never stick at Price for what they want.

But then to order the Business on Transportation of White Sugar, there ought to be 7 or 8 s. *per* Hundred Deducted at shipping of Single Refined, and for courser Sorts less, according to the Value; and because this takes from the Revenue what was not before; as there is now but 9 *d. per* Pound Remains for Raw Sugars shipt out, (the rest being drawn back) let there now be 18 *d. per* Hundred left, that is but 3 s. 6 *d.* of the 5 s. Paid back at Transportation; and I am sure that 9 *d. per* Hundred won't frighten the *Dutch* from fetching over Raw Sugars, when 'tis common for that Trade to continue, when Sugars Rise 3 or 4 s. *per* Hundred; and by this means Their Majesties will have the 18 *d. per* Hundred sure, even of all that is Transported; which, considering the small Quantities of White, in Proportion to the Raw Sugars usually shipt off, will sufficiently Compensate the Deduction, and then the 14

[5] *Vent:* Sale.

d. per Hundred added to the Duty of White spent in *England*, will, according to the former Computation, bring in upwards of 23000 *l. per Annum* to Their Majesties; the *English* Sugar-Bakers will be encouraged; and 'twill be the ready way for the Planter to find a brisker Trade for his Sugars: For if we can be able to Vye with other Nations with our Refin'd Sugars in Foreign Markets, it must needs encourage our Plantations, because it makes more room for the Vent of their Productions; but then White Sugars Imported ought to Pay at least 14 *s. per* Hundred, to make it equal with Whites Refin'd at Home, (Courser Sorts Paying less, according to their Value) and to draw back at shipping off no more than ours.

SIR DALBY THOMAS

From *An Historical Account of the Rise and Growth of the West-India Collonies*

Sir Dalby Thomas (1638–1711) stresses the wealth accruing from commodities made in the colonies, especially sugar. Arguing for the eradication of the monopoly held by the Royal African Company, he complains that slaves are overpriced and that production is correspondingly restricted. In a prescient remark, he argues that the colonies devoted to making only one commodity will never sue for their own independence, pointing to New England as a far more likely site of eventual insurrection. He concludes that the mother country should favor her Caribbean over her continental North American colonies.

Thomas published his critique in 1690, but before the turn of the century he had joined the Royal African Company, and he published a brief defense of their policies, *Considerations on the Trade of Africa*, in 1698. He went on to become commander of the RAC's Cape Coast Castle, on the Gold Coast, where he strove to implement the same kind of economically sensitive measures he discusses here. For example, when the RAC subsidized any of the costs of warfare among the African kingdoms, Thomas insisted on being reimbursed — a policy that proved counterproductive, since conflicts among the African rulers usually revolved around their alliances with one or another of the European powers. Thomas's demands drove away potential allies. At a time when Europeans showed little interest in establishing colonies within Africa, Thomas proposed that productivity might be further enhanced by establishing English plantations on the Gold Coast itself, where coffee, pepper, and minerals might be cultivated cheaply and efficiently, without the expense of transporting slaves across the ocean. His proposal was not adopted.

The text is excerpted from the first edition of *An Historical Account of the Rise and Growth of the West-India Collonies, and of the Great Advantages they are to England, in respect to Trade* (London: Printed for Jo. Hindmarsh, 1690) 8–12, 38, 39, 34–37.

I will take a short view of our Sugar-Plantations, and the nature of that Trade, to whose particular advantage and Interest after the Kingdoms, I principally sacrifice my present pains.

I therefore with all Submissiveness imaginable, desire our Legislators to Consider,

1. That the greatest Consumption of Sugar is made by themselves, and the rest of the Rich and Opulent People of the Nation, tho' usefull to all degrees of Men.

2. That the quantity yearly produced within those Sugar Collonies, is not less then 45000 Tons English Tonnage, each comprehending 20*l*. to the Ton.

3. That about the Moiety[1] of that is Consumed in *England*.

4. That the Medium of the Value of consumed Sugar at the present price Currant is 4*d* a pound.

5. That the quantity Consumed in the Nation at that price amounts to 800000*l*. Sterling, and upwards.

6. That the other Moiety sent to Forreign Markets after it has Employ'd Seamen, and Earn'd Freight, is sold for as much, and consequently brings back to the Nation in Money or usefull Goods Annually 800000*l*, which is more than any one other Commodity doth.

7. Consider too, that before Sugars were produced in our own Collonies, it bore three times the Price it doth now, so that by the same Consumption, at the same price, except we made it our selves, we should be forced to give in Money, or Moneys worth, as Native Commodities and Labour 2400000*l*. for the Sugar we spend, or be without it to such a degree of disadvantage of well Living, as that Retrenchment would amount to; We must Consider too, that the Spirits arising from *Mellasses* which is sent from the Sugar Collonies to the other Collonies, and to *England*, which if all were sold in *England* and

---

[1] *the Moiety:* Half.

turn'd into Spirits, it would Amount annually to above 500000*l.* at half the price the like quantity of *Brandy* from *France* would cost, and will yearly Increase as *Brandies* are discouraged, and by most are held wholsomer for the Body, which is observed by the long living of those in the Collonies that are great Drinkers of Rum, which is the Spirits we make of *Mellasses,* and the short living of those that are great Drinkers of *Brandy* in those parts.

The *Indico*[2] coming thence amounts to 50000*l. per Ann.*

The *Logwood* for which we formerly paid the *Spaniards* 100*l. per Ton,* now comes under 15*l.* and amounts to 1000 Ton Annually.

The *Cotton* for which we paid formerly above 12*d. per pound,* now comes at 5*d* ½. *per pound.* and amounts to 1000 Ton *per Annum,* besides the Hands it Employs in Manufacturing it.

The *Ginger* amounts to 4000 Ton *per annum,* and is not the Sixth part in price of what the Nation paid formerly for that Commodity, or for *Pepper* instead of it.

Not to speak of the many *Druggs, Woods, Cocoa, Piemonto,* and *Spices,* besides *Raw-Hides* &c. which comes from those parts, nor of the great quantity of the Gold, and Silver we have of the *Spaniards* for *Negroes,* and the English Manufactory carryed by our sloops from our Collonies to them.

So that it is demonstration, the Nation saves and gains by the People Employ'd in those Collonies 400000000*l.* Sterling *per An.*

Now if it be Consider'd that in all those *Sugar Collonies* there is not 600000 white Men Women and Children, it necessarily must follow, that one with another above what they consume each of them Earns for the Publick above 60*l. per ann.*

Whereas if the Rent be 10000000,

And the Consumption 50000000,

Then by reducing Labour and Consumption to a proper Ballance with the produce of Rents, and supporting the Imaginary Wealth of the whole Kingdom to Increase in time of Peace, the Tenth part Annually that will be but four Millions, which does not Amount to Twelve Shillings a Head clear Increase of Wealth, One with another, above necessary and constant Expences, from which it follows beyond Controversy, that hands Employ'd in the Sugar-Plantations are one with another of 130 times the value to the Common-wealth than those which stay at home.

---

[2] *Indico:* I.e., indigo, a blue powder derived from plants of the genus *Indigofera,* and used as a dye.

To this I easily foresee will be readily Objected, for want of Consideration, that those there consume nothing of Native Commodities, which if they did as these do which stay at home, their Consumption would amount to 390000*l*. Annually at 6*l*. 10*s*. 0*d*. *per Head.* as afore-said, and would consequently Increase the Rents at least a Fourth of that.

But to this I must reminde the Reader that I have demonstrated, that whatever is Consum'd by Idle Men, can never Increase either the Reall or Imaginary Wealth of the Nation, and that nothing but the Overplus or Consumption can be reckon'd Additional Wealth, which according to our Reasonable Computation cannot be above 2*s*. a head, one with another, So that if we would grant that those in the Collonies did Consume nothing of our home produce, the loss by want of them here could amount only to 1200000*s*. Annually, which is 60000*l*.

But on the contrary, this is so far from being true, that one with another each White Man, Woman, and Child, residing in the Sugar-Plantations, occasions the Consumption of more of our Native Commodities, and Manufactures then ten at home do.

This cannot be doubted by those that will Consider the great quantity of Beef, Pork, Salt, Fish, Butter, Cheese, Corn and Flower, as well as Beer, English-Mum,[3] Syder and Coals, constantly sent thither, of which Commodities for the use of themselves or Blacks, they have little or none of their own produce: Consider too, that all their Powder, Cannon, Swords, Guns, Pikes, and other Weapons, their Cloaths, Shoes, Stockings, Sadles, Bridles, Coaches, Beds, Chairs, Stools, Pictures, Clocks, and Watches, their Pewter, Brass, Copper and Iron Vessells and Instruments, their Sail-Cloath, and Cordage, of which in their Building, Shipping, Mills, Boyling and Distilling-Houses, Field-Labour and Domestick uses, they Consume infinite quantities, all which are made in and sent from *England:* Not to speak of the great number of Drudging and Saddle Horses they take off, as well as of that sort of People who would in their Youth be consumed in Idleness, or worse at home, but there become usefull to Increase the Nations, Numbers, and Wealth both.

Besides, it must be remembred, that there is in those collonies at least 5 Blacks for one White, so that allowing the Whites to be 60000, the Blacks must be 300000, all whose Cloaths and European Provisions coming from *England,* Increases the Consumption of our Native Commodities and Manufactures in a large Proportion. But the Axes,

---

[3] *English-Mum:* A kind of beer.

Hoes, Saws, Rollers, Shovells, Knives, Nails, and other Iron Instruments and Tools as well as the Boylers, Stills, and other usefull Vessells of Copper, Lead and Pewter, which are wasted, Consumed and Destroy'd by the Industry and profitable Labour of that mighty Number of Slaves, are not easily to be Computed, but must plainly and beyond all Contradiction be of great Advantage to the Nation as well as to those Industrious People Employ'd at home in making them.

If these things with the vast quantity of Shipping that those Collonies Employ, be in the least reflected on, it will open the Eyes of the most unexperienced Person in the Trade, to discern the mighty advantage the Nation receives from those People which go to those Collonies, and the great Obligation there lyes upon our Legislators to Study their due Improvement, safety and Increase.

For besides all the benefits demonstrably coming to the Nation as aforesaid, They are in some kind Maritime Armies, ever ready not only to Defend themselves but to punish the Exorbitances, Incroachments, Piracies, and Depradations of any Insulting Neighbouring Nation; Nor is it to be imagin'd in what Awe those Collonies rightly managed might keep our *French, Spanish, Dutch, Danish, Brandenburgh* and *Hamburgh*[4] Rivalls, for Wealth and Maritime Power from Entring into any Treaties, Alliances or Undertakings, to our Disadvantage.

What has been said shall serve for an Introduction in Generall to the more particular parts of the Nations Interest in the *American* Trade, and the due encouragement it ought to receive from the Laws which may naturally make us the most Rich and Florishing part, as well as the undoubted Arbitrators of *Europe,* if not of all the Maritime Nations of the World. And in the next place, I will show what Discouragements those Collonies lye under at present. . . .

For tho' to do right to the *Affrican* Company they have been wonderfully kinde in the Credit they have given the Plantations, and that rightly managed a Company is able to supply them with Negro's Cheaper than a loose Trade could, yet the Complaints the Company continually make of the Collonies bad pay, and the Complaints of the Collonies for being ill supplyed with Negro's, allow both true, it will be necessary to Enquire into the reall cause of both Inconveniencies before proper Remedies can be propos'd. . . .

It is beyond all dispute known, that the Collonies under a free, Open, and Loose Trade for *Negro's,* did flourish and Increase before the Company was Erected.

---

[4] *Brandenburgh and Hamburgh:* German states involved in the slave trade.

It is certain, that they could still be supplied plentifully at ⅔ the price the Company makes them pay.

It is as undeniable, that the Company doth not Supply them with the full Numbers they want, and could have, did not the Company shut all doors to their Supply.

And it cannot be denied, but in these few heads are included all the several Inconveniences so Complain'd of in a Monopoly.

I. For hereby a loose[5] Trade is turn'd into a Restrain'd, which lessens the Numbers of Shipping that would trade to *Guinea*.

II. That comes dear to the Subject that might be Cheap.

III. And a usefull Commodity to the Increase of Wealth is not to be had in a sufficient quantity.

It is alledged that some part of the Trade of *Guinea* considering who are our Rivalls in it, cannot be preserved without Force, and that the Castle must be maintain'd or that part of the Trade lost, and that the Castle *&c.* cannot be supported but with great Cost, And that that charge falls extreamly heavy upon so small a stock as that of the *Affrican* Company.

The consequence of which premises is, They will always be necessitated to keep up the price of *Negro's* ⅓ more than otherwise we need, (tho' the Castles are not supported, or little or no ways usefull to the *Negro*-Trade, they keeping no Forts, and seldom Factors at those places where the *Negro's* are most bought at.)

I confess a strong Argument for the Company, but a sowr one for the Collonies which seem hereby depriv'd of their Birthright, The Liberty of the Subject, and their possession which Consisted in a loose Trade.

The Premises considered, the Planters may therefore justly desire that the National Interest in the *Guinea*-Trade, The Forts, *&c.* may be equally supported by all the Nation, as our Navy's necessary Forts and Garrisons at home are, and not fall solely on their Labour and Industry: For the necessary supply of *Negro's* to the Collonies Annually should not be less than Twenty thousand pound. . . .

The beginning of our *American* Settlements were made in the latter end of Queen *Elizabeths* Reign, by the Encouragement of Sr. *Walter Rowleigh,* who undertook the Planting of *Virginia,* and first brought the use of *Tobacco* into *England;* but that nor any other Collony of ours in the *West-Indies* did promise much Success either to the Nation or Undertakers, untill the Reign of King *James the first,* whose Peace

---

[5] *loose:* Free, unregulated.

with the Crown of *Spain* restrain'd those bold Privateers who before by Harasing the *Spanish* Collonies and Mast'ring their Rich Ships of Plate, had become very Wealthy as well as Numerous: But much against the will of most of them, but Principally of such who had not sufficiently made their fortunes, this Peace oblig'd them to change the prospect of their future Conduct from Rapine and spoyl, to Trade and Planting; So that in a very short time a considerable Settlement was made in the Northern parts of *America,* to the great Increase of good Shipping in the Kingdom: By this means a gencrall Notion of having enough profitable Land in those parts of the world for nothing, so infected the whole Kingdom, that not only the Necessitous and Loose part of the Nation flockt thither, but many Non-conformists[6] did Solicite his Majesty for leave to make a Settlement together under privileges and Liberties, both in Civil and Church-Matters, by a Constitution of their own. This Combination King *James* prudently consented to, and Confirm'd by his Letters-Patents, wisely foreseeing, that tho' a *Species* of a Commonwealth was thereby introduc'd into his Dominions, yet the dependence thereof must be upon the Crown for protection, and consequently that part of his Subjects then call'd Puritans, would not be totally lost to the Nation, as they must be if driven for ever to remain in Forreign Countryes: Thus began that Numerous Collony of *New-England,* where under frugall Laws, Customs and Constitutions, they live, without applying themselves to Planting any *Tobacco* or other *American* Commodities, except for their own private use. But by Tillage, Pasture, Fishing, Manufactures and Trade, they to all Intents and purposes imitate old *England,* and did formerly much, and in some Degree do now Supply the other Collonies with Provisions in Exchange for their Commodities, as *Tobacco, Sugar, &c.* which they carried to Forreign Markets, how conveniently for the Nations Interest I shall not determine, being no Enemy to any kind of honest Industry: But this cannot chuse but be allow'd, that if any hands in the *Indies* be wrong Employ'd for Domestick Interest, it must be theirs, and those other Collonies, which settle with no other prospect than the like way of Living: Therefore if any such only should be neglected and discourag'd who pursue a Method rivalls our Native Kingdom, and threatens in time a totall Independency thereupon.

But as this cannot be said of our *Tobacco*-Collonies, much less it is to be fear'd from our Sugar-Plantations, except by gross mistakes at

[6] *Non-conformists:* Dissenters from the religious practices of the Church of England; here, the Puritans.

home we at last force them to part with their black-Slaves to the *Spaniards,* and betake themselves to the sole Planting of Provisions, and living upon their Estates, which should it happen would be the greatest blow to our Navigation, and consequently to the Rents that the Kingdom ever received since it was a Trading Nation.

This Digression I hope may be pardon'd, since it Explains a little the difference of our Nationall Interest in the severall sorts of *American* Collonies.

Nor would I be supposed to be so Ignorant, to think, that no kind of Collonies can Empty, and consequently Ruine the Nation: No, there is a naturall boundary to all worldy matters; and it becomes the Wisedom of Legislators truly to distinguish the depending and profitable, from the Detacht and Undermining Collonies, and rightly apply Lenitives and Corrosives accordingly.

To return therefore to those within the Tropicks which are principally supposed by making Sugar; The beginning of their Settlement was without the least prospect of Succeeding in that Commodity, the Art of making which, as I said before being by meer Accident gain'd in *Barbados* by a *Hollander,* something more than half a Century since: And as it was the happiness of those Islands to learn it from a *Dutchman,* so the first and main supporters of them in their progress to that perfection they are arrived to, exceeding all the Nations in the World, is principally owing to that Nation, who being eternall Prolers about, and Searchers for moderate Gains by Trade, did give credit to those *Islanders* as well as they did to the *Portugalls* in *Brasile,* for Black Slaves, and all other necessaries for planting, taking as their Crops throve, the Sugar they made: Thus with light but sure Gains to themselves, they nourisht the Industrious, and consequently Improving Planters, both before, and during the Civill Wars in these Islands: the Fame of whose good Fortune being spread at home, many ingenious Gentlemen who had unfortunately follow'd the Royall Interest Convey'd the remains of their shipwrackt Fortunes thither: amongst which Collonell *Henry Walldronds* Father,[7] with himself and other his Relations of that Family, were not inconsiderable either for Quality, Industry, or Parts: So that by theirs and many undone Cavaliers who follow'd their Example, new Improvements and Experiments were dayly added to the Art of Planting, making and Refining Sugar, which

---

[7] *Collonell Henry Wallronds Father:* Humphrey Walrond, who emigrated to Barbados in 1646, establishing a major plantation there.

were taken from them by the *Dutch* till Sir *George Askew*[8] with a Squadron of Ships remov'd the Lord *Willoughby* of *Parham* from Governing there, for his Exill'd Majesty *Charles the Second,* and Reduced the Island to the *States* Obedience: Soon after which the *Dutch War* hapining, all further Trade with that Nation ceast, by whose help they being then strong enough to subsist of themselves, their future Dealing return'd to its proper Center, which was Trading with their native Country; since which time that Island which contains but _____ Acres,[9] and not more than five and twenty thousand white Inhabitants, has produced in Commodities above thirty Millions *Sterling,* has pay'd in Duties to support the Government at a modest Computation, above ¾ of a Million which will seem incredible to those that have not Employ'd thoughts on it.

[8] *Sir George Askew:* Usually spelled Ascyue; he blockaded the island for three months in 1651–52, until the colonists finally capitulated; however, Willoughby was later reinstated as governor.
[9] *contains but _____ Acres:* Thomas left this space blank in his text; Barbados is approximately 76,360 acres (166 square miles).

THOMAS TRYON

From *Tryon's Letters upon Several Occasions*

Thomas Tryon, whose scathing criticism of the planters' way of life is printed with the British Caribbean documents (see p. 368), argues here for the virtues of sugar, which, as Sir Dalby Thomas also notes, had been a very scarce and costly commodity in England before the triangular trade, more of a condiment than the staple it was becoming by the end of the seventeenth century. Tryon situates the sugar plantations within an economic network, emphasizing not only the many culinary and medicinal uses of "this noble Juice" but also the goods and machinery required to support its production, in order to argue that sugar farming promotes international commerce in such commodities as tea and cocoa while also fostering domestic production of iron and textiles in England. As he acknowledges, however, the labor-intensive process of sugar farming was the cause for the huge influx of slaves into Barbados during the previous half-century.

The text is excerpted from the first edition (London: Printed for Geo. Conyers and Eliz. Harris, 1700) 218–21.

SIR,
After such an acknowledgement as I have made in the close of my
Letter, I hope you will believe 'tis not without reluctancy, that I would
add any thing more in this place; but not expecting to meet with a like
convenient opportunity, pray give me leave to subjoyn to the above
mentioned Uses and Excellencies of Sugar, a very few things concern-
ing the great Benefits this Commodity brings to the Nation; which
very few People are any way thoughtful or regardful of.

First then, the Manufactures of this excellent Juice is of much more importance, than all other Fruits and Spices imported to us; in respect of the improvement of our Navigation and Consumption of our Manufactures; for in King *Charles* II Reign, the small Island of *Barbadoes* Loaded yearly about 350 Sail of Ships, and most of them of considerable burden, with Cotton and Ginger, but chiefly with Sugar: (And so in some proportion did our other Sugar Islands) when it doth not contain above an Hundred Thousand Acres of Land, whereof a considerable part of that is poor and Rocky, and not worth Manuring; and at the same time there was above Twenty Thousand *English* of all sorts upon it, and 70000 *Negroes* or Black Servants; who both the one and the other, were not only Cloathed with the Manufactury of *England,* but a great part of their Eatables and Drinkables came from thence also: Besides which there were Thirty Sail of Ships employed yearly in the *Guinea* Trade, all Loaden with our Growth, to furnish this and the other Sugar Plantations with Slaves: To say nothing of the great quantities of Utensils for their Sugar Works, as Copper, Iron, and other things belonging to Building, that were constantly carryed to them. And tho' since the late War there are not above Two Hundred and Fifty Sail Loaden there or thereabouts, and not above Fifty Thousand *Negroes,* and fewer White People in *Barbadoes;* for the Island could once Muster 10000 able Men, but since not above 5000; yet both their numbers, and that Trade, is still very considerable; and surely 'tis the Nations Interest not farther to depress, but to encourage it to the highest degree.

Secondly, Sugar finds an Employment for many Thousands in *England* it self, so as common Partees,[1] Sugar-Bakers, or Distillers, Coopers, Grocers, Carriers, yes, and abundance of Ladies too; who, many of them since the common use of it, have their Closets better furnished than the Confectioners Shops were in former days.

[1] *so as common Partees:* For such people as.

Thirdly, how many Thousand Acres of Land are by the use of this noble Plant, made of five times the value and more, than otherwise they would have been? as having brought a great number of Fruits, Grains and Seeds into use, that were hardly thought of, or at leastwise but little valued formerly, such as Apples, Pears, Plumbs, Apricocks, Gooseberries, Currants, and many more of the like nature; which do all increase the Consumption of Grain: To which may be added, the many brave and exhilarating Drinks that are made of the Juices of our Fruits, by the assistance of Sugar, such as Cherry Wine, Currant Wine, Gooseberry Wine, Rasberry Wine, Cowslip Wine, and many more; nay, it renders divers things of considerable value, which of themselves are of little or none, witness, in green, raw, sharp Gooseberries, which by its sweet and friendly power, are rendred much more preferrable to those that are ripe.

Fourthly, There are but very few who are not sensible how mightily Sugar advances the Kings Customs, not only in respect to the Imports laid upon it self, but by occasioning many Foreign Commodities to be imported; which before our Sugar Settlements were not thought of, as the noble Nut called the Cocoa, of which the most equal and agreeable Pottage[3] is made, which if it were not for Sugar, would be but of little use; and several other Foreign Fruits and Drugs, as Tea, Coffee, &c.

Fifthly, Physitians and Apothecaries cannot but think themselves highly befriended by this noble Juice, since more than half their Medicines are mixed and compounded with Sugar; and a great part of our Herbs and Medicinal Flowers would be of little or no use without it, there being by a modest computation, above Three Hundred Medicines made up with Sugar; by whose assistance, their Volatile Virtues are incircled and preserved, which otherwise could not be done.

Sixthly, Then for the Confectioners, what do, or indeed can they do without Sugar? it being manifest, there are above Two Hundred several sorts of Sweet-Meats[3] made by them with Fruits of our own Growth, which are so many excellent Cordials, delicious and pleasant, and may be all eaten, to the advantage both of health and pleasure, (if order and temperance be not wanting) and confederated with things of a meaner quality; but otherwise, without Sugar they would be harsh, crude, sharp, and subject to decay; as would also great quantities of Foreign Fruits and Seeds, which are preserved by them, and which upon their Importation, pay the King considerable Customs.

---

[2] *Pottage:* A thick soup, usually with vegetables boiled until they are soft.
[3] *Sweet-Meats:* Sweet foods such as sugared cakes or nuts, pastry, candied fruit, etc.

Seventhly, It may not only be mixed and compounded with most, if not all sort of Vegetations, their several Sal Nitral[4] Virtues, all proceeding from agreeable Principles, but even Bread it self; which, with good reason, is stiled the Staff of Life, and esteemed the best and cleannest of all Foods; if it be eaten only with a little good Sugar, it inspires it with a more brisk and lively taste, and is of much easier Digestion, than if it had been eaten by it self: But give me leave by the way to insert one Caution, and that is, that Sugar is not so good mixed with the Fat of Animals, nor with Butter; that being I may say, an Heterogenious practice; for the Sal Nitral properties of Vegetables cannot so easily incorporate with the Animal Sulphurs or Fats, and consequently open the Bodies of each other; and therefore all such Foods as are made up with Butter and Sugar, are generally of an heavy, dull and cloying nature, and never fail to obstruct the Stomach, and retard Digestion: And this antipathy between Animal Fats or Sulphurs, and Vegetable Sal Nitres, is very manifest by what is practiced in the Art of Refining of Sugar; for when the Juice of the same is Boyled in Coppers with most fierce and vehement Fire, such as is necessarily required for that purpose, whereby the Liquor rises up with a much more turbulent and ungovernable motion, than either Beer or Ale, as the Syrrups do exceed in sweetness and strength, and so is subject to run over the Pan, to the great damage of the Refiner: The only Antidote they have found out to allay and quiet it, is Butter; for tho' the Copper contains 2 or 3 Hundred Gallons, Boyling and Swelling up in the foresaid manner, yet a piece of Butter put in to the bigness of a small Nut, and no more, quickly makes it fall down within its circle in the Copper, and all with an amazing Hush; and whence should this Ascendancy proceed, but that the Animal power is deduced from an higher Birth, as being made and generated from sensibility; and passing thro' all the Animal Digestions, there is a kind of an Antipathy in the Butter to the Juice of the Vegetable, as there is in other things of the like contrary kinds. But for all that is said, it must still be owned that the Juices of Sugar are of so generous a Nature, that when they happen to be mixt with any fat things, the Concoction is the easier, especially in all Milk Foods, which are more than twelve parts in fourteen Flegm.

Eighthly, The Use of this noble Juice has not only reached to our Raw and unripe Fruits, and the vast improvement of them, (as before

---

[4] *Sal Nitral:* Saltpeter, a crystalline substance with medicinal uses, and also the principal constituent of gunpowder. Tryon extols its virtues elsewhere in his writings, and seems to have regarded it as having unusually healthful effects.

noted) for common and daily Use; but proper ways have been found out to keep and preserve them for Tarts and other things all the Year round; whence as a farther Benefit, it is come to pass in the revolution of a few years, perhaps not exceeding seventy, than for every Ten Fruit Trees we had then in *England,* there are now above a Thousand.

Ninthly, Tho' Wine and Tobacco may be justly allowed to be two of the most principal Commodities Imported, that do advance Navigation and the Kings Revenue, yet the Premisses considered, they come infinitely short of Sugar, since they are not only confined (as it were) within the circle of their own Consumption; but even that Consumption may in some degree be asserted to hinder our own Growth, at leastwise in respect to one of them.

Lastly, to add no more Benefits, and to close the whole with a familiar Instance.

Does not the Queen of the Dairy; by the assistance of this noble Juice, vary or manufacture (as I may say) her Milk into more than Twenty several delicious Dishes of Food? And is it also not a Friend to the Laborious Husbandman, by encouraging the Consumption of a great quantity of fine Flower? so that in short, it spreads its generous and sweet influences thro' the whole Nation; and there are but few Eatables or Drinkables that it is not a Friend to, or capable to confederate with: And upon the whole, as there is no one Commodity whatever, that doth so much encourage Navigation, advance the Kings Customs, and our Land, and is at the same time of so great and Universal Use, Virtue and Advantage as this King of Sweets, more especially, when by Art it has been brought to its highest degree of perfection: So our Sugar Plantations should have suitable Supports and Aids from the Government, which is the hearty desire of

once more SIR,

Your humble Servant,

T. T.

On an African Prince at a Performance of Oroonoko

This selection reports the presence of an African prince at a London performance of Southerne's *Oroonoko* in 1749; it was probably the same Prince of Annamaboe whose story is told in *The Royal African,* excerpted in Chapter 3. The event described here seems to have provided Londoners with a welcome opportunity for sentimental response, judging from its coverage in both *The Gentleman's Magazine* and *The London Magazine*, the two leading periodicals of the day. Both reports focused their attention on the prince's tearful reaction to the performance. Morever, the event inspired the clergyman William Dodd to publish two poetic epistles on the subject in 1749, entitled "The African Prince, when in England, to Zara," and "Zara, at the Court of Annamaboe, to the African Prince." In the first, the prince tells of his capture and subsequent experiences, including his reaction to the play:

> O! Zara, here, a story like my own,
> With mimic skill, in borrow'd names, was shown;
> An Indian chief, like me, by fraud betray'd
> And partner in his woes, an Indian maid.

It should be noted that "Indian" was a common term, at this time, for "African." In a footnote to this passage, Dodd writes that the prince "alludes to the play of *Oroonoko*, at which he was present, and so affected as to be unable to continue, during its performance." In Zara's response, Dodd echoes Behn's treatment of the subject by emphasizing the injustice of enslaving a prince rather than attacking the institution of slavery ("Hold, hold," she tells his captors, " 'tis a prince ye bind.").

Although this story and others of kidnapped African royalty were not at first disseminated by emancipationists, after midcentury they were incorporated more frequently into antislavery arguments. Yet another version of the story would appear in John Singleton's *A General Description of the West-Indian Islands* (1767), and at the end of the century, Anna Maria Mackenzie would include an almost identical scene in her abolitionist poem *Slavery: Or, the Times* (1792), which describes an African prince weeping at a performance of *Oroonoko*.

The text is reprinted from *The London Magazine, or, Gentleman's Monthly Intelligencer* 18 (February, 1749): 94.

> A young *African* prince, and a youth of a great family,
> his companion, who were said to be committed to the care
> of an *English* C   , on that coast, to be brought over to
> *England* for their improvement, but treacherously betray'd
> by him, and about to be sold for slaves, having been
> providentially rescu'd from their design'd bondage, and
> lately arriving here, were this night at the theatre royal in
> *Covent Garden,* to see the tragedy of *Oroonoko,* with which

they were so affected, that the tears flow'd plentifully from their eyes; the case of *Oroonoko*'s being made a slave by the treachery of a captain being so very similar to their own.

THOMAS DAY

From *The Dying Negro*

Another story of a kidnapped African appears in Thomas Day's poem, spoken in the persona of a suicidal slave who, like Southerne's Oroonoko, is said to be noble and in love with a European woman. Note the thundering warning of Africa's revenge, which became a rhetorical staple of abolitionist poetry, such as Robert Southey's "To the Genius of Africa" (1795) and James Jennings's "The Prospects of Africa" (1814). Day (1748–1789) had not yet established his literary reputation when he wrote this poem, his first publication, in 1773. It sold unusually well for the work of an unknown writer, going through three editions in three years, and continuing to sell after the turn of the century. Day wrote the poem after his friend John Bicknell showed him a newspaper article concerning a slave who had run away from his master and had himself christened in order to marry a white fellow servant; apprehended and locked up in a ship on the Thames, he committed suicide. Bicknell and Day collaborated on the original text of the poem, but Day himself composed most of the supplementary material for the second and third editions, and as his career advanced, readers tended to view him as the sole author. Among the poem's enthusiasts were Erasmus Darwin, said to have been converted to abolitionism by reading it, and Maria Edgeworth, daughter of Day's friend Richard Lovell Edgeworth and author of several fictionalized portrayals of Day, who appears most famously as Clarence Harvey in her novel *Belinda* (1801), in which a black West Indian slave does marry a white servant.

After publishing *The Dying Negro*, Day continued his attack on slavery, addressing the issue in *Reflections on the Present State of England and the Independence of America* (1782) and *A Letter from ********, in London, to his friend in America, on the subject of the slave-trade* (1784). A devotee of the French philosopher Jean-Jacques Rousseau (to whom he dedicated the third edition of *The Dying Negro*), Day constantly appealed to "Nature" as the true guide to virtue. His abolitionism, therefore, is linked to the thought of Montaigne (see Chapter 2) and Tryon (see Chapter 4), as well as to that of Behn. In his arguments for abolition, Day specifically emphasizes the hypocrisy of the American slave owners, who demanded democratic self-government for themselves while treating Africans as exploitable commodities.

The text is excerpted from the second edition of *The Dying Negro, a Poetical Epistle, from a Black, who shot himself on board a vessel in the river Thames, to his intended wife* (London: Printed for W. Flexney, 1774) 9–14, 20–21.

        Curst be the winds, and curst the tides which bore
    These European robbers to our shore!
    O be that hour involv'd in endless night,
    When first their streamers[1] met my wond'ring sight,
    I call'd the warriors from the mountain's steep,
    To meet these unknown terrors of the deep;
    Rouz'd by my voice, their generous bosoms glow,
    They rush indignant, and demand the foe,
    And poize the darts of death, and twang the bended bow:
    When lo! advancing o'er the sea-beat plain,
    I mark'd the leader of a warlike train.
    Unlike his features to our swarthy race;
    And golden hair play'd round his ruddy face.
    While with insidious smile and lifted hand
    He thus accosts our unsuspecting band.
    "Ye valiant chiefs, whom love of glory leads
    "To martial combats, and heroic deeds;
    "No fierce invader your retreat explores,
    "No hostile banner waves along your shores.
    "From the dread tempests of the deep we fly;
    "Then lay, ye chiefs, these pointed terrors by.
    "And O, your hospitable cares extend,
    "So may ye never need the aid ye lend!
    "So may ye still repeat to every grove
    "The songs of freedom, and the strains of love!"
    Soft as the accents of the traitor flow,
    We melt with pity, and unbend the bow;
    With lib'ral hand our choicest gifts we bring,
    And point the wand'rers to the freshest spring,
    Nine days we feasted on the Gambian strand,

---

[1] *Streamers:* Flags.

And songs of friendship echo'd o'er the land,[2]
When the tenth morn her rising lustre gave,
The chief approach'd me by the sounding wave.
"O, youth," he said, "what gifts can we bestow,
Or how requite the mighty debt we owe?
For lo! propitious to our vows, the gale
With milder omens fills the swelling sail.
To-morrow's sun shall see our ships explore
These deeps, and quit your hospitable shore.
Yet while we linger, let us still employ
The number'd hours in friendship and in joy;
Ascend our ships, their treasures are your own,
And taste the produce of a world unknown."

He spoke; with fatal eagerness we burn, —
And quit the shores undestin'd to return!
The smiling traitors with insidious care,
The goblet proffer, and the feast prepare,
'Till dark oblivion shades our closing eyes,
And all disarm'd each fainting warrior lies.
O wretches! to your future evils blind!
O morn for ever present to my mind!
When bursting from the treach'rous bands of sleep,
Rouz'd by the murmurs of the dashing deep,
I woke to bondage, and ignoble pains,
And all the horrors of a life in chains[3]

---

[2] Which way soever I turned my eyes on this pleasant spot, I beheld a perfect image of pure nature, an agreeable solitude bounded on every side by charming landscapes; the rural situation of cottages in the midst of trees; the ease and indolence of the Negroes, reclined under the shade of their spreading foliage; the simplicity of their dress and manners; the whole revived in my mind the idea of our first parents, and I seemed to contemplate the world in its primitive state. They are, generally speaking, very good-natured, sociable, and obliging. I was not a little pleased with this, my first reception; it convinced me that there ought to be considerable abatement made of the accounts I had read and heard of the savage characters of the Africans. *M. Adanson's Voyage to Senegal, &c.* [Day's note.] Day's citation refers to Michel Adanson's *Histoire naturelle du Senegal*, published in Paris in 1757 and translated into English in 1759 as *A Voyage to Senegal, the isle of Goree, and the River Gambia.*

[3] "As we passed along the coast, we very often lay before a town, and fired a gun for the natives to come off, but no soul came near us: At length we learned by some ships that were trading down the coast, that the natives came seldom on board an English ship, for fear of being detained or carried off; yet at last some ventured on board; but if these chanced to spy any arms, they would all immediately take to their canoes, and make the best of their way home." *Smith's Voyage to Guinea.*
"It is well known that many of the European nations have, very unjustly and inhumanly, without any provocation, stolen away, from time to time, abundance of the

Ye Gods of Afric! in that dreadful hour
Where were your thunders, and avenging pow'r!
Did not my pray'rs, my groans, my tears invoke
Your slumb'ring justice to direct the stroke?
No power descended to assist the brave,
No lightnings flash'd, and I became a slave.
From lord to lord my wretched carcase sold,
In Christian traffic, for their sordid gold:
Fate's blackest clouds still gather'd o'er my head;
And now they burst, and mix me with the dead.
. . . .

    — Thanks, righteous God! — Revenge shall yet be mine,
Yon flashing lightning gave the dreadful sign.
I see the flames of heavenly anger hurl'd,
I hear your thunders shake a guilty world;
The time shall come, the fated hour is nigh,
When guiltless blood shall penetrate the sky,
Amid these horrors, and involving night,
Prophetic visions flash before my sight,
Eternal justice wakes, and in their turn,
The vanquish'd triumph, and the victors mourn; —
Then the stern genius of my native land,
With delegated vengeance in his hand,
Shall raging cross the troubled seas, and pour
The plagues of Hell on yon devoted shore.
What tides of ruin mark his ruthless way!
How shriek the fiends exulting o'er their prey!
I see your warriors gasping on the ground, —
I hear your flaming cities crash around. —
In vain with trembling heart the coward turns,
In vain with generous rage the valiant burns. —
One common ruin, one promiscuous grave
O'erwhelms the dastard, and receives the brave —
For Afric triumphs! — his avenging rage,

---

people, not only on this coast, but almost every-where in Guinea, who have come on
board their ships, in a harmless and confiding manner; these they have in great numbers
carried away, and sold in the plantations." *J. Barbot's Description of Guinea.* [Day's
note.] Day's citation refer to William Smith's *A New Voyage to Guinea* (1744) and Jean
Barbot's memoirs of his travels in Guinea, first published in England in 1732 as *A
Description of the Coasts of North and South Guinea.*

No tears can soften, and no blood assuage.
He smites the trembling waves, and at the shock,
Your fleets are dash'd upon the pointed rock.
He waves his flaming dart, and o'er your plains,
In mournful silence, desolation reigns —
Fly swift ye years! — Arise thou glorious morn!
Thou great avenger of thy race be born!
The conqu'ror's palm, and deathless fame be thine! —
One gen'rous stroke, and liberty be mine!

IGNATIUS SANCHO

From *Letters of Ignatius Sancho*

The following selections from Ignatius Sancho's letters make us mindful of the important role that Africans in England, often former slaves, played in the abolitionist movement. Some, like Ottobah Cugoano, whose writings are included in Chapter 3, were active polemicists against the trade, while others, like Sancho, served as examples of accomplished freedmen whom abolitionists could instance in support of their argument that Africans were not a naturally inferior people. Sancho (1729–1780) was born on a Spanish slave ship, orphaned, and brought to England two years later, where he was put into the service of three women who lived together at Greenwich. They opposed his attempts to teach himself to read, recognizing that such efforts would make him unwilling to accede to his bondage. However, he was noticed by John Montagu, the second duke of Montagu, who provided him with books. Sancho educated himself, and at the age of twenty he ran away from his mistresses, asking protection of Montagu's widow, who made him her butler. While in her household, he read voraciously and wrote prose, poetry, and music. His treatise on the theory of music has been lost, but many of his songs and his compositions for the harpsichord still survive. He also became an avid theatergoer, befriending such actors and writers as David Garrick and Laurence Sterne. Finally, in 1773, Sancho went into business for himself, selling sugar, tea, and tobacco in a shop in Westminster. Since the late 1760s, Sancho had been maintaining a large correspondence with politicians, abolitionists, and writers. His letters were published posthumously in 1782, and were widely read. His picture, taken from the frontispiece of that volume, is reprinted on the next page.

This engraving of the author is the frontispiece to *Letters of the Late Ignatius Sancho, An African,* 3rd ed. (London: Dilly, 1784). The engraving was done after a painting by Thomas Gainsborough.

The text is excerpted from *The Letters of Ignatius Sancho,* ed. Paul Edwards and Polly Rewt (Edinburgh: Edinburgh UP, 1994) 85–86, 121–22, 137–40.

To Mr Sterne.

July, 1776.

REVEREND SIR,

It would be an insult on your humanity (or perhaps look like it) to apologize for the liberty I am taking. — I am one of those people whom the vulgar and illiberal call 'Negurs.' — The first part of my life was rather unlucky, as I was placed in a family who judged ignorance the best and only security for obedience. — A little reading and writing I got by unwearied application. — The latter part of my life has been — thro' God's blessing, truly fortunate, having spent it in the service of one of the best families in the kingdom. — My chief pleasure has been books. — Philanthropy I adore. — How very much, good Sir, am I (amongst millions) indebted to you for the character of your amiable uncle Toby![1] — I declare, I would walk ten miles in the dog-days,[2] to shake hands with the honest corporal.[3] — Your Sermons[4] have touch'd me to the heart, and I hope have amended it, which brings me to the point. — In your tenth discourse, page seventy-eight, in the second volume — is this very affecting passage — 'Consider how great a part of our species — in all ages down to this — have been trod under the feet of cruel and capricious tyrants, who would neither hear their cries, nor pity their distresses. — Consider slavery — what it is — how bitter a draught — and how many millions are made to drink it!' — Of all my favorite authors, not one has drawn a tear in favor of my miserable black brethren — excepting yourself, and the humane author of Sir George Ellison.[5] — I think you will forgive me; —

---

[1] *your amiable uncle Toby:* A guileless, unworldly character in Laurence Sterne's *The Life and Opinions of Tristram Shandy, Gentleman* (published in nine vols. 1759–67).

[2] *the dog-days:* The hot days in July and early August, so called because they are marked by the rising of Sirius, the dog star.

[3] *the honest corporal:* Corporal Trim, Uncle Toby's assistant in *Tristram Shandy.*

[4] *Your Sermons:* Sterne published *The Sermons of Mr. Yorick* in 1760; after his death, they were supplemented and reprinted as *The Sermons of the Late Mr. Sterne* (1769).

[5] *Sir George Ellison:* A novel by Sarah Scott, published in two volumes in 1766. In the first volume, the hero, who owns a plantation in Jamaica, institutes a policy of humane treatment of his slaves, who then miraculously become twice as productive.

I am sure you will applaud me for beseeching you to give one half-hour's attention to slavery, as it is at this day practised in our West Indies. — That subject, handled in your striking manner, would ease the yoke (perhaps) of many — but if only of one — Gracious God! — what a feast to a benevolent heart! — and, sure I am, you are an epicurean[6] in acts of charity. — You, who are universally read, and as universally admired — you could not fail — Dear Sir, think in me you behold the uplifted hands of thousands of my brother Moors,[7] — Grief (you pathetically observe) is eloquent; — figure to yourself their attitudes; — hear their supplicating addresses! — alas! — you cannot refuse. — Humanity must comply — in which hope I beg permission to subscribe myself,

Reverend Sir, &c.
IGN. SANCHO.

To Mr. F'[isher]'.[8]

Charles Street, January 27, 1778.

Full heartily and most cordially do I thank thee, good Mr. *Fisher,* for your kindness in sending the books — That upon the unchristian and most diabolical usage of my brother Negroes — the illegality — the horrid wickedness of the traffic — the cruel carnage and depopulation of the human species — is painted in such strong colours — that I should think would (if duly attended to) flash conviction — and produce remorse in every enlightened and candid reader. — The perusal affected me more than I can express; — indeed I felt a double or mixt sensation — for while my heart was torn for the sufferings — which, for aught I know — some of my nearest kin might have undergone — my bosom, at the same time, glowed with gratitude — and praise toward the humane — the Christian — the friendly and learned Author of that most valuable book. — Blest be your sect![9] — and Heaven's peace be ever upon them! — I, who, thank God! am no bigot — but honour virtue — and the practice of the great moral duties — equally in the turban — or the lawn-sleeves[10] — who think

---

[6] *epicurean:* Someone devoted to the pursuit of pleasure (after the Greek philosopher Epicurus).

[7] *Moors:* See n. 7 on p. 219.

[8] *Mr. F'[isher]':* Jabez Fisher, a bookseller in Philadelphia. As the letter makes clear, Fisher had sent Sancho a copy of Phillis Wheatley's poems (see n. 11 on p. 455).

[9] *your sect:* The Quakers.

[10] *turban . . . lawn-sleeves:* The turban here stands for the garb of a Muslim, "lawn-sleeves" for that of an Anglican bishop.

Heaven big enough for all the race of man — and hope to see and mix amongst the whole family of Adam in bliss hereafter — I with these notions (which, perhaps, some may style absurd) look upon the friendly Author — as a being far superior to any great name upon your continent. — I could wish that every member of each house of parliament had one of these books: — And if his Majesty perused one through before breakfast — though it might spoil his appetite — yet the consciousness of having it in his power to facilitate the great work — would give an additional sweetness to his tea. — Phyllis's poems[11] do credit to nature — and put art — merely as art — to the blush. — It reflects nothing either to the glory or generosity of her master — if she is still his slave — except he glories in the *low vanity* of having in his wanton power a mind animated by Heaven — a genius superior to himself. — The list of splendid — titled — learned names, in confirmation of her being the real authoress — alas! shows how very poor the acquisition of wealth and knowledge is — without generosity — feeling — and humanity. — These good great folks — all know — and perhaps admired — nay, praised Genius in bondage — and then, like the Priests and the Levites[12] in sacred writ, passed by — not one good Samaritan amongst them. — I shall be ever glad to see you — and am, with many thanks,

Your most humble servant,
IGNATIUS SANCHO.

To Mr. J'[ack]' W'[ingrav]'e.[13]

1778.

Your good father insists on my scribbling a sheet of absurdities, and gives me a notable reason for it, that is, Jack will be pleased with it. — Now be it known to you — I have a respect both for father and son — yea for the whole family, who are every soul (that I have the honor or

[11] *Phyllis's poems:* Phillis Wheatley's *Poems on Various Subjects, Religious and Moral* published in London in 1773, was the first volume of poetry in English by an African American woman. As Sancho goes on to explain, a number of prominent aristocrats signed their names at the beginning of the volume to attest that Wheatley was in fact the author of the poems published under her name.

[12] *like the Priest and the Levites:* In the parable of the good Samaritan, they ignored the man who had been stripped and wounded, and only the Samaritan helped him (Luke 10.30–35).

[13] *J'[ack]' W'[ingrave]':* Son of another of Sancho's correspondents, a Mr. Wingrave who was a bookseller.

pleasure to know any thing of) tinctured — and leavened with all the
obsolete goodness of old times — so that a man runs some hazard in
being seen in the *Wingrave's* society of being biassed to Christianity. I
never see your poor father but his eyes betray his feelings for the hope-
ful youth in India — A tear of joy dancing upon the lids is a plaudit
not to be equalled this side death! — See the effects of right-doing, my
worthy friend — Continue in the track of rectitude — and despise
poor paltry Europeans — titled, Nabobs[14] — Read your Bible — As
day follows night, God's blessing follows virtue — honor and riches
bring up the rear — and the end is peace. — Courage, my boy — I
have done preaching. — Old folks love to seem wise — and if you are
silly enough to correspond with gray hairs, take the consequence. — I
have had the pleasure of reading most of your letters, through the
kindness of your father. — Youth is naturally prone to vanity — Such
is the weakness of human nature, that pride has a fortress in the best of
hearts — I know no person that possesses a better than Johnny
Wingrave: — but although flattery is poison to youth, yet truth obliges
me to confess that your correspondence betrays no symptom of
vanity — but teems with truths of an honest affection, which merits
praise — and commands esteem.

In some one of your letters which I do not recollect — you
speak (with honest indignation) of the treachery and chicanery of the
Natives — My good friend, you should remember from whom they
learnt these vices: — The first Christian visitors found them a simple,
harmless people — but the cursed avidity for wealth urged these first
visitors (and all the succeeding ones) to such acts of deception — and
even wanton cruelty — that the poor ignorant Natives soon learnt
to turn the knavish and diabolical arts — which they too soon
imbided — upon their teachers.

I am sorry to observe that the practice of your country[15] (which as a
resident I love — and for its freedom, and for the many blessings I
enjoy in it, shall ever have my warmest wishes, prayers, and blessings):
I say it is with reluctance that I must observe your country's conduct
has been uniformly wicked in the East — West-Indies — and even on
the coast of Guinea: — The grand object of English navigators —
indeed of all Christian navigators — is money — money — money —
for which I do not pretend to blame them — Commerce was meant by
the goodness of the Diety to diffuse the various goods of the earth into

[14] *Nabobs:* A nabob is the title for the governor of a town in India, and so, by extension, the term is used for rich people of high rank.
[15] *your country:* England.

every part — to unite mankind in the blessed chains of brotherly love, society, and mutual dependence: — the enlightened Christian should diffuse the Riches of the Gospel of peace, with the commodities of his respective land — Commerce attended with strict honesty, and with Religion for its companion, would be a blessing to every shore it touched at. — In Africa, the poor wretched natives — blessed with the most fertile and luxuriant soil — and rendered so much the more miserable for what Providence meant as a blessing: — the Christians' abominable Traffic for slaves — and the horrid cruelty and treachery of the petty Kings — encouraged by their Christian customers — who carry them strong liquors, to enflame their national madness — and powder and bad fire-arms, to furnish them with the hellish means of killing and kidnapping. — But enough — it is a subject that sours my blood — and I am sure will not please the friendly bent of your social affections. — I mentioned these only to guard my friend against being too hasty in condemning the knavery of a people who, bad as they may be — possibly — were made worse by their Christian visitors. — Make human nature thy study, wherever thou residest — whatever the religion, or the complexion, study their hearts. — Simplicity, kindness, and charity be thy guide! — With these even Savages will respect you — and God will bless you.

Your father, who sees every improvement of his boy with delight, observes that your handwriting is much for the better — In truth, I think it as well as any modest man can wish. — If my long epistles do not frighten you — and I live till the return of next spring — perhaps I shall be enabled to judge how much you are improved since your last favor — Write me a deal about the natives — the soil and produce — the domestic and interior manners of the people — customs — prejudices — fashions — and follies. — Alas! we have plenty of the two last here — and, what is worse, we have politics — and a detestable Brothers' war — where the right hand is hacking and hewing the left — whilst Angels weep at our madness — and Devils rejoice at the ruinous prospect.

Mr. *Rush* and the ladies are well. — Johnny *Rush* has favoured me with a long letter — He is now grown familiar with danger — and can bear the whistling of bullets — the cries and groans of the human species — the roll of drums — clangor of trumpets — shouts of combatants — and thunder of cannon — All these he can bear with soldier-like fortitude — with now and then a secret wish for the society of his London friends — in the sweet blessed security of peace and friendship.

This, young man, is my second letter — I have wrote till I am stupid, I perceive — I ought to have found it out two pages back. — Mrs. Sancho joins me in good wishes — I join her in the same — in which double sense believe me,

Yours, &c. &c.
I. SANCHO.
Very short.

OLAUDAH EQUIANO

From *The Interesting Narrative of the Life of Olaudah Equiano, or Gustavus Vassa, the African*

In this final selection, Olaudah Equiano (introduced on p. 310) recalls his arrival and initial experiences in England in 1757. Notice the contrast between his portrayal of this event and his memories of Barbados in the selection from the narrative reprinted in Chapter 4. As noted earlier, Equiano served for years as a slave shipboard, fighting in the Seven Years' War, and this selection describes the beginning of that phase in his life. When an adult and a freedman, Equiano returned to England, where he and Cugoano were both active in the attempt to return former British slaves to the coast of Africa by helping to found the colony of freedmen and -women at Sierra Leone. However, Equiano became disenchanted with the project when he saw that it was drastically mismanaged by the agents of its English patrons. The disastrous outcome of the first attempt at resettlement in 1787 demonstrated the validity of his complaints.

The text is taken from the first edition (London: Printed for and sold by the author, 1789) 1: 103–17.

All my alarms began to subside when we got sight of land; and at last the ship arrived at Falmouth,[1] after a passage of thirteen weeks. Every heart on board seemed gladdened on our reaching the shore, and none more than mine. The captain immediately went on shore,

---

[1] *Falmouth:* A port at the southeastern end of England.

and sent on board some fresh provisions, which we wanted very much: we made good use of them, and our famine was soon turned into feasting, almost without ending. It was about the beginning of the spring 1757 when I arrived in England, and I was near twelve years of age at that time. I was very much struck with the buildings and the pavement of the streets in Falmouth; and, indeed, any object I saw filled me with new surprise. One morning, when I got upon deck, I saw it covered all over with the snow that fell over-night: as I had never seen any thing of the kind before, I thought it was salt; so I immediately ran down to the mate and desired him, as well as I could, to come and see how somebody in the night had thrown salt all over the deck. He, knowing what it was, desired me to bring some of it down to him: accordingly I took up a handful of it, which I found very cold indeed; and when I brought it to him he desired me to taste it. I did so, and I was surprised beyond measure. I then asked him what it was; he told me it was snow: but I could not in anywise understand him. He asked me if we had no such thing in my county; and I told him, No. I then asked him the use of it, and who made it; he told me a great man in the heavens, called God: but here again I was to all intents and purposes at a loss to understand him; and the more so, when a little after I saw the air filled with it, in a heavy shower, which fell down on the same day. After this I went to church; and having never been at such a place before, I was again amazed at seeing and hearing the service. I asked all I could about it; and they gave me to understand it was worshipping God, who made us and all things. I was still at a great loss, and soon got into an endless field of inquiries, as well as I was able to speak and ask about things. However, my little friend Dick used to be my best interpreter; for I could make free with him, and he always instructed me with pleasure: and from what I could understand by him of this God, and in seeing these white people did not sell one another, as we did, I was much pleased; and in this I thought they were much happier than we Africans. I was astonished at the wisdom of the white people in all things I saw; but was amazed at their not sacrificing, or making any offerings, and eating with unwashed hands, and touching the dead. I likewise could not help remarking the particular slenderness of their women, which I did not at first like; and I thought they were not so modest and shamefaced as the African women.

I had often seen my master and Dick employed in reading; and I had a great curiosity to talk to the books, as I thought they did; and so to learn how all things had a beginning: for that purpose I have often taken up a book, and have talked to it, and then put my ears to it, when alone, in hopes it would answer me; and I have been very much concerned when I found it remained silent.

My master lodged at the house of a gentleman in Falmouth, who had a fine little daughter about six or seven years of age, and she grew prodigiously fond of me; insomuch that we used to eat together, and had servants to wait on us. I was so much caressed by this family that it often reminded me of the treatment I had received from my little noble African master. After I had been here a few days, I was sent on board a ship; but the child cried so much after me that nothing could pacify her till I was sent for again. It is ludicrous enough, that I began to fear I should be betrothed to this young lady; and when my master asked me if I would stay there with her behind him, as he was going away with the ship, which had taken in the tobacco again, I cried immediately, and said I would not leave her. At last, my stealth, one night I was sent on board the ship again; and in a little time we sailed for Guernsey,[2] where she was in part owned by a merchant, one Nicholas Doberry. As I was now amongst a people who had not their faces scarred, like some of the African nations where I had been, I was very glad I did not let them ornament me in that manner when I was with them. When we arrived at Guernsey, my master placed me to board and lodge with one of his mates, who had a wife and family there; and some months afterwards he went to England, and left me in care of this mate, together with my friend Dick: This mate had a little daughter, aged about five or six years, with whom I used to be much delighted. I had often observed that when her mother washed her face it looked very rosy; but when she washed mine it did not look so: I therefore tried oftentimes myself if I could not by washing make my face of the same colour as my little play-mate (Mary), but it was all in vain; and I now began to be morti-fied at the difference in our complexions. This woman behaved to me with great kindness and attention; and taught me every thing in the same manner as she did her own child, and indeed in every respect treated me as such. I remained here till the summer of the year 1757; when my master, being appointed first lieutenant of his majesty's ship the Roebuck, sent for Dick and me, and his old mate: on this we all left Guernsey, and set out for England in a sloop bound for London. As we were coming up towards the Nore,[3] where the Roebuck lay, a man of

---

[2] *Guernsey:* One of the Channel Islands, between England and France.
[3] *the Nore:* An area at the mouth of the Thames (so called because of its location in the north).

war's boat came alongside to press our people; on which each man ran to hide himself. I was very much frightened at this, though I did not know what it meant, or what to think or do. However I went and hid myself also under a hencoop. Immediately afterwards the press-gang came on board with their swords drawn, and searched all about, pulled the people out by force, and put them into the boat. At last I was found out also: the man that found me held me up by the heels while they all made their sport of me, I roaring and crying out all the time most lustily: but at last the mate, who was my conductor, seeing this, came to my assistance, and did all he could to pacify me; but all to very little purpose, till I had seen the boat go off. Soon afterwards we came to the Nore, where the Roebuck lay; and, to our great joy, my master came on board to us, and brought us to the ship. When I went on board this large ship, I was amazed indeed to see the quantity of men and the guns. However my surprise began to diminish as my knowledge increased; and I ceased to feel those apprehensions and alarms which had taken such strong possession of me when I first came among the Europeans, and for some time after. I began now to pass to an opposite extreme; I was so far from being afraid of any thing new which I saw, that, after I had been some time in this ship, I even began to long for a battle. My griefs too, which in young minds are not perpetual, were now wearing away; and I soon enjoyed myself pretty well, and felt tolerably easy in my present situation. There was a number of boys on board, which still made it more agreeable; for we were always together, and a great part of our time was spent in play. I remained in this ship a considerable time, during which we made several cruises, and visited a variety of places: among others we were twice in Holland, and brought over several persons of distinction from it, whose names I do not now remember. On the passage, one day, for the diversion of those gentlemen, all the boys were called on the quarter-deck, and were paired proportionably, and then made to fight; after which the gentlemen gave the combatants from five to nine shillings each. This was the first time I ever fought with a white boy; and I never knew what it was to have a bloody nose before. This made me fight most desperately; I suppose considerably more than an hour: and at last, both of us being weary, we were parted. I had a great deal of this kind of sport afterwards, in which the captain and the ship's company used very much to encourage me. Sometime afterwards the ship went to Leith[4] in Scotland, and from thence to the

---

[4] *Leith:* A port in southern Scotland, near Edinburgh.

Orkneys,[5] where I was surprised in seeing scarcely any night: and from thence we sailed with a great fleet, full of soldiers, for England. All this time we had never come to an engagement, though we were frequently cruising off the coast of France: during which we chased many vessels, and took in all seventeen prizes. I had been learning many of the manœuvres of the ship during our cruise; and I was several times made to fire the guns. One evening, off Havre de Grace,[6] just as it was growing dark, we were standing off shore, and met with a fine large French-built frigate. We got all things immediately ready for fighting; and I now expected I should be gratified in seeing an engagement, which I had so long wished for in vain. But the very moment the word of command was given to fire we heard those on board the other ship cry 'Haul down the jib[7];' and in that instant she hoisted English colours. There was instantly with us an amazing cry of — Avast! or stop firing; and I think one or two guns had been let off, but happily they did no mischief. We had hailed them several times; but they not hearing, we received no answer, which was the cause of our firing. The boat was then sent on board of her, and she proved to be the Ambuscade man of war, to my no small disappointment. We returned to Portsmouth,[8] without having been in any action, just at the trial of Admiral Byng[9] (whom I saw several times during it): and my master having left the ship, and gone to London for promotion, Dick and I were put on board the Savage sloop of war, and we went in her to assist in bringing off the St. George man of war, that had ran ashore somewhere on the coast. After staying a few weeks on board the Savage, Dick and I were sent on shore at Deal,[10] where we remained some short time, till my master sent for us to London, the place I had long desired exceedingly to see. We therefore both with great pleasure got into a waggon, and came to London, where we were received by a Mr. Guerin, a relation of my master. This gentleman had two sisters, very amiable ladies, who took much notice and great care of me. Though I had desired so much to see London, when I arrived in it I was unfortunately unable to gratify my curiosity; for I had at this time the chilblains to such a degree that I could not stand for several months, and I was obliged to

---

[5] the Orkneys: A group of islands off the northern coast of Scotland.

[6] Havre de Grace: A French port in the English Channel, now called Le Havre.

[7] jib: A triangular sail.

[8] Portsmouth: One of the royal dockyards for the British navy, located on the southern coast of England.

[9] Admiral Byng: Admiral John Byng (1704–1757), who suffered a defeat at Minorca in 1756 and was ultimately found guilty of neglect of duty and executed.

[10] Deal: A city on the southeast coast of England, near Dover.

be sent to St. George's Hospital.[11] There I grew so ill, that the doctors wanted to cut my left leg off at different times, apprehending a mortification[12]; but I always said I would rather die than suffer it; and happily (I thank God) I recovered without the operation. After being there several weeks, and just as I had recovered, the small-pox broke out on me, so that I was again confined; and I thought myself now particularly unfortunate. However I soon recovered again; and by this time my master having been promoted to be first lieutenant of the Preston man of war of fifty guns, then new at Deptford,[13] Dick and I were sent on board her, and soon after we went to Holland to bring over the late Duke of ———[14] to England.

[11] *St. George's Hospital:* This hospital, founded in 1733, was located at Hyde Park Corner, in what is now central London but was then close to the western reaches of the city.

[12] *mortification:* Gangrene.

[13] *Deptford:* Another of the royal dockyards, in the eastern part of London just south of the Thames.

[14] *Duke of* ——— : In later editions Equiano identifies him as the Duke of Cumberland, uncle of King George III; Cumberland returned to England in 1757 after a military defeat in Hanover.

Selected Bibliography

This bibliography is divided into two parts, "Works Cited" and "Suggestions for Further Reading." The first part contains all primary and secondary works quoted or discussed in the general or chapter introductions. The second part is a selective list of materials that will be useful to students who want to know more about Aphra Behn's life and culture or who are interested in reading critical studies of *Oroonoko*. A book or article that appears in "Works Cited" is not recorded again under "Suggestions for Further Reading." Thus, both lists should be consulted.

WORKS CITED

Acholonu, Catherine Obianuju. *The Igbo Roots of Olaudah Equiano*. Owerri, Nigeria: AFA, 1989.

Allen, Theodore W. *The Invention of the White Race*. New York: Verso, 1994.

Astley, Thomas. *A New General Collection of Voyages and Travels*. 4 vols. London, 1743–47.

Aykroyd, W. R. *Sweet Malefactor: Sugar, Slavery and Human Society*. London: Heinemann, 1967.

Ballaster, Ros. *Seductive Forms: Women's Amatory Fiction, 1684–1740*. Oxford: Oxford UP, 1992. 69–113.

Barbot, Jean. *A Description of the Coasts of North and South-Guinea, and of Ethiopia Inferior, vulgarly Angola. Now First Printed from His Original Manuscript. A Collection of Voyages and Travels.* Ed. Awnshawm Churchill. Vol. 5. London, 1752.

Baxter, Richard. *Chapters from a Christian Directory.* London, 1673.

Bean, Richard Nelson. *The British Trans-Atlantic Slave Trade, 1650–1775.* New York: Arno, 1975.

Bean, Richard N., and Robert P. Thomas. "The Adoption of Slave Labor in British America." *The Uncommon Market: Essays in the Economic History of the Atlantic Slave Trade.* Ed. Henry A. Gemery and Jan S. Hogendorn. New York: Academic P, 1979. 377–98.

Beckles, Hilary. *A History of Barbados: From Amerindian Settlement to Nation-State.* Cambridge: Cambridge UP, 1990.

Beckles, Hilary, and Varene Shepherd, eds. *Caribbean Slave Society and Economy: A Student Reader.* New York: New P, 1991.

Beer, George Lewis. *The Origins of the British Colonial System, 1578–1660.* Gloucester: Smith, 1959.

Behn, Aphra. *The Works of Aphra Behn.* Ed. Janet Todd. 7 vols. Columbus: Ohio State UP, 1992–96.

Blackburn, Robin. *The Making of New World Slavery.* London: Verso, 1997.

———. *The Overthrow of Colonial Slavery, 1776–1848.* London: Verso, 1988.

Bridenbaugh, Carl, and Roberta Bridenbaugh. *No Peace Beyond the Line: The English in the Caribbean, 1624–1690.* New York: Oxford UP, 1972.

Bush, Jonathan A. "The British Constitution and the Creation of American Slavery." *Slavery & the Law.* Ed. Paul Finkelman. Madison, WI: Madison House, 1997. 379–418.

Carlos, Ann M., and Jamie Brown Kruse. "The Decline of the Royal African Company: Fringe Firms and the Role of the Charter." *Economic History Review* 49 (1996): 291–313.

Colman, George. *Inkle and Yarico.* London, 1787.

Cowper, William. *The Poetical Works of William Cowper.* Ed. H. S. Milford. 3rd ed. London: Oxford UP, 1926.

Curtin, Philip D., ed. *Africa Remembered: Narratives by West Africans from the Era of the Slave Trade.* Madison: U of Wisconsin P, 1967.

———. *The Atlantic Slave Trade: A Census.* Madison: U of Wisconsin P, 1969.

Daaku, Kwame Yeboa. *Trade and Politics on the Gold Coast, 1600–1720.* Oxford: Clarendon, 1970.

Dabydeen, David. *Hogarth's Blacks: Images of Blacks in Eighteenth-Century English Art.* Athens: U of Georgia P, 1987.

Davidson, Basil. *The African Slave Trade: A Revised and Expanded Edition.* Boston: Little, 1980.

Davies, C. S. L. "Slavery and Protector Somerset: The Vagrancy Act of 1547." *Economic History Review* 19 (1966): 533–49.

Davies, Kenneth Gordon. *The Royal African Company.* London: Longman, 1957.

Davis, David Brion. *The Problem of Slavery in Western Culture.* Ithaca: Cornell UP, 1966.

Defoe, Daniel. *A Brief Account of the Present State of the African Trade.* London, 1713.

———. *An Essay upon the Trade to Africa.* London, 1711.

———. *The Manufacturer* (1719–1721). Delmar: Scholar's Facsimiles, 1978.

Dodd, William. "The African Prince, when in England, to Zara," and "Zara, at the Court of Annamaboe, to the African Prince." *Poems by Mr. Dodd.* London 1767. 8–20.

Duffy, Maureen. *The Passionate Shepherdess: Aphra Behn, 1640–1689.* London: Cape, 1977.

Dunn, Richard S. *Sugar and Slaves: The Rise of the Planter Class in the English West Indies, 1624–1713.* New York: Norton, 1973.

Du Tetre, Jean-Baptiste. *Histoire générale des Antilles habitées par les Francois.* Vol. 2. Paris, 1671.

Ellis, Ellen Deborah. *An Introduction to the History of Sugar as a Commodity.* Bryn Mawr College Monographs IV. Philadelphia: Winston, 1905.

"England's First Lady Novelist." *St. James's Magazine* 7 (1863): 351–580.

Ferguson, Margaret W. "Juggling the Categories of Race, Class, and Gender: Aphra Behn's Oroonoko." *Women's Studies* 19 (1991): 159–81. Rpt. in *Women, "Race," and Writing in the Early Modern Period.* Ed. Margo Hendricks and Patricia Parker. New York: Routledge, 1994. 209–24

Ferguson, Moira. *Subject to Others: British Women Writers and Colonial Slavery, 1670–1834.* New York: Routledge, 1992.

Fiddes, Edward. "Lord Mansfield and the Sommersett Case." *Law Quarterly Review* 50 (1934): 499–511.

Filmer, Robert, Sir. *Patriarcha and Other Writings.* Ed. Johann P. Sommerville. Cambridge: Cambridge UP, 1991.

Gerzina, Gretchen. *Black London: Life before Emancipation.* London: Murray, 1995.

Gildon, Charles. *Robinson Crusoe Examin'd and Criticis'd.* Ed. Paul Dottin. London: Dent, 1923.

Goreau, Angeline. *Reconstructing Aphra: A Social Biography of Aphra Behn.* New York: Dial, 1980.

Goveia, E. V. *The West Indian Slave Laws of the Eighteenth Century.* London: Caribbean UP, 1970.

Grant, Douglas. *The Fortunate Slave: An Illustration of African Slavery in the Early Eighteenth Century.* London: Oxford UP, 1968.

Grotius, Hugo. *De jure belli ac pacis libri tres.* (Bobb-Merrill, c. 1925) Trans. Francis Kelsey. London: 1625.

Harlow, V. T., ed. *Colonising Expeditions to the West Indies and Guinea, 1621–1667.* London: Hakluyt Soc., 1925.

Hewett, J. F. Napier. *European Settlements on the West Coast of Africa; with Remarks on the Slave-Trade and the Supply of Cotton.* New York: Negro UP, 1969.

Hill, Christopher. *The English Bible and the Seventeenth-Century Revolution.* New York: Penguin, 1993.

Inikori, J. E., ed. *Forced Migration: The Impact of the Export Slave Trade on African Societies.* London: Hutchinson, 1982.

Inikori, Joseph E., and Stanley E. Engerman, eds. *The Atlantic Slave Trade: Effects on Economies, Societies, and Peoples in Africa, the Americas, and Europe.* Durham: Duke UP, 1992.

Jones, G. I. "Olaudah Equiano of the Niger Ibo." *Africa Remembered: Narratives by West Africans from the Era of the Slave Trade.* Ed. Philip D. Curtin. Madison: U of Wisconsin P, 1967. 60–98.

Jordan, Winthrop D. *White over Black: American Attitudes toward the Negro, 1520–1812.* Chapel Hill: U of North Carolina P, 1968.

Kea, Ray A. *Settlements, Trade, and Polities in the Seventeenth-Century Gold Coast.* Baltimore: Johns Hopkins UP, 1982.

Keirn, Tim. "Monopoly, Economic Thought, and the Royal African Company." *Early Modern Conceptions of Property.* Ed. John Brewer and Susan Staves. New York: Routledge, 1995. 427–66.

King, Reyahn, et al. *Ignatius Sancho: An African Man of Letters.* London: National Portrait Gallery, 1997.

Law, Robin. *The Slave Coast of West Africa, 1550–1750: The Impact of the Atlantic Slave Trade on an African Society.* Oxford: Clarendon, 1991.

Law, Robin, ed. *Further Correspondence of the Royal African Company of England, Relating to the 'Slave Coast', 1681–1699.* Madison: African Studies Program, U of Wisconsin-Madison, 1992.

Léry, Jean de. *History of a Voyage to the Land of Brazil, Otherwise Called America.* Trans. Janet Whatley. Berkeley: U of California P, 1990.

Locke, John. *Two Treatises of Government*. Ed. Peter Laslett. 2nd.
  ed. London: Cambridge UP, 1967.

Lorimer, Joyce. "The Failure of the English Guiana Ventures
  1595–1667 and James I's Foreign Policy." *Journal of Imperial
  and Commonwealth History* 21 (1993): 1–30.

Lovejoy, Paul E. *Transformations in Slavery: A History of Slavery in
  Africa*. New York: Cambridge UP, 1983.

Makepeace, Margaret. "English Traders on the Guinea Coast,
  1657–1668: An Analysis of the East India Company Archive."
  History in Africa 16 (1989): 237–84.

Manning, Patrick. "The Slave Trade in the Bight of Benin,
  1640–1890." *The Uncommon Market: Essays in the Economic
  History of the Atlantic Slave Trade*. Ed. Henry A. Gemery and
  Jan S. Hogendorn. New York: Academic P, 1979. 107–41.

Meredith, Henry. *An Account of the Gold Coast of Africa: With a
  Brief History of the African Company*. London: Cass, 1967.

Milton, John. *The Riverside Milton*. Ed. Roy Flannagan. Boston:
  Houghton Mifflin, 1998.

Mintz, Sidney W. *Sweetness and Power: The Place of Sugar in Modern History*. New York: Penguin, 1986.

Mocquet, Jean. *Travel and Voyages into Africa, Asia, and America*.
  Trans. Nathaniel Pullen. London: Newton, 1696.

More, Hannah. *The Works of Hannah More*. New York: Harper,
  1852.

Nicholl, Charles. *The Creature in the Map: A Journey to El Dorado*.
  London: Cape, 1995.

Oldham, James. "New Light on Mansfield and Slavery." *Journal of
  British Studies* 27 (1988): 45–68.

Pagden, Anthony. *Lords of All the World: Ideologies of Empire in
  Spain, Britain, and France c. 1500–c.1800*. New Haven: Yale UP,
  1995.

Panday, Radjnarain Monanpersad Nannan. *Agriculture in Surinam,
  1650–1950*. Amsterdam: H. J. Paris, 1959.

Price, Richard. *The Guinea Maroons: A Historical and Bibliographical Introduction*. Baltimore: Johns Hopkins UP, 1976.

Sheridan, Richard. *Sugar and Slavery: An Economic History of the
  British West Indies, 1623–1775*. Baltimore: Johns Hopkins UP,
  1974.

Steele, Richard. *The Lover*. In *Richard Steele's Periodical Journalism,
  1714–16*. Ed. Rae Blanchard. Oxford: Clarendon, 1959.

Sypher, Wylie. *Guinea's Captive Kings: British Anti-Slavery Literature
  of the XVIIIth Century*. Chapel Hill: U of North Carolina P, 1942.

Thévet, André. *The New Found World, or Antarctike*. Trans. Thomas
  Hacket. London: Hacket, 1568.

Thomas, Hugh. *The Slave Trade: The Story of the Atlantic Slave Trade, 1440–1870.* New York: Simon, 1997.

Todd, Janet. Introduction. *The Works of Aphra Behn.* By Aphra Behn. Vol. 1. Columbus: Ohio State UP, 1992.

———. *The Secret Life of Aphra Behn.* New Brunswick: Rutgers UP, 1996.

Tree, Ronald. *A History of Barbados.* London: Hart-Davis, 1972.

Uchendu, Victor. *The Igbo of Southeast Nigeria.* New York: Holt, 1965.

Van Dantzig, Albert. "English Bosman and Dutch Bosman: A Comparison of Texts." *History in Africa* 2 (1975): 185–216; 3 (1976): 91–126; 4 (1977): 247–73.

Watson, Alan. *Slave Law in the Americas.* Athens: U of Georgia P, 1989.

Wiecek, William M. "*Somerset:* Lord Mansfield and the Legality of Slavery in the Anglo-American World." *University of Chicago Law Review* 42 (1974): 86–146.

Williams, A. M. "Our Early Lady Novelists." *Cornhill Magazine* 72 (1895): 588–600.

Williams, Eric. *From Columbus to Castro: The History of the Caribbean, 1492–1969.* London: Deutsch, 1970.

Williamson, James Alexander. *English Colonies in Guiana and the Amazon, 1604–1668.* Oxford: Clarendon, 1923.

Wyndham, H. A. *The Atlantic and Slavery.* Oxford: Oxford UP, 1935.

SUGGESTIONS FOR FURTHER READING

Bibliographies

Armistead, J. M., and Werner Bies. *Four Restoration Playwrights: A Reference Guide to Thomas Shadwell, Aphra Behn, Nathaniel Lee, and Thomas Otway.* Boston: Hall, 1984.

Hogg, Peter C. *The African Slave Trade and Its Suppression: A Classified and Annotated Bibliography of Books, Pamphlets, and Periodical Articles.* London: Cass, 1973.

O'Donnell, Mary Ann. *Aphra Behn: An Annotated Bibliography of Primary and Secondary Sources.* New York: Garland, 1986.

Studies of Behn

Ballaster, Ros. "Seizing the Means of Seduction: Fiction and Feminine Identity in Aphra Behn and Delarivier Manley." *Women, Writing, History: 1640–1740.* Ed. Isobel Grundy and Susan Wiseman. Athens: U of Georgia P, 1992. 93–108.

Dhuicq, Bernard. "New Evidence of Aphra Behn's Stay in Surinam." *Notes and Queries* 42 (1995): 40–41.

Duyfhuizen, Bernard. " 'That Which I Dare Not Name': Aphra Behn's 'The Willing Mistress.' " *ELH* 58 (1991): 63–82.

Frohock, Richard. "Violence and Awe: The Foundations of Government in Aphra Behn's New World Settings." *Eighteenth-Century Fiction* 8 (1996): 437–52.

Gallagher, Catherine. *Nobody's Story: The Vanishing Acts of Women Writers in the Marketplace, 1670–1820.* Berkeley: U of California P, 1994. 1–87.

Gardiner, Judith Kegan. "The First English Novel: Aphra Behn's *Love Letters,* the Canon, and Women's Tastes." *Tulsa Studies in Women's Literature* 8 (1989): 201–22.

Hargreaves, Henry A. "New Evidence of the Realism of Mrs Behn's *Oroonoko.*" *Bulletin of the New York Public Library* 74 (1970): 437–44.

Hutner, Heidi, ed. *Rereading Aphra Behn: History, Theory, and Criticism.* Charlottesville: UP of Virginia, 1993.

Jacobs, Naomi. "The Seduction of Aphra Behn." *Women's Studies* 8 (1991): 395–403.

Link, Frederick M. *Aphra Behn.* New York: Twayne, 1968.

Medoff, Jeslyn. "The Daughters of Behn and the Problem of Reputation." *Women, Writing, History: 1640–1740.* Ed. Isobel Grundy and Susan Wiseman. Athens: U of Georgia P, 1992. 33–54

Mermin, Dorothy. "Women Becoming Poets: Katherine Philips, Aphra Behn, Anne Finch." *ELH* 57 (1990): 335–55.

O'Donnell, Mary Ann. "Tory Wit and Unconventional Woman: Aphra Behn." *Women Writers of the Seventeenth Century.* Ed. Katharina M. Wilson and Frank J. Warnke. Athens: U of Georgia P, 1989. 341–54.

Payne, Deborah C. " 'And Poets Shall by Patron-Princes Live': Aphra Behn and Patronage." *Curtain Calls: British and American Women and the Theater.* Ed. Mary Anne Schofield and Cecelia Macheski. Athens: Ohio UP, 1991. 105–19.

Pearson, Jacqueline. "Gender and Narrative in the Fiction of Aphra Behn." *Review of English Studies* 42 (1991): 40–56; 179–90.

Spencer, Jane. *The Rise of the Woman Novelist: From Aphra Behn to Jane Austen.* Oxford: Blackwell, 1986. 42–52.

Spender, Dale. *Mothers of the Novel: 100 Good Women Writers before Jane Austen.* London: Pandora, 1986. 47–66.

Todd, Janet. *The Sign of Angellica: Women, Writing and Fiction, 1660–1800.* London: Virago, 1989. 69–83

Todd, Janet, ed. *Aphra Behn Studies.* Cambridge: Cambridge UP, 1996.

Wehrs, Donald. "Eros, Ethics, Identity: Royalist Feminism and the Politics of Identity in Aphra Behn's *Love Letters*." *Studies in English Literature, 1500–1900* 32 (1990): 461–78.

Critical Studies of *Oroonoko*

Andrade, Susan Z. "White Skin, Black Masks: Colonialism and the Sexual Politics of *Oroonoko*." *Cultural Critique* 27 (1994): 189–214.

Athey, Stephanie, and Daniel Cooper Alarcon. "*Oroonoko*'s Gendered Economies of Honor/Horror: Reframing Colonial Discourse Studies in the Americas." *American Literature* 65 (1993): 415–43.

Ballaster, Ros. "New Hystericism: Aphra Behn's *Oroonoko*: The Body, the Text and the Feminist Critic." *New Feminist Discourses: Critical Essays on Theories and Texts*. Ed. Isobel Armstrong. New York: Routledge, 1992. 283–95.

Brown, Laura. "The Romance of Empire: *Oroonoko* and the Trade in Slaves." *The New Eighteenth Century: Theory, Politics, English Literature*. Ed. Felicity Nussbaum and Laura Brown. New York: Methuen, 1987. 41–61.

Erickson, Robert A. "Mrs. A. Behn and the Myth of Oroonoko-Imoinda." *Eighteenth-Century Fiction* 5 (1993): 201–16.

Ferguson, Margaret W. "News from the New World: Miscegenous Romance in Aphra Behn's Oroonoko and The Widow Ranter." *The Production of English Renaissance Culture*. Ed. David Lee Miller, et al. Ithaca: Cornell UP, 1994. 151–89.

———. "Transmuting *Othello*: Aphra Behn's *Oroonoko*." *Cross-Cultural Performances: Differences in Women's Re-Visions of Shakespeare*. Ed. Marianne Novy. Urbana: U of Illinois P, 1993. 15–49.

Ferguson, Moira. "*Oroonoko*: Birth of a Paradigm." *New Literary History* 23 (1992): 339–59.

Fogarty, Anne. "Looks that Kill: Violence and Representation in Aphra Behn's *Oroonoko*." *The Discourse of Slavery: Aphra Behn to Toni Morrison*. Ed. Carl Plasa and Betty J. Ring. New York: Routledge, 1994. 1–17.

Giffey, George. "Aphra Behn's *Oroonoko*: Occasion and Accomplishment." *Two English Novelists, Aphra Behn and Anthony Trollope: Papers Read at a Clark Library Seminar, May 11, 1974*. Los Angeles: Clark Library, 1975. 3–41.

Hoegberg, David E. "Caesar's Toils: Allusion and Rebellion in *Oroonoko*." *Eighteenth-Century Fiction* 7 (1995): 239–58.

Pacheco, Anita. "Royalism and Honor in Aphra Behn's *Oroonoko*." *Studies in English Literature, 1500–1900* 34 (1994): 491–506.

Rogers, Katharine M. "Fact and Fiction in Aphra Behn's *Oroonoko.*" *Studies in the Novel* 20 (1988): 1–15.
Starr, G. A. "Aphra Behn and the Genealogy of the Man of Feeling." *Modern Philology* 87 (1990): 362–72.
Sussman, Charlotte. "The Other Problem with Women: Reproduction and Slave Culture in Aphra Behn's *Oroonoko,*" *Rereading Aphra Behn: History, Theory, and Criticism,* ed. Heidi Hutner. Charlottesville: U of Virginia P, 1993. 212–33.
Weston, Peter J. "The Noble Primitive as Bourgeois Subject." *Literature and History* 10 (1984) 59–71.

Adaptations of *Oroonoko*

Ferriar, John. *The Prince of Angola, a Tragedy, Altered from the Play of Oroonoko.* Manchester, 1788.
Gentleman, Francis. *Oroonoko: or, the Royal Slave.* Glasgow, 1760.
Hawkesworth, John. *Oroonoko, a Tragedy.* London, 1759.
Southerne, Thomas. *Oroonoko, a Tragedy.* London, 1696.

Credits

Aphra Behn, *Oroonoko; or the Royal Slave,* "The Golden Age. A Paraphrase on a Translation out of the French," "To the fair Clarinda, who made Love to me, imagin'd more than Woman," "A congratulatory Poem to the King's Most Sacred Majesty, on the Happy Birth of the Prince of Wales," and "The Unfortunate Bride; or, The Blind Lady a Beauty," reprinted from *The Works of Aphra Behn,* edited by Janet Todd, vol. 3, pp. 54–119; vol. 1, pp. 30–35; vol. 1, p. 288; vol. 1, pp. 297–99; and vol. 3, pp. 325–34; with permission from Pickering & Chatto Publishers and the Ohio State University Press.

Excerpt from Daniel Defoe, *The Life and Strange Surprizing Adventures of Robinson Crusoe,* edited by J. Donald Crowley (London: Oxford UP, 1972). Reprinted by permission of Oxford University Press.

Excerpts from "Dialogue between the Pagan and the Christian," in *The Travels of Sir John Mandeville,* trans. C. W. R. D. Moseley. Copyright © 1983 by Penguin UK. Reprinted by permission of the publisher.

Excerpts from V. T. Harlow, ed., *Colonising Expeditions to the West Indies and Guinea, 1623–1667.* Copyright © 1925 by The Hakluyt Society. Reprinted by permission of the publishers.

Excerpts from Ben Jonson, *The Masque of Blacknesse,* in *Ben Jonson,* vol. 7, pp. 172–75, edited by C. H. Herford and Percy and Evelyn Simpson (Oxford: Clarendon, 1941). Reprinted by permission of Oxford University Press.

Excerpts from Michel de Montaigne, "On Cannibals," In *Essays by Michel de Montaigne,* trans. John Florio (Everyman Library, London: J. M. Dent, 1910). Reprinted by permission of J. M. Dent and Sons, Ltd.

Excerpts from Robin Law, ed., *Further Correspondence of the Royal African Company of England, Relating to the "Slave Coast," 1681–1699,* copyright © 1992 by The African Studies Program, University of Wisconsin—Madison. Reprinted with permission.

Excerpt from Sir Thomas More, *Utopia,* ed. John Warrington (Everyman Library, London: J. M. Dent, 1951). Reprinted by permission of J. M. Dent and Sons, Ltd.

Excerpts from Ignatius Sancho, *The Letters of Ignatius Sancho,* ed. Paul Edwards and Polly Rewt. Copyright © 1994 by Edinburgh University Press. Reprinted by permission of Edinburgh University Press.

Excerpts from Thomas Southerne, *Oroonoko, a Tragedy,* reprinted from *Oroonoko by Thomas Southerne,* edited by Maximillian E. Novak and David Stuart Rodes, by permission of the University of Nebraska Press. Copyright © 1976 by the University of Nebraska Press.

Excerpts from John Gabriel Stedman, *Narrative of a Five Years Expedition against the Revolted Negroes of Surinam,* edited by Richard Price and Sally Price. Copyright © 1988 The Johns Hopkins University Press. Used by permission of The Johns Hopkins University Press.

Excerpts from Richard Steele, *Spectator* #11, and Joseph Addison, *Spectator* #215, in *The Spectator,* edited by Donald F. Bond (Oxford: Clarendon, 1965), vol. 1, pp. 47–51, and vol. 2, pp. 339–41. Reprinted by permission of Oxford University Press.